Daniel walked through th he compliments on his perforn

Then he spotted Linda.

She walked toward him on unsteady legs, the glass in her hand splashing liquid as she swayed. Daniel tried to ignore how drunk she was, but as she moved uncomfortably close to him, the heat of her body through her thin dress stirred an undeniable response in him.

"What room are you in, Danny?" she purred.

"Linda, forget it. I'm married. I'm almost a father. Those days are gone."

She threw back her head and laughed. "You've still got the same virgin's mind, Daniel. Don't you give a damn about the first girl you ever had? There"—she brushed his lips with the lightest, most tantalizing of kisses—"that's to show you there's no hard feelings." Then she vanished in the direction of the bar.

His accompanist appeared at Daniel's elbow the minute Linda was gone.

"Stay away from that broad," he warned. "She was trouble last time.

"And she'll be trouble again."

"AN ALL-CONSUMING SAGA . . ."
—Cynthia Freeman

"AN INTRIGUING NOVEL . . . SPELLBINDING . . . A TRIUMPH!"
—Fort Wayne News-Sentinel

". . . A GRAND NOVEL . . ."
—The Grand Rapids Press

BY LEWIS ORDE

ZEBRA BOOKS
KENSINGTON PUBLISHING CORP.

ZEBRA BOOKS

are published by

KENSINGTON PUBLISHING CORP.
475 Park Avenue South
New York, N.Y. 10016

Published by arrangement with Arbor House Publishing Company.

Tenth printing: December, 1988

Printed in the United States of America

To Ruth, Lionel and the Ross clan of
Stanmore Hill

Death is afraid of him because he has the heart of a lion.

ANON . . . ARAB PROVERB

Prologue: Rodolfo

Marcello the painter, Schaunard the musician, and Colline the philosopher had just left to celebrate Christmas Eve at the Café Momus. The garret in the Latin Quarter of Paris was silent now, and Rodolfo could continue with his work, the article he had been writing before the intense cold had stiffened his fingers and numbed his brain. For a moment, he sat contemplating the ancient pot-bellied stove in the center of the room, where, only minutes earlier, he had sacrificed one of his manuscripts for the luxury of a brief instant of warmth.

Squinting in the meager light supplied by the solitary candle on the table, he tried to concentrate his thoughts and find the elusive spark of inspiration that would allow him to finish the article. Finally, he tore up the piece of paper and threw down the pen, declaring to the empty room that he was not in the mood to write. Perhaps he should join his friends at the Café Momus. They would be waiting for him, with warmth and conviviality, laughter and wine. Yes, he decided; he should take a brief, welcome vacation from the spartan surroundings of the garret.

A timid knock sounded on the door. Eager for any diversion, Rodolfo asked who was there. A woman's voice answered. Her candle had been blown out as she was climbing the stairs and she needed assistance. Rodolfo swung back the door to see a frail young woman standing outside. The weak light from the room flicked shadows across her pale face, and she gasped for breath from the long climb up the stairs. Rodolfo stepped forward just in time to catch her as she fainted. Her key and candlestick clattered to the floor as he helped her to a chair. Under his concerned attention, she began to recover until she felt well enough to return to her own room. Regretfully, Rodolfo stood aside to let her pass.

As she stood by the door to bid Rodolfo good night, a cold, blustery draught from the stairway blew out her candle again.

Rodolfo hastened toward her, but the speed of his passage caused his candle, also, to be extinguished.

Now the room was totally dark. The girl had dropped her key, and with Rodolfo kneeling beside her, they began to search on the floor, feeling in the darkness for the cold strip of metal. Rodolfo's hand closed over the key. Instead of telling the girl, he slipped the key into his pocket, not wanting this precious interlude to end.

Guided by her voice as she asked if he were still searching, Rodolfo drew closer. His hand touched hers, almost numbed by the winter's chill that had seeped into the building. Surprised by the sudden contact, the girl stood up. Still holding her hand, caressing it gently as he tried to bring back warmth to the frozen fingers, Rodolfo also rose. His mouth opened and the first lines of Puccini's famous aria sprang easily to his lips:

Che gelida manina.
Se la lasci riscaldar . . .

The opening night audience at the opera house was resplendent in its most expensive finery. International problems, the Cold War, the squalid fighting in Korea were, for the moment, forgotten. Jewelry glittered in the Diamond Horseshoe and the starched fronts of dress shirts shone in the darkness with a luminous quality of their own. *La Bohème*, everyone's favorite, was launching the new season. Seats had been at a premium, and every square foot of standing room was jammed with opera lovers who craned their necks to improve the restricted view available to them.

As Rodolfo softly began his tenor aria, the audience was deathly silent. Their ears absorbed and stored every note, while their eyes remained riveted on the stage where two poverty-stricken figures brought to life the Paris of the 1830s. Not one person looked down at the libretto; for this, there was no need of translation.

Eight rows back from the orchestra sat an elderly couple. Despite the comfortable warmth of the opera house, the woman continued to wear an ostentatious mink jacket over her long evening dress, fearing that if she removed the sign of wealth, she would look out of place, a refugee from the Bronx who had somehow managed to become mixed up with the celebrity-studded opening night crowd. Her dark-brown, tinted hair was tightly waved, and she sat rigidly as if the slightest movement would spoil her appearance. Next to her sat her husband, an insignificant looking man of slight build, almost bald, with thick horn-rimmed glasses. As Rodolfo continued to sing, the man took off his glasses and wiped the lenses with a handkerchief, blinking back tears as he looked toward the stage. He had cried many times during his life, always ashamed that anyone might see. But they had been tears of sadness. Tonight he was crying tears of joy and he could not give a damn if the entire world bore witness. This was his night just as it was Rodolfo's. Every triumph Rodolfo would reap on stage, the elderly man would also reap. Every bravo that showered like rain upon Rodolfo's head would fall upon his own.

Realizing that the aria was nearing its end, the man sniffed back his tears. His wife turned to look at him sharply, digging him with her elbow. He ignored her, aware only of that sweet, silver voice that carried so clearly from the stage.

Rodolfo's aria finished. There was a split second of pure silence while the audience shook itself free of the music's enchantment, then the opera house erupted with noise. As one, the patrons stood to thunder waves of applause at the figures on the stage. The old man felt himself being shoved as the man on his left stood to clap wildly. He did not mind; it merely made him clap his own hands more exuberantly. This was a moment in life's weary path to be treasured. Tonight there could be no discomforts, only experiences. And each new experience—even being jostled—was enjoyable. He glanced to his right, looking at his wife. She, too, was standing, as matronly as ever, the rigid waves of her hairstyle lending an even further degree of sternness to her face.

The applause began to die. Taking this as his cue, the conductor lifted his baton to guide the orchestra into the next part of the opera. People sat down, concentrating again, not wanting to miss a single note as the seamstress Mimi made her reply to Rodolfo. The old man was among the last to sit, dropping down only when his wife tugged him by the sleeve of his tuxedo. He began to look around, then he tapped the arm of the man on his left. The man glared at him in annoyance and turned his attention back to the stage. Not to be deterred, the old man tapped him again.

"Yes. What is it?" the man finally hissed.

"You see the singer playing Rodolfo?" The old man had a mid-European accent which forty years in the United States had failed to erase.

Recognizing the accent, the other man affected a look of distaste. What was this annoying little immigrant doing here tonight of all nights? How had he managed to come by such an envied seat? "What about him?" he asked eventually.

Certain of his audience, the old man let his face crack open into a wide smile. He took off his glasses once more and dabbed at the corners of his eyes before replying, glorying in the revelation he was about to make. "That's Daniel Kirschbaum."

"Kerr," the other man corrected him. "Daniel Kerr."

The old man's smile grew even wider. "Maybe that's what it says in your program, mister. But take my word for it. It's Kirschbaum. I should know. I'm Isaac Kirschbaum, his father."

Book One

Daniel

Chapter One

Outside, it was snowing. Thick, heavy, white flakes drifted lazily downward from leaden skies to cling to the blanket of snow that stretched across the Claremont Parkway section of the Bronx. Some of the flakes settled briefly on the windows of the temple, sticking for an instant before the warmth from inside penetrated the glass to ease their grip. Then they slid slowly down, dissolving, leaving a wet trail to mark their passage. The Saturday morning worshippers paid no attention to the snow. They would worry about it only when the service was over, not before. First, they had something enjoyable to anticipate.

On the raised *bima* in the center of the temple—facing the open ark and the sacred scrolls of the Torah—stood the rabbi, eyes closed as he chanted the prayer for the Reading of the Law. In front of him, a Torah scroll was spread open, waiting for the next portion to be read. After finishing the prayer, the rabbi stepped aside and motioned for the young boy who stood behind him to come forward. Daniel Kirschbaum had turned thirteen ten days earlier; now, by Jewish law, he would become a man in the eyes of God and the community.

Daniel cleared his throat nervously. He wiped the back of his hand across his mouth and felt the beads of sweat which covered his upper lip. Fear. Stark naked fear. He had been dreading this day for the entire eight months he had been studying the portion of the Torah he would read. He was certain his voice would crack as he struggled to reach a high note. Or he would forget the words he had learned by heart and be unable to recognize anything from the Torah scroll, where the vowels were omitted and the Hebrew letters seemed like a meaningless jumble. The rabbi would glare at him. The more religious members of the congregation would call out the correct pronunciation. Instead of helping, they would only make him stumble more. That was why they did it, Daniel was sure. The old men wrapped up in their prayer shawls, taking a sadistic delight when a *bar mitzvah* boy erred, gleefully letting the entire *shul* know that he had not done his homework. Why, dear God, had he not been born a Catholic? No, that was no good either. They spoke Latin, just as difficult as Hebrew. Next time around he'd make certain his parents were Methodists; then it would be English all the way.

He found some consolation in knowing that the fear was nothing new. Each time he sang in the school choir he experienced the same pangs, the same nervousness. At home, locked away in the privacy of his bathroom, he could ham it up in front of the mirror, sing the popular hits, enjoy himself. But once he faced an audience, the self-confidence generated in his bathroom performances disappeared. Even his music teacher, who continually encouraged Daniel by telling him he had the best voice he had ever heard in the school, could not dispel the terror that an audience brought.

Stepping forward, Daniel drew in as deep a breath as he could manage and glanced down at the white card on which were printed the blessings for the Torah. Those, at least, still had the vowels intact.

"Baruchu es adonoi hamevorach . . ."

Daniel's high, boyish voice rose above the congregation as he chanted the ancient words. As the blessing continued without a mishap, he became more confident. Just like in school again, when the first part of the song was over. Maybe he should start his songs in the middle—the ludicrous thought flashed across his mind as he carried on with the blessing and served to lessen the tension even more. Glancing to his left, he saw his father in the front row of seats, eyes beaming with pride and encouragement from behind his glasses. Next to his father was fat Uncle Benny, the first member of the family to come over from Rumania seventeen years earlier, in 1911, who had sent for the remainder of his relatives within the year. He was known to family, friends and business associates alike as Fat Benny, but the appellation was somehow more affectionate and respectful than it was derogatory. Fat Benny was the successful one, with two candy stores in the Bronx and a fancy apartment in Washington Heights. Daniel knew he'd get a big present from Fat Benny, who had no children of his own and showered attention and gifts on his nephews at every opportunity.

Daniel wondered what his mother was doing. She sat behind him in the women's section, out of his sight. Nevertheless, he could feel her eyes digging into him. But she's not smiling like Pa and Fat Benny, he decided. She's probably waiting for me to make a mistake, just like those vultures with the *tallasim* wrapped around their heads. Then she can blame my father, claim that it's somehow his fault I didn't learn my lines. But she would not recognize a mistake if it jumped up and punched her squarely on her long nose. Her knowledge of Judaism extended no further than *bensching* candles on Friday night; even then, she gabbled the blessing so quickly that nobody ever knew if the words were correct. Not that his father attached much significance to religion, either. But the *bar mitzvah* was an important stage in a boy's life, he had told Daniel, and he was making certain that his son did not miss out.

For a moment, Daniel locked eyes with his eleven-year-old brother, Jack. Obviously aware of Daniel's discomfort, Jack was grinning mischievously, trying to throw his brother off or make him laugh. A minute earlier and Daniel knew he might have succeeded. Now the tension had dissipated. Daniel grinned back. Your turn's coming in eighteen months, was the unspoken message. See how the hell *you* do.

After finishing the blessing before the Reading of the Law, Daniel turned his attention to the Torah, following the silver pointer held by the rabbi as it skimmed across the lines. How different it was from the way he had learned it, when the vowels and musical directions were included in the text. But now he did not need them. His self-assurance was increasing with every syllable; he was even beginning to enjoy being the center of attention, with his listeners hanging on every word.

The end came quickly. Before he realized it, Daniel was chanting the final blessing, shaking the rabbi's bony hand and stepping down from the *bima*. His father stood up and clasped him around the shoulders, kissing him on both cheeks. Fat Benny patted him resoundingly on the back. Brother Jack shook his hand and wished him *mazel tov*. Trying his best to look duly awed with the importance of the occasion, Daniel walked solemnly toward the women's section. When he reached his mother, he leaned forward and kissed her politely on the cheek while she remained sitting stiffly erect, her expression aloof. Aunt Tessie—Fat Benny's wife—was more animated. She reached out with roly-poly arms and swallowed up her nephew, hugging him to her enormous breasts. His face turned red and he struggled to free himself.

"Let me take a good look at you!" Tessie cried, oblivious to the fact that the service had resumed. On the *bima*, the rabbi turned around crossly and hissed at Tessie to be quiet. She took no notice of him.

"Long trousers yet!" She turned to Daniel's mother. "Yetta, your little boy's a man already. I wish I was thirty years younger!" She reached out to embrace Daniel again, but this time he was quicker. He stepped back to evade her grasp and carried on to the next aunt.

When he returned to the empty seat between his father and Fat Benny, Daniel's face was covered in red and pink blotches from the kisses. Only his mother's lipstick had remained unsmudged on her lips.

After the service, the entire family and a group of close friends trudged through the snow to the five-room apartment on Claremont Parkway, just east of Third Avenue. Yetta Kirschbaum was first into the apartment and would not let anyone enter until she had set down a runner across the carpet leading from the front door *and* made her guests remove their wet shoes.

As each relative hugged Daniel again, they thrust small white envelopes at him. Self-consciously, he tucked the envelopes into the pockets of his new navy blue suit. Paper to one side—as his mother had stressed before they'd left for the temple that morning—gold coins to the other.

The extendable table in the living room was loaded down with every kind of meat, salad, bread and fruit. Daniel looked on enviously while the family attacked the feast. He was supposed to be the star of this show, so what was he doing being smothered by latecomers while his aunts and uncles, cousins and friends devoured everything in sight? Finally his father emerged from the line of scrimmage, holding a plate piled high with food.

"Here, *bar mitzvah* boy. Eat. You deserve it." He turned to Yetta as she joined them. "Did you hear how he sang in *shul?*" Isaac asked her. "Like a nightingale."

Yetta looked disparagingly at Daniel. "Too high. Everyone sitting around me said it was too high. Like a girl."

Daniel felt it wisest to remain silent, to fill his mouth with food instead of words. "Of course his voice was high," Isaac agreed. "He's only thirteen. What do you expect? His voice hasn't broken yet."

"He looks like twenty and eats enough for two. Look at that plate. You've given him too much. There won't be enough for anyone else."

Before she could remove the plate, Daniel hurriedly took a forkful of potato salad—which cascaded down the jacket of his new suit.

"Why are you eating with your jacket on?" Yetta demanded as she snatched the plate from her son's grasp. "You know how much that lovely suit cost? How much will it cost to get cleaned? You won't have to pay for it, will you? Go and get changed." Daniel began to move away but his mother pulled him back. "Give me the envelopes first. I'll look after them before you lose them."

Daniel felt in his pockets and pulled out the envelopes, passing them to his mother. Yetta stuffed them into a capacious purse, then pushed him toward the bedroom he shared with his brother. Left alone with her husband, she turned on Isaac. "Have you seen how much food's gone already? We'll have to bring out more."

"Let them eat," Isaac said wearily. "How many times does your son get *bar mitzvah*ed?"

"Look how much your family eats." Yetta indicated Fat Benny and Tessie, who sat in a corner of the room, their plates heaped with food. She failed to notice that her own family was accomplishing just as thorough an attack on the table. "They're eating like they've been on starvation diet ever since they got the *bar mitzvah* invitations."

Isaac turned around to look at his brother and sister-in-law. Fat Benny waved a fork in cheerful greeting before returning to attack his meal. "Let them enjoy," Isaac said. "Let everyone enjoy. Even you, Yetta. Try to enjoy yourself for once. Forget about what it's costing and enjoy." He walked away and sat down next to his brother, making a sandwich for himself from Fat Benny's overloaded plate.

Left alone, Yetta looked around, mentally calculating what was on everyone's plate, wondering whether they had put enough in the envelopes to cover what they ate. How her husband could blithely dismiss the cost of this occasion was beyond her comprehension. Did he make so much money tailoring that it did not mean a thing to him? That was not the way she had been brought up, her parents scrimping and saving until they could move away from Rivington Street where they had once shared a toilet with four other apartments. Yetta's family had come over from Russia in 1875, and she had been born in New York, a native American, a cause for pride. Rumanians, she thought, looking derisively at her husband's family. Gypsies. The thieves of Europe. Why did she ever marry into a Rumanian family?

She saw Daniel return to the living room, looking sheepish in short trousers, his big day already over with the removal of the long-trousered suit. How huge he was, already as tall as his father. If he carried on growing at this rate, they would go bankrupt trying to feed him. He would have to find a part-time job, bring in some money to help feed himself. Yetta winced as she realized how much Daniel was beginning to resemble Fat Benny. He was still far from being obese, but his legs were heavy and the short trousers, bought only six months earlier, already looked grotesquely tight. They wouldn't be thrown out, though. Isaac would make an alteration here, a stitch or two there, and her younger son, Jack, would fit into them. Just like the food on the table—or whatever remained of it after the Rumanians had finished satisfying their gypsy appetites. That would not go to waste either; they'd be eating it in one form or another for the remainder of the week.

"Daniel darling, come here!" The command came from Aunt Tessie, who was sitting with Fat Benny and Isaac.

Obediently Daniel walked across to her. As she had done in the temple, Tessie wrapped her arms around her nephew. "You were beautiful!" she cried out. "Your parents are proud of you. Right, Izzy?" she asked Daniel's father.

Isaac Kirschbaum nodded.

"Where are your long trousers?" Tessie wanted to know. "Why did you change?"

"Ma made me take off the suit," Daniel explained as he wiggled free. "Before I got it dirty."

"He got it dirty already," Yetta said, joining the small group. "Spilled potato salad all down the front. Now we'll have to pay to get it cleaned when he's worn it only once."

"So?" Tessie's eyebrows rose theatrically. "You never made anything dirty in your life, Mrs. Clean? Were your diapers always sparkling white?"

Daniel began to giggle and turned his face away. There were times when he felt it was wrong to love Fat Benny almost as much as he loved his own father. But with Tessie and his mother there was no contest. He often wished Tessie was his mother and not his aunt.

Yetta flushed at Tessie's words, then slowly raised a hand to her forehead. "All of a sudden I don't feel so good."

"Migraine again?" Tessie asked, instantly feigning sympathy. "You still get them?"

"I think one's coming," Yetta answered weakly. Diapers! she thought. Only her husband's family would talk about something like diapers in company; but what else could you expect from a bunch of Rumanians?

Tessie turned around and glanced at Fat Benny. Slowly, her right eyelid lowered in a conspiratorial wink. Just as secretively Fat Benny winked back. Again with the hypochondria; illness for attention. Fat Benny knew he should have kept a closer watch on his brother when he had arrived in the United States, and not let him get married to the first spinster who could get her claws into him. Fat Benny blamed himself in part for his brother's marriage to Yetta. He hadn't taken into account that Isaac lacked his own basic instinct for survival; Isaac was quieter, less self-assured. Fat Benny had let Isaac go his own way too much, even to the point of allowing himself to be introduced to Yetta by a *shadchan*, a matchmaker. Yetta, then thirty years old and unmarried, had not let go. At thirty, even a Rumanian tailor had looked inviting. Fat Benny was grudgingly forced to admit that Isaac seemed content enough having his life planned for him by a domineering wife; but it certainly didn't mean that either he or Tessie had to like Yetta.

"Sing something for us," Fat Benny told Daniel.

Daniel's stomach contracted. Hadn't he sung enough for one day already? The morning was for singing; the afternoon was for eating. "I don't feel like singing anymore, Uncle Benny."

"Come on," Fat Benny cajoled. "We all want to hear you. Right?" He turned to look at Isaac and Tessie, who nodded enthusiastically.

Daniel knew he wouldn't be allowed to get out of it now. "What do you want me to sing?" he asked Fat Benny. Daniel could never make up his mind who was fatter—Benny or Tessie. The fat was located in different places, which made it difficult to tell. Tessie was huge around the breasts and arms while Fat Benny seemed to store his excess weight in his stomach and thighs.

"Anything. Whatever you'd like us to hear."

"Ma?" Daniel turned to his mother. "What do you want me to sing?"

"I don't care," Yetta replied. "I won't be here anyway. I'm going to lie down for a while."

Isaac looked up sharply. "What about our guests?" he protested. "You can't leave."

"They're taking care of themselves very well," Yetta said sarcastically as she looked at the crowd of people still around the food table. "I'm going to take two aspirin with a glass of water and lie down."

Tessie turned to Fat Benny, who smiled knowingly. They both had a good idea what Yetta was going to do, and it had no connection with aspirin. In the privacy of the bedroom, she would open all the envelopes and count out who had given what; she would never forget who had and who had not given up to her expections.

"Daniel, you got a watch?" Fat Benny asked.

"First you should ask if he can tell time," Tessie smiled.

"Of course he can tell time," Isaac said in defense of his son.

"You got a watch?" Fat Benny repeated.

Daniel shook his head.

"Here." Fat Benny took off his own gold watch and held it out enticingly to Daniel. "You sing one nice song and this is yours."

Daniel eyed the watch eagerly. He was wise enough to know he would never see any of the money that had been given as *bar mitzvah* presents. That would be used to pay for the party, and the remainder would be put away for that rainy day his mother was always talking about. The watch he would be allowed to keep, even if it were gold. "What do you want me to sing?"

"Anything. Something you sing in the school choir."

Daniel gazed around the living room. The rabbi was still there, back at the table for his second or third helping—his mother would know exactly, down to the last piece of potato salad or slice of meat. "Anything?" he asked.

"Anything," Fat Benny encouraged.

Daniel suddenly grinned. The tiny imp inside of him, busily raking up mischief, knew exactly how to get the rabbi away from the table. Closing his eyes in concentration, he began to sing in the same clear voice he had used in the temple.

"*Ave Maria . . .*"

The sounds of conversation, of rattling cutlery and crockery in the living room, dimmed immediately. Attention was focused on Daniel, who stood alone, continuing the hymn. The rabbi was the first to react.

"What kind of music is this to sing in a Jewish home?" he demanded.

Daniel faltered, and then stopped. He had gotten exactly the reception he had expected.

The rabbi put down his plate, held his hands up toward the ceiling as though God lived in the apartment above and cried out, "For a *bar mitzvah* boy to sing a song like that, a *goyishe* hymn! May God forgive you!"

"What's the matter with a song like that?" Isaac Kirschbaum asked. "You never heard Enrico Caruso sing Eleazar in *La Juive?* It was his favorite role." He stood up and walked purposefully toward the phonograph in the corner of the room. "Here, I'll play some of the music for you," he offered, brandishing a seventy-eight record.

"Don't do me any favors," the rabbi exclaimed. "Let Caruso sing what he likes, but no Jewish child should sing *goyishe* hymns."

"Music has no religion," Isaac argued. Daniel could not remember seeing his father so animated. He knew his father loved music, adored it to the point where he would hide himself away in the corner with the phonograph and listen to Caruso for hours on end, but he had never known him to become so worked up about the subject. Daniel was enjoying the performance. "If Caruso could use his beautiful voice to portray a Jewish patriarch, what is wrong with my Daniel singing 'Ave Maria'?"

The rabbi waved aside all of Isaac's arguments. "I'm not staying in this house another second." He strode toward the bedroom where he had left his coat. Daniel, Isaac, Fat Benny and Tessie followed. Throwing open the door, the rabbi discovered Yetta Kirschbaum sitting at the dressing table, all the envelopes torn open in front of her, sorting paper money and gold coins into neat piles while she wrote down what each person had given.

"Aaah!" the rabbi screamed, horrified by what he saw. "Singing like *goyim* isn't enough for them! Now they've got to count money and write as well on *Shabbos!*"

Daniel darted past the appalled man, picked up a black coat and held it out to him. The rabbi snatched at it and rushed from the apartment.

Fat Benny was grinning as he turned to his brother. "Thank God. Now we can smoke and play some cards!" He looked around for other players, then remembered something. "Here," he said, holding out the gold watch to Daniel. "Take it. You deserve it."

Not in the least embarrassed at having been caught counting the money, Yetta returned to the living room. She was smiling and Isaac knew that they had more than broken even.

That evening Daniel lost the watch given to him by Fat

Benny. While the adults continued to play cards, Daniel took fifty cents given to him by his father and, with his brother Jack for company, walked along Claremont Parkway towards Hymie's ice cream parlor on the corner of Washington Avenue.

"How much did you make?" Jack asked, kicking snow as he walked alongside his older brother.

"Three hundred and twenty dollars." Daniel couldn't keep the pride out of his voice. In one morning of singing he had brought in more than his father earned in months. Pity there would be no repeat performances. Unless he reached eighty-three, of course, he remembered, when the real orthodox Jews had a second *bar mitzvah.* Only they wouldn't bring him gifts then; they'd give him walking sticks and wheelchairs. "And this, of course." He pulled back the sleeve of his coat and showed off Fat Benny's watch.

"How did it feel to stand up in *shul* like that and sing?" Jack wanted to know. His thoughts were on his own *bar mitzvah,* still eighteen months in the future but near enough to make him anxious.

"Nothing to it," Daniel lied. "Just like being in the school choir."

"Weren't you scared even a little bit?"

"What's to be scared about? I know I can sing," Daniel said, feeling smug now that the ordeal was in the past. "Singing's singing, doesn't matter what."

Jack took time to digest his brother's response. "I suppose it's all right for you. You can sing to begin with. I can't." He changed the subject quickly. "You shouldn't have done what you did to the rabbi, though. Ma was mad when she found out why he'd rushed into the bedroom."

Daniel gave a wry smile at the memory of his "Ave Maria." He'd sung it before, at school performances. His mother had never complained then.

At the corner of Third Avenue, streetcars and automobiles rolled past, sending up sprays of dirty, icy water. There was no break in the steady stream of traffic, and finally the two boys began to climb the steps to the elevated Third Avenue station to use the overpass. The station attendant, making change for the nickel turnstiles, watched the boys warily. When he recognized that they had no intention of taking the train, that they were using his station simply to avoid the traffic on Third Avenue, he yelled at them, sending them scurrying down the other side.

The counterman at Hymie's nodded in recognition when Daniel and Jack entered. "You got money?" he asked as they sat down.

Daniel proudly showed the half dollar.

"What do you want?"

"How much are your egg creams?"

The counterman pointed to the list behind him. "Six cents. Ten cents if you want real eggs."

"Two. With real eggs." Daniel knew he shouldn't be feeling hungry. He had eaten enough during the afternoon to fill his stomach for the remainder of the month, but the walk along Claremont Parkway had renewed his hunger. He supposed he could have stayed in the apartment and eaten more, but that would have been an unsafe course to follow. His cousins had been taken home, and the remaining adults were partnered off into various card games. Had he stayed, he was certain his mother would have sent him to bed, *bar mitzvah* boy or not.

The counterman sat down two glasses. "Twenty cents."

Daniel paid and began to drink, not stopping until he had emptied the glass. He waited for Jack to finish, then they both stood to leave.

"Where to?" Jack asked.

Daniel shrugged. "Might as well hack around for a while. They won't miss us at home."

Outside Hymie's they turned right, walking past the huge public school on the other corner of Washington Avenue. Daniel looked at the imposing facade of the school and wondered if the heat would be back on when he returned to his own school on Monday. Something had malfunctioned with the furnace on Friday morning and the entire school had been sent home early. When he had marched in with his brother, tramping snow all over the freshly cleaned apartment, his mother had clutched both hands to her heart, screaming how her sons were trying to kill her with their thoughtlessness, how she was working to give Daniel the finest *bar mitzvah* party of anyone in the entire family and all he and his brother could do was walk snow all through the apartment. He and Jack had fled, not returning until it was almost time for dinner and their father had arrived home from work.

"Hey, Cherrybum!"

Daniel stopped walking and turned around slowly. Ten yards away he recognized Tommy Mulvaney—a tall, gangly, red-haired boy from the grade above. He was with two other boys whom Daniel had never seen before.

"My name is Kirschbaum," Daniel said irritably.

"Kirschbaum, Cherrybum, what's the big difference? They all stand for the same thing," Tommy said nonchalantly. "Just so long as you know who I'm talking to, it doesn't matter." He ambled closer to Daniel and Jack, thumbs hooked into the pockets of his long trousers, winter coat held open in defiance of the cold. Daniel felt totally naked in the short trousers. "Had your big day today?" Tommy asked. "We saw you and your whole tribe leaving your temple."

Beside him, Daniel felt Jack tense up, ready to flee for his life. He held out a hand, motioning the younger boy to stop, reassuring him. "Why don't you bug out of it, Tommy? We're not giving you any trouble."

Tommy grinned good-naturedly, enjoying the confrontation. "We don't want to give you any trouble either, Cherrybum. Just want to congratulate you, that's all." As he finished speaking, he and his two friends dropped to their knees and came up with hard-packed snowballs. Before either Daniel or Jack could take evasive action, they were blasted with a salvo of white. Daniel scraped snow off his face and yelled at Jack. "Go home! Run!" Then he launched himself at Tommy.

Whatever Daniel might have lacked in years, he made up for in size and strength. He was big enough to have been chosen second-string catcher for the school baseball team, playing with boys two years his senior; next summer he would have the first team slot to himself. He hit Tommy squarely in the chest with his shoulder, knocking the ginger-haired boy into a lamp post. Tommy yelled out in surprise and pain as he was slammed into the post, then the other two boys jumped onto Daniel. One wrapped arms around his shoulders from behind, while the other pummeled his face. Daniel ducked and lashed out with his feet. One boot came in contact with bone. A ringing scream of agony followed, music to Daniel's ears, then the boy attacked even more fiercely. Back on his feet, Tommy Mulvaney also joined in, and the weight of three assailants dragged Daniel down into the wet snow. Two kicks followed, something tore at his left wrist and then he vaguely saw three figures running away.

A man helped him to his feet, dusting off the snow. Daniel's knees were scraped and bleeding. He looked up and recognized one of the old men from the temple. Jack was nowhere in sight.

"Such a thing, to fight on your *bar mitzvah* day. Is that nice?" the man chided him gently.

Daniel did not hear the words of admonition. He was too busy feeling his left wrist where the gold watch had been. The wrist was bare. He mumbled something to the old man, shook himself free and began to run toward the apartment building. When he reached Third Avenue he dashed across the road, dodging between vehicles. A streetcar's bell clanged in warning but Daniel heard nothing. All he could think of was what he would say to his parents, to Fat Benny. A gold watch. Solid gold. Given to him only that afternoon and lost already.

As he neared the apartment block, three figures emerged from the lobby and began walking toward him—Fat Benny, Isaac Kirschbaum and Jack. Isaac's face was full of fear, which disappeared the instant he saw his older son.

"What was happening with you? Jack ran in just now and said you were in a fight, that you were being murdered."

"Just a fight."

"With who?"

Thank God he doesn't know, Daniel thought. Jack had used enough sense to keep his mouth shut. "Just a fight; it doesn't matter who with." Daniel hated to think what his father would do if he knew the fight had been with Tommy Mulvaney, whose father was a police sergeant, a powerful man in the neighborhood.

"Who won?" was all Fat Benny wanted to know. It was the

obvious question for Fat Benny to ask. He was a regular spectator at the fights and loved to regale his nephews with dramatic tales of right crosses and left hooks, split eyebrows and broken noses.

"Nobody won," Daniel replied. "I ran."

Fat Benny looked disappointed, but Isaac nodded his head approvingly. "Sometimes to run is wiser than to stay and fight. Come inside and get warm. We were worried about you."

Daniel allowed himself to be escorted into the building. Only Fat Benny and Tessie remained of the *bar mitzvah* guests. Daniel asked where his mother was and Isaac replied that she was still lying down with the migraine caused by the day's excitement. She did not know about the fight, he added, and he was not going to tell her.

In the room he shared with Jack, Daniel told his brother what had happened. Jack listened anxiously, drawing in his breath when he heard about the gold watch being stolen. "What are you going to do?"

"Get it back before anyone finds out," Daniel vowed. "Tonight, when everyone's asleep."

"Ma's asleep already."

"I know. Uncle Benny and Aunt Tessie will be going soon. Then I'm going out again."

Jack looked at him apprehensively. "You'll get into more trouble. Why don't you just tell Pa and let him handle it?"

Daniel wished he could. That would be the easy way out. But his father was among the most gentle of men; he would be angry on his son's account, but not angry enough to confront Tommy's father and retrieve the gold watch. And if he were to tell his wife, Daniel would never hear the end of it. And he would probably be banned from going out for a week, a month, a year, who knew with his mother? She didn't like him out on the streets as it was, mixing with other boys. Every scratch he got playing baseball was cause for more nagging. And playing tag in the streets with the other kids could give him anything from smallpox to malaria.

While Jack watched, Daniel opened his closet. He rummaged around on the floor, pushing aside the catcher's mitt, mask and chest protector bought for his last birthday by Fat

Benny. Finally he found what he was seeking.

"What are you going to do with that?" Jack asked incredulously.

Daniel swung the baseball bat slowly through the air, a flat, level motion that would have won approval from the school coach. "What do you think I'm going to do with it?" He placed the bat on the bed, then opened the door an inch and peered out. Fat Benny and Tessie were just leaving.

Daniel waited another thirty minutes, until his father had gone to bed, then he picked up the bat and tiptoed across the living room to the front door. He closed it quietly and scurried down the stairs, out onto the street. It had started to snow again and he felt foolish carrying summer's bat in the middle of a blizzard. He tucked it underneath his coat, holding it tightly against his chest.

Behind the building where Tommy Mulvaney lived was a dark, narrow alleyway. Daniel entered it and left the bat leaning beside a garbage can, then went into the building through the back entrance, walking up to the second floor where the Mulvaneys lived. He knocked on the door and waited.

"Who is it?" a woman's voice asked.

"Daniel Kirschbaum. I'm a friend of Tommy's. Can I see him please?"

The door opened slowly and a middle-aged woman stared out. "Must you come around so late, or is it a matter of life and death? We're all going to bed." She made him wait in the hallway while she went to call her son.

"Hi, Cherrybum. What do you want?" was Tommy's greeting. Daniel saw he was not wearing the watch and wondered where he had hidden it. Bet he doesn't even know it's real gold.

"I've got to speak to you, Tommy. Not here, though. In private." Daniel put as much urgency as he could into his words.

Tommy turned back toward the living room where his mother was standing. "Got to go out for five minutes. Business." He pulled a coat from the hall closet and followed Daniel outside.

Daniel led the way through the rear of the building into the alleyway, stopping when he reached the garbage can where he had left the bat. "I want that watch back, Tommy. It was a gift and I want it back."

"A gift? For your *bar, bar* . . ." He stumbled on the word.

"For my *bar mitzvah*, that's right. I want it back right now."

Tommy squared his shoulders. "And who's going to make me give it back? You?" He put up his fists, moving them in slow circles like an old-fashioned, bare-knuckled boxer. Daniel stared, mesmerized by the older boy's big bony knuckles.

"Come on then, Cherrybum," Tommy taunted. "Make me give you back your goddamned stupid watch."

Daniel stepped back and reached out to the garbage can. His right hand came in contact with the cold, wet wooden handle of the bat and he pulled it out triumphantly. Tommy's eyes widened when he saw the weapon. Daniel swung the bat, full force, at the other boy's head. At the very moment that Tommy ducked, Daniel realized he'd come close to crushing the boy's skull. He changed his tactics, using the bat like a bayonet, jabbing instead of swinging. For all his anger, he did not want to seriously injure the other boy; all he wanted to do was scare him into returning the gold watch.

The fat end of the bat caught Tommy in the solar plexus. He doubled over, gasping for breath as the wind was slammed out of him. Daniel jabbed again, hitting Tommy on the arm, then the thighs, prodding him back along the dark, snow-covered alleyway.

"Give me back the watch! Give me back the watch!" Each frenzied demand was punctuated by a thrust of the bat. Tommy staggered back, arms flailing in a futile attempt at self-defense until his retreat was stopped by a brick wall.

"Give it back!" Daniel yelled. Seeing Tommy cornered, Daniel stopped jabbing and began to swing again, short round motions which brought the bat down with enough force to bruise but not to break.

"It's at home, for Christ's sake! I haven't got it here!" Tommy screamed. "Sweet Jesus, will you stop before you break my arms!"

"I'll break your face if you don't give me back that watch!"

Lights in the apartment windows overlooking the alleyway began to glow. A window screeched open. A man's voice bellowed down through the icy air, demanding to know what was happening. Daniel took no notice, but Tommy recognized a chance of rescue. He looked up and yelled, "Help! Police! I'm being attacked! Police!"

Daniel took one final swing with the bat, slamming wood against Tommy's shins. Then he turned around and fled, not stopping until he reached the safety of his own apartment. He staggered across the living room and into the bedroom, where he dropped the bat onto the floor and sank down on the bed, his breath coming in long, painful sighs.

"Well?" Jack asked excitedly. "Where's the watch?"

"I haven't got it."

"Didn't you see him?"

"I think I killed him." Daniel realized how loud his voice sounded and dropped it to a whisper, scared of waking his parents. "There'll be cops round here soon. They'll take me away."

Jack pulled the sheets up to his chin, alarm showing in his brown eyes. "I'll visit you in prison. I promise."

Still in his coat, Daniel lay back on the bed, staring miserably up at the ceiling. Now what the hell was going to happen? He hadn't got the watch back. He'd just beaten that stupid Mulvaney kid half to death. There wasn't even any pleasure in that. What was even worse, Tommy's father was a cop, a sergeant. What chance did he have, with a tailor for a father, when Tommy's father was a police sergeant?

Hearing sounds from the other bedroom, he realized he must have woken up his parents. Quickly, he took off his coat, undressed and slipped into bed. When the door opened and his father looked in, the light was out and both boys were apparently sleeping.

The bedroom door opened again before seven the following morning. This time, though, Isaac Kirschbaum was not checking whether his sons were asleep. His face was grim, and he called Daniel to get up.

Daniel sat up in bed, slowly remembering the events of the

previous night, associating them with the troubled expression on his father's face.

"Sergeant Mulvaney's here with his son, Daniel. They want to see you."

Daniel swung his feet slowly to the floor. Jack was also awake, witnessing the drama with frightened eyes, already wondering how old he had to be before he could visit his brother in prison. Daniel threw his dressing gown over his pajamas and followed his father into the living room. His mother was sitting on the sofa, her face pale and stern. Across from her sat Tommy with his parents. Sergeant Mulvaney, who had come off duty only an hour earlier, was still in uniform.

"This is my older son, Daniel," Isaac said softly, pushing the boy into the center of the room.

Tommy Mulvaney's father had a solid, rough-hewn face that was dominated by piercing blue eyes. As Daniel looked nervously at him, the face was set in a grim, immovable expression. Daniel had seen Mulvaney before, but never on duty; the precinct he worked out of was in Manhattan. Then Daniel noticed that the police sergeant was carrying neither his gun nor his nightstick. He began to breathe easier. It was not an official call.

Sergeant Mulvaney nodded his head a fraction at Isaac's introduction. "So you're the one my son calls Daniel Cherrybum, are you?"

"Kirschbaum," Daniel said automatically.

"I know. Cherrybum's what Tommy's been calling you ever since I got back from my shift." He pushed his son toward Daniel. "Tommy's got something to say to you."

Tommy Mulvaney shuffled self-consciously toward Daniel. A yard away, he reached into his pocket and brought out the gold watch given to Daniel by Fat Benny. "I'm sorry."

Just as awkwardly, Daniel reached out and took the watch, slipping it onto his left wrist.

"Now if you'll apologize to my son for using him for your batting practice," Mulvaney said, "I think we can wrap up this unpleasant business. Truth is," he added, in an aside to Isaac, "I couldn't find a spot to belt him that wasn't black and blue already."

Daniel looked first to his mother and then to his father, seeking guidance. Isaac nodded. "Sorry, Tommy." Daniel held out his hand, surprised when the ginger-haired boy took it.

Isaac suddenly seemed to come to life. "We were just going to have breakfast," he said cheerfully to the Mulvaneys. "Would you like to join us, perhaps?"

Sergeant Mulvaney looked speculatively at Isaac, then at his own wife. "Sure. Why not? What were you planning on making?"

"Leftovers from yesterday," Daniel said spontaneously, and burst out laughing.

Chapter Two

Daniel squatted comfortably behind home plate and pummeled the pocket of the catcher's mitt with his right fist while he waited for the pitch. One out in the final inning and the tying run was on third. Somehow they had to stop that run from coming in. The pitcher kicked and delivered. High. Daniel jerked up the glove hand and snagged the ball. The count went to 1-0.

This was Daniel's second season on the school team. Since the previous year he'd grown two inches and put on another fifteen pounds, making him a natural for the catcher's spot. So what if the coach had once laughingly remarked that his thighs looked like a couple of bouncing watermelons as he chugged around the basepaths. He was built for endurance, not speed. And when the team needed the long ball, it was to Daniel's bat that they looked for power.

The pitcher delivered high again and the count moved to 2-0. The next two pitches were fouled away, ricocheting back off the screen, and the count evened at 2-2. A fast ball, inside, which had the batter scrambling out of the box, stretched the count full. Daniel knew the decision was his. Opting to play for safety, he held out his bare right hand and called for a pitch-out, in the hope that the next batter would hit into a double play. The pitcher nodded that he'd got the signal, went into his stretch and came in with a three-quarter-speed fastball right down the middle of the plate. Behind the catcher's mask, Daniel's mouth gaped wide in amazement. The batter swung at the gift pitch and lofted the ball toward left field. On third base, the runner tagged up while he waited to see if the ball would be caught. Hands on hips, Daniel watched the ball begin to drop. Tommy Mulvaney, playing left field, was backing up, glove raised, free hand guarding his eyes against the strong sun. The ball fell and Tommy made a running grab.

As Tommy's glove swallowed the ball, the third base coach

yelled at the runner to take off. The player needed no urging. Head down, arms pumping like pistons, spikes kicking up dirt from the basepath, he came barreling in toward home plate. Tommy took two steps and threw. Pursued by the ball, the runner stretched his legs for that extra burst of speed. Daniel watched the throw bounce past third base on a true line. He stepped onto the basepath in front of home, blocking the plate as he waited for the ball. Runner and ball arrived almost simultaneously. The runner went into his slide, spikes glinting threateningly. Daniel grabbed at the ball the instant the runner slammed into him. He felt a burning pain in his left thigh and knew he'd been spiked.

"You son of a bitch!" he yelled. With as much force as he could muster, he swung around and slammed the ball into the runner's back, sending him flying.

"You're out!" screamed the home plate umpire.

The runner scrambled to his feet and leaped at Daniel, who knocked aside the first punch with his glove while he landed two short, chopping rights to the body. Other players dived in between. Daniel felt arms around him, dragging him away. He stumbled and fell, clutching at his thigh, feeling his hands wet with blood from the spike wounds. His team mates gathered around, breaking apart only when the team coach pushed his way through. He knelt down beside Daniel and examined the injured thigh. Then, with the aid of another teacher, he helped Daniel off the field and into the dressing room.

Tommy Mulvaney came by as the coach was swabbing the spike wounds with disinfectant. "Nice tag, Cherrybum," he said, grinning at him.

Daniel bit his lips as the disinfectant burned into his leg, but he managed to grin back. "Maybe the throw had something to do with it, copper." Since the incident with Fat Benny's watch, a bond of friendship had grown between the police sergeant's and the tailor's sons. Despite it, though, Daniel had never managed to persuade Tommy to call him anything other than Cherrybum. In retaliation, after learning that Tommy was intent on following his father into the police department, Daniel had tagged him with the nickname of "copper."

"You all right?" Tommy asked, looking over the coach's

shoulder as he began to apply a bandage to the injured thigh.

"I will be," Daniel grunted. "That son of a bitch must have been sharpening his spikes for a week." He saw the coach look up, surprised at his language, but paid no attention. As the injured hero of the game, he was entitled to say what he liked; he just hoped the other kid had a bruise the size of a grapefruit where he'd creamed him with the ball.

"Probably couldn't resist such a fat, juicy target," Tommy joked as he walked toward the shower. "I'll wait for you. Help the wounded get home safely."

"That's okay. Jack's outside."

"I'll still wait. Three of us will be more than your mother can handle."

Despite the fire that burned inside his leg, Daniel gave an appreciative smile. When his mother saw him limp through the front door, she'd make him swear on his life that he would never play again. But with Tommy present, she might not go into her act.

Tommy and Jack walked slowly to allow Daniel to keep up as they made their way home. Jack opened the door and the three boys walked into the living room. "Ma! We're home!" Jack shouted.

The bedroom door opened and Yetta Kirschbaum appeared, wearing a dressing gown. An icepack was held to her head. "Must you be so noisy?" she complained. "Can't you see I've got a headache?"

"Okay," Daniel said, perversely relieved that his mother was ill again. Maybe she wouldn't bother about him now. "We'll be quiet." He began to walk toward the kitchen, but Yetta called him back.

"What's the matter with your leg? Why are you limping?"

"Who's limping?"

"You. What did you do?"

"It's nothing, Ma, for crying out loud." Daniel looked to his brother and Tommy for support. "Did I do anything to my leg? Will you tell her?" Tommy and Jack shook their heads in a negative reply. "Why don't you go back to bed, Ma? You'll feel much better if you lie down some more."

"First I want to see your leg."

"Ma, it's only a scratch. That's all. Just a scratch."

She dropped the icebag to the floor and marched over to her older son. "Before it was nothing. Now it's just a scratch. Let me see."

Rolling his eyes in exasperation, Daniel pulled up his trouser leg and let his mother see the bandage.

"Why the bandage if it's just a scratch?" Yetta demanded.

"The coach bandaged it. He got carried away."

"What the matter, you were so badly injured playing your stupid game that you couldn't bandage it by yourself?" She untied the ends and began to unroll the bandage."

"Jesus, Ma, will you watch it? You're hurting."

"Don't Jesus in this house." With the bandage off, she looked in horror at the four punctures. "The doctor's coming around right now to see that, young man. You're not going anywhere until he's checked it out."

"The hell he is," Daniel protested, jumping up and hobbling away. He had an inbuilt fear of the medical profession, going back to childhood days when the doctor had been his most frequent visitor. Not because he had been a sickly child, but because every time he coughed or sneezed, itched or cried, Yetta would feel duty-bound to call the doctor. Determined to justify himself, the poor man would always prescribe some medication for Daniel; normally the cure was worse than the imagined ailment. But as far as Yetta Kirschbaum was concerned, doctors were to be revered on a plateau next to godliness.

"Tell her I'm all right, Tommy," Daniel pleaded. "Tell her how this often happens. No one's died yet."

"It happens often, Mrs. Kirschbaum," Tommy said. He wished he were enough of an actor to inject more conviction into his voice.

"Not to my son it doesn't," Yetta retorted as she reached out for the phone.

"They use a special steel for the spikes," Daniel said, clinging to even the most obvious fantasy. "It's guaranteed to be germ-free."

"That's right, Ma," Jack cut in. "The spikes are made from a specially treated steel. It's all right to get cut by them. The same metal they use for medical instruments."

Yetta's fingers spun the dial. "Doctor Oderberg? It's Yetta Kirschbaum. Could you stop by, please? Daniel's had a terrible accident. His leg's been cut to ribbons . . . Yes, that's right. Ribbons. Clean through to the bone."

"There goes the damned game this weekend," Daniel muttered.

"And while you're coming, could you perhaps bring something for my migraine headache? I've had it for almost a week. Thank you."

Tommy began to edge toward the door. Irish family life was traumatic enough, but when it came to drama and hysterics the Irish had nothing on the Jews. "See you at school tomorrow," he said to Daniel. "Got to go. The old man's taking us to the movies tonight."

"Thanks for nothing, copper."

"Goodbye, Mrs. Kirschbaum," Tommy called out. "Hope your migraine gets better real soon."

Yetta called Tommy back into the room. "Will your mother and father be attending the school's parents' night?"

"Yes."

"Give them my best wishes and tell them I look forward to seeing them there."

Daniel didn't even say goodbye. He just sat looking disconsolately at the spike wounds while he wondered what nightmare cure the doctor would dream up this time. Damn that runner! He should have tagged him in the head with the ball, not in the back. They'd play against the same team again before the summer was over. Daniel consoled himself by dreaming of the next confrontation at home plate.

Daniel fared no better at the parents' night than he had expected to. His father—after rushing home from work in Manhattan's garment district to change into his best suit—and mother sat quietly as the school principal, Ewen McIlroy, ran through Daniel's academic record.

"Have you given any thought to what Daniel will do when he leaves school?" McIlroy asked the Kirschbaums.

Yetta answered. "He's going to be a doctor. The first one in our family," she added proudly.

"I don't think so." McIlroy's voice was gentle. This was the time of year he dreaded, when all too often it fell upon his shoulders to burst parents' dreams about their children's capabilities.

"What do you mean?" Yetta demanded.

"Mrs. Kirschbaum, to go to medical school you have to attend college first. To be brutally frank, I doubt if Daniel even has the academic ability to graduate from junior high school."

Yetta's mouth sagged. There was no need for words. She just sat staring at McIlroy, waiting for him to continue.

"Do you ever read the reports your son brings home?"

"We read them," Isaac said, answering for Yetta who still sat dumbstruck.

"Daniel has finished in the bottom third of his class every time," McIlroy explained. "Jack is a completely different story. He's head and shoulders above the rest of his class. Jack is your doctor, your lawyer, your scientist, whatever he sets his mind to being. But Daniel is an academic washout."

Yetta struggled to find her voice again. "Don't call my son a washout, Mr. McIlroy. Daniel's going to be a doctor, no matter what you say or think."

"If you can find a medical school that accepts a boy who left school in the tenth grade, Mrs. Kirschbaum, please be sure to let me know."

Isaac held up a hand in a rare gesture of authority. "What would you suggest, Mr. McIlroy?"

The school principal's brow creased as he pondered the question. He felt sorry for the father, having to tell him that his older son would never amount to anything. The immigrants always took it hardest, he knew. They always put their hopes on their children, especially the European Jews. They wanted their children to do better than they had done; when the children failed, the grief was doubled. "He's good at two things, Mr. Kirschbaum."

Yetta brightened immediately at the words. "Then he'll do one of those things."

"Play baseball?" McIlroy queried softly.

"God forbid," Yetta gasped.

"And the other thing?" Isaac cut in quickly. "What's that?"
"He has the finest voice of almost anyone we've had in the school choir during my time here," McIlroy replied. "You've been here for the concerts. You've heard him sing."
Yetta wasn't impressed with this either, but Isaac smiled warmly as he remembered how beautifully Daniel had sung his *bar mitzvah* portion. Like a nightingale, every note clear, reaching into each corner of the temple with that wonderful voice. "How would one go about such a career?"
"With difficulty." McIlroy regretted instantly that the answer seemed flippant. These people were coming to him for advice. "The competition and the years of training are probably every bit as difficult as in medical school, and the chances of success are stacked against even the most talented musicians. I wouldn't really recommend it. It's not a course that promises much happiness or security."
"Then what?" Isaac asked, his dream shattered.
"Get Daniel into a trade school. He may be good with his hands, so let him learn how to use them. At a trade school he'll be given tests to determine what work he's most suited for. That's the best alternative I can suggest." Having imparted the grim news, McIlroy stood up, eager to move on to the next set of parents; perhaps he would have better news for them. Yetta pulled him back by the arm.
"You'll see," she said, standing up to wag a finger in McIlroy's face. "We've got a very influential family. You never heard of my brother-in-law, Mister Benjamin Kirschbaum?"
McIlroy shook his head. "I'm afraid I haven't." Even Isaac took a couple of seconds to identify Mister Benjamin Kirschbaum with Fat Benny.
"He's very rich, very influential," Yetta said. "He'll make certain our Daniel does well. He'll probably take him into the family business."
"What kind of business is that?" McIlroy asked.
"He's a big man in the tobacco and confectionery business. Retail. How come you never heard of him? Ah," she waved a hand deprecatingly at McIlroy. "What would you know anyway? You're just a teacher. Isaac, take me home. All of a

sudden I don't feel so good."

Isaac looked at McIlroy and shrugged his shoulders apologetically. The school principal watched the Kirschbaums leave while he wondered what the retail tobacco and confectionery business comprised. A candy store? That's where Daniel belonged anyway. He'd be better off there, where he wouldn't have to live up to impossible expectations.

Daniel was reading the sports section of the *News* when his parents arrived home. Hearing the front door open, he quickly rearranged the paper, leaving it open on a news page.

"How did it go?" he asked. "What did Mr. McIlroy have to say?"

"You'll be the death of me," Yetta said. "Why can't you be clever like your brother Jack? Now I'll never be able to hold my head up in the family because I've got a fool for a son."

Daniel switched his gaze to his father. "Didn't go well, huh?" he said quietly.

"Not at all well, Daniel," Isaac answered. "You're not a scholar. But," he added philosophically, "then neither was I."

"Is that what you want?" Yetta snapped, turning on her husband. "That he should turn out like you? Working ten, twelve hours a day, and for what? For nothing, that's what!" She looked back at Daniel again. "All the sacrifices we made for you, all the things we went without, and this is how you pay us back!"

"Leave the boy alone," Isaac interrupted, tired of his wife's nagging. "We didn't make any sacrifices for him."

"No?" Yetta swung around again. "If I hadn't married into your Rumanian family and had your children, I could have had my choice of anyone. I could be wearing furs and diamonds now, not *shmattes* like this." She indicated the dress she was wearing, brushing a sleeve distastefully. "I would have married a rich man and be living now in Riverdale, not on Claremont Parkway."

Isaac ignored the tirade. He walked away and picked up the telephone. Yetta's voice followed him, demanding to know whom he was calling. He told her he was going to speak to his brother.

"What can he do?" Yetta asked. A Rumanian turns to

another Rumanian for help; the blind leading the blind.

"Mister Benjamin Kirschbaum. Don't you remember mentioning him to Daniel's principal? Your brother-in-law? The influential man in the tobacco and confectionery business? Retail?" Isaac reminded his wife. "Maybe he can give us some advice about what's best for Daniel." He got through to Tessie, spoke a few words with her and then asked to speak with his brother. He arranged for Fat Benny to come over the following evening. When he hung up the telephone, he was smiling.

"So what if you're not a scholar," he said to Daniel. "Neither was my brother Benny. And he hasn't done too badly for himself. He'll tell you that he didn't speak a single word of English when he came to this country eighteen years ago, and now he owns two shops."

"I didn't speak a single word of English when I came to this country eighteen years ago, and now I own two shops," Fat Benny said proudly as he looked across the table at Daniel.

He stopped speaking long enough to stir the cup of tea in front of him. "School doesn't mean a thing, Daniel. It's what you've got up here that counts." He patted his head. "You want a summer job?"

Daniel leaned forward eagerly. "Doing what?"

"I've got a friend up in the mountains. Joey Bloom. He owns a hotel up there, and he takes on kids during the summer to wait tables. He'll pay you and throw in your board and lodging. You'll meet other kids your own age and have a good time."

"Joey Bloom's a gangster," Yetta broke in sharply. "Daniel's not going to work for him."

Fat Benny looked angrily at his brother's wife. "Joey's nothing of the kind. That sort of talk is a rumor put out by people who are jealous of the way Joey's got on."

Daniel listened intently to the argument. He'd heard stories about Joey Bloom, Fat Benny's friend, a small-time racketeer and bookmaker who'd been forced out of New York by bigger, tougher competition and had invested his money in the hotel in the mountains. Fat Benny and Tessie stayed there often, and Daniel had overheard them talking about whom they had met.

Jack Diamond had been there one time; another time Louie Buchalter had been staying for the week Fat Benny and Tessie were there.

"How does working the summer in your friend Bloom's hotel help Daniel for when he leaves school?" Isaac asked, eager to shut off the argument.

"Worry about him leaving school when it happens," Fat Benny answered. "Daniel's a bright boy, he doesn't need a formal education. He'll do well in whatever he chooses."

"To play ball he chooses," Yetta said.

"Then let him play ball!" Fat Benny exclaimed, as if it were the simplest thing in the world.

"You know anyone with the Giants or the Yankees?" Daniel asked.

Fat Benny considered saying yes, but then he shook his head. "Just a couple of guys on the gate, that's all. Baseball's not for a *Yiddishe* boy." He picked up the cup, saw it was empty and waited for Yetta to refill it. "Want to come into the candy store business?" he asked suddenly.

It was Daniel's turn to shake his head. He knew of the long hours involved in the candy store business, early morning until late at night, seven days a week. Fat Benny and Tessie had shared those hours until they had been able to afford part-time help. Even then, Fat Benny had put in more hours than he needed to, trying to keep an eye on his employees until one day he had resigned himself to being systematically robbed by them. "As long as they leave me enough to live on, I'm satisfied," he had once confided to Isaac; it was only then that Fat Benny and Tessie had started taking proper vacations.

"Look at him shake his head!" Yetta burst out. "He's choosy as well. You should be grateful your Uncle Benny's offering you the chance to go into business with him."

"Leave the boy alone," Fat Benny said. "You're making this whole thing sound like it's the end of the world."

"It could just as well be. All the money we've spent on him and he's going to flunk out of school. Benny, you don't know how lucky you and Tessie are not having kids of your own." She paused for breath and Fat Benny cut off any continuation with a wave of his hand.

"Stop worrying about Daniel, will you? I'll get in touch with Joey Bloom and we'll see about getting Daniel into the hotel for the summer. If he likes it, maybe he'll want to go into the hotel business. I'm sure that when Daniel finishes school, Joey'll be looking for people full-time." Fat Benny finished his tea and stood up. "Don't worry about a thing, Daniel," he said, patting his nephew reassuringly on the head. "Your Uncle Benny'll make sure you don't put a foot wrong."

Daniel left for the mountains three days after the spring semester ended. With four other boys, he waited on the corner of Fifth Avenue and 57th Street at seven o'clock on Sunday morning for the car sent by the hotel to pick up staff. Fat Benny had been true to his word. His friend, Joey Bloom, had needed extra kids to wait tables and he had taken Daniel willingly. Fifty dollars for six weeks, plus room, board and tips. Only twice before had Daniel been out of the city for more than a weekend—once to see distant cousins in Philadelphia with whom he had stayed for a week, and another time to the Jersey shore for a five-day vacation with Fat Benny, Tessie and Jack. Six weeks in the mountains stretched ahead like a lifetime of glorious adventure.

"You make sure you bring back every penny of that fifty dollars," his mother had said as she packed for him.

"Let the boy spend some, for God's sake," Isaac had argued. "What are we, paupers, that we need the boy's money? He's working for it. He's entitled to spend some."

"What's he going to spend money on up in the mountains?" Yetta had wanted to know. "He's going to fancy restaurants to eat, maybe? The food at Bloom's hotel won't be good enough for His Majesty? Or maybe he's going to take girls out every night, be a regular fourteen-year-old Mister Casanova?"

Fat Benny, waiting in the apartment to drive Daniel to the pick-up point in Manhattan, had taken his nephew aside. "Here," he whispered, thrusting two ten-dollar bills into Daniel's hand. "You bring back the fifty. If you want to spend anything, spend this."

Now the twenty dollars was folded carefully in the trouser pocket of Daniel's best suit. Fat Benny's gold watch was securely fastened on his wrist, and his clothes were in the cardboard suitcase. If he ever wanted to run away from his mother's perpetual nagging, he would never have a better opportunity, he thought rebelliously.

During the three-hour journey to Joey Bloom's hotel, Daniel became friendly with another boy, Moishe Wasserman from Brooklyn. Tall and thin with a mop of unruly fair hair and glasses that continually threatened to slip off the end of his nose, Moishe was two years older than Daniel and had worked for Joey Bloom the previous summer. Both boys were avid baseball fans, and Moishe said the hotel had pick-up games for guests in which staff members were allowed to participate. The six weeks began to look even brighter to Daniel.

After arriving at the hotel, Daniel and Moishe were assigned to the same bedroom. They unpacked and went down to the dining hall, where Joey Bloom was waiting to inspect them.

"You've got to be clean. You've got to be quick. And you've got to be polite. That's all I ask of my staff," Bloom said. "You"—he pointed at Daniel—"you're Benny Kirschbaum's nephew, right?"

"Yes, sir." Daniel wondered whether all the gangster stories were true. Bloom looked the part, that was for sure—dark-skinned, stocky, oily hair and sharp black eyes. "Yes, sir," he repeated. "I'm Daniel Kirschbaum."

"Good. Benny's an old friend of mine. We've had plenty of business dealings. You can take tables one through four. That's where my best customers sit. Look after them, and they'll look after you. You"—he switched his attention suddenly to Moishe Wasserman—"you were here last year, weren't you?"

Moishe nodded, flattered at being remembered.

"You take five through eight." Bloom ran off the other table responsibilities, then faced the group as a whole. "Remember, any of you get into any trouble, have any problems, you come and see me. While you're here, I'll be your mother, father, sister and brother. Any advice you want, come and see me."

During dinner that night, Daniel dropped a tray full of plates when he slammed into the swinging kitchen door while trying to make a fast turn. The plates were empty, but it still took ten minutes to clean up the mess. Joey Bloom stood by the entire time, tapping the toe of his patent leather shoe impatiently.

"First breakage is on the house, Kirschbaum. Next one comes out of your pocket. Watch it."

Daniel felt an overwhelming sensation of relief when the first dinner was over and the guests had left the dining hall. He was sweating from the hard work and from his anxiety at the prospect of dropping another tray; even two dropped trays a week would put him so badly in the hole that he'd end up owing Joey Bloom money when he left the hotel. He went up to his room and changed into a suit, then sat around the hotel ballroom watching the dancers and listening to the music. By ten o'clock he had tired of the pastime. Remembering he had to be up by six-thirty the following morning, he returned to the bedroom.

Moishe Wasserman was already in bed when Daniel entered the room. He was sitting up, glasses perched precariously on the end of his nose while he read a book. "Well?" he asked. "How was your first day in the hotel business?"

"Lousy." Daniel could not help the grin that spread across his face. "But I learned a lot."

"Like what?"

"Like china breaks when you drop it on the floor."

Moishe set aside the book and laughed. "You were the star of the show. How was the dance?"

Daniel picked up his pajamas and began preparing for bed. "A real bunch of ugly broads," he answered, trying to sound like a man of the world. "Except for one."

Moishe seemed interested. "Who was that?"

"Girl sitting by herself near the band. Long dark hair. Big brown eyes. Stacked." He was proud of that word, certain it made him appear at least a year older.

"That's Bloom's daughter, Linda," Moishe said. "I remember her from last year. She's his only kid. He never lets her out of his sight."

"How old is she?"

"Seventeen." Moishe looked thoughtfully at Daniel for a moment, then added, "Bet you a buck you can't get anywhere with her."

"Bet you I can." Daniel instantly regretted accepting the challenge. It would be hard enough even talking to Bloom now, after breaking the crockery; managing to be alone with his precious daughter would be next to impossible.

"Okay, bigshot," Moishe chuckled. "You've got six weeks to win your bet." He returned to reading the book, still smiling to himself.

Breakfast the following morning was another chapter in Daniel's nightmare. Everyone seemed to be calling for him at the same time, and Joey Bloom's best customers—tables one through four—were not above yelling if their orders were not taken promptly or if service lapsed because their waiter was rushed off his feet. And all the time, Joey Bloom maintained a critical eye on the proceedings from his position by the kitchen door.

"Better move it, Kirschbaum," he whispered threateningly as Daniel came spinning past, a tray held high above his head. "I get any complaints from my customers and you're out on your ear, Benny's nephew or not."

After breakfast, Bloom called his waiters for a meeting. They stood around him in a semicircle like recruits listening to the instructions of a drill sergeant. "You all took off last night after dinner when the dancing began like there was some kind of plague around here. All except you." He pointed at Daniel. "And for all the use you were, you might as well not have been here either. You just stuck around like some goddamned wallflower and watched."

None of the waiters spoke, uncertain where Bloom was leading. "Look, you're all good-looking boys, so what the hell's wrong with asking a few of the girls to dance? What's the big deal?"

"Dance?" The amazed question burst its way out of Daniel's mouth. "You mean like go up to a girl and ask her to dance?"

"Yeah, dance. You know, where you hold onto them and try to keep up with the music." Bloom wiggled his short, heavy body to add emphasis to his words. "Look, you guys, I know some of these girls are dogs. I wouldn't ask none of you to do this if it wasn't for your own good. None of the boys who come here with their parents are going to ask these dames for a dance, so they're going to feel like shit. Lonely as hell. A nice-looking guy like one of you comes along and whirls them around the floor for a few bars and their evening's made. Inside those scrawny chests, their little hearts are going to beat with joy. Mark my words, the parents will tip a hell of a lot better if their ugly daughters are kept happy."

As soon as dinner was finished that night, Daniel changed into his suit, wet his thick hair with water and brushed his teeth. Without waiting for Moishe, he went down to the ballroom and selected a strategic position by the entrance, from where he could check over each girl as she entered with her parents. He was on unfamiliar ground. The only times he had ever asked a girl to dance before had been at family functions, a cousin he'd been forced to partner, or the daughter of a family friend. Despite the bravado he'd injected into his conversation with Moishe Wasserman the previous night, he felt lost.

"What are you waiting for, Kirschbaum?"

Daniel swung around in surprise to find Joey Bloom standing next to him. "Nothing, Mr. Bloom. I'm just . . ."

"Checking out the merchandise?" Bloom asked. "What do you think this is, a goddamned market? Get out there and dance."

Daniel studied the girls again, trying to find the courage to take the first step. They all looked the same to him, homely, and self-conscious. He tried to imagine how his mother must have looked at this age. Had she been a hypochondriac even then? Always ready with a convenient malady? The idea of his mother as a fourteen- or fifteen-year-old girl made him smile despite his anxiety.

"Something funny, Kirschbaum?" Bloom wanted to know.

"No . . . no."

"These lovely girls aren't good enough for you to dance with, is that why you're laughing?"

"No, Mr. Bloom. I was thinking about something else."

"Don't waste your time thinking. Can't you hear the music playing?"

The four-piece band had struck up into a waltz. The vocalist was warbling meaningless words of romance and the saxophone player was doing his best to drown him out. And rightly so, Daniel thought. Even his performances in the privacy of the bathroom sounded better—and they were certainly more enjoyable than the task Bloom had just set him. He stepped onto the dance floor and aimed himself at the plainest girl he could see, rehearsing the lines with every step. If homeliness was what Bloom wanted his dancing waiters to look for, Daniel would make certain the hotel owner's wishes were fulfilled.

"May I have your permission to dance with your charming daughter?" he asked the girl's parents. He smiled at the girl with what he hoped was irrefutable charm.

The mother's artificial smile matched Daniel's own. She had been to Bloom's hotel before and had seen the waiters earn their money. "Of course you may," she replied.

Daniel held out his hand. The girl accepted. He led her out into the middle of the floor where Bloom could not fail to see him and began to dance. Considering that he had never taken a dance lesson in his life and had learned all he knew from watching other people, he did not fare too badly. After treading twice in quick succession on the girl's feet, he kept his steps to minute proportions.

"What's your name?" he asked.

"Sybil. Sybil Zuckerman."

Was he supposed to say that was a nice name? he wondered. He'd opened and closed his social chitchat with one question.

"Your name's Daniel Kirschbaum, isn't it?" the girl asked.

The recognition surprised him. Suddenly he felt glad he had asked this plain girl to dance, glad that Joey Bloom had forced him to. "That's right. How do you know?"

The girl began to giggle. "Everyone in the hotel knows your name after you dropped that tray of plates last night."

In Daniel's embarrassment he trod on the girl's toes for the third time. She gasped in pain and he began to apologize. "I'm sorry. Really I am. Very sorry—"

"You're a worse dancer than you are a waiter," she snapped.

"Really," he said, suddenly more angry than embarrassed.

"All I did was this . . ."

The girl flinched and cried out as Daniel's shoe crushed her toes for the fourth and final time. A second passed while she stood in the center of the dance floor, glaring at him. Then she flounced away toward the table where her parents sat.

Standing alone in the center of the dance floor, Daniel felt foolish only for as long as it took him to spot Joey Bloom's daughter, Linda. As on the previous night, she was sitting alone near the band. Daniel made a beeline for her, bowed formally from the waist and clicked his heels the way he had once seen a German aristocrat do in a movie to which Fat Benny had taken him. "I would be honored if you would have this next dance with me."

Linda Bloom looked up at him through wide brown eyes. As she began to stand, Daniel felt a firm pressure on his right shoulder, a strong thumb and forefinger squeezing painfully.

"You lay one greasy finger on my daughter, you stupid *klutz*, and Benny's going to be attending his nephew's *levoya.*"

Daniel turned around, wriggling to ease the grip. "Your daughter, Mr. Bloom?"

"My daughter, you great stupid oaf. Are you deaf as well as clumsy?"

"No, Mr. Bloom." The grip softened and Daniel backed away cautiously, but not before he had seen Linda smile at him. Whether she was smiling because she liked him or because she had enjoyed his humiliation at her father's hands, Daniel did not know. He was determined to find out, though. And not just for the sake of winning the bet with Moishe.

Chapter Three

A drenching thunderstorm forced the cancellation of the following afternoon's sporting activities. At a loss for something to do, Daniel and Moishe wandered into the empty ballroom and sat down at a table near the stage. The dampness of the storm had permeated the entire hotel. Both boys felt listless; conversation was sporadic.

Moishe looked around the ballroom, seeking a diversion. His eyes came to rest on the piano and a spark of interest came to life. "Want to hear some music?" he suddenly said, walking up onto the stage and lifting the keyboard cover.

"You play?" Daniel asked dubiously, following him onto the stage.

"Been taking lessons since I was six." He made himself comfortable on the stool and began to play. Daniel listened, at first surprised and then fascinated, as Moishe played Chopin's Nocturne in E-Flat.

"Not bad, huh?" Moishe called out. "Bet you thought I couldn't."

"You like that junk?"

Moishe shook his head. "Can't stand it. I prefer this." In the middle of the Chopin piece he switched to a jazz number and began to clown around, making faces in a parody of the music he was playing.

The guy could really play, Daniel thought. He hadn't been joking. He stood closer to the piano and watched Moishe's fingers dancing along the keyboard.

"All we need now is a vocalist and we're in business," Moishe said.

"I can sing," Daniel said tentatively.

"Yeah?" The doubt in Moishe's question was obvious.

"Better than you can play."

"Where did you sing?" Moishe never missed a note as he fired the questions at Daniel.

"School. I'm a soloist in the school choir. And I practice at home." He decided against telling Moishe that he stood in front of the bathroom mirror for hours on end, mimicking Russ Columbo.

"The school choir!" Moishe laughed, missed a note and broke off playing. "What do you sing there, 'God Bless America'?"

"I can damn well sing anything you can play!" Daniel shot back.

"Oh, yeah? How about this?" Moishe swung into "I've Got a Crush on You." Daniel listened for a few bars and then joined in, feeling his way into Moishe's accompaniment.

"Not bad," Moishe said grudgingly as he played a bridge into the second verse. "My cat sings better, but then I've got a talented cat."

"Screw you," Daniel muttered as he paused for breath.

"Watch your language. You've got an audience to consider."

Audience? Daniel turned around to face the dance floor and the lyrics dried up in his throat. Attracted by the music, half a dozen hotel guests had wandered into the ballroom and now stood looking expectantly at the stage. Daniel's face turned red in embarrassment. He prayed that the stage would open up and swallow him.

"Keep singing, you jerk," Moishe hissed. "What's the matter, you scared?" He continued playing as more guests entered the ballroom. Two couples stepped onto the floor and began to dance. "Sing," Moishe ordered.

From somewhere Daniel found the courage to continue the song. Soon, eight couples were dancing. And for the first time in his life Daniel was enjoying singing in public. This wasn't like the school choir, where singing was virtually a duty. Or his *bar mitzvah*, where he'd been certain half the congregation was waiting for him to make a mistake. This was entertaining people. Without even thinking about it, he began to snap his fingers in time with the rhythm as he looked out over the dancers. They were like marionettes, he thought, dancing to any tune he cared to sing. This beat waiting tables any time.

The song finished. The couples broke apart and a scattering

of applause rang out. He felt the deep blush returning, but now his face was warm with pleasure, not embarrassment. Bowing slightly in acknowledgment of the ovation, he stretched out an arm to Moishe, who rose from the stool.

"Ask them if they want to hear anything special," Moishe suggested.

"Any favorites you want to hear?" Daniel called out from the stage. "If we know them, we'll do them." He debated whether he sounded too cocksure; after all, one short round of applause did not make him a legend in Tin Pan Alley. Not even in Bloom's hotel.

"Someone to Watch Over Me." The request came from a young woman.

Daniel turned around to Moishe. "How about it?"

"I can fake it," came Moishe's confident reply.

Daniel held up a hand, ready to begin. Then he stopped. "Maybe you'd better not," he said to Moishe, recognizing the stocky figure of Joey Bloom standing in the ballroom entrance.

Bloom stood perfectly still for several seconds while he surveyed what was happening. Then he crooked his finger in Daniel's direction.

With legs of lead, Daniel got down from the stage and walked through the dancers toward the hotel owner. "You sing as well as you break plates, Kirschbaum?"

Daniel said nothing. There was nothing to be said. First the broken china, then the attempt to dance with Linda and now this. Bloom could demand only one sentence.

"Can you give me one good reason why you and Wasserman shouldn't be on the next bus back to New York?"

Daniel turned around to look at Moishe, who remained sitting on the piano stool, looking anxiously toward the ballroom entrance. It was bad enough he was going to get thrown out; what would Moishe do when he learned that his job was also forfeit?

"I'm waiting, Kirschbaum," Bloom said.

Out of the blue, Daniel found a reason. And a damned good one at that. The abject submissiveness he had been prepared to display as his best defense evaporated; in its place was aggressive defiance. "I can think of a roomful of good reasons,

Mr. Bloom. You ask those people who were dancing how they feel. They're your customers. They're important to you. Why don't you listen to what they've got to say?"

"Why should they stick up for you and Wasserman?"

"Because Moishe and I saved their afternoon, that's why," Daniel exclaimed. "We gave them something to do. All your outdoor activities are ruined for the day by the weather. Your guests were moping around, trying to kill time, kicking their heels till dinner."

Bloom seemed thoughtful. "Go back up on the stage and sing your songs. I'll decide afterwards whether you and your pal stay or not."

Daniel jogged back to the stage. He leaned over Moishe and whispered, "Play for your life."

Moishe took a deep breath to steady his nerves and began to play. Daniel forced himself to stare at some imaginary spot on the opposite wall and started to sing. Under the conditions of Bloom's ultimatum he was surprised he could even find his voice, let alone use it musically. Twice he stumbled as Moishe's playing failed to keep up with the words, but when he tore his eyes away from the opposite wall and looked at the dance floor he was gratified to see people dancing. A gleam of triumph illuminated his eyes as he sought out Bloom. The hotel owner was still standing in the doorway, arms crossed impassively.

Another round of applause greeted the end of the song, interspersed with shouts of "More!" The noise acted like adrenalin on Daniel. "How about some more requests?" he called out.

"What about 'How Long Has This Been Going On?' " one of the men called out. "Can you handle that?"

Daniel glanced at Moishe, who gave him the thumbs-up signal. Putting as much torch as he could muster into the performance, Daniel launched into the song. He was playing to the gallery now, even if that gallery comprised only Joey Bloom. There was no need to persuade the dancers; they were in the palm of his hand already. Bloom was the only holdout. The knowledge that he had already won over the guests spurred him on. Music was like hypnotism; he was experiencing a power he'd never dreamed existed. It was magic, nothing less; he was casting a spell over his listeners.

Another six numbers followed—requests and melodies he chose himself—before Daniel exhausted the repertoire of popular songs he'd learned by heart from the radio and practiced in the bathroom. He held up both hands to signify the end of the performance. "That's it, folks. Moishe and I have to start getting ready to serve you all dinner."

A rumble of disappointment swept over the dancers.

"Sorry, but we've got other work to do," Daniel explained. God, what he wouldn't give to stick around for another hour. If only he knew more songs, had more time to prolong this heady new sensation.

"You going to practice breaking more dishes?" one man called out.

Daniel gladly joined in the laughter at the question. He would never be allowed to forget that incident, but in his excitement over the afternoon's discovery, he wasn't at all fazed by the memory. He held out a hand to Moishe, who rose from the stool and bowed, then both boys left the stage. Some of the dancers patted them on the back as they passed, and Daniel found it even harder to leave. One more word of encouragement, one more compliment and he'd go straight back onto the stage and stay there for the remainder of his six weeks. And the hell with waiting tables.

When they reached the door, a beefy hand pressed itself forcefully against Daniel's chest, pushing him back. "I never told you to quit singing," Bloom said.

Daniel looked at him in surprise. "We've got to start getting ready for dinner soon," he answered. "I've got tables one through four to prepare."

"I'll decide whether you wait tables or sing. Or maybe you want a ride to the bus stop instead?"

"I don't know any more songs."

"So sing what you've sung already. Nobody'll know the difference. Go on, get back on that stage."

For three days, Daniel and Moishe performed in the afternoons and waited tables for the remainder of the time. Then Bloom pulled them aside. "You want to keep on waiting tables for the rest of the summer?"

"Beats hell out of spending August on Claremont Parkway," Daniel replied. Moishe nodded in instant agreement, although he had never set foot on Claremont Parkway in his life.

"You can have a full-time job singing, Kirschbaum. You and your sidekick here. Two hours each afternoon, plus two half-hour spots in the evening when the band takes a break."

"I don't know enough songs," Daniel protested.

"So learn some," Bloom suggested. "Get the scores from the band. Go over the songs with Wasserman here. If I hear you repeat one number the same day, unless it's by request, you're both back to waiting tables." He turned around to leave, but Moishe pulled him back.

"Mr. Bloom?"

"What is it?" Bloom looked distastefully at Moishe's hand on his arm before shaking it off.

"If we don't wait tables, we don't get tips."

"What?" The single word was drawn out in disbelief.

"We'll lose money by not waiting tables," Moishe repeated.

Watching the exchange, Daniel's impression of Moishe began to undergo a dramatic change. The clown with the unkempt hair had suddenly disappeared. The glasses halfway down Moishe's nose were no longer comical. Moishe had a serious demeanor now; he was an earnest negotiator bargaining for just payment.

"Are you trying to tell me you want more money?" Bloom asked, disbelief still tingeing his voice.

"We want more money."

"Twenty-five bucks a week for each of you."

It constituted a fortune to Daniel. Three times the sum he had been originally offered for the tedious work of waiting tables and dancing with ugly girls. But Moishe was still not satisified. "Entertaining takes a lot more skill than waiting tables, Mr. Bloom."

"Twenty-five's not enough for you?" Bloom's voice rose. "Who the heck do you think you are? Al Jolson?"

"Thirty a week for each of us or we don't play anymore."

"Thirty?" Bloom's mouth gaped open. Daniel spun around and stared at his partner, unable to believe Moishe was ruining a golden opportunity. Twenty-five dollars a week for singing and Moishe, the cretin, was arguing about it? Behind the glasses, Moishe's eyes glared at Daniel in silent warning.

"Thirty," Moishe repeated. "If you don't think we're worth it, go ask your guests. Otherwise we're both happy to keep on waiting tables."

Bloom looked from Daniel to Moishe, unable to believe that he was being put over a barrel by a couple of kids. Finally he said, "Okay, thirty. But you'd both better be damned good." He swung around and left them.

"Thirty!" Daniel gasped, grabbing Moishe by the shoulders and shaking him in jubilation. "I thought you'd lost him when you turned down the twenty-five. I was going to strangle you."

Moishe gave a lopsided grin. "I thought I'd lost him too. And we would have, if you'd opened your big mouth. But it just goes to show you, kiddo. Every singer needs an agent. That's what you've got me for."

"Agent?" Daniel dropped his hands from Moishe's shoulders. "You're my pianist."

"From five minutes ago, I'm your agent as well. Ten percent of whatever you get belongs to me."

Daniel did some quick calculations. "That only leaves me with twenty-seven dollars," he complained. "Two bucks better off than I would have been before."

"Don't gripe," Moishe told him. "Two bucks is two bucks."

"You can't take a commission on the entire thirty," Daniel continued. "You've got to figure out what I would have made from waiting tables and tips as well."

Moishe stood silently for an instant. Then the serious negotiator departed and the clown was back. "Tell you what. You get anywhere with Bloom's daughter and I'll pass up my entire commission. Could anything be fairer than that?"

"She's seventeen, three years older than me."

"She doesn't know that. You look old enough to have a chance. You said she smiled at you the other night. Is it a deal?"

"Deal," Daniel agreed, wondering how he was going to get past Joey Bloom. Maybe now that he was a vocalist instead of a waiter Bloom would look more kindly on him.

When Daniel sang that night, during the two breaks allowed to the band, every word was directed to Linda Bloom. After the first two songs, when she realized Daniel was communicating with her, she paid more attention, smiling at him to continue. When the second band break was over and the musicians returned, Daniel waved a hand airily at the applause he received and forgot all about introducing Moishe; he just jumped down from the stage, pulled up an empty chair and sat down next to Linda.

"Like it?" he asked.

"Like what?"

"My singing, of course."

She pursed her lips. "Not bad. You sing better than you carry plates, but you probably do most things better than you carry plates."

"Absolutely everything," he replied with a certainty he did not feel. Christ, where did he go from here? If he didn't think of something quickly he'd lose her. "Want to come for a walk by the lake?" he asked. "It's getting a bit hot in here."

"Why not?" Linda picked up her purse and stood. When she reached out and held Daniel's hand, an electric current seemed to pass between them. Daniel flinched momentarily and then relaxed; maybe it was going to be easier than he thought. As they passed Joey Bloom standing by the door, Daniel nodded an uncertain greeting. The hotel owner responded mechanically, turning to gaze after the couple as they walked away. Daniel's heart pounded and his stomach lurched. At any moment, he expected to feel Bloom's hand on his shoulder. When he reached the fresh air and nothing had happened, he wondered if he had been right. Now that he was an entertainer instead of a waiter, maybe Bloom looked on him as a different class of person altogether.

By the edge of the lake was a wooden bench. Daniel sat down and waited for Linda to join him. Now what? he asked himself. All the aids to romance he'd ever heard about were present. A balmy evening, the lake, a cloudless sky, bright moon. Even the girl. And he didn't have the faintest idea what to do next.

"Try putting your arms around me," Linda whispered. "That's always a good start."

Too concerned with his own inadequacies to be startled by the girl's forwardness, Daniel draped his arms around her shoulders, pulling her close. He began to feel even warmer than he had in the ballroom. As their bodies touched, he felt his pants tighten uncomfortably. He moved awkwardly on the bench to lessen the pressure. Linda took his right hand and guided it inside her dress. Daniel recoiled suddenly as if hit by a massive charge when his fingers came into contact with her breasts. He jumped back, rescuing his hand. In the moonlight, he could see she was laughing at him. Desperately he tried to think of something to do, some words to speak to cover his embarrassment.

"Where's your mother?" he finally blurted out. "Doesn't she work at the hotel with your father?"

"She's dead," Linda said flatly. "She died five years ago, before we came up here."

"Oh." Daniel looked out over the lake, hoping to see inspiration, like Excalibur, rising from the waters.

"Are you frightened, Daniel?"

"Frightened?" He turned to look at Linda. "Me? Frightened of what?"

"Of me. Haven't you ever been with a girl before?"

"Of course," he lied. "Plenty of times."

"How many times?"

"Plenty."

She moved uncomfortably closer. "I bet you haven't."

Daniel tried to retreat further along the bench but the armrest blocked his backward progress. "Of course I have."

Her hand snaked out and fingers performed a tantalizing dance along his thighs. If it had been a shock when he touched her breasts, it was nothing to the jolt he received when Linda's fingers began undoing the buttons of his fly. "What the hell are you doing?" he asked.

She gave no answer. Instead, she took one of his hands and pressed it against herself, guiding it up under her dress. He could feel dampness as his fingers stroked, aware all the time of Linda's own fingers as they teased and caressed. He tensed up, his body going almost rigid, as the girl's encouraging hand led him to the brink of orgasm.

Closing his eyes in ecstasy, he spurted all over his trousers.

Joy turned to dismay as he opened his eyes and surveyed his soiled clothing. "Now what the hell am I going to do?" he moaned. "I can't go back into the hotel looking like this."

Linda straightened her dress and rose from the bench. She knelt at the water's edge and rinsed her hands. "Come here," she said softly, straightening up.

Obediently Daniel stood in front of her. She put her hands around his shoulders and tilted her face. Daniel forgot about the mess on his trousers as her tongue pressed his lips apart. Then, with no warning whatsoever, she abruptly straightened her arms and sent him staggering back into the lake.

"You idiot!" he yelled at her. Sitting on the sludgy bottom, only his head and shoulders were visible above the water. "What did you do that for?"

"What's going on down there?" a voice bellowed from the hotel terrace. Moments later there was the sound of rushing footsteps down the gentle hill leading from the hotel to the lake. Daniel struggled to rise from the mud, but each attempt only seemed to immerse him more deeply. He was grateful when a hand was thrust out to him. Grabbing hold, he let himself be dragged to the bank.

"How the goddamned hell did you wind up in the lake?" Joey Bloom demanded. "Fancied going swimming with all your clothes on?" He stared in amazement at Daniel's muddy, dripping suit. "I hope you've got a change of clothes for your show tomorrow."

"I slipped."

"No, he didn't." The rebuttal of his excuse came from Linda. "He tried to kiss me, so I pushed him in."

Bloom clenched his fists, then relaxed. "Serves you damned well right, you big ox. Get back to the hotel and clean up." He watched Daniel trudge slowly up the hill and shook his head.

That night, while Daniel's suit was hanging up to dry, he sat in the bedroom with Moishe Wasserman, who was eager to hear how Daniel had progressed.

"That's all?" Moishe asked in disbelief when Daniel had finished recounting the lakeside tryst. "You copped a feel and got jerked off? And for that you wound up in the lake, the laughing stock of everyone?"

"What do you mean by that?" Daniel snapped. "The bet was if I got anywhere with Bloom's daughter, you'd forget about your ten percent. Well, I did get somewhere, so you can forget your commission."

"Getting a certifiable nymphomaniac to jerk you off isn't even reaching first base."

"A certifiable what?"

"Nympho, you stupid *schmuck!* Why do you think Bloom keeps her under lock and key the way he does? She tries to lay every guy she sees. He doesn't want her in the family way."

"Who told you that?" Daniel asked, certain that Moishe was trying to wriggle his way out of the agreement.

"When I was here last year I found out. Everyone knows. The hardest part about screwing Linda Bloom is getting her past her father. So you get past him and what happens? She jerks you off!"

Daniel sat sullenly, too ashamed to admit that he hadn't known where to begin because he was still a virgin.

"Is the bet still on?" he finally asked Moishe. "Your commission if I screw her?"

"It's still on," Moishe replied, then began to laugh. "Christ! A fucking handjob is all he can get!"

All through the following afternoon's performance, Daniel felt uncomfortably self-conscious in the dried-out suit. Thanks to the hotel laundry, the creases were all in the right place, but he was certain the fabric had shrunk drastically. No matter how much he had reassured himself by checking his appearance in the bedroom mirror before coming down, he was positive that his trousers did not talk to his shoes and that his sleeves finished a few inches above his elbows.

Linda did not show up during the afternoon performance, and Daniel began to wonder what had happened to her. Had Joey Bloom locked his daughter in her room, uncertain as to what exactly had taken place by the lake but determined that there would be no repeat? When Daniel caught his eye during one song, the hotel owner's expression was blank, giving no clue what lay behind it. Would Bloom pursue the matter? Daniel asked himself. Or would he just be glad to believe what Linda had told him? That she had pushed Daniel into the lake because he'd tried to kiss her. Fat chance of that if she really is a nympho, Daniel decided, although he was still uncertain what the word meant and was too embarrassed to ask Moishe to explain.

Linda was back that evening, sitting alone at a table near the stage as she waited for Daniel to appear during the band break. He rushed his way through the second performance, eager for the regular musicians to return. When they did, he jumped down from the stage and sat at Linda's table.

"Thanks for the bath."

"Covered that stain on your trousers, didn't it?" She smiled as he turned a deep, beetroot red. "You're still a virgin, aren't you, Daniel Kirschbaum?"

"No."

"Don't deny it. I know you are."

Daniel sought to change the subject. "What did your father say?"

"Nothing. Why should he say anything? He's got nothing to be frightened about when his daughter's with a virgin who doesn't know which way is up."

"I'm *not* a virgin."

"Yes, you are."

Daniel ignored the continued jibe. "Did he say you can't see me again?"

"He never said a word, I told you."

"Tonight then?" Daniel asked. "Now?"

"Where? Your room?"

Daniel thought quickly. "Better not. Moishe usually goes to bed early, right after we finish the final show. He's my agent, you know, as well as my accompanist," he added grandly. "What about your room?"

"It's next to my father's," she warned.

"He's down here," Daniel pointed out, feeling braver as he became more determined to compensate for his abysmal performance of the previous night. He remembered the skillful dance of her fingers, the excitement of the mounting orgasm, the sudden, blessed release. Tonight could only be better, and he'd go back to Claremont Parkway a man. The bet with Moishe meant nothing now; all Daniel could acknowledge was the driving instinct that pushed him toward a liaison with this girl.

Linda rose from the table and pushed back her chair. "I'll go up five minutes ahead of you," she whispered. "Room two-oh-nine, second floor. Good night, Daniel," she said in a louder voice. "Glad your suit dried out okay." She turned around and left. By the door, she stopped to talk for a few seconds with her father.

Daniel watched her go, then sat willing away the five minutes and repeatedly consulting the gold watch given to him by Fat Benny. Finally he stood up and walked to the door.

"Going swimming again, Kirschbaum?" Bloom asked sarcastically.

"Going to bed, Mr. Bloom," was Daniel's reply. "I'm worn out. Think I might have a cold coming after last night. I've got to watch my voice."

Bloom regarded him stonily. "Hard work singing, isn't it? You and your pal Wasserman have got it made."

"Good night, Mr. Bloom."

"Good night, Kirschbaum."

Daniel walked slowly down the hall leading from the ballroom. When he was out of Bloom's sight, he quickened his pace, taking the stairs two at a time, eager to be at Room 209. Outside, he stopped long enough to straighten his tie and pat his hair with his hands. Then he knocked twice.

"It's open."

He pushed back the door and went inside. A closet faced him. He turned left. Linda was already in the double bed, sitting upright, the sheet pulled up to her chin. "Undress," she whispered.

Faced with the inevitable, Daniel's courage almost fled. He felt awkward as he haltingly removed his jacket, tie and shirt. When he stood in front of her in undershirt and trousers, she eyed him critically.

"You're fat."

"No, I'm not," he argued, knowing she was right. "It's

all muscle."

"Looks like fat to me. Let's see the rest of you."

He kicked off his shoes and slowly began to undo his belt.

"Hurry up," Linda urged. "You won't be the first I've seen."

His heartbeat increased as he dropped his trousers to the floor and stepped out of them.

"Come here," she ordered.

Obediently he knelt on the bed. Linda threw back the sheet and Daniel looked excitedly from her breasts—remembering how he had recoiled from their touch—to the triangle of dark hair between her legs. Never having realized that women were also endowed with pubic hair, the sight of it came as a shock.

"Tell me the God's honest truth," Linda demanded. "Are you still a virgin?"

The denial was a long time in coming and she leaned forward triumphantly. "You are! I knew it!" Without warning, she snatched at the waistband of his underpants and tried to pull them down. The band snagged on his hardening erection and he tumbled forward. Sliding under the sheet, he wriggled out of his underpants and grasped the girl tightly.

"Easy, for Christ's sake!" she cried out as he gripped her even harder, rubbing against her, kissing her mouth, her neck and then her breasts in a frenzied downward plunge. "Make it last, you crud! You're not in a race!"

Daniel tried to slow down but he was too excited to control himself. He did not know which part of the girl's body to attack first, which part of his own body to use. Disappointed with his panicky fumbling, Linda began to guide him, taking his hand, opening her legs to accommodate him.

"Now!" she hissed, as he fought against climaxing under the teasing caress of her fingers. "Now!"

Following her hand, he slid inside her, welcoming the warm wetness that enveloped him and simultaneously feeling frightened by it. He began to move quickly, still unsure of himself, scared of slipping out; he felt her grip tighten as she contracted her muscles.

"Come on, you son of a bitch!" she swore hoarsely in his ear. "Work at it!"

He thrust in deeper, his initial fear giving way to the drive that had propelled him toward this girl. Linda's moans harmonized with his own rapid breathing as she arched her body up to meet his movement. His breath came even faster until it seemed like his lungs would thrust their way up through his mouth. Linda's cries became sharper, acting on Daniel like applause, bravos that spurred him on until his climax thundered forth with the roar of a grand finale.

As the strength left him, he lay with his eyes closed, breathing heavily under the strenuous performance. When he opened his eyes again, Linda was looking up at him. Her lips were curved in a satisfied smile.

"Can't call you a virgin anymore."

"I never was," he managed to find the strength to argue.

"Of course you were." She slid out from beneath him. "You'd better go. I've got to fix myself up and go downstairs, or my father will wonder what's happened to me."

As Linda swung her feet to the carpeted floor, leaving Daniel alone on the bed, the door leading to the corridor slammed back against the wall. Daniel jumped up in fright while Linda ran to the bathroom and locked herself in.

"You filthy piece of shit!" Joey Bloom roared at Daniel. "I'll teach you to fool around with my daughter!" He looked around the room, picked up a heavy chair and raised it threateningly.

Daniel dove off the bed as the chair smashed down on the pillow. He grabbed a handful of clothes from the floor, hopping about on one leg as he tried to force himself into his trousers. Bloom swung a solid but poorly aimed roundhouse punch which caught Daniel on the shoulder and sent him stumbling across the room. Before he could regain his balance, Bloom was on him, face flushed with rage, the veins in his neck and forehead popping as his powerful fists beat a tattoo on Daniel's head and chest.

Daniel did not know what to do first, protect himself from Bloom's onslaught or try to get dressed and escape. He was hopping about in the middle of the room, half in and half out of his trousers, trying to pull them up with one hand while he waved the other in self-defense.

A punch landed just below his left eye, stunning him. He

tripped over his flopping trouser legs and fell to the floor, crawling around on all fours while he waited for the bells in his head to stop their infernal ringing. When he finally coaxed himself to stagger to his feet, the clothes and the possibility of escape were forgotten.

"I'm going to tear you in two, you little punk!" Bloom screamed. Flecks of saliva spattered from his mouth into Daniel's face. "That's my daughter you're fooling around with, not some little tramp from the Bronx!" He drew his fist back for the final punch. Daniel automatically feinted with his left, ducking his shoulder into Bloom. The hotel owner dropped his guard for an instant and Daniel brought over the right, catching Bloom flush on the point of the jaw. Bloom's head snapped back. Arms flailing like a windmill gone berserk, he spun into the wall where he slid down in a barely conscious heap.

Without another look at the prostrate man—or even a thought for Linda, who had remained locked in the bathroom—Daniel wriggled into his trousers, slipped on his shirt, grabbed the remainder of his clothing and fled down the corridor to his own room.

"Schmuck!"

Moishe Wasserman spat out the word as he and Daniel carried their baggage from the bus. "Asshole! We had it made. Thirty bucks a week for doing nothing and you had to go and lay his daughter! Prick!"

Daniel ignored the tirade. It had been spewing from Moishe's lips for the entire journey, but Daniel was too wrapped up in his own troubles to react. His left eye was almost completely closed, covered by an evil-looking purple bruise, and his body ached from the battering it had received from Bloom's fists. But physical pain meant little at the moment. What would Fat Benny say when he learned that his nephew had screwed Bloom's daughter and then punched out the hotel owner in the bargain? One punch only, but what a punch! For an instant, Daniel's mood brightened as he remembered the right hook connecting crisply with Bloom's jaw. It hadn't traveled more than six inches and he'd conned the man into moving into the punch. Beautiful!

"Why in God's name did you have to bring me into it as well?" Moishe demanded. "Why did you have to open your big mouth about the bet we made?"

Daniel dropped his suitcase to the ground and spun around. "You were the one who told me she got laid by everyone!" he shot back. "It's your fault just as much as it's mine."

"Fine! I told you!" Moishe admitted, raising his voice to outshout Daniel. "But you could at least have had the sense to lock the fucking door! You invited him in, you stupid asshole! And he caught you *in flagrante delicto.*"

"In what?"

"Never mind," Moishe said disgustedly.

Daniel forgot all about Moishe when he recognized the Ford sedan waiting near the bus stop. Only one person in the Kirschbaum family had an automobile, and Daniel could see Fat Benny sitting behind the wheel.

"Hi, Uncle Benny," Daniel said lamely as he reached the car and Fat Benny got out.

"Joey Bloom called me," Fat Benny said, explaining his presence. "You did a terrible thing, Daniel."

"I didn't mean it to happen the way it did," Daniel tried to explain. "It was just something I couldn't control."

"This your *shitfes?*" Fat Benny asked, looking at Moishe Wasserman for the first time. "Your partner in crime?"

"I'm his agent," Moishe said proudly. "I had him up to thirty bucks a week till he went and blew it."

"You want a ride to the Bronx?"

"I live in Brooklyn."

"So take the subway then. Get in the car, Daniel. I'll take you home."

Daniel put his cardboard suitcase in the car and turned around to face Moishe. "Sorry I got you into this mess."

Moishe held out his hand, the earlier animosity forgotten. "Don't worry about it, Danny boy. I'm still your agent, remember? Next time I'll get you into a better place. See you around." Moishe picked up his bag and began walking toward the subway entrance.

During the long drive back to Claremont Parkway, Fat

Benny hardly said a word, leaving Daniel to mull over the reception that awaited him. Entering the apartment building, he trudged up the stairs, carrying the case. His mother opened the door.

"Hi, Ma."

She slapped him hard across the face. Daniel stood his ground, blinking back tears, making no attempt to defend himself. "Pig!" Yetta screamed. "Is this how you repay Uncle Benny for getting you a job?" She slapped him again.

"Take it easy, Yetta," Fat Benny cautioned. "It's not all his fault."

"No? Whose fault is it then? Mine? I told him he should do filthy things with that gangster's daughter?"

Fat Benny put a protective arm around Daniel and led him into the apartment. "Sit down, I've got to talk to you." He waited for Daniel to wipe his eyes, then continued. "The black eye's nothing, Daniel. You were lucky. Nobody does what you did to Joey Bloom and his daughter and gets away with it like this. Anyone else he would have crucified. Because of me, you and your *shitfes* got out of there in one piece."

"How?"

"Joey owes me a few favors. He called to let me know what had happened because he remembers the favors. Otherwise you'd be in the hospital by now."

"But it wasn't all my fault," Daniel protested.

"I know. Joey's daughter's ill. It's a disease, like someone who depends on alcohol or drugs." Daniel had never heard Fat Benny speak so seriously about anything before. "With Linda, it's sex. You were there so you provided the outlet. That's why Joey keeps such a close eye on her. She's been to doctors but they can't help. They think it has something to do with her mother."

"But she told me her mother was dead."

"Did she tell you how her mother died?"

Daniel shook his head.

"Someone left a bomb in Joey Bloom's car. Only that day his wife used the car instead. That's when Joey took Linda and ran away from the city to open that hotel. Linda's never been right since."

"Does Pa know about all this?" Daniel asked. "You know, what happened with me at the hotel?"

"He knows. But I spoke to him already. He won't say a word about it." Fat Benny put a gentle hand on Daniel's black eye to see how bad it really was; he shook his head sadly. "Whose idea was it to fool around with Linda? Yours? Or did that Wasserman kid put you up to it?"

"Half and half," Daniel replied honestly. "I said I could and Moishe egged me on. He promised he'd let me off his commission if I made it."

"Commission?" Fat Benny had not paid any attention to the way Moishe had introduced himself at the bus station.

"Ten percent of what he got out of Mr. Bloom for my singing."

"Boy, you can sure pick winners." He snapped his fingers as if an idea had suddenly registered. "You interested in another job for the remainder of the summer?"

"Doing what?" Daniel asked suspiciously.

"Helping out in the stores. Jack's there already. No singing, no waiting tables, and no agents like that lunatic Wasserman."

Daniel did not even need time to think about it. Working for Fat Benny was a plane removed from staying in the apartment with his mother for the entire summer.

Chapter Four

"Kirschbaum! Would you please be kind enough to explain to the class what a seam is?"

Daniel raised his eyes slowly from the workbench and looked apprehensively at the instructor. For almost a year, Joe Ozegowsky had been teaching tailoring to Daniel's class, and Daniel had loathed every single minute of it. Now Ozegowsky was holding up the jacket sleeve over which Daniel had labored. The instructor's bushy white eyebrows were raised and his nose was wrinkled to demonstrate his distaste. The other pupils in the class set down their work, eager for the diversion they knew was coming.

"Well?" Ozegowsky prompted. "Would you tell us what a seam is?"

"Two pieces of material sewn together," Daniel answered.

"A line where they are sewn," Ozegowsky corrected him. "A line of predetermined shape. This"—he held up the offending sleeve for all to see, dangling it like some soiled, objectionable rag—"must have been sewn with an orangutan in mind!"

The class collapsed in a fit of laughter, delighting in the misfortune of someone else. Daniel gritted his teeth in suppressed anger until his gums hurt. "Goddamned bastard," he muttered. "I'd like to turn you into a predetermined shape."

Ozegowsky bundled up the sleeve, drew back his arm and flung the fabric across the classroom. It unrolled in mid-flight and dropped two benches in front of Daniel. The boy sitting there flicked it onto the floor and made a disgusted face to trigger another burst of laughter.

"Undo it and sew it again, Kirschbaum," Ozegowsky ordered. "See if you can manage to follow the pattern this time."

Daniel retrieved the sleeve and began to cut the sitches, wondering what cruel twist of fate had decreed that he should earn his living as a tailor, like his father. That was if he could earn a living at all when he left school. All kinds of business—not just clothing firms—had foundered in the wake of the previous October's crash. Rich men had become poor overnight; and the poor had become destitute. If it had not been for Fat Benny coming to the rescue when the bank where Isaac kept his savings had gone under, Daniel did not know what would have happened to his family. But through it all, Isaac had displayed a sense of optimism. There would be jobs, he said. When Daniel finished trade school, business would have picked up again; his diligence would be rewarded.

During his first week in the trade school, Daniel had taken a number of aptitude tests—cabinet making, building, plumbing, mechanics. At each of them he had proved inept. At last, the principal—in mounting desperation—had asked Daniel what his father did for a living. When Daniel had replied that Isaac was a tailor, the relieved principal had clapped his hands in satisfaction. "Good, Kirschbaum. You can follow in your father's footsteps. Make him proud. At least with tailoring you won't be responsible for electrocuting or drowning anyone."

Then Daniel had met Joe Ozegowsky, who instructed the tailoring class. Ozegowsky worked as a tailor for a dress company in Manhattan until five years before, when a heart condition had forced him to retire from active work and become an instructor. A middle-aged, bitter man, whenever he found a pupil who lacked ability, instead of helping the boy he would make him the butt of insensitive jokes. In Daniel, Ozegowsky had found a source of amusement which had lasted for almost a year and showed every sign of continuing into the distant future.

"Your father's a tailor, isn't he, Kirschbaum?" Ozegowsky asked, then continued without waiting for an answer. "Is this the kind of work he turns out? Does hamfisted sewing run in your family? Is it a congenital trait?" He smirked as each biting question was received with a snigger by the class.

Mention of his father ripped away the control Daniel had been exercising throughout the instructor's tirade. "My father's a better goddamned tailor in his sleep than you ever were awake!" he shot back. "You wouldn't be fit to sit on the same bench with him!" He stood up and dared the instructor to bait him further.

Ozegowsky eyed Daniel warily, momentarily startled by having a student face him down. "Pity you didn't inherit some of his skill," Ozegowsky said, closing the subject. "Now"—he directed the words to the entire class—"for those of you have mastered the relatively simple art of sewing in a straight line, we'll be finishing off the sleeves this afternoon. All except for one of us," he added, "who will be starting his sleeve all over again."

Daniel was the last to leave the classroom. He sat picking at the stitches of the aborted sleeve until everyone but Ozegowsky had left. Then he stood up, walked purposefully over to the instructor's desk.

"Yes, Kirschbaum?" Ozegowsky asked. "Are you staying behind for some extracurricular instruction? It's a marked improvement in your attitude if you can admit you need it."

Daniel glared ferociously at the instructor. "Say all you like about me, if you need to get a few cheap laughs that badly. But leave my father out of it."

"Are you threatening an instructor?" Despite the calmness he managed to inject into the question, Ozegowsky felt fear. His stomach tightened uncomfortably and he had to force his voice to remain level.

"No," Daniel replied, careful not to overstep the mark. "I'm asking you politely not to make fun of my father. You've never met him. You don't know anything about him. You've got no right to poke fun at him. He works a goddamned sight harder than you do, and he knows a lot more than you ever will."

"So why doesn't he teach you to sew in a straight line?" Ozegowsky began to feel on firmer ground. With words, he could defeat this clumsy, overweight boy.

Daniel could not remember where he had heard the quote. Perhaps he had read it somewhere, or maybe it was something that Fat Benny had once said. Either way, the words came readily. "Those who can, do, Mr. Ozegowsky. Those who cannot, teach."

The instructor slowly stood up, staring in disbelief at the boy in front of him, shocked by his insolence. "I teach only because I am no longer healthy enough to work in a factory, young man." Every few words were punctuated by a jabbing motion with his forefinger into Daniel's chest. "If I had my health, I wouldn't be wasting my time, skill and experience teaching morons like you."

"Stop pushing me, Mr. Ozegowsky."

The instructor took no notice. "I'm trying to help you make something of yourself, and this is the gratitude I get. All I've seen of you, Kirschbaum . . ."

"Don't push." Despite a conscious effort to control himself, Daniel's voice began to rise. Why had he ever started this when he knew there could be only one outcome?

". . . tells me that you're going to finish up as a bum, scrounging off other people because you'll never be able to support yourself with a respectable job."

"What job?" Daniel fired back. "There are no jobs out there."

"For a good tailor there are. But you'll never be a good tailor. You wouldn't even be able to hold down a job in a full employment market."

"Neither would you," Daniel snapped. He tried to hold himself back. Having come this far, though, he found it impossible. "If it wasn't for the school, you'd be on the breadline as well."

"How dare you speak to me like that?" Ozegowsky exploded. He continued to jab Daniel in his chest.

"Keep your damned hands to yourself!" Daniel yelled back.

"You're useless, Kirschbaum! Useless! Do you hear me?" He gave Daniel a final jab in the chest to emphasize the last word. Unable to restrain himself any longer, Daniel brushed aside Ozegowsky's hand and jabbed him back, hard, sending the instructor staggering into the desk.

"You struck me," Ozegowsky said, lowering his voice in wonder. "You hit an instructor."

Daniel stared in horror at the older man, then he swung around and ran from the classroom, holding his breath until he had slammed the door. Heart pounding uncontrollably, he stood against the corridor wall and let out his breath in one long sigh. Possible consequences of his action flitted across his mind as he wondered what Ozegowsky would do. Daniel had no doubt the instructor would pursue the matter; he would never be willing to let it rest and allow Daniel back into the classroom as if nothing had happened. He would go to the principal and claim he had been assaulted. Daniel had seen it happen once before, to another boy who had been the butt of Ozegowsky's vindictive sarcasm. The boy had pushed the instructor in the chest, no harder than Daniel had just done. The parents had been called in and the boy removed.

Daniel cursed himself for allowing Ozegowsky to goad him into such a senseless action. He should never have let himself get riled up like that. But no one was going to speak about his father like that!

Daniel began to think about his father, how Isaac would react when he learned his son had assaulted a teacher. Like the old man doesn't have enough on his plate already, he thought miserably. Not a penny in the bank because the bank went belly-up; living from day to day with help, when he'd accept it, from Fat Benny. His mother wasn't much comfort either. She couldn't seem to get it through her head that everyone was being hit by the hard times. She seemed to think that her husband was the only one who had had an account at the defunct bank; he was the only one having trouble making ends meet.

He turned around and hammered his fist against the wall in self-directed fury. Now he'd only added to his father's worries. Should he return to the classroom and apologize . . . ? Ozegowsky was probably waiting for him to do so; that was why the instructor had not yet emerged. He was gloating in anticipation, expecting Daniel to crawl back and seek forgiveness. The hell with it! He wouldn't give him the pleasure of an apology. He'd rather get thrown out of the school than eat humble pie before that creep! He wouldn't go back. Instead, he'd cut school for the rest of the day and go to the ballgame. He had enough money in his pocket. Maybe Tommy Mulvaney would want to cut classes as well.

Daniel gazed at the classroom door for a long time while he debated whether to go back inside and apologize. Then he spun around and marched determinedly out of the school. The hell with them all.

Together with Tommy Mulvaney, Daniel spent the afternoon watching the Yankees beat the Philadelphia Athletics. He found little to interest him in the contest, though; he was too preoccupied with his own immediate problems. Even a towering home run into right field by Babe Ruth did little to relieve Daniel's depression. Normally he would have been out of his seat, jubilantly cheering each jogging step his hero took around the base paths; this time he sat quietly, chin clasped dejectedly in his hands while the rest of the stadium erupted around him.

"What's eating you, Cherrybum?" Tommy asked.

"School," was the simple answer.

"No good?"

"I hit an instructor."

Tommy's eyes widened. "What did he do? Try to steal your stupid watch?"

Daniel managed to raise a wry grin. "The guy kept picking on me, so I picked back on him a bit."

"You punched him good?"

"No." Daniel shook his head regretfully. "I should have but I didn't. I just poked him in the chest with my finger because he kept doing it to me."

"That's nothing, Cherrybum. Everything'll be all right. You'll see."

"Not with this guy, it won't. He's a worm."

"Will you quit worrying about it? He probably deserved whatever happened to him."

"He did and worse. But that doesn't help me, though. Bastard's got it in for me because I told him my father had forgotten more about tailoring than he'd ever learn. Told him in front of the entire class." He related to Tommy how Ozegowsky had picked on his father. Tommy listened sympathetically, and when the story was finished, he clapped Daniel on the shoulder.

"You did the right thing, Cherrybum. I wouldn't let anyone badmouth my father either."

"How is he?" Daniel suddenly asked. He had been so taken

up with his own dismal future he'd completely forgotten to ask Tommy about his own family. "Made lieutenant yet?"

"Any day," Tommy answered proudly. "Top of the list."

"What about you? When are you going in?"

"Soon as I graduate from high school. Then I go to the academy and join the family business."

"Copper." Daniel smiled.

"Better watch your ass when I'm in uniform. I'll lock you up and throw away the key. Else I'll stick you in the same cell as this Ozegowsky character." Tommy stood up, hooked his thumbs into his belt and tried to do an impersonation of his father's granite face. "Beating up on a poor defenseless teacher, eh, Cherrybum? You're under arrest. Are you coming quietly, or do you want to make me use force?"

Faced with Tommy's clowning, Daniel laughed and began to forget about Joe Ozegowsky and the trade school. He joined in with his friend's joking mood, thankful that Tommy was around.

When Daniel arrived home after the game, his father was already there, sitting in an armchair while he read the newspaper and listened to his Caruso records. His mother was in the kitchen preparing dinner, and Jack was doing his homework in the bedroom.

"Why so late?" Isaac asked, putting aside the paper.

Daniel mumbled something about being kept after school to finish off a sleeve and then entered the bedroom. Jack was sitting at a small desk Isaac had bought secondhand, poring over a book, pen in hand; ink smudges decorated his lips where he had been chewing on the pen in concentration. He looked up when Daniel entered.

"What's Pa doing home so early?" Daniel asked.

"No work. They cut back at the factory as of today. Put everybody on short time."

Daniel's heart plummeted. The day was getting worse by the minute. First the fight with Ozegowsky and now this. It was as if he was being punished for flaunting his father's work in Ozegowsky's face. Sure, his father had spoken about the possibility of being laid off or put on short time. But it was something his father had pushed to the back of his mind, as if by ignoring it the catastrophe would never happen. If he could have expected sympathy from Yetta, perhaps he would have talked about it more often. Ignored or not, though, it had happened. What would the family do now? Perhaps Fat Benny would come riding in like the cavalry again, Daniel mused. He remembered clearly the morning when Isaac had lost all his savings. He'd watched his father dejectedly join the long line of people outside the bank's local branch, all braving the snow and icy weather in the desperate hope that they would be able to get their money. When Isaac had trudged home, empty-handed, with the bitter knowledge that he had also lost a day's work, he had gone to the bedroom and laid down for almost three hours. Even Yetta had not dared to disturb him. Finally he had emerged and telephoned Fat Benny. His brother had come within half an hour. Pulling a roll of cash from his pocket, he had handed it to Isaac, shooing away the earnest promises to repay.

"That's what you get for trusting banks," Fat Benny had joked in an effort to lighten the awkward situation. "Bank-ruptcy."

"Didn't you keep your money in a bank?" Isaac had asked, the wad of bills still in his hand.

"Me?" Fat Benny had burst out laughing. "I never put a penny away in the bank. I run a cash business. Once you start dealing with the banks, the government gets hold of you."

"Where do you keep it then?"

"At home," Fat Benny had explained. "Everything's at home. Under the floorboards, hidden in the bathroom, stitched into the furniture. Wherever you sit, walk or lie in my house, you're doing it on Benny Kirschbaum's *gelt.*"

Unable to resist a faint smile as he recalled Fat Benny's preposterous claim, Daniel left the bedroom and ventured into the living room. His own troubles were forgotten momentarily as he said to his father. "I hear things are bad at work."

Isaac folded up the newspaper, dropped it onto the floor and turned off the phonograph. "They're not good, Daniel. I'm only working three days a week now. But they'll pick up again," he added, trying to maintain his optimism.

"How will we manage?"

Isaac smiled patiently at the question. "We've managed before when things were rough. We'll manage again, you'll see." He leaned forward and Daniel thought he could see tears glistening in his father's eyes. "You know something, Daniel? People are good."

"They put you on three days a week. That's good?"

"No, not those *mamzerim.*" Isaac made a disgusted face as he thought about his employers. "I mean the landlord. He's good, a kind man. When I came home I called him to let him know what had happened. I told him we might have to move. And do you know what he said?"

Daniel shook his head.

"He said we weren't even to think about moving. The landlord said this to me, can you believe it? He's going to lower the rent from forty-five dollars a month to thirty until things get better. Who would think he would do something like that?"

"Why would he?" Daniel was struck by the strangeness of the gesture. The landlord wasn't given to making such charitable acts. He had always demanded his full rent on the first of the month, and Daniel could even recall two families being evicted for nonpayment of rent. So why was a distinction being made when it came to his own family?

Isaac rewarded the question with another patient smile. "Times are hard for everyone, Daniel. I think the landlord understands this. He feels, perhaps, that if we go he will get some family who will pay his full rent for a month and then not pay any more. The two months or so it will take him to evict them will be money out of his pocket. He's making allowances, tightening his belt. We all have to now."

"And Ma? How's she?"

"She's like your mother always is," Isaac replied philosophically. "No worse and no better. But enough of *tsouris.* How did you do at school today? You said something about staying late because of a sleeve when you came in. Did you have trouble with it? After dinner I'll show you . . ."

Daniel broke in. "I hit the instructor."

Isaac didn't seem to hear, as if by talking he could push out of his mind the reality of a short work week. He carried right on as if Daniel had not spoken. ". . . an easy way to make a perfect sleeve."

"Pa. Will you listen to me, please?" Daniel's voice became urgent, cutting into his father's words. "I hit the instructor, Mr. Ozegowsky."

"You . . . ?" Isaac blinked back his amazement as the impact of his son's words flooded over him. "You hit the instructor?" He gripped Daniel's shoulder tightly. "Why, for God's sake? Why?"

"He kept pushing me. Calling me stupid. Saying I was no good."

"And for that you had to hit him?" The lean times at work meant nothing to Isaac now, not when they were compared with the enormity of what his son was telling him. "Everyone you have to hit, Daniel. Is it because you're so big you think you can push people around? Is that how you're going to live your life, a little bully turning into a big bully?"

"He said some bad things, Pa."

"You told me he said you were stupid. Maybe you were."

"He said other things. About you."

"About me?" Isaac released his grip on Daniel's shoulder. "How can he talk about me? He's never met me."

"He wanted to know if I took after you. He asked if I was hamfisted like you, if I'd inherited it from you."

"Hamfisted!" Any anger Isaac felt toward his son transferred itself into a growing rage against Joe Ozegowsky. "I can sew straighter seams with a blindfold than your instructor could with his eyes wide open! And in half the time!"

"That's what I told him."

"Was that when you hit him?"

"Later. After the class. He kept jabbing me in the chest with his finger, so I jabbed him back."

"When was this, this afternoon?"

"This morning. I cut classes after that."

"Where did you go?"

"To the stadium, with Tommy Mulvaney." Daniel heard footsteps coming from the kitchen and looked around to see his mother. He wondered if she had heard the last few sentences.

"Very nice," she said sarcastically. "Your father's on short time. I'm working myself sick to keep a clean home. Your brother's studying and you're watching your stupid baseball games. Is this why we send you to school? To play truant with that Irish kid?"

Isaac cut in quickly. Perhaps his own employment problems were beyond his control at the moment, but he could still avoid having his home turned into a battleground between his wife and son. "You'll have to apologize to Mr. Ozegowsky when you return to school tomorrow," he told Daniel, forgetting his own anger at the man.

"I can't, Pa."

"What do you mean, you can't?"

"I can't go back."

"Why not?" Yetta asked. "Did you do something so terrible that you're scared to go back?"

"I just can't."

"Why can't you?" Yetta demanded again. "You must have a reason. Is it something else you've done that we must be ashamed of?"

Daniel felt his face beginning to burn. Tears sprang to his eyes as he tried to make his parents understand. "Ozegowsky won't let me come back. He'll report me to the principal and that'll be that."

Isaac held up a placating hand. "We'll talk to your Mr. Ozegowsky. We'll talk to your principal. You'll see, Daniel. Everything will be all right."

How could he make them understand? Daniel jumped up from the chair, rushed past his mother into the bedroom and slammed the door with such force that the entire apartment reverberated. Jack's head shot up from his homework at the sudden explosion of noise.

"What's the matter with you?"

"Nothing!" Daniel screamed at him. "Will you leave me alone?"

Jack gazed pensively at his brother for a moment, then he picked up his homework and walked slowly from the bedroom. Left alone, Daniel threw himself onto the bed, buried his face in his hands and did something he could not remember doing for years. He cried.

Ten minutes passed while he lay sprawled on the bed. Then

the door opened and his father tiptoed in. He stood uncertainly, looking down at his son. Finally he sat down on the edge of the bed, his hand resting on the back of Daniel's head. "What is it?" he asked softly. "Was there something else besides this *mamzer* Ozegowsky?"

Daniel tried to sniff back the tears, ashamed that his father should see him like this. He sat up on the bed and turned to face Isaac. "I can't go back to that school, Pa. Not tomorrow. Not ever."

"So you kept saying before. Why not? There must be a reason," Isaac said patiently.

"I don't think you'd understand."

"Me not understand?" Isaac chuckled. "I understand Rumanian, English, Polish and Yiddish. What's so difficult about you that I wouldn't understand?"

"I hate that school!" Daniel burst out. "I'm not a tailor. I'm not like you. I'm useless with my hands."

Isaac nodded in understanding. "So that's your problem. You think you're wasting your time at that school, is that it?"

"I'm wasting everyone's time. I'd rather be out working. *Shlepping* a dress rail through the garment center, running errands, any job I can find. But I'll never be a tailor no matter how many years I stay at that stinking school!"

"So? Is it the most tragic event in the world if you don't become a tailor?"

"What else can I do?"

"Do you want to work with Uncle Benny? He said he'd take you in with him. Candy stores are a good business. It's hard work, but it's good. Look how well Benny does."

Daniel took a long time to think over the proposition. "Pa," he said at last, "I don't want to work for Uncle Benny either."

"Then what do you want to do? You're fifteen. You should know by now what you want."

"I want to be a singer."

"A singer?" Isaac repeated doubtfully.

"Remember when I worked in the mountains at Joey Bloom's hotel? I sang there. They liked me. They applauded. I can do it, I know I can."

"Daniel, you're only fifteen," Isaac reasoned, reversing his logic of moments earlier. "Tell me, where does a fifteen-year-old boy earn a living by singing?"

"I don't know, but I can do it somewhere. If I get the chance, I can do it."

Isaac spread his hands helplessly, hating to destroy his son's dreams with the realities. "Daniel, to sing properly you need lessons. What you did in the hotel was like an amateur. The people applauded you because you were young, a child who had the courage to stand up there and sing."

"I got paid," Daniel protested.

"You got paid, yes, because you and your friend were a novelty act and your singing was convenient for Mr. Bloom. It saved him spending a lot more money for proper entertainers. You have a nice voice, I know, but I don't have the money to send you to a singing teacher."

"What about Uncle Benny?"

"I've never asked Benny for anything," Isaac said firmly. "He's given but I've never asked for it. Nor will I ask him for money in this instance. We pay our own way."

"Then I'll leave school, get my working papers and start with Uncle Benny in the candy stores," Daniel decided. "I'll do anything but go back to that school."

"Nobody's going to force you to return there if you don't want to."

"What about Ma?"

"Don't worry about your mother. I'll call Uncle Benny now, and he can come over and ask you to work for him as if it's his idea. So wipe your eyes and come outside."

Daniel never returned to the trade school. While Isaac went up to see the principal and arrange for his son's removal from the school and issuance of working papers, Daniel began working in Fat Benny's candy store on Fordham Road, close to the intersection with Jerome Avenue.

The Fordham Road store was the first that Fat Benny had opened, back in 1918, and the daily regimen of Daniel's job brought him a totally new outlook on life. His day started at six in the morning, when he and one of Fat Benny's part-time employees would arrange the newspapers for people to pick up on their way to work. Aunt Tessie would bring in breakfast at seven-thirty and stay in the store for the remainder of the day, until Fat Benny drove her home at five-thirty. Fat Benny divided his time between the second store on University Avenue and the Fordham Road store, where he would often lock himself away for three or four hours at a time in the small office at the back. Daniel watched representatives from tobacco and candy companies arrive, knock on the office door and identify themselves before being admitted. It all seemed very secretive to him, and when he questioned Tessie about it, she just smiled and told him it was the way Fat Benny liked to conduct his business.

Although the University Avenue store closed at six each evening—with the exception of Saturday, when it stayed open late for Sunday newspaper delivery—the Fordham Road operation was kept open until eleven each night by more of Fat Benny's part-timers. Daniel was required to work only one evening, Saturday, although he was given the remainder of the day off. At the end of the first week, his body ached in almost every conceivable spot. Muscles groaned in protest under the unaccustomed strain of lifting cartons, moving stock and standing for long periods behind the counter. But it was better than trying to learn tailoring at the hands and caustic wit of Joe Ozegowsky.

"What do you think of the business now, *shitfes?*" Fat Benny asked on Saturday evening as he helped Daniel to bundle the following morning's newspapers.

"Hard work," Daniel gasped. He glanced toward the counter at the long line of people waiting for their Sunday papers and quickened his pace.

"Builds muscle," Fat Benny said.

Daniel spared a moment from his battle with the volumes of newspapers on the floor to look incredulously at his uncle.

"This is muscle," Fat Benny protested as he understood the reason for his nephew's amazed stare. He offered Daniel his arm. "Solid. Like a rock. Feel for yourself."

Daniel laughed but refused the offer. He hoisted the bundle of newspapers he had just collated and dropped them on the counter where the customers could help themselves.

"Ever hear from that lunatic friend of yours?" Fat Benny asked as Daniel got down to work again. "Wasserman."

Daniel thought back to the disastrous few days in the mountains which had witnessed the birth and death of his singing career. "No, he's probably up to something else by now."

"Good," Fat Benny muttered. "Stay away from *meshuguyim* like that. You don't need them."

"He did me a favor."

"Sure he did," Fat Benny said sarcastically. "He got you the best black eye I've ever seen. Some favor."

"No, I don't mean that. He got me the chance to sing."

"With your voice, you'd have got the chance anyway. Wasserman or no Wasserman."

There seemed to be an underlying meaning to Fat Benny's outwardly simple statement, but before Daniel could think of a tactful way to mention it, his uncle had to leave for the University Avenue store to supervise the newspaper delivery there. Left alone with Tessie—who also worked Saturday nights—Daniel collated the remainder of the newspapers. Finished, he pulled up a stool to the counter and sat down with a chocolate malted and tried to regain his energy.

"Want anything else done, Aunt Tessie?" he asked when the glass was empty.

She looked at the clock over the office door. Ten-fifteen. "You can sweep up if you like, then you might as well go home." She reached into the cash drawer. "Here, don't forget to take this with you."

Daniel looked uncertainly at the ten and two fives his aunt held out to him. "Uncle Benny said fifteen."

"I know what Benny said. So does he. Give the fifteen to your parents. Spend the five on whatever you want. You earned it, darling."

Gratefully, Daniel pocketed the money and began to sweep the floor, clearing up the debris from the newspaper delivery. He cleaned the small washroom in the back of the store, then tugged at the handle of the office door and found it was locked.

"What about in here?" he asked Tessie.

"Don't worry about the office," she called back. "I clean it out once a week for Benny."

"It's no trouble, Aunt Tessie. While I've got the broom I might as well sweep it."

"Don't give yourself work, silly boy. It's Saturday night. Go home. Besides, Benny doesn't like anyone going in there. He's scared his papers will get messed up or something."

Daniel shrugged his shoulders, deposited the garbage in an empty carton and left the store, stopping to kiss Tessie on the cheek as he passed her. She wrapped her arms around him and kissed him back. Waiting until he was on the sidewalk, he began to rub feverishly at the lipstick marks with his handkerchief.

When he got home, he proudly presented the fifteen dollars to his father. Isaac's eyes lit up with pride. "Look, Yetta!" he cried. "Another breadwinner in the family."

Daniel's mother looked at the fifteen dollars with undisguised contempt. "Some giver, your brother Benny," she said to Isaac. "The boy works all week, early morning till late at night, and this is what Benny gives him. Better he should have stayed at school."

Daniel felt in his trouser pocket and pulled out the other five dollars. "Aunt Tessie gave me this on top."

"For yourself?" Isaac asked.

Slowly, Daniel nodded his head.

"Then we don't need it. You keep it. You're a working man now. You need money in your pockets."

Daniel looked deeply into his father's eyes. He pocketed the money, leaned forward and, as if embarrassed by the action, quickly kissed his father on the cheek.

The following afternoon, Daniel went to another ballgame with Tommy Mulvaney. This time, however, he was up on his feet with the rest of the crowd when Ruth slammed another shot down the rightfield line for a home run.

"How does it feel to be a working man?" Tommy asked. He could not help noticing the change in his friend's behavior. If he wasn't exactly self-confident about his new status in life, at least he wasn't as unhappy as he had been in the trade school.

"Working in a candy store isn't really work," Daniel

replied, affecting a blasé attitude about the idea of having a job. "It'll do, though, till something better turns up."

"Anything in sight?"

"Not yet, but I'm looking." Talk was ridiculously easy, Daniel decided. He had the only job available to him in these hard times, and right now it looked as if he'd spend his entire life behind the counter of the candy store. He supposed that when Fat Benny and Tessie eventually died, they might even leave him the stores if he was still working for them. Fifteen years old, and already the heir apparent to a thriving candy store business. The idea brought a huge smile to his face. "You know something, Tommy? One day, if I play my cards right, I might just become the candy store king of the Bronx."

"Just make sure you spare a passing thought and a free cup of coffee for the patrolman who staggers in frozen during the middle of winter."

"Nothing on the arm for coppers," Daniel retorted, turning to grin at the ginger-haired boy. "First rule of the house is that all cops get charged double the price."

"And I'll get all your stores so plastered with violation notices you won't be able to see out of the windows. Come on, let's get out of here," he added as the final out was made on the field.

On the way home, Tommy invited Daniel up to the apartment for a cold drink. As they arrived, they met Sergeant Mulvaney coming home from his shift. In the living room, Daniel watched in fascination as Tommy's father removed his gun and belt, wrapped them into a tidy bundle and locked them away in a closet, pocketing the key.

"You ever used that, Mr. Mulvaney?" Daniel asked, pointing to the closet.

"Only for pistol qualification," Mulvaney answered. "And that's the way I'd like to keep it till I turn my gun in. How's your father doing?"

"Not too good. They cut back at the factory, put him on a three-day week."

"Tough," Mulvaney sympathized. "But Tommy tells me you're out working now, left school and found a job."

"Soda jerk and floor sweeper at my Uncle Benny's place on

Fordham Road."

"Uncle Benny?" Mulvaney seemed to become more alert, to take more interest in what Daniel was saying. "Benny . . . Kirschbaum?"

"Yes, that's him," Daniel answered, pleased at the police sergeant's recognition of Fat Benny. "He's my father's older brother. How do you know him?"

"His name used to . . ." Mulvaney stopped talking and gazed oddly at Daniel.

"Used to what?"

"I used to be on a nodding acquaintance with him, that's all." Mulvaney tried to switch the subject, asking about the day's ballgame, but Daniel refused to be put off.

"Tell me about how you know Uncle Benny," he pressed the police sergeant. At first he had been pleased that Mulvaney knew him; now he was concerned.

Mulvaney pursed his lips in thought, as if questioning his judgment. "You fond of your uncle, Daniel?"

"He's like a second father to me."

Mulvaney glanced at his son, who was watching the exchange in bewilderment.

"Will you please tell me?" Daniel said.

"Okay." Mulvaney sighed deeply. Couldn't do any real harm to tell the kid, he reasoned. What happened in the old days was all water under the bridge now. "Your uncle used to keep some pretty strange friends. I used to run into him when I had a beat in the Bronx."

Daniel relaxed, convinced that he had been worrying for nothing. "You mean Joey Bloom?" The hotel owner's name sprang automatically to his lips.

Mulvaney nodded. "Among others. You know Joey Bloom?"

"I worked for him last summer, at his hotel."

"How did you get that job? Through Benny?" When Daniel nodded, Mulvaney's eyes narrowed almost imperceptibly. So, they're still bosom buddies, he thought. "What were you doing? Waiting tables?"

"That, and"—an edge of pride crept into Daniel's voice—"some singing."

"How did you get on with Bloom?"

"Not too well," Daniel admitted ruefully. "He threw me out because he caught me making a pass at his daughter."

"He did you a favor." No expression crossed the police sergeant's face as he spoke; no grin appeared as it would have if he were joking. "A big favor."

Tommy interrupted. "How do you mean he did Cherrybum a favor?"

Mulvaney moved in the chair to look at his son. "By the time you come into the department, Tommy, I'd like to believe that scum like Joey Bloom won't still be around. But they will. If not Bloom himself, then some other creep just like him."

"What did he do?" Daniel asked.

Mulvaney swung back to Daniel, his mind made up to tell him everything. The kid could take it; and it might do him good to know the kind of people with whom his uncle associated. "Your uncle and Joey Bloom were partners, Daniel. Along with a couple of other guys called Mickey Bentley and Abe Hirsch. They used to run a bookmaking operation, a big one. From what I could gather, it was strictly on the up and up. They paid out the bets, and no one ever complained. But Bloom had other ideas. He wanted to spread his wings, be the Napoleon of crime. He wanted more money, more power. He wanted to challenge the big boys. So he went into the protection rackets. Small shops that didn't pay up got wrecked by Bloom's thugs, their owners were beaten up, the families threatened."

"Was Fat Benny in with him?" Daniel was so appalled at Mulvaney's revelation that he did not even realize he had let the nickname slip.

"No," Mulvaney said firmly. "Your uncle and the other two broke off the business connection when they realized what was happening. But your uncle stayed in touch. We think it was Benny Kirschbaum who hid Bloom when the mob was looking to pay him out for muscling in on their territory. Stashed him away somewhere until the heat cooled."

"Was that after Bloom's wife was killed?"

"Who told you about Bloom's wife? Your uncle?"

"He said Bloom's wife started the car and there was a bomb in it, meant for Bloom," Daniel replied.

Mulvaney gave a sour grin. "You're making it sound like a terrible accident, Daniel. Like we should all feel sorry for Joey Bloom. Don't be fooled. Bloom always had his wife start the car for that very reason. She was more frightened of that little runt than she was of the possibility that something might happen to her. Now do you understand what I mean by saying Bloom did you a big favor by kicking you out?" Mulvaney finished by asking.

Daniel could think of nothing to say in reply. He was too horrified to speak. If Fat Benny had known all about this—and he must have—then it was no wonder he'd told Daniel how lucky he had been to get off with only a black eye. His uncle must have used every piece of influence he had with Joey Bloom to get him out of the mess. The thought of what might have happened to him had Fat Benny not intervened made Daniel's blood turn to ice in his veins.

That night, listening to his brother's regular breathing as he slept across the room, Daniel lay awake in bed, going over the conversation with Sergeant Mulvaney. Was it really true what he had said about Bloom, or was he exaggerating? Had it really been no accident that Bloom's wife had been killed by the bomb? Had Bloom been so callous as to send her out each morning to start the car when he knew it might be booby-trapped? And if all this were true, how much did Fat Benny know about it?

And most important of all—the question hammered away inside Daniel's brain, terrifying him—what was Fat Benny's continuing involvement with the gangster?

Chapter Five

Isaac Kirschbaum had promised his older son that the family would manage, although its major earner had been put on a three-day week, and he intended to honor that vow. He quickly found a second job—doing alterations for a small tailoring shop within a mile from home—which filled in the missing two days and enabled him to bring home an additional ten dollars to supplement the reduced income from the factory in Manhattan. By far the biggest boon to the family, however, was the fifteen dollars which Daniel continued to bring home each week from Fat Benny's candy store, as well as the extra few dollars Tessie handed him each Friday night for pocket money. After the first week, when he had kept all the five dollars for his own enjoyment—spending as if he had inherited a fortune—Daniel insisted on turning over the money to his father to be put toward the family's upkeep. He continued to tell Tessie he kept the money for himself, but she smiled knowingly each time, easily seeing through the transparent deception.

By the end of August, with eight full weeks of experience behind him, Daniel was certain he could run the Fordham Road store on his own. His mind had become retentive to a degree that would have simultaneously thrilled and shocked the same school teachers who had criticized his lack of ability and concentration. After a day in the store, he would reel off to Fat Benny which cigarette and confectionery brands needed replacing, how many newspapers had been left unsold and which ice cream flavors and syrups needed reordering. At first, Fat Benny had checked the inventory to see for himself, unwilling to trust the memory of his fifteen-year-old nephew. After a week of double-checking Daniel's mental calculations, he began to take his word.

The last Friday in August began with a brief but heavy summer shower, drenching Daniel as he dragged the morning newspaper delivery in from the sidewalk. By the afternoon, however, the sun's searing heat had made him forget about the rain. The temperature was in the nineties, the broad-bladed electric fan circulating above the counter was doing its best to move the sticky air, and Daniel was doing a record business in ice cream sodas. Tessie occupied her customary position by the cash drawer, fanning herself lethargically with a newspaper, moving only when it was absolutely necessary to make change for a customer. Sweat had gathered under the arms of her short-sleeved dress and spread across her back; the ends of her hair were soaking wet. Occasionally she would glance at Daniel behind the counter, watching as he wiped his sticky hands on the white apron that protected his trousers. The apron reminded Tessie of an artist's abstract interpretation of a rainbow, stained with different colors from the various syrups. Only the rich brown of coffee was missing, she noticed; on a day as hot as this one, nobody in his right mind was going to order a cup of coffee.

"Want to take a break, darling?" she called out to Daniel.

He turned around at the sound of her voice and she saw his face was shining with sweat. "In a while, Aunt Tessie."

"Suit yourself." She moved on the seat, trying to unstick herself from the plump cushion that protected her flesh from the hard wood, and looked out through the plate glass window to the street. As he watched, Fat Benny's Ford sedan drew up to the curb. Her husband climbed out, accompanied by two men, and walked toward the store entrance. All three men carried their jackets. Their shirt sleeves were rolled high and their collars were undone. One man carried a bulky, well-worn leather briefcase.

Hearing the sounds of voices, Daniel looked up from his work. He watched Fat Benny pause long enough to kiss Tessie. As he passed Daniel, he leaned across the counter and pinched his nephew's cheek affectionately. Then all three men disappeared into the back office.

"DeNobili cigars," Tessie said without hesitation.

"Both of them?"

Tessie shrugged. "Maybe one of them's new, learning the route, meeting the customers. I couldn't tell you."

That didn't seem likely, Daniel thought; both men had seemed like pros. He gazed speculatively at the closed door to the office and wondered why it took two men to handle Fat Benny's order. Even stranger, why did his uncle bring the men to the store? Didn't DeNobili representatives have their own transportation? The concern raised by Sergeant Mulvaney's revelations reasserted itself, gnawing at Daniel while his imagination ran riot, forming liaisons between Fat Benny and all kinds of unsavory characters. He stopped daydreaming only when the man waiting to be served rapped in exasperation on the counter top.

The two men from DeNobili cigars left fifteen minutes later and Fat Benny appeared at the office door, looking out into the store. Behind him, Daniel could make out a desk with two telephones. Two telephones? Why did Fat Benny need two telephones in the office when he had one outside in the candy store? One of the phones began ringing and Fat Benny closed the office door to answer the call.

Representatives from various companies continued to come and go throughout the afternoon. Sometimes Fat Benny had as many as three men from different firms in the office at the same time. Each time a man walked through the shop and knocked on the office door to be admitted, calling out his name, Tessie would have a company with which to link him.

"How come he's got travelers from competing companies in there at the same time?" Daniel eventually asked. "One shouldn't know what business the other one's doing."

"End of the month scramble," Tessie explained easily. "They're all rushing around like chickens without heads to get their orders in or their accounts settled. Poor Benny's almost exhausted, but they all leave it so late it's criminal."

Daniel did not bother asking any more questions. He turned on the small radio, found a popular music station he liked and increased the volume. When he recognized a song, he joined in.

"Who's that with the stammer?" Tessie wanted to know.

"Bing Crosby," Daniel answered, tapping his foot in time with the crooner's rhythm.

"Crosby? Don't know him."

"He's new," Daniel explained, eager to share his knowledge of the popular music scene. "A vocalist with Paul Whiteman."

"Whiteman? A *Yiddishe* boy?" Tessie wondered aloud. "Maybe he changed it from Weitzman?"

"Why should he?" Daniel wanted to know. "We never changed ours from Kirschbaum."

"Your Uncle Benny was lucky when he came over to this country, darling. He had an immigration officer who could speak Yiddish. Otherwise we'd have been called something *goyishe* like Kerr." She became interested in the radio again. "Why does this man Crosby stammer all the time, with this bu-bu-bu-bu-business?"

Daniel could not help laughing at the question. "That's not a stammer, Aunt Tessie. That's his style, See? I can do it, too." While Daniel performed his best impersonation, Tessie eyed him cynically.

"Some *meshuggeh* world we live in," she said as he finished. "When a speech impediment is a singing style."

Another man walked in from the street and Tessie pointed toward the back of the store. As the office door opened, Daniel could hear the ringing of both telephones; one was answered by Fat Benny, the other by one of the men in the office with him. Before the door was closed, Daniel thought he heard the second man who had answered the phone shouting at someone. He shrugged his shoulders and returned to his work; it was none of his business.

By five-thirty, all of Fat Benny's visitors had left. He came out of the office, locked the door and slipped the key into his jacket pocket. "Want a ride home?" he asked Daniel.

"Sure."

Fat Benny waited for the woman who would mind the store for the remainder of the evening, then he, Tessie and Daniel went out to the Ford.

"Coming up?" Daniel asked when the Ford stopped outside the apartment building on Claremont Parkway.

"Your father home yet?" Fat Benny asked.

"Should be."

Tessie and Fat Benny followed Daniel up to the apartment. The table was set in the living room for the Friday evening meal. Candles were ready for lighting at the top of the table next to the bottle of wine and plaited *challah*, and the best cutlery gleamed. At the sound of the apartment door closing, Yetta Kirschbaum emerged from the kitchen. Dusting flour from her hands onto her apron, she eyed her brother-in-law and his wife and wondered what could be the cause of their visit.

"Hi, Yetta." Fat Benny stepped forward and kissed her on the cheek. "How you been keeping?"

"Very well," Yetta replied stiffly. "Anything you want in particular?"

"Isaac around?"

"In the bedroom. Changing. He's just home from work." She nodded to Tessie, who had remained by the door.

"How's things at the factory?" Fat Benny asked.

"So-so." Yetta made a noncommittal gesture. "Still only three days a week."

"You getting by?"

"We get by. It would be nicer, though, if we had our own business like you, but I suppose we mustn't complain."

The bedroom door opened and Isaac emerged. His face brightened when he saw his brother and sister-in-law. He hugged Fat Benny and kissed Tessie, glad to see them both. Then he hugged his son. "Is being a merchant in his blood?" he asked Fat Benny, indicating Daniel.

"Being a soda jerk's in his blood," Yetta said sourly. "That's all he'll ever be, leaving school like he did."

Fat Benny took no notice of his sister-in-law. "He's got a mind like a steel trap, our Daniel. I don't have to keep records anymore of what's been sold. I just wind Daniel up and he reels off figures like he's got an adding machine between his ears. He could be an accountant—even if he did leave school when he did," he added loudly for Yetta's benefit.

"Do you want to stay for dinner?" Isaac asked. "Yetta's made *perchar.*" He smacked his lips exaggeratedly.

Fat Benny was tempted, as he imagined a plate of calf's foot jelly in front of him, a piece of sliced egg on top, the subtle flavor of garlic, but he shook his head. "No, we've got to go out. Another time." He could swear he saw a look of relief flash across Yetta's face. As much as he liked the cooking of the *heim*, he did not think he could sit through a meal with Yetta for company, knowing she was totting up every bite he took, begrudging his every mouthful. He pulled Isaac aside.

"You need anything?"

"No. With two jobs and with what Daniel brings home we're making ends meet better than before."

"Are you sure? All you've got to do is say the word. Don't be frightened to ask."

"Benny, don't worry about us. We've got food on the table. The rent's paid and we're clean and dry. What more can we possibly want?"

"Your tastes were always too simple." Fat Benny did not know whether Isaac understood the double meaning.

Isaac gave his brother a little smile. "Yetta's all right. She's just difficult to understand sometimes. After all these years I'm used to her."

"Okay. I just prefer my women to be big and jolly like Tessie." Fat Benny reached out a hand to straighten Isaac's shirt. "Take the family away for the weekend. Get out of the city, out of the heat." Isaac felt something being pushed into his shirt pocket. He stiffened up, then relaxed; it was useless to fight against Fat Benny's generosity.

"Thank you."

"Don't thank me. Thank your son. He's saving me money the way he's working. You've got a lovely boy there, Izzy. I'm jealous of you."

"The truth—he's working out well?"

"Too well. I don't know how long I'll be lucky enough to keep him."

"What do you mean?"

Fat Benny just smiled, leaving Isaac to dwell on the statement.

Daniel continued to sit at the dinner table long after the meal was over. His stomach was heavy with food and his senses were dulled. His brother was helping to wash up in the kitchen, while his father was slumped in his favorite chair, listening dreamily to a Caruso record. As the music washed over Daniel, he felt he had to get out of the apartment. The heat and the heavy dinner were joining forces to form an uncomfortable combination and he needed fresh air desperately. It had to be cooler outside. Besides, as much as he loved his father he could not tolerate the music he continually played. Caruso! The man had been dead for almost ten years and his father had still not found a replacement. On top of that, you couldn't understand the words, and the man sounded like he was trying to give himself a hernia the way he reached for those high notes. Wop singing!

"I'm going out, Pa."

"Be back late?"

"Probably."

Isaac smiled at the answer. "Look at my son, the working man. A dollar in his pocket, it's Friday night and he's going to hit the town."

"No work till tomorrow evening."

"Be careful how you go."

Daniel promised that he would. He said good night to his brother and mother and left the apartment. Outside, he stood uncertainly, not knowing where to go. He decided to try Tommy Mulvaney. The ginger-haired boy was out, and Daniel began to walk along Claremont Parkway, stopping to look in shop windows. At Hymie's he had a soda, spending fifteen minutes there while he waited to see if anyone he knew would come in. Finally he picked up his change and left.

An hour of aimless walking brought him to the intersection of Fordham Road and Jerome Avenue. What about popping into the candy store? he wondered. Maybe Fat Benny had come back for something. He'd have someone to talk to. With more purpose to his stride he started to walk in the direction of the store.

"What are you doing back here?" the woman employed by Fat Benny inquired as Daniel entered the store. "You like it here so much you can't stay away?"

"Nothing to do, Millie," Daniel answered. "You need any help?"

"Never goes to waste, that's for sure." The woman studied him for a moment. "You really want to do me a favor, Daniel?"

"Sure."

"There's just an hour or so until we close. Would you take over for me and lock up so's I can go home? I've got a lot to do."

"No problem," Daniel said grandly. He moved behind the cash drawer, watching the woman as she swept the floor and cleaned up before leaving. There would be little for him to do now, sell the occasional pack of cigarettes, make a soda or two. It was better than strolling blindly around the streets in search of something to pass the time, or going home to the stifling atmosphere of the apartment and his father's Caruso records. A eunuch, that Caruso must have been. Only someone with no balls could reach that high and sound like a woman. Give him Russ Columbo and this new guy Crosby anytime.

Daniel experienced a certain peace as he sat behind the cash drawer, king of all he surveyed until Fat Benny came back and reclaimed rightful possession of the realm of candy stores. The remaining hour passed swiftly while Daniel alternately listened to the radio and daydreamed. Precisely at eleven o'clock, he turned off the lights and prepared to lock the heavy glass-and-wood front door. Some instinct made him stop. He stepped back into the store and locked the door from the inside. In the darkness, he hesitated for a moment, knowing that what he was doing was wrong. Then he walked toward the office in the back.

His breathing sounded loud enough to deafen him as he tried the office door handle. If someone walked by on the street they'd hear him. They had to. They'd call the police and he'd be arrested. He suddenly smiled, knowing how ridiculous the idea really was. Nobody could hear his breathing from outside. Besides, he had every right to be in the store. He worked there; his uncle owned it.

The door to the office refused to move. Daniel retreated to the cash drawer and felt around blindly in the dark as he tried to find a spare key. Was there one? Or did Fat Benny have the only key? He found nothing and began to question his determination to see what really lay in that rear office. It was none of his business anyway. If Fat Benny had wanted to involve him in that part of the operation he'd have invited him in there by now. No, the office was Fat Benny's private domain, and should remain so.

Having reached that decision, Daniel walked toward the front door, ready to leave. But halfway there, he changed his mind again, unable to rid himself of the suspicion and anxiety aroused by Mulvaney. Damn Tommy's father. Why the hell did he have to tell him about Fat Benny's past? And why did all those men have to come into the shop today, the reps from DeNobili, and all the others that followed them?

Daniel returned to the cash drawer and felt around underneath the counter. His hand came in contact with a strip of springy metal, a cigarette advertisement that now lent its straight edge for use as a ruler. Picking it up, he returned to the office door. He slid the strip of metal into the crack of the door and jiggled it about. To his surprise there was a soft click. The door swung back. Feverish with the excitement that comes with knowingly crossing the threshold between right and wrong, Daniel dropped the strip of metal onto the floor and stepped into the office. Closing the door, he switched on the light. There were no windows and he felt safe.

With his first glance around the room, nothing he saw showed it to be anything other than an ordinary office—a desk, four chairs, the telephones he had seen, and cupboards piled high with papers. On the cheaply carpeted floor was a carton of empty seltzer bottles.

Daniel almost felt cheated for a moment, but more than anything else he felt relieved. Fat Benny wasn't involved in anything other than running the two candy stores. Mulvaney's words had triggered unwelcome visions in Daniel's mind, visions that had combined with the secrecy that Fat Benny insisted on maintaining and prompted Daniel to peek inside the office. Now he was inside, there seemed to be nothing to warrant that secrecy. But still that nagging doubt continued to plague Daniel. Until he had seen the contents of the desk, of the cupboards, he would not be able to relax. He opened a drawer of the desk and pulled out a set of papers, scanning them quickly. They were orders and receipts, all pertaining to the candy stores, from tobacco and confectionery companies. Another file he skimmed through concerned newspaper and periodical distribution. He replaced everything in the correct order and closed the desk drawers. Next, he went to the cupboards. Dust covered a hardbound ledger. He leafed through the pages, relieved when he recognized Fat Benny's handwriting in what was obviously an old set of the company's books.

So far he had found nothing extraordinary. Not that he had really expected to, he told himself. But the memory of the conversation with Tommy's father made him press on. Another hardbound ledger came to light, tucked away in the bottom of one of the cupboards. Daniel opened the pages to see more columns of figures in his uncle's unmistakable handwriting, some in red ink, others in black. But this time there were no familiar names to coincide with the entries. There were dates, but instead of names there were numbers. And some of the entries were far larger than any he had seen in the other set of books. There was even a four-figure entry, in red ink, amounting to more than fifteen-hundred dollars.

Although he understood nothing of the figures in front of him, Daniel became apprehensive. All he knew was that they had nothing to do with the candy store operation. He set down the book and explored further. A large cardboard carton was next, filled almost to the brim with scraps of white paper. Seeing they were in no specific order, Daniel tipped the contents onto the carpet. The first one he held up to the light made him suck in his breath. At the top was the letter B; underneath was the number 2 and another letter, G. At the bottom was written the sum of five dollars, followed by a large W with a name. All of it was clearly in Fat Benny's handwriting.

The name at the bottom of the piece of paper meant nothing to Daniel, but he could figure out the remainder. The B stood for Belmont. The number was the race, the letter signified the selected horse, and the bet was five dollars to win.

Sergeant Mulvaney was right. Fat Benny was a bookie. Although he had broken off his business association with Joey Bloom when Bloom had expanded the operation, Fat Benny had carried right on with the bookmaking, using the candy stores as his front. No wonder he and Tessie always had money to spare, spending it and giving it away like they could grab handfuls of the stuff out of the air whenever they needed it. From what he had seen of the two candy stores, Daniel could never understand how Fat Benny came by so much money. Now he could.

Taking great care to put everything back the way he had found it, Daniel turned off the light and pulled the door closed. The lock snapped back on. After he had locked the store and started to walk back toward Claremont Parkway, he thought anxiously about the men who kept visiting Fat Benny in the back of the store.

Company representatives or gamblers?

Or worse?

The Sunday morning newspaper delivery was ten minutes behind schedule on Saturday night. Daniel stood around idly, waiting for the truck, while Fat Benny busied himself rearranging the display of periodicals. A line of people stood by the counter, ready to snap up the first newspapers.

"You putting in some overtime last night?" Fat Benny asked his nephew.

The boy looked up sharply. Fat Benny's face showed nothing other than sweat from his exertions. "What do you mean?"

"You came back here just before ten and helped Millie out. She told me all about it. Said you were a sweet kid for taking over and letting her go home early."

Daniel's heartbeat, which felt as if it had doubled its rate, subsided to a near-normal pace. "I had nothing to do. Pa was playing his Caruso records so I had to get out of the house. I dropped by here, thought that you might be around."

Fat Benny's entire body wobbled as he laughed at his nephew's reply. "Must be something important missing from you, Daniel. When I was your age, I had better things to do with my spare time. Come on, look sharp. Here comes the truck."

Daniel transformed his body into a machine, arms moving in robot fashion as he stuffed the different sections into the correct order and pushed the completed papers along the counter top toward the waiting customers. The telephone in the shop rang and Tessie answered it, indicating to customers that they should leave the correct change if they had it. After a moment, she waved to Fat Benny. Daniel looked up. Over the noise and confusion in the shop, he could swear that she mouthed a single word to her husband.

"Joey."

Disturbed, Daniel went back to sorting the newspaper sections. He tried to push the name out of his mind. Surely Fat Benny knew more than one Joey; it didn't have to be Joey Bloom. He looked up again to see Fat Benny replacing the receiver, then he went to his jacket and pulled out the key to the office door. Daniel's heart began to race again as he tried frantically to remember if he had left everything as he had found it. The door closed and Daniel attempted to concentrate on sorting the newspapers. One customer complained when he got a paper with a section missing, and Tessie chided her nephew, smiling to take the bite out of her words.

When the office door opened again, ten minutes later, Daniel suddenly paled. Fat Benny's normally jolly face was puzzled. In his hand he held the springy strip of metal that Daniel had dropped onto the floor and forgotten all about.

A week slipped past, during which Fat Benny made no mention of finding the metal strip on the floor of his office. Gradually Daniel allowed the memory of his uncle's perplexed face to fade from his mind. As busy as his uncle was, he probably could not remember whether he had taken the strip into the office himself, Daniel reasoned. It was used as a ruler in the store; why shouldn't Fat Benny have taken it into the office with him for that very purpose? Despite calming his own fears, though, nothing could ease the shock and disappointment he felt discovering Fat Benny was still a bookie.

The following Saturday night, shortly after ten, Tessie complained of a headache. Fat Benny told Daniel he would take her home, but would be back by eleven to help close up. Just before eleven, when Daniel was preparing to close up, Fat Benny returned.

"Stick around for a while, Daniel, I want to speak to you."

Daniel stared into his uncle's face as he tried to read what lay behind the invitation. He could see nothing, but deep down he knew the reason for the unexpected request.

"Lock the front, Daniel," Fat Benny said as he opened the office door. "Then come in here."

Obediently Daniel locked the front door and turned off the store lights. When he entered the office, Fat Benny was sitting at the desk. "Take a seat," his uncle invited. "Make yourself at home. You're not a stranger to this room, are you?"

Daniel did not say a word. He perched nervously on the edge of a chair, waiting to see what would happen next.

"You left something here the other night, didn't you?" Fat Benny picked up the metal strip, which was lying on top of the desk. "You'd make some lousy kind of housebreaker, leaving clues lying around for the cops to nail you."

Still Daniel said nothing. He swallowed a couple of times and tried to speak, but each time he opened his mouth his throat went dry. Words simply refused to come.

"Is that why you came back here last Friday and took over from Millie?" Fat Benny asked. "To find out for yourself what was back here?"

Slowly Daniel shook his head. "Not at first," he whispered, his voice choking off in the back of his throat. He had to speak, had to find some words with which to defend himself before Fat Benny damned him.

"Not at first," his uncle repeated. "But then you slipped the lock and you looked around? What did you find? Company records? Order forms? Receipts?"

Daniel managed to find his voice at last. "Betting slips!" he burst out. "You had a cardboard box full of betting slips! And more ledgers that had nothing to do with the candy stores!"

Fat Benny glanced toward the cupboard where Daniel had unearthed the betting slips. "That box of slips was a mistake," he admitted. "We were so busy that day I forgot to clear them out. Normally I do it every day, throw them down the incinerator at home."

Daniel seemed not to hear him. He rose from the chair and pointed an accusing finger at his uncle. "You're a bookmaker!" he shouted. "You're a crook! A criminal!"

Fat Benny's huge, moonlike face seemed to sink in pain as he stared at the teenager with the pointing finger; a physical blow could not have injured him more. "I'm not a criminal, Daniel. Being a bookie's not the same as being a crook."

"What is it, then?"

"I've never cheated or robbed anyone. All my winners get paid out. I don't welsh on my bets."

"But it's against the law!" Having burst through the dam of silence, Daniel could not stem the angry words that flooded out. "You're breaking the law so you're a crook!"

"Whose law?" Fat Benny sat up in the chair as straight as his body would allow. "Some stupid jerk in government who thinks it's immoral for people to gamble?"

The simple questions stymied Daniel. He felt a burning anger with himself for challenging the ethics of a man who had done so much for himself and his family, but he was even more furious with that man. He'd adored Fat Benny all his life, and now he had discovered that his uncle was nothing but a crook. "What about those other things?" he shot back, perversely trying to deepen the anguish he knew his uncle felt. "What about the partnership you used to have with Joey Bloom? His protection racket?"

Fat Benny's face paled. "Who told you about me and Joey Bloom? Who's been spreading that kind of poison around? Your mother, God bless her?"

"No." Daniel bit his lip, not wanting to implicate the Mulvaneys. "I . . . I just heard it from somewhere, that's all," he finished weakly.

"I suppose that now you think you're entitled to an explanation of my association with Joey Bloom," Fat Benny said. "Although I don't know what right you have to expect anything. Anyone in his right mind would beat the hell out of you and throw you out on your ear." He waited several seconds, deciding what, if anything, to tell his nephew. Then he said, "Joey Bloom and I used to be partners in this thing. With two other guys."

"Mickey Bentley and Abe Hirsch," Daniel murmured.

"You should have done your homework so good at school. That's right, Mickey and Abe. We split up from Joey when he became too big, too ambitious for his own good. Joey wanted too much. He wanted a piece of all the other action that was going on. Being a bookie, earning a good living without hurting anyone wasn't enough for Joey. So we split up the money and called it a day." He broke off for a moment, and his voice was solemn, quiet, as he said, "Daniel, I swear this on my own life, and God is my witness, I had nothing to do with Joey when he started muscling in on the protection rackets."

"What about when you hid him out?"

Fat Benny regarded his nephew with a new awareness. "You've really got an in somewhere. Sure as hell your mother never told you that. Nobody knows about it. Someone put the finger on Joey's car and his wife got blown to bits instead. So he had to hide out 'til the pressure was off."

"Why you?" Daniel asked. "Why didn't he go somewhere else?"

"You don't pal around with a guy like Joey Bloom and then shrug him off like some old coat, Daniel. I had to hide him for my own sake. I was scared he'd take me down with him. Joey and Linda stayed right here—she was a little kid then—in this room. For two weeks. Then they both skipped town. Since then I've had no business dealings with him."

"But you still see him?"

"Sure. Tessie and I go to his hotel. We get the best service and the best rates. He owes me, and this is the way he pays off. But that's all."

Daniel looked away, unable to face his uncle. He felt ashamed of himself. Fat Benny was right. Being a bookie wasn't so terrible. Everyone had some fiddle going; why shouldn't his uncle?

The carton of empty seltzer bottles was still on the floor. Daniel rose from the chair and lifted the carton. "Guess these should go outside with the rest of the collection," he said.

"Been meaning to do that for a couple of weeks," Fat Benny remarked. "Got so hot in here one day that we went through a complete case in one afternoon. Me and a couple of guys who come in here sometimes to help answer phones."

"Those men who come to see you?"

"Some are just friends. Some are gamblers, or other bookies laying off heavy money. I get a lot of action from small bookies who get too scared to handle big bets."

"Who was the guy with the briefcase last Friday?" Daniel asked. "He got out of your car with another man. Aunt Tessie said they were from DeNobili."

Fat Benny burst out laughing. "She said that? That's a scream. That guy wouldn't know a DeNobili cigar if he saw one. It's Cuban cigars or nothing for him. That's Callahan, a detective from the precinct. He's the bagman. I pay him off for peace and quiet, protection money." He watched Daniel carry the seltzer bottles to the door. "Are you still disgusted with me?"

Daniel turned around and looked at his uncle. "It'll pass."

"Not everyone in life can afford to keep up high ideals, kid."

"I'm learning."

Fat Benny stood up and followed Daniel out into the darkened store. "Hungry?"

"A bit."

"I know a good delicatessen. Coming?"

Daniel felt his stomach tighten at the thought of food. It was a long time since he had eaten dinner. He could already envision a steaming pastrami sandwich on a plate before him. Any animosity he might still have harbored toward Fat Benny disappeared as he realized how close he was to his uncle—both in family ties and in appetite, if not yet in girth.

"See that man sitting in the corner?" Fat Benny asked as he entered the delicatessen with Daniel.

Daniel looked and saw a middle-aged man, newspaper in one hand, a cup of coffee in the other. As if by telepathy, he looked up as Fat Benny pointed him out, then lowered his head again quickly. "Who is he?" Daniel asked.

"Larry Kahn. Ever listen to 'Music for Dreaming'?" Fat Benny asked, naming a popular local radio show. Daniel nodded. "Kahn's the producer. He's also a customer of mine. I'll introduce you to him." Fat Benny walked directly toward the producer's table. Suddenly Daniel realized that his uncle had not chosen this delicatessen or this hour by accident; he had a purpose in asking Daniel here.

"How's it going, Larry?" Fat Benny asked.

Larry Kahn looked up slowly, unwilling to take his attention off the newspaper or to acknowledge the large man who stood over him. "Hi, Benny," he said at last. "What's new? Been meaning to give you a call, honest."

"What's been keeping you then?"

To Daniel, watching the interchange intently, the radio producer looked frightened. It was a new experience for Daniel. He'd never imagined anyone being frightened of Fat Benny, yet this man was almost visibly quaking.

"I know," Kahn said. "I owe you about two—"

"No abouts needed, Larry. You owe me exactly two hundred and eighty-five dollars," Fat Benny said quietly. He pulled out a chair. "Mind if we join you?"

Kahn waved a hand in invitation. The chair groaned as Fat Benny's immense bulk tested its strength. Daniel took the seat next to him.

"I'll be able to pay you off in a couple of weeks," Kahn offered, the newspaper and coffee now forgotten. "I've got a couple of things going for me, no problem."

Fat Benny did not appear to hear the man's protestations. "Larry, I want you to meet my nephew, Daniel Kirschbaum."

"Hi, kid, how's it going." Kahn uttered the few words and dismissed Daniel as being of no importance.

"Daniel's got a great voice, Larry," Fat Benny pressed. "You should hear him sing. He's a born crooner."

"I believe you," Kahn agreed quickly, trying to understand why Fat Benny was bothering him with some overweight kid. "Just give me a couple of weeks and I'll straighten myself out with you, Benny. You can take my word."

"I've already got a fistful of IOU's that are worthless, Larry. What the hell would I do with your word? Anyway, I'm not interested in money right now. I just want you to listen to my nephew sing."

Kahn's face showed more animation as he understood the offer that was being made. "Here? Now?"

"Of course not. Give him an audition during the week at your studio."

"Hey, Benny! Look, you know I'm always willing to swing a favor for you because I like you, but—"

"And because you owe me two hundred and eighty-five

dollars," Fat Benny pointed out.

"That, too," Kahn agreed. "But I can't put the kid on the air just on your say-so. He's got to be good enough to warrant a spot. We've got a million kids out there who think they're Russ Columbo, for Christ's sake. I can't do it."

"All I'm asking you to do is give him a fair chance to show how he can sing," Fat Benny said. "And if he's as good as anyone else, make sure you give him a spot."

"How much does he want?"

"How much do you want?" Fat Benny asked.

Daniel had been listening with growing amazement. His uncle and a radio show producer talking about putting him on the air . . . and now he was being asked how much he wanted? He couldn't believe it. "I don't know. I haven't decided yet."

On more familiar grounds now, Kahn dropped his contrite manner and became businesslike. He saw a way out of his dilemma. Fat Benny was willing to write off the gambling debt if he gave the kid a chance. Fine. As far as Kahn could see there was little possibility of the kid being any good. What did Fat Benny know about music? So he'd give his nephew a shot. The kid would be so thrilled just to get the audition that Fat Benny wouldn't even question why he never got any further. "If you're any good, kid, I can pay you five bucks for a one-hour spot. Maybe have you on a couple of times a week if you catch. We've got some bums filling time now that we can ditch. That okay with you, Benny?" he added, switching back to the deferential manner.

"Sounds fine by me. You just make sure you give him an equal break." Fat Benny stressed the word *equal*, just to put Kahn properly in the picture.

"Yeah, sure, Benny. You got an accompanist you want to bring along for the audition, kid?"

An accompanist? Who had an accompanist? Daniel opened his mouth to reply and saw Fat Benny screw up his eyes in resignation, as if he could sense what was coming. "I used to work with a guy up in the mountains," he said. "Studied classical piano but he can play anything." Daniel was surprised how easily the words were coming to him. He was selling himself, building himself up in the producer's eyes. All right, so Fat Benny had opened the door for him, leaning on the producer with the promise of wiping clean his gambling slate. But from here on in, Daniel was going to make his own mark.

"What's this guy's name?" Kahn asked.

"Wasserman. Moishe Wasserman from Brooklyn." Daniel could swear he heard Fat Benny groan. When he dared to look around, his uncle's face was half covered by his hand. "He'll need paying, too." The roles would be reversed this time; maybe he'd get Moishe to cough up ten percent.

"Get hold of this Wasserman. If the pair of you are any good, we'll pay you five bucks each. Come by on Tuesday evening, around seven. Ask for me." Forgetting about what remained in the coffee cup, Kahn pushed himself back from the table and stood up. "I'm doing just like you asked, Benny. Don't forget."

"I won't. Your markers are as good as flushed down the toilet." He watched Kahn leave the delicatessen, then he turned to Daniel. "What the hell's the matter with you? I get you a shot at something, a foot in the door, and you bring in that lunatic. Do you think I want to write off almost three hundred dollars to let that *meshuggeneh* make five?"

"I don't know anyone else who can play the piano," Daniel protested. "Anyway, he lives in Brooklyn. Maybe it's too far for him to come. Or maybe he's busy Tuesday night."

"He'll come," Fat Benny said with disconsolate certainty. "A stupid klutz like that don't know enough to stay away."

Daniel did not arrive home until almost two in the morning. Fat Benny accompanied him up the stairs, his heavy footsteps sounding inordinately loud in the early morning silence. When Daniel opened the apartment door, he saw the lights were on. His parents were waiting up for him.

"What time do you call this?" Yetta Kirschbaum demanded. "A fifteen-year-old boy staying out so late? It's disgraceful!" When she saw Fat Benny's figure looming in the doorway behind Daniel, she lowered her voice and pulled her dressing gown tighter.

"He was with me, Yetta." Fat Benny nodded to Isaac, who sat quietly in the armchair by the phonograph. "There's nothing to get excited about. We had a business appointment."

"What kind of business is it that has its appointments when honest people are asleep?" Yetta spat out contemptuously. "No-good business, that's what!"

Daniel let his mother finish. She'd probably been working herself up to this crescendo, mentally rehearsing each word she would say. Let her enjoy it. Besides, he wanted silence for what he had to say. "I've got an audition for a radio show," he finally said. "Singing. Uncle Benny arranged it for me through a producer he knows."

"You?" Isaac asked excitedly, jumping up from the chair. "On the radio? When?"

"Not yet." Daniel grinned at his father's reaction. "I have to audition first. If that works, I'll get my own show, maybe twice a week if I'm lucky."

"What do you mean, if?" Isaac said exuberantly. "Of course it'll work!"

"How much are they going to pay you?" Yetta asked suspiciously. "And what station needs a singer so badly that they're willing to audition a child?"

"Only five dollars a show to begin with."

After digesting that lowly figure, Yetta did not even want to know the station. But Isaac's interest waxed. "How did this wonderful thing come about?"

"Through Uncle Benny. He knows a producer there, Mr. Kahn. We met him tonight after the shop closed and he's agreed to give me an audition." Only after the words were out of his mouth did Daniel realize how conveniently he had omitted all reference to Kahn's gambling debts; he'd accepted Fat Benny's bookmaking activities because he was benefitting from their influence.

Isaac's face stretched into a wide smile as he regarded his older brother. He held out his arms and tried to wrap them as far as possible around the huge body, kissing Fat Benny on the cheek. Tears began to form in Isaac's eyes, dribbling down his cheeks till at last they stained Fat Benny's face. It was the first time Daniel had ever seen his uncle blush; his face looked like an enormous beetroot as he struggled to free himself from Isaac's grasp.

"Enough already!" he cried after pushing Isaac away. "I haven't done a thing for the boy. He's doing it all for himself. If he gets the spot, it'll be because his voice is good enough. It'll have nothing to do with me. And if he doesn't get the show, it'll be because his voice is no good. It'll still have nothing to do with me." He opened the apartment door to leave, then turned around to look at Daniel.

"You get plenty of practice so you sound good on Tuesday. Don't let me down. And when you speak to that cretin Wasserman, tell him from me that if he messes up I'll jump on his head with both feet."

For ten minutes after Fat Benny had given his warning and left, Daniel sat up with his father, relating everything that had happened with Larry Kahn—everything except the lever that Fat Benny had used to get him the audition. Now Isaac had two reasons to be proud. His son, and the brother who would go to such lengths for his nephew.

"Did you ever say anything to him?" Daniel asked.

Isaac shook his head. "I told you I would never ask Benny for anything. He must have known you wanted the chance. Tell me the truth, Daniel." Isaac leaned forward as he spoke, his voice little more than a whisper. "Do you know if Benny paid anything for this chance of yours?"

Daniel was uncertain how to answer the question. "No. But it cost him."

Isaac nodded understandingly. "He called in outstanding favors, is that it? Like with you and Joey Bloom's daughter that time? He made people pay off favors they owed him?"

The question brought a sad smile to Daniel's face. His father had no idea about the kinds of favors that Fat Benny called in. With Isaac's gentleness, he probably thought people were constantly repaying his brother for good turns he'd done. "Mr. Kahn owed Uncle Benny for a favor he once did," Daniel replied ambiguously.

Isaac nodded, satisfied.

When Daniel finally went to bed, he found his brother fast asleep. Somehow, Jack had managed to remain undisturbed throughout the entire commotion. Daniel prodded him awake.

Jack sat up slowly, rubbing his eyes as he tried to force them to focus.

"What is it? What's the matter?"

"I'm on the radio," Daniel exclaimed.

"Now?" Jack looked in disbelief at the clock on the table between the two beds. "At two in the morning?"

"No, you idiot! Of course not. Next Tuesday, I've got an audition for a singing show."

"You asshole!" Jack shouted. "For that you woke me up?" He picked up the pillow and threw it at his brother. Daniel caught the pillow in midair, laughing as he threw it back.

"Show some respect for a radio star," he shouted happily.

He undressed, put on his pajamas and slid under the sheet. For almost an hour, he stared at the ceiling, his mind too full of questions to allow him to sleep. The day had been a crossroads in his life. Not just because of the offer of the audition. It was more than that. Today he had added a new perspective that made him feel older, somehow stronger, and yet it saddened him. He had realized that nothing was plain black and white. You had to compromise. Even Fat Benny had compromised, and with the exception of his father there was no one better than Benny. Maybe that was the whole secret of living. The art of compromise. The ability to juggle what you had to obtain the best results.

Moments before he finally fell asleep, Daniel decided that today had been the most important in his life.

Chapter Six

The radio station's offices and studios were located on the top floor of a three-story building on the Grand Concourse in the Bronx. The first floor of the building was given over to stores, the second floor to commercial offices. On the roof, directly above the station, was the transmitter which relayed a moderately weak signal to a tiny band of space at the top of the radio receiver dial.

Shortly before seven o'clock on Tuesday evening, Daniel and Fat Benny stood on the sidewalk outside a hardware store. Neither uttered a word as they waited for Moishe Wasserman to arrive. Unable to ascertain whether Moishe's family had a telephone, Daniel had made the arduous trip to Brooklyn on Sunday afternoon. Moishe had been amazed to open the apartment door and find Daniel standing outside; not having heard from him since the escapade in the mountains the previous year, he'd never expected to see him again.

"Remember my uncle who picked me up from the bus?" Daniel had asked. "He's got me a singing audition on a local Bronx radio station. I need an accompanist. You interested?"

Moishe had pushed back his glasses as he pondered the proposition. Finally he had laid a reassuring hand on Daniel's shoulder. "You came to the right place, kiddo. I'm going into law, specializing in the entertainment field, representing singers and musicians. What do you think of that?"

"I want a yes or a no," Daniel had said impatiently. Jesus Christ! The guy hadn't changed a bit in all that time. He was still gushing forth ideas of self-advancement like a volcano spewing out hot lava.

Faced with Daniel's anger, Moishe had said yes.

"There he is," Daniel said, pointing along the street. Fat Benny shuffled around to look. Strolling toward them at a leisurely pace, hands thrust deeply into his trouser pockets, was Moishe. Under his arm was gripped a cardboard folder containing sheet music. The glasses were perched halfway down his nose and his fair hair, grown unfashionably long, blew about in the light summer breeze. When he recognized Daniel, he waved the folder in greeting. Sheets of music flew out of it to blow along the sidewalk. Moishe turned around to give chase, collecting them gratefully from pedestrians who stooped to pick them up.

"*Golem*," Daniel heard Fat Benny mutter. "Goddamned lunatic."

"This the place?" Moishe asked, once more in control of his music.

"Third floor. We'd better get up there quick," Daniel told him.

"Had a hell of a job getting out to this godforsaken neck of the woods," Moishe explained, guessing correctly that Daniel was tactfully chiding him for cutting the time so close. "Change here, change there, take this train, that train. I just hope these people are paying expenses." He laughed abruptly. "I'll tell them I took a cab."

Daniel started to lead the small group into the building, but Moishe pulled him back. "You didn't mention anything about money on Sunday. What's the score?"

Fat Benny answered the question. "Five bucks for each of you. *If* you do well in the audition."

Moishe pushed the glasses back up his nose and assumed the serious demeanor Daniel remembered when he'd argued money with Joey Bloom. "Five bucks? That's all? It's not even worth my while coming all the way here from Brooklyn for that kind of dough."

"Then you should have stayed put in Brooklyn," Fat Benny replied coldly.

Moishe chose to ignore the gibe. Instead, he turned to Daniel. "I can do better for you, Danny boy. You've got a voice that's worth more than five stinking bucks. You just watch my style when we land this crummy spot."

Moishe might have intended saying more. Just then, Fat Benny reached out and grabbed him by the shirt front, lifting him clean off the ground. "You open your big mouth in there, except to ask Daniel if he's ready, and I'll bust every bone in your stupid body. Understand?"

The glasses slipped down to the end of Moishe's nose as he stared first at Fat Benny's bunched fist screwing up his shirt front, then at the man himself. "Okay," he said defensively. "I was just trying to help, that's all."

"The only way you can help is by keeping your big dumb mouth shut." Without warning, Fat Benny released his grip and Moishe staggered backwards. "Now we've got that straight, let's go see about this audition."

Larry Kahn was working in his small office when Fat Benny marched in. Daniel immediately noticed the change in Kahn from when he had first seen him in the delicatessen. There, he had been nervous, frightened when confronted by Fat Benny's huge bulk and the reminder that he owed money. Here, he seemed more sure of himself, knowing he was in charge. Even the Sword of Damocles that Fat Benny held over his head meant little here in his own kingdom.

"You Wasserman?" Kahn asked.

Moishe nodded.

"There's a piano you can use in"—he checked his watch—"about twenty-five minutes. It's being used right now. We can fit you and Daniel in for the audition while the seven-thirty news flash goes on."

"How long do we get?" Daniel asked.

"Ten minutes. Five minutes for warm-up, five minutes for the audition."

"That's ridiculous!" Moishe exploded. "That only gives us time for one song. What the hell can you tell from one song?"

"All I need to know," Kahn replied. He was convinced that he did not even need one song to know that the fat kid and the skinny accompanist who looked like he was going to lose his glasses at any minute were not going to come through the audition as winners. What did it matter though? Kahn wondered; he would have wiped his slate clean with Fat Benny.

Moishe refused to quit. "I didn't come all the way from Brooklyn to this backwater to get in one lousy song."

"Here, bigshot." Fat Benny cut into the argument. "Here's a dime. Cover your subway expenses."

Moishe swung around belligerently to take on Daniel's

uncle. His gaze dropped to the proffered dime, then up to the pudgy face. Some expression he recognized in Fat Benny's eyes told him it was useless to continue the fight.

"Come with me," Kahn said. He led Fat Benny, Daniel and Moishe along a corridor until they reached a door at the end. A red light was shining outside. Kahn held his fingers to his lips and opened the door gently. It swung back noiselessly on well-oiled hinges. Daniel, Fat Benny and Moishe peered inside. A pretty, dark-haired girl was sitting at a piano, smiling serenely as her fingers danced along the keyboard. Next to her was a microphone. The girl turned to look as the door was opened and Kahn smiled at her. She smiled back as if glad of the interruption to her solitude. Through the glass panel beyond the girl, Daniel could see two technicians in the control room.

"Tosti," Moishe whispered knowingly. "It's an Italian song called 'Ideale,' but you can do it as a piano piece as well." Kahn closed the door as quietly as he had opened it and Moishe spoke louder. "That kind of music would go even better in Brooklyn than around here."

"Italian music—both opera and Neapolitan folk songs—is still very popular everywhere," Kahn said. "Even in the Bronx."

"You're not expecting us to do that kind of stuff, are you?" Daniel asked in a horrified tone. He was terrified that Kahn might be expecting him to sing the kind of music his father insisted on playing on the phonograph.

"We're looking for modern music. That's why we're auditioning you and your friend."

Oh no, it's damned well not, Daniel thought. It's because you owe my uncle a bundle of money which he's willing to write off if you give us this chance. "Who's the girl?" he asked.

"Lucia Sforza," Kahn answered. "She plays here three times a week, half-hour spots. Sings as well."

"Doesn't play badly either," Moishe grudgingly acknowledged. "Almost as good as me."

With Kahn, they sat in the control room and watched Lucia Sforza through the glass panel until her half-hour program was finished. As the music ended, Kahn checked his watch again. "There's ten minutes of news coming up, then there's a drama

I want to supervise. Make it snappy."

With Moishe leading the way, they retraced their steps along the corridor. As they reached the room with the piano, the door opened and Lucia Sforza came out, clutching some sheets of music.

"Nice going, kid," Moishe congratulated her. "Stick around and pick up a few pointers." He marched past her into the room, settled himself at the keyboard and began playing. The girl joined Kahn and Fat Benny, who stood by the wall watching as Daniel walked across to the piano.

Fighting down an increasing attack of nerves that started deep in his stomach and infiltrated every single part of his body until he was certain his hands and legs were shaking with fear, Daniel bent close to Moishe. "What are we going to do?" Panic tinged his voice.

"How about the girl?" Moishe quipped while he carried on practicing.

"Quit fucking around."

Moishe shook his head. "Nope, can't say I know that one. You hum it and I'll catch on."

Daniel's anxiety disappeared in the face of Moishe's clowning. "You screw this one up and I'll stomp your head in," he threatened lightly. "And when I've done with you, my uncle'll finish you off."

"He really your uncle?" Moishe gazed at Fat Benny for a moment.

"Yes, and he's worked damned hard to swing this deal."

"How about 'I've Got a Crush on You,' dedicated to your uncle?" Moishe joked. "We did it in the mountains. Remember the words?"

Daniel nodded, closing his eyes while he mentally rehearsed the lyric. "Ready whenever you are."

Moishe broke off what he was playing, paused for an instant, then came in with the same introduction he had used for Daniel at Joey Bloom's hotel. The nerves returned. Daniel felt as though his chest would burst; his heartbeat accelerated and his head pounded. Desperately he sought a release valve for the panic he knew was setting in. He looked to where the small group of spectators stood. His eyes settled on Kahn, who stared back stonily. Then Fat Benny, who smiled encouragingly, just as he had when Daniel had been *bar mitzvah*ed. Finally the girl, Lucia Sforza. With a physical jolt, Daniel saw that she was wearing a silver Star of David around her neck. Why was a girl with an Italian name like Sforza wearing a *camiah?*

"Come on, for Christ's sake," he heard Moishe mutter. "You just missed your damned cue."

Daniel tore his eyes away from the girl's throat and tried to concentrate on the music. His foot tapped gently on the wooden floor as he waited for Moishe to come around again. Then he opened his mouth and began to sing.

The girl nodded her head in approval as Daniel looked again in her direction. Sforza with a *camiah?* The question flashed once more across his mind and he almost staggered on the words, catching himself just in time to avoid repeating a line. Moishe hissed some unintelligible obscenity and Daniel gathered up his faculties, keeping his eyes away from the girl until the song was over.

To Kahn, the quality of Daniel's singing came as a surprise. He had agreed to the audition only to humor Fat Benny, never thinking for one moment that his bookie's nephew might possess real talent. The voice was sweet, too sweet for Kahn's personal taste, but the kid could put across a song. And Kahn was sure he could get Daniel and the pianist for even less than he had originally offered; they'd be so thrilled to be offered a spot that they'd do it for nothing.

At the end of the song, Moishe added a little flourish for effect. Daniel fidgeted nervously, uncertain where to put his feet or his hands. While he had been singing, his hands had been a part of his expression. Now they were useless appendanges. Thrusting them into his trouser pockets, he turned to Moishe.

"We did okay, kiddo," Moishe whispered. "A-okay."

"Let's hope Kahn thinks so." Daniel turned around to face his jury. His eyes hit the girl first. She clapped her hands and cried "Bravo!" He switched to Fat Benny, who gave him the thumbs-up sign. Lastly, he looked to Kahn, who complimented the performance with a single, curt nod.

"Not bad," the producer said as he walked over to where

Daniel stood. "I can give you and your pal a one-hour spot on Friday nights. Eight till nine."

Daniel let out a triumphant whoop of joy. He swung around to Moishe on the piano stool and grabbed him by the shoulders. Then he pounced on Fat Benny and hugged him ecstatically. Next he shook Kahn by the hand, after which he looked around to see who else could share his joy. Only the girl remained—Sforza with the *camiah*. Without hesitation, Daniel reached out, squeezed both her hands and kissed her on the cheek.

Kahn was content to stand back and watch the scene of celebration for a moment before he drew Fat Benny aside. "Can I see you in the office for a minute?"

Caught up in his nephew's moment of triumph, Fat Benny beamed at the man. "Forget all about your markers, Larry. They're gone, forgotten about. You never made such stupid bets."

"It's not about the markers. It's about something else."

The smile dropped from Fat Benny's face as he sensed a problem. Telling Daniel he'd be back in five minutes, he followed Kahn along the corridor to the producer's office. "Okay, what is it, Larry?"

"Money," Kahn said simply. "This station's run on a shoestring budget. I can't afford to pay your nephew and his pal five bucks each."

"What? Five bucks isn't exactly a fortune. Ten lousy bucks are going to break you?"

"Maybe it's not a fortune to you, but times are tight for the rest of us. Benny, I can take my choice of a million singers and piano players for that kind of money."

"But Daniel's good."

"Yeah, so are the other million. They're all looking for a break, and most of them need the money more than Daniel does. They all haven't got you for an uncle."

"How much are you paying the girl?"

"Not that it's any of your concern," Kahn answered, "but she gets five dollars for three half-hour spots during the week. She sings as well, lovely soprano voice. She's a big favorite with the listeners."

Fat Benny let a deep sigh of resignation escape from his

lips. "Okay, how much can you give Daniel and his *shitfes?*"

"I can go up to five bucks between them for the hour."

"Five bucks between them?" Fat Benny repeated. He weighed up the offer for what seemed like an eternity to the anxious Kahn. "Good enough. I'll put up the other five to round it up to ten dollars. But you say one word about half the money coming from me and I'll find those goddamned markers again."

Kahn nodded eagerly. "It's a deal. I'll make out I'm paying the full ten."

The two men returned to the room where Daniel waited with Moishe and Lucia Sforza. "You two can start this Friday," Kahn said. "Your hour follows Lucia's thirty-minute spot. And bring your own music. Maybe if anyone's deaf enough, they'll think they're listening to Russ Columbo."

Fat Benny took two dollars from his pocket and passed them to Daniel. "Here, bigshot. Go out and celebrate your victory. Just don't stay out too late because you're opening up in the morning."

Daniel took the money, motioned for Moishe and the girl to join him and fled from the building, still unable to believe his stupendous luck. A radio star! A singer on the air! With his own show, yet! He strutted along the sidewalk, lightheaded, chest thrown out as if he had just landed the biggest contract in radio history. Hell, he had! How many other fifteen-year-olds had a radio program?

"You got a radio, mister?" Daniel stopped an elderly man to ask.

The man stared at Daniel as if he had just escaped from a lunatic asylum and was still wearing the straitjacket. "Sure," he eventually said. "Sure, I got a radio. I got an automobile and a summer home, too. What kind of stupid question is that to ask? There's a depression on. I'm making ten bucks a week if I'm lucky and you're asking if I got a radio!"

Daniel waved away the protests. "Get one. And listen in on Friday night at eight. That's when I'll be on, Daniel Kirschbaum. And my accompanist, Moishe Wasserman. You listen out for me, you hear?"

The man turned to stare after the three youngsters, shaking

his head in bewilderment.

They stopped at a small ice cream parlor. Still excited, Daniel sat down, threw a dollar on the counter and called noisily for service. He swiveled on the seat and looked at his two companions. "Well, is this the start of a glorious career or is this the start of a glorious career?"

Moishe took off his glasses and wiped them carefully. "It might be, if someone would take the trouble to remember the damned lyrics," he said caustically.

Recalling why he had almost stumbled in the middle of the audition, Daniel looked at Lucia. "If you ever want a better spot, I can always let you have Moishe's job."

"He plays well," the girl said. Moishe inclined his head in false modesty. "How much is Mr. Kahn paying you?"

Immediately Moishe held up his hand, but Daniel chose to ignore the warning. "Ten dollars between us for the hour."

Lucia raised her eyebrows. "That's a lot more than he's paying me," she said, clearly impressed.

"There's two of us," Moishe cut in, angry at Daniel for his indiscretion in revealing salary. "And we've been around a bit."

"How come your name's Sforza?" Daniel suddenly asked. "When you're wearing one of those things around your neck?"

Instinctively the girl felt at her throat, fingers toying with the *camiah*. "My real name's Lucy Feltz. Mr. Kahn didn't think it was a very appropriate name for the kind of music he wanted me to play and sing."

"Guess it makes some kind of sense at that," Daniel concurred. "If you're doing wop music, you might as well have a wop name to go along with it."

Lucy's face changed dramatically. Her lips tightened into a thin line and she glared at Daniel through narrowed eyes. "Don't you dare speak like that!" she snapped.

"Hey! What did I say, for crying out loud?" Daniel appealed to Moishe. "What did I do?"

"You wouldn't like it if someone called you kike, would you?" Lucy said sharply.

Daniel wilted under the ferocity of the unexpected

onslaught. "No," he faltered. "I . . . I wouldn't."

"Then have the same respect for others."

He stared down at the counter for a long time before meekly saying, "I'm sorry. I didn't think."

Daniel didn't see Moishe's look of discomfort, couldn't know that his seemingly brash and self-confident friend was feeling like an outsider, the third person at a party—despite the argument—for two. Daniel had invited him along and now he'd forgotten completely about him. He was doing it all over again, the mountains and Joey Bloom's daughter revisited. Moishe just hoped the stupid twerp had the sense to lock the bedroom door this time. Argument or no argument, he had the feeling that was where this was heading. "I've got a long way to go," Moishe said, picking up his folder of music. "See you people on Friday."

Daniel raised a hand in a half-hearted farewell, too immersed in furthering his relationship with the girl to even notice that Moishe was leaving. "Where do you live?"

"Near here," Lucy answered casually.

"Where near here?"

"Do I have to tell you where I live just because you bought me a soda?"

"If I faithfully promise never to call anyone a wop again, will you tell me?"

She regarded him thoughtfully, studying his features with deep blue eyes. "How old are you, Daniel?"

"Fifteen. But I'll be sixteen at the beginning of next February," he added quickly.

"I'm sixteen already."

"Still at school?"

"Yes. You're not, are you?"

"How do you know?"

"That fat man you were with. He said something about opening up in the morning."

Daniel felt he had to explain about Fat Benny, who was responsible for getting him the audition. "He's a friend of Larry Kahn's," he said blithely. "Who helped you get in?"

"My father. He also knows Mr. Kahn. I'm studying music and my father got Mr. Kahn to listen to me. I've been with the station for eight months now." She looked at the empty glass in front of her, then said, "I have to go home. I live off Tremont Avenue if you want to take me."

When Daniel held her arm, she made no attempt to resist. "You've got a nice voice," she complimented him. "Melodious. You carry a tune well."

"I know. Uh, I mean I've been told," he corrected himself. What was he trying to do? Make an impression on this girl? Show her he was not conceited? Ridiculous! If anyone had a right to be conceited it was he. "What does your father do that he knows Larry Kahn?"

"He's a musician."

Daniel's interest quickened. "Where?"

"He plays violin in the orchestra of the Metropolitan Opera House."

Daniel's interest plummeted as quickly as it had risen. "Oh," was all he could think of to say.

Lucy could not help smiling. "He plays a lot of what you used to call wop music," she teased. "What does your father do?"

"Tailor," Daniel mumbled, as if regretting his father occupied no higher position. Even a violinist playing opera music was more glamorous than a tailor on a three-day week.

"Don't be ashamed of your father," Lucy said as she read Daniel's thoughts.

"I'm not," he replied defensively and hated himself for lying about it. He'd never been ashamed of his father before, of the man or of the way he made his living. Now, faced with the background of this girl, Isaac's means of existence seemed very mundane.

"We're here," Lucy said suddenly as they arrived outside an anonymous apartment block. "Coming up?"

"Who's there?"

"Nobody. My father's working at the Met tonight."

"What about your mother?"

The question brought a faintly wistful expression to the girl's face. "She doesn't live with us. She's not well."

Curious as he was, Daniel decided not to press the matter. He pondered the invitation and shook his head. He wanted to go home, to tell his own family about the good news. "Will you wait for me after the show on Friday?" he asked. "Maybe we can go out for another soda."

"All right." She grinned impishly at him, stood on tiptoe and gave him a light, brushing kiss on the cheek. "That's my congratulations. You'll do well."

Daniel rushed home, forgetting all about the girl in his haste to tell his family how he had progressed. They would all be waiting for him, eager to hear. Even his mother would want to know. Maybe he shouldn't have seen the girl home; he should have gone to his own home instead, let his family in on the good news. There wasn't that much of it around that you could treat it so casually.

"I did it!" he yelled, bursting open the front door and charging into the living room, arms raised above his head in victory. "I'm going to be a radio star!"

Isaac got out of his chair and hugged his son. "We know. We know. Benny called us up with the wonderful news. He said you wouldn't be home for hours yet because you were out celebrating your new career."

"I met a girl. She's also on the radio. Lucia Sforza."

"Sforza?" Yetta Kirschbaum made a dubious face. "It's not enough that you've got to have an Irishman named Mulvaney for your best friend, now you've got to have an Italian girl?"

"Her name's really Lucy Feltz."

"So what's with this Sforza nonsense?"

"She plays piano on the air and sings Italian songs."

"And if you sing American songs, are they going to give you an American name?" Yetta demanded. "Kirschbaum won't be good enough for you anymore? I won't even be able to ask my friends if they heard Daniel Kirschbaum on the radio?"

"Leave the boy alone," Isaac said. "You'll drive him mad. When do you start?" he asked Daniel.

"This Friday. And every Friday after that. For an hour."

Isaac turned away from his son and looked at the old Emerson receiver on the table next to the phonograph. "Better make sure we can pick up your station." He switched on the set and began fiddling with the tuning knob. A rumble of static erupted from the speaker as he spun the control, finally yielding to the sound of raised voices—the drama that Kahn had wanted to supervise. "I'll go to *shul* tomorrow morning, put on my *tefillin* and pray the set holds out till Friday,"

Isaac joked.

"Don't worry about that old thing," Daniel said expansively. "We'll save from my radio money to buy a new set."

"Every cent of that money gets put away," Isaac said firmly. "To buy you a good suit for when you appear in front of an audience. To appear on the radio you can look like a bum. But when you get better jobs, you'll need to look the part."

Daniel did not argue. He was overjoyed that his father was talking about his future as a singer. So what if he refused a gift now? One day, when he could afford more—after appearing in front of audiences in those good clothes—he'd buy something so grand that even his father would be unable to refuse it.

The following three days seemed like three centuries to Daniel. At the candy store, customers came and went. Fat Benny's special visitors paraded through the store, and Daniel went about his chores like an automaton, his mind on only one thing—that first show on Friday night.

Twice when Fat Benny came out of his back office, Russ Columbo was on the radio. Each time he pointed to the set and asked Daniel, "Why aren't you singing along? Are you already so wonderful that you don't need to practice?"

Disregarding the customers, Daniel opened his mouth and joined in. When he finished, the people in the store applauded him. He loved every single second of it.

On Friday he left work early, arriving home as two deliverymen were manhandling a huge carton into the apartment. Isaac stood by, bewildered, stating over and over again that he had ordered nothing, nor was he going to pay for it.

"Nothing to pay," one of the deliverymen assured him. "It's all been taken care of." They had him sign a receipt, then they left.

"What is it?" Jack asked, roused from his homework in the bedroom by the noise surrounding the delivery.

Isaac shook his head numbly. "I didn't order anything," he repeated. "There must be some mistake."

"It's addressed to you."

"I know, but I didn't order anything."

"Why don't you open it?" Yetta suggested. "You won't find

out what it is any other way."

Daniel fetched a knife from the kitchen and set about separating the heavy, protective packing. Light fell on mahogany polished to a luxuriant luster. He ripped back the remainder of the packing to reveal a Stromberg-Carlson radio receiver.

"Daniel . . ." Isaac began.

"I don't know anything about this." Daniel leaned forward to pluck a white envelope from the set. Inside was a card that read, "Good luck, Benny and Tessie."

Isaac studied the radio like a child with a new toy, turning the controls, buffing the highly varnished surface with his handkerchief, taking care not to leave finger marks. Satisfied, he plugged it into the outlet and fiddled with the dial. The sound of the ancient Emerson was like chalk scratching across a blackboard when compared with the smooth reproduction given by the Stromberg-Carlson. Isaac stood listening for a moment, then he walked quickly to the door, throwing it open.

"Where are you off to?" Yetta called after him.

"I'm inviting all my friends to a party!" he yelled back.

"It's Friday night!"

"Good. This is the way we should spend Friday night. By listening to my son give his debut performance on my new Stromberg-Carlson."

By seven, when Daniel was preparing to leave, the apartment was almost full. Friends, neighbors, even Sergeant Mulvaney was there with his wife and Tommy. From somewhere, Isaac had found enough folding chairs to put around the walls of the living room and accommodate all the guests. As more people came, Isaac guided them to their seats like an usher in a theater. Yetta and Jack were handing out cups of tea and coffee, and plates of sandwiches. The entire apartment had an atmosphere of festivity.

"Looks like we're making a *simcha*," Isaac said to his wife.

"Good. Maybe they'll all get the message and leave presents." She returned to the kitchen, bringing out a full teapot, seeing who wanted refills.

The doorbell rang yet again. Isaac opened the door to allow the latest guest to enter. Outside stood Fat Benny. He peered over Isaac's shoulder in amazement. "What have you got going in there, a party?"

"We're listening to the new Stromberg-Carlson someone sent us," Isaac replied. "Come in. Have a cup of tea."

"No time. I'm driving Daniel to the studio." Nevertheless, Fat Benny stepped in for a better look at what was happening. "You charging admission for this shindig?"

"Should I?"

"Who knows? Depends if the talent's worthwhile. Where is he, anyway? You ready yet?" he asked, spotting Daniel.

"A minute." Daniel disappeared into the bathroom, the sudden victim of stage nerves. When he returned, Isaac was introducing Fat Benny to the guests. As they neared Tommy Mulvaney and his family, Daniel edged closer to listen.

"Sergeant Mulvaney," Isaac said, "this is my older brother, Benny. He's the one who made everything possible for Daniel tonight."

Mulvaney stood up to shake Fat Benny's hand. The police sergeant's face remained as stolid as ever, but Fat Benny's expression seemed to alter momentarily. His eyes opened a fraction wider and his body stiffened slightly.

"How's everything going, Benny?" Mulvaney asked.

Fat Benny shrugged philosophically, suddenly more at ease, as if he had placed Mulvaney's name and face. "Mustn't complain. But sometimes I wish I had a nice secure job like you."

"Take the entrance examination," Mulvaney suggested, and both men laughed.

In the car on the way to the studio, Daniel was unusually silent, waiting to see whether Fat Benny would mention Mulvaney. He did not have to wait long.

"Is that your informant, Daniel? Sergeant Mulvaney?"

"Informant?" Daniel feigned ignorance.

"The one who told you about my association with Joey Bloom."

Daniel nodded glumly, realizing it had been a mistake for his father to invite the entire neighborhood. "You know him?"

"Used to. He was a beat cop years ago in the Bronx. Honest cop, too."

"Is that bad?"

Fat Benny gave a cynical chuckle. "It is when everyone else

in the division's on the take. That's why he was moved. He didn't want any part of the payoff action that was going on, so they moved him out of the division. Right out of the borough." Fat Benny chuckled again, like he'd seen some private joke. Moments later he decided to share it. "Mulvaney could be a rich man now if he'd played the same game as the others. Do you have any idea how much I pay out each month to be allowed to stay in business? Two hundred and ninety dollars, that's how much. Mulvaney could have had a piece of that action, just like he could have had a percentage of all the other rake-offs if he wasn't so damned straight."

A vision flashed in front of Daniel's eyes. Tommy's father in a suit, walking through the candy store with a well-worn leather briefcase swinging from his hand and rapping on the office door. With Tessie shouting out that he represented DeNobili cigars. The absolute absurdity of the idea made him laugh to himself.

Moishe was waiting in Kahn's office when Daniel arrived with Fat Benny. Sheet music was spread out in front of him as he went over the songs they would perform. Quickly, Kahn took them on a tour of the studio, starting with the control room from where he would supervise the hour-long program. Through the glass panel, Daniel could see Lucy Feltz at the piano. He waved to her and was gratified when she smiled in response.

For fifteen minutes, while Fat Benny stood around and watched the technicians at work, Daniel conferred with Moishe. Before, the time had dragged. Now, when he needed just another few minutes to make certain everything was prepared, there was no more. Before he realized it, Lucy Feltz had finished her Lucia Sforza show, and Kahn was beckoning urgently to him.

Daniel heard a voice from the speaker on the wall announcing a sensational new singer, then he was rushing past Fat Benny and down the corridor, with Moishe close on his heels. When he got into the room, Kahn was on the other side of the glass panel, holding up a card that read thirty seconds. Moishe settled himself quickly, spread out the music and watched Kahn for instructions. As the producer's fingers counted off the seconds, Moishe's own fingers flexed themselves. Daniel watched as if he were somewhere else, viewing the drama from a safe, impersonal distance. At this moment, he wished he was a listener, too. He wished he was anywhere, anyplace but here in front of the bulky square microphone. Then he remembered his father and mother, all of Claremont Parkway gathered around the new Stromberg-Carlson in the living room. He knew there was nowhere he could run.

As Kahn counted off the last seconds, Moishe began to play a simple little melody. Daniel gulped, stepped closer to the microphone and began to speak.

"Good evening, ladies and gentlemen. This is Daniel Kirschbaum with Moishe Wasserman on piano inviting you to listen with us every Friday night."

He glanced toward the glass panel to see how Kahn was reacting. The producer was waving his arms in a frenzy. Daniel stared at him, blankfaced, while he carried on with the introduction over which he and Moishe had labored. Finally, Kahn pulled out a pen and scribbled in block capitals on a piece of paper which he then held up to the glass:

NEVER MIND THE TALKING!!! I'M PAYING YOU TO SING!!!

Daniel swallowed hard and looked to Moishe for assistance. Kahn's agitated arm-waving had driven every thought from his head. Right now he wasn't even certain he could remember his own name, let alone what song he was supposed to start the show with. Moishe pointed frantically to the sheet in front of him. Sweat poured off Daniel's brow into his eyes, blinding him. He blinked to clear his vision, but the smarting film of sweat refused to go.

"'Always'," Moishe whispered, praying as he had never prayed before that Daniel would remember the words.

From deep within himself, Daniel plucked up the courage to face the microphone again. He took a deep breath, letting it out slowly while his right foot kept time with Moishe's playing. When his entrance came around, he began quietly, letting the momentum build up by itself. The panic on Kahn's face subsided gradually as Daniel's voice went out over the air. The producer held his thumb and forefinger together to form a circle as he tried to reassure his newest performer. Next to Kahn stood Fat Benny, clapping his beefy hands together in time with the music. Daniel looked past his uncle as the door to the control room opened and Lucy Feltz entered. As Daniel had done to her, she waved. He waved right back, feeling more confident with each bar that he would carry the night.

After three songs, Kahn held up his hands to signify a break for advertisements. Daniel poked a finger in his shirt collar and pulled it open. "How are we doing?" he asked Moishe.

The piano player immediately adopted his businesslike pose by pushing back his glasses. "All right, so long as you remember your goddamned lyrics." He thought over what he had said, then added, "Lyrics, hell. It would be nicer if you could even remember the title."

"How was I to know that Kahn didn't want us to introduce ourselves?"

"That doesn't excuse what you did. There's no excuse for behavior like that. You froze. Look"—Moishe became intensely serious, pushing his glasses up to the top of his nose—"I don't want anything to do with amateurs. You either act and sing like a pro, or you can find yourself another accompanist.

"Okay. Okay." Daniel began to feel flustered as he saw Kahn going through his countdown again. "What's the next number?"

Moishe pointed to the sheet. "Get it right this time, for God's sake. I don't want to have to run through the intro five or six times till you remember what you're supposed to be doing."

Kahn dropped his hand and Moishe began to play. This time Daniel came right in on cue, feeling totally at ease. He'd found the secret: watch the microphone and don't let anything distract you. He refused to look through the glass panel into the control room. For all he knew Kahn could be having a heart attack out there, or one of the technicians could have gone berserk and slain everyone in the room. All Daniel had eyes for was the microphone. He sang to it, smiled at it, seduced it. That was his audience, through there. He was singing to them, putting all the emotion at his command into a sweet fifteen-year-old voice.

By the time the show was over, he was drenched in sweat. The studio was hot, but his own exertions had caused the flood of perspiration which had soaked his clothing. As Kahn signaled the program's close, Daniel clapped his hands and turned around to embrace Moishe, almost dragging him off the stool, before rushing from the room. In the corridor leading back to Kahn's office, he hardly even noticed Fat Benny and Lucy, so intent was he on hearing what Kahn had to say.

"How did we do?" Daniel asked.

"Not bad," Kahn replied. He counted out ten dollars in singles, passing five to Daniel and five to Moishe.

"Same time next week?" Moishe asked as he counted the money carefully.

"Same time."

"You liked the show?" Daniel pressed. He didn't bother counting the money; he just thrust it into his trousers, certain that Kahn would not shortchange him. After all, Fat Benny was still his uncle.

"I told you, you weren't bad. The nerves will go away after another show or two. You might even get to become regulars."

"Will you pay us more then?" The question, obviously, came from Moishe.

"Be glad you're getting what you are."

When they emerged from Kahn's office, Fat Benny was waiting outside. Daniel looked around as if he had lost something. "Where's Lucy?" he asked his uncle.

"She left," Fat Benny replied.

"Left?"

"You walked straight past her like she wasn't there," Fat Benny said. "So she went home. What do you expect, you treat her like that?"

Daniel cursed himself for not sparing a moment to acknowledge the girl. She'd been waiting for him, and he'd ignored her. "Wait for me," he told his uncle. He waved farewell to Moishe, shouted that he'd see him the following Friday and ran down the stairs, the triumph of his first broadcast forgotten in the urgency of his quest for the girl. It wasn't his fault he'd ignored her. She must have been excited, too, her first time. Surely she could understand that.

He reached the street and skidded to a halt while he looked left and right. Fifty yards away he saw Lucy. He chased after her, slowing down to a quick walk as he drew close.

"Going somewhere?"

"I didn't think you knew I was there," she replied, glancing at him coolly before looking forward again.

"I'm sorry. I really am." He hoped he sounded apologetic enough. "I was excited, out of my head."

She carried on walking as if he were not there.

"Lucy, I said I'm sorry. What do you want me to do?" He stepped up his pace to get in front of her, blocking her way. "Were you cool, calm and collected when you finished your first show?"

She stopped walking and her features softened. "I guess I wasn't at that."

Daniel's face lit up with a smile as he recognized the change in attitude. "We've got a big party going at home. How about coming?"

"Will your Uncle Benny be there?"

"He's waiting back at the station to drive me. Come on." He took her hand, tugging gently. "I'll make sure you get home afterwards."

Lucy seemed to debate the wisdom of accepting the invitation. Then she smiled in acceptance. "All right. Let's see how the famous entertainer's family welcomes him home."

"You really figure I'll be famous?" he asked eagerly. Maybe the girl had a sixth sense; he hoped so.

"If you can concentrate enough to remember the lyrics, you might be."

"Everyone's entitled to one mistake."

"Wait till you start singing in Italian instead of English," she teased.

"Never happen," Daniel said confidently. "None of that—" He stopped himself from calling it wop music just in time. "None of that highbrow stuff for me. I'm strictly popular music."

"We'll see," Lucy said. She recognized the cause of his hesitation and felt pleased. In two meetings she had changed his vocabulary.

When they arrived back at Claremont Parkway, the

apartment was still packed. As Daniel entered, a rousing ovation started, catching him completely off guard. He stood still, acknowledging the applause, enjoying it. To his surprise, he did not blush. A professional singer—that's what Moishe wanted, right?—didn't blush when he was applauded, he told himself. He stood there, accepting the adulation as his rightful due.

"How did I sound?" he asked his father.

"Like a singer, you sounded! How else should you sound? It was the greatest thrill of my life to hear my son's voice coming so beautifully out of my new Stromberg-Carlson. Who's this?" he asked, noticing Lucy for the first time.

"A friend, Pa. Lucy Feltz. I told you about her. She sings and plays piano at the station."

Isaac took the girl's hand gravely, uncertain how to act. This was the first time his son had brought home a girl. At fifteen he was already grown up. "Welcome, welcome. Are you and my son going to sing a duet for us?"

"You'll get on well with her, Pa," Daniel broke in. "She likes your kind of music."

Lucy smiled as she shook her head. "I'm afraid I haven't prepared anything, Mr. Kirschbaum. Perhaps some other time."

"I'm holding you to that, young lady," Isaac said. "Come, meet our family and friends."

It was almost eleven-thirty when Daniel got Lucy home. She invited him in, and this time he accepted, guessing that she needed an alibi for being so late. Opening the apartment door, she ushered him inside. Her father was waiting up, sitting in an armchair, lovingly polishing a violin.

"This is Daniel," Lucy said. "He follows my show. Did you hear him?"

Joe Feltz set down the violin on the carpeted floor with exaggerated care. "Do you have a good reason for bringing my daughter home at such a late hour, young man?" Like Daniel's own father, he spoke with an accent. Daniel tried to place it, but failed.

"We were having a party at my house, sir. To celebrate my debut on the radio. I'm sorry." Damn! he swore to himself. He was saying sorry to everyone tonight. To Lucy; to her father. A night of triumph was turning into a night of lame apologies.

Debut or not, the excuse was lost on Joe Feltz. He got out of the chair—a short man with a pot belly and steel-rimmed glasses—and approached Daniel. "In future, when you're with my daughter, please be kind enough to return her home by eleven. Is that understood?"

Daniel looked to Lucy, who shrugged helplessly. "Yes, sir."

"I'm glad you understand. Good night." Feltz returned to the chair, picked up the violin and continued to polish it.

"I'll walk you downstairs," Lucy offered, certain that Daniel had not realized he had been dismissed from the apartment. When they were safely outside, she apologized for the way her father had acted.

"He's very strict with me about coming home late. What with my mother, and being an only child, I suppose he's right."

"You should have told me. I'd have got you home earlier," Daniel remonstrated. "What about your mother, anyway? You said the other night she's not well."

It was a moment before Lucy replied, and when she spoke it was in a subdued tone. "She's in a sanitarium. She's been there for almost eight years. She's sick."

"What's the matter with her?"

"Nobody knows," Lucy answered quietly. "She just sits in a room and stares at something she thinks she sees. Daddy kept her at home for two years, but he couldn't cope. Then he had her committed. He travels up to Binghamton every week to see her at the sanitarium. When he comes back he's crying. It breaks his heart."

"I'm sorry," Daniel mumbled. He felt totally inadequate and wished he hadn't asked the girl about her mother. "But what about your father, though? Will he let me see you again after tonight?"

"Daddy's made his point and he's certain you'll abide by his wishes in the future. Russian Joe's bark—that's what they call him at the Met—is a lot worse than his bite. He's really a very gentle man, but he tries to protect me too much."

Daniel was happy to see the sad expression pass from Lucy's face. "What about Sunday then? If it's nice, we can go to the beach in the afternoon when I get off from my uncle's store."

"Sounds great. Got a pen?"

Daniel produced a pen and a scrap of paper. Lucy scribbled her phone number on it. When he tried to kiss her good night, she angled her face slightly and he was forced to settle for kissing her cheek.

"Tell Russian Joe I'll be back," he called out as he walked down the street.

Lucy held her hand up in a gesture of silence, scared that her father would hear Daniel's farewell. But she laughed all the same.

On Saturday night, as the Sunday morning papers were unloaded in the store, Daniel pushed the memory of his evening of triumph to the back of his mind. Fat Benny's candy store came first. If it hadn't been for Fat Benny, he'd never have gotten the chance at all; he could only pay him back by working hard. While he collected sections of the newspaper, Daniel wondered to whom he should feel more gratitude. To his father, who had given him a home? Or to his uncle, who was providing all the openings and advantages which his father could not? Through means his father would never have dreamed of.

Just after ten-thirty, Fat Benny entered the store with another man. Daniel looked up with quickening interest. His uncle's companion was not the kind of man who normally walked through the shop to knock on the office door. He was in his fifties, with a short, well-trimmed beard and warm brown eyes behind gold-rimmed glasses. What struck Daniel most was the suit and homburg Fat Benny's visitor was wearing, despite the heat.

"This is my nephew, Daniel," Fat Benny said to his companion.

The man extended his right hand. "I've heard a lot about you, Daniel. A lot of good things."

Daniel accepted the man's hand while he looked to his uncle for an explanation.

"I'm Cantor Eli Kawolsky from B'nai Yeshurun in Washington Heights," the man continued. "Your uncle tells me you'll lend your beautiful voice to my choir if I give you singing lessons."

Chapter Seven

As the mourner's *kaddish* brought to a close the *N'elah* service, Daniel looked down from the choir balcony over the packed temple. He felt like a combat veteran, a soldier who had come unscathed through countless battles. This was his third *Yom Kippur* in the B'nai Yeshurun choir under Cantor Kawolsky, although the first one, two years earlier, did not really count. Then he had not had the time to learn the entire service and had been pressed into use only for certain outstanding passages. By the time the second *Yom Kippur* came around, Kawolsky's careful tutelage had forced the complete service into his head and his voice had carried the entire choir.

Daniel shrugged off his *tallis* and black gown as Kawolsky picked up the *shofar* and blew a long, clear note to signify the end of *Yom Kippur*. A collective gasp of relief escaped from the congregation. Men shook hands and wished each other health and happiness for the coming year. Daniel could see Fat Benny gripping the hands of those around him. Next to his uncle were his father and brother, who had made the long journey from Claremont Parkway to be present at the temple in Washington Heights. He switched his gaze to the women's section. His mother had already left, on her way home to prepare the meal that would break the fast. But it was Lucy for whom Daniel was searching, Sforza with the *camiah* who had given up going to the temple in the Bronx with her father so she could attend the B'nai Yeshurun service and listen to Daniel sing in the choir. He knew she would never be able to identify him through the mesh that surrounded the choir balcony, but he waved anyway.

As Daniel bent forward to fold his *tallis*, an ominous growl erupted from his stomach to remind him that he had not eaten for more than twenty-six hours. Twenty-six hours was an eternity for Daniel to be without food and he wondered what his mother would be preparing. But more than food, he needed a glass of water. His mouth was dry, his throat parched from the day of singing. An ice-cold soda would be even better, but right now he would settle for the tepid water from the washroom tap.

"Nice performance, Daniel," the choirmaster commended him. Daniel nodded at the praise. Gone were the days when he would blush at any compliment; now he accepted them as just reward.

Like the other boys in the choir, Daniel attended the weekly classes given by the choirmaster, but his prime instruction came from Cantor Kawolsky. From time to time it would raise dissension among other members of the choir who felt that Daniel was being favored, especially when choice pieces of the service were allocated to him. Once, the dissension had erupted into violence, after a rehearsal for the previous year's *Rosh Hashanah* service. Two of the choirboys had waited in the yard adjoining the temple after the rehearsal, attacking Daniel as he emerged from the building. Hearing the commotion, the choirmaster had rushed outside to break up the fight. By the time he succeeded, Daniel had bloodied one boy's nose and blackened the eyes of the other. After that display—with the subsequent lectures from both Kawolsky and his own father—Daniel had ignored the taunts; in turn, the other choirboys had vented their frustrations through vague mutterings and threatening looks. Never again did they try to use force to intimidate him.

The three hour-long lessons Kawolsky gave him each week—on Monday, Tuesday and Thursday, combined with the Wednesday night session conducted by the choirmaster—ha brought out vocal powers Daniel had never realized h possessed. As well as preparing him for the short Friday nigh service and the three-hour Saturday morning service—plu the High Holy Days—his performance on the weekly show with Moishe Wasserman had improved dramatically. But singing in the choir had also brought its share of problems. As soon as he had taken up Kawolsky's offer, Daniel had spoken with Larry Kahn about changing the radio spot to Sunday evening, as he would be unable to work on Friday evening anymore. Kahn had complained bitterly. Daniel had appeared in just one show, and now the producer would have to juggle his schedule around to compensate for some kid who was having an attack of religion. He'd threatened Daniel with dismissal from the station, but when Fat Benny had intervened on his nephew's behalf, Kahn had complied. Relations between the producer and Daniel, however, had deteriorated from that point. If Daniel turned up the least bit late, Kahn would have a pocket watch in his hand, pointing angrily to its face. If the selection of songs was not to his liking, he would complain. Daniel and Moishe had accepted the constant criticism for more than two years because they still needed the money, unaware that half of it was continuing to come out of Fat Benny's pocket.

Most important of all, though, Kawolsky had taken it upon himself to provide Daniel with an understanding of music, how to read and interpret it. The only restriction the cantor had placed on him concerned the amount he could use his voice at full strength. Initially, Kawolsky had wanted him to discontinue the radio performances, telling Daniel to rest his voice as much as possible until he was eighteen. The suggestion had almost caused a mutiny. Daniel resisted for two reasons. Money was an obvious one; and Kawolsky soon came to realize that his pupil needed the recognition he received as a radio performer, the sensation of having a public that knew his name and listened to him regularly. As a compromise, Kawolsky had made Daniel agree that he would seek no other commercial engagements until he was eighteen, when his voice would be able to cope with the added strain. "Crooning, I suppose, can't hurt you," he had admitted. "But when you do croon on your radio show, Daniel, please croon *pianissimo*."

Daniel left the choir balcony down the back stairway and entered the main area of the temple. He kissed his father and shook hands with Jack and Fat Benny. Then he joined the long line of worshippers waiting to congratulate Cantor Kawolsky on the day-long service. The cantor eyed him with amusement as he held his hand.

"Are you trying to take away my job from me, Daniel?"

Daniel stiffened slightly at the remark, uncertain how Kawolsky intended it.

"Your singing is becoming better than mine," Kawolsky explained. "Very soon, the management of this *shul* is going to realize that the sweetest voice here comes not from the *bima*, but from the balcony."

"It's the way you taught me," Daniel replied, glad to see that Kawolsky was joking. After a close relationship of more than two years, he was still unable to always judge the cantor's mood accurately. He visited his home three times a week, had met his wife and family, and was still unsure that he knew the man. On the surface, Kawolsky was a man totally wrapped up in his family and his religion; nothing outside mattered. His vibrant tenor voice was a gift from God, and he would use it only to serve that God.

During the lessons, Kawolsky was a stern teacher, forcing Daniel to go over exercises again and again until he was satisfied. When the lessons were finished, and Daniel sat down for a cup of coffee and a piece of cake before going home, Kawolsky seemed to change. He would joke with Daniel, commend him on his aptitude for learning and tell anecdotes of his career as a cantor. Once he had even gone into depth about his association with Fat Benny, informing Daniel how his uncle had helped to raise one thousand dollars to buy new Torah scrolls for the B'nai Yeshurun. Daniel had been unable to conceal his surprise at the revelation. Fat Benny was about as religious as his own father, only attending services on important holy days, or when someone got *bar mitzvah*ed, married or buried. Kawolsky had thrown another shaft of light on Benny Kirschbaum, a man who made it his business to help his community as well as his own family. Daniel wondered how much of the money for the Torah scrolls had come out of Fat Benny's own pocket. Or had he leaned on other people to make donations? It was becoming more difficult for Daniel to keep track of the favors Fat Benny had called in or bought on his own behalf. First there had been Joey Bloom, then Larry Kahn; and now, to a degree, even this cantor who was helping him with the singing lessons. So what if he was singing in the choir for nothing when the other boys were picking up pocket money? Kawolsky would never have made the offer to teach him had it not been for Fat Benny's influence.

"It's the way I taught you," Kawolsky repeated as he stepped down from the *bima* and shook hands automatically with other members of the congregation. "Daniel, the finest compliment for a teacher is when the pupil surpasses him."

Daniel forgot all about the drink of water he so desperately needed as Kawolsky placed a gentle arm around his shoulders and guided him to where his father stood. "Your son has the ability to become a great *chazan* if he wishes, Mr. Kirschbaum," Kawolsky said. "He will have the voice, he will have everything. You can be very proud of him."

Isaac looked first at the cantor, then at Daniel. "We're proud of him already. Every Sunday night we're proud of him."

"Crooning." Kawolsky injected a gentle irony in the word. "I've also heard him. But that kind of singing anyone can do. Your Daniel is destined to reach a much higher level."

"Like opera?" a girl's voice asked.

Daniel turned around to see Lucy standing behind him, laughing as he shook his head so vehemently that his *yarmulke* flew off. She stooped quickly to recover it while Daniel held a hand over his head.

"You should live so long," he shot back.

"I intend to." She held out both hands for Daniel to take. He accepted and leaned forward to kiss her warmly on the cheek.

"Coming back with us?"

Lucy nodded eagerly. "Only for a few minutes, though. It's bad enough that I didn't go to *shul* with my father, but I promised I'd be there to break the fast with him."

Fat Benny joined the small crowd, patting his nephew on the back, shaking hands with Kawolsky. Daniel regarded his uncle fondly while he debated whether the enforced fasting had affected his weight at all. Fat Benny looked the same as always, although his jowls were hidden to a degree by the day-old stubble. Daniel felt his own chin and the slight growth of prickly hair which festooned it. Not even eighteen years old yet and forced to shave daily. He hated the morning ritual almost as much as he loathed going without food for an entire day. The thought of food reminded him how thirsty he was. He excused himself and went to the washroom, where he cupped his hands beneath the cold tap and stooped over to drink.

After leaving Fat Benny, Daniel took the bus back to Claremont Parkway with Lucy, his father and Jack. Jack had brought along money for the fare, depositing a different coin in each pocket so there would be no treacherous jingling when he moved in the temple. Inside the apartment, Daniel stayed only long enough to take a piece of cake and a cup of coffee before escorting Lucy home.

"Mr. Kawolsky's perfectly right, you know," Lucy said as they began to walk.

The unexpected comment threw Daniel. He was thinking about Lucy and the last thing on his mind was the cantor's opinions. Despite a desire not to do so, he had more and more frequently found himself comparing Lucy with Linda Bloom, the only other girl with whom he had shared any kind of relationship. Total opposites, he had decided. Linda had encouraged him into a sexual adventure from the moment they had met. With Lucy, all he'd managed to achieve was a kiss on the cheek each time they said good night, and he had been seeing her regularly for more than two years. Although their shows no longer followed each other, he was always waiting for her whenever the Friday evening service at the B'nai Yeshurun terminated early enough to allow him the privilege. In return, she waited for him on Sunday evenings. Recognizing the closeness between the two young people, Kahn had tried to capitalize on it by suggesting an additional show where they sang duets while Lucy played piano. At first, the idea had appealed to Daniel, even if it meant only a means of bridging the rift between himself and Kahn. When he had remembered Kawolsky's advice about not straining his voice, however, he had turned it down. The refusal had added fuel to the animosity Kahn already felt toward the young singer.

"Kawolsky's right about what?" Daniel asked.

"About your voice being too good for popular singing. Popular singers don't need the range and depth you're acquiring. You'll be wasting it. You should think seriously about being a cantor."

"Do me a favor," Daniel said, then repeated the expression in Yiddish. "*Titz mir a tovah.*" For some reason, he had always liked that particular Yiddish expression; perhaps it was because it sounded vaguely obscene. "Cantors make a living, that's all. Popular singers make a fortune."

"Not all of them," Lucy pointed out. "And it's a much tougher life. A cantor's a respected member of the community, while a popular singer's in a perpetual rat race."

Daniel let his mind wander over the possibilities while he walked silently, Lucy's hand clasped in his own. If he was honest with himself, he envied Kawolsky for the praise that was heaped on the cantor's head at the termination of each service. Sure, some compliments were thrown his way, but the lion's share always went to the cantor. Kawolsky was entitled to it, certainly, but Daniel knew it was his own faultless performance during each service that helped to make Kawolsky sound so good. They were like a team of comedians—he played straight man to Kawolsky's punch lines. But was Hebrew liturgical singing really the kind of music he wanted to perform all his life? It had a definite appeal, now that he had come to understand it. And a good *chazan* like Kawolsky held the congregation in the palm of his hand, just like a good entertainer would do with his audience.

Lucy broke into his thoughts as she pushed on with her argument. "You've been working for Larry Kahn for more than two years, and where has it got you? You're still making the same money."

"I've been told not to take on any more work," Daniel argued. "Moishe could get us better bookings, but I'm following Kawolsky's advice." He knew he could have fired a similar question at Lucy, but it would have been unfair. She was still studying. The radio sessions gave her both practice and a small amount of money. Daniel was actively working on his career, and he knew Lucy was right. He was in a rut.

"Sorry." She squeezed his hand as she spoke. "I guess that was a bit of a low blow."

He stopped walking and pulled her around to face him. "What do you think I should do?"

"Are you really asking me, or are you just being polite?"

"I'm really asking you."

"Kawolsky's done a lot for you already. Keep right on taking his advice. If he thinks the best future for you is as a cantor, then you should give it some serious thought."

Daniel wondered what Moishe Wasserman would say about that. After all, it would affect his job, too.

"You're mad!" Moishe said emphatically when he met Daniel the following Sunday evening for their show. "You're a stark, staring, raving lunatic!"

Daniel had expected the abuse. Whenever Moishe disagreed with a certain course of action, he could be relied upon to launch into an invective-ridden salvo.

"I've been patient with you, kiddo," Moishe continued, not in the least fazed that his dramatic outburst was having no effect on its target. "I haven't pushed you. I've been content to let you stick with this one crummy job because your cantor friend tells you to spare your voice. I just figured the time would eventually come when you'd want something better, when you'd be ready to push on. But now this!" Moishe raised his hands to the heavens. "Deciding to be a cantor yourself! You're wasting a gift, boy!" he ranted, gaining strength and fire with each accusation. "Christ! You're not even religious. You care as much about Jewish lore and tradition as the Pope does!"

"I've given it a lot of thought since Lucy suggested it," Daniel said quietly. "Kawolsky, my father, Lucy—we all think it's the right course to take."

"Lucy!" Mention of the girl's name triggered the final explosive outburst. "Suddenly she's the expert on how you should run your life? Listen to me, for heaven's sake. I've got the contacts. I'm the one that's going to specialize in entertainment law. What the hell can Lucy do for you?" He looked in desperation at his friend, then his face mellowed. "How long have you been seeing her, Danny?"

"Two years. A little more. Since we started here."

"Get anywhere yet?"

Daniel's expression tightened. For an instant, Moishe feared he might have overstepped the bounds of friendship. He was two years older than Daniel, but age meant little when he was outweighed by fifty pounds. Daniel's hands turned into tightly bunched fists and his face darkened threateningly.

"You've got five seconds to apologize for that remark," Daniel said between clenched teeth, the long friendship totally forgotten as he thought about Lucy.

"Bet you a buck you can't get anywhere with her." The words sprang spontaneously from Moishe's lips, the same challenge he had used to spark the calamitous series of events in the mountains.

The menacing scowl remained etched on Daniel's face for as long as it took him to recognize the source of the challenge. Then his hands relaxed and he began to laugh, amazed that he could have allowed himself to become so upset by Moishe's fooling; he should be used to it by now.

"Once Kawolsky gives you the green light to use your voice fully, we can moonlight while you're doing your religious number," Moishe pointed out eagerly, relieved that the crisis was over.

"I know. I thought about that as well. Even mentioned it to Kawolsky. He was unhappy about the idea." Unhappy was about the last word Daniel could have chosen to describe the cantor's reaction. Kawolsky had come close to tears as he pleaded with Daniel to forget popular music altogether, to concentrate instead on becoming a fine cantor instead of one of many mediocre entertainers. "There is only one way you can repay God for giving you such a wonderful voice," Kawolsky had stressed, "and that is to use that voice in His praise as I do. To take that voice and mumble inane words into a microphone, for people who are not even listening attentively, is blasphemy."

"What does Kawolsky know?" Moishe asked derisively. "I'm surprised that he hasn't asked you again to pack it in here."

Daniel waited a long time before replying. "He has," he finally said. "And this time I'm going to."

For once the impossible happened. Moishe was lost for words. He stood gaping stupidly at Daniel, wishing he could disbelieve what he had heard. Ignoring the dazed expression on Moishe's face, Daniel carried on talking.

"I was going to bring it up around Christmas time, the end of the year. You brought it up first." He shrugged helplessly, suddenly feeling very sorry for his friend.

"Thanks. Thanks a million," Moishe said sarcastically. "What the hell am I supposed to do now?"

"What about all those contacts you're going to make when you get out of law school? Can't they help you, entertainment lawyer?" The spite which crept into Daniel's voice was unintentional. But when he recognized it, he made no attempt to change his tone.

Moishe breathed deeply and tried to control himself. "Don't worry yourself about me, kiddo. I made you," he said, forcing a smile onto his face, wanting this spasm of unpleasantness to disappear, "and I can break you. You'll be back on all fours asking for my help, *chazan*."

If Daniel had not been ready to tell Larry Kahn that he was quitting, the radio producer would have done him the favor following the poor performance both boys turned in. The memory of the short but nonetheless ugly quarrel lingered over the show like a malevolent shadow. Moishe fumbled a number of notes, his confidence and normally skillful playing shattered, and Daniel's singing was one note ahead of his accompanist for most of the night. Kahn was furious when the performance was over. In the privacy of his office, he told them exactly what he thought of their efforts.

"Neither of you deserve this," he growled, holding out their money. "You both stunk tonight."

Moishe took his share of the money immediately, not prepared to argue with the producer about the performance. Once the money was safely in his pocket he'd pick a fight. But Daniel's temper began to rise. He knew he'd sung badly, that his timing had been abysmal. It had been a lousy night all around—the argument with Moishe, the poor performance and now this. But he'd be damned if he'd accept Larry Kahn's abuse.

"Keep the money," he said, his voice low with anger. "Keep it and shove it, right up your asshole."

Kahn stared at the youth, unable to believe he was refusing the money. No one refused money in Kahn's world. They would accept whatever treatment he handed out as long as he paid them.

"You can keep your stinking show as well," Daniel went on. "I'm finished with craphouse outfits like this!" Daniel saw Moishe close his eyes in horrified resignation, but he didn't care anymore. All he wanted to do was get out of Kahn's office and see Lucy, who would be waiting outside for him. She would understand why he had taken this course of action; she supported him.

"Just remember that you walked out on me," Kahn yelled after him. "Don't come running back here for work. I've paid off your uncle. He's got no more favors coming from me."

Daniel spun around and faced the producer. "You didn't do my uncle any favors! He did you one by getting Moishe and me to play on your shithouse station!"

"What the hell's going on here?" Moishe cried out, witnessing the clash without understanding any of it. "What favors?"

Too late Daniel realized that Moishe knew nothing about Kahn's gambling debts, how Fat Benny had used them as a lever to get the audition. He debated the wisdom of putting Moishe in the picture and knew he had to. Moishe had been involved for too long to be left out. "How do you think we landed this job in the first place?" he asked quietly. "Mister Producer here owed my Uncle Benny almost three bills on gambling markers. Benny wrote them off to get us the audition. He bribed our way in here."

"That's a lie!" Kahn yelled, looking first at Moishe then at Daniel. "Don't believe a word of it!"

"I want to believe it," Moishe said in delight. "I want to believe every single word. Jesus Christ! It makes this shitty job halfway glamorous. Hold on there, Danny boy! I'm coming right along with you." He raced after Daniel, who was halfway out the door.

On the sidewalk, Daniel told Lucy everything that had happened between himself and Kahn. Moishe hovered nearby, occasionally interjecting his own comments. Lucy listened soberly until Daniel had finished his account.

"You did the right thing," she said. "You don't need Larry Kahn."

"What about you?" Moishe asked. "You're buddy-buddy

with Daniel. How's Kahn going to feel about you?"

Daniel had been afraid to ask the question himself. Hearing Moishe voice it gave him the courage to speak. "You're going to be at the bottom of his popularity poll, Lucy. It's my fault and I'm sorry."

Lucy dismissed his apology with an impatient shake of her head, then drew herself up and tightened her jaw as if coming to a decision. She marched into the building, determination in every small step. Two minutes later, she reappeared, dusting her hands symbolically. "I don't know what you said to him, but I guess I just told him the same thing. Now he's got another spot to fill." Her eyes danced mischievously as she witnessed the surprised expressions of the two youths.

Daniel was the first to react. He lifted up the girl and swung her around and around, while Moishe yelled exuberantly. Pedestrians stopped to watch the three youngsters, convinced they had taken leave of their senses.

"I guess this is the parting of the ways again," Moishe said when the celebrations had run out of steam. "Seems like we're always splitting up after one disaster or another."

Daniel went quiet as he weighed Moishe's words. Then he grinned. "At least it lasted longer this time."

"Keep in touch," Moishe advised as he began to walk away. "Even a *chazan* needs an agent and a lawyer." He waved jauntily and quickened his pace, eager to leave Daniel and Lucy by themselves. Although Moishe refused to show it, Daniel was certain he was upset about losing the job. It had been a steady, if unspectacular, source of income for more than two years, and the experience had been invaluable.

"Beginning to think you made the wrong move?" Lucy asked as she sensed his flood of self-doubt.

Daniel waited until Moishe had disappeared, then he turned to face the girl. "I don't know what to think right now, and that's the honest truth. My mother will have a screaming fit because I won't be bringing home five dollars a week anymore. And my father . . ." He stopped as he tried to think what his father's reaction would be.

"Your father will tell you it's what's in here that counts," Lucy said, patting her heart. "If you feel that you did the right thing for yourself, that you're continuing to do the right thing by wanting to become a *chazan*, then it is the right thing."

"You're making it sound pretty simple."

"I wish it were," she said, linking arms with him. "But first you have to come home with me and tell my father that I did the right thing by quitting as well."

"You tell my family and I'll tell yours," Daniel offered.

The girl laughed and squeezed his arm affectionately.

Isaac Kirschbaum looked disparagingly at the Stromberg-Carlson radio receiver given to him two years earlier by Fat Benny. "To tell you the truth, Daniel, I never thought your voice sounded that marvelous over this radio. Maybe to others it sounded good, but to me, who knows how you really sound, it was . . . *nisht aher, nisht ahin*," he said, lapsing into Yiddish. "Neither here nor there." He studied his son closely, wondering if Daniel understood his meaning. "In a *shul*, where your voice doesn't have to travel through miles of cable and wire, you'll sound a million times better."

"You'd like me to be a *chazan*, then?" Daniel asked, finally catching on to his father's rambling approval.

"I could think of nothing finer. Who knows?" Isaac puffed up his chest with pride. "I might even become a regular *shul* goer." He put one arm around Daniel's shoulders and the other around Jack's. "I have one son who'll be a *chazan*, and my other son will be an engineer. A professional and an artist. You," he said, looking at Jack, "start making plans to build the finest *shul* in the world for the finest *chazan* in the world." He hugged them both tightly.

Yetta Kirschbaum decided it was time to inject a dose of cold reality into the festivities. "And where is all the money going to appear from? For Jack's education? How's Daniel going to get along? He's already lost his five dollars a week from the radio station."

Daniel eyed his mother with a growing animosity. She was doing what she always tried to do, put a damper on the good times. Any happiness, she'd sour it. God, there were times when he hated her. "I'll keep on working at Uncle Benny's store," he answered, holding his irritation in check. "And in three years' time I'll be earning good money as a *chazan*."

"I should still be alive in three years to hear you," Yetta prayed, closing her eyes. "That's if we don't all starve to death by then."

Isaac released his sons and turned his attention to his wife. "Yetta, will you please stop? I'm working. Daniel's got a job. Besides, this thing won't last forever, this depression."

"Al Jolson said in the newspapers that you shouldn't call it a depression," Jack remarked.

"When did he say that?" Daniel wanted to know.

"Earlier this year. He was in San Francisco," Jack replied smugly, pleased that he knew something about a popular singer that his brother did not. "He said to call it a panic."

"He's rich enough to call it a panic if he likes," Isaac said. "To everyone else it's still the depression. But it won't last forever. And *I* said that."

"So, the engineer and the *chazan* have got an economist for a father now, have they?" Yetta remarked. "Let's place an advertisement in the newspapers. Isaac Kirschbaum the famous economist says the depression can't go on forever. Maybe everyone will find work again."

"At least he manages to keep a smile on his face."

Those few words, spoken by Daniel in a flat, level voice, opened the floodgates. He had never openly taken sides before, but now that he had started he could not restrain himself. He reveled in the shock that flashed across his mother's eyes. His voice rose and his face became flushed with anger. "You were scowling and whining even when things were good."

"Daniel!" Isaac's voice was sharper than either of his sons had ever heard it. Daniel did not seem to notice as he maintained the attack on his stunned mother.

"Everything you have to criticize! Nothing's ever good enough for you! Even when I was *bar mitzvah*ed, you complained that I sang too high. Like a girl, you said. Everyone else loved it or said they did. But not *you*. *You* had to complain."

"Daniel!" Isaac tried again. "Stop this kind of talk at once!"

"You criticize Uncle Benny, Aunt Tessie, everyone. Are you so goddamned perfect?"

"Daniel!" A third time Isaac roared at his son. Then he grabbed hold of him by the shoulder, swung him around and slapped him hard across the face. The swift, stinging blow brought tears to Daniel's eyes. "Don't you ever speak like that to your mother again!"

Daniel blinked back the tears as he stared in amazement at his father. He looked at Jack, who was as stunned as himself, then at his mother, who had a hand raised to her forehead, massaging her temple in a motion Daniel knew well. Another of her migraines was on the way. Pity it hadn't arrived half an hour earlier.

"Apologize to your mother at once!" Isaac demanded. "To me as well, for behaving like that."

"Apologize?" The thought of apologizing to his mother hurt Daniel more than the slap had done. He could not bring himself to understand the command. Why should he have to apologize? He had defended his father, and he'd been beaten for his support. "She should apologize to you. To all of us!"

"We're waiting," Isaac said.

"You can keep on waiting! I'll never apologize to her as long as I live!" Daniel charged at the door, slammed it back against the wall and rushed outside, flying down the stairs to the street. How could it all have gone so wrong so quickly? One moment his father was hugging him. The next moment there was an argument and his father was hitting him. Daniel knew where the fault rested. With his mother. If she hadn't opened her sour mouth like always, none of this would ever have happened. Now what was he going to do? Go back inside and make a fool of himself by apologizing?

Head down, completely oblivious to the people he passed, he strode along the sidewalk. At Third Avenue, he became the target for horn-hitting motorists by crossing against the lights. On the other side, he brushed hurriedly past a figure in a navy blue uniform. The patrolman grabbed him by the arm and pulled him to an abrupt halt.

"You trying to get yourself killed, mac? Do it somewhere else, huh? I don't need the paperwork."

Daniel scowled ferociously while he struggled vainly to free himself from the patrolman's iron grip. "Leave me the hell alone! Why don't you do what you're paid for—catch crooks?"

The patrolman's grip relaxed a fraction. "Cherrybum! For Christ's sake, it's me! Don't you recognize me?" He pulled off the hat to reveal a closely cropped head of bright ginger hair.

"Tommy!" Daniel forgot all about the argument with his parents as he stared in delight at the uniform Tommy Mulvaney was wearing. "Where on earth did you get that monkey suit?"

"From a little Jewish tailor," Tommy joked. "You want one just like it?"

"When did you graduate?"

"Last week. My old man pulled a few strings to get me assigned to the local precinct. And who turns out to be my first full emergency but Daniel Cherrybum? What's with all the rushing around? What's the problem?"

The anger began to settle heavily on Daniel's shoulders again. "I just had a huge fight with my parents and I don't know what to do."

"Tell your local peace officer all about it," Tommy suggested. He pointed down the street toward Hymie's. "Over an egg cream. I'm buying."

"What about your beat?"

"I just signed off my shift. I was on my way home when I saw you impersonating a runaway truck."

Daniel allowed himself to be shepherded into Hymie's, sitting morosely at the counter while Tommy ordered. Then he began to talk quietly, going over the events of the evening. How he had quit the radio station, the celebration at home over his decision to study for a cantorial career, and the fight which had started with his mother.

"You sound surprised your father hauled off and hit you," Tommy observed. "I know damned well that if I behaved like that to my mother, my old man would take his belt to me. Even now," he added drily, "when we're both working for the same firm."

Daniel said nothing, content to stare moodily into the glass as if he could find some answer there to his dilemma.

"Better go back and make it up while you still can," Tommy suggested. He licked his straw clean, then tipped back the glass to capture any drops he might have missed. "The longer you leave it, the tougher it's going to get to patch it up. Pat me on the back, quick. I've just helped solve my first family dispute." He grinned widely, trying to lift Daniel's depression.

Daniel failed to see any humor at all. "It's not that easy, Tommy. Why should I apologize? The whole damned problem's my mother's fault."

"Because they're your parents," Tommy said simply. "There's an old, unwritten law that says parents are always right, no matter how wrong they might be."

"That the advice they taught you at the academy?"

"Nope. That's what my old man said when he first took his belt to me. Go home and say you're sorry, Cherrybum. Knowing your father, he's probably more worried than mad right now."

Daniel pushed himself away from the counter. "I want to walk around for a while. Give myself the chance to cool off."

"Good idea. But don't leave it too late."

Walking slowly, Daniel returned to the apartment building. He stood in the lobby for fully five minutes, trying to pluck up the determination to climb the stairs and apologize to his parents. His father would be easy. By now Isaac's anger would have passed, turned to increasing anxiety as Tommy had guessed. But his mother was different. She was probably well into her migraine by now, not caring what happened to her son just as long as he returned home to humble himself in front of her. Then she'd keep on at him for weeks, how he had made her ill.

With that thought planted firmly in his mind, Daniel walked out of the apartment building and waited at a bus stop. He knew what to do. He'd go to the people to whom he always turned for advice; they'd intercede on his behalf as they had always done.

Tessie was wearing a dressing gown over her nightdress when she opened the door. "Daniel, my God! It's past midnight. What are you doing here?"

"I had a fight with Ma. I left home."

Tessie gave a deep, resigned sigh. "Come in and tell us about it, darling."

Fat Benny's voice came rumbling out of the bedroom,

demanding to know who was calling so late. When Tessie told him it was Daniel, in trouble, the big man appeared; the dressing gown flapped around him like an ill-fitting tent.

"What's the matter?"

"I had a fight at home," Daniel repeated.

"So what the hell are you doing here?" Fat Benny asked incredulously. "Did your parents throw you out?"

"No. I ran away."

"Why?"

"Because Pa wanted me to apologize to Ma. And he hit me when I shouted at her."

"I'd have hit you, too. And you'd have felt it a damned sight more from me than you did from your father."

Fat Benny's instantaneous condemnation of his behavior shook Daniel almost as much as the slap from his father. If there was one person in the world he knew he could always rely on, it was his uncle. Hadn't he gone to bat for him every time he needed help? Now even he was against him. Fat Benny went to the telephone, and Tessie asked whom he was calling. When he told her Isaac, she protested, saying the family would be asleep by now. Fat Benny shook his head.

"Knowing my brother, he won't go to sleep until His Majesty over there comes home. He's probably frightened out of his mind about what's happened to him by now."

The telephone was answered almost immediately. Fat Benny spoke quietly, in Rumanian, which Daniel did not understand. When he came off the phone, the lines of his face were tightly drawn.

"There's the door, Daniel. Go home this minute and apologize to your parents. They're waiting for you. Otherwise you can spend the night sleeping in the gutter for all I care. Suit yourself. But just make damned sure you're at the store to open up in the morning, otherwise I'll find some other help."

"But—"

"Get out!"

Without another word, Daniel left the apartment, convinced that everyone in the family hated him. Even Fat Benny and Tessie had turned on him, siding with his mother and father. How could Fat Benny justify allying himself with his mother? Daniel knew his uncle could barely stand the sight of Yetta Kirschbaum, and yet now he was taking her part.

Although he walked quickly, it was almost two in the morning when he arrived back on Claremont Parkway. The light from his parents' living room shone out into the darkness, and he could imagine them sitting up there, two righteous judges waiting for the accused to plead his case and beg forgiveness—Fat Benny, Tessie, even Tommy Mulvaney. He thought about the two other people who had any hold on his life, Kawolsky the cantor, and Lucy. What would they advise him to do? He did not have to think for very long. He knew.

Each step he took up the stairs toward the apartment seemed to take an hour. His feet dragged and he was certain the landing would never come into view. When it did, he willed himself to approach the apartment door. He couldn't find his key and realized that he had run out in such a panic that he had forgotten it. He bunched his fist and rapped once upon the wood. Maybe they would not answer. They'd just leave him out there to stew in his own recriminations.

He heard the sound of the lock being turned. The door swung back and Isaac looked out curiously, a man wondering who could be banging on his door this late at night.

"Yes?" he asked quietly. "What do you want?"

"I've come home."

If Daniel had expected the statement to create a welcome for him, he was mistaken. Isaac did not move from the doorway, blocking his son's entrance into the apartment.

"You're not setting foot in this house until you're ready to apologize."

The words were a long time coming, sticking in Daniel's throat while he tried desperately to force them out. Finally he managed to say, "I want to say I'm sorry to you and Ma. May I?"

Isaac stepped aside and ushered his son into the apartment. Yetta was sitting in the living room, eyes half-closed from fatigue, head nodding. Daniel coughed and his mother opened her eyes, startled at the noise.

"So? You've decided to come home? Very nice of you."

His mother's tone aggravated Daniel's already smarting

pride. The blood began to simmer in his veins again, preparing him for another outburst. But his father's voice cut short any retaliation.

"Yetta!" Isaac was as sharp with his wife as he had been earlier with his son. "Daniel has come home to apologize because he knows he was wrong. The very least you can do is listen and accept it."

Yetta sniffed defensively under her husband's onslaught, astounded by its savageness. Even Daniel was amazed. Twice in one night his father had lashed out, once at himself, then at his mother. A gentle man trying to establish himself, after all these years, as the undisputed head of his household.

"Go on," Isaac prompted his son. "We're waiting."

Daniel's gaze took in both his parents, but his words were meant solely for his father; and he knew that Isaac realized it. Something had happened tonight. The little respect he had harbored for his mother—if there had been any at all, and he doubted even that—had been destroyed beyond redemption. He felt nothing for her anymore, not even the slightest gratitude for giving him birth, or for looking after him before he was old enough to take care of himself.

"I'm sorry," he said simply.

"That's all?" Yetta demanded.

"That's enough," Isaac countered. "Go to bed," he advised his son. "You've got to be up soon to open Benny's store."

Daniel walked past his father into the bedroom he shared with Jack. His brother was sleeping soundly, unaware of the final stages of the night's drama. Daniel undressed quietly and slipped into bed, knowing he would never be able to fall asleep. He was too pent up, digging furiously into his memory to reconstruct the entire evening. His mother, damn her. It was always his mother who started these things, with her negativity, her sarcasm, her constant needling. She was a leech intent on sucking any possible enjoyment out of a situation, on trying to make everyone around her as bitter as herself.

Damn her again. Whatever he did, Daniel vowed, whatever he became, he would do it for himself and for those people about whom he cared. But he'd roast in hell before he ever let his mother derive one scrap of enjoyment from him.

Chapter Eight

For the first time since he had become a cantor many years earlier, Eli Kawolsky did not look forward to leading the arduous series of devotions beginning with that morning's *Rosh Hashanah* service and ending ten days later with *Yom Kippur*.

Standing in the bathroom of his home, he opened his mouth wide and peered closely at the reflection in the mirror as he tried to locate the cause of the scratchiness in his throat. Probably he had a cold coming; that would account for the hot and cold flushes he'd been experiencing, and for the numbing ache centered in his chest and spreading out to his arms. God only knew that the weather had been contradictory enough to make even the strongest sick, burning heat following chilly dampness as autumn began. Kawolsky had protected himself as best he could against the elements, but now he had to acknowledge defeat.

He rummaged around in the medicine cabinet until he found the throat spray, pointed the nozzle into his mouth and gave himself the benefit of three long squirts. When he swallowed hard, he was grateful to find the discomfort had lessened. He would take it easy today, he promised himself. The congregation might be upset to miss the lyrical high notes of the special melodies he saved for *Rosh Hashanah*, but this way he would save something of himself for the following morning's service. By *Yom Kippur*, he would have had time to recover completely.

As he replaced the throat spray and closed the medicine cabinet, Kawolsky chided himself for not taking his own advice. He should have cared more for his voice when he was young, as he had instructed Daniel to do. A voice was a muscle, that was all; and like all muscles it had to be protected, otherwise it would simply wear out. Daniel would have to work harder over the next few days, that was the answer. The younger voice from the choir balcony would have to compensate for the aging voice on the *bima.*

Kawolsky smiled contentedly as he thought about his protegé. If he could be remembered for only one thing, he would want it to be as the man who had persuaded Daniel Kirschbaum to forget about a career in popular music and to concentrate instead on becoming a *chazan*. Kawolsky was only too aware that after six years in the choir and the concurrent four years of intensive studying, Daniel could have created for himself a comfortable niche in a small temple somewhere, a cantor in his own right. There were always advertisements for cantors appearing in the Jewish newspapers, and Kawolsky was certain that Daniel would encounter little difficulty in filling any of them, despite his youth. But Daniel had stayed with the B'nai Yeshurun, lured by the unspoken promise from the temple's board of management that one day he would take over as cantor. Daniel had already substituted at some of the Sabbath morning services when Kawolsky had been indisposed, like now, with a sore throat and the hot and cold spasms. Daniel would not take this one, though. Like the star of a Broadway show, Kawolsky had worked too hard and was too egotistical to turn over his chance of a show-stopping performance to an understudy.

As he finished dressing and prepared to leave for the temple, he began to cough again—a dry, hacking torture which began deep down in his chest and left his throat scarred and weak. His wife protested that today he should rest; she begged him to stay at home. Kawolsky smiled good-naturedly at her concern and brushed it aside.

Nothing would keep him from praising his God on the New Year.

On the choir balcony, Daniel closed his eyes as the reading of the Torah began, glad of the opportunity to relax. He had been up until past one the previous night, talking with Lucy about the direction of their respective careers. Each wanted to strike out alone, Daniel to follow up the advertisements which appeared in the Jewish newspapers and Lucy to finally take up her audition for the Metropolitan Opera chorus which her father had arranged for her.

Although he was grateful to Kawolsky for the time and effort the elderly man had put into his training, Daniel felt the temple's *gontzer machers* were stringing him along, using his younger, stronger voice to back up Kawolsky's performance while continually dangling the carrot of his succession as cantor. If the situation at home had been more acceptable, Daniel would have been content to stay with B'nai Yeshurun, singing for nothing in the choir while he absorbed everything he could from his mentor. The study under Kawolsky of *chazanuth*—the Hebrew liturgy—had created a flexibility in Daniel's voice that would serve him well in any branch of singing. And Kawolsky had not been above using underhanded trickery to improve his pupil's capabilities. Daniel remembered with amusement one ruse where Kawolsky had hit an A on the piano and told him it was an A-flat. "Match it," the cantor had ordered. If he had been told it was an A, Daniel doubted whether he would even have come close; he would have been too nervous about trying. But an A-flat he knew he could manage. Kawolsky had not admitted his deceit until almost two years later, after he had coaxed Daniel into reaching a respectable high-C. Then he had rolled back on the piano stool like a delighted child, laughing while he tried to tell Daniel how he had misled him.

Unfortunately, the situation at home was, if not actively deteriorating, certainly stagnating. Daniel and his mother barely acknowledged each other's existence, while his father tried his best to divorce himself from the problem. With Jack away most of the time for the engineering company with which he had found work, Daniel was forced to bear the brunt of his mother's bitterness. Whenever he felt he could take it no longer, he would leave the apartment and stay overnight with either Fat Benny and Tessie or the Mulvaneys, all of whom were sympathetic to his problem. Never again, though, would he raise his voice to his mother. It was not for fear of retaliation from his father. Instead, it was prompted by a desire not to aggravate his father; he knew how much Isaac had been injured by that first fight and he loved him that much to spare him further hurt.

Daniel's father attended services regularly at Washington

Heights to hear his son sing in the choir, but his mother satisfied herself by attending the High Holy Day services at the local temple on Claremont Parkway. Maybe he should try to land the *chazan*'s job at that temple if it ever became open, Daniel thought. Then what would his mother do? Go somewhere else? Or would she sit and *kvell* as she told everyone about her son the cantor? She'd do it anyway, Daniel knew. Treat him like dirt in private and brag about him in public. But he'd never give her the opportunity.

The only way to solve the problem was to move out on his own. To do that, though, he needed money. Working for Fat Benny in the candy store and singing for free in the choir would barely pay for a roof over his head. He was twenty-one years old and should be on his own. A *chazan*'s position in another temple would reward him with enough to take care of himself. Money, he and Lucy had both agreed, was the overriding factor in looking beyond Kawolsky and B'nai Yeshurun.

He became so lost in his thoughts that the choirmaster nudged him to pay attention. He looked up, startled, trying to orient himself.

"Wake up!" the man hissed.

Daniel looked over the balcony to where Kawolsky was preparing to step down from the *bima*, leading the small procession to return the two sacred scrolls to the ark. Hurriedly, Daniel picked up his prayer book and turned to the correct page, rehearsing mentally for the duet he would sing with Kawolsky when the cantor placed the scrolls in the ark and sang the poignantly beautiful, "*Eytz chaim hee.*"

With the care and tenderness that parents reserve for tiny, beloved children, Kawolsky placed the first sacred scroll in the ark and stood back while the second scroll was set alongside it. His throat was raw. Only by tremendous willpower had he managed to stop the hacking cough from erupting again. His chest hurt with the strain of singing, and he wondered if vanity would be his undoing, or whether he would be able to recover in time for the following morning's service.

While he waited, he closed his eyes for an instant in rest. To his horror, the prayer book slipped from his left hand and landed on the carpet in front of the open ark. Ashamed, he knelt down and lifted the book to his lips, kissing it. His hand was weak, too limp to even grip the book tightly. And his head felt light from standing too quickly. More than that, Kawolsky could feel the cold sweat breaking out under his robe again.

Kawolsky forced himself to breathe deeply, consoling his tortured body with the knowledge that soon would be his chance to sit and rest, when the ark was closed and the rabbi would deliver his sermon. But first would come one of the highlights of the service, a piece that was eagerly anticipated by both the congregation and himself. If he had to choose one part of the service that he held high above everything else, it would be this portion, this plaintive prayer before the ark was closed, when he beseeched God to renew the Children of Israel's days as of old. In the final lines—beginning with the words "*Eytz chaim hee,*" the tree of life—Kawolsky's voice would reach sweetly into every corner of the temple, caressing the senses of his congregation with a beauty that could never be equalled by any other song in any other language. And with Daniel on the choir balcony to harmonize with him, the effect would be doubly impressive.

A hush settled over the congregation as Kawolsky prepared for the prayer. He faced into the open ark, eyes still closed, the prayer book held closely to his chest.

Then he began.

From the choir balcony, Daniel's voice echoed that of the cantor's, singing softly to create a perfect harmony, something else Kawolsky had taught him. Yet there seemed to be a difference this time. Nothing was wrong with his own technique; he had practiced this particular piece too often to make mistakes. It was as if Kawolsky's voice was receding. Some of the sweetness and strength were missing.

Daniel toned down his own part even more, frightened of overpowering the cantor. He glanced anxiously at the choirmaster. The man was staring down from the balcony at Kawolsky, also aware that something was wrong. His left arm went up and down automatically in guidance, but his attention was riveted on the cantor. Kawolsky's voice was going, there was no longer any doubt about it. It was cracking as the cantor searched desperately for the high notes, fading as he struggled to recover from them.

The choirmaster turned around agitatedly and waved at Daniel. "Louder!" he whispered urgently. "Cover for him!"

Daniel lifted his voice and let it ring full. It carried clearly across the temple until it almost drowned out the weakened, feeble singing from below.

Too late Kawolsky realized that something far more serious than a simple cold had him in its grip. He had sung with colds before, but never had he lost his voice to the humiliating extent where the choirmaster had been forced to call in Daniel or some other member of the choir to cover for him from the balcony.

The pain in his chest. The alternating hot and cold waves that washed over him. The way the prayer book had fallen from his numbed hand. This was no cold . . . Suddenly it occurred to Kawolsky that he was dying, that he would be struck down on *Rosh Hashanah* in front of the ark. There was no other place he would wish to die, no other occasion. To allow him to pass on like that would be a just and true reward from God for the manner in which he had served Him all his life.

The thought gave strength to Kawolsky's ravaged body. He fought back the pain and stood erect, eyes focusing clearly on the shiny frontplates of the Torah scrolls, the silver pointers dangling down in front of them. He was almost finished. Another few words and he would be able to step down and take that break while the rabbi addressed the congregation.

"*Hasheevanu adonoi aylechoh. Venoshuvoh. Hadaish yomainu*"—the voice became stronger with each word, showing a tone and depth that Kawolsky could not remember enjoying for many years; it was like listening to Daniel sing, the youngster's voice emanating from his own throat—"*kukedem. Hadaish yomainu*"—Kawolsky gathered up his remaining strength, ready to launch himself onto that final word of the prayer and the high note it contained. He did not want to use guile to ease himself up there this time, using the preceding notes as a stepladder. He was certain he could take off from low down and land precisely on the note, as he had done many years earlier before age and use had taken their toll on his voice.

"Ku'ke'eh'dem!"

The high note soared across the temple like a swallow in flight, a smooth, intoxicating sound that Kawolsky—with a professional performer's appreciation of effect—let linger for just an instant longer than necessary before he finished off the prayer with the final syllable.

The echo of the note resounded in his ears like a triumphant fanfare of trumpets. His eyelids dropped again, and, with the prayer book still clutched tightly to his chest, he toppled forward into the open ark.

The *Rosh Hashanah* service resumed almost an hour later.

The rabbi—still ashen-faced and unable to recover completely from the trauma of seeing his colleague stricken in the middle of the service—kept his sermon short. He had planned to discourse at length on how a Jew should view the days leading up to *Yom Kippur*. Instead, he spoke briefly on the joyous way Eli Kawolsky had been selected to die, while worshipping his God.

Daniel was seated on the *bima*, dressed in Kawolsky's spare *kittel*—the white ornamental robe reserved for the High Holy Days—which was far too small for him. He listened uneasily to the sermon. He felt stunned by the events of the morning. One moment, the choirmaster had been urging him to sing louder to compensate for Kawolsky's weakness; the next moment, he was on the *bima* and Kawolsky was dead.

In the commotion following Kawolsky's dramatic plunge into the ark—and the appearance from the congregation of a doctor who had pronounced the cantor dead—a hurried discussion between the choirmaster and the temple president had led to Daniel donning the white *kittel* and hat and preparing to take Kawolsky's place. Daniel still couldn't accept the enormity of what had happened—twenty-one years old and leading the *Rosh Hashanah* service at a temple as prestigious as B'nai Yeshurun. It was unbelievable.

Daniel knew it was his duty to complete the service faultlessly. It would be a tribute to Kawolsky, to the man himself and to the way he had selflessly passed on his art, made certain that another would be ready to continue the tradition.

As the rabbi continued with the sermon, Daniel glanced to where his father and Fat Benny sat. He needed their support and encouragement more than ever. He had told himself he was ready to find a congregation of his own; now that he had been dramatically thrust into the forefront he was again uncertain. His uncle and father stared back expressionlessly, as stunned by Kawolsky's death as Daniel was. He turned his head toward the women's section. When he finally managed to spot Lucy, she responded by lifting a gloved hand to the level of her face and giving him the tiniest wave of support. She realized what must be taking place inside of him. She would not fail him; and she would not let him fail himself.

The sermon finished and Daniel stood up hesitantly, knowing the eyes of the congregation were upon him. He stepped forward to the dais and prepared to take the congregation into the next part of the service. He knew what he had to do. Kawolsky's spirit was still present in the temple, as it would be until the walls were torn down and the building demolished. He would show Kawolsky how much he had learned. He would make Kawolsky proud of him.

And at the same time—the feeling began to grow stronger inside him—he would serve notice on the B'nai Yeshurun board of management that they need look no further than their own choir for the next cantor.

When the service finished, the rabbi was the first to congratulate Daniel. He left his pulpit by the side of the ark and hastened to the *bima*, where Daniel occupied the position for which he had so often envied Kawolsky—standing by the two steps while he waited for the good wishes of the congregation.

"Daniel!" The rabbi grasped him by the hand. "Under the circumstances you were magnificent."

Daniel accepted the praise with genuine humility. Although the service was over, he knew he was still on display. Possibly even more so now. The quality of his voice and his ability to lead the service had never been in doubt. It was his character that would now be under scrutiny, he suddenly realized. He dare not be seen as a grasping opportunist, capitalizing on the tragic death of Kawolsky to further his own career. Any overtures had to come from the temple management; all he could do was wait.

"*Shekoyuch,*" another voice said. Daniel swung around to see Sam Grossman, the temple's president. "Kawolsky would have been proud of you, the way you sang."

"Thank you, Mr. Grossman," Daniel replied modestly, shaking the president's hand. He could never make up his mind whether he liked Sam Grossman or not. The B'nai Yeshurun had been expanded from a small *shul* to a major temple twenty years earlier, mostly with Grossman's money, and Grossman had been unanimously elected as president. An elderly man, almost as tall as Daniel but considerably thinner, Grossman always reminded Daniel of an undertaker with a perpetually drawn, anxious face.

Grossman had made his money in the garment business before retiring to move into city politics, always reliable to swing a block of Jewish votes for any piece of legislation he favored. Like Fat Benny, Grossman had a host of outstanding favors he could call in at convenient times. Daniel could never put his finger on the reason—maybe it was the garment business connection and the way his own father had been put on short time in 1930—but something about Grossman irked him.

"Can you find time to come around to my home this afternoon?" the temple president asked. Daniel caught the deferential tone in the man's voice and enjoyed it. "For a drink? For a toast to the New Year?"

"I've already got other arrangements." Daniel indicated Lucy, who was approaching from the women's section. "Some other time, perhaps."

Grossman hesitated, as if uncertain how to continue. He had expected Daniel to jump and he'd remained firmly rooted to the ground. "It's urgent," he finally said. "About tomorrow's service."

"Only tomorrow's service?" Daniel regretted the question immediately. Natural ambition had shoved aside humility.

Grossman took the question in his stride. He was on safer

ground now; he knew what he was up against. "That's what we have to talk about, Daniel. We're all greatly shocked about Kawolsky, but the *shul* has to continue."

"Lucy." Daniel held out a hand. "Say hello to Mr. Grossman, the president of B'nai Yeshurun."

Lucy smiled politely. She'd met Sam Grossman before. "Should I wait outside for you, Daniel?" she asked.

"No, it's okay. I'll be through in a minute."

"Perhaps you'd like to bring your friend along this afternoon?" Grossman suggested.

Daniel looked at Lucy, who nodded her approval. "Thank you."

"We'll be by around three," Daniel said. Then he turned his back on Grossman and began shaking the hands of congregation members, accepting their good wishes and praise and commiserating with them over the morning's tragedy. He thought he'd handled Grossman well. Too bad about that one slip of the tongue, but perhaps it was not so disastrous after all. It would do Grossman good to know that the choirboy was interested in nothing short of a full-time position as cantor.

Before going to Sam Grossman's home, Daniel visited the Kawolsky apartment with Lucy, staying for an hour with a dozen friends and relatives of the family. Kawolsky's widow refused to let her grief show, as if she had expected something like this when her husband had left for the temple that morning. Very matter-of-factly, she told her listeners of the way Kawolsky had behaved that morning, how he had refused her advice to rest because he was so intent on taking the service. There was pride in her voice as she recalled the years Kawolsky had been with the temple. Then she looked directly at Daniel, the old king's widow addressing the successor in front of the assembled court.

"Remember everything he ever taught you," she said. "He loved you like a son because of that gift God gave you. When you sing at B'nai Yeshurun, I'll hear Eli sing again."

Daniel was relieved to get out of the apartment to keep his appointment with Grossman. Although it was gratifying to have Kawolsky's widow recognize him as the next cantor of B'nai Yeshurun, there was something distinctly unnerving about being compared with a dead man. Perhaps it was just as well for Kawolsky to have died when he did. At least he was spared the hurt that would have been inevitable had Daniel sought a position with another temple.

With Lucy on his arm, he arrived at Sam Grossman's home a little after three. Grossman's wife opened the door. She showed Daniel and Lucy into the living room, where Grossman waited, and then left them in private.

"Sit down," Grossman invited, and carried on talking before either Daniel or Lucy could decide which seats they wanted. "Tea? A drink? Something to eat?"

Daniel shook his head. He had come to Grossman's home in anticipation of being offered the position of cantor; he was not paying a social call.

"*Rosh Hashanah*'s hardly the right time to be discussing this, I suppose," Grossman began hesitantly. "But we're facing an emergency at B'nai Yeshurun. The show—for want of a better comparison—must go on."

Daniel sat alertly, saying nothing, content to let Grossman say whatever he had to.

"You filled in well this morning. Everyone said so. I doubt if anyone else could have carried it off like you did. You must have nerves of steel."

You should only know, Daniel thought, as he remembered how tensed up he had been. If he hadn't forced himself to think about Kawolsky's spirit he would never have managed to get through the service. "I learned my trade from the best teacher available."

"Sure you did." The modesty was completely lost on Grossman. "That Kawolsky, he had a whole lot of respect for you. He was grooming you for when he packed it in; he let it be known all over the place that he wanted you to succeed him."

Listening to the man, Daniel could only think that Grossman fitted the part perfectly for this type of conversation. The funereal face. He was even wearing the heavy, navy-blue, double-breasted suit he had worn that morning in the temple. Daniel would not have been surprised to learn that Kawolsky lay in a coffin in the next room, and that Grossman was handling the burial arrangements.

"Getting to the point," Grossman continued, "I guess you could say that Kawolsky decided to pack it in this morning. Your turn's come, Daniel."

"Are you officially offering me the position?"

Grossman nodded. "Some break, eh, kid? How old are you?"

"Twenty-one."

"Twenty-one," Grossman mused. "And the offer of being *chazan* of a *shul* like B'nai Yeshurun." He surprised Daniel by suddenly grinning, if the slight upward elongation of his mouth could be termed a grin. "I'm all for youth. When I was your age I had a successful clothing business."

And you were probably putting people like my father on short time, Daniel felt like saying. "We have to discuss terms, Mr. Grossman. Even on *Rosh Hashanah.*" Daniel was amazed at how businesslike he had suddenly become. Yesterday he would have given ten years of his life for this opportunity. Now that it was being offered to him, he could only think of money. He knew why. With money he could leave home, find his own apartment, finally get away from his mother.

"Seventy-five dollars a week."

Daniel felt Lucy's hand tighten on his arm. Seventy-five dollars a week! That was more than his father could ever hope to earn. More than anyone in the family made, with the exception of Fat Benny. It was a fortune. And for singing!

"That includes Friday night, *Shabbos* morning and evening, plus all the *Yomtovim,*" Grossman said, reeling off conditions of the contract. "Also, you'll be expected to officiate at funerals and *shivahs,* turn up at *shul* functions and keep control of the choir. Attending *simchas,* saying grace and so on, is your own affair. Kawolsky used to accept whatever was given to him."

There was no need to think about the offer, no cause to consider it in the light of other possibilities. Daniel knew what his answer would be even before Grossman had asked the question. Nevertheless, he turned to Lucy, searching for the answer in her eyes. She smiled encouragingly at him and he swung back to face the temple president. "I accept your offer, Mr. Grossman."

"Good. We'll settle everything formally after *Yomtov* goes

out." Grossman stood up to signify the meeting was over. "See you in *shul* this evening."

Daniel kept his jubilation bottled tightly inside himself until he reached the sidewalk. Then he threw his arms around Lucy and hugged her tightly. She shrieked, half in fright, half in delight as he crushed her to him.

"Independence!" he yelled exuberantly. "Now I can do whatever I damned well want!" Kawolsky was momentarily forgotten. So was the offer of the position at B'nai Yeshurun. All Daniel could think of was being able to afford to leave home.

"When are you going to tell your family?" Lucy asked.

"Right now. Then as soon as *Yomtov* goes out I'm going to look for an apartment of my own. Get a little peace into my life at last."

"Where?"

"Around here, I suppose." Daniel fell quiet as he started to ponder the ramifications of being the cantor at B'nai Yeshurun. "I'll have to live within walking distance of the *shul*. Taking the bus from Claremont Parkway when I was in the choir was one thing. Doing it while I'm *chazan* would give a few people heart attacks." He became silent again and stared at Lucy, his eyes wide open.

"What is it, Daniel?" she asked softly.

He did not answer immediately. He was too busy remembering how he had turned around in the temple that morning, seeking her support, the way she'd lifted a gloved hand in encouragement. He had been seeing her for six years, sharing his bad times and good with her. When he had doubt, she'd given him strength; she had shown that she believed in him continually. He wondered what he would have done if Lucy had not been around. With the way he'd studied with Kawolsky and worked for Fat Benny, there was hardly ever the time to go out and meet girls.

"Want to help me look for an apartment?" he suddenly asked. "Come with me and choose the furniture?"

She gave Daniel a long, speculative glance. "Can't you do it yourself?"

It was then he realized that he could not. He was so used to having Lucy by his side that doing anything without her seemed out of the question. "I don't want to do anything by myself," he replied eventually. "I want to do everything in the future with you."

"Do you think I'd make a good wife for a *chazan?*"

"I just know you'd make a good wife for me." Daniel began to laugh as he thought of the good fortune that had been bestowed on him in one day. For a fleeting instant, the horrifying image of Kawolsky toppling forward into the ark flashed in front of his eyes to temper his happiness, but it was replaced immediately by the events that had followed in such quick succession that he had difficulty in sorting them into the proper order. Unanimously selected to complete the service in Kawolsky's place; the talk with Grossman; and now Lucy. With a jaunty spring to his step, he began to walk toward the bus stop. Sensing his intention, Lucy pulled him back.

"Better walk back to the Bronx," she suggested. "Just in case Grossman's looking out of the window or someone else from the *shul* sees you getting on the bus. You're the *chazan* now, remember?"

"See how much I need you!" he exclaimed. "I'm lost without you." He wrapped his arm around her waist, not caring if Grossman or the entire B'nai Yeshurun congregation saw him. There was nothing in the Jewish religion that forbade a man—even a cantor—to hug his fiancée on *Rosh Hashanah.*

A cantor's wedding was the social event of the year for any temple. Daniel's marriage to Lucy carried additional weight. Not only were the leading members of the B'nai Yeshurun congregation present, but there were several musicians of the Metropolitan Opera House orchestra, invited by Joe Feltz. And somehow, when preparing for the ceremony, Daniel had managed to instigate his first crisis at the temple by his choice of best man. Even Isaac had been upset to the point of questioning his son's selection.

"You could have Jack as your best man," Isaac had argued. "You could have anyone. What's so special about this *goy* Tommy Mulvaney that you have to choose him?"

"Because he's my best friend," Daniel had insisted in

defense of Tommy. He'd known it was going to raise hell, but he was confident enough of his own popularity and position after five months as cantor of B'nai Yeshurun to override any objections.

Sam Grossman had also questioned his integrity when Daniel had casually let it be known that he wanted a Catholic for his best man. Politically astute, however, Grossman had kept his complaints to a token sentence or two when he learned that the best man was a police officer, with a father who was a lieutenant in the department. Such events could not harm the temple, he had reasoned.

Standing under the *chuppah* on a bitterly cold Sunday afternoon in early March, Daniel took his eyes off the rabbi to look around. Lucy stood next to him, the white veil of her headdress partially hiding her face. Past her, Daniel could see Joe Feltz—Russian Joe—smiling benignly. Feltz's sister was next to him, taking the place of his wife who still languished in the sanitarium. Feltz never spoke of his wife or her illness to Daniel. The few times Daniel had asked how she was, Feltz seemed to ignore the question. After a while, Daniel had stopped asking, understanding that was what Feltz preferred. His wife was a closed subject and any grief he felt was his own affair. Lucy, though, had told Daniel that doctors held little, if any, hope for her mother; she was literally nothing more than a vegetable and would remain that way until she mercifully passed away. She had always been vulnerable to bouts of intense depression. Over the years they had occurred more frequently and lasted longer until they reached the stage where they ran into each other. Feltz had tried for two years to nurse his wife by himself before finally being forced to commit her to the sanitarium in Binghamton.

Daniel turned his head the other way and checked his own parents. If his father's smile had been any wider, it would have split his face in half. His mother, though, wore her habitual aloof expression, as if she were witnessing a distasteful scene of which she wanted no part. Thank God he didn't have to live at home anymore. He couldn't have taken it another day. Within two weeks of accepting the B'nai Yeshurun position, Daniel had moved into a two-bedroom apartment on Cabrini

Boulevard in Washington Heights, overlooking the Hudson River and the Jersey shore, two blocks away from Fat Benny. Knowing his family missed the money he used to bring home from the candy store, Daniel made up for it by slipping his father ten dollars every Thursday night when he and Lucy dutifully went to Claremont Parkway for dinner.

"The ring?"

Daniel snapped his wandering attention back to the rabbi who was waiting for the wedding band. Tommy Mulvaney, looking self-conscious with a white silk *yarmulke* crowning his ginger hair, reached into the jacket of his brown suit and pulled out the gold band. He rubbed it on his sleeve for luck before passing it across. Daniel took Lucy's left hand and placed the ring on the third finger.

"Charay ut m'kudeshet lee b'tubu'us zu c'dus Moshe v'Yisroel," he recited, following the Hebrew with the English translation. "Behold, thou art consecrated unto me by this ring, according to the law of Moses and of Israel."

After the seven marriage benedictions, a box containing a cloth-covered glass was placed on the floor in front of Daniel. He turned around to grin at his best man, knowing how strange the ceremony must appear to Tommy, then he raised his foot high above the box.

"Go on," the rabbi encouraged.

Daniel brought his foot down hard, but with the excitement of the moment instead of crushing the glass he caught his heel on the edge of the box, tipping it over. Realizing what he had done, he blushed an instant crimson. He had seen the marriage ceremony performed countless times, but never had he seen a groom fail to break the glass.

"Nerves," the rabbi said quietly as he stooped down to straighten the box. "Take your time."

When Daniel plunged his foot down again, he was rewarded with the noise of shattering glass. A roar of *"mazel tov!"* went up around him. Lifting Lucy's veil, he kissed her on the cheek. Tommy pounded him enthusiastically on the back. Isaac was beaming happily. Through all the festivities, though, Daniel could think of only one thing.

According to Jewish superstition, failure to break the glass was an omen of ill luck.

At nine-thirty that evening, while the wedding guests danced, ate and drank the health of the newlyweds, Daniel and Lucy bade a quiet farewell to their parents and slipped away from the hall. Parked outside was the shining black Packard that Fat Benny and Tessie had given as a wedding present. Daniel slipped into the driver's seat and guided the big automobile toward his apartment on Cabrini Boulevard. As he pulled away from the curb, a loud clattering erupted from behind the car. He started to slow down and then stepped on the gas once more. The hell with it! The string of empty cans could stay there until he reached the apartment.

"Tommy," he explained, as if Lucy needed to be told who had played the practical joke. "A copper's sense of humor."

Lucy stared out of the window as pedestrians gazed after the source of the noise. "We'll spend our wedding night in jail if you don't take those things off," she warned.

"When we get home, I'll do it." For all Daniel cared, the string of cans could clatter until the Messiah came. He had waited six years for this moment and Tommy Mulvaney's warped humor was not going to make him wait a moment longer than was necessary. He glanced sideways at Lucy and smiled at her in the darkness, wondering if she were as anxious to be home as he was. "Nervous?" he asked suddenly.

"About what?"

He laughed and told her to never mind. He could already feel his own pants beginning to tighten uncomfortably. Six years! He could hardly believe it. Six years he'd waited for Lucy and finally it was all going to happen. The long period of waiting had sharpened his senses to a keenness that would make it all the more enjoyable.

An odd thought struck him and he forced himself to choke back a chuckle. When choosing Tommy Mulvaney for his best man, Daniel had told his father that Tommy was his best friend. He realized now that the statement wasn't completely accurate. His best friend had been Lucy, always there with support, always ready to help him push for what he wanted.

When they arrived at Cabrini Boulevard, Daniel cut the

string attached to the back of the Packard and left the chain of cans in the gutter. Maybe some other lunatic had a friend who was getting married; he could use the cans!

"What time do we have to be up in the morning?" Lucy asked as they entered the apartment.

"Six." The train for Niagara Falls—where they would spend a four-day honeymoon—left at eight. Daniel would have preferred a longer break but he was needed for Friday night at the temple; he had not been cantor long enough to qualify for a full vacation.

"We'd better get to bed then," Lucy suggested, giving him an arch smile. "Get some sleep before we miss the train."

Daniel picked her up as if she weighed no more than a feather and carried her unprotestingly into the master bedroom. He dropped her onto the center of the bed and leaned over her.

"Is there a *borucha* for this, *chazan?*" she asked impishly.

"*Shehechiyonu, vekiyemonu, vehigiyonu, luzmun huzeh,*" he replied immediately. "The blessing for tasting fruit for the first time in a new season."

"Daniel Kirschbaum, you're disgusting!"

Daniel lay awake until past three in the morning, feeling Lucy's warm body snuggled up to him, listening to her regular breathing.

He felt cheated, as though the wedding night had not been worth waiting for all these years. More than that, he felt confused and hurt, unable to understand the transformation that had come so abruptly over Lucy. When they had arrived back at the apartment from the hall, she had instigated their lovemaking by joking about going to bed straightaway in case they missed their train the following morning. When he had joined her in bed, though, it was as if another woman was waiting for him, a woman who was terrified either of him or of the act of making love.

She had been scared of him. He was certain of it. He had been as gentle as he knew how and it had still been like making love to a plank of wood. And because he knew it unsatisfactory for her, it was frustrating for him also.

She would change, though, he told himself. It was up to him

to help bring about that change, to make her more responsive. He had been patient for six years; a little longer could not possibly hurt.

He felt Lucy stir beside him, stretching as she woke. "You asleep, Daniel?" she asked.

"Yes," he joked.

She nuzzled closer to him, seeking the warmth of his body. "What time is it? Do we have to get up yet?"

"Quarter after three. Another three hours." As she moved closer, he felt himself beginning to harden again. He twisted around and pressed against her, letting her know what he wanted. This time would be better, much better.

To his dismay, she withdrew. "Not now, please."

It sounded like someone begging. He shrank immediately and rolled onto his back again, staring futilely at the ceiling. He wished it were morning already.

"Tomorrow," she said softly, sensing his disappointment. "I'll feel better tomorrow night when all the excitement's worn off."

She dozed off again, leaving Daniel lying miserably awake. After another ten minutes he got out of bed, put on his dressing gown, went into the kitchen and brewed coffee. He found a day-old newspaper, turned to the sports section and began to read. Tommy and the rest of them must be thinking he was having the time of his life, he reflected gloomily. Another big joke. Just like the string of cans tied to the back of the Packard.

Daniel could even imagine the story going around Tommy's squad room. Did you hear the one about the cantor who spent his wedding night sitting in the kitchen, drinking coffee and reading the hockey scores? It didn't even need a punch line, Daniel thought miserably.

Damn! he swore silently. Maybe I should have taken better aim at the fucking glass!

Chapter Nine

The telephone rang five times before the noise penetrated Daniel's deep slumber. He sat up groggily in bed, brain confused as he tried to shake himself alert.

Doorbell? No; wrong sound.

Telephone? Had to be.

What time was it? He looked at the clock and saw ten after six. As he started to bound up, the ringing ended abruptly. He cursed and sat down heavily on the edge of the bed, feeling his way into his slippers.

He swung around and looked across the room to the twin bed where Lucy continued to sleep, undisturbed by the phone. Maybe her insistence on buying twin beds once she had become pregnant had been an unintentional blessing. Without her warm body pressing against him during the night, he had less reason to become aroused. To his bitter disappointment, Lucy had not softened since their disastrous wedding night. If anything, she had become even more frigid, submitting her body but never herself to his needs. What continued to perplex him most of all was that during the day she was the girl he had always known—sweet, considerate, a joy to be with. At night, when they prepared for bed, though, a tall fence suddenly grew between them. He became the enemy and she the besieged. She would defend her territory against his attacks until at last his superior forces overpowered her, only to find that she had laid waste what he desired most—herself.

Initially he had tried hard to understand her abhorrence of physical contact. He had sought to discuss it with her, but each time she had begun to cry and Daniel had felt guilty, as if his attempts to sympathize with her problem were the cause of her tears. Then he had even given up talking about it; he merely accepted whatever she decided to offer him, and according to her timetable.

When she had become pregnant, a distinct change had

occurred. She had blotted Daniel out completely and centered her entire life around the unborn child. She had insisted immediately that they buy twin beds. She wanted no sexual contact at all during her term, scared that harm might befall the baby. Daniel had argued with her. He had sought the aid of doctors. Their advice that sex during a normal pregnancy would have no effect on the child had fallen on Lucy's deaf ears. She had made up her mind and nothing was going to budge her from that decision. In desperation—not so much for himself but for what he considered Lucy's well-being—Daniel had even contemplated the ridiculous idea of seeking help from Joe Feltz and asking him to intercede; perhaps Lucy would listen to her father's advice where she would not heed doctors. He had given up the idea without even trying, uncertain even how to approach such a sensitive subject. And the only person on whom he had relied constantly for assistance and advice, Fat Benny, certainly had no role to play in this kind of situation.

The telephone began to ring again. Daniel stood up and walked quickly into the kitchen. "Yes?"

"Danny Kirschbaum, the wonder cantor?"

"What?" Was someone playing a gag? "Who is this?"

"Me, *klutz!* I told you you'd need an agent or a lawyer one of these days. That day has finally arrived."

"Moishe, are you aware what time it is?" It didn't matter to Daniel that he had not heard from Moishe Wasserman since the breakup of the radio show almost six years earlier. All he could think about was being dragged out of bed in the middle of the night. "What the hell do you want?"

"You should thank me, not curse me!" Moishe shouted excitedly. "I have just arranged"—he drew the words out proudly—"the biggest and best deal in the world for you."

"What are you talking about, for God's sake?" Daniel made a conscious effort to lower his voice. He didn't want to wake Lucy, but it was difficult to talk quietly and rationally when he was dealing with a certifiable lunatic. "Where are you?"

"Brooklyn. I've just driven back from the Catskills. Got in a few minutes ago after hammering out this fantastic deal for you."

"What fantastic deal?" Daniel asked suspiciously.

"You're signed up to conduct the *seder* night services during Passover at the Cavenham Hotel. You're getting five hundred bucks for the two nights. What do you think of that?"

"You're crazy, that's what I think!" Daniel wondered why he didn't hang up and go back to bed; it was the sanest thing to do.

"Look, kiddo." Moishe's voice became low, his tone serious. Daniel could not help the grin that spread across his face as he pictured Moishe pushing the glasses back up his nose while he glared belligerently at the telephone. "I've been following your career closely, reading some of the reviews you've been getting in the Jewish rags. You're a big-time *chazan* already and you're only twenty-three. Capitalize on it. Don't let all that talent and reputation go to waste. The Cavenham's willing to pay a lot of dough for the right cantor to do the *seder* night services because they can pull in all the rich Borscht Belt customers. I went up there and asked them if they wanted you. Did they ever! It's signed, sealed and delivered, so don't let me down."

"The next sound you hear will be the sound of me letting you down," Daniel said and replaced the receiver. He walked back into the bedroom, puzzling over the call. Had he done right by cutting Moishe off so curtly? It didn't matter. If Moishe was that serious, he'd call again.

Lucy was sitting up in bed, regarding him inquisitively. "Who were you shouting at?"

"Moishe Wasserman."

"Your pianist friend?"

"That's the one. I don't hear from him for about six years and then all of a sudden he pops up with some lunatic deal he's arranged on my behalf, to take the *seder* night services at the Cavenham Hotel. Now he's got whatever reputation he's built for himself riding on the deal, and he expects me to say yes."

"The Cavenham?" Lucy's face reflected a quickening interest. "That's one of the top hotels."

"I know. But I like to be asked if I'm interested before someone says I'll do it. Especially when *Pesach*'s only two months away. It's too sudden."

"Did Moishe mention money?"

"Five hundred dollars." Daniel felt an erection beginning under his dressing gown as he gazed down at Lucy. He couldn't understand why. Now in her sixth month, Lucy's appearance was doing what she had tried to do since the day they were married—make him lose interest in her sexually. He moved closer to the bed. The bright look of curiosity on Lucy's face changed to one of wariness as she realized what was happening.

"Not now, Daniel. Remember what we agreed."

Not now. The words he had grown to know so well. Once he had thought fondly of Lucy as Sforza with the *camiah;* these days he thought of her as "not now."

"Lucy, it can't do any harm to the baby. The doctors told you that."

"I don't care what the doctors say," she responded angrily. "It's my child, and I don't want anything to happen that could possibly affect its health."

Her words struck him like a stinging slap in the face. Now it's my child. No longer our child but my child. It was as if she was intent on using the baby as a shield to block out everything else. Daniel opened his mouth to continue the protest, but the telephone rang again, cutting him off.

"Are you so stinking rich these days that you don't need five bills?" Moishe's angry voice yelled from the earpiece. Daniel guessed he had been standing by the telephone while he worked himself up into enough of a righteous fury to call again. "Or couldn't you give a shit if your old buddy doesn't make fifty bucks out of the deal to keep himself alive? Think of me, huh? I spent a fortune in gas going up there to fix this deal. I've been up all night long on your lousy behalf!"

Daniel turned his attention back to the bedroom, feeling his erection harden even more. It was the mention of money, the chance of performing in front of a paying audience that was doing it to him. But there was nothing Moishe could do to help quench the desire that grew stronger with each passing second; even the biggest audience in the world could not do that for him. "You doing anything tonight?"

"No."

"Come over for dinner. Eight o'clock. Thirty-six Cabrini Boulevard. We'll talk about it then." He hung up again and walked quickly back toward the bedroom. As an afterthought he retraced his steps and took the receiver off the hook. Let Moishe dial until he wore his finger down to the bone.

"Lucy, we've got to sort this out once and for always!"

She pulled the covers up around her chin as he reentered the bedroom. Despite a powerful desire to look elsewhere, her eyes were drawn magnetically from Daniel's face down to his groin where the telltale bulge in the dressing gown confirmed her fears.

"I don't want to talk," she cried. "I'm tired. Besides," she added, grabbing at the most convenient excuse, "you've got to go to *shul* soon. It's Saturday; you've got to be there at eight-thirty."

Disregarding her frantic attempts to sidetrack him, Daniel perched on the edge of the bed and pressed Lucy back against the pillow. "There's plenty of time." He tried smiling. Anything to help put her at ease, to get her out of this miserable pit she had dug for herself. Maybe doctors weren't enough. He should go the whole route and persuade her to see a psychiatrist. Or would she ignore his advice as well, claiming as always that she knew best?

Lucy closed her eyes and lay back in resignation, a martyr about to be sacrificed for her belief. Daniel tried to blot the entire scenario out of his mind, to drive away the urge to take her. He failed as he knew he would. Abstinence was for Catholic priests; it was not for cantors. Knowing he would receive no pleasure from the encounter—but desperate for relief at any price—he slid in between the sheets. When he held her close, he could feel the small, hard lump of the unborn child pressed against his stomach. He heard Lucy's muted whimpering as he entered her, then her cries were stifled as she clamped down with her teeth on her lower lip.

When he left the bed, he felt filthy, degraded. According to Jewish lore, a man was supposed to feel uplifted by making love to his wife. It was a reward from God. Daniel felt besmirched. But then he had not made love to his wife.

He had raped her.

Daniel was sitting in the apartment building lobby when

Moishe arrived shortly before eight o'clock that evening. Instead of taking him upstairs, Daniel led him to the Packard and drove to a nearby delicatessen.

"Lucy's not feeling well," Daniel explained, unwilling to tell Moishe that she had hardly spoken a word to him all day long. When he had left for the temple that morning, she was still in bed. At one, when he had returned home, she was walking around the apartment in a dressing gown. She had served him lunch and returned to bed immediately afterwards. Daniel had spent the afternoon at Fat Benny's home, until his uncle had left for Fordham Road to supervise the Saturday evening rush.

"Lucy?" Moishe looked mystified. "Who's Lucy?" Daniel realized that Moishe did not know he had married Lucy Feltz.

"From the show. Lucia Sforza, remember?"

Moishe shoved out a hand in congratulations. As he took it, Daniel could not help but notice the heavy gold ring on the pinkie finger; he wondered if Moishe needed him to fill the Cavenham bill to help pay for the expensive piece of jewelry. "*Mazel tov*, Danny. Always thought she was a classy girl. So she's the *rebbitzin,* eh?"

"The *rebbitzin*'s the rabbi's wife," Daniel corrected him. "I'm just the cantor."

"Same difference." Moishe waved away the mistake. "What's the matter with her?"

"Pregnant. Expecting in June and having a rough time of it," Daniel explained easily.

"All the more reason you need this job at the Cavenham. You need money for kids, Danny boy. And believe me, this gig'll bring you in bigger and better things." He pulled out a wallet and withdrew a card which he threw across the table. "That's me."

Daniel picked up the card and scrutinized it carefully. Maurice Waterman, it read, attorney-at-law. "Whatever happened to good old Moishe Wasserman?"

"Too ethnic. A name like Maurice Waterman's got more class. You can still call me Moishe, though. Now, about this job I've got for you."

Daniel rested his chin on his hands, thinking about Lucy while he listened to Moishe. He wished he could turn back the clock to when Moishe had first called that morning. It was the sudden flush of animation on her face as he had talked about Moishe's proposal that had made him want her. She had come alive, stirring a responsive chord within himself that he could not ignore. He knew what to do. He'd accept the job and take Lucy along. It would do her the world of good to get away for a couple of days, leave the city and go into the mountains. She'd be almost eight months gone by then, but it would be all right if he took the journey in easy stages.

"I'll do it," he said, cutting into the middle of Moishe's sales pitch.

"You haven't heard everything I've got to say," Moishe protested.

"Five hundred bucks for two nights, right? Plus room and board for Lucy and myself."

"Minus ten percent for me. Don't forget that."

"How could I?" Daniel asked, "when your greedy legal face is sitting right opposite me?" He stood up, ignoring the sandwich in front of him. "I'll run you back to your car."

"We just got here!" Moishe exclaimed, pointing unhappily to his unstarted sandwich.

"Ask for a doggy bag. Take it with you. I want to get back to see how Lucy is." He began to feel even more guilty about his conduct during the day. Not only had he forced himself on her, but he had left her alone in the apartment at night without even telling her where he was going or what time he would be back.

"I'll call you with the details once they're ironed out," Moishe offered. He grabbed the sandwich, stuffed a pickle into his mouth and followed Daniel out into the street. He continued munching in the Packard, spraying the interior with crumbs every time he spoke.

"This is just the beginning for you, Danny boy. Your job in the temple is going to seem like peanuts compared to what I can set up for you." He rolled down the window and threw out the crust. "I can see it now. Big placards. Lights. Cantor Kirschbaum sings Gershwin."

Despite his anxiety about Lucy, Daniel could not help laughing as Moishe continued to outline his career for him.

Everyone should have a Moishe Wasserman when they're depressed, he thought; this lunatic can come up with enough *meshuggeh* get-rich-quick schemes to drive away even the blackest clouds. Just as long as Sam Grossman and the board of management at B'nai Yeshurun didn't hear him. They'd start the search for a new cantor straightaway. And Kawolsky would roll over in his grave. He decided to put his foot down before Moishe became enthusiastic enough to put one of his bizarre plans into operation.

"*Seder* nights only. All I'll do is singing connected with religion. I've got a career and reputation to consider. And in future, ask before you make a commitment concerning me. I get kind of nervous when you call up after six years and say you've landed something and expect me to turn up."

He pulled up next to Moishe's car, a white Dodge studded with chrome and assorted ornaments. "Call me when you've got some definite news."

"See you," Moishe shouted and banged the roof of the Packard. Daniel shuddered as he watched the Dodge swing out of the parking spot and scream up the street, its lights off. The car jerked to a halt at the intersection and then swung hard right and screeched around the corner. Fat Benny had been right about Moishe. He was a *golem*. He even drove the way he carried on his life. Like a *golem*.

Daniel parked the Packard and went upstairs. Lucy was sitting by the phonograph in the living room, still wearing her dressing gown. A man's syrupy-sweet voice filled the apartment with music.

"That's nice," Daniel said. He recognized the piece, having heard Lucy play it a number of times. Since Kawolsky had taught him about singing and music, he had come to appreciate the art of the lyric tenor, although he still found little to like in opera. "Who is it?"

"Gigli. It's called 'Cielo e mar', from *La Gioconda.*"

"What does that mean?"

"Sky and sea. It's an aria sung by a ship's captain as he prepares to set sail. Daddy played several times at the Met with Gigli before he left America six years ago to return to Italy."

"Nice voice."

"He sobs too much," Lucy criticized. "It's the fault of a lot of Italian tenors. They go too much for the dramatics. Listen to this and you'll see what I mean." She replaced the record with another. Daniel pulled up a chair and began to listen. The new record was "Vesti la giubba," from *Pagliacci*. He nodded in understanding; the tenor's voice was tinged with sobbing as if he would break down and cry in the middle of the recording.

"It's a sad aria," Lucy explained, "but he goes overboard. Most of these tenors are stinking actors on stage, so they try to cover their dramatic shortcomings by putting something extra into their singing. It doesn't always work."

As Daniel listened to her, he remembered how he had always run out of the apartment on Claremont Parkway whenever his father started playing the Caruso records. Now it was a generation later, and it was Beniamino Gigli. "Play that other Gigli record you have."

Lucy looked at him questioningly. "I have dozens of Gigli recordings."

"You know the one I mean. The song about the frozen hand."

Lucy burst out laughing at his description. "'Che gelida manina'! Your tiny hand is frozen."

"That's it." She was happy. Good. Even listening to music he did not particularly like was worthwhile if it put a smile on Lucy's face. "I think I've heard that song enough times to know it off by heart. I bet I can go higher than Gigli can. And hold the notes longer."

"There's a lot more to operatic singing than hitting high-Cs," Lucy said. Nevertheless, she pulled out the record and handed Daniel a sheet of paper. "That's the libretto, the words. Follow it a couple of times, then try." She replaced "Vesti la giubba" in its folder and sat down again. Daniel studied the libretto while he listened to the music, trying to follow the pronunciation of the Italian words. Twice the record played, then Daniel held up his hand.

"If you promise not to laugh at my Italian, I'll have a shot at it." He waited for Lucy to reset the record. There was the scratching noise of a steel needle on the disc, followed by the long single note that introduced the aria. Keeping his eyes on the libretto, Daniel began to sing, feeling his way slowly into the unfamiliar piece as he sang half a note behind Gigli.

Lucy watched and listened intently. When Daniel glanced up, she reminded him of Kawolsky during the singing lessons. Her hands moved to guide his phrasing, lengthening or shortening a syllable, turning a word to run into the next line. He stumbled once where a repetition was not indicated on the libretto but recovered quickly, relying on memory.

Toward the end of the aria, Lucy waited, holding her breath expectantly as Daniel approached the lines where a tenor's mettle would be tested with a cluster of high notes.

Poichè, poichè v'ha preso stanza.
La speranza.

Daniel reached the high notes with consummate ease, clearly, faultlessly, before falling back from them to end the aria with a subdued "*Vi piaccia dir?*"

"Bravo!" Lucy clapped her hands in delight. "You'd have brought the house down!"

"Was I that good?" Daniel was surprised to see how quickly Lucy's depression had departed, but he knew it was not he who had chased it away. It was the music. Her beloved opera. And a rare exhibition of interest in it by himself.

"You were marvelous, Daniel! You sing as well as Gigli. Why don't you let my father arrange an audition for you at the Met?"

Daniel shook his head. In the same hour, Moishe was ready to point him in the direction of a jazz career, and Lucy was pushing him toward opera again. "I'll stick with being a *chazan*. Those words, at least, I can understand. What about you, though?" he asked. "You had your heart set on the Met."

"I'll get to it," she replied confidently. "Didn't you know that sopranos are supposed to sing better after they've had a child? There's supposed to be more depth, more clarity in their voices."

"Does that go for tenors, too?" Daniel quipped and was gratified to see her laugh. Now was the perfect time to unload his guilt of the morning. "I'm sorry about what happened today," he said, taking her hands. "I'd do anything to start today all over again, I'm that ashamed of myself."

The mask of happiness brought on by music fell off Lucy's face in a flash. "I don't want to talk about it, Daniel."

"I won't touch you again until after the baby," he promised.

"I told you, I don't want to discuss it."

"I took that job at the Cavenham, conducting the *seder* nights," he said, knowing now it had been a mistake to remind her of what had happened. He should have remained quiet about it in the hope she might forget. "We'll go up there for a couple of days, you and me, get a break."

"I can't."

"Why not?"

"I'll be too close to full term by then. I don't want to travel. It'll be uncomfortable and dangerous."

"Then I'll have to go by myself," he said after a pause, surprised and hurt that the brief moment of sympathetic feeling had evaporated so completely.

Looking at his watch, he saw it was past ten. He wanted a newspaper, something to read before he fell asleep. There was certainly no other way he'd be able to relax.

Early the following morning, Daniel drove to Claremont Parkway to tell his father about the Cavenham offer. He asked Lucy to accompany him, but she declined, saying she wanted to clean the apartment. He decided not to push the issue. He just hoped that she would keep her word of the previous night and return to chasing her operatic dream once the baby was born. It would help bring her out of the shell she'd created for herself, put her in touch with other people. Or, he wondered, would it cut him out of her life completely while she concentrated solely on two loves? The baby and opera?

"What are you doing here?" Isaac Kirschbaum asked in surprise as he opened the door.

"I've got some good news." He walked into the living room and sat down. "Where's Ma?" he asked dutifully.

"Lying down. Doesn't feel too good."

The information had little impact on Daniel. He didn't even ask what was wrong with her. He felt sorry for his father, though, having to carry the load by himself. Jack no longer lived at home; he was working for a construction company in

Virginia, now that the economy had begun to expand and building was picking up. "I've been booked to conduct the *seder* night services at the Cavenham Hotel," he told his father. "Moishe Wasserman fixed it up for me."

"All of a sudden that madman springs up?" Isaac asked dubiously. "Is the money good?"

"Five hundred. Coming along to listen?"

"What about Lucy?"

"She doesn't want to travel. Too close to the baby."

Isaac shook his head sadly. "Daniel, I would love to come. But we'll have our *seder* nights here like always. Jack will probably be back for *Pesach*. And we'll invite Lucy and her father. That way, perhaps, she won't miss you so much."

"Thanks. It'll be the first *seder* I've missed, but it's too big an opportunity to turn down."

"I understand," Isaac said. "If it were me, I'd do the same."

Daniel left the apartment an hour later without ever seeing his mother. He heard her call out once, wanting to know who was visiting, but she never showed herself. As he walked away from the building to where he had left the car, a police cruiser pulled up. Two men were inside, a sergeant and the driver. The sergeant swung his door open.

"Mr. Kirschbaum?"

Daniel swung around as his name was called, instantly worried that a police officer should know him. Then he recognized the driver. It was Tommy. He started to wave a greeting, but the sergeant cut him off.

"Would you get in the car, please, sir?"

"Hey! What is this?"

"Just get in, please."

"Tommy!" Daniel sought out his friend, who sat immobile behind the steering wheel. "What the hell's going on here?"

"Do as he says, Cherrybum. It's important."

"Is it Lucy?"

Tommy shook his head. "She told us where to find you. We were just round at your apartment. Now will you please get in? This is as urgent as all hell."

Without another word, Daniel entered the car. It sped off, crossing over into Manhattan and then heading toward midtown. When it screeched to a halt outside a precinct house in the Times Square area, Daniel decided he had been patient with Tommy's evasiveness for long enough.

"Look, Tommy, you'd better tell me what the hell is going on here. I don't like the idea of being abducted on a Sunday morning by the police."

Tommy swung around to face his friend. "My father wants to see you. There's big trouble brewing." He got out of the car and opened the rear door for Daniel to get out. With the sergeant leading the way and Tommy bringing up the rear, Daniel allowed himself to be escorted into the building. He climbed a long flight of stairs, walked through a detective squadroom and stopped outside a wood-and-glass door on which was printed: Lieutenant James T. Mulvaney, C.C.U.

"You brought me all the way down here so I could see what your father's first name is, right?" Daniel joked with Tommy as he tried to dispel the tension. "What does C.C.U. stand for?"

"City Crime Unit. It's a new outfit, maybe a year old, that's all. Trying to crack down on the gangs."

The sergeant knocked on the door. Mulvaney yelled, "Enter." Daniel opened the door and went inside, surprised to find that neither Tommy nor the sergeant followed him. Mulvaney was seated behind a scarred wooden desk, working his way through a pile of papers. He pointed to one of two straight-backed chairs.

"Good to see you, Daniel. Sorry we had to drag you down like this."

"If you were trying to scare me, you did a damned thorough job."

Mulvancy smiled grimly. "Maybe it's just as well. We got a whisper last night about something taking place that affects you."

"What?"

Mulvaney stood up and pointed to one photograph among many that were pinned to the wall. "Recognize him?"

Daniel saw a middle-aged man, almost bald, with ears that looked like jug handles. "Never seen him before in my life."

"That's Abe Hirsch."

"Uncle Benny's old partner?"

"That's right. He was killed two weeks ago. Shotgun blast

from a passing car as he left an all-night automat on Broadway. How about him?" Mulvaney pointed to another photograph. Daniel shook his head. "That's your uncle's other partner, Mickey Bentley. He got his five weeks ago. Pushed under a subway train in the Bronx during a rush-hour stampede."

"What's all this got to do with me?" Daniel asked, still perplexed.

"Joey Bloom—your uncle's third partner—has sold his hotel. We've had a tip that he's getting ready for a comeback. We believe Bloom was responsible for the murders of Hirsch and Bentley, and your Uncle Benny's the next one on his list."

"That's crazy!" Daniel gasped. "He wouldn't touch my uncle, even if what you think is true. Benny saved Bloom's life that time! He hid him and his daughter! He told me!" Daniel felt a knife twisting in his stomach, wrenching at him as he thought of Fat Benny and Tessie being in any kind of danger. "Why don't you pick Bloom up?"

"Because we don't know where he is. We checked with the hotel and found that he's taken the money and run. He could be anywhere, using that money to bankroll his comeback."

"But my uncle never did him any harm," Daniel protested. "He helped him, saved his life!"

"Save a snake's life and he'll still bite you," Mulvaney said philosophically. "All I'm asking is that you talk to your uncle, warn him first and then ask if he knows where Bloom is. Maybe you can even persuade him to cough up a motive for Bloom to kill Hirsch and Bentley. Let me know." He sat down and returned to his paperwork, indicating that the brief meeting was over. Feeling stunned, Daniel left the office. Tommy and the sergeant were sitting outside, smoking.

"Want a lift back to Claremont Parkway, Cherrybum?"

Daniel nodded, too shaken to speak. He sat in the car, thinking of Bloom, wondering where the gangster was, what he was planning, and if it were true that Fat Benny could be the next target. Outside his parents' apartment building, he transferred to the Packard and sped to Fordham Road. Tessie was behind the cash drawer when he entered the store.

"Come to help?" she asked, hugging him affectionately.

"I want to see Uncle Benny."

Tessie was taken aback by her nephew's abruptness. "He's

in back. Something wrong?"

"No." He walked through the shop and banged loudly on the office door. "It's Daniel! Let me in!"

Fat Benny opened the door. "What's the matter?"

"I've got to speak to you. It's urgent."

"Come in." He closed the door behind Daniel and waited for his nephew to speak.

"Abe Hirsch and Mickey Bentley are both dead," Daniel said. "Murdered."

"You been talking to Mulvaney again?" Fat Benny asked.

"Never mind who I've been talking to!" Daniel exploded. "Your two ex-partners are dead, murdered by Bloom."

"Says who? Mulvaney?"

"Yes, Mulvaney. But it doesn't matter who says it because it's true."

Fat Benny did not show the least sign of concern when he asked, simply, "So?"

"Where is Bloom?"

"How the hell should I know?" Fat Benny gave him an exasperated look. "Daniel, you come in here like a whirlwind throwing all kinds of crap around. What do you want of me?"

"I want to know where Bloom is."

"I don't know. He sold his hotel and skipped with the money."

"Where to?"

"What's it to you?" Fat Benny asked. "Suddenly you're so concerned about his welfare?"

"The police—Mulvaney—want to know where he is so they can stop a third murder. Yours."

"What?" Finally Daniel seemed to be getting through to his uncle. Fat Benny reached out for a chair and sat down heavily. "What did you say?"

"Bloom's wiping out his old partners, Uncle Benny. Can't you see that? You're the only one left."

Daniel had expected Fat Benny to laugh, to protest the allegation as ridiculous. He did neither of these things. Instead he sat silently while he mulled over his nephew's words. "Abe and Mickey crossed Joey up. That's why they were hit."

"How?"

"When we all split, Joey had a quarter of the money coming

to him. We had quite a stash put away. Abe and Mickey wanted to share the money only three ways, by selling Joey out. They fingered Joey's car for the hoods who were after him. Only his wife used it that morning. That's when I hid Joey and Linda. He swore he'd come back and get them. Looks like he did."

"But you're next!" Daniel tried again to drive home the message. "He thinks you held out on him as well, tried to set him up."

"The hell he does!" Fat Benny dismissed the idea with contempt. "I made sure he got his share. The only thing Joey's got on me is that I heard him say he'd get Mickey and Abe. And that was so long ago that only an elephant would remember." He laughed suddenly. "Guess that's why I remember it so clearly, huh?"

"Do you know where he is?"

"No. And I'm not worried either. If he wants to get back into the rackets, that's his concern. Abe and Mickey are no skin off my nose. And if you want to tell Mulvaney something, tell him the last place to look for Joey Bloom is here."

Daniel turned around to leave, but his uncle called him back. "Do me a favor, will you?"

"What?"

"You're a good kid. You've always been my favorite nephew. But stick to singing, will you?" Fat Benny began to grin, an expression that grew wider with each word. "Quit trying to break into my office to see what I'm up to all the time. Otherwise I'll start coming to *shul* regularly. And I'll make sure I sing louder than you do."

The grin remained on Fat Benny's face until the office door had closed behind Daniel. Then he became thoughtful. He pulled open one of the desk drawers and withdrew a well-lacquered wooden box. Inside was a small-caliber automatic pistol and a spare clip of ammunition. Fat Benny weighed the gun in his hand, unused to its feel. The last thing he wanted was to wear it. Guns weren't for him. And God forbid that Tessie should ever catch him with it.

But if even the cops had got the word that Joey Bloom was on the rampage, maybe it was about time he started thinking less about what Tessie would say and more about himself.

Chapter Ten

Daniel drove cautiously to the Cavenham Hotel. There was still some snow on the road, coupled with the ever possible danger of a sudden squall in the mountains. He hadn't wanted to drive at all, feeling he needed to rest before singing the long service that night. When he had suggested Moishe should drive, his friend had refused emphatically. "You're making a pile more money out of this gig than me," Moishe had argued. "You can pay for the gas."

"I'll pay for the gas, for crying out loud. Just take your car."

"It's wear and tear on the car as well," Moishe had continued to protest. "You can afford it a damned sight more than I can. Besides, the Packard's more comfortable. It's got more class than my Dodge."

Daniel had debated letting Moishe drive the Packard. Then he remembered the way Moishe drove his own car and decided against it. The Packard was a status symbol, to show everyone he had arrived. The last thing he needed was a dented status symbol.

"Tell me about these guys you worked the deal with," Daniel said.

"Sol and Harry Leishman? They're brothers. Never out of each other's sight. Eat together. Even take their vacations at the same time."

"That close, huh?"

Moishe gave a sarcastic laugh at the question. "They don't trust each other, that's why. Each one's scared what the other one will do if he gets the chance."

Daniel laughed also as he pictured the scene. "They even go to bed together as well?"

"They probably draw the line at that. While they're sleeping, they can't rob each other blind."

The act of driving became mechanical, allowing Daniel time to let his mind wander. He thought about Lucy, getting as big as a house as she neared the end of her pregnancy. Maybe she was carrying twins, although there was no history of multiple births on either side of the family. Perhaps she was planning to drop another Fat Benny on the world, or a smaller version of himself. Instinctively he took a hand off the steering wheel and patted his stomach. He'd have to watch that, otherwise he would wind up looking like his uncle. But weren't all the great singers fat men? They had to get that resonance and timbre from somewhere. Nonetheless, he promised himself to go easy on food while he was at the Cavenham; as much as he loved Fat Benny, he did not want to be able to wear his clothes.

He thought of Sam Grossman as well, while the heavy Packard coasted along Route 17 into the mountains. The temple president had not been thrilled when Daniel had told him he would be absent for the first two days of Passover. He had pointed out to Grossman that he was due for a vacation, and had promised to be back for the final two days of the festival. Besides, what about the prestige of having a *chazan* who conducted the *seder* services at the Cavenham? Grossman had wilted, yielding to Daniel's wishes. Already Daniel was in the position at B'nai Yeshurun to demand special consideration. If he chose to go elsewhere, the offers would be phenomenal. Grossman could not afford to lose his star attraction.

When Moishe had arrived at Cabrini Boulevard earlier that day, Daniel had driven with him and Lucy over to Claremont Parkway. They stopped long enough to have lunch, which Yetta Kirschbaum prepared. There was company—Moishe—and Yetta wanted to show how highly she regarded her son. Moishe had not been impressed; he'd been too busy talking about his plans for Daniel and himself to even notice what he was eating.

"Remember this?" Isaac had asked as Daniel and Moishe prepared to leave for the mountains. He held up an old, well-worn seventy-eight. "Caruso in *La Juive?*"

"I remember running out of the apartment whenever you used to play it," Daniel had replied.

"What did you know when you were a child?" Isaac had chided. "Do you realize what this opera means? As well as being the last one Caruso took into his repertoire, it was a milestone in operatic history. During the course of it, Caruso conducted the *seder* service. It was beautiful. Caruso had a *Yiddishe* quality to his voice that made it real. You do as well tonight, then you'll know you're a great *chazan.*"

Daniel grinned at the memory of his father's words and switched his thoughts to two months in the future, when the baby—his child—was due. He'd have to be even more patient with Lucy while he continued to pray for change. Would she change? Or would she become even more terrified of physical love once she'd been through childbirth?

"Watch it!" Moishe lunged across the car and grabbed at the steering wheel. "Look where the hell you're going, for Christ's sake!"

Daniel swung the wheel to the right as the Packard strayed into another lane. A Cadillac coming up fast behind them blasted savagely on the horn before flashing by. "Sorry," Daniel muttered. "Lost in thought."

Moishe muttered an obscenity, then curled up on the seat, staring out of the side window as if frightened to look out of the front. Daniel reached out and patted his friend reassuringly on the shoulder. "Don't worry. I'm back again."

"Stay there," Moishe grumbled, unconvinced.

"You like boxing?" Daniel suddenly asked.

"Why?"

"My uncle's got tickets for the Joe Louis-Max Schmeling fight on June twenty-second at Yankee Stadium. Want to come?"

"Didn't know you were a fight fan."

"I just want to see this kraut superman get the shit knocked out of him. Interested?"

"Sure." Like Daniel, Moishe had been following the events that were taking place in Germany. Joe Louis was going to be an American hero, the Black *untermensch* who was going to whale the living daylights out of the master race's champion. "Count me in."

"Be cause for a double celebration," Daniel prophesied. "I'll be a father and we'll get to see the Brown Bomber knock this Nazi goon on his big fat ass." The prospect filled him with savage joy. Pity Joe Louis wasn't Jewish as well; the krauts would never forget it.

Sol and Harry Leishman were everything Moishe had

promised. The two brothers arrived together to greet Daniel at the Cavenham's registration desk, each trying to outdo the other as they welcomed him. They reminded Daniel of a comedy act, two of the Marx Brothers suddenly flung into managing a Borscht Belt hotel.

Sol was in his late forties, short and plump with thick dark brown hair—Daniel suspected it was tinted—which was heavily greased and parted in the center. His screaming-for-attention royal blue suit was shabby, without the slightest vestige of a crease, and his brown shoes were scuffed. Harry was about six inches taller and just as fat, a man in his early fifties who tried his best to look as though he had just left his tailor. His brilliantly shined shoes and impeccably pressed charcoal grey suit contrasted strongly with his younger brother's slovenliness.

"It's an honor for the Cavenham to have you here, Cantor Kirschbaum," Harry said, then added in an aside to his brother which Daniel could not help but overhear, "He seems very young, Sol. Do you think he's really the Kirschbaum from B'nai Yeshurun?"

Sol looked over Daniel like a man studying a piece of merchandise while he pondered his brother's question. "Mr. Waterman, this is Cantor Kirschbaum from the B'nai Yeshurun temple, isn't it?"

Moishe nodded emphatically while Daniel tried to figure out who Mr. Waterman was. Finally he remembered it was Moishe's professional name.

"Of course, this is Cantor Kirschbaum from Washington Heights," Moishe protested. "That's the deal I made with you."

"Let me handle it, Moishe," Daniel said. He hadn't driven all the way up from the city to have his authenticity questioned by two brothers who looked like they had escaped from a fat farm. Turning to the Leishmans he said, "My car's outside. The engine's still warm. If you're worried about my age, I'm perfectly prepared to leave now."

"No!" Sol and Harry replied in chorus.

"We're just accustomed to seeing older cantors, that's all," Harry explained quickly. He exchanged glances with his brother while Daniel waited patiently. What would they do if the cantor walked out? All those people who'd paid money for the *seder* nights, and no cantor to conduct the service? Such a possibility was terrifying to dwell on; the hotel would be ruined.

"The boy will show you to your room," Harry said. He snapped his fingers and a bellboy appeared and took the bags. Daniel and Moishe followed him upstairs to two adjoining rooms which overlooked the Cavenham's eighteen-hole golf course.

"Not bad," Moishe commented as he examined one room, opening closets and drawers, bouncing up and down on the mattress.

"You won't have much left of your fifty with this kind of room," Daniel remarked, watching Moishe with amusement.

"All part of the deal. Room and board for me as well."

"You should have brought a girl with you," Daniel said. In all the time he had known Moishe, during their on-again, off-again relationship, Moishe had never mentioned an interest in women, except to egg him on.

"I've got no time for fripperies like women," Moishe answered. "Business, that's all I'm concerned about." He walked into the other room and tried the bed there, bouncing on it like it was a trampoline.

There was a knock on the door. Moishe answered. Sol and Harry Leishman stood outside. Sol's hands were jammed deeply into his trouser pockets, accentuating the slovenly effect. In contrast, Harry's arms were folded precisely across his chest.

"The *seder* service begins precisely at seven," Harry said. "We'd like you to be in the dining hall by six."

"To check that everything's to your satisfaction," Sol added.

Harry glared down crossly at his younger brother. "And to meet a few of our most important guests. Your being here to conduct the *seder* service has aroused a great deal of interest."

"How many people will be attending the service?" Daniel asked.

"We have reservations for six hundred," Harry replied. "I trust that you're in good voice."

A spark of mischief ignited itself within Daniel. "Just the

back-end of a cold, that's all." He coughed hoarsely to demonstrate his claim. Both Harry and Sol blanched.

"He's kidding," Moishe protested. "Tell them you're joking, Danny boy. Please."

"I'm kidding." Daniel cleared his throat and sang the first two lines of *Adon Olom,* the prayer which terminates Sabbath and High Holy Day morning services.

Sol and Harry relaxed as Daniel's clear voice filled the room. "Very nice," Harry complimented him. "I'm certain our guests will not be disappointed with our choice."

"Me, too," Sol added, which drew another disapproving glance from his brother.

"Chico and Harpo," Moishe said, echoing Daniel's earlier thoughts as the Leishman brothers marched away.

Daniel nodded in agreement. "What bothers me is what Groucho's going to do when he turns up."

"He's here already." Moishe pointed an accusing finger at Daniel. "Back-end of a cold, that's all. Jesus Christ, you scared the life out of me, you bastard."

The Cavenham's massive dining hall was set out in preparation for a gigantic feast. The top table—a row of small ones joined together—was almost twenty yards long, with Daniel's place in the center. Running from it at right angles were ten even longer tables, covered in sparkling white linen, gleaming crockery and shining silverware. Each place setting had a name card, and at the far end of the hall, by the main entrance, was a notice board with neatly typed seating arrangements.

"Happy with the set-up?" Harry and Sol Leishman asked together.

Daniel surveyed the area of the table directly in front of where he would sit. Everything was where it was supposed to be. All the ritual objects connected with the service—bitter herbs, parsley, roasted egg, basin of salt water and the rest of the paraphernalia—were within easy reach.

"There's something missing," Harry said, looking at Daniel. "You're wearing a suit. Our cantors don't wear suits."

"My *kittel*'s in my room," Daniel told him. "I'll change just before we're ready to start. If it's all right with you, I prefer to make my entrance when all your guests are in their places."

"Prima donna," Sol muttered.

Harry took Daniel by the arm and guided him toward the far end of the hall. "There are some people who'd like to meet you. The Cavenham's most cherished guests."

Daniel allowed himself to be led to a small cocktail lounge which was crowded with the Leishmans' most cherished guests. Names were given to him. He repeated each one in the vague hope of remembering it; within seconds, he had forgotten most of them. His hand was shaken continuously, pumped up and down like a lever or just delicately grasped. He nodded politely at everyone.

"Mr. and Mrs. Robert Beinstock," Harry said.

"How do you do, Cantor?"

"Very pleased to meet you," Daniel replied. "Hope you enjoy the service."

"Mrs. Betty Seidman and her son, Milton."

"Looking forward to hearing you, Cantor Kirschbaum."

"Very pleased to meet you," Daniel replied again. "Hope you enjoy the service."

"Mr. and Mrs. Lou Markowitz and their son, Sidney."

"Glad to see you here, Cantor. Our son's especially looking forward to tonight. He wants to be a cantor as well. What do you think of that?"

Daniel didn't think anything about it at all. "Very pleased to meet you. Hope you enjoy the service."

"Mr. and Mrs. Irving Goldberg."

By now, Daniel was in a virtual trance. All he had to do was hear a greeting and he would automatically stick out his right hand and mumble, "Very pleased to meet you. Hope you enjoy the service."

A woman's voice stopped him as he prepared to go on to the next of the Leishmans' most cherished guests. "I hope you don't break any dishes tonight."

Daniel spun around, suddenly alert. He saw a heavily made-up young woman with bleached blond hair; by her side was a man in his late fifties.

"Linda?" he asked incredulously.

"Never expected to see me again, did you?"

"No." Daniel felt Sol and Harry tugging at him—one to each

arm—to move on to the next guest. He shook them off. "Staying for the service?"

"Wouldn't miss your voice for anything in the world. That's why we came. See you later."

Daniel allowed the Leishmans to drag him away. He shook hands and mouthed platitudes, but all the time he was thinking of Linda. Had she not spoken to him, he would never have recognized her. The bleached hair, the make-up; he would have walked straight past her. Mrs. Irving Goldberg. It was one of the few names he had managed to retain from the mass of introductions. The old guy must be her husband; she'd married a man old enough to be her father.

Her father . . . Maybe she knew where Joey Bloom was. Daniel struggled to free himself from the Leishmans and made his way back across the lounge. He was just in time to see Linda and her husband walking into the dining hall.

"You'd better get changed," Harry said when Daniel returned. "It's almost six forty-five."

"Wait a minute. One of your guests, Mrs. Goldberg."

"What about her?" The question came from Sol.

"I know her. Knew her, I mean. Who's the guy she's with, her husband?"

"That's right. Irving Goldberg's an importer of Oriental art. They're very frequent visitors to the Cavenham. Mrs. Goldberg's father used to own a hotel himself."

"I know." Daniel didn't have time to follow Linda into the dining hall; he would have to speak to her after the service. Excusing himself, he returned to his room. Moishe heard him enter and came in from the adjoining bedroom.

"Your stuff's all laid out." He indicated the white robe and hat.

"Thanks. You go on downstairs. I want to make a phone call first." He asked the operator to connect him to his parents' home in the Bronx. They'd be getting ready to sit down for the *seder* now, just like the guests in the Cavenham's dining hall. When Isaac came on the line, Daniel asked to speak to Lucy. After ascertaining she was all right, he asked if his uncle was there.

"Guess who I bumped into?" he greeted Fat Benny.

"Who? *Eliyah Hunovi?* Turned up to drink his glass of

wine?" Fat Benny asked. "How the hell am I expected to know who you bumped into?"

"Linda Goldberg. Linda Bloom who was. She's staying here."

"Good! Maybe she knows where her father is."

"I'm going to ask her just that."

"Daniel." Fat Benny lowered his voice until it was no more than a whisper that his nephew had to strain to hear. "You get off this kick with Bloom before you scare the life out of Aunt Tessie. You hear me?"

"Tommy's father would like to know."

"Do what you like. Keep playing copper, amuse yourself. But I'm not interested, remember that!" Fat Benny hung up and returned to whatever he had been doing. Daniel held the receiver for a few seconds while he wondered why his uncle had been so abrupt. Before he had treated Daniel's anxiety and warnings as a huge joke; now he had become curt. The joke had worn thin. Probably, Daniel decided, because there was no reason to worry.

"Come on," Moishe yelled from the doorway where he had been standing during the entire call. "It's two minutes to seven. My performers make their entrances on time."

Daniel put down the receiver and slipped into the white robe. He held the hat until he was just outside the dining hall, then he placed it carefully on his head. A round of applause began as he entered the huge hall. He acknowledged it by briefly raising his right hand before going directly to his position at the center of the top table.

On either side of him was a Leishman brother with a wife. Moishe's place was far off to the side, almost at the end of the top table. Looking around, Daniel spotted Linda and her husband. She waved to him. He nodded in response before letting his gaze wander further. Waiters were stationed at regular intervals, ready to begin distributing the jugs of water and towels for the traditional blessing and washing of the hands. Mountains of wine bottles were neatly stacked at strategic points, ammunition for the four glasses of wine that every adult was expected to drink.

"Ready?" Daniel whispered to Harry Leishman.

Harry nodded.

"Ready?" he asked Sol, not wanting the slovenly, younger brother to feel omitted.

"Ready."

Daniel filled the silver goblet in front of him with wine, lifted it high into the air and began the *seder* night service with a blessing. *"Baruch ata adonai eloheinu melech ho'olam borai peree hagophen."*

"Beautiful," he heard Sol Leishman whisper to his wife as the diners responded with "Amen." "Beautiful."

Daniel held back a satisfied grin and got on with the service.

The *seder* service finished at ten after eleven. The meal which split the service into two parts had taken two hours, and Daniel had wanted to spin the formalities out until midnight; he was enjoying the experience that much. As he had prepared to say the Grace After Meals to begin the second part of the service, however, Harry Leishman had whispered a request that he speed up. The hotel guests wanted time to play cards after dinner.

Daniel had responded positively. He had buzzed through grace and the following prayers, only slowing down to a more leisurely pace when he came to the group of joyful songs at the end of the service. This was the part of the *seder* he had always enjoyed at home. The plea to the Almighty to rebuild His temple in Jerusalem, the thirteen questions, the song about the kid bought for two *zuzim*. Hotel patrons who wanted time to play cards before they went to bed—even the Leishmans' most cherished guests—were not going to force him to speed through those songs.

As the final notes of the service died away, Daniel leaned back in the upholstered chair and smiled broadly. He was satisfied with his performance and now he awaited audience reaction. The applause began quietly, a few guests brave enough to be the first to show their appreciation of his efforts. It began to grow steadily in volume, sweeping toward the top table like a tidal wave until it completely engulfed those who sat there. Daniel made no attempt to move, to raise a hand in response, to try to stop it. He wanted to enjoy it, to savor every moment.

"You were great!" Sol Leishman yelled in his ear. "Listen

to that!"

"Fantastic!" Harry roared in his other ear. "We've never had a response like this."

Daniel let the applause ring out for another thirty seconds. Then he stood up slowly, both hands raised.

"Thank you." The clapping began to lose strength. "Thank you very much. I'm thrilled that you all enjoyed the service." He felt the words were feeble. Perhaps they were enough for his listeners but for himself they could never express the triumph that surged through him. Another peak climbed and conquered. Applause ringing in his ears and rightly so. He deserved it, every single clap. This was what had been missing from his performances at B'nai Yeshurun. In Washington Heights, the congregation expected miracles from every service; they were satisfied with nothing less. Here, the people had paid top dollar for the privilege of hearing him; and they believed in expressing their appreciation.

"I look forward to seeing you all again tomorrow night."

Harry Leishman grabbed him by the elbow. "Wait a minute. You're not finished yet."

"What do you mean I'm not finished?"

"Our cantors always put on a show in the cocktail lounge after the *seder*'s finished. A lot of our guests like to hear them sing while they're having a drink. A few requests, stuff like that."

"That's the first I've heard of it." Daniel glared along the length of the top table to where Moishe sat. His friend was engaged in an earnest conversation with the man next to him.

"Mr. Waterman said you would. It was part of the deal."

"Just a moment." Daniel forgot all about the applause as he tore himself loose from Harry's grasp. He stormed along the table until he stood behind Moishe. "What's all this crap about me singing in the cocktail lounge? Requests, yet?"

Moishe looked up, immediately fearful of what he saw in Daniel's face. "Relax, will you? Just a couple of songs they can get drunk to. It's part of the deal."

"Deal, hell!"

"Danny," Moishe pleaded, "don't let me down. I told them you'd do it when I set this thing up. I didn't think you'd mind. Their cantors always do it."

Daniel bunched his fist and brought it close to Moishe's face. "I ought to bust you, you four-eyed squirt! You conned me."

"A few stinking songs," Moishe pointed out, more confident that the worst had blown over. If Daniel were going to hit him, he would have done it already. "Can that hurt?"

"You louse," Daniel murmured, smiling at the people on either side of Moishe as he pretended he was having an amicable conversation.

"I'll pay you back, you'll see."

"Damned right you will! With your hide you'll pay me back, you worm. Here—" He took off his hat and robe and threw them at Moishe. "Put these back in my room."

When Daniel walked into the cocktail lounge, graciously accepting compliments on his performance, he spotted Linda. She walked toward him on unsteady legs, the glass in her hand splashing liquid as she swayed.

"Were the four glasses of wine too much?" he asked.

"Never enough." She lifted the glass and emptied it. As Daniel watched, she dropped the glass onto the floor between them. It shattered into a thousand tiny fragments. "For old time's sake," she explained as a waiter knelt down to clear up the debris. "Whenever I think of you I hear things go smash."

Daniel tried to ignore how drunk she was. "Where's your husband?"

Linda made a disgusted face as if the question was beneath her answering. "Where all old men should be at this time of night. In bed."

"Am I supposed to make some remark about that? To sympathize with you?"

"If you had any feelings you would. Or if you gave a damn about what happened to the first girl you ever screwed." She moved uncomfortably close to him and he could feel the heat of her body burning through the thin dress she wore. It stirred an undeniable response within him. "What room are you in, Daniel?"

"Linda, forget it. I'm married. I'm almost a father. Those days are gone."

She threw back her head and laughed. "You've still got the same virgin's mind, Daniel. There"—she brushed his lips with the lightest, most tantalizing of kisses—"that's to show there's no hard feelings." She walked away in the direction of the bar.

Moishe suddenly appeared at Daniel's elbow. "Stay away from that broad. She was trouble last time. She'll be trouble again."

"You recognized her?"

"Sure. I heard you mention her name on the phone before as well." He looked around the cocktail lounge, gauging the crowd. "We might as well get this part of the gig out of the way."

"We?"

"You and me. Another part of the deal," Moishe added as sheepishly as he could manage. "I'm your accompanist. Couldn't resist a tiny share of all this glory for myself."

Daniel heaved a deep, martyred sigh. One day, he promised himself; one day he would take Moishe's glasses and twist them ever so tightly around his scrawny neck.

Daniel selected his songs carefully, ballads he could handle easily even if he'd had the cold he had used to frighten the Leishmans. He kept his voice low, realizing as he sang how much he had taken out of himself with the lengthy *seder* service. He wished now that he had paid more heed to Harry Leishman's request to speed up the service and saved something of himself for this imposition.

"Any requests?" Moishe called out cheerfully from the keyboard as Daniel finished his fourth and—he had hoped—final song.

"Are you out of your mind?" Daniel swung around and looked poison at Moishe.

Moishe ignored Daniel as he looked around the crowded lounge. A woman—Daniel vaguely remembered her as Mrs. Betty Seidman, with the half-witted-looking son, Milton—waved a hand enthusiastically.

"Your chance to own the fabulous Kirschbaum voice for a few minutes, lady!" Moishe called out. "What's it to be?"

"Do you know any operatic arias, Cantor Kirschbaum?"

A beautiful vision appeared in front of Daniel's eyes. After he had twisted the glasses around Moishe's skinny neck until he was blue in the face and gasping for breath, he'd tear his ears clean off his head and stuff them down his throat. "I'm afraid that opera's not an interest of mine, Mrs. Seidman."

"Oh." There was no disguising the disappointment contained in the single word. "Not even a teensy-weensy one?"

"Give her one, for Christ's sake," Moishe muttered.

"I don't know any, you asshole!" Daniel hissed back.

"You must! Your goddamned apartment's full of the junk. Whenever I've been up there Lucy's playing the muck. Keep that stupid old broad happy and you'll make the Leishmans delirious."

Daniel dug through his memory, trying to think which of Lucy's Gigli arias or his father's Caruso arias he might be able to muddle his way through. Even if he couldn't remember the exact words he'd be able to bluff. These people spoke English and Yiddish, not Italian. Then he remembered that Caruso hadn't sung only in Italian. He'd sung English lyrics as well. Daniel bent down and whispered something to Moishe, who shook his head.

"I can't do it without the music," Moishe said. "You're on your own, pal."

Daniel recognized his escape in Moishe's answer. "Sorry," he said to Mrs. Seidman. "Mr. Waterman, my accompanist, is unfamiliar with the Caruso favorite I'd like to do." He grinned smugly. For once in his wretched life Moishe had said the right thing.

"That's all right," Mrs. Seidman replied in a tone that registered instant anxiety within Daniel. "I teach piano. I'll be able to accompany you."

"Did you put her up to this?" Daniel whispered to Moishe.

"Not me." Moishe got up from the stool and walked quickly away.

"What is your selection, Cantor?" Mrs. Seidman asked as she sat down on the vacated stool.

"I'd like to sing 'Because,'" Daniel answered.

"That's hardly opera."

"It's all I know."

"Very well." The woman decided to make the best of it and began to play. Daniel closed his eyes in concentration and his mind went suddenly blank. He could not even visualize the first line. He'd heard the song a thousand times and not a word would come to him.

The piano playing stumbled to an uncertain halt. There was a complete silence in the cocktail lounge. Daniel stood with his mouth open, his mind empty as he stared helplessly at his expectant audience. He turned around, face turning crimson as he mumbled an incoherent apology to Mrs. Seidman and rushed from the lounge. Moishe followed, yelling at Daniel to stop and return to the cocktail lounge. Daniel took no notice. He reached his room, slammed the door and locked it. Then he locked the interconnecting door to Moishe's room.

"Let me in!" Moishe yelled from the corridor. He banged on the door with his fist.

"Go to hell, you four-eyed bastard! You made me look like a damned fool!"

"You made yourself look like a fool! I didn't tell you to forget the goddamned words! The Leishmans are hopping mad!"

"Let them hop. I contracted for two *seder* services," Daniel shouted through the door. "Not for a freak show; singing to a bunch of drunks." He threw himself, fully clothed, onto the bed. After a while, Moishe's protests ceased and Daniel fell asleep.

Something woke him. A noise. Daniel sat up on the bed and looked at his watch. It was ten after two and he'd been sleeping for two hours. He wondered what he was doing fully dressed until he remembered the disaster in the cocktail lounge. Moishe. He'd kill him. Maybe the Leishmans had torn up the contract? He'd lose four hundred and fifty bucks and Moishe would lose fifty; but Moishe would feel the loss more than he would. Good! He hoped they had ripped it up.

He heard the noise again and realized it came from the door. Someone was trying the lock. As he watched, the key on his side was pushed through, landing on the carpet. Without a sound, he crossed the room and stood behind the door. As it opened, he reached out and grabbed the intruder around the throat.

"Let go!" a woman's voice spat at him. "It's me!"

"Linda! What are you doing here?"

She closed the door quickly and brushed her hair away from her face. "I bribed the guy on the desk for your room number and the house key."

"What do you want?"

"What do you think? Your wife's at home, pregnant, no good to you. My old man's out like a light. He's no good to me."

"Go away, Linda. Go back to your room."

"Act your age, Daniel." She flounced past him and sat on the edge of the bed, kicking off her shoes. "Too bad you made a big fool of yourself downstairs." She began to unbutton her dress. Daniel watched, fascinated, knowing he should throw her out but unable to force himself to do so.

"You want to take the lead this time, or are you still shy? Don't worry if you still feel a bit shook up about what happened downstairs."

He managed to find his voice. "Linda, you've got a husband here."

"He'll never know. And even if he did, it wouldn't bother him." The dress joined the shoes on the floor. "You want to know why I married him, Daniel? Because he's got a lot of money and he's too old to bother me. As long as I'm there when he wants to show me off, he couldn't care less what I do." She continued to disrobe, throwing her clothes haphazardly onto the floor. Daniel stared hungrily at the twin bands of white flesh above the tops of her nylons, unable to tear his eyes away. "He used to come to my father's place a lot, that's how we met."

"What happened to your father?" Daniel asked. His uncle's reaction had reassured him there was nothing to fear from Bloom, but there was no harm in finding out what he could. "I heard something about him selling out."

"That's right." She undid her garters and rolled down her nylons. "He travels a lot. In Chicago this week, out West next week. He's looking for a new place somewhere."

Daniel hardly heard a word she said as an irresistible force propelled him toward the bed. His legs moved as if he had no control over them until he was standing by Linda, looking down at her. When was the last time he had been with Lucy? That Saturday morning, the morning Moishe had telephoned with the preposterous idea about the Cavenham Hotel. That time didn't count, though. But then again, it seemed as if none of the times with Lucy had ever counted; they'd all been like making love to a robot.

Linda looked up and recognized the desire in Daniel's eyes. Victorious, she removed her bra slowly, tantalizing Daniel as he stood over her. Finally, she rolled down her panties and lay back on the bed invitingly. "Unless that fiasco downstairs really threw you, I'd bet you've got the biggest hard-on in the world under that suit," she teased. "Get comfortable." She patted the bed next to her.

Daniel did not remember undressing. All he recalled was a flurry of breathless activity. Then he was on the bed beside her, arms around her, mouth covering hers. He felt her hand caressing him, making him stronger still. A horror gripped him that he would climax under her hand. He backed away, breathing heavily as he tried to get his body under control.

"Turn out that fucking light," she whispered. "I hate to see who I'm screwing. It might be my husband," she giggled.

Daniel reached out to flick off the bedside lamp, plunging the room into blackness. She moved underneath him, grinding upward, pressing her damp mound against his thigh. Then she enveloped him, drawing him on, riding him like a jockey gauging a race to perfection. Suddenly her fingers clawed bloody furrows in his back. She arched her body and gasped in frenzy as he drove in deeper. Then she seemed to collapse as his own liquid spurted out.

"Jesus, you've improved," she complimented him.

"I was a kid." His back smarted furiously and he wondered how noticeable the scratch marks were. Not that he should be concerned; there'd be plenty of time for healing before he ever went to bed with Lucy again.

"You still are." She slid out from underneath him and kissed his cheek affectionately. Turning on the light, she began to dress, hardly sparing a glance at Daniel, who remained naked and exhausted on the bed.

"Want to know where to reach me?" she asked.

He said nothing. His eyes were closed as if he were trying to shut out the memory of what had just taken place. He'd cheated on Lucy. Even if she had given him reason to cheat, the realization came as a damning shock. Cheated on her with a drunken whore who'd barged her way into his room, laid him and dressed immediately afterwards. Should he offer Linda money? That was all she'd done for him.

"Keep this." She tossed a piece of paper on the bedside table. "That's Irving's card. The home number's on it. Call me there if you get the urge. See you." She turned off the light and left the room.

Daniel woke shortly after eight the following morning, snuggled warmly under the blankets. As he sat up in bed, he noticed the card on the bedside table. He picked it up and saw Irving Goldberg's name with a Park Avenue address. Very nice, he thought before screwing up the piece of paper and tossing it into the trash can. Seconds later, he dove into the can and retrieved it, straightening it out and placing it carefully in his wallet.

He took a long time showering, aware that it was a symbolic act meant to wash away the contact with Linda. Pity he couldn't wash it so easily out of his mind, but if he really wanted to do that, why had he kept the card? When he finally went downstairs for breakfast, Moishe was waiting for him.

"Don't worry about last night," Moishe greeted him. "I straightened everything out with the Leishmans."

"Last night? You mean Linda?" The words came out inadvertently, escaping before Daniel could cut them off.

"Linda?" Moishe's face dropped. "Oh, Christ, you didn't, not again. How could you?"

"How could I what?" Daniel demanded, springing to the offensive. "I spoke with her for five minutes, what else?"

"Oh." Moishe's face resumed its habitually cheerful expression as he tried to believe Daniel. "I meant about running off like that. Sol and Harry agree with me that you're not expected to sing junk like that, just regular standards. I talked it over with them after you locked yourself in your room."

"Protecting your investment?" Daniel remarked drily.

"Protecting you, Danny boy. You're getting nine hundred percent more than me out of this caper, and I'm the one that's getting the ulcers."

"Look." Daniel leaned across the table, keeping his voice low. "I'm packing this afternoon. As soon as tonight's service and the sing-song in the cocktail lounge are over, I'm driving back to New York. I'm not staying here another night."

"That's crazy," Moishe argued. "Driving through the middle of the night."

"You can take the bus tomorrow, or bum a ride with someone, but I'm leaving tonight," Daniel reiterated.

Moishe shook his head sadly. "Okay, I'll tell the brothers grim. Make sure they're ready to hand over the cash tonight."

"You do that. I'll do a few stupid ballads after the service, and we'll get the hell out of here."

Moishe looked across the table, his expression curious. "It's nothing to do with that crazy broad, is it? Linda?"

Daniel glared back angrily. "You mention her name again, and I won't even bother waiting till tonight."

Daniel managed to avoid all eye contact with Linda during that night's service. He kept his concentration strictly on the *Haggadah*, the special prayer book for the *seder* service. When the service was over, he carefully folded his white robe across the back seat of the Packard, and then joined the other guests in the cocktail lounge. Moishe had already selected half a dozen songs he knew Daniel could skip through. By midnight, they were ready to leave.

"Here." Moishe handed Daniel a white envelope. Daniel looked inside and counted nine fifty-dollar bills. "You earned it."

"Thanks." Daniel stuffed the envelope into his jacket pocket and looked around. "Where are the Leishmans?"

"Don't worry yourself about them," Moishe said casually. "I already said goodbye for you. They liked you, believe me. Asked about the chances of you coming back for next *Pesach*."

"I should still thank them and say goodbye myself." He shook off Moishe's protests and went back into the cocktail lounge. Sol and Harry were sitting with their wives and some other people, laughing as if someone had just told a joke.

"I'm leaving now, have to get back to New York," Daniel explained as he interrupted the conversation.

Sol and Harry stood up together, two Siamese twins joined together for life, one incapable of moving without disturbing the other. "Didn't expect to see you again tonight, Cantor," Harry said. "Mr. Waterman said you weren't feeling very well and were lying down in the car."

"I feel fine," Daniel assured Harry, all at once wondering what was going on.

"Good. We're glad. We enjoyed your services a lot. Pity you couldn't stay over till tomorrow."

"Yeah," Sol added, shaking Daniel by the hand. "All being well, we'll have you back next year. Might even arrange to jack up your ante from six hundred to seven or seven-fifty. All our guests said they'd be back next year if you were here."

"Thanks." Now Daniel understood why Moishe had not wanted him to say goodbye personally to the Leishmans. He shook hands and left the group to find Moishe still waiting in the lobby.

"Ten percent of the take isn't enough for you, Mr. Waterman?"

Moishe turned a shade whiter and licked his lips nervously. "You've got to understand, Daniel. I took off the extra hundred for legitimate expenses. I laid out a lot of money to set this thing up."

"You're a *gonef*, Moishe. A thief." Daniel smiled suddenly, reached out and touched Moishe's glasses as if he wanted to adjust them. Instead, he pulled them off and dropped them to the ground. Moishe blinked in panic as his vision became distorted. There was nothing wrong with his hearing, though, and there was no way he could mistake the sound of glass being crunched as Daniel drove his heel savagely into the lenses.

"That's another expense for you, *gonef*. A new pair of glasses."

"Bastard," Moishe muttered in the direction of the hazy blur that Daniel had become. "Stinking, ungrateful bastard. That's the thanks I get for landing you this job, for putting you on the road to fame and fortune."

"Quit trying to give me a guilt complex. You're beginning to sound like my mother." Daniel opened the front door and looked outside. "I'm going to start the car, Moishe. I'll give you a minute to find your way to it. Otherwise, I'm taking off and you can play blind man's bluff on the bus tomorrow. Better hurry, Mr. Waterman." He let the door swing to and walked toward the Packard.

Chapter Eleven

Daniel ducked his face down behind his hand and yawned luxuriously. None of the Saturday morning congregation noticed his surreptitious action. Most of the worshippers had their attention on the rabbi as he delivered his sermon. Those who did not were dozing themselves, taking the opportunity of the break in the service to close their eyes and use the Sabbath in the way it was really intended—as a day of rest.

Often, after the service finished, the rabbi would ask Daniel how he had enjoyed the sermon. Daniel fervently hoped that today would not be one of those occasions; he had not taken in a single word the poor man had said. All of Daniel's concentration and willpower had been brought into action to keep his eyes open during the first part of the service. More than once he had to clamp down before a treacherous yawn could develop fully and destroy a note.

At three o'clock that morning, Lucy had woken Daniel and calmly asked to be taken to the hospital. Panic-stricken, Daniel had hastily grabbed the suitcase Lucy had prepared a week earlier and helped her down to the Packard. Then he had driven at breakneck speed to the Jewish Memorial Hospital in Washington Heights. He had stayed there until six-thirty, sitting in the waiting room with three other nervous expectant fathers, talking and drinking coffee to stay awake. Finally, the smoke from the other men's cigarettes had forced him to leave. In a few hours, he would be expected to sing, wife in labor or not; any further exposure to the cigarette smoke and his throat would be as raw as if he gargled with acid. A doctor had assured him that he would be notified immediately if anything happened. Satisfied, Daniel had gone home to shower and change. At seven-thirty, an hour before the B'nai Yeshurun service was scheduled to begin, he had presented himself at Fat Benny's apartment for breakfast.

The temple door opened and Daniel looked around, glad of any diversion that might help him stay awake; after all, how would he feel if the rabbi fell asleep while he was singing? The Irish janitor entered, looked around uncertainly as if he were on unfamiliar ground, then bent down to the nearest man and whispered something in his ear. He repeated the procedure to two other men before backing out of the temple and quietly closing the door. When Daniel saw him again, the janitor was in the women's section, repeating his secretive performance.

A low murmur began to permeate the temple as the janitor's message was passed from one member of the congregation to another. Daniel watched in bemused fascination while he wondered what was going on. The murmur gradually turned into a growl so intense that the rabbi—wrapped up in delivering his weekly lecture—noticed it. He stopped talking and looked around inquisitively, wondering who would enlighten him as to the cause of the disturbance. Sam Grossman stood up and walked quickly across to the rabbi. He cupped his hand and whispered a few words. The rabbi began to smile appreciatively.

Watching the pantomime, Daniel's initial curiosity became tinged with annoyance. Fine, he thought, now everyone in the place knows but me. What had happened? It couldn't be a World Series score—not on a Saturday morning in June. World Series results were usually passed around during the *Yom Kippur* afternoon service, to either lift the solemnity of the day or plunge it irretrievably beyond the threshold of agony. Anyway, that wouldn't make the rabbi smile; he didn't know the Yankees and the Giants from the Royal Canadian Mounted Police.

Daniel looked across the temple to where his father sat. The message had reached that section. Isaac was talking animatedly to the man sitting next to him. He was even chuckling, Daniel could swear to it; even stranger, the other man was shaking Isaac by the hand and patting him on the shoulder. What in God's name had come over this normally staid congregation? To see his father laugh and joke during a service did something to Daniel. He stood up on the *bima* and looked angrily around the temple.

"Would someone mind telling the *chazan* the reason for all these interruptions?" he demanded. "Has our traditional decorum flown out the windows?"

All eyes turned to Daniel, standing alone on the raised

platform in the center of the temple. And still the buzz continued. It was the rabbi who answered from his pulpit.

"*Mazel tov!* What are you going to call your daughter?"

"Daughter?"

"Your daughter. Your wife had a little girl half an hour ago."

Daniel felt his stomach churn. His head floated a foot above him. He was a father! Lucy had given him a daughter. Taking the two steps from the *bima* in one giant stride, he dived into the congregation to embrace his father. Next he sought out Grossman. The question he was about to ask the temple president was unnecessary.

"Of course you can go!" Grossman exclaimed. "Why ask? Run!"

Daniel seemed to be nodding and shaking hands with everyone as he rushed from the temple. Faces passed in front of him, hands grabbed at his own, messages of goodwill echoed in his ears.

The walk from B'nai Yeshurun to the Jewish Memorial Hospital normally took between eight and ten minutes. Daniel covered the distance in six, half-running, half-walking, darting across intersections with only the barest awareness of car drivers who honked in desperation, or pedestrians who stared in confusion after the rushing figure still clad in the black robe and hat, with the fringed *tallis* flying from his shoulders.

The same three expectant fathers were still pacing the waiting room floor of the maternity ward when Daniel arrived, out of breath, the hat in his hand. Only when they stared at him in amazement did Daniel realize he was still wearing the accoutrements of his profession. He grinned feebly and tried to explain that he had rushed from the temple as soon as he had heard the news.

"You a priest?" one of the men asked.

"I'm sort of a Jewish one."

"Good enough. Put in a good word with Him for me. Tell Him to hurry up. I'm losing money by being stuck here."

Daniel laughed, his own anxiety and excitement momentarily forgotten.

"Mr. Kirschbaum?"

He swung around as his name was called. A nurse was

standing behind him. "That's me. Where's my wife? Is she all right? How's the baby?"

The nurse held up a hand to defend herself against the rapid-fire questions. "Take it easy, please. Your wife had a little girl—"

"I know. Is she healthy?"

The nurse smiled broadly. "Of course she is. Big and healthy. Just over eight pounds."

"And Lucy, my wife?"

"Doing just fine."

"When can I see them?"

"Very soon," the nurse promised. "But why don't you sit down while you're waiting? I'll get you a cup of coffee."

Daniel accepted gratefully. Only after he had sat down and sipped from the cup did he think about removing his robe. Before anyone else in the hospital mistook him for a priest and asked him to perform last rites.

"Hi, Lucy." He'd managed to rush out and purchase a large bunch of red roses, after explaining to the amazed florist that he would pay for them later; it was the Sabbath and he had no money in his pockets.

Lucy's face was white and puffy and she looked exhausted. When she saw Daniel and the bunch of roses that loomed out of his hand, she raised a tired smile. "It's a girl," she greeted him.

"I know. I saw."

"Are you unhappy because it's not a boy?"

"Of course not. Just as long as the baby's healthy. How do you feel?"

"Worn out." She stared down at the blanket, avoiding Daniel's eyes. "I'm sorry about the last few months. I must have been pure hell to live with."

"Forget it."

"No, I mean it. I've been a bitch because of the baby. I was just . . . just scared of something terrible happening."

"I understand."

"No, Daniel. You don't understand." The way she said it wrenched away his joy. "You don't understand at all."

"What do you mean?"

"My mother." She brought her eyes up from the blanket and searched Daniel's face for the compassion she needed to explain. "I lied to you about my mother."

"You lied?" he asked incredulously. "You lied about her being in a sanitarium?"

Lucy shook her head weakly. "She's there all right." She took a deep breath before continuing, steeling herself. "I had a sister who would have been eighteen now."

"Would have been?"

"She was stillborn. I was only six when it happened but I remember it so clearly and I wish I didn't. When my mother came home from the hospital without the child, she acted as if everything was as it should be. Daddy had prepared a nursery and my mother wouldn't let him touch it. She wanted it left just the way it was." Tears began to form in Lucy's eyes but she struggled on. "She even got up during the night at regular feeding times and went into the nursery. Doctors advised my father to be patient with her. The way she was acting was a buffer against her own grief, they told him. A release valve. Daddy did everything he could for two years. By then he was becoming ill himself. He couldn't cope anymore. When he forced himself to realize that she was still deteriorating, he did the only thing he could."

Daniel put down the bunch of roses and sat on the edge of the bed. Now he could understand. It was no wonder she had acted so coldly. What she must have gone through; a child being forced to watch her mother slowly driving herself mad. But if only she'd told him earlier . . . The unpleasantness that could have been avoided . . .

"Why didn't you say anything about it before? I would have understood."

"I wanted to, Daniel. God, how much I wanted to. But you might have thought . . ." She was unable to finish the sentence. Turning away, she burst into tears, a pain-wracked bout of sobbing that shook her entire body.

Daniel reached out, turned her face toward himself and kissed her on the forehead. "I would have been the same if it was me having the baby," he managed to say. "I wouldn't have let you near me."

The very stupidity of his words was therapeutic. The tears

stopped and Lucy coaxed a weak smile onto her face.

"We've got to give this kid a name," Daniel said. Give her something to think about, anything as long as it takes her mind off what happened to her mother. "We can't be the first parents on the block with a no-name kid. She'll get a complex."

"I like your father's idea," Lucy said. "It's a nice name and a nice thought."

"Rachel?"

"Rachel. Eleazar's daughter in *La Juive.*"

"What about a middle name?" he asked eagerly. He almost had her. Another minute and she'll be back to realizing she should be happy.

"I'll leave that to you," Lucy offered.

"Sforza," Daniel said with immediate certainty. "It'll sound like she's descended from Italian nobility, and it'll remind me of a girl I once knew at a tacky radio station."

"I'm too tired and too sore to laugh, Daniel. Go away. While I get my strength back you can think about a real middle name."

He stood by the ward door for a second, looking back at her. "No more crying, okay? I can't afford to pay for too many sets of clean sheets on a *chazan*'s pay."

Daniel was ready with a middle name when Lucy came home from the hospital a week later. He had decided on Elaine, as close as he could come to finding a feminine derivative of Eli, in memory of Kawolsky. Knowing what the cantor had done for Daniel, Lucy was thrilled with the choice.

Lucy's return was marked by a massive day-long party in the apartment on Cabrini Boulevard. Friends, relatives, people Daniel hardly even knew from B'nai Yeshurun trooped into the apartment during the afternoon and evening. Some stayed for only a few minutes, to deposit a gift and wish the new parents well; others stayed longer. The local delicatessen conducted a roaring takeout trade on sandwiches and salads. Fat Benny was on the telephone constantly, checking the buffet table with a practiced eye to see what needed reordering.

By eleven o'clock, only a few people remained. Lucy's father had left just after ten and Daniel's parents had followed suit a few minutes later. Taking this as a signal, most of the other guests had also departed. Tessie remained—cleaning up the apartment—while Moishe, who had brought the baby the biggest teddy bear Daniel had ever seen, carried paper plates and cups to the incinerator. Daniel watched them for a while, too exhausted to even offer to help, then he went into the bedroom to see Lucy, who had gone to lie down half an hour earlier.

"Was it too noisy for you?" he asked.

"No. I loved every sound of it. See?" She pointed to the crib where the baby slept peacefully. "She wasn't even disturbed."

Daniel crept over to the crib and peered inside. His daughter's eyes were closed, and her tiny chest moved up and down in a regular rhythm. He stood entranced, unable to believe that he could have had anything to do with such a delicate creature.

"Proud of yourself?" Lucy asked quietly.

"Prouder than I've ever been before," he answered truthfully. All the applause in the world paled into insignificance when compared with his daughter.

"You've every reason to be." She looked toward the bedroom door. "Who's left?"

"Moishe and Aunt Tessie, cleaning up the mess. Uncle Benny's around somewhere—probably ordering more food."

"Shoo them away," Lucy said. "We can clean up the rest in the morning."

Daniel eyed the twin beds. "When can we shoo them away as well?"

"Give me a couple of weeks, Daniel. I'm still a bit sore."

"Okay." He left the bedroom and returned to the living room. "The lady of the house has given me explicit instructions to throw you all out," he told Tessie and Moishe. "Where's Uncle Benny?"

"Maybe in the bathroom, darling," Tessie replied. She gave Daniel a hug and a wet kiss on the cheek. "So how does it feel to be a father? Seems like only yesterday it was your *bar mitzvah.*"

"Feels fine." He'd wipe his cheek when he was out of Tessie's sight. She meant well and he didn't want to upset her. "How does it feel to be a great-aunt?"

"Don't get fresh!" Tessie shot back, laughing. "I can still give you a *k'nuck.*"

Calling out Fat Benny's name, Daniel looked in the kitchen and then the second bedroom. He tried the bathroom last. The door swung open and he walked in. Fat Benny was by the basin, jacket off, vest open and shirtsleeves rolled up while he washed.

"I'm chucking you out," Daniel said unceremoniously. "We need some rest around here."

"We were going." Fat Benny reached out for the towel and turned around to face his nephew. "Don't forget about a week from Wednesday."

"What's a week from Wednesday?"

"I pay thirty bucks each for ringside seats and all you can ask is what's a week from Wednesday?" Fat Benny said disgustedly. "The fight, *golem!*"

Of course, the Louis-Schmeling rematch. "Shows what being a father can do to you," Daniel joked. "Slipped my mind completely." He forgot all about the fight again as his eyes came to rest on the waistband of Fat Benny's trousers; they were held there by a sinister, rectangular piece of metal. "What have you got there, Uncle Benny?"

Fat Benny's face froze. Too late he tried to button his vest and hide the butt of the gun he wore in his trouser waistband.

"What is it?"

"It's a pistol, what does it look like?" Fat Benny retorted gruffly.

If he had not been so surprised at seeing his uncle with a gun, Daniel would have been tempted to laugh. Fat Benny with a gun? The Keystone Cops would be doing Shakespeare next. "What are you, of all people, doing with a pistol?"

"I've got a permit to carry it," Fat Benny said. "You want to see it? It's in my wallet. I'm not breaking any laws."

Daniel kicked the bathroom door closed. "I don't give a good goddamn whether you've got a permit or not. Who do you think you are to bring a weapon into my home?"

Fat Benny backed away until the edge of the bath stopped his retreat. He had not seen Daniel this mad since he was a fifteen-year-old boy accusing him of being a crook. "I have to carry it. I'm walking around with a bundle of cash most of the time. Look," he protested, drawing a huge roll of bills from his trouser pocket, "I've got to protect myself. The boys at the local division made sure I got the permit without any trouble."

"Don't give me that crap!" Daniel had learned a lot about vocal expression from Kawolsky. Keeping his voice low, he managed to inject more fury than he ever could have done by shouting. "You've always walked around with wads of cash. You never carried a gun before, so why now?"

Fat Benny sat down on the edge of the bath and looked dejectedly at the floor. "I'm scared, Daniel," he whispered. "Shit scared. That's why I carry a gun."

"Scared of what?" His uncle wasn't making any sense at all.

Fat Benny looked up sharply at the question. "What do you think I'm scared of? Ghosts?" He laughed at his own question, an abrupt, shrill noise which was choked off almost immediately. "Yeah, it's ghosts at that. The ghost of Joey Bloom."

Daniel's anger wilted as he recognized the genuine fear that had his uncle in its grip. "Tell me."

"Your friend Mulvaney's right all along," Fat Benny admitted. "Well, almost right. So close it doesn't really matter. We all cut Joey up. Abe Hirsch, Mickey Bentley, even me. I didn't finger his car—don't get that idea—but I wasn't against sharing his percentage of the take once he'd cut and run. But because I'd hidden him and his daughter, he never suspected me."

"Then you lied to me about making sure he got his share of the money." It was an accusation, not a question.

"I lied. We split Joey's share three ways. Abe, Mickey and me. But I was clever. Joey knew they'd fingered him, so I let him think all the time that they'd beaten me out of my share as well. When I heard he was coming back to the city, it didn't bother me. I didn't even know where Abe and Mickey were; hadn't seen them for years. Joey found them, though."

"You sold your partners out?" Daniel gasped. "Put the finger on them like they'd done to Bloom?"

There was no need for Fat Benny to answer.

"So if you shifted the blame onto them, why do you think Bloom's coming after you now?" Daniel wanted to know. "All the time you've been telling me that I was crazy, that Mulvaney was crazy. Why the sudden change?"

"Joey called me a few weeks ago at the shop, just before you went up to do your *seder* services at the Cavenham. He was gloating over what he'd done to Abe and Mickey. Said he'd spoken to Mickey before he shoved him under the train. Mickey was like me—he scared easy. Maybe he thought by making a clean breast of it, by throwing me to Joey, he'd get off the hook."

"So?"

"Joey called me up to let me know he wanted to see my eyes when he gave it to me, just like the other two. And now he's making me sweat it out."

Daniel started to turn away. Fat Benny grabbed him back. "Where are you going?"

"To call Mulvaney, where do you think?"

"Don't!" The panic began to rise in Fat Benny's voice. "Tessie doesn't know a thing about this. It'll kill her if she finds out anything."

"It'll kill her if you get murdered."

"Never happen. Bloom will never be expecting me to be wearing this. I'll surprise him."

"Uncle Benny, you've never used a gun in your life. Bloom has. He's a maniac, a murderer. Can't you understand that?"

Fat Benny waved aside the rationalization. "Don't worry. The boys in the division are keeping an extra watch on my place. Joey couldn't get within a mile of Fordham Road without getting picked up."

Some chance, Daniel thought. Mulvaney's got better men out looking for him and he's got nowhere. "Don't wait till then," he told his uncle. "I can find out where he is right now."

"From his daughter?" Fat Benny grinned and Daniel recognized someone resembling the uncle he knew. "Very smart, Daniel. And give Lucy an idea you've been fooling around with some other broad?" He watched Daniel wince. "That's right. You should never have told me you'd seen Linda. No healthy guy with a seven-months pregnant wife is going to pass up a walkover like that."

"Shut up, for Christ's sake!"

"I will. On one condition. You let me handle this my way, okay?"

Daniel had no alternative. "Okay," he agreed, opening the

bathroom door. "I just hope you know what the hell you're doing."

"I do." Fat Benny rolled down his shirtsleeves, put on his jacket and checked his reflection in the mirror before leaving the bathroom to ensure the pistol did not show. "If I don't see you before, just make sure you don't forget a week from Wednesday."

Daniel walked Tessie, Fat Benny and Moishe downstairs to their cars. When he returned to the apartment, his brain was in a turmoil of conflicting loyalties. He knew what he should do, go straight to Mulvaney with the news of Bloom's threat against Fat Benny and let Mulvaney's special squad handle it. They'd guard Fat Benny better than his pals in the local division could ever hope. Besides, what would happen once Fat Benny left the comparative safety of his candy stores? How would the local cops protect him then from Bloom? Or was he really planning to defend himself? The image of Fat Benny pulling out a gun to fight off a thug like Bloom shook Daniel; he was certain his uncle did not know which end of the weapon was which.

Above all—and far more pertinent to his own well-being—how serious had Fat Benny been when he made the threat about mentioning Linda Bloom should Daniel contact Mulvaney? It was ludicrous that his uncle should even consider such a ploy, stooping to blackmail. Then again, maybe it wasn't so strange when Daniel considered the threat in light of what else his uncle had told him. Fat Benny had cheated Bloom; it was as simple as that. Conned him and then helped to set up two other guys to take the fall.

Daniel remembered clearly his first disappointment with his uncle, when he'd learned that Fat Benny was a bookmaker. He recalled the anger he'd felt, the disgust that the man he'd looked up to could be involved in such an activity. When he'd talked it out with Fat Benny, he'd realized it wasn't such a sin. This time, though, the feeling of shock was greater, the stakes higher. Daniel knew what he had to do, though. No matter how upset he was, he'd stick by Fat Benny, help him as much as he could. A cheat he might be, a man who'd betrayed others. But, above all, he was still Daniel's uncle, the man who'd given more than anyone.

Fat Benny would always be Fat Benny.

Chapter Twelve

Daniel checked a second time to ensure he had locked the Packard's door; sporting events were notorious for car thefts. Satisfied, he ran to catch up with Fat Benny and Moishe Wasserman for the quarter-mile walk to Yankee Stadium.

The entire area had a carnival atmosphere. Food and soft drink vendors served customers and made change as fast as they could. Long lines marked the locations of souvenir stands. People were shouting. Not only was it a world title fight—with the German Schmeling attempting to wrest away the heavyweight title from Joe Louis after defeating him two years earlier in a non-title fight—there were the political overtones as well. Schmeling, to the minds of many fight fans converging on Yankee Stadium, was a pseudonym for Adolf Hitler. So what if he had an American manager called Joe Jacobs? Schmeling was still the Nazi's champion, and the Brown Bomber was going to destroy him, annihilate him so completely that they'd need a vacuum cleaner to sweep the kraut up from the canvas when it was all over. Hadn't the German government gleefully tagged Louis as subhuman after Schmeling had beaten him two years earlier? The same government whose chancellor had stalked off the podium at the Berlin Olympics rather than give a gold medal to the Negro runner Jesse Owens? The same government, again, which had succeeded in persuading the United States to omit Jewish athletes for those very Olympics? Daniel was certain there wasn't a Negro or a Jew in the entire world who did not want Louis to win.

"Wouldn't want to try a *Heil Hitler* here," Moishe remarked drily as they waited to enter the stadium. He pointed to a noisy circle of demonstrators carrying anti-Nazi placards.

"More power to them," Fat Benny grunted. "Should be a few more like them, before Hitler gets too big for his jackboots."

Daniel laughed at his uncle's words. "You worry too much."

"Sure I do." Fat Benny gave him a skeptical glance. "Try telling that to all the poor bastards spilling out of Germany. Or don't you read anything in the papers but the baseball results? What are those people running from like scared rabbits? Nothing?"

What about you? Daniel felt like asking. What are you running from? He'd thought a lot about Fat Benny since his uncle had sat on the edge of the bathtub in the Cabrini Boulevard apartment and confided his fears. He'd even considered taking a rain check on the fight to avoid being with his uncle, his disappointment in the man had been so shattering. He'd looked up to Fat Benny all his life as some kind of god, seeking his advice and guidance more often than his own father's. Now it turned out that Fat Benny was a cheat and a robber; and to compound the evil he'd tried to sacrifice two others to save his own skin.

Daniel only half believed the excuse Fat Benny had given him about Tessie learning the truth if he sought Mulvaney's protection. It seemed that in some confused way, his uncle was trying to square his own conscience by inviting a one-on-one showdown with Bloom. Maybe that made it better, Daniel reasoned. Or perhaps it just added stupidity to Fat Benny's other shortcomings.

"You got that gun with you?" Daniel asked quietly, making certain that Moishe could not hear.

Fat Benny patted just below his huge stomach. "You bet."

"You're mad."

"I've got to be to put up with a pestering nephew like you. Will you leave it alone?"

Eventually they reached their seats close to the ring. Daniel forgot about Fat Benny's gun as he studied the card. In one six-round preliminary bout there was an Argentinian heavyweight called Jorge Brescia fighting a man named Al Kettles from South Bend, Indiana. Another six-rounder featured Carmen Barth of Cleveland against Al Coccozza of Harlem. There were two more six-round fights on the card, as well as two four-rounders, but Daniel paid little attention to the combatants' names. Like everyone else in the stadium he had come to see just one fight. Everything that came before it was dressing. He was impatient. He wanted the meat.

The eighty thousand crowd packed into Yankee Stadium grew steadily noisier as the preliminaries ended. Schmeling entered the ring and from somewhere nearby Daniel heard isolated shouts of *"Unser Maxe! Unser Maxe!"* He bit his bottom lip and hoped whoever had shouted the encouragement got his head kicked in.

"Over there!" Moishe dug him hard in the ribs and pointed his finger. Daniel looked but saw nothing other than people around the ring.

"Max Baer," Moishe said excitedly. "He's come to feel Louis out. He wants next crack at him if he wins."

"Oh." Daniel looked at Baer for an instant before switching his gaze back to the ring. Another figure was climbing through the ropes—a tall, brown-skinned man who seemed to walk on the balls of his feet, moving with the threatening grace of a predator. A terrifying roar swept up to the skies as Joe Louis acknowledged his fans. Daniel shot to his feet, shouting, clapping his hands together, jumping up and down.

Slowly, unwilling to relinquish the moment of magic, the spectators returned to their seats. The adulation was over; now they were eager for the fight to begin. Daniel held his breath, too excited to even think about letting it out. He could not push from his mind the noise, the pandemonium associated with a champion. What did it feel like for Joe Louis, alone in the ring with the referee and the challenger? He remembered what it had been like when he sang for the first time in front of an audience. A handful of people had applauded his earnest efforts, a scattering of noise which then had sounded like thunder. How did Louis feel now? Nervous that he might lose the fight? Or nervous in case he let his people down?

The referee stepped back. The bell sounded. Louis came out of his corner and met Schmeling in the center of the ring.

"Watch his right, Joe!" a voice screamed near Daniel. He turned around, surprised to find it was Moishe, hands cupped to his mouth as he yelled advice to the champion. "It was the kraut's right that did him last time," Moishe added for Daniel's benefit.

Louis's sharp, powerful left went to work, snapping like the end of a whip into Schmeling's face, jerking his head back as he drove him to the ropes.

"Watch his right!" This time it was Daniel who shouted, horrified as Schmeling threw a right over Louis's left guard.

The champion retreated to long range, using his left to force an opening. Daniel clasped his hands together and prayed, almost afraid to look as Schmeling lunged forward and connected with a right to the head. Louis scowled, shook off the effects of the blow and sent the challenger reeling back to the ropes with a tremendous right. Then he was on Schmeling like a tiger, a flurry of stunning punches that ended with a crushing right to the German's jaw. Daniel was on his feet, banging Moishe on the back as Schmeling toppled to the canvas.

"You got him, Joe!" Daniel screamed. "You got him!"

Even Fat Benny was standing, clapping his hands above his head in jubilation as he sensed an early and spectacular end to the contest.

Schmeling got up at the count of three. Louis straightened him with a left and then landed another blasting right. Schmeling dropped a second time but got up almost immediately.

"Put him away!" Daniel yelled, his voice lost in the frightening clamor that surrounded him. "Put that kraut bum away!"

Maybe Louis heard the frantic plea, separated it from the tidal wave of noise that swamped the ring. He tracked Schmeling as the black-haired German staggered drunkenly backwards, hammered him with a blistering series of straight lefts and left hooks before finally—and mercifully—bringing up the right. Amid the most tumultuous explosion of noise Daniel had ever experienced, Schmeling dropped in a headlong dive, unconscious.

Two minutes of the first round had elapsed.

"They've thrown in the towel!" Fat Benny shouted. At the count of three, a white towel had sailed into the ring from Schmeling's corner, hurled by his trainer, who did not want to see his fighter take any more punishment.

"Doesn't count!" Moishe yelled across Daniel to Fat Benny.

"Towels don't matter over here! Got to be a full count! This isn't Europe!"

The referee ignored the symbol of surrender and tossed the towel out of the ring while the count continued. It reached to five when the referee decided that the remainder of the count was unnecessary. He spread his arms to signal the end. The timekeeper continued counting to ten, but it was meaningless. Yankee Stadium erupted.

"What did I tell you?" Daniel shouted joyously. He looked at Fat Benny, who was standing quietly. "What's the matter?"

"I paid thirty bucks a seat for a stinking two-minute fight? I got to be crazy!" Then he burst into laughter, his beefy hands gripping Daniel's shoulders. "If it had lasted ten seconds, it would have been cheap at twice the price."

"Be a lot of noise in Harlem tonight," Moishe said, as the excitement began to drain away. "Lots of parties, dancing in the street."

"And a lot of krauts crying into their beer in Yorkville," Fat Benny replied. "Hope those *mamzerim* drown."

As the delighted crowd began to filter out of Yankee Stadium, Fat Benny pulled Daniel and Moishe back. He pointed to a hot dog stand. "Let's wait for a few minutes. I'm too old and fat to fight the crowd." He led the way over to the stand and ordered three frankfurters, pushing one each to Moishe and Daniel.

"These won't make you any thinner or younger," Daniel said.

"I'll worry about that." Fat Benny took a huge bite out of the hot dog and gulped it down. Daniel watched, amused by the vast appetite of the man; it made his own, which was far from inconsiderable, seem like that of a child. One day Fat Benny would just go bang. There would be an enormous explosion and all that would be left of Benjamin Kirschbaum would be a large crater in the ground where the detonation had taken place. That, and the fallout from the million pastrami and corned beef sandwiches he must have eaten during his lifetime.

Fat Benny finished off the hot dog and turned back to the counterman to order another. As the man handed it over, Fat Benny seemed to hesitate. Reaching out for the hot dog, his fingers froze in mid-air as if he had suddenly lost his hunger. The next moment he was scrambling frantically at his waistband as he tried to rip open the vest buttons and pull out the gun.

Daniel spun around to learn what had caused Fat Benny's panic. Five yards away, emerging like a wraith from the passing crowd, was a short, stocky man. The hair was turning white at the sides, no longer the oily black that Daniel remembered, but the eyes still retained their dark, smoldering fire. Bloom's hands were clasped together in front of his face. Something silver and shiny was grasped in them.

"Here's for you, Judas!"

The next instant Bloom squeezed the trigger. A tongue of flame blossomed out from the pistol and Fat Benny screamed in pain as he staggered back into the hot dog stand. A second time the pistol's report rang out, then Bloom thrust the gun into his jacket pocket and dived back into the crowd. In a fraction of a second, before Daniel or Moishe even had time to realize what had happened, Bloom was swallowed up by the horde of celebrating fight fans. The two shots were of no significance, lost in the continuous sound of exploding firecrackers.

"Benny!" Daniel shouted. He pushed Moishe out of the way and dived to the ground, holding his uncle's head. Blood was pouring from a wound in the neck; more blood seeped from a wound in the chest. "Benny!"

"What happened?" Moishe yelled. The hot dog was still raised to his mouth, as it had been before Bloom had appeared.

"He's been shot! Call a cop!"

The shouted request was unnecessary. The crowd of curious onlookers which had started to gather around the hot dog stand parted reluctantly. Two police officers pushed their way through. "What's going on?"

"It's my uncle." Daniel wiped the back of his hand across his eyes in a futile attempt to stem the tears. "He's been shot. Will someone call an ambulance?"

The older of the two patrolmen knelt down alongside Daniel and lifted Fat Benny's wrist. He shook his head sadly. "Too late, son. Your uncle's dead."

* * *

Daniel was numb. There was no other way to describe it. He couldn't feel, couldn't see, couldn't even think. With Moishe, he sat stupidly in Lieutenant Mulvaney's office, staring dazedly at the wall behind Tommy's father.

"Was it Bloom?" Mulvaney asked.

Moishe looked uncomfortably at Daniel before he decided to answer. "I never saw a thing. It all happened so quickly. One moment we were standing by the hot dog stand. Then there were two loud cracks and Mr. Kirschbaum was on the ground, bleeding."

Mulvaney fingered his chin while he debated what to do. Moishe's testimony was useless; it wasn't even a testimony. He needed a witness who could positively identify Bloom. He stood up and walked around the desk. "You want a drink?" he asked Daniel. From a cupboard he produced a half-bottle of bourbon and a smeary glass. "Here."

Daniel took the glass and lifted it to his mouth. The whiskey burned his throat and he began to cough. Tears sprang to his eyes as he bent forward, choking, while Mulvaney slapped him on the back. The shock to his system worked and his senses began to clear. Fat Benny was dead. Big and impregnable. There forever and now he was gone, a victim of his own deceit and fear.

"What about my aunt?" Daniel spluttered as he regained his breath. "How's she taking it?"

"Tommy's on his way round there now," Mulvaney replied. "He went to see your father first, and to let him know you were okay."

"Oh, my God," Daniel muttered, envisioning how the news would shock his father and aunt.

"You feel up to telling us what happened? Or do you want a few minutes longer?"

"I'm okay now." He took a deep breath and began to talk, hesitantly at first. Then he began to pick up speed. Grief and shock pushed him along until he was unable to control the flood of words that gushed from his mouth. He described the argument he'd had with Fat Benny following Lucy's return from the hospital. How he had found his uncle carrying a gun.

The telephoned threat by Bloom to gloat over what he'd done to the other two men, and the promise that he would avenge himself on Fat Benny as well. And then tonight, at Yankee Stadium. The sudden, chilling appearance of an older but still recognizable Bloom. The two shots that had rung out. Fat Benny crashing back into the hot dog stand, fatally wounded.

"Did you catch him?" Daniel asked.

"No. He was clean away before we even knew about it. But we've got two hundred men out looking for him now."

"Have you any idea where he is?"

Mulvaney shook his head. "Have you?"

He hesitated for a moment, thinking of the card Linda had given him, then said, "No."

The police lieutenant studied Daniel for a long time. "Daniel, I remember coming round to your parents' apartment on Claremont Parkway one Sunday morning. With Tommy. To give you back that gold watch. You still got it?"

Daniel lifted his sleeve to show the watch. "My Uncle Benny gave it to me. It was a *bar mitzvah* present."

"I always liked you, Daniel. You were a tough kid. You had to be, to do what you did to my Tommy. But you had respect, that was important. This time, though"—he shook his head sadly—"I think you're lying your head off to me."

"I don't know where he is," Daniel reiterated stiffly.

"But I'm willing to bet my pension you know how to damned well find him. You're as stupid as your uncle was, ignoring help from the police. Benny Kirschbaum could have been alive now if he'd come to us—or if you'd have come to us and said he'd been threatened. You're almost as much to blame for him getting killed as he is."

"Don't say that!" The protest did not come from the heart. Daniel knew Mulvaney was right. He'd kept quiet to protect himself. Fat Benny had blackmailed him, and he'd been the willing victim. The stupid victim was more like it. It was suddenly difficult to believe that his uncle would really have told Lucy about Linda Bloom. And even if he had, it now seemed a small price to pay for Fat Benny's safety, for his life.

Mulvaney looked at Daniel sitting sullenly in the chair. "Tell you what I'm going to do, Daniel. I'll give you forty-eight hours. If you haven't told me by then where Bloom is, I'm locking you up for protective custody."

Daniel sat bolt upright in the chair. "You can't do that to me. I've got a wife and a two-week-old baby."

"I can. And I promise you I will!" Mulvaney's voice had acquired a steely ring that invited no argument. "You're my only witness, Daniel. You've got a wife and a baby? Tough! I've got three murders to worry about."

Daniel recognized that there was nothing to be gained by continuing the argument. "You give me forty-eight hours, then. I'll deliver him to you on a silver platter."

"No heroics," Mulvaney warned. "Don't forget that wife and baby you're so concerned about."

"No heroics," Daniel agreed. He knew how to find Bloom, all right. Linda would know where her father was, and Daniel had a piece of paper in his wallet with Linda's address and phone number. He knew he should turn it over to Mulvaney, but the police officer would never get the information out of her that Daniel would. She wouldn't give Mulvaney the time of day. But she'd tell Daniel. She'd tell him everything he wanted to know. Even if he had to beat the living daylights out of her.

Daniel wanted vengeance for his uncle's death. He wanted it on Joey Bloom and on anything that Bloom touched. And that included Linda.

It rained two days later, on the Friday that Fat Benny was laid to rest in a New Jersey cemetery. Daniel had handled all the funeral arrangements, aware that his father and Tessie were too shattered by the violent tragedy to function normally. Only his mother seemed unaffected. If anything, she was quietly reveling in the notoriety that the shooting had focused on the Kirschbaum family. When visitors came to the apartment to offer their sympathy, Yetta would confide—out of her husband's and Daniel's hearing—that she had known all along that Fat Benny was involved with gangsters; she'd predicted such a stormy end for him.

Tiny rivers of rain washed down Daniel's face to mingle with his unchecked tears as he conducted the graveside service. He knew the words by heart, from other burial services, but it was different this time. A part of himself was lying in the casket with Fat Benny. As he prayed, he looked around the small group of mourners standing with heads bowed, hats dripping with water. At his father, who looked forlornly at the muddy earth. At his brother Jack, who had caught the train up from Virginia. At Moishe, who had driven over from Brooklyn for the service and was now nervously pushing his glasses back up his nose.

Daniel looked down at the coffin, glistening in the downpour. The coffin did not seem any bigger than others he had seen. The undertaker must have worked all night to squeeze Fat Benny's huge bulk into such a confined space.

The service came to a close and the mourners filed past the open pit to shovel a token spadeful of earth onto the casket. Daniel put a comforting arm around his father as they walked back to the chapel. They washed their hands and entered the car that would take them back to Claremont Parkway where the week-long *shivah* period would be held, beginning the following night after the Sabbath had terminated.

"You feeling all right?" Daniel asked his father as they crossed the George Washington Bridge from Jersey into New York.

Isaac sniffed and wiped his eyes. "Not really. You know, I was thinking before, during the service."

"What about?" Daniel decided to let his father ramble. Perhaps it would help to blunt the sorrow.

"About Benny. If it hadn't been for him, our lives would be totally different."

"How do you mean?"

"He brought me over to this country, for one thing. And if Benny hadn't got himself involved, where would you be?"

The simple question made Daniel feel ashamed for the animosity he had shown toward his uncle. How dare he have thought of Fat Benny as a cheat and a crook? What right did he have to judge his uncle? Fat Benny had given him everything, every opportunity he'd ever had; he'd opened every door for him. In return, Daniel had damned him, made him crawl the one time he had asked for support.

"Daniel." Isaac placed a hand gently on his son's knee.

"You were closer to Benny than any of us were. Did you know anything about this? About this gangster looking for Benny, wanting to kill him?"

"No," Daniel lied. He stared out of the window, looking down the Hudson for the midtown Manhattan skyline; it was completely obliterated by the low clouds. "He never said anything to me."

"It's funny, but you know a man all your life and you think you know something about him," Isaac muttered as if speaking to himself. "And when he dies, you wonder how much—if anything—you really knew about him. That's life, Daniel. Life."

Daniel stayed in his parents' apartment for only an hour before driving home to Cabrini Boulevard. He was no longer so worried about his father. Isaac was beginning to come to terms with his brother's death, accepting it with the fatalistic philosophy that ruled his life. But the sight of Tessie unnerved Daniel completely. He guessed she had been sedated by her doctor, but that knowledge didn't help; all she did during the entire time he was in the apartment was sit in a chair with her eyes closed. Daniel wondered what she would be like the following evening, when the *shivah* period started. The prayers. The visitors. All reminding her bitterly of the husband she had lost.

Lucy heard his key in the door and let him in. "How was it?"

"Must you ask?" The question sounded abrupt and he regretted it immediately. "It was terrible, like putting a piece of us all into the ground." He threw off his sodden raincoat and slouched down in a chair. Lucy picked up the garment and put it on a hanger to dry.

"Something to eat?" she asked.

Daniel shook his head. For once his stomach could take no food. All he could think of was Fat Benny. The man who had sat on the edge of the bath confessing how frightened he was. The blood gushing from the wound in his throat. The shiny, dripping casket. Daniel loathed himself as he remembered shouting at Fat Benny that night in the bathroom, demanding to know what right his uncle had to bring a gun into his house. His home! It was a sick joke. Without Fat Benny's help, he would never be living here. He'd be in some menial job, sweeping a floor or mending a road, with no hope of ever achieving anything higher.

Lucy knelt down beside Daniel's chair. "Do you want to talk about it?" she asked. "Get it out of your system?"

"There isn't anything to talk about. My father's broken up but surviving, and Tessie's sitting over there like a zombie."

"What about you?"

"I'll get over it." He looked into her face and realized how concerned she was. "How's Rachel?"

"Sleeping."

"That's what I'd like to do right now, but I can't." He stood up and walked to the phone, dialing the home number of Sam Grossman, the president of B'nai Yeshurun. When Grossman's wife answered that her husband was out—he'd gone straight back to work from the funeral—Daniel left a message that he would be unable to conduct the Sabbath services that weekend. Grossman's wife mouthed the traditional condolences and promised that she and her husband would attend the services every night of the mourning period. Daniel hardly heard her. Another matter was occupying his mind. The forty-eight hours Mulvaney had given him would expire at midnight.

"I've got to go out," he said to Lucy after hanging up the reciever. "Be back soon."

Without another word of explanation, he left the apartment and walked quickly to the nearest pay phone. While he waited for Linda to answer, he wondered if she knew about Fat Benny's murder. Did she know Fat Benny had been his uncle? Would she associate his death with Daniel's sudden call? The murder had merited nothing more than a few lines in the newspapers, about a man called Benjamin Kirschbaum being shot to death after the Joe Louis–Max Schmeling championship fight; there had been no mention of any connection with Joey Bloom. Police had said simply that they were following a certain line of investigation and hoped to make an arrest soon.

"Linda?" he asked when a woman's voice finally answered.

"Yes. Who's this?"

The voice sounded distorted. Daniel thought he might have a bad connection until he remembered how he'd seen Linda at the Cavenham Hotel. She had been drinking heavily then; obviously she hadn't lost her taste for it. "It's Daniel. I finally got around to calling that number you gave me."

"I knew you would."

He loathed the smug certainty of her answer. It was as if she wielded power over him—the first woman he'd ever made love to, and the first woman who'd made him cheat on his wife. But there was no trace of suspicion in her voice. She thought he was calling her for one reason only. The grief for his uncle intensified as Daniel spoke to the daughter of the man responsible. There was power in that grief which Daniel transferred to the vengeance he'd wreak on the Blooms. He'd pay them back for what they'd done to Fat Benny. In spades, he'd pay them back. "What are you doing later on tonight?" he asked, forcing down his bile.

"What have you got in mind?"

From somewhere, Daniel managed a suggested chuckle. "Maybe a drink or two. A little conversation. Who knows?"

"Sounds promising. Irving's away for a change, out of the country on one of his buying trips. And I'm bored out of my mind."

"I'll be there around about ten." He heard the kiss she blew into the mouthpiece. Instead of sickening him, it hardened his hatred even more.

Chapter Thirteen

At 9:30 that evening, Daniel drove Tessie to her home in Washington Heights. He had agreed with his father that the best course would be for Fat Benny's widow to stay at Claremont Parkway for the entire *shivah* period. When they had broached the subject to Tessie, though, she had been adamant about returning to her own home. She had recovered somewhat from her dazed state and was starting to show some of her customary energy as if she were determined to resume the business of living.

"You going to be all right?" Daniel asked, watching while Tessie searched through her purse for the key. He still was not happy about leaving her alone in the apartment.

"I'll be all right, Daniel." She located the key and opened the apartment door. "I'll cry a little bit over Benny and I'll remember a lot of the good things I did with him. But I'll be fine. You go home and look after your wife and baby."

Daniel stood still for a few seconds while he looked deeply into his aunt's face; her eyes were red from the tears she had already shed. "Anything I can do for you before I leave?"

"Pray, darling," she answered quietly. "Pray the cops find the *mamzer* that did this terrible thing to my Benny. Pray they catch him and burn him to a crisp."

I'm going to answer your prayers tonight, Daniel thought. I'm going to find that sonofabitch tonight and deliver him to the cops, trussed up like a Christmas turkey. He forgot about his aunt for a moment as blind rage at Bloom consumed him. He wanted to see Bloom spread out on the ground like Fat Benny had been, blood gurgling out of his mouth.

"Go home already," Tessie said, mistaking her nephew's agitation for a desire to be with his wife and daughter. "Lucy needs you more than I do."

Daniel shook his head to clear it. "Good night, Aunt Tessie." He kissed her on the cheek. Suddenly she wrapped both arms around him and held tightly.

"You're a beautiful boy, Daniel. If I'd ever had a son, I would have wanted him to be like you." She began crying again. Embarrassed by the new outburst, Daniel retreated.

"See you tomorrow, Aunt Tessie. I'll pick you up, take you to Claremont Parkway in the afternoon."

"All right, darling. Now, for God's sake, will you stop worrying about a fat old lady who wants to cry by herself and go home to your wife."

Daniel walked slowly down to the car, thinking over what he had to do, steeling himself. During the twenty-minute drive, his hands gripped the steering wheel so tightly that his knuckles turned white. When he parked near the intersection of East Seventy-fifth Street and Park Avenue, he had to force his hands free of the wheel.

"Thought you were going to stand me up," Linda greeted him when she opened the door.

Daniel said nothing. He walked stiffly into the plush apartment and looked around. The entire place reeked of money. Delicate furniture, thick carpeting, ornate crystal and silver. Along one wall of the living room was a glass-fronted cabinet in which were displayed several beautiful vases.

"Irving's hobby as well as his livelihood," Linda explained as she followed Daniel's gaze. "He lives, breathes, eats and sleeps art and antiques."

"You don't, huh?"

"Not me. I hate the way he stands around for hours and admires his paintings and statues. I prefer to collect live things, like you." She moved closer and Daniel could smell the alcohol on her breath. "Why did you make me wait so goddamned long before you decided to call?" Clasping her fingers behind his neck, she drew his head down and tried to force open his lips with her tongue.

Daniel felt the first gentle probe and almost succumbed to its spell. Linda's body was warm, burning through his clothes, starting to melt his resolve. He pushed her away and stepped back. His breath came in uneven gasps as he demanded. "Where's your father, Linda?"

"My father?" Astonishment illuminated Linda's face at the

question, so completely out of context. "Why are you asking about my father all of a sudden?"

"I want to know where he is."

"How the hell should I know?"

"Your father killed my Uncle Benny two days ago, at Yankee Stadium, right after the big fight. Shot him twice."

The bluntness of the statement had the desired effect. Linda's mouth opened in surprise and her eyes widened. "You're crazy! Get out of here before I call the cops."

"I saw your father do it," Daniel said. "I was there with my uncle when it happened. Now, where is he?"

Linda's lips, so inviting seconds earlier, tightened into a thin, vicious line. "Get out!" she screamed.

Daniel's hand came up quickly, flashing across the intervening space to slap Linda hard across the mouth. "Where's your father?"

Linda reeled backwards under the force of the blow. She fell onto a couch, her legs sprawled in the air, skirt riding up past her thighs as she struggled for balance. Daniel reached down and dragged her roughly to her feet, shaking her in mounting anger.

"Where is he? Tell me before I bust every bone in your body!"

"You're mad!" Linda screamed hysterically. She saw the next blow coming but could do nothing to avoid it. With one hand, Daniel held her by the neck while he slapped her with the other. Her head jolted back and Daniel struck her again and again, slapping her from side to side.

"Where is he, Linda? Where is your father?"

It was like Tommy Mulvaney in the alleyway all over again. Then it had been Fat Benny's watch, important at the time but of little consequence when compared with this. Now it was Fat Benny's murderer. Aided and abetted by him.

"I don't know! For Christ's sake, will you believe me?" She scratched futilely at his face. The defiance added fuel to Daniel's fury. He bunched his free hand into a fist, drew it back and slammed it into Linda's stomach. As he released his grip on her neck, she collapsed onto the floor, clasping her stomach in agony, retching. When she saw him lift his foot, she threw herself at his legs, pleading for mercy.

"Where is he?"

"Here!" Linda cried.

"In New York?"

"The Bronx," she managed to gasp out. "He's got an apartment. Calls himself Joey Budd."

Joey Budd. He knows enough to change his name but he's too conceited to change it by much. Daniel gave a final, disgusted look at the figure on the floor before walking across to the telephone. He dialed Mulvaney's office number. Late as it was, Mulvaney would still be there, waiting to hear from him. Unless he'd already gone out to look for him and make good the threat of protective custody.

Mulvaney answered and Daniel identified himself. "Your time's almost up," the police lieutenant said. "What about it?"

"I know where Bloom is."

"Where?"

"We do it my way or I don't tell you a damned thing."

"What do you want now?"

"Get over here right away." Daniel gave him the address. "I'll deliver him to you. But be quick." He jabbed the receiver to break the connection, then looked at Linda. "What's your father's number?"

"Fuck off!" she spat at him.

He dropped the receiver and leaped across the three yards separating him from the girl. Dragging her upright, he gave her two ringing slaps across the face. "You pick up that phone right now and call him. Get a wrong number or a busy signal and I'll break both your arms, so help me."

Linda staggered to the phone and dialed. When it was ringing she handed the receiver to Daniel. His heart was pounding savagely when a man's voice answered.

"Bloom?"

"Who wants him?"

"This is Daniel Kirschbaum." There was silence from the other end as the name registered. "I'm with your daughter, Bloom. I'm with Linda. Listen to what she's got to say to you." He grabbed Linda by the hair and dragged her face close to the phone. She cried out in pain as Daniel tugged her hair viciously. "You hear that, Bloom? That's your daughter screaming."

"You bastard!" Bloom yelled. "I should have done you in as well as that fat double-crossing son of a bitch!"

Daniel spoke slowly. He wanted every word to be clear. He wanted to give Bloom every reason for revenge, every reason to come out from where he was hiding and drive like a crazy man across the city. "You haven't heard the half of it, Bloom. Do you want to know what I made Linda do?"

"What?"

"She's got a sweet mouth, Bloom. Your daughter's a real good cocksucker. Did she learn that from your wife? Or did you make her practice on you?"

"I'll kill you!" Bloom's roar erupted from the earpiece. "You made my daughter do that, I'll rip you in two!" Then there was silence. Bloom had not even bothered to hang up the receiver in his haste to leave. Daniel prayed that Mulvaney would come soon.

He sat for a couple of minutes, unaware of Linda who lay sobbing on the carpet. Then he called Lucy. By now she must be worrying about him; she'd probably called his parents and learned that he had left there more than an hour earlier.

"Where are you?" she asked.

"Midtown."

"What are you doing down there?"

"Business. To do with Uncle Benny."

"The police?"

"Yes. I don't know what time I'll be home."

"All right." She sounded anxious. "I'll wait up for you."

"Don't. It might be very late." He replaced the receiver and turned to Linda. Her right eye was swelling and blood trickled from her nose and the corner of her mouth. His stomach rebelled as he wondered how he could have worked himself up to such violence.

"I'm sorry, Linda." He bent down next to the girl and reached out to make her more comfortable. "I didn't want to do this to you."

She spat at him, striking him on the jacket. "Fuck off, you bastard. I hope my father gets here before your friends do.

He'll kill you."

Daniel wiped his jacket with a handkerchief. Then he turned his attention to the door. Ten minutes passed while he waited nervously, his thoughts alternately centering on Bloom and Mulvaney. Had he given Mulvaney enough warning, enough time to get from his office? Should he have delayed calling Bloom until later, after Mulvaney had arrived? God, why had he rushed into it like this instead of thinking it out carefully?

Five minutes later, there was a rapid series of knocks on the door. Daniel breathed out in relief when he heard Mulvaney's voice calling for him. He opened the door slowly. Mulvaney stood outside with Tommy and two uniformed police officers. Daniel waved them inside quickly.

"Did you do this?" Mulvaney walked across the living room and knelt down beside Linda to examine her. "Are you crazy?"

"That's Bloom's daughter, Linda. I had to find out where her father was."

Mulvaney looked around as if expecting to find Bloom already in the apartment. "Where the hell is he then?"

"He's coming. Right now." Using a minimum of words, Daniel recounted his conversation with Bloom. Mulvaney listened intently while he worked out a plan of action. He ordered one police officer to take Linda into a bedroom and stay with her. Next he deployed Tommy and the second uniformed officer inside walk-in closets, ordering them to leave the doors ajar. "I'll be in there." He pointed to the bathroom. "When he arrives, open the door and get the hell out of the way."

If someone had told Daniel two days earlier that a man might point a gun at him, he would have been frightened out of his wits. Fists he could understand; he'd used them often enough himself. But a gun was beyond his comprehension. The sight of Fat Benny's life blood spilling onto his clothes, though, had driven all fear from him. If need be, he'd face Bloom alone and unarmed.

Hurried footsteps came from the hallway, a man striding from the elevator, a man in a hurry to reach an apartment door. "Someone's coming," Daniel said to the empty room.

"We've got you." Mulvaney's assuring voice came from the

bathroom. "Throw the door open and duck."

Daniel's heart took off, pounding faster as the footsteps grew louder. The sound came nearer, then stopped outside the door. Waiting for the knock, Daniel began to quiver with anticipation.

There was no knock.

The lock splintered and the door flew inward as Bloom kicked it in. The next instant he was inside the apartment, a pistol grasped in his right hand as he looked around to orient himself.

"You filthy piece of shit!" he screamed when he saw Daniel. "You scumbag!" The hand holding the pistol flashed up to eye level and a loud roar blasted across the room, amplified a thousandfold by the confined space. Daniel threw himself behind a chair as the glass front of the cabinet shattered into a million pieces. From somewhere Daniel heard another voice. Mulvaney. Doors banged back against their stops. A second shot ripped out from Bloom's pistol. There was a grunt of pained surprise before a salvo of three explosions—so close together that they seemed like one—answered Bloom. Daniel cowered on the floor, trying to crawl under the thick carpet as he jammed his hands over his ears to blot out the deafening, terrifying din.

A highly shined black shoe planted itself next to Daniel's head. A hand tugged gently at his arm to pull him up. Opening his eyes, Daniel recognized Tommy bending over him, his face a mask of sweat.

"It's over, Cherrybum."

Daniel rose groggily and stared about the room. Mulvaney was holding his arm; blood seeped between his fingers. By the broken door, Bloom lay like a shattered rag doll. One bullet had struck him squarely in the face, smashing his features to a bloody, unrecognizable pulp. The other two had torn into his chest. A pool of blood was forming steadily on the carpet beneath him.

"You all right?" Tommy asked.

"Fine. What about your father?"

Mulvaney heard the question and lifted his hand. Daniel saw a tear in the sleeve of his jacket. "A scratch," Mulvaney assured him. "Nothing to worry about."

Daniel nodded weakly. Then, as reaction set in, he doubled up and was sick all over the carpet.

Mulvaney called out a name and the fourth police officer appeared. Linda followed him. When she saw her father lying by the door, she shrieked wildly and ran across the room. Ignoring the crowd of neighbors who had rushed from their apartments at the sound of gunfire, Linda cradled her father's head in her lap for fully a minute while she sobbed convulsively. When she stood up, blood smeared her skirt and blouse. She looked at the four policemen, taking great care to study the features of each. Then, with no warning, she flung herself on Daniel. Too weak to resist, Daniel stumbled backward, feeling burning pain as her fingernails raked his face. Mulvaney leaped forward to drag the girl away. Daniel regained his balance unsteadily and felt his cheeks. Blood came away on his fingers.

"You bastard!" Linda screamed. "You stinking shitbag bastard! I hope you burn in hell! I'll get you, so help me I'll get you."

Mulvaney ordered Tommy to disperse the onlookers. Then he grabbed hold of Linda and unceremoniously threw her into the bedroom and locked the door. "Daniel, we're going to need a statement from you. I'll help you put it together so we can cut out everything about her"—he gestured toward the locked bedroom door—"except the bare essentials."

"Thanks." Daniel was too exhausted to even care anymore. He saw the telephone and wondered if he should call Lucy again. No matter how carefully Mulvaney worded the statement, Lucy would have to be told what had happened. She'd see the scratches on his face. He'd have to tell her about Linda. But what could he tell her? Everything—except what had happened at the Cavenham Hotel.

A hand was placed on his shoulder. "Why don't you go in the bathroom and clean up?" Tommy suggested sympathetically. "We'll wait for you."

"What about Bloom's daughter?"

"She'll come down with us. We'll get a doctor to check her over. Whatever you want to say about her getting hurt is fine by us; we'll back you up. She stinks of booze anyway. Tripped and fell while blind drunk. You name it and we'll say the same."

"Thanks, copper."

Tommy winked. "That's what we're here for, Cherrybum."

It was dawn when Daniel arrived home. He opened the front door quietly and tiptoed into the apartment.

"Daniel?"

Lucy was sitting up for him, waiting in the kitchen. "I couldn't sleep for worry." She noticed the strips of plaster on his face to cover the scratches Linda had made. "My God, what happened to you?"

"It's over." He pulled out a chair and dropped into it gratefully. "Joey Bloom's dead."

"I heard on the radio. But what happened to your face?"

Daniel's fingers strayed uncertainly to the strips of plaster. "Bloom's daughter. She went mad and attacked me. Blamed me for her father being killed. I . . ." Here it comes, he thought dismally. "I used her to set Bloom up for the police."

Lucy's eyes narrowed. "How?"

"I went round to see her. I got her to call her father. I . . ." Again he paused.

"Yes?" Lucy waited.

"I beat the hell out of her first of all because she wouldn't tell me where her father was. Then I beat her some more to make him come running. Lieutenant Mulvaney had a squad of men waiting in the apartment."

Lucy took a while to digest the information. "How did you know Bloom's daughter?"

She had asked the one question he had been fearing; now he had to answer it. "When I worked for Bloom up in the mountains, waiting tables with Moishe. Nine years ago. We met there."

"You said it, Daniel. Nine years ago. A lifetime. How did you know where to find her after all this time?"

He was too tired, too emotionally stripped to answer any more questions. "I just did," he retorted sharply. "Now let it go at that."

He managed to sleep for three hours before the events of the previous night attacked his subconscious. He woke up, shaking and covered in sweat. He got out of bed and walked outside. Lucy was bathing the baby. Daniel watched in the hope that his daughter's innocence might drive away the fearful memories.

"Your name's been on the radio, Daniel," Lucy greeted him.

"What about?"

"You're the number one story in the news programs. All stations. Gangster killed by police. Set up by his daughter's . . ." Lucy stopped in mid-sentence and stared at Daniel seeking some expression that might betray him. "Set up by his daughter's lover."

"What?" he asked incredulously. Mulvaney had promised to keep Linda's exposure to a minimum. What had gone wrong?

"That's what Bloom's daughter is saying."

"Never mind her. What are the police saying?"

"Just that Joey Bloom was shot and killed during a gunfight with police. One police officer was slightly wounded. But all the news stories are quoting Bloom's daughter; she's better copy."

"It's a lie," Daniel said without managing to inject much conviction into his voice. "She threatened last night to get even with me. Maybe this is how she thinks she can do it."

Lucy carried on bathing the child. "Perhaps I believe you, Daniel. But what will Sam Grossman and everyone else at B'nai Yeshurun think?"

The disquieting thought had occurred to Daniel as well.

Sam Grossman telephoned shortly before two in the afternoon to request an urgent meeting with Daniel. After the Sabbath morning service, the B'nai Yeshurun board of management had met hurriedly to discuss the news stories, Grossman said. While sympathizing with Daniel and the subsequent series of traumatic events, the board was committed to protecting and pursuing the temple's best interests. With Lucy's promise to stand by him echoing in his ears, Daniel left the apartment to visit Grossman's home.

In the same living room where Grossman had originally offered him the position of cantor at B'nai Yeshurun, Daniel explained what had happened the previous night. Grossman listened sympathetically and admitted that neither he nor any of the board's members believed for an instant the claims made by Bloom's daughter. However, they could not allow even the slightest whisper of scandal to tarnish B'nai Yeshurun.

"I'm afraid, Daniel, that we're forced to let you go. Believe me, our loss is greater than yours. You'll find another position quickly. We won't be so fortunate to find another *chazan* of your quality so soon."

Grossman walked him to the door, all the while explaining how regretful he was to take this step. Daniel hardly heard him. All he could think of was how quickly Linda's wild threat had come true.

He walked around aimlessly for the better part of two hours before deciding he should return home. He stared idly into shop windows while he contemplated his future. He had no doubt that he would find another cantorial position that paid just as much as B'nai Yeshurun had. There would be no financial strains.

It was the damage to his ego that needled him. To be let go by B'nai Yeshurun wounded Daniel's pride. But then it was largely because of his pride that he had let himself believe his uncle's threat about telling Lucy, he thought bitterly.

When he eventually arrived home, Lucy was in a panic, demanding to know where he had been for so long. She was so upset that she did not even ask what had transpired at the meeting with Grossman. When Daniel asked her what was wrong, she burst into a torrent of tears.

"What's the matter?" he repeated. "Is the baby all right?"

"Your father called for you. He wanted to speak to you. It was urgent and I couldn't find you. I tried Grossman's home, but you'd gone already. Where were you?"

"What's the matter, Lucy?" he asked yet again. "Will you tell me?"

She did. In halting phrases she told him how the superintendent in Tessie's apartment block had been called to trace a gas leak. Unable to get a reply from Tessie, he had broken down the door to find Fat Benny's widow lying in the kitchen with the gas fully turned on.

Chapter Fourteen

Three months of summer drifted past while Daniel was content to remain unemployed. He knew of vacant cantorial positions he could have filled on the strength of his two years with B'nai Yeshurun, but he was in no hurry. He wanted to let the ugly memories of Fat Benny's murder and Tessie's suicide pass—along with the awkward whisper of scandal evoked by Linda's claims to newsmen.

He was the main beneficiary of his uncle's will. With the inheritance had come the responsibility of disposing of the candy stores. Daniel did not even waste a moment's consideration on the possibility of taking over the business; he'd had more than enough of running the Fordham Road store when he was a teenager. Through a real estate agent, Daniel sold both stores as going concerns, complete with stock and goodwill. Then he had turned his attention to Fat Benny's apartment in Washington Heights. One Sunday morning, with his father's reluctant assistance, Daniel turned the apartment inside out. They had agreed that the furniture was to be sold, but Daniel remembered Fat Benny's preposterous boast about walking, sitting and sleeping on cash in his home. Morning turned into afternoon and stretched into evening as Daniel and his father searched every drawer, every closet, unscrewed whatever could be unscrewed, even checked the hems of drapes. By eleven that night, when they were both exhausted, they had discovered close to twenty-eight thousand dollars secreted away in eleven separate cashes. If any more money remained, they had decided, whoever found it was welcome to it.

Daniel had insisted on dividing the money into two equal portions, one for his father, the other for his brother. He refused Isaac's insistence that he take a share for himself. The money from the sale of the stores, plus what he had found in Fat Benny's safe deposit boxes, came to far more than what they had found in the apartment.

During the first weeks after he had been let go by B'nai Yeshurun, Daniel had been hesitant about venturing outside the apartment in case he was spotted by congregation members. Even their sympathy at his situation would have been uncomfortable. He decided that he and Lucy would have to move, but there was no point in searching for another home until he decided to resume work.

"Why don't you take Rachel out in the carriage?" Lucy suggested one morning when she was fed up with seeing Daniel walking gloomily around the apartment as he tried to find things to do. "It's a beautiful day; give her some sunshine."

"Can't you?"

"I'd like to take a rest, too, sometimes. What else have you got to do?"

"Nothing," he agreed. He placed the baby in the carriage, stood by while Lucy checked that she was all right, then took her down to the street. He walked around for fifteen minutes, smiling benignly at unknown women who insisted on looking at the baby, feeling stupid as he thanked them for their compliments. He never understood what peculiar attraction there was in a baby carriage that drew total strangers and forced them to make the weirdest faces and noises. If he did such things, it was perfectly understandable; Rachel was his daughter, after all.

Stopped at a busy intersection, he leaned over the carriage and tickled Rachel's tiny button nose with his finger, laughing while she gurgled happily. When he stood up and saw two amused women watching him, he turned scarlet and marched stiffly away. He had put up with enough. Five minutes later, he was back home.

"Daniel, as long as you're going to be around to keep an eye on Rachel, I'd like to get out of the apartment," Lucy told him.

"Where to?" he asked.

"I also had a career, remember? I'd like to start taking singing lessons again. My father's been on at me about all the time I wasted by not studying. He's perfectly right."

"Lucy, we don't need the money. You don't have to worry about that."

"Daniel, I need some independence. Money doesn't enter into it. You have a career—when you choose to go back to it. I was hoping to have one, too."

"Do you think you've still got a chance?"

"My father thinks so, if I don't leave it too late. He's knowledgeable enough to know what's good or bad. He always thought you did, too."

"Don't start that again," Daniel warned.

Lucy chose to ignore his tone of voice. "Why not?" she cried. "You're doing nothing now, just letting that marvelous gift go to waste while you sit back and live off your uncle's money. Tell me something. Did you ever enjoy a single service you conducted?"

Lucy had managed to strike aside his complacency. It was the remark about living off Fat Benny's money that made Daniel realize how right she was. He opened his mouth to say yes, that he had enjoyed them all, but he couldn't. "Two," he said at last. "I enjoyed two of them. Those two *seder* nights at the Cavenham when you were expecting Rachel."

"Two out of how many?"

"I don't know."

"Why those two?"

Because I screwed Linda Bloom, he thought, loathing himself for even remembering the bitch. "Because I knew I was appreciated. They clapped for me. They applauded me. They made me feel like I was a king."

"They won't clap for you in a *shul*," Lucy said.

"I know. Look, Lucy, if you want to sing your silly little songs in a language you don't even understand, go ahead. I'll stick with being a *chazan*. I can live very nicely without singing about frozen little hands and becoming a grown man sobbing in time with music."

"Would you mind looking after the baby then?"

"Not as long as it's only a couple of hours here and there. But I'm not taking her out for any more walks."

"Fine. I'll go back to my old teacher, then. At least one of us will be making a step in the right direction as far as a career is concerned," she said bitingly.

Daniel understood the message and acted swiftly on it. In

the afternoon, he drove into Manhattan, parked the Packard on West Forty-fifth Street between Sixth Avenue and Times Square, and entered a narrow building. In the lobby he checked the list of name plates. Maurice Waterman, Attorney, Room 202, one read. He took the stairs two at a time and entered Moishe's office. A mousy middle-aged woman guarded the small reception area, seated behind a rickety desk on which was set a typewriter and a telephone.

"May I help you?"

"I'd like to see Moi . . . Mr. Waterman, please."

"Do you have an appointment?" She opened a desk drawer and extracted a diary, looking into it. "He's very busy at the moment."

"No. But he'll see me. Tell him it's Daniel Kirschbaum."

"I'll check for you."

Daniel watched the woman leave her desk and go through a glass-fronted door. Then he checked the diary. The page was blank. He replaced it, feeling guilty at his curiosity. He also felt guilty about leaving it so long before contacting Moishe. The man he'd derided and abused each time he had put something Daniel's way had proved to be a staunch friend, as strong as Tommy Mulvaney. Between the two of them, they had helped to pull Daniel through the most difficult period of his life. Moishe had spent days straightening out the legal tangles caused by the death of Daniel's aunt and uncle. He had become almost a permanent fixture in the apartment as he perused papers with Daniel and contacted the proper authorities for each piece of the puzzle.

The woman returned to her desk, sat down and looked primly at Daniel across the top of the typewriter. "Mr. Waterman will see you."

"Thanks." Daniel walked past her into Moishe's office. A blast of warm, humid air from a window fan greeted him. Moishe was sprawled in a chair, feet on the desk, a newspaper open at the sports pages lying untidily in front of him.

"Greetings," Moishe said. "Summer's almost over so you've decided to come out of hibernation." He stood up and shook Daniel's hand. "Bet you didn't even get to see one good ball game."

"Didn't even think about going."

Moishe sighed unhappily. "If I could have afforded to take the summer off like you, I'd have seen every Dodger home game. Truth is, I almost did. Business ain't that busy."

"Bad, huh?"

"Ah!" Moishe gave a deprecating wave of his hand. "I should be grateful I'm getting by, but I'm a long way from the millions I always anticipated. How's Lucy?"

"She's the reason I'm down here."

"How come?"

"She's nagging me. She wants to resume her musical career, and she dropped a few subtle hints that it's about time I got off my ass. I need encouragement."

Moishe pointed to a sign pinned to the wall behind his desk. "A lawyer's time and advice are his stock in trade, that's what Abe Lincoln said, but he never mentioned anything about encouragement. What are you looking for?"

"I suppose I'll get a cantor's job again. There's plenty advertised."

Moishe seemed thoughtful. He took off his glasses and massaged his eyes gently. "Ever hear of a place called Paterson?"

"Should I?"

"It's about ten miles west of you, other side of the Hudson in New Jersey." The glasses went back on again, pushed up high as Moishe roused himself into action. He searched through his desk drawers and threw a tattered copy of an English-language Jewish newspaper to Daniel. "Here, read this."

Daniel glanced at the story. A new temple had been founded in Paterson following a split among the members of the main house of worship. Competition between the two temples had almost reached a state of war. The new temple, calling itself Adath Yisroel, had managed to poach the cantor of Temple Isaiah, the existing synagogue. Left without a cantor, with the High Holy Days only a few weeks away, the president of Temple Isaiah was forecasting the end of what remained of his congregation.

"Danny boy," Moishe said enthusiastically, "you could ask Temple Isaiah for the universe and they'd be only too happy to give it to you. If you're interested, I'll call them and set something up."

Daniel mulled the proposition over in his mind. He was certain Moishe was right. Moishe was always right—up to a point. His failure was that he became too carried away with his projects and let blind optimism interfere with common sense. But Paterson, New Jersey? Did he really want to leave New York? Come to think of it, he had heard of the place. A small city twenty or twenty-five minutes by car from the George Washington Bridge. Large Jewish community—there had to be to afford another temple, although one of the existing ones looked in imminent danger of closing its doors. "Give it a try," he told Moishe. What could he lose?

"What's the president's name?" Moishe asked, the phone already balanced in his hand. "It's in the story."

"Feldman. Harry Feldman."

"Got you." Moishe told his secretary to find out the number and connect him. "Good thing you came in, Danny. I thought about you when I read this article last week."

"Last week? Why didn't you call me?"

"I wasn't going to call you. I wasn't going to do a thing until you got in touch with me. The phone works both ways, kiddo, same as friendship."

"Sure of yourself, aren't you?" Daniel could not help grinning. Inwardly he flinched at the truth contained in Moishe's statement.

The phone rang and Moishe snatched at it. "Mr. Feldman? Good afternoon. My name's Maurice Waterman, an attorney in New York. I understand you're having a little difficulty in filling the position of cantor for your temple."

Daniel sat back and listened. He needed Moishe, he knew that. Or someone just like Moishe, if there were any carbon copies—and that was doubtful. Left to his own devices, he would have mooned around the apartment for an eternity. With the legacy from Fat Benny there was no need to work. He would have just grown lazier with the passage of time until it would have taken an earthquake to move him. And where would his voice have been when that happened?

"Your cantor went to Adath Yisroel," Moishe was saying.

"That's right, Mr. Feldman, he's a traitor. You said that in the newspaper story. Unethical, that's it, that's right on the money. Anyway, let me get to the point. I take it that you've heard of Cantor Daniel Kirschbaum? From Washington Heights, that's correct." He looked across the desk and winked at Daniel. "He's been on three months' leave, family problems, but I believe he'd be interested in discussing the vacant position with you. How about"—Moishe riffled the pages of the newspaper on his desk—"sometime tomorrow afternoon. Obviously Cantor Kirschbaum would like to look around Paterson as well, to decide if it's the kind of city in which he'd like to raise his family. Yes, I'm sure it is a very pleasant place, but that would be up to the cantor. See you tomorrow then. Good day." He put down the receiver and beamed at Daniel.

"We've got him, Danny boy. The hook's in so deep he'll never be able to wriggle free."

"What did he say?"

"He said he's interested. He'd like to meet you."

"That's all? You sounded like he was frothing at the mouth with anticipation."

"It's not what he says," Moishe pointed out. "It's what he thinks. Up there"—he touched his forehead—"our Mr. Feldman's thinking that not only will he get a cantor in time for *Rosh Hashanah* and *Yom Kippur* and save his *shul* from going under, but he'll get Kirschbaum, the boy wonder from Washington Heights. I bet you anything Feldman's already scheming his revenge on the other *shul*."

"And how much are you hoping to get out of this?" Daniel asked, confused by Moishe's keen interest. "Ten percent of my paycheck every week?"

Moishe smiled smugly and leaned back in the chair, hands clasped behind his head. "I don't want your money this time, Danny. I want you. I've got other plans. By the way, you are still interested in making some bucks on the side, aren't you?"

With the baby carriage folded up in the trunk of the Packard, Daniel drove Lucy, Rachel and Moishe to Paterson the following afternoon. They arrived half an hour before the appointed meeting with Feldman. Daniel used the spare time to drive around. He liked what he saw. The town was green. Trees dominated the sidewalks, except for the central business core. Houses—not cramped apartments—boasted large gardens. It was a far better place for his daughter to grow up than Washington Heights.

Harry Feldman was a short, paunchy man with only a fringe of dark hair around his shining head. He welcomed Daniel's party eagerly, recognizing salvation. First he showed them around the temple—almost as large as B'nai Yeshurun—then he ushered them into his office.

"Why don't you take Rachel out for a stroll in the carriage?" Daniel suggested to Lucy. "You don't want to sit in the office with us while we're talking business."

"Don't you want me in there?"

"It's not that. You and Rachel might be uncomfortable sitting around for a long time."

Lucy gave him a quizzical look before taking the baby outside. Moishe and Daniel sat down, facing Feldman.

"Does our temple meet your expectations, Cantor Kirschbaum?"

Daniel took his time answering. He had been coached carefully by Moishe on how to react to any possible question. "It's not as large as I'm used to, and I don't think the architecture will provide such excellent acoustics as I've had in the past. But"—he let the word hang for a second—"I want to get out of New York, so I suppose I'll have to make some sacrifice."

Moishe was watching Feldman intently, gauging his reaction. He was elated when Feldman's face first dropped then lifted again at Daniel's answer. "I think we can get down to business fairly quickly, Mr. Feldman. As I mentioned on the phone yesterday, as Cantor Kirschbaum's attorney I'm representing his interests."

"You represent him?" Feldman had never heard of a cantor being represented by anyone before. They came, they sang, and they got paid; it was as simple as that. Now he had one with a representative? "I'm afraid I don't understand."

"It's simple," Moishe insisted. "Cantor Kirschbaum's an artist and is entitled to the best possible representation. Just like any other artist. Probably better." Moishe produced a neatly folded contract which he spread out on Feldman's desk. "If you'll go over this, I believe you'll find it's a fairly standard contract."

"A contract?" Feldman's eyes rose in question. "We've never had a *chazan* on contract before."

"It's a new age, Mr. Feldman. If you'd prefer to stick with your traditional methods, I'm certain that Cantor Kirschbaum will have no trouble finding a temple that accepts contracts."

"No, no, I'm a firm believer in progress," Feldman protested. He scanned the contract, clause by clause. "Three months notice by either party, fine. Paid vacations, fine. Expenses toward occupation-related clothing, fine. Permission for outside work not associated with liturgical singing . . . what does this mean?" He looked at Daniel for an answer.

Daniel did not have the slightest idea. He hadn't even known that Moishe was carrying a contract with him.

"My client, as well as being an outstanding cantor, also has a rewarding career in popular music," Moishe replied quickly. "Of course, we wanted you to know about that facet of his career, as we did not wish to inflict any surprise on you."

"What comes first?" Feldman demanded suspiciously. "Gershwin or God?"

Daniel felt it was time he brought himself into the discussion before Moishe could get carried away and make promises on his behalf that he would never be able to honor. Already he was stunned by the sudden appearance of the contract and the mention of the other career. "My cantor's position always comes first, Mr. Feldman. I would never let my popular music career interfere with it. However, where there is no conflict, I would like to be at liberty to accept other engagements."

"Very well." Feldman passed on to the other clauses. Daniel wondered what other surprises the contract had in store for him, but Feldman raised no more questions. He simply muttered "fine" every few seconds, then he scribbled his name on all three copies. "You can begin for *Rosh Hashanah*, of course?"

"Of course." Daniel scribbled his own signature on all three copies before passing them to Moishe for witnessing. "Can you recommend a real estate agent around here, Mr. Feldman?"

Feldman seemed to change. The businesslike attitude disappeared; in its place was a friendly, jovial local merchant. "Myself," he said proudly. He gave Daniel a card. "Come to think of it, I've got a four-bedroom house that's more than perfect for a growing family. And it's only two hundred yards from the *shul.*"

"You were much to quick buying that house," Lucy complained as they drove back to the city. "You don't buy a house like you buy a piece of cheese. Look at it once and say you'll pay cash."

Daniel concentrated on driving, letting Lucy's protests sail over his head. He knew what was eating her. It wasn't the house or the way he'd bought it. It was being asked to take the baby for a walk while he had discussed business with Feldman and Moishe. Lucy felt he had cut her out, chosen Moishe over her. Maybe it had been a mistake, but it was too late now. Besides, it was a business arrangement. Moishe had set it up and was going to do his talking for him. Lucy did not need to be there.

She continued to complain until they dropped Moishe off at his car. Daniel had invited him inside for something to eat, but Moishe had declined, able to recognize the brewing fight. He wanted no part of it.

"I'll be in touch with you about some club dates," he said as he shook Daniel's hand. "Give you plenty of notice, don't worry about it." He kissed Lucy on the cheek, made a face at the sleeping baby and jumped into his car.

Daniel watched the Dodge scream up the street in Moishe's normal driving fashion, then he followed Lucy into the building. She started into him as soon as he closed the door.

"Don't you think I'm entitled to hear what's being offered to you?" she demanded.

"You had no business in that meeting," Daniel replied evenly. "It was between me, Moishe and Feldman."

"I thought a wife was supposed to be interested in her husband's work, to be supportive of him. I was there when they offered you the position at B'nai Yeshurun—and I wasn't even your wife then."

Daniel remembered the day well. After the trauma of Kawolsky's death, he'd needed someone that day. But today was different, he told himself. "When you get back on the tracks with your singing, I promise I won't butt in," he said at last, knowing the reply was weak; he had avoided Lucy's point of contention completely.

"Who are you calling?" Lucy asked as she saw Daniel go to the telephone and begin dialing.

"My father. To tell him the good news."

"Make sure you tell him how you cut me out as well."

"Knock it off, Lucy," he pleaded. "Yesterday you as good as told me to get up off my rear end and find a job. I did. I found us a lovely house as well, so we can stop being cooped up in an apartment. I did everything you wanted and more, so will you get off my back?"

Lucy picked up the baby and began crooning. Rachel woke up and gurgled happily. While he waited for the phone to be answered, Daniel watched mother and child, aware of what was going on. Lucy was using the baby against him, taking affection from him and showering it on the infant as if to say the baby cared about her even if he did not. Isaac finally answered the telephone and Daniel forgot all about the problems at home as he related the news.

Daniel waited until the end of November, when the autumn leaves had been cleared from the garden, before he threw a housewarming party. In two months he had come to like suburban life, almost out in the country but close enough to New York to be able to get to the city with ease. He was not certain that he liked the responsibility that came with owning such a big house, but an army of local workmen were available to maintain the property. Daniel began to feel as close as he ever had to being lord of the manor.

The move suited Lucy, too. The social life of the temple in Paterson was far more active than it had been in Washington Heights. As the cantor's wife, she was invited to join every level of the women's circle. She became a center of attention as Temple Isaiah, led by president Harry Feldman, waged war against the upstart Temple Adath Yisroel and its management. Temple Isaiah had Cantor Kirschbaum, Feldman boasted. And both the cantor and his wife were talented musicians. Prompted by curiosity, the rebels began to return. After Daniel had been at Temple Isaiah for two months, the congregation was larger than it had been before the old cantor had left. Feldman was pleased with his acquisition, contract and representative or not.

Daniel invited everyone he knew to the housewarming party. The guests began to arrive shortly after midday. His mother and father were among the first. Although Isaac had been initially upset by his son's decision to leave New York, he was more enthusiastic each time he saw the house. It was a far cry from the apartment on Claremont Parkway. Isaac was happy to remain living there, but whoever thought his son would own a house like this?

"Which of us ever thought we'd be able to buy something like this for cash?" Isaac joked as he looked around. Daniel followed him, enjoying the ritual his father pursued whenever he visited. "Lots of bedrooms. Plenty of room for more children. You are thinking of more children, aren't you?"

"Maybe later, when Rachel's a bit older," Daniel replied. He didn't have the heart to tell his father that there would be no more. Lucy had said she would never go through another pregnancy. Knowing what he now did about her mother, Daniel respected her wishes. Besides, she'd told him, she had a career to pursue; another child would be an encumbrance.

"You fill these rooms with my grandchildren and you won't be able to keep me away," Isaac promised. "You'll never need a babysitter. I'll even learn to drive so I'll be able to get here more quickly."

Daniel hugged his father and then turned to his mother. "What do you think of it?" he asked politely.

"You're a rich man now," she answered stiffly. "You want everyone to know how rich you are, so you live big."

"That's right, I'm a rich man now. Aren't you proud to tell all of your acquaintances"—he purposely refrained from using the word *friends;* he wasn't certain Yetta had any—"how well off your son is?"

"I don't talk about you. In case they remember all those disgusting things the girl said about you in the papers."

"Yetta!" Isaac said sharply. "Will you be quiet?"

Daniel felt like kissing his father.

By three in the afternoon, more than one hundred people were wandering through the house. Daniel felt like a tour guide as he explained to each group what he—or some local builder—was planning to do with each room.

"Which room will you be using as your office?" Moishe asked.

"Office?"

"Sure. I'm getting together those dates for you. You'll be self-employed; you can write off some of the house expenses."

"I'll worry about taxes when I see the money." He took Moishe's arm and guided him through a small group of people. "You remember Harry Feldman, don't you?" He left Moishe with the temple president and went to talk with the Mulvaneys. The only bright spot to come out of the entire Fat Benny-Joey Bloom affair was the promotion of both Mulvaneys within the police department, Tommy to sergeant and his father to captain.

"Where's the baby?" Tommy asked.

"Upstairs. Somehow managing to sleep through this racket."

"Can I have a look?"

"Sure. But you wake her up and you're not leaving till she's asleep again."

"Deal." Tommy loped up the stairs, a huge grin on his face, leaving Daniel alone with Mulvaney.

"Congratulations. You're doing well for yourself."

"Thanks."

"It's none of my business, but did your inheritance from your uncle help to buy this house?"

Daniel grimaced. "Every cloud has a silver lining, huh? He and my aunt left me almost everything."

"Don't feel ashamed. You deserved it."

"By the way," Daniel said, "I never did get the opportunity to thank you for playing down any relationship between

Bloom's daughter and me."

Mulvaney smiled wryly. "Didn't help much, did it? She blabbed to the papers anyway. How much harm did she do you?"

"Cost me the position in Washington Heights, but I'm happier here anyway. Nothing else. Your refuting her allegations kept me out of it."

"Glad we could help." Mulvaney drew Daniel away from the main body of guests. "How about a small favor in return?"

"Buy a ticket for the policemen's ball?" Daniel joked.

"Almost. With a captain's bars comes added responsibility. I'm chairman of some *ad hoc* committee put together to honor the commissioner who retires in a few months."

"You want me to sing?"

"Well . . ." Mulvaney seemed almost embarrassed at asking the favor. "I was speaking to your pal Waterman. He was going on about arranging club dates for you, how he was going to put your name in lights. I mentioned the commissioner's night and he said he was sure you wouldn't mind doing a freebie for the police."

Daniel began to laugh. Moishe had struck again. Mulvaney wanted to know what was so funny. "The last time he did this to me I broke his glasses and gave him a minute to find his way to the car in the middle of the night. Okay, Captain Mulvaney, I'll do it. Who knows, maybe I'll want another favor sometime."

Tommy returned from the baby's room, a worried look on his face. "What's the matter with the kid, Cherrybum?"

"What do you mean?" Daniel forgot all about Mulvaney's request.

"She looks out of it. She's awake, but I tried playing with her and she didn't want to know. Sort of apathetic."

"Oh." Daniel felt relieved. "She's been like that for a few days. Lucy had the doctor in. He said it was just a cold and we should keep her wrapped up warm and the rest of it."

Tommy seemed satisfied with the explanation. "Thought it was just a reaction to me. Must be rotten to have a cold when you don't even know how to sniff or blow your nose."

Daniel laughed, slapped Tommy on the back and told him about his father's invitation to sing at the commissioner's party.

"I guess that makes us permanent residents now," Daniel said to Lucy after he had seen the last of the guests to their cars. "We've had our first party."

"It was nice. Everyone loved the house."

"Even you?"

"I always did," she admitted. "I was just upset with you that day because you left me out of your stupid meeting. I liked the house enough to have bought it as quickly as you did, but I was too mad at you to say so." She bent down to collect glasses that had been left on the table.

"Tommy noticed the baby didn't seem well," Daniel mentioned as he watched Lucy clean up.

"It's beginning to bother me," Lucy admitted as she carried the glasses into the kitchen. "The doctor says Rachel's only got a cold, but I don't think she should be this lethargic." She began to rinse the glasses, stacking them neatly on the draining board. "Daddy knows a really good specialist in New York. He's going to fix up an appointment."

"Are you that worried?" He moved up close behind her and wrapped his arms around her waist, nestling his face on her shoulder.

She didn't seem to notice his presence, preoccupied as she was with thinking about Rachel. "A second opinion can't do any harm, and it'll make me feel easier."

He gave up trying to coax her into bed early. She had too much to do in tidying up after the party, and Daniel knew she would never leave the mess around until the morning. He thought about helping her, then changed his mind. Instead, he returned to the living room and switched on the radio. If Mulvaney was expecting him to sing at the commissioner's party, he might as well begin doing some homework.

Unless the commissioner was really expecting some Hebrew hymns, and Daniel was certain he was not.

Chapter Fifteen

The doctor forced himself to smile encouragingly at Daniel and Lucy as they sat nervously in his office while he completed the series of tests on Rachel.

"Well-behaved baby," he remarked cheerfully. "Usually by this time they're kicking and screaming blue murder."

Neither Daniel nor Lucy made any reply and the doctor returned his attention to the child. He wished she *would* kick and scream blue murder. He'd feel happier, then, knowing that he had a healthy baby on the table, not a lethargic, almost inanimate object. The infant's muscles were abnormally weak and she followed his slow, deliberate movements with her eyes as if she had difficulty in seeing clearly.

Feeling steadily more certain that his initial, disturbing diagnosis was correct, the doctor picked up an opthalmoscope and peered again into Rachel's eyes. The cherry-red spot was clearly visible on the baby's retina. He put down the opthalmoscope and turned to face the parents.

"I assume you're both Jewish?"

Daniel started at the totally unexpected question. "What the hell is it to you?"

The doctor held up a placating hand. He felt suddenly tired, now that his worst fears were confirmed. "It has nothing to do with me, Mr. Kirschbaum. But it has a lot to do with your child's illness."

"Is it serious?" Lucy asked slowly.

"I'm afraid it is." The doctor looked down helplessly at the baby, lying so still on the examination table. "Please tell me one more thing. Is either of you descended from Russian immigrants?"

"My mother's side of the family," Daniel replied, not understanding a thing that was happening except that Rachel was ill, suffering far more seriously than the local idiot doctor had claimed.

"My father's Russian," Lucy replied.

"I see," the doctor said.

"Would you mind telling us what you see?" Daniel asked.

The doctor forced himself to look up, to face the child's parents. "I think your daughter is suffering from Tay-Sachs disease," he answered quietly. There was a tremor in his voice which he was unable to control; he'd never yet learned to be unemotional when confronting parents with tragic information about their children.

"Tay what?" Daniel and Lucy asked simultaneously.

"Tay-Sachs," the doctor repeated. "Amaurotic family idiocy."

Daniel gripped Lucy's wrist tightly as he goaded himself to ask the question for which he was certain he already knew the answer. "But it can be treated?" He could feel Lucy beginning to shake, sobs that started deep inside her and struggled to find their way to the surface.

"I regret to say it's terminal." The doctor looked away uncomfortably as Lucy burst into a flood of tears. Daniel put his arm around her, trying to bring comfort while the doctor called in his nurse. He held a whispered conversation with the woman, then she led Lucy from the office.

"My nurse will look after your wife, Mr. Kirschbaum. She'll be fine."

Daniel nodded numbly. "What about Rachel and this Tay-whatever it is?"

"Tay-Sachs," the doctor said again. He spared a moment to glance down at Rachel on the table; she hadn't moved. "It's a hereditary disease. Almost without exception—and I realize how unbelievable this must sound—it afflicts Jewish children of Russian ancestry. It's selective. It's tragic. And there is nothing we can do about it."

"Nothing?" Daniel buried his face in his hands and began to weep, trying to blot out the doctor's words. Why us? The question hammered away at his brain. Why us? Some goddamned freak disease I've never even heard of has to hit us! Russian Jews! It was impossible that a disease could have been invented solely for them.

The doctor knew he had to explain further; to leave it like

this would be criminal. "You each have a parent of Russian origin," he said quietly, watching Daniel while he tried to gauge the intensity of his reaction. "Both you and your wife are carriers. Together you have produced a child with the disease."

Hidden behind his hands, Daniel cursed his mother quietly and fluently. Goddamn her! She'd even picked her parents' place of birth to spite him.

The doctor carried on, speaking softly. "A carrier and a noncarrier will have perfectly healthy children. But the children, as normal as they appear, might be carriers themselves."

Daniel fought back his anguish and lifted his head to look at the doctor. "So what happens now?"

"As a rule, the baby will progress normally until four or six months old, as Rachel has done. Then the infant will begin to exhibit signs of retarded development. Blindness. Apathy. Weakness of the muscles."

"And later?"

The doctor coughed nervously. "Convulsions. Loss of weight."

"And?"

"Spasticity. And finally, mercifully, death."

Daniel bit his bottom lip as he looked across the office at his daughter. Some favor we did you, he reflected bitterly. Gave you life and made damned sure you wouldn't live it long. Jesus, there must be a million or more bastards out there who deserve this, and it has to hit some sweet, innocent kid. "Is anything else known about it?" He was surprised at how level his voice had become. By rights he should be outside with Lucy, bawling his eyes out. But someone had to take charge.

"Basically, it's caused by a defect in the child's metabolism, Mr. Kirschbaum. The child is unable to utilize certain fatty substances which are taken in with the food. These fatty substances then accumulate in the brain and destroy the normal healthy brain cells."

"But why only Jews, for God's sake? And why only Jews of Russian descent?"

The doctor spread his hands helplessly. "Perhaps if we knew

that we'd be a lot closer to solving the mysteries of the disease. Tay-Sachs occurs in about one of every six thousand Jewish births, and in one of every six hundred thousand non-Jewish births, a hundred-to-one ratio. So you can see it's primarily a Jewish disease, with the infants having Russian ancestry."

"How long will Rachel be . . . ?"

Daniel could not find the strength to find the question. He leaned forward and held his head in his hands again, weeping openly. The doctor sat quietly, staring helplessly at his hands which lay clasped on his lap. A minute passed before Daniel could raise his head again; his eyes were red and streaks from tears made his cheeks shine.

"She can live for another two years, possibly three," the doctor said, anticipating the end of Daniel's unfinished question. "But she'll become steadily worse."

"And finish up as a vegetable. That's what spasticity means, doesn't it?"

"I'm afraid so."

"Would you recommend a hospital?"

The doctor shook his head. "The decision to hospitalize your daughter would have to come from you and your wife. Frankly speaking, though, I would advise against it. Such a step would be a waste of money as there is nothing that can be done in a hospital that cannot be done at home. However . . ."

"Yes?" Daniel prompted him, eager for any ray of hope, no matter how slim.

"Having such a child at home, in certain cases, can have an extremely negative psychological effect on other children . . ."

"We have no other children. Rachel's our first."

"I see. What I intended to add was that such a situation can also be very damaging to the parents. You might be better off—as callous as this might sound to you—to put Rachel into a hospital for chronic diseases."

Daniel shook his head in firm rejection of the idea. He and Lucy had given life to the child; it was their responsibility to care for her.

"I feel it would be to your wife's benefit if she understood the complete picture, much as I've given it to you," the doctor said. "Would you rather tell her, or shall I?"

"You." Daniel felt sickeningly weak. He did not possess the strength to repeat the doctor's words to Lucy. "I'll go outside and make sure she's all right." He stopped by the door and turned back into the surgery. "One thing, doctor. I've got one question that might sound idiotic to you, but I've got to know."

"Go ahead and ask. You're entitled to every assistance I can offer you."

"Would making love to my wife while she . . . ?" The question tailed off as Daniel realized how absurd it sounded. He knew the answer. Other doctors had assured both Lucy and him that sex during pregnancy was safe.

"I'm listening," the doctor urged him. "And I'm sympathetic to your problem, believe me."

Daniel reached out to hold the door frame for support. "Lucy didn't want me to make love to her while she was pregnant," he burst out. "She was scared of something happening to the baby, like being born deformed. Doctors told her it was crazy but she insisted she was right." He rolled his eyes up to the ceiling, then looked back to the doctor. "I made love to her once. I forced myself on her. Would that one time have caused this?"

"Tay-Sachs is a genetic disease," the doctor replied gently. "A hereditary deficiency. Nothing else can cause it. Don't punish yourself by even dwelling on that possibility, Mr. Kirschbaum."

Daniel breathed out deeply as relief flooded through him. "Thanks. Will you please tell that to my wife?"

The doctor slowly nodded his head. "I will."

The return journey to Paterson passed in complete silence. The route flashed by as Daniel drove automatically, his concentration completely absorbed by the news the doctor had imparted. Tay-Sachs. Something he'd never even heard of. A rare disease, one in six thousand Jewish babies. Why him? For God's sake, why him? Why Lucy? Why Rachel?

From time to time he glanced in the rearview mirror at Lucy, who occupied the back seat, cradling Rachel. She was as shocked as he was, more so. A cold, the local doctor had said.

The baby was lethargic because she had a cold. Keep her warm and she'd be all right. And now it was a fatal disease, a throwback to some genetic accident in Russia a million generations before.

He crossed over the Hudson from New York to New Jersey without even realizing it. All he could think of was Rachel, and the torment he knew Lucy must be enduring, even more anguished than he because of what had happened to her mother. Why did it have to happen to them?

When they arrived home, Lucy took Rachel straight upstairs to the nursery and stayed there for almost an hour while Daniel sat dejectedly in the living room trying to think of something to do; anything that might somehow alleviate the misery. Another doctor? A second opinion? Then a third and a fourth and a fifth? What good would it do? They would be deluding themselves each time they wrapped Rachel up for another journey and another examination, carting her from specialist to specialist in the vain hope that one of them would say she was suffering from some other ailment, a minor illness that could be cured with careful treatment. There was no cure, the doctor had said. Nothing to look forward to but a lingering death. At least the child would not suffer, Daniel thought. Some consolation. She would be like a vegetable, unable to understand what was happening to her and therefore unable to feel suffering. But what of himself and Lucy? They would suffer in her place, a hundredfold, a thousandfold.

He heard footsteps coming down the stairs and looked up. Lucy's face was ashen, drawn. She passed Daniel without a word and walked into the kitchen. Daniel waited a minute before rising from the chair to follow her. Lucy was standing by the sink, hands holding the edge rigidly for support as she stared down.

He walked up behind her and wrapped his arms gently around her waist. "Lucy, we have to talk about this sometime. We can't ignore what's happening in the hope that it'll go away."

She spun around with such abruptness and ferocity that Daniel jumped back in surprise. "Get away from me!"

"Lucy!"

"Don't you ever come near me again," she hissed.

"Lucy, for crying out loud! What's the matter?"

"What do you think is the matter? You did this to Rachel. That morning when Moishe called you about the hotel. Remember?"

He moved his head from side to side. "No, Lucy. No," he repeated, unable to believe the venom in her voice, or the loathing that shone in her eyes. "It had nothing to do with it. It's a genetic disease."

"Like hell it is!" she spat out. "I warned you, I begged you, and still you didn't care. All you could think of was yourself. Now see what you've done!"

"Didn't the doctor speak to you?"

"I don't care what you asked him to say. I don't care what he thinks. I know why Rachel's ill. It's because of you and what you did."

Daniel sought words of reason, gentle words that would make her understand. Nothing came, and he knew why. There was nothing he could say that would help her understand. All he could do now was leave her alone and hope she would bend. "I'm going out," he finally said. "I don't know when I'll be back."

Taking a coat from the closet, he left the house. Outside he turned left and started to walk toward the temple. There would be nobody there now except the janitor. The building would be empty, silent, exactly the kind of atmosphere he needed. He stopped by the janitor's hut and explained that he wanted to look at something inside the building. The man let him in and then returned to his work. Daniel looked around before choosing a seat close to the ark. He sat down and undid his coat.

A sensation of insignificance descended over him as he realized that he was completely alone in the huge building. It was as if he didn't matter, as if the building were an entity unto itself that had allowed him entrance because his presence would disturb nothing. He had never been inside the temple before when it was like this, the lights out, empty, totally silent. It seemed to generate a kind of peace. He sat perfectly still for fifteen minutes, while the atmosphere erased everything from his mind to leave it blissfully blank.

The temple became darker as the light filtering through the windows diminished with the coming of twilight. Daniel reached out and picked up a prayer book lying on the seat next to him. He flicked through the pages, seeking a prayer for sick children. There was nothing that fitted the description; the closest he could find was a prayer to be said by a sick person. Setting down the book, he closed his eyes, leaned back in the seat and let his mind wander. That first meeting with Lucy rushed out at him from his memory. The radio station in the Bronx. Sforza with the *camiah*. Then he recognized Kawolsky's gentle face, and the hundreds of lessons that had started him on the road to this place, to this temple where he now sat so peacefully.

As it grew completely dark, Daniel realized he would have to leave soon. The janitor would be going home and would want to lock up the premises. But he was reluctant to move. The initial feeling of tranquility had expanded into a harmony he had never known before. How many times had he been inside a temple? He could not even begin to count. Each time, though, he had always been active, participating in the service or leading it. This time was different. He was alone. Sitting inside the darkened temple for no reason. Or was there a reason? There was the desire to be by himself, yes, but why should he have chosen the temple? He could just as easily have locked himself away in one of the spare bedrooms in the house and pulled down the shades.

He fastened his gaze onto the only light in the temple, the dim red bulb over the ark that must never be allowed to go out, the everlasting symbol of the holy oil that burned in the biblical temple. Daniel had never considered himself to be deeply religious. He knew more than enough to competently fill a cantorial position, but he had never let religion become the motivating factor in his life. He was not even certain that God existed; he had an open mind about it, neither willing to totally believe or disbelieve. To his way of thinking, Judaism was a tradition more than a religion. It was the way you were brought up, educated to attend the temple services, to be *bar mitzvah*ed to observe certain laws. Now, for the first time in his life, Daniel sensed a different meaning in the building where he earned his living. Perhaps the purpose of a temple was to instill harmony into those who worshipped there; peace was the result of worship.

He sat for another twenty minutes, luxuriating in the total silence. His eyes had become accustomed to the darkness and he could make out the familiar shapes, the *bima*, the rows of seats, the women's section. The temple would be full when he next came, bright and alive with the energy of its congregation, with his own energy. He supposed he would have to tell people about Rachel; there would be sympathy for himself and Lucy. The congregation would gather together in support, trying to ease them over this most difficult period. Lucy would need their help more than he would, he was certain. He would be able to carry the tragedy on his own. He'd shed his tears in the doctor's office; there would be no more. And if he found he could not cope, he would come back to the temple and sit like this again, alone in the darkness with just the dim red glow of the lamp above the ark to remind him where he was.

The temple lights suddenly shone bright and Daniel blinked his eyes in surprise, shielding them from the unexpected glare. "I'm closing up now," the janitor called out. "Do you want me to leave you the keys?"

Daniel stood up and buttoned his coat. "No. I'm leaving." He walked toward the exit, nodded to the janitor and passed into the street.

He walked home slowly, hands deep in his pockets, coat collar pulled up around his neck to ward off the chilly breeze. He wanted to tell Lucy about his experience in the temple, to share with her the tranquility he had found. It had helped him to come to terms with the shattering, tragic news given by the doctor. It would help him again, just to sit there in the silent, empty temple, alone with his thoughts. Or had he really been alone, finally, with the God whose praises he sang during each service? Able to communicate with Him at last through a different perspective, a one-on-one meeting instead of praying on behalf of an entire congregation?

Lucy was in the kitchen, preparing dinner, when he entered the house. Purposely he refrained from trying to kiss her in greeting. Instead, he watched her from a distance.

"Where did you get to?" she asked. "You were gone for more than an hour."

"The *shul.*"

"What were you doing there?" She did not look at him as she spoke; she continued to busy herself with the food.

"Thinking. That's all." Daniel was glad to answer her questions. Only with communication would she ever soften.

"Thinking about what?"

"About nothing and everything. Just sitting there by myself with the lights out. It was peaceful."

"It'll be peaceful upstairs as well," Lucy said, turning away from the food to face him. "When it gets worse, she won't even make a sound. She'll just lie there, like a doll. No movement. No sound. No nothing. She'll be the perfectly behaved child—we won't even know she's there." She began to laugh, quietly at first, then growing louder until Daniel realized she was hysterical.

"Lucy!" He stepped forward and shook her. She fought back at him, pummeling his chest with her fists, kicking at his legs. He lifted a hand and slapped her sharply across the face. She stumbled backward, grabbing at the table for support. Daniel stared at her, horrified by what he had done.

"Be proud, Daniel!" Lucy cried out. "You forced yourself on me and doomed Rachel. Now show what a man you are by beating me. Like you did to that other woman." She wiped saliva from her chin. "Why couldn't you have done this to that slut as well? Or wasn't she pregnant when you screwed her?" she demanded, determined to hurt Daniel as she believed she had been hurt.

"Lucy! Will you listen to reason?"

"What reason? I believe that whore more than I believe you. You knew where to find her all right when you wanted her father. Of course you knew! You were screwing her!" She spun around and raced from the kitchen, the food forgotten. Daniel listened to her footsteps hammering on the stairs, then along the corridor. Seconds later, he heard the bedroom door slam. He stared helplessly at the food before leaving the kitchen and slowly climbing the stairs. When he tried the bedroom door, he found it was locked.

"Go away!" Her voice screamed at him from inside the room. "Go to hell!"

He walked into the nursery and turned on the night light. The baby slept. To Daniel's eyes, she seemed as normal as any other baby. Bending over the crib, he kissed her on the forehead. Then he crept out and turned off the light. He returned downstairs to the kitchen, where he picked up the food Lucy had been preparing and dropped it into the garbage can. Finally, he put his coat back on and left the house.

"There is nothing that can be done?"

The distraught question came from Isaac Kirschbaum as he sat looking miserably at his son. "This is a tragedy. My granddaughter."

"Nothing, Pa." Daniel related the conversation he had shared with the child specialist. "We've just got to sit back and wait for it to happen. And try to pretend that nothing's wrong, otherwise we'll drive ourselves into the insane asylum."

Isaac shook his head very slowly. Even Yetta Kirschbaum, for once, seemed affected by someone else's misfortune; maybe she was even accepting a portion of the blame for passing onto Daniel the defective genes which had afflicted the child. She sat silently on the couch. Not a word had passed her lips since Daniel had broken the news.

"How is Lucy?" Isaac asked eventually. "How is she taking all this?"

Daniel debated how to answer. The truth? Or a palatable version which would not upset his father more than he was already. "She's broken up about it, what else?"

"You should be with her," Isaac advised. "Your place at a time like this is with your wife, not with your parents."

"Pa, she doesn't want me around. She's locked herself in the bedroom and won't let me near her. She hates me."

"Why?"

"Because she blames me for it."

Again Isaac asked why, and Daniel haltingly explained. He did not even look at his mother as he spoke; he couldn't care what her reaction was to his story.

Isaac's face grew even more somber as he listened. "This I

cannot advise you about," he said when Daniel had finished. "The only thing I can say is what I said before. You should be with her. Somehow—if you love her—you must help her through this tragedy."

"And who's going to help me?" Daniel asked selfishly.

"You are stronger than she is, Daniel. You have enough strength for two. Go home and help her. It might take time, so you must be patient."

"Sure. I'll try." He stood up and walked to the phone.

"Are you calling Lucy?" Isaac asked.

"No. Someone else." He spun the dial furiously. Moishe answered on the third ring. "Moishe, Daniel. I need your help."

"What do you want, old buddy?"

"Pull your finger out right now and get me all the club dates you can. Anything and everything. Got it?"

"Why the sudden rush? I thought you wanted to wait a while."

"Never mind. Just do it." He hung up and left the apartment without saying another word to his parents.

While Daniel slept in the guest room, Lucy maintained an all-night vigil with the baby, staring disconsolately at the crib. Each time Rachel moved, Lucy would lean over the child, hoping against hope that the specialist would be proven wrong. Rachel would start crying. She'd kick and scream. She'd be as normal as any child.

When the light of dawn crept through the windows, any optimism Lucy might still have harbored was shattered. It would be like this for two years. She would have to watch her child die, minute by minute, breath by breath. A living death that would be shared by her. She did not think she would be able to cope. Each day she would die a fraction with the child. Even if the treacherous cherry-red spot were not present in her own retina, she would waste a little every day, physically and mentally, until she would be unable to take care of herself, let alone the infant.

Two years. Possibly three. It stretched out until eternity. Torture, sentenced to watch her daughter die. And Daniel?

What would happen to him? He had brought this catastrophe on her, no matter what lies he persuaded doctors to tell. He'd triggered off the disease that morning when he had attacked her. She'd begged him to leave her alone, but his selfishness, his need to prove his masculinity had driven him on, deaf to her pleas. Daniel would be all right; that same selfishness that had destroyed her and the child would insulate him from any grief.

The child was hers and hers alone, a part of her own body. To Daniel, it represented nothing more than a five-minute game, a spell of pleasure to remind him that he was a man. To her, the child meant nine months of growth, nine months of her own life as she had felt it swell up inside her. Daniel would have his work to cushion himself with. She would have nothing. Even the singing lessons would have to be canceled while she sat at home and helplessly watched her daughter die.

Hearing Daniel move around the house as he got up, she stopped dwelling on the future. She was still the cantor's wife and held a position within the community. She had to keep up appearances. Even if inside she was slowly dying along with her child.

Chapter Sixteen

Daniel returned home from the temple at the conclusion of the Saturday evening service to find Lucy setting the table for dinner. He ate quickly, without taste or enjoyment, prompted by the need to get out of the house as quickly as possible. It was no longer a home. The house he had bought on impulse had turned into a virtual prison, with an unwitting warden who lay almost inanimate in the nursery on the second floor; the sick child's presence was as oppressive as that of any guard.

"Will you come with me tonight?" Daniel asked. He pushed aside the half-full plate, no longer interested in toying with the food.

"I've got other things to do," Lucy replied.

Daniel did not ask what. "This is a big one tonight. One of the top clubs in Harlem. Moishe sweated blood to land this deal. Come with me. Get out of the house."

"I have to look after Rachel."

"We'll get a babysitter."

"Rachel needs her mother, not a sitter," Lucy said, picking lethargically at the food in front of her; her appetite was as blunted as Daniel's.

"Okay, suit yourself." Daniel made no attempt to carry the discussion further. Life with Lucy had become peaceful coexistence. He slept in one room, she in another and they met at mealtimes. Lucy's terms for living together had been simple. She would continue to fill her social duties as the cantor's wife but she would acknowledge no other claim on her by Daniel. If they were to have anything in common at all, it would be to watch their child die. Daniel had fleetingly considered a separation, but he'd pushed the idea from his mind. He'd talked about it with Moishe, who had quashed the idea immediately. Separation or divorce at this stage of his career—no matter what the grounds—would be another scandal. He had managed to survive the trouble at B'nai Yeshurun, but another episode might ruin him. Even without Moishe's advice, Daniel knew that he would never seriously contemplate such a step. He couldn't leave Lucy now. No matter how much he tried to tell himself that the baby's illness wasn't solely his fault, he was unable to wash away the feeling of guilt that Lucy had embedded in his mind. He knew he had to stay with her until the end.

Finished with dinner, he turned on the radio. He was eager to hear news of the situation in Europe. A special prayer had been said that morning by the rabbi, a plea to God to look kindly on the forces of His Majesty's Government which, two days earlier, had declared war on Nazi Germany following the attack on Poland. As he had listened to the rabbi, Daniel remembered the Louis-Schmeling fight at Yankee Stadium. He had closed his eyes and offered up his own prayer to God, asking for a repeat dose and just as quick.

There was nothing new on the radio so Daniel went upstairs to shower and change. In place of the sober, dark gray suit he had worn for the temple, he chose a black tuxedo and a floppy bow tie. He shaved off the beard which had been allowed to grow over the Sabbath and then stood admiring himself in the bedroom's full-length mirror; his hands caressed an imaginary microphone as he pretended he was already at the club. The dates that Moishe had got for him so far would be nothing compared with tonight. The Deuces Wild was one of the real Harlem jazz clubs. Gain acceptance there, he said out loud to his reflection in the mirror, and your foot's well and truly planted on the ladder.

Before leaving the house, he stopped in at the nursery. The pleasure of anticipating the welcome he'd receive at the Deuces Wild evaporated as he looked at his daughter. The doctor had been sickeningly right in his diagnosis nine months earlier. Where other babies were flourishing, growing chubby and healthy, Rachel was receding. Her flesh was almost paper thin. Daniel could feel the bones sticking through as he touched her. The convulsions had also come. The first time he'd witnessed them, he had been physically sick, unable to watch the child shudder and jerk, arms and legs shaking uncontrollably, a marionette with the strings pulled by disease-ridden nerves.

He bent down and kissed the child's forehead before hurrying from the room. As much as he fought against it, he hated being in the same room with Rachel. Charged with a father's duty to love and protect her, he was unable to do a thing. He loathed himself for his cowardice in running away, but it was preferable to the grief caused by staying.

"I'll be back late," he called out to Lucy.

"Good luck," she said automatically. She stood by the window and watched him drive away. Then she went upstairs to sit with the baby. For half an hour she stayed next to the tiny crib, never taking her eyes off the child, watching Rachel's chest rise and fall with each labored breath. Finally, she lifted the baby from the crib and took her downstairs.

The child's body was warm against her own as Lucy leaned back in an armchair. For a moment, she managed to delude herself into believing she was holding a healthy baby who would grow up into a beautiful woman. Then the child began to shake, shuddering as if she were having a bad dream. Lucy gripped the pathetic bundle tighter and began to sing softly. After a while, the shaking stopped.

It grew even darker outside and Lucy wondered how Daniel would fare at the club. She envied him for his outside interests, for his apparent ability to divorce himself from what was taking place at home. He was selfish, and she was jealous of him for it. If she, too, had only been selfish, she would never have allowed herself to forsake her own career for marriage.

The memory of her own singing prompted a response within her. She set the baby down on the carpet and knelt down by the phonograph next to the chair. From the record rack, she selected a handful of seventy-eights, scanning the titles before she found the ones she wanted; the others she replaced. Putting on the first record, she resumed her position in the armchair, the baby once more protected in her arms.

A man's voice, incredibly sweet and clear, filled the room, singing the "Flower Song" from *Carmen*. Lucy closed her eyes and let her body sway gently in time with the music. She remembered seeing *Carmen* at the Met, long before she had met Daniel. A child she had been, but she had still appreciated the poignancy created by Don José as he sat gloomily in his prison cell and recalled the events that led to his downfall. Lucy could not even remember the name of the tenor who had sung the role that night. Whoever it was, though, had not been as good as the tenor to whom she now listened. Jussi Bjoerling was a new voice to her—not even Italian but a Swede. Her father had spoken in reverent terms of the tenor's debut at the Met the previous year, as Rodolfo in *La Bohème*, and Lucy had gone out to buy as many of the Swede's recordings as she could find.

As she listened to one record after another, losing herself completely in the tales woven by the voice from the phonograph, she thought again of Daniel. A voice that could have been just as sweet; that was just as sweet when he performed in the temple. Perhaps not as pure as Bjoerling's, but then who did have a voice that could compare with the Swede's silver tones? Daniel's was darker and less educated, but with the proper drive and tuition he would not have been put to shame. And where was Daniel now? Wasting his voice, abusing his gift in some dingy, smoke-filled nightclub. He didn't care about his voice, that it was a gift in a million. He didn't care about anything. Just as long as he could enjoy himself.

She tried to remember what had attracted her to Daniel. Was it the promise she could see in his voice, or Daniel himself? It didn't matter. All that mattered was that he was being selfish as usual. Instead of using his voice for a purpose that would bring enjoyment to all who appreciated good music, he was prostituting it to mimic popular singers for a few dollars and a round of drunken applause.

Her father had promised to get her into a dress rehearsal when Bjoerling sang. The possibility enthralled her. To be almost alone in that magnificent monument to music, with Jussi Bjoerling singing just for her, was more than she had ever dared dream. Had she followed her career, she could have been Mimi to his Rodolfo, Aïda to his Radames, Tosca to his Cavaradossi. She would have been any and all of opera's tragic heroines for just one chance to sing in company with that voice.

The baby began to shudder again. Lucy forgot about the

records while she tried to comfort the child. Each spasm seemed to shoot right through her own body, making her cry out in pain. She clutched the baby tightly to her breasts while she stared up at the ceiling. The convulsions ceased and the child became quiet. Lucy waited for several minutes, then she went once more to the phonograph. She sought a particular record, one of the new ones by Bjoerling. Finding it, she set it carefully on the turntable, replaced the steel needle and switched on the machine.

This was the aria she loved more than any other. Puccini's "E lucevan le stelle" from the third and final act of *Tosca.* The doomed artist Cavaradossi alone on the ramparts of the Castel Sant' Angelo in Rome, an hour before his scheduled execution, sadly remembering his lover, the singer Tosca, and crying from his heart that he had never loved life more.

The record ended and Lucy reset it. Bjoerling's voice began again and Lucy imagined herself as the subject of the aria. The ill-fated Cavaradossi's lament. A song that recalled shining stars, sweet-smelling earth, the creak of an orchard gate and the light step of his lover that would sound on the path. She would come into his arms, soft, fragrant. Sweet kisses, languorous caresses. Trembling, he would free her lovely body from its garments.

Bjoerling reached the climax of the aria. Lucy felt her body arch and stiffen. A warm sensation flooded through her as the tenor sang the final, despairing line. Stunned, she reached down and felt the dampness seeping through the fabric of her dress, a wetness that both shocked and thrilled her. In all the times she had tried to make love to Daniel, she had never been aroused, never satisfied, always treating it as some loathsome act. Now, listening to a singer bemoan his lost love in an operatic aria, she had achieved her first orgasm.

Moving only to reset the disc again, she let the dampness seep into the chair's upholstery as she cradled the child and listened yet again to the aria. Was it only music that could excite her so? Could music triumph where Daniel had failed? She shifted in the chair, feeling the damp clothes cling to her. How long would the needle last? It was supposed to give a minimum of twelve plays. Good, she would not have to fiddle with it for almost half an hour. She could just sit and listen, reaching out each time the record ended to reset the arm.

What happened after this? She ran through the story of *Tosca*, slotting the aria to which she was listening into its place in the sequence of events. In return for her favors, Tosca had persuaded the Roman chief of police, Scarpia, to reverse the sentence of death pronounced on her lover; there would still have to be an execution, but the soldiers' muskets would contain only powder and no shot. Once in possession of safe conduct passes signed by Scarpia, Tosca had stabbed the police chief and fled to the Castel Sant' Angelo to tell Cavaradossi the news. But the promised fake execution—in a macabre game of bluff and double bluff—had been real, and Tosca had flung herself from the battlements of the fortress as Scarpia's men tried to arrest her for the police chief's murder.

It was defiant, heroic, what life and love should be about, Lucy reflected. The ugliness of the world—the Scarpias—would still be present, but their threat would be overshadowed by vibrant music, thrilling voices.

She should never have married Daniel. She should have continued with her studies. Taken the audition her father had promised to arrange instead of being chained to the house with a fatally stricken child. But that, too, was heroic. Operatic heroines, almost without exception, were tragic figures. Martyrs as well as heroines. What composer, though, would write a score about Tay-Sachs? Or what librettist could sufficiently pen the words that could express the anguish of a mother as she watched her child waste away?

Lucy thought again of Tosca, plunging to her death from the battlements with a final, defiant cry of "*O! Scarpia, avanti a Dio!*", a spine-chilling wish to meet before God with the evil chief of police, where he would be judged and damned for his treachery. Then she stood up and returned the child to the nursery, while Bjoerling continued to sing.

"Big time, Danny boy," Moishe whispered excitedly as he guided Daniel along 137th Street in Harlem. "The other clubs I got you were small stuff."

"You're not kidding." Daniel grinned as he looked along the

unfamiliar street and wondered how safe it was to leave the car there. In one glance, he could see more Negroes than he had ever seen in his entire life, including that fateful night at Yankee Stadium. Moishe wasn't concerned about parking his battered Dodge in the neighborhood, but who would want to steal that—dents and all—when they could take a Packard instead?

"Those dates helped you, didn't they?" Moishe protested. "Without those under your belt, you'd never have got into the Deuces Wild. Your fame's beginning to spread, my boy. And it's all thanks to me."

Daniel placed a hand on Moishe's shoulder. "I was pulling your leg, that's all. Those clubs were great; they gave me something to do with myself."

"And they paid you a lot more than the commissioner's party, right?"

Daniel nodded. The favor to Mulvaney had cost him nothing more than an evening, and he had been glad to do it. To some degree, it repaid Mulvaney. They reached the club and stood off to the side of the entrance for several minutes, watching the customers enter. Daniel liked the look of the crowd. Well-dressed. Rich. Leaving their comfortable houses and apartments to listen to good music in Harlem. They'd listen to him as well, even if he was one of the few white faces on the billing.

"What did I tell you?" Moishe yelled exuberantly. "Louis Armstrong's here tonight."

"Where?" For the first time, Daniel noticed the billboard outside the entrance. He followed Moishe's finger as it pointed out Satchmo's name. "Where's my name?"

"Right at the bottom." Moishe pointed again and Daniel bent lower, trying to read the small print in the light from the streetlamps.

"What is this?" he cried out.

"What's what?" Moishe asked innocently.

"The way I'm billed. Daniel Kirschbaum, the jazz cantor?"

"Well . . ." Moishe began, "it was the only way I could get them to take you, Danny boy. I needed a gimmick to hang the act on, some *shtick* to get you in here."

"Why? And why that, for God's sake?"

"Because there's a city full of white guys trying to get a break in a place like this, that's why. You were different. You're a cantor. You've got novelty value."

"Feldman will hit the roof when he hears about this," Daniel complained, thinking about the temple president.

"He won't hear," Moishe assured him. "Louis Armstrong'll get any reviews that are going, not you. And when you get up in the billing, we'll get rid of the cantor handle."

Daniel allowed himself to be mollified by Moishe's explanation. He had little doubt that Feldman—or anyone else from the Paterson temple—would ever learn of his being billed as a cantor. But what were the customers expecting? Those rich, well-dressed people he had watched entering the club. What did they think they were going to get? A jazzed-up "Kol Nidre"? "Eli Eli" to a Dixieland beat?

Still worried, he followed Moishe into the club. Two tall Negroes were standing at the bottom of a steep flight of stairs. Moishe seemed to know one of them and began talking.

"This is the man," he said, indicating Daniel.

"Hi, I'm Jake Joyner. Deuces Wild is my club."

Daniel shook his hand. "Good to meet you."

"Your man here's been telling us a whole lot about you," Joyner said. "We're willing to give you a shot. Float around till your spot comes up."

Moishe pushed Daniel inside. He was assailed at once by the smoky club atmosphere he had become accustomed to, and his ears throbbed with the vibrations of a five-piece band on the small stage.

"Give me your coat," Moishe yelled in his ear.

Daniel shrugged himself out of the lightweight coat, feeling instantly conspicuous in the tuxedo, as if an arrow were pointing directly at him which labeled him as a performer and not a customer. "Where to?"

"Head for the front." Moishe pushed his way through and found two empty seats at a table. A Negro couple occupied the table, the woman clapping her hands in time with the music, the man sitting quietly. Moishe rattled the two empty chairs and the man nodded his head.

"Where's Louis Armstrong?" Daniel asked.

Moishe shrugged. "Probably backstage. Top-line artists get dressing room privileges. Bums like you sit in the crowd till they're ready to go on."

A waitress came by and Daniel ordered drinks. He looked around the club and tried to gauge the mood of the crowd. This was definitely one of the better establishments Moishe had booked him into. The first, a sleazy hole-in-the-wall operation on Fifty-third Street had been filled with obnoxious drunks who, when they weren't shouting at the singer to get off the stage, were drowning him out by joining in. Daniel had been upset, professional enough to care about his performance. But Moishe hadn't given a damn. He'd just presented Daniel with his share of the take after the show, clapped him on the shoulder and exclaimed, "Experience, Danny boy. Experience. It's invaluable." Daniel often wondered if Moishe had any other clients. He had to. He'd moved out of his parents' home in Brooklyn and taken his own apartment in Greenwich Village; he must be doing something right, somewhere, although Daniel could never figure exactly what.

Before the drinks came, Moishe got up from the table and disappeared. Left alone, Daniel fidgeted uneasily until the man opposite pointed to his tuxedo and asked if he was on the bill. When he gave his name, the man looked puzzled. Daniel's confidence sagged a little.

Moishe returned to the table. "You're on right after Louis Armstrong. Fifteen minutes while the band takes a break. You and me, like usual, pal."

"Right after?" Daniel's ego suffered a massive blow. "Everyone'll be going home when Satchmo's finished. They'll have seen what they came for and they'll split."

"Satchmo'll be coming back later on. The crowd'll stick around."

"I hope so." Daniel gazed gloomily into his drink as he envisaged singing to an empty club; even the drunks on Fifty-third Street were a better audience than empty chairs and tables.

He looked up from the drink to spot a flurry of activity on the other side of the club. Louis Armstrong was weaving his way between the closely set tables, stopping to talk with people he knew, laughing, shaking hands. Daniel watched the man closely, envying him his popularity and the way he accepted it. Royalty, born to adulation and expecting nothing less. Satchmo would get a reception on stage like Joe Louis had received in the ring that night. He wouldn't even have to play or sing to warrant the applause; just by appearing he was assured of his subjects' love.

Satchmo stopped by one table and bent low to talk to a white man. Daniel thought he recognized the man; there was something familiar about him but he could not place the face. He asked Moishe, who squinted through his glasses before shaking his head. Then he asked the man opposite.

"That's Al Jolson," the man said after swinging around in the chair to look.

"Jolson!" Daniel stared in disbelief and the Negro laughed.

"Doesn't look the same without his blackface, does he? Looks just like you and your pal."

Daniel grinned at the pointed barb. "He just looks older, that's all."

Applause broke out as Louis Armstrong climbed onto the stage, clutching a gleaming trumpet. Daniel clapped so loudly that the performer stared down at the table.

"Nice suit you got there, boy! Gonna get a job with Stork Club as a waiter?"

The audience's applause turned to good-natured laughter. Red-faced, Daniel joined in. Before the merriment could die away, Satchmo started to play. The club suddenly became quiet; even the haze from the cigarettes seemed to disappear. Daniel listened, absolutely entranced. His feet tapped and his fingers snapped quietly with the rhythm of the music. He glanced over to where Jolson was sitting, but the entertainer had disappeared. Shame, Daniel would like to have talked to him for a while, find out what it was really like when you'd made it to the top. Even if you couldn't manage to stay there all the time.

Moishe told Daniel later that Louis Armstrong had played and sung for an hour, but it seemed like no more than five minutes. Before Daniel knew what was happening, Moishe was pushing him toward the stage that Satchmo was vacating.

Satchmo, face gleaming with sweat, stopped when he recognized Daniel preparing to get up onto the stage.

"I didn't order anything!" he yelled out, and the audience broke up again. "Wait a minute, you must be the guy in the small print at the bottom of the bill." He held out a hand to help Daniel onto the stage. Then he turned to the audience, a wide, beautiful smile lighting up his face.

"Give a big welcome to a newcomer. He's a cantor by trade—that's Jewish gospel music—and now he wants to see what real music's like. Otherwise, he's going back to waiting tables. Daniel Kirschbaum!" He shook Daniel's hand and wished him luck.

Daniel fruze in the middle of the small stage as Louis Armstrong walked away. He'd shaken hands with Satchmo, been treated as an equal by a living legend! Wait till he got home and told Lucy, told his father, told everyone he knew!

From a distance, he heard Moishe's introduction, but he could not tear his eyes away from Satchmo. Only when the trumpet player disappeared through a door on the other side of the club could Daniel begin to sing.

The words came by themselves. He didn't even have to think. He looked around the club, trying to find a woman, a receptive face to which he could relate while he sang—give the words that extra emotion and make one of the paying customers feel special for a few minutes. He saw that Jolson had returned, and he remembered reading somewhere that the entertainer's father had been a cantor in Russia or Rumania or somewhere. Did Jolson have Tay-Sachs in his family, too?

By the end of the first song, Daniel had found the woman he wanted to serenade that night, an attractive brunette sitting at one of the tables clustered around the stage. There were six people at the table, three men and three women. The men looked drunk, the women bored, except for the one he had chosen. Daniel decided to liven it up. Moving to the edge of the stage, he dropped to one knee—so what if Jolson got mad at having his style copied?—and crooned to the woman. She responded with a warm smile, but one of the men glared at him belligerently. A spark of anger crossed his eyes when he realized why Daniel was so close. He waved a hand at the singer to move back. Daniel took no notice. While he was on stage, he was undisputed boss; nobody could push him around. He'd even been introduced by Louis Armstrong, hadn't he? He was a somebody.

"Fuck off before I push your face in, buddy," he heard the man mutter.

Daniel got to his feet and stepped back, but he never took his eyes off the woman. When the last song was over, he winked at her, slowly and deliberately. Something inside of him gave a small shout of triumph when she winked back.

"Thank you very much," he said, signaling Moishe to stand up and take a bow. "See you later." There was an uneven scattering of applause as he jumped down from the stage and headed for the table. He got three steps when a hand grabbed the front of his jacket.

"You making eyes at my girl, pal?"

Daniel swung around to see the man who had sworn at him. "Someone has to," he answered flippantly. "You're too smashed, so I did." He saw the right coming even before the man thought about throwing the punch. Ducking, he let the clumsy blow whistle over his head and stepped back as the momentum of the punch threw the drunk off balance. People at nearby tables moved uneasily, but Daniel held up his hands.

"No problem," he called out. "Tarzan here just had too much to drink."

"Danny, watch it!" Moishe yelled.

Daniel spun around. His heart skipped when he saw the drunk holding a heavy chair aloft. As it swung down, he jumped aside. The chair smashed across a table, shattering glasses. A woman screamed in terror as liquor and slivers of glass showered over her. Daniel leaped forward and dropped his right shoulder. Drunkenness slowed his opponent's reactions, but he still managed to make the correct counter, bringing up his own right hand to block the anticipated left hook. Instead, Daniel straightened up and launched his right. The tightly bunched fist swung in a short, vicious arc and caught the drunk flush on the jaw. He twisted sideways like a spinning top and fell across the table he had been sharing with his friends.

Instantly, the area surrounding the stage became a battleground. While the drunk struggled to lever himself off the table, his two friends charged at Daniel. He blocked one punch, then reeled backwards as another grazed his temple. Moishe jumped off the stage and threw himself into the fight, screaming like a banshee as he climbed onto the back of the man who had hit Daniel and locked his arms around his throat. The man tried to shake him off, but Moishe clung tenaciously as the man whirled around in an attempt to shake him loose. More men joined in, some trying to break up the fight, others swinging indiscriminately at anyone within range.

Moishe was finally flung off and landed in a heap on the stage. The man he had been holding jumped up after him, picked Moishe up and tossed him through the air. Moishe landed across a table, breaking it under his weight. He slid down to the floor, body bruised and aching, mind alert enough to know when not to move; by some miracle, his glasses were undamaged.

Daniel saw a face come into sight and he drew back his arm. The punch stopped in mid-flight as he recognized Jake Joyner, the club owner. Joyner grabbed Daniel and tried to hustle him away from the center of the fight, pushing past grunting, struggling men who did not have the least idea why or whom they were fighting.

"Rule number one," Joyner panted. "Never hit the paying customers." He might have said more, but a body crashed into him and he stumbled forward. Daniel shook himself free and dived back into the fray. Moishe was somewhere in the thick of it. He could not leave him there. Moishe had stuck up for him.

Above the din, a woman's voice screamed "Cops!" Everyone seemed to freeze, then a concerted rush for the exit began. Suddenly left alone, Daniel spotted Moishe lying motionless on the floor beside a broken table and scattered chairs. He knelt down next to him.

"You all right?"

"I will be when these lunatics have gone."

Daniel looked at the last of the stragglers as they raced toward the door. Past them, he could see four uniformed patrolmen pushing people back into the club. "It's over. You can get up."

Moishe rose to his feet unsteadily. With exaggerated tenderness he examined the growing lump on the back of his head where he had struck the floor. "I think we've blown our chances with Deuces Wild," he said ruefully.

"The hell with that," Daniel replied. He felt elated for some reason. His face was flushed with pleasure and his body seemed ready to burst right out of the tuxedo. "It was worth it. Did you see the punch I gave that guy? I knocked him clean across the table."

"You two! Over here!" one of the patrolmen shouted at Daniel and Moishe. One arm around Moishe to support him, Daniel joined the small crowd of people herded into a corner of the club by the police. The drunk who'd started the fight was not among the crowd, Daniel realized. But he saw the brunette to whom he had sung, the woman who had aroused her boyfriend's jealousy enough to make him swing.

"Where's your friend?" Daniel asked.

"He left. Got the hell out in the first rush that managed to get past the cops."

"Real Sir Galahad."

"He can't afford the bad publicity," the woman said. "His father's a newspaper publisher. Millionaire and friend of the church. He'd cut his son off without a cent if he knew he was in a place like this."

"Hope he does." Daniel began to take more interest in the woman. Before, when he'd been singing to her, he had used her as a sounding board, hardly even noticing what she looked like.

"Like what you're looking at?" she asked, understanding Daniel's appreciative glance. She stepped backward as one of the police officers walked past, counting out loud.

"Anything wrong if I should?" She came up to his shoulder, with dark curly hair and the deepest, brownest eyes he had ever seen.

"I guess not. I'm Sandra. Sandra Dean. But you could have found that out from the police blotter in the station house anyway."

"Are they really going to arrest us?"

"Depends how busy they are. If it's quiet, they'll send down a few wagons and take us all in."

"You make it sound like you're an old hand at being arrested," Daniel joked as he tried to cover his own fear. Arrest? That would take care of everything. Better Feldman and the Temple Isaiah *gontzer machers* should read his reviews as the jazz cantor than hear of his arrest.

"I am," she said, smiling mischievously. "How's your friend?"

Daniel turned around to look at Moishe. "I'll live," Moishe muttered, although he did not sound as if he believed a word he said.

A fleet of police wagons drove up to the club within ten minutes, accompanied by more patrolmen. Daniel got into a wagon with Moishe and Sandra for the short ride to the station house. The desk sergeant looked glumly over the mass of heads in front of him as he anticipated the paperwork. Daniel glanced around and saw that neither Louis Armstrong nor Al Jolson were among those detained. Neither was Jake Joyner, the club owner. Just the noisy and the slow, Daniel reflected. If he hadn't gone back for Moishe, he could have got clear away as well.

"Don't you people have anything better to do?" the desk sergeant complained.

"Can I make a phone call?" someone yelled.

"Sure you can make a phone call. You can all make a phone call. Soon as you're booked."

"I'll call my lawyer," Sandra whispered to Daniel. "He'll get me out of this in a minute."

"I'd call mine," Daniel said, "but he's right here with me." He pointed to Moishe. "Wait a minute, I've got a better idea." He pushed forward through the crowd until he stood in front of the desk sergeant.

"You going to a wedding, mac?" the sergeant wanted to know.

Daniel ignored the reference to the tuxedo. "Can I have a word with you, please?"

"Save it for the night magistrate."

"It's important. It won't wait." Daniel leaned closer. "I've got to make a phone call straightaway. Urgent as all hell. To Captain James Mulvaney. Know him?"

The sergeant's eyes opened a fraction wider. "He a personal friend of yours?"

"Yes. A very close one."

"How many are in your party?"

"Two. No, wait," he added, remembering the woman. "Three. Mr. Maurice Waterman, Miss Sandra Dean and myself."

The sergeant debated what action he should take. Maybe this guy in the tux was a friend of Mulvaney; maybe he was bluffing. The sergeant wasn't about to call Mulvaney up in the middle of the night to find out, though. Anyway, it would be three less heads to process. He called over a patrolman. "Get this guy and his two friends out of here. Take them where they want to go."

"Deuces Wild," Daniel said immediately. "I left my coat there."

Ten minutes later Daniel, Moishe and Sandra were standing by the Packard on 137th Street. "Where do you live?" Daniel asked the woman.

"Central Park West."

"I'll give you a lift. It's on my way home," he lied. He winked at Moishe, who understood. Moishe said good night, climbed into the Dodge and drove off.

"Are you really a cantor, or is that just a gimmick?" Sandra asked as Daniel drove south.

"I'm really a cantor. At a temple in Paterson, New Jersey."

"Then Central Park isn't on your way home."

"No sense of direction," Daniel admitted. "Tell me, what do you do that you're so used to being booked?"

Sandra did not answer immediately. Turning on the interior light, she pulled out a make-up compact from her purse and studied her face in its mirror, touching up her lipstick. "I'm a call girl. Expensive, and worth every penny of it, so I'm told."

Daniel looked at her in shock, and the Packard swerved toward the sidewalk until he glanced away and brought the car back into his lane.

"Are you serious?"

She nodded. "Jason—that was the slob you punched out—was my date for the night. Looks like you took his place. Or is there a Mrs. Cantor somewhere in New Jersey looking after all the little cantors?"

"There is and there isn't."

"You make about as much sense as Jason did, but at least he had the excuse of being drunk most of the time."

Daniel did not understand why, but he started to tell the woman about Lucy and about the child. He hadn't ever managed to discuss the tragedy in any depth with Lucy; he even found it difficult with his own family and friends. Now he was telling all his troubles to a self-confessed whore he'd met an hour earlier. She was a good listener, though, not saying a word until he was finished. Perhaps, he reasoned, that's what made her such a good and expensive whore. She was sympathetic.

"Sounds tough being a Russian Jew," she remarked. "Over there." She pointed to a building. "That's where I live."

Daniel parked the car and waited.

"Coming up?" she asked.

He looked at Fat Benny's gold watch and saw it was past one. He started to feel guilty about leaving Lucy alone in the house with the baby.

"Only for a drink," Sandra prompted him. "No business."

Daniel grinned at the invitation. "I probably couldn't afford your prices."

In the darkness she smiled back at him and squeezed his hand. "You don't know my rates to begin with, so don't even try to guess." She continued to hold his hand as she led him into the building. A uniformed doorman greeted her with a practiced touch of his cap. Daniel wondered what the man must think, whether he knew about the tenant's profession.

"What do you drink?" she asked after Daniel had settled himself comfortably in a leather wing chair.

"Whiskey'll do fine."

She brought two drinks from the cabinet, Scotch and soda for him, a whiskey sour for herself. "How did you work the miracle at the station house?"

"I've got a friend who's an influential cop." He began to tell her about Mulvaney and only stopped when he realized he was blurting out his entire life story. Fat Benny. Bloom. Everything.

"When's the last time you really spoke to someone?" Sandra asked. "Really had a heart-to-heart chat?"

"Does it show?"

She nodded. "Carrying on a conversation with God doesn't have quite the same effect, does it? I used to go to confession when I was a kid. That didn't help either." She patted the sofa next to her. "Why don't you come a bit closer, talk some more?"

Daniel spared a single thought for Lucy at home with Rachel. He sat down on the couch next to Sandra. An electrifying tingle coursed through his body as her thigh pressed against his. He reached out and took her in his arms, lips hungrily seeking her mouth, then sliding down until they were stopped by the high collar of her dress. She responded just as fiercely, hands sliding under his jacket, beneath his shirt to caress his back.

"Inside," she whispered, feeling his fingers tugging at the fastening of her dress. "Inside."

He followed her into the bedroom, watching hungrily as she sat in the middle of the chintz bedspread. She held her arms out to him. Very slowly, wanting to enjoy every second of anticipation, he lowered himself into them. He undressed her, sliding each article of clothing over the side of the bed; his own clothes joined them.

"You should have hit him harder," she said suddenly.

"Who?"

"That creep Jason. At least I won't have to spend the night with him."

"You'll lose a customer." He teased her nipples with his tongue until they grew hard.

"I might gain a friend instead." She placed both hands on top of his head and pushed down, moaning softly as his tongue traced delicate patterns along the insides of her thighs. A ridiculous idea sped across Daniel's mind, that it was Lucy with whom he was in bed, Lucy allowing him to act out the fantasies he'd harbored, Lucy with a smile of pleasure on her face instead of the mask of painful endurance she saved for bed.

He felt the pressure of hands pulling him up. But they were not Lucy's hands; they were Sandra's and the illusion disappeared. Long fingernails trailed tantalizingly across his stomach. A soft-skinned hand held him tenderly, squeezing, sliding back and forth until it seemed that nothing could stop him from exploding. Slowly she guided him into her. Teeth nibbled on his ear. Her arms wrapped themselves tightly across his back. Her legs crossed themselves behind his thighs to imprison him. Their grip increased like the jaws of a vise, driving him deeper into her, penetrating until she cried out loud.

His climax began deep within him, a quiet murmur that quickly gained strength and became a rushing, unstoppable torrent. He was the dam. He had to hold back the flood until he could extract every last measure of enjoyment from it. He tried, and he could not. The climax burst over him like a raging fury, washing away everything in its path, taking the last ounce of strength from his body.

Vaguely he was aware of Sandra's anguished, pleasure-filled cries as his body collapsed.

Sandra prodded him awake. "You'd better go home."

Daniel opened his eyes slowly and saw her standing beside the bed, a housecoat covering the body that had given him so much release. She was holding a steaming cup of coffee.

"Drink this and go home. Before Mrs. Cantor begins to wonder what's happened to Mr. Cantor."

"What time is it?"

"Just after five."

He took a cautious sip from the cup. "Thanks for waking me."

"That's okay. You saved me a bundle of trouble last night with the cops. I'm returning the favor."

The same doorman was on duty when Daniel left the building, coat held loosely over his arm. The doorman touched his cap again and Daniel could swear he saw a knowing smile lurking behind the respectful, uniformed facade.

The sky was already bright when he reached Paterson. He left the car in the street rather than make noise by opening the garage and let himself quietly into the house. A scratching sound greeted him, a radio that wasn't tuned properly to a channel. He traced the sound to the living room. The phonograph was on, its needle worn right down to a stub which was somehow managing to follow the end of the groove of the record on the turntable. Lucy must have left it on and forgotten all about it, he decided. The record was ruined, not that he really cared. He glanced at the title: "E lucevan le stelle," sung by Jussi Bjoerling. Who the hell was Jussi Bjoerling? Another of Lucy's sobbing tenors? This one wouldn't sing or sob again, he thought; not on this record anyway.

He tiptoed up the stairs and stopped by the nursery door. When he crossed the room to peer into the crib, his heart stopped beating. Rachel's face was covered completely by a pillow. Panic mounting, he threw the pillow onto the floor and felt the child's cheeks. They were ice cold. His brain on fire, he spun around and raced toward the bedroom, shouting Lucy's name with every step.

"Lucy!"

He tried the door. It was locked.

"Lucy!"

He lifted his foot and kicked in the lock. The door swung back and he shouldered it out of the way. The room was completely empty. He turned to leave when a gentle movement attracted his attention. One of the drapes was moving, blowing gently in the breeze from the open window. Daniel ran across the room and looked out of the window. Twenty feet below, lying perfectly still on the concrete patio, was Lucy.

A loud noise filled the room, the grief-stricken, terrifying scream of a man suffering pain he had never dreamed existed. Daniel clapped his hands to his face and fell backwards onto the bed, sobbing loudly. For ten minutes he lay crying until the tears would come no more. Then he stood up and forced himself to think. While he had been out, satisfying his own needs, Lucy had reached her breaking point. First the baby, and then herself. While he had been with Sandra, or even before, when he had been sitting at a table with Moishe—maybe even while Louis Armstrong was shaking hands with him—Lucy had smothered the baby and then jumped from the window. But why the window? Why that? The drop wasn't enough to guarantee suicide. Why did she choose that?

As he walked past the dressing table, gathering his courage to return downstairs and go out on the patio, he was dimly aware of a message scrawled in lipstick on the mirror. "*O! Scarpia, avanti a Dio!*"

It made no sense to him at all.

Chapter Seventeen

Daniel listened to the news of the war in Europe with half an ear while he concentrated on dressing. He was surprised that the tuxedo he had worn to the date at the Deuces Wild—on the night Lucy killed herself—still fitted. Maybe he hadn't put on any weight in those two years and three months, but, to his dismay, he had not lost any either.

The news continued to be depressing. British and Commonwealth troops were getting it in the neck wherever they met the Germans. And the Nazis were pushing on relentlessly to their east as well, driving back the Red Army as if it wasn't there. Just as well the British had been able to rescue the bulk of their expeditionary force from the Dunkirk sands the previous year, otherwise it might have been all over by now and Hitler would have been addressing some puppet government from the British throne. Where would that have left the British Royal Family? Daniel asked himself. He had no doubt that they would not have stayed around long enough to find out. Canada, he decided; or the United States. They had enough friends here, God only knew, and Roosevelt was doing his damnedest to convince his countrymen that America should join in. As far as Daniel was concerned, that day could not come soon enough.

He did up his bow tie and stood back to admire the knot. He was looking forward to the *bar mitzvah* party he was attending tonight. The kid hadn't sung as well that morning as he had done almost fourteen years earlier, but he hadn't made a bad job of it either. Almost professional in the way he had attacked the task. Nothing fancy, just get up there, do the piece and get out in time to count the presents. This *bar mitzvah* was one of the temple's big events of the year, the oldest grandson of Harry Feldman, the president. Daniel realized he was not expected to give a present when he was invited to a function for the purpose of conducting the Grace, but he'd put something in an envelope for the kid anyway. Feldman had been wonderful to him following Lucy's suicide. So had the entire congregation, for that matter. They had all been on his side from the very beginning, when he had made public the news that his daughter was suffering from Tay-Sachs. When Lucy had smothered Rachel and then jumped to her death, the community had gathered behind him like an invincible army. Whatever assistance they could provide, they had provided willingly.

After allowing a respectable period of time to elapse, Feldman had found a buyer for the house and Daniel had moved from homeowner to lodger, settling in with an elderly widowed member of the congregation, a woman of sixty who looked after him as if he were her own son. His father had wanted him to return to Claremont Parkway until he was over the tragedy, but Daniel had vetoed the suggestion immediately. You could never look back, he told himself, and close proximity with his mother for any length of time would have been unbearable. The woman in whose home he now boarded looked after him with more care and consideration than Yetta Kirschbaum had ever done.

He finished dressing and turned sideways to view his profile. After sucking in his stomach and cinching it with a cummerbund, he decided it looked better. The profile was more appealing than the front view, he thought. The straight nose and solid jaw looked good; if only he could do something with his stomach, something more permanent than pressing it back with a cummerbund. Maybe he should turn sideways when he sang Grace at the *bar mitzvah*, and give his listeners a profile view instead of the customary fleshy front view.

After putting on a coat, he left the house and drove the short distance to the temple hall where the party was being held. What woman would they have lined up for him tonight? He was certain there would be a single girl seated next to him at dinner. There always was at these functions. A long string of coincidental seating arrangements that left him to fend off some unmarried girl in the community whose parents wanted her married off to the cantor. Whoever arranged the seating had to be raking in a fortune, Daniel concluded. Unless they were being paid by results, in which case they were well on the way to the poorhouse. Marriage was most definitely not in his immediate future. Since Lucy, he had not been out with the same woman for more than a month. A month was safe, he'd decided some time earlier. Four weeks gave him long enough to enjoy whatever the relationship had to offer, and it was not quite long enough for the girl to get firm ideas. He had no intention of making another commitment just yet.

The knowledge that his marriage to Lucy had been unsound from the beginning had not helped to ease the shattering impact of her death. They had naively mistaken the camaraderie of all the years they had known each other for love. He realized now, all too late, that Lucy's place in his life should have been that of a trusted friend, along with Moishe and Tommy Mulvaney.

Although he knew that marrying her had been a tragic mistake, never a day passed without him thinking of her. Always to the front of his mind came that cryptic message she had left for him, scribbled in lipstick on the dressing table mirror. "*O! Scarpia, avanti a Dio!*" It had been Moishe, of all people, who had taken it upon himself to find out what the words meant, and their place of origin. At first, the translation had made as little sense to Daniel as the original message. But then he had acquired the libretto from *Tosca*. After wading through it, the meaning had become much sharper. He was not the evil Roman chief of police, but through Lucy's tortured logic he knew he must have appeared every bit as destructive as Scarpia. By marrying Lucy—and chaining her to the house with a terminally ill child—he had thwarted her own ambitions and turned her into a prisoner. Wrapped up in operatic tradition, poor Lucy had found disturbing similarities between herself and the tragic heroines she loved. In one traumatic instant, she had stepped over the bounds of reality into the shadowy world of illusion, carrying the affinity she saw between herself and the singer Tosca to its inexorable and terrifying conclusion.

Daniel wondered if Lucy had any way of knowing that he had unraveled her riddle; and if she had, did it afford her any consolation?

His prophecy had been correct. There was a single girl sitting next to him at the table. She was waiting, a smile of anticipation covering her face as the guests filed in from the reception for dinner. Daniel identified the smile, cataloging it among those he had come to call I'm-going-to-marry-a-cantor smiles. He smiled back graciously and waited for the girl to introduce herself.

"Good evening, Cantor. I'm Sylvia Prashker, Harry Feldman's niece."

"How nice to meet you. I noticed you in *shul* this morning." He hadn't, but she'd never know that.

"It was a lovely service."

"Thank you." Daniel looked toward the top table and saw that the *bar mitzvah* boy's immediate family were in their places. He joined them, recited the blessing for the traditional handwashing and turned his attention to the plaited *challah* loaf. He cut off the crust and quickly chanted the blessing over bread. If the remainder of the guests were as hungry as he was, they would be waiting impatiently to start the meal. Afterwards, when they were sated, he would take his time, and ease their digestive systems with a beautifully performed Grace.

"You've got a wonderful voice," the girl said when he returned to his seat.

Daniel, an hors d'oeuvre already raised halfway to his mouth, turned to look at her. He couldn't even manage to remember her name, so why didn't she just leave him to eat in peace? He glanced down at the card she had pushed from her plate. Sylvia Prashker. Now he remembered. She was Harry Feldman's niece.

"Thank you." He gobbled down the hors d'oeuvre before she could interrupt him again.

"I heard from my uncle that you sing at night clubs as well."

"I used to," he replied; another hors d'oeuvre was halted in mid-journey. "Haven't done too much lately." The truth was that he had not done a thing since that night with Moishe at the Deuces Wild. Following the brawl and the mass arrests, the club owner had informed Moishe that his client would not be required for any return engagements. But the deciding factor was that Daniel did not have the heart for any more club dates, as if that one engagement had pushed Lucy another few inches along the path that led to her jumping from the window.

In an act of charity that surprised him, Daniel made up his mind to be nice to this girl, even if she was the biggest *mieskeit* he'd seen in years. After all, she was Feldman's niece, and Feldman had been one of his main supports during his worst moments of depression. "Where are you from?" he asked.

"New York. Brooklyn."

"Nice." The only times he had ever visited Brooklyn were when Moishe was still living with his family. Since Moishe had moved to the Village, Daniel had not set foot in Brooklyn.

"I think Paterson's nicer," Sylvia said. "I come over here only twice a year, but it's much more pleasant than living in Brooklyn."

Daniel looked away, finding some imaginary object on which to focus his attention for a moment. Feldman's niece or not, he was about to stop being nice, before she saw him as a means of moving from Brooklyn to Paterson.

"Brooklyn has a lot more life," he said eventually. "You're probably better off there. Paterson's dead." What was it that made single women—and their mothers!—look on cantors as fair game. If he had been a lawyer or a doctor without a wife, he could understand it. But a cantor? Especially a young, overweight cantor with one screwed-up marriage behind him? He supposed whoever had briefed this girl—Feldman, probably—had mentioned that his wife had committed suicide after killing their sick child. He could even visualize the conversation that must have taken place between Feldman and his niece. Be gentle, Daniel's just getting over a wretched experience. And be patient. You've got to make him understand how badly he needs a wife. Had Feldman even picked out the house he was going to sell them?

"Maybe," the girl said uncertainly. "But I'd still like to give Paterson a try. My uncle said he could always get me a job here."

"Oh? What do you do?"

"I'm a nurse."

"What made you decide to be a nurse?" He was not even

sure why he was bothering to continue the conversation. Something to do between courses, he supposed; a bout of social chit-chat to pass the time between the chopped liver and the chicken soup.

"I like to help people."

Daniel smiled at the reply. If she was looking to help him, she was on to a loser. He didn't want any help right now. "Even to the point of cleaning out dirty bedpans?" He applauded himself mentally as the girl turned away, her lips curling in distaste. Score one for the fine art of suitable dinner conversation. Thinking about dirty bedpans would keep her busy until the meal was over. By then he would have said Grace and disappeared into the crowd. She'd never find him again.

Sylvia Prashker had a stronger stomach than Daniel had given her credit for. After a pause of a few seconds, she replied, "Someone has to clean them out. It's all part of helping people to get better."

So, Daniel decided, she wasn't that easily put off. He'd have to fight a delaying action until he could get clear of the table. He made up his mind to ask the waitress for second helpings of everything. With his mouth permanently full of food, he could not be expected to carry on a conversation, only to listen and occasionally nod. The ruse succeeded through two bowls of soup and the first helping of the main course. Then it began to come unstuck.

"You shouldn't eat so much," Sylvia chided him gently as he attacked the second portion of the entrée. "I think you're a little bit overweight as it is."

"I need the weight to sing well. It gives me resonance." He ducked his head back towards the plate.

"Are you certain that's why you eat so much? Or is it nervous tension?"

He decided against answering until he'd cleaned the plate. Just dessert now, and he'd be off to the top table to sing Grace. "I've got nothing to be nervous about."

"Did you eat this heavily before what happened to your wife and baby?"

Daniel waved the waitress away. Suddenly he did not want any dessert. "Will you excuse me?" he said to Sylvia. "I have to go somewhere." He rushed out of the hall and into the washroom, where he locked himself in a cubicle. Ten minutes passed while he remained there, sitting on the commode lid and staring morosely at the gray-painted door. Dessert would have been served by now, and it would be safe for him to return. He would not have to go back to his own table, where Sylvia Prashker sat, obnoxious bitch; he'd go straight to the top table and say Grace. Then, maybe, he'd excuse himself and go home.

It had been almost pleasant for a while but then Feldman's niece had broken the rules by mentioning Lucy and the baby. That wasn't in the script, although he should have seen it coming, the way she asked about nerves. She'd hit it, all right. Not about the eating, but about the nerves. Try as he might, he could never rid himself of the guilt, the possibility that he had contributed to Lucy's death. What had happened to Rachel had not been his fault, no matter what Lucy talked herself into believing. But he might have been able to prevent Lucy's death if he had tried harder to help push aside her doubts and worries. He had not supported her in the least; he'd tried just once and given up all too quickly, content to leave her alone while he gallivanted around the clubs with Moishe in an attempt to forget his own troubles. Lucy had wanted to be the grieving mother, he had decided, so he'd let her get on with it in the stupid, selfish belief that she recognized her own best course. It had been a cop-out for him, an easy avenue of escape. Why the hell hadn't he sought more help for her? Nagged her, forced her to see psychiatrists, instead of letting whatever malignancy that had been smoldering inside her ignite into destructive flame?

Hearing voices in the washroom, he realized that the meal was over. They'd be looking for him. He opened the door and let himself out, washed his hands and returned to the party. Feldman was standing at the top table, one hand on his grandson's shoulder while he scanned the hall. Daniel quickened his pace.

"Wondered what happened to you," Feldman said.

"Washroom."

"You all right now? Saw you rush off."

"I'm okay."

"How did you like Sylvia, my niece? Nice girl, nice parents. Nice family," Feldman added in a self-congratulatory postscript.

"Some other time, Harry," Daniel answered.

"Pity." Feldman looked at the table where Sylvia sat. "She likes you. Rushed up here when you took off, wanted to know if she'd said anything wrong."

"She said plenty wrong. Leave it at that."

"Don't worry about it, Daniel. I've got plenty more nieces dying to meet you." He grinned sheepishly and leaned closer, dropping his voice to a whisper. "You can't even begin to imagine what it's like being president of a temple that has a young, eligible cantor, and having a dozen unmarried nieces."

Daniel began to laugh, the discomfort of a few minutes earlier forgotten. Feldman wouldn't mind if he gave Sylvia Prashker the brush-off for the remainder of the evening; he'd content himself with the thought that it was arithmetically impossible to strike out all twelve times.

By the following morning, Feldman's niece was almost forgotten about, back home in Brooklyn, wondering where she had gone wrong, what she had said to send Daniel scurrying off to the washroom and make him ignore her for the rest of the evening. Just once Daniel thought of her as he drove from Paterson to Claremont Parkway. Maybe she'd learned something for the next time she was seated next to an unmarried cantor, and her evening would not have been a complete waste.

Isaac opened the apartment door. Lunch was already on the table and Daniel sat down, hungry again despite the vast quantities of food he had eaten the previous evening in an effort to stave off conversation with Feldman's niece.

"Busy?" Isaac asked.

"*Bar mitzvah* last night. Wedding later this afternoon."

"Then you shouldn't eat so much now," Yetta Kirschbaum broke in. "You won't leave enough room for anything tonight."

Daniel finished a mouthful and washed it down with a swallow of coffee. "Don't worry, Ma. This is work. I don't have to give a present so I don't have to make sure I eat enough to cover it."

Yetta snorted. "Listen to him, the bigshot! A little money in his pocket and he's trying to make out we were paupers."

The doorbell rang and Daniel got up to answer it. "That'll be Moishe."

"Is he eating here as well?" Yetta wanted to know.

"I'll take him around the corner to the deli for a sandwich if you've got nothing left," Daniel shot back. He was pleased to see his father smile at the remark; maybe the old man was winning more of the battles these days. He opened the door and admitted Moishe, bundled up in a thick coat and a fur hat. They shook hands and Daniel invited him into the living room. Moishe looked around and nodded a greeting.

"You going into the nightclub business again?" Isaac asked, associating Moishe with Daniel's forays into popular singing.

Daniel shook his head. "Just a bite together. You're halfway between where we both live. Gives us the chance to get together."

The reply brought a frown to Yetta's face. So now her home was a halfway house for her son—whenever he decided to visit—and his friend.

"Captain Mulvaney was asking after you," Isaac mentioned. "I met him in the street the other day."

"I should go over and say hello," Daniel admitted. "Tommy was by a few weeks back, that's the last I've seen of them. Hear from Jack?"

Isaac rummaged around in a drawer and produced a tattered, well-read letter which he handed to Daniel. It was two weeks old, mailed from Chicago. Jack was well, busy in construction and considering marriage. "You'll have to go out there," Daniel said.

Isaac nodded happily at the prospect, but Yetta frowned again. "Where are we supposed to get the fare for the trip?" she asked. "Why he couldn't find a girl from here is beyond me."

Money was no longer a problem, Daniel knew, and he could not resist aiming another barb at his mother. "I'll buy the tickets for you."

"Bigshot," she called him again. "We can pay our own way. We don't need your charity."

When he was ready to leave, Daniel decided he had time to visit the Mulvaneys before he drove back to New Jersey. With Moishe for company, he left the apartment and walked slowly along Claremont Parkway. Nothing seemed to have changed from the time Daniel had wandered its length as a child. The faces that smiled at him were the same, older now but still recognizable. He found himself wondering why Tommy had never left the neighborhood, or at least found an apartment of his own. He decided the reason was money; not everyone had it to throw around like he did. They crossed under the Third Avenue line and entered the Mulvaneys' building. Daniel had to ring three times before Tommy opened the door.

"Deafness an occupational hazard of the police department?" Daniel quipped.

It might as well have been. Tommy did not answer. Nor did he even seem to recognize Daniel and Moishe standing in the hallway. He just swung around and raced back into the apartment. Daniel looked questioningly at Moishe, then went inside. The Mulvaneys were clustered around a radio in the living room, all listening intently. Captain Mulvaney and his wife were sitting, Tommy crouching; none of them seemed to notice they had visitors.

"Good afternoon," Daniel said. Tommy turned around and waved agitatedly at him to be quiet.

"What's going on?" Moishe asked.

Tommy's father turned away from the set. His face was grim as he looked at Moishe and Daniel. "Japanese planes just bombed Pearl Harbor in Hawaii. We're going to be at war."

Daniel felt sorry for the bride and groom that afternoon. He felt even sorrier for the bride's parents. They had dreamed of this day since their daughter had been a child, putting away money whenever they could so that nothing would be spared for their daughter's wedding. And now, instead of celebrating, the wedding guests were overcome by the thought of war. Finally the United States would be forced to enter the conflict. All plans were put aside, shelved indefinitely. Daniel did not even worry about who would be sitting next to him at dinner. He was too busy thinking about the following day.

Tommy and Moishe had both agreed that there would be increased conscription into the armed forces. By enlisting immediately, they would stand a better chance of getting the jobs for which they were best suited—Tommy in the military police, and Moishe in the judge advocate's office as a military lawyer. Both expected a commission. In their enthusiasm to enlist, they had roped Daniel in as well. Fine for them, he thought, but what does a cantor do in the army? Sing reveille? If he had been a rabbi, he could have become a chaplain. But for a cantor, there were no set paths.

"Harry, I've got to talk to you." He pulled Feldman aside after the dinner.

"What is it? Terrible news today. Terrible." Feldman had uncomfortable visions of the price of real estate tumbling as it had during the depression.

"I'm joining up."

"You're what?" Feldman stepped back in horror at what he had heard.

"Enlisting. Tomorrow. With a couple of friends."

"You're crazy! You're running away from all this?" Feldman spread his arms to encompass the wedding party, the temple, all of Paterson.

"No, Harry. I'm suddenly sane." Watching Feldman, Daniel realized why he had agreed so readily to join Moishe and Tommy. Enlisting gave him an excuse to leave Paterson, an opportunity to divorce himself from his present life and give it some cold, hard thought from a safe distance. He had become too comfortable at Temple Isaiah. The position fitted him like a favorite piece of clothing. Without this chance for a break, he would be content to stay in Paterson until he was old, singing for one generation of worshippers after another, and out of sheer desperation eventually marrying one of the women they sat next to him. Life seemed to stretch out in front of him as an endless tedium. Once he had dared to dream. Of applause. Of his name on people's lips. Of being a someone, an entertainer in an arena far more vast than all of Paterson, or all of New Jersey. He'd compromised the dream after Lucy had died, as if punishing himself by staying in one place and stifling his ambitions.

The war would give him time to rethink his attitudes, time to plan, time to decide what he wanted. God bless Hirohito, he thought; but not too much, he added hurriedly.

"Where am I going to find another *chazan* so soon?" Feldman wanted to know.

Daniel took a long time to think about the question. "Better you should ask yourself where you're going to find a congregation," he told Feldman. "Or enough men to make up a *minyan*. I'll be seeing more of them than you will."

"What about that three months' notice clause your lawyer friend Waterman put in the contract?" Feldman said triumphantly.

"I'm not quitting you, Harry. I'm taking an extended leave of absence."

Feldman knew when not to fight. "Go. Good luck and God bless." He stuck out his hand and Daniel shook it. "I'll make sure all of your stuff in the house is looked after. And the job'll still be here when you get back."

"Quit making a big deal out of it, will you?" Daniel urged. "I'll be back before you know it."

"Sure you will," Feldman said caustically. "That's what I said when I put on a uniform for the last one. *Gey gezunter heyt!* And keep your head down!"

Chapter Eighteen

Daniel looked to his left, saw that nothing was coming and stepped out into the street. The frantic, deafening blast of a horn sent him scurrying back to the safety of the sidewalk. A black taxi whipped past from the other direction, its wheels sending a spray of dirty water from the gutter to splash over Daniel's uniform trousers. Damn, he swore softly. How long was it going to take him to get used to traffic driving on the left? Goddamned lunatics these British drivers were. Why Hitler wanted to waste men and ammunition trying to subdue them was beyond Daniel's understanding; given time, the British would all kill each other off trying to cross the street.

"Hey, Yank!" a voice called. Daniel turned around to see an elderly man watching him in amusement. "Someone ought to teach your mob how to cross the road properly."

Daniel smiled good-naturedly. No matter what happened to him in London, he found it difficult to stay mad for any length of time. The British possessed a stoic sense of humor which had rubbed off on him. Whatever befell them, they could take it and still come up smiling and confident of winning through.

"There's a cleaner's shop a hundred yards down the road, Yank," the man said, bursting into a fit of delighted laughter. "Maybe they can give your trousers artificial respiration."

Daniel looked helplessly at the sodden trousers which clung irritatingly to his legs. "That's okay. Thanks. I'll change when I get home." Deciding to risk his life again, he looked right this time, saw that it was safe and ran quickly across the road. After reaching the other side, he waved cheerfully to the elderly man before continuing on his way.

He arrived back at the small hotel on Baker Street where he was billeted to find a message waiting. Changing his sopping wet trousers, he went to the room adjacent to his own and knocked on the door.

"Come in!" a voice called.

Daniel pushed back the door and walked inside. First Lieutenant Harvey Berman, the Jewish chaplain to whom Daniel was assigned, sat at a small table, writing a letter. He looked up as Daniel entered, waved him to a chair and quickly penned the last few lines. Glad of the opportunity to sit and rest, Daniel waited patiently for Berman to finish.

Easy life, they'd told him in personnel services division back in Camp Blanding, Florida. Chaplain's assistant is one of the plum jobs. Just make sure your chaplain doesn't get into any trouble and you're made for the duration. Only those morons at personnel had not reckoned with First Lieutenant Harvey Berman. This guy had to be the Black Jack Pershing of the religious ranks, determined to visit every Jewish G.I. stationed in and around London. Daniel already knew the streets as well as any home-grown taxi driver and was able to jostle for position in his open jeep with the worst of them. Even if he could never manage to remember which way the traffic went while he was on foot.

Chaplains are inherently stupid, the personnel specialists had told Daniel before sending him to be Berman's assistant two years earlier. Catholic, Jewish, Protestant, it doesn't matter what branch of God they're representing; they've all been hit in the head with the same idiot stick at birth. Your job is to make sure your particular idiot gets where he's supposed to be going and comes through the war in one piece. You know the kind of thing, Kirschbaum. Don't let him conduct any services in the middle of a minefield.

Only Berman was the exception to the personnel division's stereotyped chaplain. In his thirties and as tall as Daniel, but far more muscular—he'd played college football and had even considered an athletic career before deciding God was a better prospect—Berman had a zest for life which even Daniel found difficulty in matching. He had set aside a good-sized congregation in Chicago to throw his considerable weight into America's war effort, and Daniel had lost all of ten pounds just trying to keep up with the man.

If Daniel had been surprised to learn that Berman was exactly the opposite of what the personnel specialists had predicted—and the opposite of his own conception of rabbis—

Berman had been just as happily amazed to find himself assigned an assistant who not only knew something about Judaism but who was a cantor in his own right. Not that Berman had ever heard of Daniel before they met in London. Berman had a deep pride in the Chicago Jewish community and had refused initially to believe there were any good cantors in New York. Daniel had protested that he sang in New Jersey, to which Berman had shrugged his linebacker shoulders and said it was the same difference—New Jersey was nothing more than a suburb of New York. After the first Saturday morning service that Daniel had persuaded Berman to let him conduct, the Chicago rabbi's opinion had altered dramatically. He had agreed to allow Daniel to take all the services, while he concentrated on other duties.

"We've got orders," Berman said, the letter finished.

"Where to?" Daniel hoped it might be back to the States. He was beginning to forget what his family looked like.

"France. We're being assigned to the Third Army. There's a Jewish chaplain's slot open. I've got it, which means you've got it as well."

Daniel nodded. He was not certain whether he should be pleased or not at the news. Third Army meant Patton. If what he'd heard was to be believed, there would never be enough time to put down roots in any one place. Third Army just kept on moving and moving. At least, it was moving in the right direction. "Maybe we'll be in Germany in time to do a *Kol Nidre* service from Nuremberg."

"I'd rather do a burial service," Berman replied.

Daniel understood the chaplain's meaning. "I never came across a prayer for planting your enemies."

Berman smiled at the thought. "I'll settle for doing a tap dance on their graves."

"When are we moving out?"

Berman consulted a scrap of paper on the table. "Report to Third Army headquarters at eight in the morning"—Berman refused to submit to military jargon when it came to time or anything else—"on August twenty-ninth. A week from now. Although God only knows where Third Army headquarters will be by then." Berman picked up another sheet of paper from the table and passed it across to Daniel. "This also came through. *Mazel tov.*"

Daniel glanced at the orders promoting him from corporal to sergeant. About goddamned time! Especially so when he knew that Tommy Mulvaney and Moishe Wasserman were both captains. Tommy was company commander of an MP unit already in Europe, going in on D-plus-two; and Moishe was an army lawyer in Washington D.C.

"Better get all your new stripes sewn on before we go over," Berman advised. "You'll be in the real army over there. Got to look the part."

Daniel just grinned at the thought. The hotel had a tailor who would do the work. So what if a sergeant's stripes were not as pretty as a captain's gleaming silver bars? He had earned them, and he would wear them just as proudly.

Early Sunday morning, Daniel and Berman left the hotel in Baker Street and drove towards the East End of London. No longer were they appalled by the devastation they saw, the constant reminders of the savage bombardment from the air to which Britain had been subjected. They had become used to it, immune to the sight of ruined buildings, and to the thought of what had happened to those who'd lived there. Daniel remembered the method he had first used to find his way around London—turn left at this bombsite, right at that gutted building, keep on straight past the next two bombed-out blocks; and just hope that nothing landed before you got home, otherwise you'd be lost forever.

Half an hour after leaving the hotel, they pulled up outside a terraced house in the East London section of Hackney. Berman reached under his seat for a small parcel which he tucked under his arm as he and Daniel climbed the steps to the front door. A young boy in short gray flannel trousers opened the door. Berman patted him on the head and handed him the parcel. The boy ran inside the house with the parcel, calling out to his mother that Uncle Harvey and his friend had arrived. The boy's mother appeared, a woman in her early thirties. She kissed Berman on the cheek and shook hands with Daniel; then she turned to her son to see what Berman had given him. When the boy opened the parcel to reveal bars of chocolate and packets of candy, the mother looked crossly at Berman.

"Why did you do that? You're going to spoil him rotten."

"We've got more than we can use, Betty. Besides, what's family for if you can't help out?"

Daniel turned away to hide his smile. He wondered what would have happened had he looked up every Kirschbaum in the London telephone directory and started calling them to see if there was any family link to the American Kirschbaums. That's what Berman had done as soon as he had landed in London. Of the many Bermans he had contacted, the family he was now visiting knew of ancestors who had left Poland fifty years earlier and had split up, one group going to the United States, the other to England. Betty Berman's husband, Phil, and the American chaplain had worked out when they first met that they were second cousins. Or maybe third. Or maybe nothing at all. But it was just great to have someone with the same name in a strange city, the chaplain had declared, and he had adopted the London Bermans as his own cousins. That was before Phil Berman had been conscripted into the British army and stationed in Scotland. Since then, Harvey Berman had become even closer with the family, dragging Daniel along to the meetings and making him, too, feel at home.

"Afraid I've got some bad news," Berman said, following the woman into the breakfast room, where the table was set for four people.

"Oh? What's that?"

"We're moving out in a few days. Got orders to do some spiritual salvation in Europe."

Betty Berman gave the chaplain a sad little smile. "Phil wrote to me that he's also going. Maybe you'll run into one another."

"I doubt it. The British are way to the north of where we're going. Still," Berman added, optimistically, "you never know. Once the Berman clan's together, it'll take more than a Hitler to tear us apart." He picked up the cup of tea that had been poured for him and stretched out a hand before Betty could add milk. "None of that, thanks."

"I forgot."

"That your American side of the family has some strange customs, like black tea?" He looked away from Betty to the boy. "Want a ride in a jeep?"

The boy nodded eagerly and jumped out of the chair. "What do you say?" his mother asked.

"Please."

"That's better."

"Just run him around the block," Berman whispered to Daniel. "Stay off the main streets in case an MP patrol wanders past."

Lovely, Daniel reflected. The officer hands out the treats and the noncom carries the can. "Okay." He finished off the tea and called the boy outside. Ten minutes later they were back. The boy's face was glowing with excitement as he rushed to his mother to tell her about his journey.

"He's going to miss you, both of you," she said, holding the boy close to her.

"You make sure you look after your mother, you hear?" Berman demanded of the boy. "You're the man around the house now. You need anything?" he added to the woman.

She laughed at the question and led them into the kitchen where she opened a cupboard. It was filled with canned food. "What would my neighbors think if they saw this?" she asked. "With Phil up in Scotland and all."

"They'd reckon you were having an affair with a couple of good-looking G.I.s," Berman replied with a straight face. Daniel did not even bother trying to hide his grin this time. It wasn't so much the remark that struck him as funny; it was just that a rabbi had made it. No other rabbi in Daniel's memory would have dared to dream of a line like that, let alone come right out and say it. But then none of them had been Harvey Berman.

They took folding chairs out into the garden. While Berman and Betty talked and enjoyed the summer sun, Daniel played with the boy. It was a strange game the boy wanted to play, and Daniel was certain he would never get the hang of it. There was a bat and a ball, that much he understood. But the bat was strangely shaped, flat and wide. And instead of home plate, the target comprised three ridiculous sticks which the boy planted proudly in the lawn.

"What kind of game is this?" Daniel asked, bewildered by the ritual.

"Cricket," the boy explained solemnly. "You bat first. I'll bowl."

"I thought cricket was played with hammers and hoops in the ground," Daniel said.

"That's croquet," Berman cut in, laughing as he watched the exchange.

"I'm ready!" the boy yelled.

Daniel adopted a baseball batting stance, legs slightly bent, the bat held rigidly by his shoulder. This was a cinch. With a bat this wide it was harder to miss the ball than hit it. He wondered if he could clear the roof of the house.

The boy threw the ball so that it bounced just in front of Daniel. Judging it to be out of the strike zone, Daniel made no move, content to watch it go past. When it struck one of the three sticks, the boy leaped exuberantly into the air. "You're out!" he shouted. "You're out! My turn!"

As he handed over the bat, Daniel didn't even bother to ask why he was out; he was certain he'd never understand anyway. He just looked at Berman and the woman and shrugged his shoulders fatalistically.

"You'd make a wonderful father," Betty Berman remarked. "You've got patience. You should have children of your own."

"One day," Daniel replied. The chaplain didn't know about his marriage to Lucy. Nobody did. And for a while, Daniel had almost forgotten it himself. The woman's friendly words had brought the memories flooding back. With difficulty, he pushed them to the darkest recesses of his mind and turned to face the boy. "I've got to hit those sticks, right?"

The boy nodded.

Daniel decided on a fastball. No point in trying to baffle the kid with a curve when a straightforward fastball would do the trick. He went into a cut-down wind-up and pitched. The boy swung the bat in a futile gesture as the ball whipped past him and shattered the stumps. "You're out!" Daniel yelled. "Give me back the bat!"

To his surprise, the boy threw the bat onto the ground and

jumped up and down in childish anger. "No-ball!" he shouted back at Daniel. "No-ball!"

"Of course it wasn't a ball," Daniel agreed, wondering just what was going on. Patton and the entire Third Army looked like a well-ordered routine in comparison with this game. "It was a perfect strike."

"It's a no-ball!" the boy repeated, tears of frustration beginning to glisten in his eyes. "It doesn't count."

"Why not?" What kind of lunatic game was this where you made up the rules as you went along?

"You're supposed to bowl with a straight arm, not throw the ball like you did." The boy calmed down and demonstrated the correct bowling action. "Like this, see?" Satisfied that Daniel finally understood, he tossed back the ball. Daniel turned to look at his audience again.

"You want to try your hand at this?" he asked Berman.

"What do you take me for, a madman?" Berman's eyes moved away from Daniel, searching for something in the sky. Daniel listened keenly and heard the faint roar of a single-engined aircraft. He swung his eyes skyward and saw an RAF Spitfire at two thousand feet, nose up in a steep climb.

"What's he up to?" he muttered. There were no other planes in the sky that he could see.

"Over there," Berman said quietly.

Daniel followed the chaplain's pointing finger. At first he saw nothing. Moments later, the game of cricket was forgotten as he recognized the small, sinister shape that flitted threateningly across the calm blue sky. Above the rasping note of the climbing Spitfire could be heard a high-pitched, menacing drone.

"Keep on buzzing, you bastard," Daniel whispered between clenched teeth. "Keep on buzzing, you son of a bitch."

He tore his eyes away from the approaching V-1 rocket just long enough to look at those in the garden with him. Even the boy was gazing skyward, mesmerized by the rocket as flame shot out of its rear and its short, stubby wings kept it on a true course. What the hell was the Spitfire pilot planning to do? Ram the damned thing? Daniel recalled reading about one Spitfire pilot who had played chicken with a V-1, touching wings to steer it away from a hospital. The buzz bomb had crashed and exploded on waste ground, and the Spitfire's heroic pilot had lost control of his aircraft and been killed.

Daniel watched the lone Spitfire close in on the V-1. The terrifying drone became louder as the rocket approached. The Spitfire made a single pass before pulling clear, as if the pilot had decided there was nothing he could do that would alter events. No matter where he tried to guide it—at risk of his own life—the buzz bomb would still fall on a populated area; better to leave it alone and pray it had enough fuel to pass clear over the city.

As the V-1 came almost directly overhead, the buzzing began to peak toward a nerve-rending crescendo. Another mile, Daniel prayed. Another half mile. Keep buzzing for another half mile, you fucking kraut bastard. Keep buzzing till you're overhead, then do whatever you damned well want.

Then the buzzing stopped.

In the eerie silence that followed, the Spitfire's straining engine note also seemed to disappear. Birds became silent. The sounds of traffic from the street beyond the house stopped. Everything ceased to exist but that chilling, streamlined shape high in the sky above their heads.

Propelled by impetus alone, the buzz bomb continued on a level course for a few seconds after the flame had burned out. Suddenly the nose dropped. The rocket started to tumble earthward, gaining speed with every second, plummeting swiftly and surely as if it had selected the very spot where Daniel stood as its point of impact. Daniel stared, hypnotized, as the flying bomb grew larger in his vision until it seemed to block out the entire sky.

"Get down!" Berman screamed.

Daniel spun around to see the chaplain wrap his arms around Betty Berman and throw her to the ground, covering her with his own body. Daniel looked for the boy. He was standing rooted to the ground, eyes riveted on the onrushing rocket. Daniel launched himself at the child and pulled him down with a football tackle. A shadow passed over them, a whispering rush of wind as the buzz bomb just cleared the top of the house and crashed into the street beyond.

A tremendous, deafening explosion filled the air. Daniel felt his eardrums smashed inwards. He was lifted off the ground and flung through space. Bricks, stones, blasts of hot air pummeled his body unmercifully. He screamed in fright and pain, and the sound was swallowed up immediately in the roar of the explosion. Through closed eyelids, he saw a vision of the house erupting like a furious volcano. The roof and walls disappeared. Concrete spewed out in all directions. Flames leaped high into the sky. Brighter and brighter still, until it seemed to Daniel that he was being pushed into the very heart of the sun.

Then a second bomb detonated inside his head, and the lights were abruptly extinguished, leaving everything black.

Daniel regained consciousness to the sound of a man screaming for help. He recognized his own voice. He was screaming! He was still alive! By some miracle, he had survived the buzz bomb's blast.

He opened his eyes slowly and saw a shattered pile of rubble where the house had been. Bricks and debris littered the garden. An elm tree lay on its side, sheared off just above the ground. Fences were smashed flat. Houses on either side were damaged, but the Berman's house seemed to have borne the brunt of the explosion.

He tried to stand up. An excruciating pain ripped through his right leg and he collapsed. Clutching his leg, he could feel blood seeping through his trousers. He gritted his teeth against the pain and crawled across the lawn to where the small boy lay sleeping.

"No-ball!" Daniel gasped. "You're still in. It was a no-ball, don't you understand?" He reached the boy and shook him by the shoulders. Blood leaked from his ears and nose. A flying brick had crushed his skull like an egg. Daniel eased the body back to the grass and looked around. Berman was still lying on top of the woman to protect her. Daniel crawled towards them.

"Harvey, get up! We're going to France! Get up!" He shook the chaplain like he had shaken the boy. Berman rolled off the woman and Daniel saw that half of his face was missing. He didn't bother to look at the woman. There was no point; he knew she was dead. He fell onto his back and gazed up at the sky from where death had abruptly appeared. All he could see was cloudless blue, and the Spitfire circling lazily.

The same man's voice screamed again. The sky darkened, royal blue, then indigo and finally pitch black. No stars. No moon. Only an inky darkness that Daniel's tired eyes could not penetrate. He gave up trying. Letting his eyelids slide closed, he surrendered gratefully to the blackness.

When he woke again, the blackness had been replaced by a pristine white. So white that it hurt his eyes. He sat up sharply and pain flooded through his head. Where was he? In bed? Who'd put him there?"

"Feeling better?" a man's voice asked.

Daniel looked around, willing the pain in his head to disappear. He saw a leg, swathed in white plaster, suspended in traction. Beyond the huge, ugly clubfoot, he saw a tall, sallow-skinned man with jet-black hair. "Who are you?"

"Doctor Martinelli. Enzo Martinelli. And you would be Sergeant Daniel Kirschbaum?" The man's accent was almost musical. Daniel struggled to place it.

"How long have I been here? Where am I, anyway?"

Martinelli walked slowly around the side of the bed. "You've been here for two days. And here is a United States Army hospital, near Hitchin, which is northeast of London."

"You Italian?" Daniel asked suspiciously.

"I am."

"What are you doing here?"

"I am not an admirer of *Il Duce*, that is why I am here. I am a refugee." Martinelli gripped Daniel's wrist lightly and checked his pulse. "Are you interested in what happened to you, or would you like to know more about me?"

"What happened?"

"God must love you because you survived. A mild concussion, but very fortunate considering that twenty-eight people died in that V-1 explosion."

"What about that?" Daniel pointed anxiously to the leg suspended above the bed.

"Your leg was broken in two places. Here"—Martinelli

tapped his thigh with a pencil—"and here," he added, touching the ankle.

"Will it be all right?"

"In time. Treatment. Therapy. Exercise to rebuild the muscles that are wasting away right now."

Daniel remained sitting up in bed while he attempted to focus on the events that had put him in the hospital. Two days? Had he really been completely out of it for two days? He ran a hand across his face and fingered the rough beard. Harvey was dead, he remembered that much. So was the woman, Betty Berman, and her son. What would happen to that vacant Jewish chaplain's slot with Third Army now? "Was I brought straight here?"

Martinelli shook his head. "No, you were taken with the other casualties to the nearest civilian hospital. In Dalston, the German Hospital. A good choice of name, yes?"

"Yeah, very good. Then what?"

"The German Hospital notified American military authorities. You were in a coma, but it was decided that you were safe to move. Besides, they needed your bed for civilian casualties. You were brought here."

"How will it look?"

"The leg?" Martinelli smiled thinly. "You will never be asked to model swimwear. Other than that, it will be perfectly serviceable. In perhaps two weeks, you will be able to walk around on crutches. Until then, you must stay in bed and be a model patient."

"Can I write letters?"

"Certainly. I will get pen and paper for you."

"Thanks." Daniel let his head fall back onto the pillow. He'd write to his father. To Moishe and Tommy as well. Those two would be jealous as anything; with this leg, he was going back to civilian life.

Two weeks later, with the aid of crutches Daniel began to walk around the grounds of the military hospital. The weather was warm and he sat in the country setting and played chess or talked with other patients. Often Doctor Martinelli would accompany him on short walks, interested to learn how his patient was progressing.

They talked, and Daniel learned about the doctor's background. Martinelli had practiced for ten years in Milan before clashing with Mussolini. Because of his opposition to the Fascists, Martinelli had been forced out of the medical profession and eventually thrown into jail for a year. After his release, he had slipped across the border into Switzerland, leaving behind his family. Only the burning hope that one day he would be able to return and be reunited with his family kept him interested in living. Each day that passed, as the news from Europe grew brighter, Martinelli became more animated, as if he sensed that soon his exile would be over.

"You play a solid game," Martinelli complimented Daniel after watching him destroy an opponent at chess. "Unimaginative, but very, very solid."

"My father taught me when I was a kid."

"Do you enjoy chess?"

"Not really. Just something to do." Daniel got up from the table and began to hobble across one of the hospital's magnificent lawns.

"Bored already?" Martinelli asked.

"And how. When can I get out of this place and go home?"

"Patience." Martinelli stroked a hand across his chin while he thought. "I am off duty tomorrow. If you are that bored, would you like to spend a day at my house?"

"Why?" Daniel asked. None of the other doctors got that friendly with the patients.

"Perhaps I could teach you to be more imaginative in your approach to chess. Besides, I think we have a lot in common."

"Like what?"

Martinelli smiled and spread his hands disarmingly. "I am an Italian. I love good music. I love to talk about music. A place like this is a wasteland, a cultural wilderness for me. The people who pass through here have a musical education that begins with Tommy Dorsey and ends with Glenn Miller. But you, you were a cantor. A cantor, too, must like music, otherwise he would do something else for a living."

Daniel could see it coming a mile away, like the flying bomb that had put him in this hospital. It was inevitable. It was his father all over again, with the Caruso recordings. Lucy and her Gigli. Now it was Martinelli. Why did everyone try to force it down his throat? But he found it impossible to refuse. Martinelli was as lonely and frustrated as he was; a kindred spirit crying out for company with which he had something in common.

"All right," Daniel agreed. "But I warn you right now, I'm not interested in that kind of music."

Martinelli affected an air of amused disbelief. "Everyone is, Daniel. It just takes some people longer than others to realize it."

The following morning Martinelli picked Daniel up at the hospital and drove him to the house he rented three miles away. Daniel was glad to get out of the hospital grounds, but the ride made him homesick. Autumn was just beginning, and the leaves were starting to turn; the golden brown colors reminded him disquietingly of fall back in the States. Soon, he assured himself. Just a little bit longer while this damned leg heals and I'll be back there.

He had already written to Harry Feldman at the Temple Isaiah in Paterson to say he would be returning soon. It was a letter acknowledging defeat. He had gone away wanting to use the time to think about his career; instead, he had become even more deeply entrenched in the field of religion. Perhaps he was fated to grow old in Paterson and marry one of Feldman's nieces.

"We have arrived," Martinelli said grandly as he swung the rickety Austin into the drive of a large farmhouse. Daniel had never seen anything like the house. The grounds seemed to extend forever, and the house looked like it had been painstakingly built by hand. The walls were made of odd-sized pieces of dark gray stone, and the roof—he couldn't believe it!—was thatched.

"Rustic is how a house salesman would describe this piece of property, I believe," Martinelli said, reading Daniel's thoughts.

"Doesn't the roof leak?"

Martinelli's expressive face creased up into a broad smile.

"Only when it rains. Come inside, Daniel. Really, it is quite civilized."

Daniel followed the doctor into the house. It was exquisitely furnished with solid, old-fashioned pieces that had been lovingly polished until they shone with a luster from deep within the wood. Martinelli proudly explained that one of his hobbies was restoring antique furniture.

"A glass of wine?" he asked Daniel.

Daniel accepted. As he looked further around the house, he marveled at the weeks and months that Martinelli must have spent in restoring some of this furniture. He played a few notes on a gleaming mahogany grand piano, then he wandered into another room where he saw an oak dresser that was awaiting attention. The wood was badly scratched, the varnish almost gone. Daniel tried to guess how much time Martinelli would spend restoring this piece—and even more important, where did he find the time to locate all these old pieces and restore them? He always seemed to be at the hospital. Did the man never sleep?

"Ready for a game?" Martinelli asked. "We shall learn if Italian inventiveness is any match for solid American play."

"Sure."

Martinelli set out the chess pieces and invited Daniel to sit down. Before he joined him at the table, he went to the phonograph and selected a record.

The sound of a clarinet, very quiet, very slow, came from the phonograph. Automatically, Daniel tapped his foot in time with the familiar piece of music. "'Avalon,'" he said. "Al Jolson had one hell of a hit with this number."

Martinelli sat down and studied the chess board. "Mr. Jolson also paid out a very substantial plagiarism settlement—I recall it was twenty-five thousand dollars—to the estate of Giacomo Puccini. Listen more closely, Daniel."

Daniel paid more attention. It wasn't "Avalon" after all, although the first notes had sounded exactly like it. It was something else, a piece of music so terrifyingly familiar that it made his skin go cold. "What is this called?" he asked Martinelli.

"'E lucevan le stelle.'" Martinelli did not notice the

different mood that had settled over Daniel. "Sung beautifully by, of all people, a Swede. Bjoerling."

"From *Tosca.* The third act."

"Very good." The Italian doctor looked at Daniel with a new awareness. "I think that you know more about opera than you are willing to admit." Only then did he notice the change in Daniel. "Is something wrong?"

"My wife left this record, by Bjoerling, playing on the phonograph when she smothered our baby daughter and then committed suicide," Daniel explained simply. "She threw herself out of the window and broke her neck."

Martinelli got up quickly to reject the disc, but Daniel told him to leave it playing. "When did this happen?" the doctor asked, returning to his seat.

"Four years ago, no, five now. Exactly five years ago. Lucy, my wife, was disturbed. We had a terminally ill child and Lucy had taken it really badly, much more than I realized at the time." He paused and looked hard at Martinelli. "Do you really want to hear all this?"

"Only if you really want to tell me."

Daniel found it easy to talk. Something about the Italian inspired trust and confidence. "Lucy had been wrapped up in this kind of music all of her life. Her father's a violinist with the Metropolitan Opera House in New York, and she'd been planning a career of her own before we got married. I think one thing led to another with the baby, until illusion took over from reality. Lucy saw herself as a tragic figure, like the singer Tosca. She identified so much with the character that I'm certain she didn't know what she was doing. She even left me Tosca's farewell words scrawled in lipstick on the dressing table mirror in the bedroom before she jumped."

"'*O! Scarpia, avanti a Dio*'," Martinelli murmured. "What was wrong with the child?"

"Tay-Sachs disease. Lucy smothered her with a pillow, then took her own life. All while this goddamned record was playing away."

"I see. Where were you?"

Daniel felt sweat break out on his forehead and above his mouth. He considered lying. Martinelli would never know. But he could see that Martinelli expected the truth; to tell him anything else would be an insult. "I had a club date that night. In Harlem, singing at a joint called the Deuces Wild. Afterwards, I spent the night with a woman I'd met there. You see," he added quickly, trying to justify his confessed infidelity, "Lucy wouldn't let me near her. She hadn't for ages because she blamed me for the baby's illness. I met this other woman and . . . you know."

"Tragic," Martinelli said quietly. "Tell me something, do you feel guilty about it? Do you feel it would not have happened had you stayed with her?"

"I don't know what I feel anymore. At first, I probably felt more sorry for myself than anything else. Now, I don't know. It's like a dream. Something that never really happened."

"Until you heard that recording again?"

Daniel nodded. "That's about it." He tried to lighten the mood by adding, "He's got a beautiful voice, though."

Martinelli caught on; there was nothing to be gained by delving further into such a sensitive subject. He leaned back in the chair, relaxed as he recognized safer ground. "In my opinion, for what it is worth, Bjoerling is the finest tenor since Caruso."

"Caruso was my father's favorite," Daniel said, smiling as he remembered his father citing Caruso's career when he had defended Daniel against the rabbi for singing "Ave Maria." "My father would sit in the corner by the old phonograph and listen for hours on end."

"What was his favorite aria?"

"'Rachel, quand du seigneur', from *La Juive*," Daniel replied. "Lucy named our daughter—at my father's suggestion—Rachel, after the opera."

"Halévy. French opera." Daniel could swear a disparaging note had appeared in Martinelli's voice. "Not bad, mind you, but nowhere near as fine as Italian opera."

"What others are there?"

"Austrian." Martinelli shrugged his shoulders to dismiss that country's contributions. "And, of course, there is German opera and Wagner."

"No good?"

"Wagner was a Nazi a long time before Hitler's name was known," Martinelli replied. "Wagner is a patron saint of

Nazism. He had even given them the music to do their obscene goosestep by." He stood up, the chess game forgotten. Walking to the phonograph, he selected another record. "Is this aria familiar?"

Daniel listened. There was no mistaking the voice; he'd heard Caruso too often in Claremont Parkway not to be able to recognize him. "*Aïda?*" he asked hesitantly.

"*Aïda,*" Martinelli concurred. "From the first act, 'Celeste Aïda', by Giuseppe Verdi." He said the composer's name with a flourish, reveling in its pronunciation. "The warrior Radames has been chosen to lead the Egyptian army into battle with the Ethiopians. And in his moment of supreme glory, all he can think of is Aïda, the Ethiopian slave girl whom he loves. It was the grandest of all grand operas. Tell me, Daniel, do you know why Verdi was the greatest operatic composer who ever lived?"

Daniel shook his head. He could not even think of another opera written by Verdi. If Martinelli had not told him that Verdi had composed *Aïda*, he wouldn't have known that either.

"Verdi filled his operas with human conflict and emotion as well as glorious music. Look at Radames. He is in love with an Ethiopian girl and thrilled to be leading his country into battle against the Ethiopians. Puccini makes you listen, but Verdi, the master, makes you think." Martinelli walked around the room as he spoke, hands clasped behind his back like a schoolteacher instructing a class. Daniel watched in fascination.

"Did you ever study Shakespeare at school, Daniel?"

"Only when I couldn't cut classes."

Martinelli chuckled at the honesty of the answer. "Too often subjects are taught before a pupil is old enough to appreciate them. They are forced on a child until he grows to detest them." He caught himself as he realized he was digressing. "Verdi's finest moment in dramatic opera came when he made use of Shakespeare's *Othello* and wrote *Otello*. There is one part of the opera—when Otello the Moor is being manipulated by Iago, the man he believes is his friend—where Verdi surpasses Shakespeare for drama and tension. To do that, a man must be more than mere genius, Daniel. He must be a god. And Verdi was a god."

To his surprise, Daniel found himself enjoying the lecture. He had become infected by Martinelli's quiet but forceful enthusiasm for the subject. Lucy, with her pointed nagging, had only served to alienate him from opera. Sure, the music was nice sometimes, there was no denying that, but in between the big numbers he had always found it boring, heavy going. Even his father had failed to generate any interest in him. Somehow, Martinelli was succeeding where all others had failed. The Italian doctor had so much genuine love for opera that his listeners could not help but be swayed.

"What other examples are there of this conflict?" Daniel asked.

"With Verdi? In *Rigoletto*, of course," Martinelli replied. "Rigoletto, the court jester, plans revenge against the man he hates, the Duke of Mantua. But Rigoletto's daughter, Gilda, unknown to him, is in love with the duke. When she finds that her father has arranged for the duke's murder, she takes his place under the assassin's knife."

"Puccini doesn't have this?"

"Puccini has love and sadness. But Verdi mixes in enough internal conflict to keep Sigmund Freud busy for a century."

"Who else is there? Composers, I mean?"

"How many days do you have to sit there and listen to the answer?" Martinelli asked in reply. "Italy breeds magnificent composers like America grows wheat."

Daniel inclined his head in acceptance of the reply. "Who else do you like, then, other than Puccini and Verdi?"

"All of them," Martinelli replied frankly. "There are the *bel canto* composers such as Donizetti and Bellini, where wings are given to song."

"What's *bel canto?*" Daniel asked, his interest growing in spite of himself.

"Precisely what it sounds like. Beautiful singing. It is really a term to describe the Italian operas composed during the first half of the last century, where the music allowed the singers the opportunity to reach every high note as many times as possible. Before Wagner and his heavy-handed Germanic nonsense assaulted our eardrums."

"What else is there?"

"*Verismo*," Martinelli replied. "Realism. *Pagliacci* by Leoncavallo is *verismo*. A group of strolling players, minstrels, clowns—on the surface they laugh for their audiences, while underneath is burning tension. Here, I will show you." He reached into the records and selected another aria. Daniel recognized Caruso again. "'Vesti la giubba,'" Martinelli explained. "A clown crying inside because his wife is unfaithful, while all the time he must show his clown's face to the public."

Daniel cupped his chin in his hands while he concentrated on the music. There was no need to understand Italian to know what was happening. The meaning was unmistakable. The depth of expression contained in Caruso's voice put across the message as clearly as if he were singing in English.

"You like it?" Martinelli asked, pleased by Daniel's rapt attention.

"I've never listened to this music in quite this way before," Daniel admitted. "You should be a teacher, not a doctor. You give it meaning."

"Could a cantor sing like this? With this depth? With this warmth? With this"—Martinelli clenched a fist—"feeling? Could you?"

Daniel was uncertain how to answer. He sensed that the Italian was goading him. "In a temple, yes."

"But you are not in a temple now," Martinelli said quietly. "You are standing alone in the center of a magnificent stage. You are in La Scala, in Covent Garden, in your own country's Metropolitan Opera House. Out there"—he indicated an imaginary audience with a wave of his hand—"are thousands of people, sitting, waiting. They are not waiting to hear a cantor, Daniel. They are waiting to hear a tenor, an operatic tenor with such brilliance in his voice that he is going to thrill them to the bottom of their boots. Could you do this?"

The gauntlet had been thrown down, the challenge made. Daniel knew there was no way he was going to refuse it. He struggled to his feet, leaning heavily on his crutches as he glared defiantly at Martinelli.

"You're damned right I could!"

Chapter Nineteen

Had Daniel ever given any serious thought to reincarnation, he would undoubtedly have placed Eli Kawolsky's soul into the body of Enzo Martinelli. Working with Martinelli was like being with Kawolsky all over again, starting from the very beginning and learning the basics before he could proceed to the next step.

Martinelli arranged with the hospital administration for Daniel to be allowed leave whenever the doctor was off duty. Daniel ate in the farmhouse with the thatched roof, worked in it and sometimes even slept in it. He listened to Martinelli's recordings for hours on end, wearing out needles by the boxful, reading each corresponding libretto, memorizing words, phrasing, pronunciation. When he had mastered one aria sufficiently, Martinelli would switch off the phonograph and turn to the grand piano to accompany Daniel as he rehearsed. Sometimes the Italian would smile. At other times he would scowl and scold his pupil, cajole him into improvement. Always there was encouragement, though, a compliment, a pat on the back that somehow made the arduous and unfamiliar work bearable.

The plaster cast came off Daniel's leg and he began to hobble around with a walking stick while he underwent therapy to rebuild the wasted muscles. As Martinelli had promised, the right leg would never be seen in a beachwear advertisement, but Daniel was not unduly concerned about the scars that marked where bone had pierced the skin. His only concern was that the leg was functional. It was sore, but it worked.

"Your period of convalescence is almost over," Martinelli said one morning as he examined Daniel's leg in the hospital. "In two weeks' time, you should be fit enough to go home, back to America for your discharge."

"Bet you wish you were going home as well, eh?"

"My time will come," Martinelli promised. "Very soon.

What will you do when you return home?"

"Hack around for a while, I guess," Daniel answered. "Till I get the feel of things again. Then I suppose I'll start working. I had a letter from the president of the temple where I worked, saying they were waiting for me."

"A cantor." Martinelli shook his head sadly.

"What's that supposed to mean? What else can I do?"

Martinelli looked up at the ceiling and closed his eyes in resignation. "If you have to ask me a question like that, Daniel, you deserve to remain a cantor all your life."

"Hey, come on," Daniel protested angrily. "You got me interested in opera, okay. You gave me a reason why it should be taken seriously. Leave it at that and don't push your luck."

"Daniel, do you believe that I would ever look at another sick person again if I had a gift like yours?"

"A gift!" Daniel shook his head in exasperation. "If I had a buck for every time someone told me I had a gift, I'd be the richest man in the world."

"Daniel," Martinelli said quietly, "it is a gift. From the same God who decreed that you would live through that explosion. If it were mine, I would keep on trying, even if I knew I might eventually die penniless and starving. I would chase the dream until I either caught it or my heart gave out trying. A million people can stand up in a church or a temple and lead a congregation in prayer, but only one person in that million can sing a 'Vesti la giubba' with such fire and passion that only the deaf would not break down and cry. You know what grief is, Daniel. You've lived through it. You know what triumph is as well. Translate those emotions into action, sing like you sang for me, and you can catch that dream."

Daniel was frightened by Martinelli's passionate outburst. Not fear caused by the doctor's intensity, but a nagging, gnawing apprehension that Martinelli was right. Uncertain how to reply, he sought refuge in sarcasm. "What am I supposed to do about it? Turn up at the Metropolitan Opera House and say that Enzo Martinelli sent me along for an audition?"

Martinelli ignored the gibe. He pulled a sheet of paper from his pocket and began to unfold it. "This hospital is holding a

Thanksgiving Day party two days before you are shipping out. After the meal, there will be entertainment. Some of the staff and patients play instruments. There will be a USO show. And you"—Daniel dreaded what he knew was coming next—"will sing. I will accompany you."

"I can't! For Christ's sake, I'll forget the goddamned words!"

"Too late." Martinelli showed him a piece of paper. "There it is, in irrevocable black and white. Official. Top American and British brass will be present. So will local dignitaries. You cannot back out." He dropped the paper onto Daniel's lap and stood up to leave. By the door, he turned around. "If you are worried, I will rehearse with you. We will be doing four arias. From *Bohème, Tosca, Rigoletto* and *Pagliacci*. You know them well enough by now."

"What if I screw up?" The possibility terrified Daniel. It didn't matter that he would never see any of these people again; but he would have to live with the memory of failure.

"Then you will remain a cantor for the rest of your life," Martinelli replied coldly. "And I think that is what you fear most. But you would have had your chance."

The day before Thanksgiving Daniel sat quietly in the hospital's recreation hall, reading a reference book of opera loaned to him by Martinelli. He scanned each page quickly, seeking familiar mentions. Most of the contents were foreign to him, with only the Italian composers and some of their works sounding familiar. Of the three tenors he knew—Caruso, Gigli and Bjoerling—only the first two were listed. Daniel surmised that Bjoerling's omission was a deliberate snub by the book's Italian editors of a non-Italian. Only when he read the copyright notice at the front of the book did he realize it had been published in 1929, before Bjoerling had made his debut.

Setting down the book, Daniel began to think about the Swedish tenor, recalling the records Martinelli possessed. The doctor had several famous arias recorded by all three tenors, and Daniel had compared styles with the thought of copying one of them before deciding to create his own style. He knew he was in no position to make such a judgment, but he always seemed to enjoy Bjoerling's performance more than those of Gigli and Caruso. The Swede's voice had a clear beauty to it, like the ring of fine bone china or expensive crystal when a fingernail is flicked against it. Bjoerling, Daniel decided, would have made a fine cantor.

He heard footsteps crossing the recreation hall and looked up, expecting to see Martinelli checking up to ensure he was studying. Instead, he saw a soldier with captain's bars striding across the hall; as he walked, he pushed heavy glasses up his nose as they threatened to slip off.

"Moishe!" Daniel got out of the chair to greet his friend. "What are you doing here?"

"I got transferred to London, Staff Judge Advocate's office. Had to get up to see you before they sent you home, you lucky bastard. Let me look at you." He stepped back to inspect Daniel. "You've lost some weight, which is a vast improvement; otherwise you're as ugly as ever."

"How long are you staying for?"

"Why?"

"I'm giving a concert tomorrow. After the turkey."

"Yeah?" Moishe's face split into a huge grin. "Want an accompanist, kiddo?"

"I've already got one, an Italian doctor who's been treating me. Besides, I don't think it's your kind of music." He took Moishe's arm and guided him to the bulletin board. "Take a look."

As Moishe began to read, his mouth dropped. "You're putting me on," he finally said. "What are you getting mixed up in this kind of garbage for? A bet?"

"No bet. It's a long story. Sit down and I'll tell you all about it." Daniel began to explain about Martinelli, the first visit to his house and the way the doctor had fired him up. Moishe kept shaking his head and muttering that he didn't believe it; they'd both become entangled in each other's bad dream, and when they woke up they'd be back in the States.

"Will you at least stick around and listen to me?" Daniel begged. "I'm dreading it. But it'll go a damned sight easier with one familiar face in the audience."

"Kiddo, this familiar face is going to be laughing itself sick," Moishe promised. "How could you do this to me? Being a *chazan* was bad enough. I nearly gave up on you then. But this, this . . ." The impossible had happened. Words, at last, failed Moishe.

"Moishe, you're not going to believe this, but . . ."

"Carry on and tell me," Moishe said resignedly. "After this, I'll believe anything. Tell me Hitler's a Jew and I wouldn't bet a plugged nickel against it."

"I'm getting to like the stuff, Moishe. There's meaning to it, excitement."

"Where do you keep your brains? In your legs?"

"What's that supposed to mean?"

"That's where you wrote and told me you'd been hit, wasn't it?" Moishe asked. "Because something sure as hell messed up your brain, whatever there was left of it."

"Just stay and listen to me, that's all I ask."

"Okay. I'll stick around for the comic relief. But if I walk past you on the street without saying hello once we get home, you'll know why."

"And don't laugh while I'm singing, or I'll bust your glasses again."

The threat had no impact on Moishe. "Danny boy, while Uncle Sam's paying my medical bill, you can bust all the glasses you like. If I feel like laughing, I'll damned well laugh."

"You laugh just once and I'll break your scrawny neck," Daniel promised. "See if Uncle Sam foots the bill to replace that!"

During the Thanksgiving dinner, Daniel made two unscheduled excursions from the table to the bathroom. The first time Moishe followed him, standing by while Daniel locked himself in a cubicle, the victim of a nervous stomach. The second time Moishe just let him go. If he was worried about singing real music, Moishe could understand. But to be nervous about singing this crap? The turkey and cranberry sauce needed Moishe's undivided attention far more than that turncoat did.

White-faced and sweating uncomfortably underneath his

uniform, Daniel returned from the bathroom. He looked at the head table where Martinelli sat. Intent on conversation with the red-robed mayor of Hitchin, the doctor did not even notice Daniel's beseeching glance. It's all right for you, Daniel thought, pushing away the remainder of his meal. You're not going to stand up there and make a fool of yourself. All you've got to do is play piano; you can cackle with the rest of them if I miss a high note or fluff a line. Yet deep down, Daniel recognized this to be a lie. Martinelli was as nervous as he was; he just refused to show it. He was Martinelli's protegé, the teacher's prize pupil about to show what he had learned. If he failed, the teacher, too, would share in the shame.

After the meal, while hospital staff and patients mixed in the recreation hall with the visiting dignitaries—Daniel counted two American generals, a British brigadier and a flock of colonels and majors—Martinelli introduced Daniel to the mayor. "This young man is going to prove, alas, that my own country does not have exclusive rights on beautiful singing."

Listening to Martinelli build him up, Daniel's confidence rose. His nervous stomach had subsided and the perspiration had dried. "I thought a Swede had already proved that."

Martinelli smiled hugely. "Any man who can sing like Bjoerling has to have at least one pint of Italian blood coursing through his veins. Perhaps he had a transfusion when he was a child, who knows?" Martinelli glanced at the mayor and realized the worthy gentleman was having difficulty in following the conversation; it didn't matter. "What about your parents and grandparents, Daniel? Who was Italian among them?"

"Nobody. My mother's family's Russian . . ."

"Of course," Martinelli nodded. "Your baby."

"My father's from Rumania."

"That explains it," Martinelli said with the air of Sherlock Holmes solving an almost unsolvable case. "Rumanian, like Italian, is a romantic language. They are very much alike. Do you speak Rumanian?"

Daniel shook his head.

"Perhaps it is just as well. As an American, you will bully Italian pronunciation a little. As a Rumanian, you would crucify it."

Martinelli remained effusive while he introduced Daniel to other guests. Daniel prayed silently that he could live up to the doctor's expectations. He knew the four arias Martinelli had selected by heart, as well as two more he could use as encores. Encores? The idea struck him as ludicrous. Would anyone be that desperate to hear him sing again? That was one worry he would not have with Moishe.

As the first part of the show was about to begin, Daniel took a seat next to his friend. "When are you on?" Moishe whispered.

Daniel stared at a Negro sergeant on the stage who was playing the piano in a respectable imitation of Fats Waller; the poor bastard had lost a leg in France. "Last. After the USO show."

Moishe's eyebrows lifted at the significance of the reply. "Top billing, Danny boy. Couldn't have done better for you myself. Mind you, if you're lucky, everyone might have left by then."

"Shut up!" Daniel hissed.

Halfway through the USO show, Martinelli came over to Daniel and tapped him gently on the shoulder. Daniel nodded, stood up and discreetly left the hall. He walked to the other end of the hospital, where the sounds of the USO show were so faint as to be inaudible, then he locked himself in a small room which the nurses used for coffee breaks.

For all of a minute, he stood perfectly still, enjoying the total silence. Moishe would be wondering where he'd gone, rushing off like that. Maybe he'd think he had been taken sick again, and go chasing off to the bathroom to find him. Daniel pushed the thought from his mind as he concentrated on Martinelli's instructions. Loosen up your voice. Do ten minutes of exercises right before you go on; there's nothing more embarrassing than a tenor with a tight voice that cracks the moment he opens his mouth.

Daniel hoped that nobody was passing by the small room. If they heard him preparing for the recital, they'd break down the door or call the MPs because someone was being tortured to death inside. He began to practice scales, softly to start with, gradually giving them more air. Kawolsky had made him do this as well. Up and down. Down and up. The voice became stronger, more confident. The noise that battered back at Daniel from the walls sounded like anything but a lyric tenor limbering up his vocal chords before a performance. Did Bjoerling go through this ritual each time he performed? Did Gigli? Had Caruso? He had never done it before a service in the temple, so why now? It all seemed so foolish and unnecessary.

Despite his doubts, Daniel persisted. From slow scales, he switched to *arpeggios*, chords whose notes follow in swift succession, then he sang the opening lines of each aria he would perform.

A knock sounded on the locked door. Martinelli's voice called Daniel's name. Daniel stopped singing and opened the door.

"I think you are ready," the doctor said.

"How long have you been listening outside?"

"All the time. I wanted to be certain that you did your exercises and did not cheat." The smile that Daniel would have expected with such a comment did not materialize. Martinelli was deadly serious. "You are loose enough. Let us go back into the hall."

Daniel followed the doctor back to the recreation hall. The USO show was almost over. Daniel took an empty seat next to the aisle. He saw Moishe look at him and give the thumbs-up signal; he grinned in response.

The USO show ended and Martinelli climbed onto the stage. "Honored guests," he began, inclining his head respectfully toward the mayor and the high-ranking British and American officers, "hospital staff members, patients. Ladies and gentlemen. You all know Sergeant Daniel Kirschbaum. He has been here long enough to become part of the staff. We are glad that he is leaving this hospital in a few days to return home. Before he departs, however, he is going to give us something that we will remember him by for as long as we live." Martinelli stopped talking and looked at Daniel while he let the audience's anticipation build up.

"I am delighted that I may have been instrumental in guiding Sergeant Kirschbaum along the first steps of a road that will—and I am certain you will agree with me after hearing him—eventually lead to the most famous opera houses of the world. Daniel, will you come up here, please?" Martinelli waved him toward the stage.

A muted, uncertain round of clapping greeted Daniel as he walked carefully up the steps to where Martinelli stood. He had discarded the walking stick for the day, and could move comfortably as long as he put no excess strain on the injured leg. Lifting a hand to acknowledge the applause, he watched Martinelli settle himself at the piano.

"Remember, you are on the stage of an opera house, Daniel. You are not in a temple," Martinelli whispered. "No cantor tricks here. Think of Bjoerling. Keep it clear, keep it simple, and do not be afraid to let your voice ring full. *In bocca el lupo.*"

Daniel turned to face the audience. Somewhere out there was the only friendly face he knew, Moishe, with captain's bars gleaming on his shoulders. If he had been sitting in the very center of the front row, though, Daniel would not have recognized him. All he could visualize were the hills of Rome, as he looked out over the ramparts of the Castel Sant' Angelo. It was the hour before dawn. He was no longer Sergeant Daniel Kirschbaum; he was Mario Cavaradossi, the artist, scheduled to face a firing squad at dawn. Now, when death approached with unfaltering steps, he would lament that he had never loved more deeply in his life.

As he began "E lucevan le stelle," he clasped his hands together. They fell away almost immediately, back to hang motionless at his sides as he remembered Martinelli's advice. Let the audience hear you mentally, not see you visibly. Do nothing that might detract their attention from your voice. In an opera you act; in a recital you stick to singing.

Before he realized it, the aria was finished. He stood perfectly still before looking back over his shoulder at Martinelli for the verdict. The Italian slowly nodded his head in satisfaction. From the audience came the sound of chairs scraping on the wooden floor. The applause was louder this time, but to Daniel it still sounded alarmingly faint. Quickly he crossed the stage to where Martinelli sat.

"What's wrong?"

"Nothing is wrong. You were perfect."

"What about them? They're clapping like zombies."

"Most of them have never heard opera," Martinelli explained. "They were not sure what to expect. Be patient. Give them time to adjust."

"How much time, for God's sake? I'm only doing four songs."

"Four arias. There are no songs in opera. There are arias." Martinelli thought for an instant. "Change around. Instead of leaving 'La donna è mobile' until last, do it now. Liven them up."

Daniel returned to center stage. Martinelli's sprightly introduction began and Daniel launched himself into the opening lines. This was an aria he had particularly enjoyed learning, one that bounced with zest and fire. He changed his technique and focused on the audience instead of trying to think himself into a character. His eyes sought out Moishe . . . and he could not believe what he saw. Moishe was moving his head up and down in time with the music. And he was smiling encouragingly.

That was all Daniel needed to restore the confidence that had dropped after the mediocre reception to "E lucevan le stelle." Daniel put more into the song. The acoustics in the hall were bad, but he didn't care. If he had Moishe wrapped up enough to keep time with the music, there was nobody in the hall he could not reach.

He was right. A loud, spontaneous burst of applause greeted the end of the aria. Daniel took a step backward in amazement at the strength of the ovation. He sneaked a look at Martinelli. The Italian doctor was sitting stiffly at the piano, his face devoid of all expression. Then, very slowly, he moved his head toward Daniel. "See?"

Daniel stretched his arms wide in recognition of the applause. He wanted to embrace the audience, to hug each member, to make love to each and every one of them. Never before had he experienced a thrill quite like this one. There had been applause at other times, but never like this.

Gradually the ovation began to die. Before it could peter out into a single embarrassing handclap, Martinelli cut it short by playing the introduction to "Che gelida manina" from *La Bohème*. Daniel dropped his arms and fixed his attention on a pretty blonde nurse in the front row, singing to her alone. At first she blushed and looked around awkwardly, perplexed by the attention. Daniel smiled inwardly and carried right on. Soon he had her total attention. She was unable to tear her eyes away from his face as he sang beautifully of the Bohemian poet's life, his hardships, his aspirations.

Again the applause increased in volume and duration. Martinelli took advantage of it to call Daniel to the piano. "Listen carefully to me. You spiced up their lives with 'La donna è mobile.' You thrilled them—especially that blonde nurse, I saw—with 'Che gelida manina.' They are yours, Daniel. You own them all. Now make them cry. Wring tears from their eyes. Twist their hearts and tear them apart."

"Vesti la giubba." Daniel took a few seconds to think himself into the role of Canio, the clown who must hide his sorrow and anger from an audience which expects nothing but entertainment. Daniel's own audience was out there beyond the stage, but his heart was not full of sorrow. It was full of joy. He had ascended a new height, climbed it with ease. How could he feel sorrow, know what Canio was supposed to feel when the only sensation he had was delirious happiness? Triumph instead of bitter grief?

He looked down at the blonde nurse as he sought the inspiration needed to feel grief. She was gazing raptly at him. Moishe? His friend had his glasses off, wiping them. When he replaced them, pushing them back up his nose in that characteristically businesslike manner, Daniel's memory flashed back to a hotel in the Catskills. Moishe arguing finances with Joey Bloom and winning. Fat Benny and Tessie, Bloom's friends and finally his victims. Daniel looked down at his wrist and saw Fat Benny's gold watch. That was enough, all that he needed to find the proper mood. He swallowed hard, choked back his feelings and signaled to Martinelli that he was ready.

More passion went into that single aria than Daniel had ever realized he possessed. As he sang, a series of haunting, painful flashbacks unrolled across his vision. Fat Benny's funeral when he had cried like a baby while conducting the funeral service. And Tessie, when he was too worn out to cry anymore. The baby, and Lucy lying still and cold on the concrete patio. Lieutenant Berman and the family he had found in London. The child who'd thrown down his bat in disgust and screamed that Daniel had thrown a no-ball; the same child who seconds later was lying dead. Daniel wondered what had happened to Phil, the woman's husband, the child's father.

The aria died away into complete silence. Daniel wiped the back of his hand across his eyes and was not surprised to find them damp. He swung around to check with Martinelli. The Italian smiled while he gently dabbed his own eyes.

"*Bravo*," he whispered. "*Magnifico.*"

Daniel held up both hands like a triumphant boxer to ward off the devastating applause. It had been slow in starting, a lag of a few seconds while the audience shook off the aria's bewitching spell. Now people were pushing back their chairs to stand up and clap. Daniel saw the mayor, the British and American officers, the pretty blonde nurse. As one, they were clapping him enthusiastically, shouting to demand more.

Sensing that Daniel was confounded by the tumultuous reaction, Martinelli left the piano, walked to the front of the stage and held up his hands for silence.

"Daniel," he whispered as the audience began to settle. "You have admirers. Speak to them."

Shaken far more than Martinelli had imagined by the response, Daniel found it impossible to say a word. He tried to speak but his throat closed up. Simple words of gratitude that could never express his feelings refused to leave his lips as easily as the arias had flown from them. In desperation, he bowed stiffly and walked hurriedly from the stage, leaving Martinelli alone.

The Italian leaped after Daniel and caught him in the corridor outside the hall. "They are calling for you, Daniel. Listen."

Daniel paid attention to the noise which swept out of the hall into the corridor. A steady rhythm of applause had taken over, and the word "Encore!" was repeated again and again.

"They will not allow you to go," Martinelli said. "Give them an encore, and only then will they be happy."

"I'm scared," Daniel confessed. "I'm terrified of going back in there to sing again."

"Why?"

"Because . . ." Again Daniel could not find the words. "I've never known anything like this. It's awesome. Look at me, will you? I'm a full-grown man and I'm almost blubbering like a little kid."

"That's the cantor speaking, Daniel, not the lyric tenor. A cantor is not used to applause; it frightens him. A tenor expects it as his due. Blow your nose and go back inside," Martinelli said sternly. "The people in there expect it of you, and you cannot—dare not—disappoint your audience." He marched away and reentered the hall. Daniel watched him go, debating whether to follow him or turn tail and run, hide until it was time for him to be shipped back to the States. Taking a handkerchief from his trouser pocket, he wiped his eyes, blew his nose and steeled himself to return to the stage.

As he appeared in the doorway, the noise increased. He stared straight ahead, not daring to look at the audience in case his nerve cracked. He climbed onto the stage and the roar became deafening. Only when he reached the center of the stage and looked out over the audience did the noise begin to subside.

"'Nessun Dorma,'" Martinelli whispered.

"Nessun Dorma," from *Turandot.* Puccini's final opera, Daniel remembered reading. The composer had died before finishing it and the score had been completed by someone else. None shall sleep until the Chinese Princess Turandot learns the real identity of the Unknown Prince.

The audience became still as Daniel's voice rang out once again. They were satisifed. They had refused to let him go until he had sung one more aria; and now he was back, offering them another piece of music that would help them forget for a few seconds, a few minutes, the war that raged across the world.

The roar of "Encore!" erupted again as the aria finished. Helplessly, Daniel looked to Martinelli for guidance. He only knew one more aria.

Martinelli nodded. "*Aïda.*"

It had been a wise judgment to leave this particular aria until last, Daniel decided. Nothing in the world could climax "Celeste Aïda." Even without the trumpet fanfare that went with the score, it was the most glorious of all the arias he had learned. Martinelli was right about the opera—it was the grandest of all grand operas. The cast alone would more than fill this hall. The scenery Daniel had studied in Martinelli's reference book would dazzle the eyes of even the most jaded spectator; massive, imperious structures that brought alive the might and splendor of ancient Egypt. He sought out the nurse again. She would be his Aïda, just as she had been his Mimi. He wondered if she understood a single word of what he was singing.

"Thank you. Thank you very much," he said simply after finishing the aria. There were demands for more encores which Daniel rejected with a weak shake of the head. Even if he knew any more off by heart, he was certain that he no longer possessed the strength to get through them. His leg hurt and his entire body seemed numb, as if he had taken a physical battering. Never before—not even during the day-long *Yom Kippur* service—had singing exacted such a price.

Martinelli took over. The doctor clapped his hands loudly until he had the audience's attention. "Ladies and gentlemen, I urge you all to remember this day well. In ten years time—no, in five, even—you will have to give Daniel Kirschbaum the entire City of London to make him sing those six arias in a recital." He gripped Daniel by both hands and looked deeply into his eyes. For an instant, nothing else existed for either of them. There was no audience, no sound of continuing applause and echoing demands for yet another encore.

"Daniel, you have repaid your teacher abundantly. God gave you a wonderful gift. I am grateful that it was my privilege to teach you how to unwrap that gift."

"I'll remember."

"Be certain you do." Martinelli's eyes crinkled into a half smile, but Daniel knew the Italian was not joking when he said, "Otherwise I will come after you with a sharp scalpel to remove those wonderful vocal cords and give them to a man who is more appreciative."

"You're really going to do it, aren't you, kiddo?" Moishe said as he climbed into the taxi that would take him to the station in time for the London train.

"Damned right. I'm going back to New York and I'm going to hammer on the doors of the Metropolitan Opera House until the bastards let me in."

Moishe studied his friend and shook his head emphatically. "There you go again. Act first and think afterwards. Do you want some advice? Really good advice?"

"What?" Daniel asked suspiciously as he saw Moishe trying to cut himself in for another ten percent. Even with three thousand miles of water between them, Moishe would still want to run his career.

"Don't hammer on any doors." Moishe closed the taxi door and leaned through the open window. "Just stand outside the Met and sing like you sang in there. They'll send out a squad of strong-arm goons to drag you inside before you can get away from them." The taxi moved off and Daniel waved.

"See you Stateside!" Moishe yelled. "You're still going to need a good agent, you classical creep!"

Chapter Twenty

A dismal, bone-chilling rain swept across New York City as Daniel limped cautiously down the gangplank of the U.S. Navy transport ship which had brought him from Southampton in England. Seeing the walking stick in his hand, the cluster of people on the dock stepped aside respectfully to let him through. Sympathetic glances were sent his way; complete strangers patted him on the shoulders and back, and said, "Well done, buddy. Welcome home."

Daniel paid scant attention; he nodded automatically and smiled every few seconds. He had spotted his father from the rail of the ship, standing alone by a Cadillac limousine; now he pushed his way through to the spot.

Isaac Kirschbaum blinked back tears as he watched his son emerge from the knot of people and approach. Behind the glasses, his eyes flicked painfully to the walking stick that Daniel used. He felt the burning fire himself, the pain that his son must have endured when the bomb exploded so close to him. Thank God he was going to be all right. Isaac closed his eyes and offered up a silent prayer of gratitude to the good Lord who had seen fit to bring his son home safely.

Five yards away, Daniel dropped the stick to the ground and opened his arms wide to embrace his father. Unaware of what was taking place around them—of other just as joyful reunions—father and son hugged each other tightly, each, at last, acknowledging the reality of this long-anticipated meeting.

"You look wonderful, Daniel. I could hardly tell which leg was the injured one," Isaac lied.

"In a few weeks time, you won't be able to see a thing." Daniel studied his father for a long moment. Isaac had aged considerably in the two years since he had last seen him. "How's Ma?"

"As usual. She would be here but she was scared there would

be a big crowd. You know how she is about crowds."

Daniel said nothing. Yetta Kirschbaum would have found an excuse to avoid meeting him even if he was arriving alone. She had not changed a bit, not that she ever would. If she could not be the center of attention, she would much rather be somewhere else. "What do you hear from Jack?"

"A very busy man, your brother. A captain in the engineers. Somewhere in Europe. He wrote that he tried to get leave to visit you in England while you were in the hospital, but too much was happening with his unit."

"I'll bet it was," Daniel said. "They're running around repairing all the bridges the Nazis are blowing up as they retreat." So Jack was also a captain. Everyone in the world was a captain except him. But he was home. "Moishe came up from London to visit me."

"Good. You must have been happy to see him." Isaac motioned to the limousine. "Get in the car. We can talk on the way home."

"You drove?" Daniel asked in amazement. "And a Caddy?"

"Sure. Without a license I drove down here," Isaac answered, and Daniel noticed the uniformed chauffeur for the first time. His father was making certain that his homecoming was accomplished in style. "Mr. Feldman's been telephoning every day," Isaac said as the limousine cleared the dock gates and picked up speed. "Do I know exactly when you're coming in? he asks. Do I know if you'll be able to go back to Temple Isaiah straightaway? Do I know if you'll be able to stand up for an entire service? Thank God you're home, Daniel, because I'm running out of answers for the poor man."

"I'm not looking forward to seeing Harry," Daniel said softly. "Something else has come up."

"What do you mean?"

"Long story, Pa." Daniel smiled wearily and laid his arm affectionately around his father's shoulders. "You remember the old vaudeville line, a funny thing happened to me on the way to the theater?"

Isaac nodded, although he had no idea what Daniel was talking about.

"Well, an even funnier thing happened to me on the way to

the hospital."

Daniel was content to loaf around for a month while he exercised his leg and became accustomed to civilian status again. When he traveled to Paterson to see Feldman, he told the temple president he needed at least another two months to recuperate properly. That way, Daniel saw himself as carefully hedging his bets. Two months would be more than enough to learn whether he had the glorious career in opera that Martinelli believed he did. And if things did not work out, he would be able to resume at the Temple Isaiah where he had left off, without Feldman being any the wiser. If he was successful? Daniel was certain Feldman would not want to stand in his way. Not that he could.

Daniel was so glad to be back in the United States, even living in the same apartment as his mother was bearable. Yetta Kirschbaum cooked for him, cleaned for him and left him alone, with barely a word exchanged. When friends visited the apartment, though, she was quick to point out how her son had sacrificed himself for his country.

By the end of the month, the leg was strong and the limp had disappeared. Daniel could run up the stairs without difficulty, and long walks around the old neighborhood had toned up the wasted muscles. Soon, he told himself; soon he would begin to pursue Martinelli's dream. But right now, it was easier to sit in the apartment's living room and listen to his father's records, those now familiar arias, and bask in the still warm memory of the reception he had been given in the army hospital in England.

When he returned from one of his walks, a Western Union cable was waiting. Puzzled, Daniel opened it. The message area contained a one-word query. "Well?" The signature block just read, "Enzo."

"Pa, I'm going to need your help," Daniel said to his father when Isaac returned home from work that evening. He showed him the cable. "Enzo's trying to light a rocket under me."

"Good!" Isaac exclaimed, nodding his approval of the Italian's message. "I was wondering when you would decide to do something. You think that you can pursue this grand career you spoke of by sitting around here all day listening to real tenors? What help do you want?"

"I've got to see Joe Feltz."

"Why? You've hardly spoken a word to him since Lucy passed away. Why now?"

His father was right, and Daniel knew it. Since Lucy's death, he had cut all ties with her family. "I need him, Pa. He's the only person I know who can give me a push in the right direction, open a door or two for me. I need an introduction from him, and I'm too scared to go in alone and ask for help."

"I don't think you're scared, Daniel. Ashamed is the word you should be using," Isaac reminded his son. "All this time you haven't bothered with the man. Now, when you want something, you decide to knock on his door."

"Will you come with me or not?"

"What help could I be?"

"If you're with me, maybe he'll think twice before slamming the door in my face."

"Daniel, have I ever refused you anything when it was in my power to grant it?" Isaac asked. Daniel shook his head. "This time I must. If you want that man's help, you must go alone to ask him. You are taking the first step toward what your Italian friend believes will be a marvelous career. It is a step you must take all by yourself."

The noise of the bell echoed inside the apartment, then Joe Feltz opened the door. He looked at Daniel without the faintest sign of recognition. "Yes?"

"Mr. Feltz, it's me, Daniel. Daniel Kirschbaum."

Feltz began to close the door.

"Mr. Feltz, I have to speak to you urgently." Daniel moved a foot into the opening before his father-in-law could swing the door shut. "It's about Lucy," he added quickly, seeing a way he could get Feltz to receive him. If he wouldn't listen for Daniel's sake, he'd listen because of a wish his late daughter had once cherished.

The door opened wide again. "What about Lucy? Didn't you do enough to her already?"

"Please, may I come in and speak with you?" Daniel asked. He felt foolish standing in the hallway while he tried to plead his case.

"What is it about Lucy?" Feltz asked. "Tell me before I let you in."

"She always wanted me to follow a certain direction with my singing. I've learned that she was right."

Feltz's face assumed a puzzled expression. Daniel decided to press his attack harder.

"Opera, Mr. Feltz. Lucy was right when she said I should try for an operatic career."

"So you come to me hoping that I might know someone who'll give you a good break, is that it? I should put in a good word for you?" Despite Feltz's negative response, the door remained open. "We've already got Jan Peerce, and his brother-in-law, Tucker, is making his debut in a few days in *La Gioconda*. I don't think the Met has room for any more New York Jewish tenors."

Daniel selected his next words very carefully. Feltz was the only contact he had within the mysterious world of opera. Without Feltz's assistance, he would be forced to use normal channels—and God alone knew how long it would take to meet anyone who mattered through normal channels. If his own personality was any criterion, all musicians had egos the size of the Empire State Building. Didn't Feltz love to perform, to hear the applause just as he did? Wouldn't he want to be the man who could say he had introduced a shining new talent? "Okay, Mr. Feltz. I guess I'll have to try my luck with the 'Metropolitan Opera Auditions on the Air' that Sherwin-Williams sponsors." He turned around and walked slowly toward the stairs.

"Wait!" Feltz stepped out into the hallway. "Come inside. I want to know what made you change your mind."

Daniel entered the apartment and walked down the long, familiar hallway into the living room. Pictures of Lucy were everywhere, interspersed with photographs of Rachel before the disease had struck and wasted her away. He picked up a photograph taken of Lucy in her wedding gown as he gazed into her face, so serene and guileless, a face that could never mirror the tragedy that lay behind it. Was it guilt he still felt? he asked himself. Guilt that he had really been responsible for Lucy's plunge from the window? Guilt that if he had stayed in that night—and not gone to the Deuces Wild with Moishe and bedded the woman he met there—Lucy would not have jumped? Or would she have chosen a different time? Another day when she was left alone to consider her broken dreams?

"Please don't touch the photographs," he heard Feltz say. "It was bad enough that you touched my daughter. At least leave her memory alone."

Daniel replaced the picture gently on the sideboard. "Mr. Feltz, I didn't push your daughter out of the window. It wasn't solely my fault that we had a sick child. Sure, I'm sorry everything turned out the way it did—I'd be a sad case if I wasn't—but I don't carry all the blame."

Like Daniel's father when he had seen him at the dock, Feltz looked older. His face was more lined, the hair thinner, and his breath was labored as he sat down and looked at a group of photographs, forgetting that Daniel was even in the room with him. "You know," he said in a quiet voice as if thinking out loud, "Lucy had her heart set on being a soprano at the Met." He turned around in the chair and gazed up at Daniel. "When she married you, she gave it all up. I begged her to carry on, but by the time she started lessons again it was too late. It's only because of Lucy that I'm even listening to you. Lucy believed you had the talent, the voice to become a great tenor. I thought you did, too. Maybe we were right, maybe we weren't. But what I want to know now is why you changed your mind."

"Someone had the time and patience to spend a few weeks explaining opera to me," Daniel answered simply. "The way they told it to me, everything made sense for the first time in my life."

"Pity you couldn't have seen the same sense half a dozen years ago," Feltz murmured. "Then maybe Lucy would have been able to live her dreams through you." Feltz's eyes became sharper as he shrugged off the painful memories. "So, you turn up here expecting me to fix you up with an audition, is that it?" He did not bother waiting for Daniel to answer. "Just what makes you think you wouldn't show yourself up if the Met gave you an audition?"

"Because I'm good."

"Who says? What companies have you sung with?"

"None."

"On the strength of a cantorial career you want to walk

straight into the Met, is that it?"

"I had a very successul recital in England."

"Where? Covent Garden?"

"In the hospital where I was recovering from injuries I got in an air raid."

Daniel's reference to being wounded made no impression on Feltz. "A hospital? Are you serious? You want me to approach a man like Edward Johnson, the general manager of the Metropolitan Opera Company, and risk my good name on what you felt was a successul recital in a hospital concert? You're mad."

"Sorry I bothered you, Mr. Feltz." Daniel turned toward the door. Now he knew why Feltz had invited him in. To poke fun at him, to gain revenge in some small way for losing his daughter and grandchild. Daniel hoped the old man had enjoyed it.

"But . . ."

Feltz let the word hang in the air as he waited for Daniel to turn back. "My Lucy, *olova sholom*, thought you had it in you to make the grade. That means more to me than any review you could bring."

"You'll help me then?"

"Yes, I will. But not at the Met. At the Grand, instead. I know the manager there, Hammersley, very well."

Daniel had heard of Roger Hammersley, an English-born tenor who had sung with Covent Garden before moving to the Grand Opera Company of New York as general manager eight years earlier. Before Hammersley had arrived to take control, the Grand had been in imminent danger of going under in the face of competition from the Met. The legends had all appeared there—Caruso, Galli-Curci, Gigli—but the Grand's glory had been in its illustrious past, with very little in its future. Hammersley had altered the swing of the pendulum. As an immigrant, he had decided to show how fond he was of his new country by encouraging American talent, grooming domestic singers. While the Met had continued to display mainly European stars, Hammersley's Grand had successfully promoted Americans.

"I'd be very grateful for any help you could give me," Daniel said.

"You can thank Lucy, not me," Feltz retorted. "It was her dream. What you want is incidental."

The Grand Opera Company of New York had been established in 1895 to compete with what were then the two major companies—The Academy of Music and the Metropolitan Opera Company.

The company's original building, Grand Opera House, had stood for thirty years in Union Square before a fire—started accidentally during the ship-burning scene in Act Two of *La Gioconda*—had gutted the building in 1925. Following this, the company had ceased production for two years while new premises were located and refurbished. In 1927, the new Grand Opera House was opened on West Thirty-fourth Street and Herald Square. What had been a deserted warehouse was reconstructed internally on the lines of the original Grand Opera House with donations from wealthy patrons.

The entrance to the opera house on Thirty-fourth Street was unimpressive. Daniel stood uncertainly outside the row of glass doors as shoppers and office workers filed past. Peering into the lobby, he could see ticket offices and the highly buffed marble floor, but he had been expecting more. This was an opera house, a center of culture. There should be beautifully sculpted cornices, stained glass windows, an atmosphere of history and legend that you could see, that you could feel with your bare hands.

He looked for a final time at the billboard outside the entrance—which announced that evening's performance of a new production of Puccini's *La Fanciulla del West*—then gathered up the courage necessary to push open the door and enter. The woman behind the ticket cage looked optimistically at him. Daniel paid her no attention. He walked up the stairs to the left side of the opera house and entered the auditorium. When he emerged in the second ring, the view was breathtaking. A sea of red velvet and gold trim greeted his eyes. He stood perfectly still, taking in everything in one awestruck glance. The pictures he had seen of opera houses, the scenes his own imagination had conjured up, paled into insignificance beside his first real view. Even empty of patrons it was magnificent. Like a temple, yes! But like a temple that had been designed by God himself.

The gold curtain was down. Cleaning staff wandered along the rows of seats and through the boxes, making certain everything was prepared for that night's performance. Daniel pulled down a plush red velvet seat and dropped into it. He closed his eyes and pictured the opera house full of people, the excited buzz before the curtain rose, the rousing applause that followed each aria and act, flowers tumbling from the boxes onto the stage, rousing chants of "bravo" from an ecstatic audience that would not allow a singer to leave without one last bow.

"Who are you?"

A man's brusque voice intruded into Daniel's reverie. He turned around and saw one of the cleaners.

"I've got an appointment with Mr. Hammersley."

"You won't find him here," the man said. "Now, would you mind moving yourself so I can sweep along this row?"

Daniel stood up to let the man pass. "Where is Mr. Hammersley's office?"

The cleaner gestured toward the opera house's vaulted ceiling with a thumb. "Go up to the next floor. You'll find the executive offices there."

Daniel left the second ring, climbed another flight of stairs and followed a broad red arrow that pointed to the offices. In the reception area, an elderly man sitting behind a desk looked up as Daniel approached. "Can I help you?"

"My name's Daniel Kirschbaum. I've got an appointment with Mr. Hammersley."

The man rang through on a telephone. He spoke for several seconds, then looked at Daniel. "You're early. Sit down over there. Mr. Hammersley will call you when he's ready."

Daniel sat down heavily in an overstuffed armchair, dusty and splitting at the seams. On the table next to him was a disorganized pile of old opera programs. He looked at one, then tossed it back, preferring to watch the seemingly never-ending procession of people who rushed along the corridor to offices he could not see. Some were carrying sheets of music, others cowboy costumes; one man even struggled with a heavy table which Daniel could hear banging along the walls until its carrier finally reached wherever he was going. All looked panic-stricken, as if their own particular problem was the only one that mattered. A woman scurried past holding two six-guns. Daniel remembered that *La Fanciulla del West* was opening that night, and the guns and costumes he was seeing must belong to the set; the table, too. He grinned as he imagined himself wearing one of the costumes.

"Mr. Kirschbaum?"

He looked around as his name was called. A young woman had appeared in the mouth of the corridor. She beckoned to him. "Mr. Hammersley will see you now."

Daniel got up from the chair, dusted off his suit and followed the woman. She turned into a clutter-filled room, leading Daniel across it to the general manager's office. Opening the door, she ushered him inside.

The small office was almost a replica of what Daniel had seen outside in the reception area. Costumes littered nearly all of the available space; they were draped over part of the desk and covered all of the filing cabinets. Cardboard cartons occupied a complete corner of the room. As Daniel looked around in confusion, Roger Hammersley pushed a pile of costumes off his desk to create some space and stood up to greet his visitor.

"If you weren't in this business yourself, Kirschbaum, I'd apologize for the mess. But you obviously know what a new production's like."

Daniel had no idea what a new production was like, or any production, for that matter. But he was not about to air his ignorance. He shook the hand Hammersley offered and looked around for a seat. Hammersley told him to throw a mass of costumes onto the floor and use the armchair they had been occupying.

"So, you're a tenor, Joe Feltz tells me." Hammersley placed his hands together and rested his chin against them while he studied Daniel. "What operas do you have in your repertoire?"

"None as yet," Daniel replied. "I've been sticking to recitals."

"Recitals, eh?" Hammersley's startlingly bright blue eyes twinkled merrily beneath bushy white eyebrows. His hair was as white and shaggy as his eyebrows, but his face was surprisingly unlined. Daniel guessed him to be no more than fifty. "Isn't that something like learning to run before you can walk?"

"One recital only," Daniel said quietly. And there goes this interview, he thought dismally. "But I suppose Mr. Feltz told you that."

"No. He didn't tell me very much at all," Hammersley admitted. "All he said was that you were a young cantor with an exceptionally beautiful tenor voice, and that you had suddenly discovered opera."

"That's about the size of it," Daniel agreed. "And I think I'm good enough to create an outstanding career for myself."

"Confidence! That's what I like to hear," Hammersley laughed. "Never knew a good tenor yet—even myself—who didn't have more than his fair share of it. How well do you know Joe Feltz?"

"He was my father-in-law. I thought he would have mentioned that."

"No, he didn't." Hammersley took a while to digest the news. "That would be Lucy?"

Daniel nodded, but he made no attempt to enlighten Hammersley further.

"Terribly sad affair, that," Hammersley murmured. "Tragic." He perked up and looked directly at Daniel. "I'm prepared to give you an audition because I'm always interested in new American talent. What selection from your recital career would you like to do?"

"'La donna è mobile' and 'E lucevan le stelle.'"

Hammersley waved a hand airily. "One will be sufficient."

"'La donna è mobile.'"

"Very good. Come downstairs and we'll set it up."

In the auditorium, Hammersley led Daniel up onto the stage and placed him in front of the lowered gold curtain. Daniel gazed out into the dimly lit opera house. The only movement came from the cleaners who went about their work as if nothing extraordinary was taking place. To them it wasn't, Daniel realized. They had seen and heard some of the greatest while they were pushing their brooms. What does the name of Daniel Kirschbaum mean to them?

"I'll find someone to accompany you on the piano." Hammersley walked quickly from the stage, leaving Daniel entirely alone. As he looked up at the closest boxes, his imagination started working again. They were filled with people, faces leaning over to watch and listen just to him. Musicians were seated in the orchestra pit, strings, brass and percussion, all looking at the pied piper in white tie and tails whose magical baton gave them direction. Behind the conductor, the seats were filled as far as the eye could see. And above, in the second, third and fourth rings.

A movement in the orchestra pit broke Daniel's concentration. The filled opera house disappeared and the cleaners were back again. A woman slid behind the piano and lifted the keyboard cover. Daniel suddenly wished it were Moishe who was accompanying him. Where was Moishe now, anyway? Still in London, handling courts-martial, and probably slicing ten percent off anyone he got acquitted? With Moishe here, he'd feel more at ease. Or Martinelli. The Italian doctor would know the music better than Moishe did. Instead, it was a woman he'd never seen before in his life, and Hammersley was sitting out in the opera house, a dozen rows back from the orchestra. Daniel's whole career could be shot down before it even got off the ground because of a woman he'd never seen before.

"Kirchbaum!" Hammersley called up to the stage. "We're ready whenever you are. Haven't got all day, you know."

Behind Hammersley, Daniel saw the cleaners turn to look at the stage. They would compare him with the others they had heard, Gigli, and Caruso for those who could remember back that far. His first audience inside an opera house consisted of a woman who might or might not be able to play the piano, a bunch of menial workers and a general manager who wanted to get back to his office so he could chase after other, more important affairs.

"I'm ready." Daniel closed his eyes to gather concentration. The last things he wanted to see were the cleaners leaning on their brooms while they judged him. He heard the standard introduction to the aria and coughed quickly to clear his throat. Martinelli, where are you? Daniel's heart screamed out as his lips began to sing the words of Verdi's buoyant, lecherous duke. Help me, Enzo! For God's sake, help me!

Hammersley was out of his seat before the last notes had left Daniel's mouth. "Thank you, Kirschbaum, very nice!" he called out, clapping his hands. "We'll be in touch with you."

Daniel was numb as he watched Hammersley stride from the auditorium, followed by the pianist. He'd blown it, ruined the chance he'd been given. Not a word of praise, not a single syllable of encouragement. He didn't know if he'd sung well or not; he'd been so keyed up he had not heard a single note. What was the point in wondering how he'd sung, he told himself. He knew. It must have been lousy, judging from the way Hammersley had rushed out.

On leaden legs, Daniel climbed down from the stage and started to walk toward the exit to the lobby. For all the attention the cleaners paid to him, he might just as well not have been there at all. They didn't even notice as he passed by.

Outside, on the street, he pulled up his coat collar against the blustery wind and headed for the subway. He'd go back to Claremont Parkway from where he would call Harry Feldman in Paterson. It was time to become a cantor again.

And Enzo Martinelli? The Italian's dream was for someone else, some other tenor. It was not for Daniel Kirschbaum.

That first Sabbath morning service as cantor at Temple Isaiah was like putting on a favorite coat again. Daniel just slipped into it as if he had never been away. His former landlady still had his room waiting for him, and Daniel eased gently back into the community. There were new faces, and the familiar faces were older, but the overall atmosphere of the community was as comfortable as he remembered it.

"Nice service," one member of the congregation said as he shook Daniel's hand.

"Glad to have you back."

"Missed your voice."

"Thank God you're back in time to sing at my son's wedding."

Daniel accepted the compliments gratefully. He needed them, needed every assurance he could get. Here, at least, he was wanted; he had a home. He should have seen that earlier on, before chasing after some dream that he could never hope to attain. Operatic tenors didn't suddenly appear. They started young, brought up in the lore and tradition of Verdi and Donizetti. Nobody abruptly switched from being a cantor to a

Radames or a Turiddu, without the slightest background to help make that change.

Another face appeared in front of Daniel, one of the new members whom Daniel did not remember from his early days at Temple Isaiah. Wearing an expensively cut pinstripe suit with an unusual black derby hat, the man extended his hand as all the congregation members had done.

"You conduct a beautiful service, Kirschbaum. Didn't understand a single word of it, mind you, but it was beautiful."

"Mr. Hammersley! What are you doing here?"

"You gave me an address on Claremont Parkway in the Bronx. I expected to find you there."

"I went back to my old job."

Hammersley looked around the quickly emptying temple. "So I see. Your father told me where I could find you. I thought I might as well see how you performed in your own environment."

"Why?" Daniel gave a wry smile. "Are you thinking of putting on *La Juive?*"

"Not yet. In fact I don't even know where I could use you yet, but I'm blasted certain I could use you somewhere. I'd like to discuss contracts with you."

"I didn't think you were interested."

"I most certainly was. Your voice is an exceptionally clear instrument which carries a wealth of expression. It's a little rough around the edges, but careful tuition will cure that. I rated your performance at the audition very highly, but when you've only got a few hours to unscramble a year's worth of problems with costumes, scenery and prima donnas, I'm afraid you don't give very much time to aspiring tenors who are suddenly shoved through your letter box. You will forgive me, I trust?"

Forgive the man? Daniel was ready to throw himself on bended knee and kiss Hammersley's highly polished wingtips; he was prepared to worship and give thanks to another human being in the very place where he normally worshipped God.

Hammersley waited in the temple foyer while Daniel changed from his robe, then they walked together toward the town center. "Do you have a good memory?" the general manager asked. "There's a lot more to opera than just learning the big arias."

"I'll study."

"And as I said before, you need tuition. Do you have a good voice teacher?"

"Not at the moment."

"I'll fix you up with a good one. And there's one other thing, of course." Hammersley twirled a rolled-up umbrella as he walked. Daniel watched, amused as he thought what other people must be thinking about Hammersley; they'd never seen anything quite like him in Paterson before.

"What's the one other thing?"

"Your unfortunate allocation of a last name, my dear fellow. I'm afraid that Daniel Kirschbaum doesn't have quite a dramatic enough ring to it. No offense, of course," he added quickly.

"What's wrong with Kirschbaum?"

"Nothing, nothing at all!" Hammersley exclaimed. "For a cantor it's a simply marvelous name. But the Grand doesn't want a cantor—we want an outstanding American tenor. Look at Jan Peerce over at the Met. Did you know his real name is Jacob Pincus Perelmuth?"

"A Jewish name's no good then?"

"It's as good as any other if it has the right ring to it. Did you ever hear of Jean de Reszke?" Daniel shook his head. "Turn-of-the-century tenor, sang everywhere. He had a Polish name I wouldn't want to pronounce even if I could. He tried a couple of other names before he settled on de Reszke. A good name helps to give stage presence."

Daniel remembered the old candy store on Fordham Road and a conversation he'd once had with Aunt Tessie. "How about Kerr?" he asked Hammersley. "Daniel Kerr."

"Daniel Kerr. Let me see, Daniel Kerr." Hammersley tried the name a few times for effect. "Not bad. Not bad at all. Any particular reason why you chose that one?"

"Ellis Island."

"Ellis who?"

"Ellis Island, where they used to process the immigrants," Daniel explained. "If the immigration officer who processed my family hadn't spoken Yiddish, I'd have been called Kerr now anyway."

Hammersley started to laugh. He clapped Daniel delightedly on the shoulder and rocked back and forth on his heels. "Very good. That's where we English have an advantage when we come to the Colonies. We speak almost the same language. Come to my office on Monday morning, about ten. We can talk contracts then."

Hammersley saw a passing taxi and waved with his umbrella. "Don't forget, ten on Monday," he called out as the cab began to move. "See you then, Daniel Kerr."

Daniel waved as the taxi drove off. He'd made it after all. Wouldn't those cleaners at the Grand get the shock of their mundane lives when he appeared there again. They'd all given him up for lost, and now he was going back. He quickened his pace, eager to be home. First he would write a letter to Martinelli. Then, after Sabbath had terminated and he'd finished his cantorial duties for the weekend, he would drive over to Claremont Parkway and share the marvelous news with his father. Even with his mother. What about Feldman? Thought of the temple president diminished the elation Daniel felt. If he had never returned to Temple Isaiah there would be no problem. But he had returned; he'd shown the community he had come back for good. How could he tell Feldman that he no longer wanted the position?

By the time he arrived home, Daniel had reached a decision. It was a compromise but a decision nonetheless. He would sign the contract Hammersley was offering, and he would arrange to continue as a cantor. Only when he was forced to a decision regarding the cantorial life did he realize how much he loved and relied upon it for his strength. Obviously, the run-of-the-mill Sabbath services would be out. He'd be expected to save his voice for the Grand. But he would still be able to conduct High Holy Day services. And Feldman—pragmatic businessman that he was above all else—would revel in having an operatic tenor as his cantor for *Rosh Hashanah* and *Yom Kippur*.

Easier in his mind, Daniel sat down to write the letter to Martinelli. After a few lines he threw down the pen. He'd cable Martinelli instead. There was no sense in making the Italian wait for up to a month to learn how right he had been.

Part Two

The Bent Nail

Chapter One

The tea had been allowed to grow cold.

Roger Hammersley picked up the dainty Royal Adderley cup and looked suspiciously at its contents. The ring of congealed milk floating on the top deterred him from drinking. With a faint expression of disgust he replaced the cup in the saucer and pushed it away. Then he lifted his eyes to glare across the desk at his visitor.

"Daniel Kerr, exactly one year ago a promising young tenor entered this office because he had suddenly discovered the beauty of opera. So far, The Grand has offered you three roles in this season's productions and you have yet to accept one. Exactly what, in the name of all that is holy, are you interested in doing?"

Daniel mulled over the question while he tried to think of the best reply. He had known immediately why Hammersley had called him to the office. His constant refusal to accept any of the roles that the company had offered him during his first season with the house. "I'm not interested in minor parts," he said eventually.

Hammersley blinked at the audacity of the answer. "Just because a certain role is small in volume does not mean it is minor in impact," the general manager pointed out. "The lamplighter in *Manon Lescaut* is hardly minor when one recalls that Jussi Bjoerling used it for his debut in Stockholm in 1930. Unless, of course, you regard Bjoerling as a minor artist."

Daniel shook his head vehemently. "No, sir. I do not. He's an exceptional artist." He had gone to see Bjoerling at the Met following the Swede's return to the United States after the end of the war. What he had listened to on Martinelli's records in England had been nothing short of an insult to the power and clear quality of the barrel-chested Swede.

"What about the other two roles we offered you?" Hammersley asked. "Parpignol, the toy vendor in *La Bohème?*

Or Borsa, the courtier in *Rigoletto?* Are they also too minor for your consideration?"

"Who debuted in them?" Daniel wanted to know.

"I made my Covent Garden debut as Parpignol." Hammersley's bushy white eyebrows bristled threateningly for an instant. "Daniel, I am forced to be brutally frank with you. This house's board of management is becoming increasingly impatient with a contracted tenor who simply refuses to perform. You are being paid one hundred and twenty-five dollars a week while you are permitted to continue your career as a cantor. We have bent over backward to accommodate you. So what is it you want from us?"

"I want a lead role." Daniel realized he was playing a dangerous game as he pushed brinksmanship to its extreme limit. At the end of the New York season in April the Grand Opera Company might simply choose not to renew his contract. When the others went away on tour, he would be left behind; a cantor in Paterson, still no further along the road to an operatic career than he had been when he'd returned from Europe. If he accepted a smaller role, though, he feared that he would be stuck forever in a rut. He was in a win or lose situation; for him, place and show did not exist.

Since being accepted by the Grand, Daniel had studied diligently with a voice teacher recommended by Hammersley—Enrico Rosati, who had coached Gigli and Lauri-Volpi. He had learned the lead roles of Chevalier des Grieux in *Manon Lescaut* and Rodolfo in *La Bohème*—two of the current productions—in the hope of being chosen. But despite his constantly improving artistry and his obvious willingness to learn, Daniel had only been offered supporting roles by Hammersley. The major parts had been given to established tenors. Other newcomers to the company had accepted the minor roles eagerly, but Daniel remained a stubborn holdout. It was a calculated gamble on his part; he would settle for nothing less than the best.

"As I have stressed to you countless times there are no lead roles available this season," Hammersley told Daniel. "Now that the war is over, we are settling down to something approaching normality and are planning our productions a year in advance. There is nothing for you this season. Look"—he softened his voice as he tried to place himself in Daniel's position—"I also wanted a lead role when I started. Who doesn't? But the Covent Garden management was not about to push some established tenor out into the cold to make room for me. I had to wait my turn, work for it, just as you will have to." Against better judgment, Hammersley reached out for the cup and drank the cold tea. He grimaced sourly at the taste.

"Daniel, I thought that by concentrating on American talent—with only the minimum imported—I would be able to avoid the problems that have plagued the Met in recent years. Prima donnas who feel they're too important for such mundane events as rehearsals, a complete breakdown of discipline. You're going all out to prove me wrong." Hammersley spread his hands on the desk top and smiled sympathetically. "I hired you because I believed you had the potential to become an outstanding tenor, given hard work and the time to mature. But this cuts both ways. You have to bend a little as well. Leads will come, I promise you."

"I'm sorry, Mr. Hammersley, but I'll settle for nothing less. Tucker over at the Met got a lead role the first time out, as Enzo Grimaldo in *La Gioconda.* And he was a cantor as well."

"Then I suggest that when your contract at the Grand expires at the end of this season you approach the Met. I'm sorry too, Daniel," Hammersley said, closing the discussion, "but we cannot allow you to run before you've learned how to walk."

After leaving Hammersley's office, Daniel trudged disconsolately down to the auditorium. The same cleaners who had been working when he had taken the audition a year earlier were still pushing their brooms, and he was still unknown to them. Just being among the cast would not have helped either. Who knew anything about a tenor singing Parpignol? Who gave a damn? Only the lead artists were known and admired, talked about and celebrated. Nobody except the immediate family and a couple of close friends cared about who sang the lamplighter.

The knowledge that he would have to write to Enzo Martinelli in Milan increased Daniel's dismay. A reply to the

Italian's last letter was almost a month overdue, put off again and again as Daniel waited in vain for a break. What would he tell Martinelli this time? That the Grand's management was still saving him for something special? Or that his career with the company was almost through? Visions of Martinelli stepping off an ocean liner in New York with a shining scalpel in each hand did nothing to ease Daniel's misery. Even his father said nothing now, but Daniel knew that his continuing refusal to accept a minor role aggravated Isaac Kirschbaum as much as it did Hammersley.

He left the opera house and looked along West Thirty-fourth Street for a taxi. Seeing none, he walked toward the subway entrance at Herald Square, momentarily cheered as he recalled a story Hammersley had once told him about the conductor Thomas Beecham trying to find a cab to take him to the Met for a rehearsal during the war. The cab driver had explained that because of gas rationing he was forbidden to take anyone to a place of entertainment, to which Beecham had frostily replied that going to the Met was not entertainment—it was a penance. Obviously Hammersley still regarded it as such, constantly criticizing the Grand's competing house for its lack of discipline and control over its artists and technicians.

Daniel changed his mind about the subway and started to walk the ten blocks north to Times Square. He went slightly out of his way to pass the Metropolitan Opera House on Thirty-ninth Street and Seventh Avenue where he stopped to look at the aging yellow brick building. The sidewalk was almost completely blocked with theatrical sets; pedestrians were forced to walk in the gutter as the opera company's technicians prepared for that night's production. Daniel looked at the label stuck on the back of one set—*Il Trovatore*, it read—then he tried to peek inside the building. A burly man in a worn suit barred entrance. Hands jammed deeply into his coat pockets, Daniel walked away, irked by the knowledge that had Hammersley given him one of the leads that season, the man in the worn suit would have been more respectful.

In a few days, he would be thirty-one years old. That was almost ancient for an operatic debut. Bjoerling had been only nineteen. At nineteen, he could afford to accept a minor role like the lamplighter. Even then, that small part had been followed a few weeks later by a starring role as Don Ottavio in *Don Giovanni*. At thirty-one, Daniel could not afford the luxury of starting at the bottom. He had to begin high up the ladder. There was no longer the time to make it step by step.

Entering the lobby of a building on West Forty-fifth Street, between Sixth Avenue and Times Square, Daniel ran up the stairs to the second floor. He still found it amazing how Moishe had managed to get back his original office after closing up the law business for four years. Having enlisted so early, Moishe had been among the first to be discharged, as a major; he had even turned down the opportunity to participate at a junior level in the war crimes tribunal. Back in New York, he had taken a lease on his old office, traced his former secretary and persuaded her to work for him again and gone back to civilian life as if he had never been away.

"What's doing in the world of highbrow wailers?" Moishe greeted him.

"Nothing. And that's the problem." For the first time, Daniel noticed how sparse Moishe's hair was becoming on top. When he had seen him in England, at the hospital over Thanksgiving, Moishe's hair had been cropped short, disguising the onset of baldness. Now that the hair was growing back to its normal, unfashionably long style, the patch of scalp in the center was more noticeable. The sight of the bald spot confirmed Daniel's earlier feelings. They weren't kids anymore; and he could not settle for a minor role. Time just wasn't on his side.

"Pull up a chair," Moishe invited. "This lawyer's time and advice are at your disposal."

Daniel sat down and let out a long, painful sigh. "I've been given what amounts to an ultimatum."

"Take whatever the company offers you or get the hell out?" Moishe guessed.

Daniel nodded. "I've turned down three roles so far this season. Walk-ons in *Bohème*, *Rigoletto* and *Manon Lescaut*." He knew the names meant little to Moishe. "And I sweated blood to learn the major roles in *Bohème* and *Manon Lescaut*."

When he paused, Moishe waved a hand at him to continue.

"So I'm being given a last chance. To do the lamplighter in this season's final production of *Manon Lescaut,* or get lost."

"When's the production?"

"Two weeks' time."

"So take the lamplighter, then," Moishe suggested to Daniel's amazement. "At least it'll get you on the stage."

"For a minute or two, that's all." Daniel felt as if he was arguing with Hammersley all over again. He had expected support from Moishe. Support for his own point of view, not for the company's. "I don't want the lamplighter, Moishe. Any cretin can do that. I want des Grieux, the hero of the opera, the main tenor role."

"Who's singing des . . . des . . . ?"

Daniel helped him out. "Des Grieux. Cesare Scarlatti, an Italian tenor. Which makes the whole damned business even more ridiculous. Hammersley's always going on about pushing domestic talent, yet he hires Scarlatti as soon as he returns from Europe."

Moishe knew of the Italian tenor, but not through any operatic fame. Cesare Scarlatti had sung in New York during the thirties before going home to Italy at the start of the war in 1939. In the fall of 1945, he had returned to New York to resume his career, expecting the same adulation he had received before. Instead, his first appearance had caused near riot-level demonstrations outside the opera house and police had been called to escort the terrified tenor into the building.

"Daniel"—Moishe pushed the glasses to the top of his nose—"tell Hammersley that you're willing to sing the lamplighter or whatever. Make your peace with the man. You need him right now a hell of a lot more than he needs you."

"Are you serious?" Daniel spluttered. "Whatever happened to the grandiose schemes that were the hallmark of Moishe Wasserman?"

"I buried them with the name of Moishe Wasserman," Moishe answered quietly. "Maurice Waterman thinks with his head, not with his heart. And it wouldn't be a bad idea if Daniel Kerr did the same thing. Just suppose that something comes up? Someone falls ill, maybe, and they need an understudy? How can they call on you if you're not there? Go back and tell your man that you'll take whatever he gives you. Go on, beat it. I've got other work to do."

As Daniel left the office, he heard Moishe tell his secretary to telephone an inspector at the immigration and naturalization service. Now Daniel understood. Moishe Wasserman—the kid who was going to be a big show business lawyer—had ceased to exist. Maurice Waterman handled immigration cases, something Moishe Wasserman would sooner have starved than do.

Sadly, Daniel decided that he liked the impractical lunatic he'd known before the war a lot more than the pragmatic lawyer who worried more about meeting his overhead than anything else.

Daniel returned to the Grand and informed Hammersley that he would accept the lamplighter role for the season's final *Manon Lescaut.* With his contract for the following season assured—providing he did not fluff the role—he went to the one-bedroom apartment he rented in Greenwich Village, close to where Moishe lived. The last letter from Martinelli beckoned to him and he sat down to answer it.

The first few words made him stumble as he attempted to disguise his disappointment at being forced to accept a minor role. Finally he recognized a way around the predicament. He would cable Martinelli instead of writing. He'd send him a telegram just as he had done when Hammersley had first offered him a contract to sing with the Grand. He'd cable Martinelli the simple message of "Debut February 26, Grand Opera Company of New York, *Manon Lescaut.*" That way, the Italian would not know that Daniel had been cast in the lowly role of the lamplighter.

Daniel visited a Western Union office to send the cable. When he returned to the apartment he called his father with the news. Isaac Kirschbaum said that he was glad to see his son had finally decided that humility was also an asset.

Standing deep in the wings, arms folded grimly across his chest, Daniel watched the first two acts of the rehearsal for *Manon Lescaut.* His envious eyes followed the short, dumpy figure of Cesare Scarlatti as the middle-aged Italian tenor strutted pompously around the stage, playing the Chevalier des Grieux to Manon, a young attractive soprano called Anna Markova. When he had first seen the soprano, Daniel had thought that Hammersley had thrown away his policy of emphasizing domestic talent and gone completely overboard with imported singers; then he had learned that Anna Markova was really Annie Markowitz from Brooklyn. It made Daniel feel happier—but not much—that one native New Yorker had made it to stardom at the Grand.

Hearing his cue, Daniel stepped out onto the stage and sang the few lines allotted to the lamplighter before wandering off down the narrow street built into the set of a square near the French port of Le Havre. Behind, he could hear Scarlatti and Anna continuing their duet. Just great, Daniel reflected gloomily; nobody in the audience will even notice me. If they choose that exact moment to sneeze or blink they'll miss my debut. Walk on. Sing a few words. Walk off. Swallow your pride to ensure next year's contract and pray like hell that there's something better in it than this stinking role.

He returned to the wings and looked out onto the stage. When he could bear to look and listen no longer, he switched his attention to Hammersley in the auditorium, sitting between the Grand's musical director and stage manager. What was Hammersley thinking now? That Daniel's voice merited more than the lamplighter? Or that such a small role was all he was really worth? Daniel chuckled grimly as the most unwelcome thought of all slipped into his mind: maybe Hammersley had chosen that goddamned moment to blink.

As Daniel watched and wondered, Hammersley's secretary made her way along the row of seats, followed closely by two men dressed in almost identical dark grey suits. They spoke a few words with Hammersley, and one of the men showed something that he held cupped in the palm of his hand. Hammersley's smooth face creased up in annoyance as he listened. After a few seconds, he excused himself to his two colleagues and followed the secretary and the two men in dark grey suits out of the auditorium.

Five minutes later, Hammersley returned by himself. He clapped his hands and called for silence. "Thank you very much, ladies and gentlemen. That will be all the rehearsing for today. Signor Scarlatti"—he beckoned to the Italian tenor—"would you please be kind enough to come with me?"

Everyone involved with the rehearsal stared in amazement at the retreating figures of Hammersley and Scarlatti. Rehearsals at the Grand were sacred. Maybe at the Met nobody bothered to turn up, but attendance at Grand rehearsals was on a level only slightly below a presidential summons. Nothing short of war or plague could be allowed to interrupt them. An excited buzz began as members of the cast tried to guess what had happened.

Eager to stop any speculation, the musical director yelled out for silence. "Please clear the stage. Rehearsals are over for today."

"Wonder what the hell that was all about?" Daniel mused, falling into step beside Anna Markova as they returned to the dressing rooms two floors up from stage level.

Anna turned to see who had spoken to her. Recognizing Daniel, she smiled warmly, disregarding the unspoken tradition that established singers did not socialize with aspirants. Her own background in Brooklyn's Crown Heights was too close to Daniel's to allow any divisions, and she admired the way he had stood his ground against the Grand's management before finally being blackmailed into accepting a minor role. "God only knows," she replied. "I'm just glad it happened. There's no need to keep rehearsing this production. We've already done it four times this season."

"You might have done it four times," Daniel said. "But it's my first shot at it. Maybe they're rehearsing for my benefit."

"Keep dreaming, Daniel." Anna squeezed his arm affectionately in case he took offense. "The Grand's not that loaded with money to pay technical staff and musicians overtime so a walk-on can rehearse. Anyway, you sounded good enough to me."

"Thanks," he said, then quickly added, "Short but good."

"They'll get longer. Give yourself time."

"How much time, for God's sake?" He remembered asking the same question of Martinelli after that first aria had blown a gasket in the hospital recital in England. Anna could talk quite blithely about time. She had been only twenty-two when she had been recommended to the Grand four years earlier. The two years she had spent—first in the chorus and then in supporting roles—before being cast as Gilda in a production of *Rigoletto* had not mattered at that age.

Before Anna could think of an answer, a woman's strident voice called after them. "Mr. Kerr! Phone call!"

Daniel turned around to see one of the office staff waving at him. "Who?"

"A Mr. Waterman. He said it's urgent. You can take it in the dressing room."

"Excuse me." Daniel left Anna on the stairs and hurried up to the crowded communal dressing room that was used by the minor players. A telephone extension was located next to a loudspeaker which piped in sound from the auditorium.

"Moishe? What do you want?"

"Anything happening, Danny boy?"

"What do you mean, anything happening?" Now what was Moishe on about? Did he want a blow-by-blow description of how it felt to rehearse the lamplighter?

"In the opera, *schmuck!*"

"I don't know what you're talking about, for Christ's sake!"

"I can't make it any plainer," Moishe hissed. "We're on an open line. Think!"

"You mean about Cesare Scarlatti?" That was all Daniel could think of, but he failed to see how Moishe could know about it, or how it could interest him. "Those two men who came . . ."

"Jesus Christ! You bigmouthed jerk!" Moishe snapped. Then he slammed down the receiver.

Daniel looked in bewilderment at the dead telephone before replacing it. A hand touched him gently on the shoulder and he wheeled around. Hammersley's secretary was standing behind him.

"Mr. Hammersley would like to see you in his office, Mr. Kerr."

"Now?" So he'd blown the lamplighter role, and Hammersley was going to throw him out.

"Right away, if you please. It's extremely urgent."

That's what the woman had said about Moishe's phone call as well, Daniel remembered. And that had not been as urgent as it had been confusing. Why had Moishe snapped at him and suddenly hung up? It didn't make any sense. He just hoped that Hammersley's idea of urgency was better defined.

"Close the door and sit down, please," Hammersley invited from behind the desk.

Daniel pushed the door closed and sat down, facing the general manager. For once, the office looked reasonably tidy. The only costumes that were visible were piled neatly in a corner, and Hammersley's desk was almost clear.

"Do you know anyone in the Immigration and Naturalization Service, Daniel?" Hammersley asked conversationally.

"Where?" Hammersley was making about as much sense as Moishe. Moishe? Wait a minute. Forgetting that Hammersley was waiting for a proper reply to his question, Daniel forced his memory to unwind. Moishe handled immigration cases. Moishe had just called him. Now what scheme had that harebrained madman dreamed up?

"Never mind," Hammersley said. "More to the point, we have an emergency. An emergency of tremendous consequence."

"We?"

"The royal 'we'," Hammersley explained. "Like Queen Victoria, I am speaking on behalf of everyone. At this precise moment, Signor Scarlatti, our Chevalier des Grieux, is being escorted to the offices of the Immigration and Naturalization Service to be interviewed, pending possible deportation proceedings against him."

"What?" Daniel fervently wished that his conversation could consist of something more substantial than amazed, one-syllable questions; he also wished he could make some sense out of what Hammersley was saying, although a bizarre idea was beginning to take shape in his mind.

"Those two gentlemen who interrupted our rehearsal were immigration investigators. Although Signor Scarlatti was allowed back into the United States after the end of the war, so he could continue his operatic career, it now appears that certain discrepancies have arisen concerning his claim that he disassociated himself from the Fascist party of Mussolini. He contributed—or so the immigration people are saying—more than was necessary to the party's welfare."

As Hammersley continued to talk in a low, even, accented voice, Daniel at last fully understood the meaning of Moishe's phone call. Moishe had put in the fix. He worked on immigration cases. He knew people in the service. As Daniel had left his office that day, Moishe had told his secretary to call some immigration inspector. It had to be. There was no other possible explanation. Coincidences like this didn't just occur; they were carefully planned. Whether or not there was any truth in the claim against Scarlatti—that he had been a supporter of Mussolini's Fascist party and, therefore, an enemy of the United States—was of little concern. The Italian tenor's appearance as des Grieux in the season's final *Manon Lescaut* would be ruined. Newspapers would get hold of the story. They'd tie it in with the original controversy over his return and have a field day fueling public indignation and emotion. They would crucify him. Just as they'd crucify the Grand if Hammersley took the foolish step of having him back.

"How can I help?" Daniel asked.

"Need you ask?" the general manager replied cynically. "Or are you seeing if I'll crawl to you and beg?"

Daniel stared blankly at the man. The reality of the situation had still not fully penetrated his brain; he was too busy thinking about Moishe.

"You've told me countless times you want a lead for your debut," Hammersley continued. "You've told me that you've studied for des Grieux. Now you have the opportunity to stand or fall by your claims."

"What about the lamplighter?" It was the most inane question Daniel could have asked, yet he could think of nothing more constructive.

"Let him light blasted lamps!" Hammersley said irritably. "If push should come to shove, even I could fill in for those few lines. I need a des Grieux. The Grand Opera Company of New York needs a des Grieux. The role is yours."

Daniel stretched his hand across the desk. "Mr. Hammersley, you'll never regret this. I promise you." Words of gratitude bubbled uncontrollably from his mouth. "It'll be the finest *Manon Lescaut* the Grand has ever put on."

"I'll make that judgment only after the end of the final act." Hammersley gazed at the outstretched hand and decided to ignore it. "To be very honest with you, Daniel, this entire business is extremely repugnant to me, although for you it is a fortuitous coincidence. I asked you before"—despite himself he began to smile—"if you know anyone working at the Immigration and Naturalization Service. Do you?"

"No, sir!" Daniel protested vehemently. But he could not stop the blush that spread quickly across his face to damn him as a liar. "I don't know anyone there at all."

"It doesn't matter," Hammersley said, finally taking the hand which Daniel continued to hold out. "I am a fatalist. To my way of thinking, whatever happens, happens eventually for the best. You were fated to debut in a lead role. Fate has indeed smiled on you, even if it has chosen to scowl most ferociously upon the unfortunate Signor Scarlatti. Do not disappoint fate, or me."

The performance was due to begin at eight. Daniel left his Greenwich Village apartment just after five and rode the subway up to Herald Square. For fully a minute he stood outside the opera house to admire the poster—Anna Markova as Manon, and introducing Daniel Kerr as des Grieux.

There it was. In black and white. Nothing could change it now. His operatic debut would be in a lead role!

Office workers on their way home walked past Daniel as if his existence were solely in his own mind, just as they had when he had first visited the Grand to audition for Hammersley. Now he felt like grabbing one of them by the arm and pointing to his name. That's me! he wanted to yell. See! I'm going to be on that stage tonight! The applause you'll hear will be for me!

What was the use? he finally decided. These lemmings streaming past him into the subway didn't know who he was. They didn't know who des Grieux was. Nor did they care. But tonight, at eleven o'clock, the people inside the opera house—the only ones who mattered—would know the name of Daniel Kerr. And the following morning, after the reviews had been read and discussed, his name would be on everyone's lips.

He entered the building and walked to the ticket cage. "Do you have my tickets, please?"

The woman looked at him questioningly. "What's the name?"

"Kerr," he said slowly, enjoying the consternation that suddenly flashed across the woman's face. "Daniel Kerr."

"Oh"—the woman hesitated, obviously embarrassed—"you're Daniel Kerr. Here you are, sir." She handed him an envelope containing three complimentary tickets.

"Thank you." He returned to the sidewalk and looked around. When he checked Fat Benny's gold watch he saw that it was only five-thirty. Moishe was not due until six; he had half an hour yet to wait.

Standing alone, he could feel the nerves beginning to build up, the same way they'd done at the hospital. Tendrils of fear that started deep in the pit of his stomach and slowly spread out until their icy touch had affected every part of his body. Despite the cold, he started to sweat. He needed company, a warm, friendly atmosphere to see him through the next half hour.

He walked across the street to a bar and sat down with a rye and ginger, trying to nurse the drink to make it last. He shouldn't be drinking now; that would only dull his concentration, not sharpen it. Inwardly he smiled as an odd idea struck him. Everyone else wanted the clock to go back, to turn back the years. He wanted to advance the clock. He wished it were eight already, more than two hours in the future. No. He changed his mind. Not eight. He wished it were eleven o'clock, when the fourth and final act would be over and he would be standing in front of the Grand's gold curtain, side by side with Anna Markova, bowing graciously in acceptance of the applause for which he'd hungered all his life. And for which so many others had worked and made sacrifices—Fat Benny, Kawolsky, Martinelli. Now, even Moishe. Daniel thought back to the conversation he'd had with Moishe following Scarlatti's abrupt disappearance from the opera house and his own instant elevation. Moishe had simply shrugged his shoulders and said that a lot of Germans and Italians tried to hide their wartime records when they came to the States; when he could find the time, he'd look into Scarlatti's case through contacts in the immigration office.

To his surprise, the glass was empty. He ordered a second

drink and began to sip it, enjoying the relaxation it brought while he spared a thought for Joe Feltz, Lucy's father. After he had been given the contract at the Grand, he had gone around to Feltz's apartment to thank him. Feltz had opened the door just wide enough to see who it was. He had listened expressionlessly to Daniel's thanks and closed the door again, without inviting him inside. Later, when he had gone to listen to Bjoerling at the Met, Daniel had waited outside after the performance for Lucy's father to leave. Carrying his violin case, Feltz had completely ignored Daniel, walking straight past him as if he were not there. Since then, Daniel had not even bothered trying to make contact.

There had been a good side to that evening, though. After Feltz had left him standing in front of the opera house like a fool, Daniel had gone around to the stage door in time to catch Jussi Bjoerling leaving. Daniel had pushed his way through the crowd of well-wishers until at last he was face-to-face with the Swede. Bjoerling had looked amused as Daniel blurted out that he was a tenor with the Grand. Knowing that Bjoerling had never heard of him, Daniel felt like an idiot. But the Met tenor had eased the situation by clapping him on the arm and inviting a fellow artist for a drink. They'd parted company two hours later, after Bjoerling had regaled Daniel with anecdotes and tales of his career. Daniel had willingly picked up the tab as the Swede only had enough money in his pocket for the cab ride back to his hotel.

Halfway through the second drink, Daniel glanced through the bar window and spotted Moishe on the other side of Thirty-fourth Street, outside the opera house. He gulped down what remained of the rye and ginger and hurried to join his friend.

"Three tickets," he said, passing the envelope to Moishe. "Two for my parents, one for you. Don't lose them."

"Are your parents that hard up for a good laugh?" Moishe joked.

"Knock it off," Daniel warned. "I'm shit scared as it is without any wisecracks from you."

"You can handle this, kiddo," Moishe assured him, still grinning. "Anyone who can take on the Leishman brothers like you did can get away with mumbling a few words in Italian. Just make sure you don't start singing in Hebrew instead, not that half of them would know the difference."

"Including you?"

"Especially me!" Moishe roared. "Good luck."

"Thanks. See you after the show." Daniel ducked into the building and made his way up to the dressing room. No more shared dressing rooms for him; as the lead he rated his own. He knew he would be among the first to arrive, but he needed time to think, time to prepare himself. There were no worries about the role, but he was more frightened now than he had been eighteen years earlier when he had stood on the *bima* of the *shul* in Claremont Parkway to sing his *bar mitzvah* portion. In the eyes of a thirteen-year-old boy, the *bar mitzvah* had loomed as the most terrifying prospect in the world. In retrospect, it was nothing to fear. What he faced now—four acts to a full opera house with his triumph or failure splashed across the reviews the following morning—was sheer unmitigated terror.

To hell with dreaming about accepting applause gracefully. First he had to earn that applause. Tonight was his real audition for the Grand Opera Company of New York. What he had done for Hammersley the previous year had meant nothing. This performance—the tenor lead in a four-act opera—would make or break him.

His costume and wig were lying on the chair. First he tried on the white, powdered wig and made preposterously serious faces at himself in the mirror, anything to drive away the nagging tension that had him in its unrelenting grip. The two pre-performance drinks hadn't helped. Maybe he had time to slip downstairs for another one? He dismissed the idea as folly.

Taking off the wig, he slipped into the costume. Panic screamed from deep within him as he tried to stand up. He could not. He felt like Quasimodo, the hunchback of Notre Dame. The costume was too short, and billowed out at the sides like a shapeless sack. It made him look deformed. Des Grieux was a handsome, young aristocrat, not a hobbling, amorphous cripple. The panic turned to near hysteria as he imagined himself staggering onto the stage dressed like this. The audience would howl with laughter. They would think Rigoletto had gotten drunk and turned up on the wrong night. Or that the Grand was staging *Die Fledermaus* instead of *Manon Lescaut* and Richard the Third had dropped in as one of the surprise guests.

Daniel bellowed for the wardrobe mistress.

"What is it?" she wanted to know.

"What is it?" he repeated, unable to believe the woman had to ask. "What the hell do you call this?" He pointed furiously at his deformed shape.

"The costume was altered to fit Signor Scarlatti," the woman tried to explain.

"That doesn't help me! I'm a mile taller than Scarlatti. I can't go on looking like this."

The wardrobe mistress refused to be cowed. She had dealt with temperamental tenors before. "Take it off. I'll see what I can do with it." She took the costume and walked away, leaving Daniel standing miserably in his underwear.

The make-up man appeared. Unaccustomed to the procedure, Daniel allowed himself to be pushed back into a chair while the man went to work. Watching the reflection in the mirror, Daniel marveled at the man's skill as he transformed the fleshy face, changing the shape of eyebrows, rouging cheeks, giving the nose an aristocratic, aquiline curve. When the wig was in place, Daniel was certain he could have passed himself on the street without the barest trace of recognition.

The wardrobe mistress returned with the silk and brocade costume. She had pinned in the trousers at the waist, lengthened the legs and let out the jacket seams. Fearfully Daniel tried on the costume again. It fit well enough to be passable. The woman stood studying him for several seconds before adding more pins to the trousers, all the while explaining that the costume had been altered to fit Scarlatti. Scarlatti was much fatter around the thighs than Daniel. Scarlatti had shorter legs. Scarlatti had a broader, squatter body. Daniel began to wish that Scarlatti were here, that Moishe had not set the INS on the Italian. The role of the lamplighter was becoming more attractive with each pin the wardrobe mistress inserted.

"What about my shoes?" Daniel asked, pointing to his white-stockinged feet.

"Shoes?"

"I can't go on without them."

"I'll find some for you." The woman disappeared again.

Daniel took a break from his own concern to wonder if his parents had arrived yet. Had they found Moishe and gotten the tickets? His father had been ecstatic about Daniel getting the lead, first laughing with the joy of it, then crying because Fat Benny and Tessie—who would have given anything for this day—were no longer here, and then laughing and crying simultaneously. And Harry Feldman from Temple Isaiah in Paterson was supposed to be coming, Daniel remembered. He'd been as happy as Isaac about Daniel's good fortune. Not only did the temple have a tenor from the Grand Opera Company as cantor, but an important tenor! Just don't bring any of your nieces, Daniel prayed. Leave them in Brooklyn.

The wardrobe mistress reappeared, holding a pair of brown shoes with elegant silver buckles. Daniel tried them on. They were at least a size too large and rattled on his feet like empty boxes. "Who wore these, an elephant?"

"Signor Scarlatti . . ."

"Yes, I know. Signor Scarlatti had bigger feet than I do." How on earth did a fat midget like Scarlatti manage to have size thirteen feet? "Can you do anything with them?"

The woman stuffed wads of cloth into the toes. "Try them now. Just be careful how you walk in them."

Daniel slipped on the shoes and turned to admire himself in the mirror. If nothing else, he looked the part of des Grieux, a young nobleman in eighteenth-century France. Providing none of the wardrobe mistress's hastily inserted pins fell out. Then he'd look like a huge tent flapping in a hurricane.

What time was it? Seven-thirty. Time for his exercises. Vocalize to loosen up the cords. He'd started early that morning, right after breakfast. The voice had sounded bad but he hadn't pushed it. He'd waited until after lunch before trying again, a one-minute workout that was more satisfactory. Before he had left the apartment he had vocalized again. The voice had come easily and he had continued for two minutes. Now he was certain that it would be there, loud, clear and perfect.

From other dressing rooms he could hear his fellow artists going through the ritual. Basses, baritones, tenors, all sounding like a herd of distressed cattle. Above them all, Daniel heard Anna Markova's pure soprano, and the darker mezzo-soprano of the woman who would play the role of the madrigal singer in the second act. Daniel joined in, no longer self-conscious as he had been when conducting the warm-up session in the English hospital.

After a minute he was satisfied and turned to singing the first lines of "Donna non vidi mai," his major aria of the first act. How far could his voice carry? A few blocks north to the Met? Was Bjoerling—his drinking partner of that night, his inspiration—even now shaking as he recognized the voice that would push him off the top of the heap? Was Tucker trembling? Was Gigli?

Watch out! Daniel felt like screaming. Make room for me or get trampled in my passing!

Hammersley entered the dressing room, resplendent in white tie and tails as he made his customary round of the dressing rooms to wish his artists good luck. He stood in front of Daniel and inspected the costume closely. Then he held out his hand. "Your sudden replacement of Signor Scarlatti has created a tremendous amount of interest, Daniel Kerr. Live up to it."

"I intend to, Mr. Hammersley."

The general manager pulled a sheaf of papers from his pocket and passed them to Daniel. "Read them before you go on."

Eyes wide in pleasure, Daniel snatched the telegrams from Hammersley's grasp. The first one he tore open was from Harry Feldman. Another was from Jack, his brother in Chicago. From his parents. From Moishe. Even one that read: "Now I know who you are," and was signed by Jussi Bjoerling. But one was missing.

"Is that all?" Daniel asked, trying hard to keep the biting disappointment out of his voice.

"Five aren't enough for you?" Hammersley asked in amusement.

"There was one I was kind of expecting . . ." Daniel tried to explain and then gave up. Hammersley wouldn't understand, just as Daniel himself could not understand why Enzo Martinelli had neglected to wire him. Maybe there was something wrong with the overseas cable service, he reasoned, trying to ease his disappointment. He couldn't imagine the Italian forgetting an occasion like this.

"Maybe it will come later," Hammersley said. "Good luck. I'll be listening carefully."

"Thank you."

A uniformed figure appeared in the doorway, blocking out the activity that bustled along the corridor outside the dressing room. Daniel recognized one of the doormen from the front.

"There's some guy outside to see you, Mr. Kerr. Says he's got to talk to you before the performance."

"Who?" The opera started in fifteen minutes. He didn't have time to talk to anyone now. It would have to wait.

"He wouldn't give his name, sir. Just told me to pass this on to you"—the doorman held out a thin object wrapped in white tissue paper—"and you'd know who it was."

Puzzled, Daniel took the package, unwrapped it and began to laugh. In his hand was a gleaming surgical scalpel. "Where is he? Quick, take me to him."

Enzo Martinelli was waiting in the corridor outside the dressing room. His darkly handsome face lit up with a delighted smile when he recognized the bewigged, costumed figure approaching him. He clasped Daniel around the shoulders and hugged him warmly.

"What are you doing here?" Daniel asked, completely forgetting the disappointment over not receiving a good-luck cable from Martinelli.

"Nothing in the world could have kept me away from your debut, Daniel. Not even another Mussolini."

"When did you get in?"

"Two days ago."

"Why didn't you call, for God's sake?"

"I did not want to call you. I wanted this to be a surprise. And imagine my surprise, Daniel, when I find that you are cast in the role of des Grieux. I thought Edmondo, perhaps, if you were very lucky. Or even the lamplighter. For any of those roles I would have come, but the lead? *Magnifico!*" He hugged Daniel again.

"We're almost ready to go," Daniel said, unwilling to break off the conversation but knowing he had to. "Can we get together afterwards? We've got a celebration planned in Wheeler's, the Grand's restaurant. Say you can join us."

"I would be delighted. *In bocca el lupo.*" A third time he hugged Daniel and kissed him on both cheeks. "Do not forget to vocalize. I will be listening."

"I already did. And watch out for my make-up!" Daniel joked. "Do you want your scalpel back?"

"It is yours, a souvenir. I am convinced I will never need it."

Daniel shook the Italian's hand and returned to the dressing room as one of the stage staff walked past calling out that only ten minutes remained. From the auditorium he could hear the orchestra warming up; an even stranger sound than his own vocalizing; the musicians didn't want their instruments to be tight either.

He left the dressing room and began the long walk downstairs, almost unaware of other costumed figures that accompanied him.

"Worried?" a woman's voice asked as he stood in the wings, fidgeting while he waited for the overture to begin and the curtain to rise.

He turned to see Anna Markova standing beside him, dressed in a high wig and an elaborately embroidered dress. "Out of my goddamned wits," he answered truthfully.

"It'll pass."

"That's just what it feels like it's going to do any second now," he answered flippantly. As he said the words, his stomach began to churn and he wished he'd kept quiet. That was all he needed now, a trip to the washroom. Once he went, he'd never return.

He looked away from Anna to the stage where the scene was set for the first act of the opera—a spacious square near the Paris Gate at Amiens, an inn with a porch under which were tables, and an avenue leading off to the right. Students, soldiers and villagers strolled around the square, or stood together talking. One of the students, Edmondo, was preparing to address his colleagues.

Applause sounded from the auditorium. "The conductor," Anna whispered. "Whatever you feel like doing right now, hold it in for twenty-five minutes."

The lively overture began. Majestically the heavy gold curtain rose. Edmondo's words—"*Ave, sera gentile, che descendi*"—began the first act.

Daniel clenched his fists and pressed them against his stomach as he listened carefully, waiting for his cue to enter. The rumbling in his stomach refused to diminish. Why the hell hadn't he gone before? He'd had plenty of time. He couldn't go now, that was for damned sure. His cue would come and go and he'd be sitting on the toilet. And down that same toilet would go his entire career. Desperately he sought an object on which to focus his attention. He gazed beyond the footlights, past the orchestra pit and tried to see the audience. It was black out there, like night. Would he be able to see anyone once he stepped onto the stage? He'd even forgotten where Moishe and his own family were sitting. And Martinelli, where was he?

Martinelli! He hadn't even asked the Italian whether he had a ticket for the performance. Daniel forgot all about his troublesome stomach as he cursed himself for his thoughtlessness. Of all people, Martinelli should not have to pay.

"Be ready," Anna whispered.

Daniel nodded, concentration straining for the cue. He felt Anna's warm, drying hand clasp his own damp one and squeeze gently. Sweat broke out beneath the make-up on his face and over his body. He turned to look into Anna's wide brown eyes and murmured, "Pray for me."

"Like I've never prayed before," she promised.

His cue drew closer and he fretted like a greyhound in the traps when the hare goes streaking by. As he started to move forward, Anna continued to hold onto him. With her free hand she swatted him playfully across the buttocks. "Give them hell, Daniel," she told him. Then, in the most atrocious parody of a Brooklyn accent that Daniel had ever heard, she added, "Show dose bums out dere dat New Yawk can sing like Naples!"

It was all Daniel could do to choke back a laugh.

On cue, he stepped out of the wings and onto the stage. A chorus of "*Ecco des Grieux!*" erupted from the students while a round of applause from the audience greeted his debut appearance.

Daniel glanced down into the prompter's box. The sight of the prompter waving an arm gaily in time with the music while he sang quietly along drove the tension away. This guy had to know every operatic score by heart. And he was probably the only person in the world who could truthfully claim that he had sung every role of every production the Grand had staged during the last ten years.

Daniel's stomach settled down. The perspiration dried. Never had he felt more at ease, more at home. He fitted into the action around him as if he had been born solely for this occasion. The lines flowed surely and musically from him and each time he looked into the wings he saw Anna nodding encouragingly.

The ovation that greeted his bantering serenade, "Tra voi, belle," warmed Daniel, lingering in his memory until he heard the sound of a horn announcing the arrival of the coach from Arras. Daniel joined the group of students and villagers who clustered around the coach to view the new arrivals. Anna as Manon stepped down, accompanied by her brother, Lescaut, and Geronte, her elderly suitor. As she passed close by Daniel on her way to the inn, she went far outside the score by winking quickly at him.

The act continued smoothly until it reached the point where Manon stood on the balcony of the inn with her brother. Then Daniel turned away and gazed out into the blackness of the auditorium. Reality had taken over from enchantment. His moment of truth had arrived. His first major aria that would either stamp him with greatness or expose him as a fraud. He thought of the five telegrams he had received, four that had wished him luck and the one from Bjoerling that had said, "Now I know who you are." When this aria was over, everyone would know who he was. Daniel opened his mouth and began to sing.

Donna non vidi, mai simile a questa!
A dirle; io t'amo,
a nuova vite l'alma mia si desta . . .

His voice felt wonderfully loose. It seemed to float above his head as if he were singing out of his body, on a plane removed. He stole a quick look at the prompter. The man was still singing along, smiling broadly as he waved his hand up and down. Daniel knew in that single moment that nothing could go wrong, nothing could ruin the moment he had dreamed of since returning from Europe.

"*. . . deh! non cessar! deh! non cessar!*"

The applause that greeted the end of the aria was both instantaneous and overwhelmingly deafening.

Daniel stood perfectly still, a statue as he reveled in the adulation. This was what it was all about. Applause ringing out from an audience that had hung enraptured on every word, every note. He wished for an instant that he were in Italy, in one of the small provincial opera houses where singers took bows after each aria. Such displays were strictly forbidden by Hammersley, who wanted nothing to interfere with the dramatic continuity of the performance. Bows were fine at curtain calls, the general manager had stressed; but at the Grand they had no place during the actual performance.

At the end of the first act, Daniel stood in front of the gold curtain, first by himself, then with the act's major characters, and finally with just Anna, holding her hand while he let the continuing ovation flood over him.

"They must like you," Anna whispered out of the side of her mouth. "They can't all be from Claremont Parkway."

From one of the boxes a single rose was thrown down. It dropped in front of Anna and she stooped to pick it up, presenting it to Daniel. "Here, it'll be the first of many."

Another rose dropped down onto the stage. As Daniel bent to retrieve it, intent on returning the compliment to Anna, he heard the sound of cloth tearing and felt a ripping sensation in his trousers. He heard Anna starting to laugh. He stood up quickly, the rose forgotten, and felt pins jabbing him painfully in the back of his right thigh.

"Exit backwards," Anna advised. "And make sure you take small steps or we'll be closed down on an obscenity charge." She pulled him through the gap in the curtains and gave in to helpless laughter as she examined the gaping hole in the back of his trousers. Daniel looked around for the wardrobe mistress. All he could see were technicians changing the scenery for the next act. Finally he spotted the stage manager.

"I'm falling apart, for Christ's sake!" Daniel cried out.

"Don't worry. We'll get you fixed up." The stage manager sent off his assistant to find a seamstress while Daniel limped carefully up two flights of stairs to the dressing room, clutching the errant folds of fabric in his hand. Anna followed, laughing every step of the way.

By the end of the final act, Daniel's costume was soaked—not with the sweat of fear but with the sweat of exertion. He reckoned he had worked off at least five pounds, an admirable side effect he'd never even considered. Each time he tried to leave the stage, curtain calls encouraged his return. The ovation lasted for fifteen minutes before Hammersley appeared backstage to signal the end.

"Bravo," he congratulated Daniel. "A magnificent debut. You were right. Fate was right. And I gratefully acknowledge that I was wrong. You would have been wasted as the lamplighter."

"Thank you, Mr. Hammersley."

The general manager followed Daniel up the stairs to the dressing room. "By the way, I have a snippet of news that might be of interest to you. Before the performance, I spoke with Signor Scarlatti's lawyer. Apparently the investigators at the immigration office have dropped the case. It appears that Signor Scarlatti was the victim of mistaken identity."

Daniel swung around at the words, towering over Hammersley from the step above. "So now what happens?" Surely they couldn't relegate him to the bench after he'd turned in such a debut? Hadn't Hammersley taken any notice of the applause? The audience had loved him; they hadn't wanted to let him go.

Hammersley shrugged philosophically. "Absolutely nothing happens. Signor Scarlatti has refused to ever again set foot on American soil. He's leaving for Europe tomorrow."

Daniel turned back up the stairs so that Hammersley would be unable to see the gleam of triumph that flashed across his face. There was no longer any competition.

After he had cleaned up and changed, Daniel walked slowly down to the empty auditorium. He knew that his family and friends would be waiting in the restaurant for the post-performance dinner that was a tradition at the Grand. They would have to wait a few moments longer, he decided selfishly. First he needed time alone to come to terms with such sudden success.

Choosing a seat in the front row of the orchestra stalls, he gazed up at the massive gold curtain and tried to imagine how he must have looked onstage. His entrance; had he still been clasping his stomach? That magnificent first aria. And the curtain calls after the first act when his trousers had given way.

Somehow he could not picture any of it. No visions came to mind, nothing but the mute gold curtain and the auditorium empty as he had first seen it, a shell that only hinted at the glory it contained.

"Daniel?"

The spell was broken. He moved in the seat and recognized Moishe walking down the aisle.

"Get the lead out, Danny boy. We're all waiting for you in the restaurant. Your parents. Martinelli. The champagne's going flat."

Reluctantly Daniel rose and followed his friend into Wheeler's. As he entered the crowded restaurant which adjoined the auditorium, the maître d' grabbed him by the hand and congratulated him on the performance; loudspeakers had carried the opera into the restaurant. Diners set down their cutlery to applaud as Daniel made his way to the table where Martinelli and his parents sat. Even his mother stood up to greet him.

Daniel shook hands, clapped people on the back, kissed. His father was crying again, tears running unashamedly from his eyes as he tried to tell his son how beautifully he had sung. Words collided with each other and Daniel gently pushed him back into the chair. He felt awkward at the praise. From his audience he expected it. It was his due, as Martinelli had once pointed out. But from his own father it embarrassed him.

"Well?" He let his gaze run over the people at the table. "What's the verdict?"

"Every bit as good as Caruso," Isaac announced. He held out his glass to the bottle of champagne Moishe was lifting from the ice bucket. "A toast to the second Caruso!"

Martinelli, who had been observing Daniel's reception with a quiet enjoyment, felt it was time to speak. "No, Mr. Kirschbaum. Not to the second Caruso." When he saw Isaac's face sag at the contradiction, he raised his own glass. "The correct toast should be to the first Daniel Kerr."

Delighted by the toast, Daniel lifted his own glass in response. Then he looked at Moishe. "And to the immigration office," he whispered so that only his friend could hear him.

"You might have to sing for their pension fund," Moishe replied just as quietly.

"And fork over ten percent to you, I suppose, *gonef*." Daniel looked up as the maître d' hovered over the table, offering another bottle of champagne. Attached to the bottle was a small white envelope. Daniel read the note inside, written in a dainty script: "See how hard I prayed . . . Anna."

Laughing, Daniel accepted the bottle and looked across the crowded restaurant to where Anna sat with a small group of people. When she saw him looking in her direction, she waved happily. Daniel excused himself to his guests and walked to her table.

"You must have a direct line to God to get prayers answered like that," he said. "Thanks. And thanks for the champagne."

"Enjoy it. You only get one debut." Anna introduced the people at her table as friends. Daniel nodded to each one, thanking them as they congratulated him. He seemed to be thanking everyone tonight, and he was loving every moment of it. They had thanked him the way they had applauded; now it was his turn.

"Do you want to come over and join us for a while?" Daniel asked Anna. "If you can bear the din and the tears."

Anna shook her head. "Celebrations are private affairs. You don't get too much privacy in this game so enjoy it while you can."

"Okay, see you later." He returned to his own table.

"Who was the girl?" Yetta Kirschbaum wanted to know.

"Anna Markova. The soprano who sang Manon."

"So young," Yetta mused. "What kind of a name is this Markova anyway? Russian?"

"It's Markowitz."

"Jewish girl?"

Daniel looked helplessly around the table until his eyes rested on Martinelli. The Italian was chuckling quietly. "Yes. A Jewish girl. Happy now?"

"Why did you both have to change your names?"

"Enzo, do me a favor and answer that question." For once

Yetta Kirschbaum had said something funny and Daniel knew he would never be able to reply without laughing.

Martinelli gazed at his long slender hands for a moment, then he looked across the table at Yetta. "Mrs. Kirschbaum, can you even begin to imagine what effect it would have on an opera-loving public if the Grand Opera Company of New York staged a production of Puccini's *Manon Lescaut* and the two leading singers were named Markowitz and Kirschbaum?"

Moishe, busy pouring more champagne, stopped to think about the question. "Sounds as crazy as a lawyer with a name like Moishe Wasserman," he grunted to himself. He pushed back his glasses and continued to pour.

As they drank coffee after the meal, the maître d' stopped by the table once more. This time he cleared a space in the center and set down copies of that morning's early editions. Moishe's hand snaked out and grabbed the *Times*, while Daniel scrambled frantically through the *Herald*.

"'Cesare Scarlatti was not missed,'" Moishe began to read aloud, "'because in his place as des Grieux was Daniel Kerr, a young American tenor whose voice—if not his tailor—will assure him of popularity.'" He threw down the newspaper and burst out laughing.

"Wait!" Daniel cut in. "Wait till you hear this gem. 'The most exciting noise of all was not Mr. Kerr's high notes—which he reached with impeccable ease—nor the well-deserved if lengthy ovation which followed Act Four. It was, instead, the unusual sound of Mr. Kerr's trousers ripping at the seams.'"

Martinelli reached out for the newspapers and smiled broadly as he read the reviews. "Next time, Daniel, you will be able to ensure that your costume fits properly. That, and that alone, is the mark of a star."

Isaac took off his glasses and wiped his eyes. He felt tired from all the excitement and his eyes ached. "Maybe you should hire me as your personal tailor. Did I ever do an alteration for you that split?"

Daniel laughed again. Then he collected all the newspapers together and carefully tore out the reviews, folding them neatly into his wallet.

It was time to start his scrapbook.

Chapter Two

Dropping the score of *Tosca* onto the top of the grand piano, Daniel walked thoughtfully across to the living room window and gazed out over Washington Square. Traffic around the square was sparse because of the blanket of snow that covered the streets. The few people braving the early afternoon cold were wrapped up like Arctic explorers, faces invisible behind thick woolen scarves, hats pulled down low, earflaps fastened. All wore trousers bundled tightly into boots; there was no way of identifying men from women.

Daniel was grateful for the eerie silence brought by the snow. He needed the quiet to concentrate. Any other opera, any other score he could have studied despite the noise of traffic which drifted up from the street to his fourth-floor apartment. But *Tosca* held more difficulties for him than memory alone could conquer.

In the four years since he had debuted at the Grand in *Manon Lescaut*, Daniel had twice turned down the tenor lead of Mario Cavaradossi in *Tosca*, a steady favorite which Hammersley insisted on including every season. This time, though, the general manager had demanded that Daniel undertake the role. It was a special performance for which Hammersley had obtained the services of Italian soprano Claudia Rivera and was being billed as the finest *Tosca* ever produced by the Grand. Hammersley had spent countless hours drumming into Daniel that he was perfect for the role, how vital it was for him to sing this one performance with Claudia Rivera. It would establish him internationally.

Realizing that Hammersley was right—and that he would be unable to avoid the role forever—Daniel had chosen to study for the part. It would be some consolation—no matter how minor—that when Claudia Rivera sang the fateful words of "*O! Scarpia, avanti a Dio!*" Daniel's Cavaradossi would already be dead. Wrenching memories of that lipstick-scrawled message on the dressing table mirror would not cause him to choke on his words.

A figure in the snow stumbled and fell, sending a brown paper bag of groceries skidding across the sidewalk and road. Daniel watched sympathetically while the unfortunate pedestrian staggered upright and tried to collect the groceries, then he returned to the piano and picked up the score. As always, morbid curiosity forced him to turn to the final page. The closing words of the opera loomed menacingly at him from the page. As he looked, the page became indistinct until he could no longer see words, notes or staff. All he could see was what he prayed each night to forget. Lucy lying on the patio, the baby cold in its crib. God, would he never be allowed to forget that night, to wash it from his memory? Or was it to be forever etched into his mind, an eternal, indelible punishment for going to the club in Harlem and making love to the woman he'd met there, while he left Lucy to nurse her agony by herself?

Throwing down the score again, he went to an old-fashioned mahogany secretary which occupied a small alcove in the living room. From a drawer he pulled out a large book and began to leaf through the pages. Those first reviews from *Manon Lescaut* were frayed at the edges, turning yellow, and Daniel knew he should buy transparent sheets to protect them; but who had time for such everyday tasks in between rehearsals, performances, tours and recordings? He smiled as he remembered his trouser seams splitting and Anna Markova pulling him back through the gap in the curtains at the end of the first act.

Daniel knew he would feel a lot easier about doing *Tosca* if Anna were playing opposite him. Anna gave him confidence. She could sense when he was nervous before a performance, which occurred more frequently than he liked to admit. Everything was fine once he had taken that first step onto the stage, sung that first note. But until that time . . . the waiting drove him to distraction. Even the two drinks he'd made a custom of having before a performance did not help; they had merely become a part of his ritual, a superstition. His stomach still churned before each production, and then the anxieties magically disappeared once he became involved. When he worked with Anna, she knew this. Her bantering and joking helped him through. In this production of *Tosca*, though, he'd be working with Claudia Rivera, an aging, overweight prima donna who specialized in upstaging everyone around her. The woman even employed a claque in case the applause was not quick enough in coming.

Taken with the scrapbook and the wealth of memories it contained, Daniel turned the pages. *Cavalleria Rusticana*, which he had sung in his second year at the Grand—"A spirited, full-voiced Turiddu," one critic had written. *Rigoletto*, which he had conquered the following year—"A suitably lecherous Duke." Only in Verdi's *Un Ballo in Maschera*—done that same year—had the critics come down on him; not for his singing but for his acting. He had kept the review anyway because he thought it was amusing—"If everyone died as smilingly as Mr. Kerr's Riccardo did in last night's final act, then heaven must indeed be a wondrous establishment." The next time he had sung Riccardo, Daniel's acting abilities had been of no concern. It was in a two-part recording broadcast under Toscanini—after Daniel's voice teacher Enrico Rosati had recommended him—in Studio 8-H with the NBC Symphony Orchestra. The soprano who had played Amelia opposite him, under the baton of the white-haired, fiery Toscanini, had been Claudia Rivera.

It was the success of the Toscanini broadcast and recording which had prompted Hammersley to sign up the Italian soprano for one special performance of *Tosca*. She and Daniel had created magic on record; the sorcery they would produce together on stage would be unmatched.

For Daniel, though, the recording and the live production were two totally different worlds. In the studio he had sung to Toscanini, obeying the instructions of the baton. He had not sung to Claudia Rivera. In comparison, the first rehearsal of *Tosca* at the Grand had been a nightmare. Daniel had sung well enough, but he had found it impossible to think himself into the part. How could he be in love with a woman who weighed almost two hundred pounds and was twenty years older than he was? No matter what miracles the wardrobe staff and make-up artists performed, nothing could change that. He had sung of love in the *Tosca* rehearsal not because of Claudia Rivera, but despite her. On a recording, where he would be judged by voice alone, he would be found faultless. On stage, where he had to react visibly and emotionally with the soprano, was a different matter.

To exacerbate the situation, the soprano had taken it upon herself to give Daniel acting lessons. He was never to stand in front of her, she told him firmly; he was never to shield her from the audience. When she sang, she always stood slightly forward of the man playing opposite her. That was the way she had always performed and she would change for no one; she was the star and deserved the most exposure. Daniel had looked to Hammersley for help. For once, the general manager was anything but master in his own house. To get Claudia Rivera to appear at the Grand, he had been forced to compromise himself by submitting to her contract demands. If he tried to clamp down on her, she would flounce off the stage and probably never return.

Daniel realized he had been spoiled by his many performances with Anna Markova. She was the rarest of all operatic singers—an attractive, slim, untemperamental soprano. Working with her was a joy. There were no tantrums, never a sharp word. She applied herself diligently to the task at hand and encouraged everyone around her. When things started to fall apart she was always the first with a humorous line to dissipate any tension. Claudia Rivera was somewhere beyond the other end of the spectrum, a tempestuous butterball whom Daniel could not stretch his arms around, even if he had wanted to.

The bell on the small alarm clock set on top of the piano began to ring, signaling to Daniel that it was time to go to the opera house for the dress rehearsal. Sticking to his ritual, he poured himself a shot of rye and downed it quickly, shuddering as if it were unpleasant medicine. Before he left the apartment, he lifted the piano lid and played part of his third-act aria, "E lucevan le stelle," so reminiscent of Al Jolson's "Avalon."

He was honest enough to know that he dreaded only one thing more than today's dress rehearsal.

And that was the performance itself.

* * *

Long lines of people shivered in the biting cold outside the Grand Opera House while they waited to enter for the paid dress rehearsal. As the taxi for which Daniel had waited fifteen minutes deposited him on the icy sidewalk, the orderly lines broke and he was besieged by autograph hunters. He stopped long enough to sign a dozen of the pieces of paper that were thrust at him. Then he pushed his way through, smiling at everyone, grateful when he saw the doorman coming to his rescue. He knew he could have entered secretively by the stage door, but he enjoyed the sensation of being besieged by his fans. If such things could happen to a skinny singer with a limited range like Frank Sinatra, why couldn't they happen to him? The smile split into a wide grin as he pictured a group of paid bobby-soxers in the front seats screaming with hysterical delight every time he opened his mouth. That would outdo any claque that Claudia Rivera might organize.

There was little for the make-up man to do. Daniel had grown a full beard for the role of Cavaradossi. After four weeks, he decided that he liked it so much he would keep it after the production. It covered his fleshy skin and lengthened his face. Anything that made him look thinner should be considered in a permanent light, he decided. Maybe he should pay more attention to his diet instead and lay off the calorie-ridden delicatessen food that was his favorite. During his four years with the company his weight had seesawed between one ninety-five and two thirty-five. But he was tall; he could handle the excess weight with ease.

The telephone rang as the make-up man finished his work. It was Anna, calling from her apartment on Fifth Avenue, overlooking the park.

"There's something for you in the drawer," she said.

Jamming the receiver to his ear with his shoulder, Daniel rummaged through the dressing table drawer. He found a white envelope with his name on it and shook the contents onto the table. A bent nail soldered to a fine gold chain dropped out. He laughed delightedly.

"It's beautiful!" he exclaimed. "For good luck?"

"What else? Unless you want to stick it into the *diva* if she gets on your nerves," Anna suggested. "Has she turned up yet?"

"I don't think so. She makes a habit of being late." Although he had come to expect Anna's encouragement, Daniel was especially glad that she had called. Anna fitted comfortably into his life. Her interests and goals were the same and they complemented each other, both onstage and off. Sometimes Daniel wondered if she fitted in just a little too comfortably. Often he had compared her with Lucy but it was a difficult match to make. Lucy had been a child, a girl who had led a totally sheltered life, while Anna was a woman mature enough to handle herself under any conditions. Being exposed to the glare of a constant spotlight did not bother her. And when the time came for her to reestablish her privacy, she retained the attributes Daniel had first admired—her consideration toward others and her supportiveness for any project she deemed worthwhile.

"Being late's a woman's privilege," Anna remarked lightly.

"Don't you dare turn out like her," Daniel warned.

"I don't eat that much. You should worry about yourself, though." She laughed and hung up.

Daniel placed the chain around his neck, shivering as the cold metal of the nail touched his skin. He felt immensely cheered by both the call and the thoughtful gift. The woman who had prayed for him on his debut as des Grieux was still standing by him; even if she wasn't appearing in the same production, her presence was felt. He was never certain how he felt about her. He knew he needed her. Sometimes he even thought he loved her, but then the specter of the tragic relationship with Lucy intervened and he questioned whether he knew what love even was.

He checked his appearance once more in the mirror, then began his vocal exercises, stopping when there was a knock on the door. Roger Hammersley stood outside.

"Has madam arrived yet?" Daniel asked after inviting the general manager into the dressing room.

"She's changing now." Hammersley pulled out a chair and sat down. "Daniel," he said quietly, "do me a big favor and be nice to the woman. You've only got two performances with her—today's dress rehearsal and Saturday's performance. After that, she'll be out of your hair forever."

"And yours, too, eh?" Daniel chuckled.

Hammersley nodded in agreement. "Mine, too." He knew now that it was a mistake to have hired Claudia Rivera, but he had been so swept away by the success of the *Ballo* recording that he could only see the triumph the Grand would reap with the same pairing; he had been blind to the pitfalls. Now that he had worked with Claudia Rivera, he knew that his heavy reliance on American singers had been the correct path to take. There was no doubt that the pairing would be an artistic success, but he was wondering if the price he would have to pay would be too high.

"I won't stand in front of her," Daniel promised. "I'll let her blot me out completely."

Hammersley just grinned sourly.

Five minutes before the curtain was due to rise, Daniel stood in the wings talking ice hockey with two stagehands. A flurry of activity announced the arrival of Claudia Rivera. She was preceded by her manager, a voluble rake of a man who had been flown over from Italy at the Grand's expense as part of the soprano's contract, and her favorite New York hair stylist; the one supplied by the opera company was not good enough for Claudia.

Daniel watched the procession with a degree of amusement. When Claudia spotted him, she crooked her finger imperiously.

"You, come here."

Daniel obediently ambled over to her.

"Remember, in duets I always stand in front of you. You are never to stand in front of me."

"I'll remember," Daniel promised and backed away a few steps. If he had his choice, he'd stand as far away from her as he possibly could. Never mind about behind. Viewed from close quarters, the make-up artist's work usually looked grotesque, a clown's face, heavy cosmetics which seemed normal from the other side of the orchestra but not from a yard away. With Claudia Rivera, even the clown's mask was an improvement if it only served to disguise the double chins and puffy eyes.

Claudia paced after him, unwilling to let him escape so easily. "And do not breathe over me, either. I do not want your germs," she warned. "Although I have protected myself by taking garlic."

From somewhere behind, Daniel could hear the stagehands laughing. As well as being repulsive to look at, the damned woman would be blasting garlic fumes all over him. He fondled the bent nail resting on his chest. If it were really a good luck talisman, Claudia would be struck down with terminal laryngitis before the overture began.

The soprano dismissed Daniel and waddled over to the stage manager. "Is my mattress ready?"

"Extra soft as you requested." He led her around the back of the stage to where the sets for later acts were stored. Daniel followed, watching as the stage manager pointed out the mattress that would cushion Claudia's fall after she had jumped off the ramparts of the Castel Sant' Angelo in the final moment of the opera. The drop was only four feet, after which she would crouch below the level of the parapet, out of the audience's sight. When you were as heavy and ungainly as the soprano, though, four feet could be as dangerous as forty. As he watched Claudia examine the mattress, wickedness began to form in Daniel's mind. He drew one of the stagehands off to the side.

"Just the one mattress?" Daniel asked conversationally.

"Sure."

Daniel looked earnestly at the man and shook his head. "Look, far be it from me to tell you guys how to do your job, but I think you'd be a lot safer using two, maybe even three."

"Why?" The man seemed perplexed.

"She's a very heavy lady. She's vain as well, won't admit that she needs more than one mattress. We've got the proper performance coming up on Saturday and I'd hate to see anything happen to Miss Rivera today, like breaking her neck because one mattress wasn't enough."

The stagehand looked doubtful. During the first rehearsal, Claudia hadn't bothered to jump; they hadn't even had the set completely erected. But surely the woman knew how many mattresses she wanted? "I don't know, Mr. Kerr. We were told just the one."

"I'll give you twenty bucks if you use two or three. Make it three, just to be on the safe side."

The prospect of money for nothing more strenuous than finding two additional mattresses convinced the stagehand that Daniel was right. "Sure, Mr. Kerr. Miss Rivera will be happy to know that she's got friends like you."

As the volley of musket shots rang out across the stage, filling the area with acrid smoke, Daniel dropped to the floor, fervently grateful that his active participation in the opera was over. Standing close to Claudia Rivera had been a waking nightmare. Not only did her breath stink of garlic, but he was certain the soprano had not taken a bath for at least two days. Maybe that was her good luck charm, he reasoned; her bent nail. Dirt. A body odor that would have felled Scarpia just as surely and swiftly as the knife she had used at the end of the second act.

He was surprised at how easily he had managed to sing "E lucevan le stelle." The memories of Lucy and the child that had plagued him when he was studying the score had disappeared. That was what working with Claudia Rivera was doing for him, he thought; making him forget everything else but her. Didn't Hammersley have any control over the soprano at all? Or was it also written in her contract that she could take as many bows as she thought fit after each aria? Daniel felt especially sorry for the baritone who had sung Scarpia. The man had been left to stand alone, looking like a fool while Claudia took bow after bow following her "Vissi d'arte." Sure she could sing, but so could Anna Markova. And with the Brooklyn soprano they would all be spared the histrionics that went with the Italian's performance.

Daniel tried to shut down his senses as he felt Claudia's sagging body hanging over him, crushing his head to her overabundant bosom while she sang in anguish at his death. He didn't know what was worse, the nauseating odor that oozed from her pores or the garlic on her breath. But soon, if the stagehand had earned his twenty bucks, Daniel would have his revenge. And the house would have a grand finale it had not reckoned on.

Daniel only breathed out when his Tosca stood up and ran to the ramparts to escape from the police. Without moving his body, he opened his eyes and watched in fascination. Standing on the parapet, Claudia sang Tosca's final line. Then, with what she considered to be a dramatic touch, she threw both arms high above her head and leaped to her death.

A gale of laughter swept through the opera house when Claudia's head and shoulders reappeared as she bounced up from the three mattresses, accompanied by a loud, terrified shriek that Puccini had never intended to be included in the score.

It took every ounce of determination in Daniel's body for him to lie still and not curl up in a fit of laughter. Maybe he'd give the guy thirty bucks instead of twenty.

Isaac Kirschbaum shook his head slowly in admonition, but he found it difficult to keep a smile off his face. "A joker, you are. A practical joker. Daniel, how could you? Miss Rivera's an internationally famous opera singer. Before the war, she sang with Gigli."

"I'm also a famous opera singer, Pa," Daniel defended himself. "I'm entitled to some respect as well."

"Of course you are. And you'll get it without playing silly tricks like that. The poor woman might have been seriously injured." When he saw Daniel cross his fingers, Isaac shook his head again. "Aw, what's the use of talking to you anyway? You don't listen. You know best."

"Pa"—Daniel grabbed his father's hand as he tried to communicate his own high spirits—"if you'd have heard the audience laughing when she came back up, you wouldn't be complaining."

"Daniel, an opera like *Tosca* is not a comedy. That final act is very tense drama. That last scene, when Tosca jumps to her death and the orchestra plays the refrain from 'E lucevan le stelle' is supposed to send shivers down your spine. It's not supposed to make you laugh."

"Hammersley said the same thing," Daniel admitted.

"And the stagehand lost his job because of you, huh?"

"No. I took all the blame." Daniel stood up and looked out of the window. It was snowing and he could barely see Van Cortlandt Park. Without the view, his parents might just as well have stayed in Claremont Parkway. "You getting out at all?" he asked his father.

Isaac shrugged. "A little bit. When the weather's not too bad."

"You should try to get out more."

"Daniel, I'm not a youngster. When the winter comes, I stay indoors. Your mother has places to go, but I'll wait for the spring."

It was not Yetta Kirschbaum about whom Daniel worried. Since he had persuaded his parents to leave Claremont Parkway a year earlier and move into a house he had bought for them close to Van Cortlandt Park, his mother had immediately launched herself at the local women's committees, eager to be the center of attraction as she had been in the old neighborhood. But his father, retired from work, no longer had a routine to force him out of the house. Daniel feared that without the friends from Claremont Parkway who would drop in on the off-chance, Isaac would simply sit at home and waste away. During the warm weather, the problem had not been so critical. Although he had been deprived of going into the city every day, Isaac had made the trip to Claremont Parkway to keep up his friendships; and he had walked in the park, meeting people there, finding games of chess and cards in which he could join. With the advent of winter, however, he had shut himself away in the house, only venturing out when Daniel took him somewhere.

The move had affected Daniel as well. No longer a visitor to the Claremont Parkway section of the Bronx, he had almost lost all contact with Tommy Mulvaney. The last time he had seen Tommy had been a chance encounter in the Village. He had been on a dinner date with Anna, and Tommy had been with his wife; Daniel was ashamed that he could not even remember the girl's name. Both Tommy and his father had left the police department. The older Mulvaney had retired and gone south and Tommy had switched from one law enforcement agency to another—he had joined the FBI and was working from the bureau's New York office. During a jubilant reunion, Daniel had promised to send Tommy two tickets to one of his performances, a promise that was forgotten as soon as the two couples had parted company. Occasionally Anna would remind him and Daniel would feel guilty at his neglect; and each time he would push it to the furthest recesses of his mind again. After all, what cop was interested in opera? It was best this way. He and Tommy had gone their separate ways. Happened all the time, close childhood friends drifting apart once they grew up and split in different directions. They'd be an encumbrance to each other now.

"Pa, if I leave tickets for you at the box office, will you be able to get down to the opera house by yourself on Saturday night?"

"So we can see you play practical jokes on your soprano?" Isaac queried.

"No tricks, Pa. I promise you. This is the real thing, not some crummy dress rehearsal."

"We'll take a cab," Isaac said grandly. "And arrive in style just like the lead tenor's family should arrive. Where will you be that you can't see us before?"

"I'm having dinner with Anna before the performance."

Isaac smiled happily at the answer. "I think, perhaps, that you would rather have Anna as your Tosca instead of this Italian mattress prima donna."

"You bet." Daniel took his coat from the closet and put it on, preparing to leave. Isaac called him back.

"Daniel, I'm very proud of you. I hope you know that."

"Of course I know." He opened the front door, wanting to leave before his father became sentimental. He knew that Isaac did not want him to go, leaving him alone in the house. His mother had adjusted to the move from Claremont Parkway, but his father—although continually praising Daniel for buying the house—had not. The open spaces of the park frightened him. Walking upstairs to go to bed frightened him. The whole new environment frightened him. Combined with the absence of the routine imposed by going to the garment center each morning, he was becoming lost.

"Your mother, too."

Again Daniel said he knew. The funny thing was, he realized that his father was right. Maybe Yetta had mellowed with age; perhaps he had. She still watched every single penny as if it were her last, and she was still prone to the sudden illnesses that would assure her of attention and sympathy. But she was no longer the virago to whom Daniel had promised to deny any pleasure from his achievements. It was his own maturity, he decided. He viewed his mother now in a different perspective, no longer dependent on her for his well-being. And he realized that with Jack and his family firmly entrenched in Chicago, he was the only close relative his parents had. He remembered well the private vow he had taken after deciding to become a cantor. It was a promise that was impossible to keep. To deny his mother any enjoyment, he would have to harm himself; to make her miserable, he would have to forsake his own career. Above all, to do so he would have to hurt his father.

"Sure, Pa." Christ almighty! he wished his father would stop. But whom else did he have to talk to?

"Daniel, come back here a minute. I want to ask you something."

Daniel pushed the door shut and moved close to his father. "What is it, Pa?"

"On Saturday night, make a big show of your mother. Do it for me."

"I'll be with Anna. I'll have time to say hello and goodbye after the performance."

"Then make it a fond hello and goodbye. Please?"

"Okay, Pa. We'll grab a bite to eat in Wheeler's afterwards." He leaned forward to kiss his father on the cheek, then he got out of the house as quickly as he could.

Daniel tried his hardest to picture Claudia Rivera in the full-length mink coat that Anna was wearing. He gave up. Probably there were not enough minks in the entire world to make a coat that would fit that gargantuan body.

Damn! All he could think of was that bitch. It was bad enough that he'd have to sing with her in a couple of hours, with the garlic on the breath and the stink of unwashed flesh, but did he have to ruin his precious time with Anna by thinking about her?

"Penny for them," Anna said.

Daniel switched his attention from the Fifth Avenue shop windows to look back inside the cab, to Anna sitting beside him. "Give you one big fat stinking guess."

"La Rivera?"

"Who else? The b.o. and the whole *schmear.*"

"Try stuffing wads of cotton up your nose," Anna suggested brightly.

"Interfere with my singing. Pity that something doesn't interfere with hers."

Anna leaned back and laughed. Then she became serious. "Daniel, watch out for her," she warned. "She'll want to get back at you for the other day. I know that if someone pulled a trick like that on me, I'd want to get my own back on them, sure as hell."

Daniel dismissed Anna's warning out of hand. "I know the stagehands better than she does. Rivera couldn't pay them enough to put real powder and shot into the firing squad's muskets." He smiled suddenly and took Anna's hand. "Do you mind a snack with my parents after the performance? I promised my father."

"No problem."

"I'll make it quick," Daniel promised. "Then we can go to a club."

She squeezed his hand fondly. "Sounds great."

Claudia Rivera ignored Daniel completely as they stood together in the wings before the opening curtain. As far as she was concerned, Daniel did not exist; he was on a level with the technicians who rolled the scenery on and off the stage. Claudia Rivera did not stoop to acknowledging the presence of such people.

Hammersley appeared, dressed in his customary white tie and tails. He whispered in Daniel's ear that President Truman and his daughter were in the audience, seated in Hammersley's own grand tier box. Daniel flinched, but before he could make any reply, Hammersley had moved on to Claudia and her manager. Daniel watched while a white envelope was passed across. Payment before performance, another trick of the

Italian soprano. Daniel knew what he'd do if he were in Hammersley's shoes. He wouldn't give Claudia a check; he'd pay her in dollar bills. See what she'd do with a parcel that size! But you'd think with what she was getting paid she would be able to afford a bar of soap and some deodorant.

"Next time she sings here put something in her contract about taking a bath at least once a year," Daniel whispered as Hammersley walked by, on his way to his box and the President.

"Try not to breathe too deeply," was Hammersley's reply.

Daniel thought of Lucy just once during the performance, while he walked along the ramparts and sang "E lucevan le stelle." As applause for the aria rang out, he closed his eyes and pictured what Lucy must have seen the moment she jumped from the window. No mattress. Only a cold stone patio. No lifeless Scarpia or Cavaradossi behind her. Just a mercifully dead child and an uncaring husband. He fondled the bent nail hanging under his shirt and thought about Anna instead. Sitting in the audience, waiting for him. And about the President up in Hammersley's box. During the interval before the second act, he'd peeked through the curtain and seen him. Hammersley was probably planning to introduce the cast to Truman after the performance. The unwelcome vision of Lucy passed.

Claudia appeared on stage to tell him how she had deceived Scarpia into signing two safe conduct passes and how she had then killed him. Daniel delicately angled his head away to avoid the smell as he sang "O dolce mani"—sweet hands that would kill for him. Anna's warning of revenge had been for nought. Notwithstanding the odor, Claudia was behaving perfectly. Never had there been even the slightest hint of her trying to upstage him. She must have learned something from the mattress episode, Daniel decided. That he had more friends at the Grand than she did.

More applause followed "O dolce mani" and Daniel's confidence reached new heights. The Grand was his opera house. Claudia Rivera was a guest, nothing more. When she and her tantrums and her God-awful smell had gone, he would remain firmly established.

American tenor and Italian soprano played against each other beautifully as they neared the climax of their duet, discussing how wonderful life would be in exile after the mock execution had taken place. Until at last they joined voices for the four words "*armonie di canti diffonderem.*" Daniel closed the final note on cue, ready for the pause that preceded "*Trionfal*" and the last verse. He was startled and then horrified when Claudia held onto the note for a full second after he had finished.

"You fucking Italian bitch!" he hissed at her.

She smirked back at him.

He caught himself quickly and picked up the duet again. Sheer professionalism kept his voice singing while his mind raged at the soprano. She had held onto the note and made him look short of breath! In front of thousands of people! In front of the President of the United States!

The duet ended among cries of "*Brava*, Rivera!" And hisses and catcalls which Daniel knew were directed at him. The audience had turned on him, and Daniel knew that Claudia's paid help—the leader of the claque she had organized—was responsible. If he knew who the guy was, where he was sitting, he'd leap off the stage and plaster him against the nearest wall, President Truman in the audience or not. The slimy little bastard would never lead applause or catcalls again.

Hammersley would realize what had happened. The orchestra would. The cast. So would everyone at the Grand who had worked on the score. But the audience would have only one thought, a single idea that had allowed them to be led into hissing him. That he had been physically unable to hold onto the note for as long as necessary.

They would forget all about his successful arias of the night, where he had held onto more difficult notes for far longer. Only the question mark surrounding that one short note would remain.

Daniel left the curtain calls to Claudia. As soon as the curtain dropped, he stormed off the stage and raced upstairs to his dressing room. Hammersley was there less than a minute later, closing the door, cutting the two of them off from the rest of the opera house.

"Daniel, I know what happened out there. I promise you that she will never work here again."

"Are you going to tell that to the audience? To the critics?" Daniel snapped. "To the President and his daughter? They sure as hell don't know. All they know is that I screwed up monumentally."

Hammersley stood patiently, letting Daniel finish. "President Truman and his daughter have left. And they know what happened."

"Fine!" Daniel spat out, not even bothered that now he would not get the chance to meet Truman. "What about everyone else? That bitch made a fool out of me."

"She cut you up like a professional, Daniel," Hammersley replied evenly. "You should take it the same way. After all"—a slight smile illuminated his smooth face—"you did manage to make her look like a complete jackass during the rehearsal."

"Looking like a jackass and looking like a rank amateur are two totally different things," Daniel retorted. "What she did to me is unforgivable."

"I told you, she'll never work here again while I am general manager," Hammersley repeated. "If she were under contract for further performances, I'd tear up the contract and send her packing. Do you think we can leave it at that?"

Daniel did not answer. He looked in the dressing room mirror and started applying cold cream to his face. Some of it stuck in his beard and he rubbed furiously with a towel, transferring his anger from Claudia Rivera to the cold cream. God, what wouldn't he give to get one final crack at that fat bitch! He could have had his revenge when she was sprawled on top of him in grief after the firing squad had done its work. A sharp jab with the point of Anna's bent nail, a pinch, a grab at her tits; something upstage, out of the view of the audience that would have ruined her lines. She'd have croaked instead of singing. Or she'd have hit a note she never dreamed she could reach. But it was too late to think about it now. The performance was finished, and the joke had been played on him.

"Daniel." Hammersley watched warily as Daniel threw off his costume and began to clean up. "May I please have your word as a gentleman that you will take this unfortunate incident no further?"

"How the hell can I take it any further?" Daniel swung around to face the general manager. "You said it yourself—we're not appearing together any more."

Hammersley inclined his head in acceptance of the words. "Perhaps it's just as well. I'll go to see Rivera now and explain how disappointed I am with her behavior."

"Make sure you tell her how pissed off I am as well!" Daniel yelled after him.

"I imagine that your feelings on the matter go without saying, which, from your choice of language, is just as well." Hammersley closed the door on the way out. Two seconds later there was a knock.

"Come in!"

Anna entered the dressing room with an exaggerated display of caution. "Are you going to shout at me as well?" she asked meekly.

"Did you hear what happened out there? In front of Truman, everyone, that fat bitch pulls a stroke like that."

"She did a job on you," Anna said unnecessarily. "It was disgusting."

Hearing Anna agree so readily with his own thoughts had a soothing effect on Daniel; the woman's own steady calmness influenced him. "What do you think I should do?" he asked.

"Be a pro and forget about it. I'm sure that Mr. Hammersley will talk to the critics about what happened. He wouldn't allow you to get a black mark like that. It would be bad for both you and the company."

Daniel thought about it before finally conceding that Anna was right. He reached out to embrace her. She recoiled as his cream-clotted beard brushed against her face.

"Hurry up and get ready," she told him. "I saw your parents before. They're waiting for you in Wheeler's. Your father's a bit upset by the reception you got."

"Great!" Daniel said sarcastically. "Even he thinks I screwed up." He washed and dressed quickly, then accompanied Anna down to the restaurant. When he entered Wheeler's, the customary polite round of applause was missing. In its place was a subdued buzz, the sound of cutlery on china. Face turning crimson from embarrassment and rage, he looked at the nearest diners. They turned their heads away. Daniel knew why. Rivera and that goddamned note she'd hung on to. They all thought he'd blown it. Choked and missed the note. Timed his breathing so badly that he couldn't hold on. Nothing Hammersley could say or do would be able to change it.

"Don't worry, Daniel," he heard Anna whisper. "You'll live through it."

Daniel nodded grimly as he led Anna between the tables to where his parents sat. Remembering what he had promised, he bent down and kissed his mother. Then he clasped Isaac by the hand.

"What happened?" his father asked. "In that last duet?"

"That Italian whale held onto the note for longer than she was supposed to."

"Why would she do a thing like that?" his mother asked.

"Why? To make people think exactly what you're thinking. That I blew it."

"She got you back for the other day, huh?" Isaac said. "Picked her moment well, in front of the President and all. That will teach you to play schoolboy tricks."

"Yeah, sure." Daniel looked around the restaurant uneasily. Tonight he didn't feel at home. Wheeler's was suddenly enemy territory. "Can we get out of here? Go somewhere else?"

"Sit down," Anna told him firmly. "You belong here. If you don't stick this out, you'll lose in the long run."

"Okay, I'll stay." At least Anna was standing by him. He started to sit, then stood up again. "I've got to go somewhere first." He walked quickly to the washroom and locked himself in a cubicle, certain that everyone in the restaurant was talking about him now that he had gone. He needed time to think, time to cool off. The way he was feeling right now he would antagonize everyone. His parents. Even Anna. That would be all he needed to cap a disastrous night.

Five minutes later he emerged from the cubicle, his mind set to accept the embarrassment. Anna was right. His next performance would knock this evening to the back of his history books; the short note would never be remembered.

The washroom attendant brushed his jacket. Daniel tipped

the man and prepared to rejoin his party in the restaurant. As he opened the door, he had an idea. He spoke a few words to the attendant, who took something from the storage cupboard and passed it to Daniel. Daniel slipped it into his pocket and reentered Wheeler's.

"Did you wash your hands?" Anna asked lightly as he sat down.

"Before and after," he replied. "See?" He showed her his hands, back and front.

"Feel better now?"

"Yes." He picked up a menu. "Let's order."

As the waiter appeared, a single cry of "*Brava*, Rivera!" rang out through the restaurant, magnified as other diners took it up. Daniel swiveled on the chair and looked toward the restaurant entrance to see the Italian soprano entering like a triumphant Caesar returning to Rome with the spoils of victory, beaming in pleasure at the reception, waving a fat, beringed hand in recognition of the praise. Daniel knew whose voice had started the cries. The same worm who had instigated the applause during the performance and who—he was certain—was responsible for the hissing and catcalls that had followed the short note. Now he could see who it was. He got up from the chair and took one step away from the table. Anna pulled him back.

"Daniel, leave it alone," Anna whispered. "Rivera will be gone by tomorrow. You'll still be here."

"It's not her I want. It's that little *vuntz* over there." He pointed to the claque leader, a tall, skinny, middle-aged man dressed in a tuxedo. As Daniel watched angrily, the man stood up and clapped his hands enthusiastically, leading the restaurant customers into a louder, more sustained ovation. He stopped clapping long enough to pull out a chair at the table he was occupying, holding it for Claudia.

"Leave it alone," Anna repeated.

Daniel chose not to hear the warning. He shook himself free and marched across the restaurant. About to sit down in the chair being held for her, Claudia stopped halfway when she saw Daniel.

"A word of advice!" Daniel called loudly to the claque leader over the suddenly silent restaurant. "Use two chairs. One for each buttock!"

Chairs scraped as people moved to better witness the eruption of the volcano. Claudia straightened up, the pudgy face drawn tightly. "A pity you do not sing as well as you shout, Mr. Kerr. Perhaps you would then draw the applause a true artist deserves."

Daniel kept his eyes on the claque leader. "I don't like paid applause. Especially when it's led by a creep like the one you hired."

The man took his hand off Claudia's chair and squared his shoulders. Daniel moved swiftly and grabbed the man by the lapels of his tuxedo jacket, lifted him clear off the ground and deposited him firmly in the center of the table, sitting him in a bowl of iced water which held two bottles of champagne. The claque leader's screams drowned out the anguished cries of the maître d' who was trying to stop his restaurant from being turned into a battlefield.

Turning from the stricken claque leader, Daniel reached into his jacket pocket and presented to Claudia the wrapped bar of soap he had been given by the washroom attendant.

"Madam," he said loudly enough for everyone in the restaurant to hear. "In the United States we call this soap. I would suggest that you try using it. It will stop your body from singing as powerfully as your voice."

Then he turned to address the entire restaurant. "I, too, can hold a note for an unnecessarily long time. '*Armonie di canti diffonderem!*' "

He held the last note for seven seconds. Then, with a wide grin of satisfaction that mirrored his pleasure at the ovation he received, he walked triumphantly back to his own table. He covered three steps when something smashed into the back of his head and he fell to the ground, unconscious.

A face topped by a shock of white hair swam drunkenly into his vision, alternately sharp and fuzzy as Daniel tried to bring it into focus. Daniel blinked three times in rapid succession, and Hammersley's face stabilized.

"What the hell happened?"

"Rivera crowned you with a bottle of Dom Pérignon, which you wholeheartedly deserved from what the maître d' told me."

Daniel sat up, surprised to find himself in Hammersley's office. Anna was sitting in a chair, her concerned face beginning to relax as she saw that Daniel was all right. "Where are my parents?" he asked. "How did I get up here?"

"I sent them home in a taxi," Anna replied. "Your mother was hysterical." She would be, Daniel thought. "Fortunately there was a doctor in Wheeler's. He took care of her."

"Then we brought you up here," Hammersley continued. "So Wheeler's could return to normal. Fat chance of that," he added quietly.

Daniel struggled to his feet, feeling his head to be sure it was still there. A lump the size of a golf ball greeted his questing fingers. "Jesus," he muttered, half in shock, half in admiration. "Rivera did that? Where is she?"

"Forget about Rivera," Hammersley answered. "She left."

"Can I press charges?" Daniel asked hopefully. "Assault?"

"For the good of the company I would prefer it if you did not. Besides, her friend could do the same to you, remember?"

"But I only dumped him in a bowl of ice water!" Daniel protested. "She creamed me with a full bottle."

Hammersley waved away the justification as having no significance. "Stealing five cents and stealing five dollars is still theft. So you can forget all about pressing assault charges. There is, however, one matter I would like to discuss with you if you feel well enough."

"What?"

"My artists do not make a habit of insulting each other in private or in public. An apology is in order."

"To Rivera?" Daniel asked incredulously. "You're kidding!" He looked to Anna for support, but he could find no expression in her face to give him comfort.

"No," Hammersley said. "Not to Rivera. To me. To Anna. To everyone who witnessed that disgraceful exhibition in Wheeler's. And to all of our patrons. I would suggest a public apology in the columns of the New York *Times*."

"That's crazy!" Daniel burst out. "Rivera's the one who should apologize."

"If she were under further contract to the Grand, she would. Otherwise, she would no longer work for me," Hammersley explained. "You, however, are still under contract."

"If I apologize, I'll admit I was wrong."

"You were. You made a fellow professional—no matter how obnoxious a person she might be—look a complete and utter ass in front of a restaurant full of patrons. And you physically assaulted one of her party."

"He deserved it," Daniel muttered.

Hammersley ignored the comment. "I leave the choice to you," he said with an air of finality. "A public apology to our patrons against the continuation of your contract. Think about it over the weekend. I'll expect your decision first thing on Monday morning."

Daniel watched sourly as Hammersley held open the office door. Then he took Anna's hand and left.

"I'll see you home," Anna offered as they stood outside the empty opera house and looked along West Thirty-fourth Street for a taxi.

"You don't have to," Daniel said half-heartedly. "I'm not an invalid."

"I never said you were. But I think you need company more than you're willing to let on." She flagged down a passing cab and helped Daniel inside. His head ached abominably and he felt nauseated. Far above the physical discomfort, though, rose a sensation of horror that he would have to apologize in public for the mayhem in Wheeler's.

The cab turned south toward the Village and Daniel slumped back in the seat, angry at Hammersley for demanding an apology as a condition for continuing with the Grand, and even angrier with himself for disregarding the advice of both Hammersley and Anna that he should conduct himself like a professional and not be provoked by Claudia's antics. But didn't they understand that she had made him look like a rank beginner? That she'd harmed the reputation he had worked so hard to establish? Even his father—and what stronger supporter did he have?—had thought he'd fluffed the note. It was ingenious, though. He had to admit that. Claudia Rivera—that fat stinking bitch—had chosen her moment of revenge well. Insults, abuse he could have taken and still laughed. But to be left stranded, apparently short of breath while she continued the note, had been like a dagger thrust between his shoulder blades. Grudgingly he forced himself to admit that the Italian soprano's revenge bore the trademark of a real professional at the game. She'd picked her audience well—everyone from Harry S. Truman on down—and she'd picked her method well. Daniel was still learning the business.

The cab stopped outside his apartment house. Anna paid the driver and helped Daniel out. "Keep the cab," he told her. "I'll be all right from here."

She shook her head firmly, brooking no argument. "Nothing doing, pal. I'm tucking you in tonight."

He managed to grin. "Are you going to undress me as well?"

"I've seen you in your underwear before." She put an arm around him for support. "Come on, you wounded soldier. The war's over for today."

Unprotesting, Daniel allowed himself to be helped up to the apartment. In the living room, he dropped heavily onto the divan, not even bothering to remove his topcoat.

"Where do you keep the aspirin?" Anna asked.

"Bathroom. Medicine cabinet."

Anna disappeared, returning seconds later with a bottle which she held upside down. "Empty," she said needlessly. "Why do you bother keeping empty aspirin bottles?" She threw the bottle into the trashcan in the kitchen, put on her coat and opened the door. Daniel asked where she was going.

"There's an all-night drug store over on Sixth Avenue. I'll be back in a few minutes." Before Daniel could stop her, she left the apartment. He stood up and put away his coat, then he went into the kitchen to make some coffee. By the time it was perking, Anna was back with a large bottle of Bayer aspirin.

"How's the head?" she asked, measuring out three tablets into the palm of her hand. She gave them to Daniel, who swilled them down with a glass of water.

"Still there. Aren't you going home? It's past one."

"Before I leave tonight we're going to write that apology for Mr. Hammersley," Anna said evenly.

"I'll do it in the morning."

"Like hell you will. You'll sit up all night long and work yourself into a frenzy, find a thousand and one reasons why you shouldn't have to apologize. And you know damned well you should." She watched him pour the coffee and take two cups into the living room. "Where's the notepaper?"

Daniel pointed to the mahogany secretary. Anna pulled open the doors, took out a pad of notepaper and began to write.

"What are you putting down there?" Daniel asked, alarmed by the speed with which the words flowed from her pen. "He wants an apology, not a book."

Anna held up her hand for him to be quiet. A minute passed while she continued writing, crossing out words, substituting new ones. Finally she held the pad away to read off the message. "To Mr. Roger Hammersley, the members and patrons of the Grand Opera Company of New York: Following the disturbance in Wheeler's Restaurant on Saturday night, I wish to apologize for my unprofessional behavior. Although I was provoked, I now realize that my unfortunate response was ill-conceived and I regret any embarrassment or discomfort I may have caused." She paused and then added, "Sign it, Daniel."

Daniel exploded. "I can't sign that!" he yelled, instantly regretting the force of his words as the anvil chorus in his head picked up pace. "Rivera will bust a gut laughing. So will everyone."

"Daniel, Rivera's career is almost over; she's got another five, maybe ten years tops. Yours is just starting. She'll have damned good reason to laugh if your career ends right here. Then she would have won."

Anna's logic cut through his pride and anger. She was right. She had been around far longer than he had, knew the ropes more. Despite his successes in *Manon Lescaut*, *Cavalleria Rusticana*, *Rigoletto* and *Ballo*, he was still a virtual newcomer. If he refused to apologize, Hammersley would terminate his contract at the Grand and let him go. He knew the general manager well enough by now to realize that he would stick to his word, even if it meant losing one of his top tenors. Hammersley was a man of unyielding principle who demanded complete loyalty and obedience from his artists.

"Give it here," Daniel said quietly. "I'll keep you happy and sign the damned thing."

Anna rewrote the apology neatly, then passed it across for Daniel to sign. When he had finished, she took back the sheet of paper, folded it carefully and deposited it in her purse. "Just in case you change your mind by Monday morning."

Daniel grinned and was pleasantly surprised to find that his headache had subsided slightly. He held out his hands to Anna. "You're a doll."

She shook her head but took his hands nonetheless. "I'll be an Aïda, a Mimi or a Gioconda. But I refuse adamantly to be a doll. Another apology, please."

"Uh-uh. That's one I'm not apologizing for." He pulled her onto the divan beside him and kissed her lightly on the lips. "That's how my speechwriter gets paid."

"Speechwriter, hell!" she shot back. "I'm your career-saver." She ran her hand across the back of his head and tenderly felt the bump. "That Rivera should have been a boxer," she murmured. "A heavyweight contender. She punches her weight and then some."

"Smells it as well."

"You'd better go to bed, Daniel. Make yourself a cold compress and get some sleep."

"You mean you're going to leave me?" Daniel asked plaintively. "Leave an invalid, a dying cripple all alone? How can you? Where's your sympathy?"

"In my purse with your apology. Daniel"—she leaned forward to kiss him—"if I don't leave now, it's going to be very tough for me to leave at all. Some other night." She stood up and walked to the closet for her coat.

"Where did your family come from?" Daniel asked out of the blue.

"My family? Why do you want to know about that?"

"I'm curious about the name Markowitz, that's all."

"Poland," she said. "Two generations ago."

"Good."

She looked at him strangely, but he made no attempt to clarify the comment. She let him help her into the mink coat, then he walked her down to the street to find a cab. When he returned to the apartment, he waited for half an hour—enough time for her to have gotten home through the snow—and dialed her number.

"How do I make a cold compress?" he asked.

Chapter Three

The telephone rang shortly after eight o'clock in the morning, disturbing the Sunday tranquility.

Daniel reached out to lift the receiver from the bedside extension, grateful for the diversion. He had hardly slept at all, kept awake by the dull throbbing pain in his head and the even sharper pain that a public apology about his behavior would surely bring.

He hoped it was Anna calling to find out how he was feeling. After last night's debacle, the soprano was about the only bright star on his horizon; he was convinced he was in love with her.

Instead, it was his mother.

Yetta did not ask Daniel how he was feeling. She did not ask what had happened after she and Isaac had been sent home in a taxi by Anna. All she said was, "Your father's been taken to the hospital."

Daniel sat up in bed, suddenly alert, the ache in his head forgotten. "What's the matter with him?"

"He was up all night, complaining about chest pains . . ."

"What's the matter with him?"

Yetta carried right on, dramatizing the situation until Daniel felt like screaming at her. "He thought it was indigestion. He took some seltzer for it, but the pain wouldn't go away."

"For Christ's sake! What's the matter with him?"

"He's had a heart attack."

Holding the receiver to his ear, Daniel jumped out of bed and began looking around the room for his clothes. "Where did they take him? Which hospital?"

"Montefiore. On Gun Hill Road and Bainbridge—"

"I know where Montefiore is. Are you there now?"

"Of course."

"I'll be there in half an hour."

Without bothering to wash or clean his teeth, Daniel dived

into the clothes he'd worn the night before and rushed downstairs to the garage where he kept his car. Because of the snow and cold, he had not used the car for two weeks, but he knew he had little chance of finding a cab to take him to the Bronx at eight on a snowy Sunday morning. When he turned the ignition key, his efforts were rewarded with nothing more encouraging than a dull click. The battery was dead.

He jumped out of the car and, in blind frustration, lashed out savagely at the fender with his foot, leaving a deep dent. The icy wind that whistled around his unprotected head and throat held no discomfort for him. All he could think of was the damned car, and his father lying in a hospital with a heart attack. How ill was he? Critical? Dying? Daniel prayed that his mother had transferred some of her own hypochondria to Isaac. Maybe it was just indigestion and his mother had done what she used to do to him—called in every doctor and ambulance within a ten-mile radius.

Of course it wasn't indigestion. His father had suffered a heart attack and the car was useless! Now, how was he going to get to the Bronx? Subway? Daniel started running toward Sixth Avenue and the closest station. He slipped on the ice and fell, skinning his hands and knees, tearing his trousers. Tears of anger almost froze as they sprang to his eyes and started to roll down his cheeks.

Moishe! That *meshuggeneh* would drive in this kind of weather. He wouldn't even see it had been snowing. He'd get Moishe to run him up to the Bronx. Mind made up, Daniel walked quickly but cautiously over the icy sidewalk to Moishe's building and ran up the stairs. Moishe opened the door in pajamas and dressing gown, sleep-filled eyes widening in shock as he surveyed the tattered figure of Daniel.

"What happened?"

"Get dressed!" Daniel snapped. "I need you to run me to the Bronx. My father's in the hospital with a heart attack."

"Where's your car?"

"Dead battery. Jesus, are you going to take me or not?" Daniel demanded.

"Okay, okay. Give me five minutes to throw some clothes on, will you?"

Daniel paced the living room while Moishe dressed. What was taking him so long? Was he taking a shower? Cleaning his teeth? Shaving? Daniel wanted a driver, not a tailor's dummy! When Moishe came back, fully dressed, less than two minutes had elapsed. To Daniel, it seemed like two hours.

"Where is he?"

"Montefiore. Gun Hill Road and Bainbridge Avenue."

"You'd better direct me." Moishe led the way downstairs and started the car. The rear wheels spun on the icy road surface and then gripped. Daniel held on tightly, hoping there would be no traffic. Moishe was dangerous on dry roads; on ice it would be like flying co-pilot with a Kamikaze.

"What happened to your father?" Moishe asked, gripping the wheel as tightly as he could. Thirty yards ahead, a traffic light changed against him. Moishe debated about whether he should brake and decided not to. He gave the engine gas, sending the car speeding through the intersection moments after the lights had turned to red. A chorus of angry honking applauded his efforts as cars coming across braked wildly to avoid an accident. Daniel screwed his eyes shut and prayed.

"I asked you what happened," Moishe repeated, oblivious to the multiple accident he had nearly caused.

Daniel forced himself to open his eyes again, amazed to find that the windshield was still intact. "Last night I had a run-in with Claudia Rivera in Wheeler's after the performance. Didn't you read anything about it in the newspapers? I imagine it was in them."

"I haven't seen a paper. I was in bed when you tried knocking the door down." Moishe pressed harder on the gas pedal as he sensed the next light about to change. The car's speed rose to forty-five miles an hour in his quest to catch all the lights along East Houston Street to the East River. The car swayed drunkenly as it hit potholes left by the winter, and Daniel felt that he was going to be sick at any minute.

"I got hit over the head with a bottle," Daniel explained. "It must have upset my father. Now he's in the hospital suffering from a heart attack."

"Quit worrying. It's probably minor," Moishe said hopefully.

"How can a heart attack be minor?"

From a hundred yards behind, a siren began to wail. Daniel swiveled in the seat and saw a patrol car gaining on them. "Pull over," he told Moishe.

Moishe ignored Daniel's instruction. "This is an emergency," he pointed out.

"Pull over, you idiot, or we'll wind up in a hospital, too." Daniel reached across and turned off the ignition, pulling out the key. The engine died and Moishe guided the car to an abrupt halt. The police cruiser pulled to an angled stop in front of them, and the driver climbed out. He pulled his coat collar up around his ears and went to Moishe's window.

"You in a hurry to get to church or something?" His breath left clouds of vapor hanging in the freezing air.

Daniel leaned across Moishe to answer. "My father's just been taken to the hospital with a heart attack. We're trying to get to the Bronx to see him."

"What hospital?" the police officer asked dubiously; he hadn't heard this excuse for almost two days.

"Montefiore."

"What's his name?"

"Kirschbaum. Isaac Kirschbaum."

"Wait a minute." The officer returned to his car. Three minutes dragged by while he spoke on the car's radio. Then he rolled down his window and signaled Moishe to follow him. Lights flashing, siren blasting, he led the way uptown, over the Harlem River and into the Bronx. When the police car pulled up in front of Montefiore, the driver waved to Moishe and Daniel, executed a wide u-turn and headed back to Manhattan. Daniel left Moishe to lock the car while he hurried into the building. A woman at the reception desk told him what ward his father was in. Unwilling to wait for the elevator, Daniel ran up the stairs to the third floor.

Yetta Kirschbaum was sitting in the corridor outside the ward. She stood up when she recognized Daniel running heavily from the stairway.

"How is he?" Daniel asked.

"The doctor's in with him now."

Daniel peeked into the ward. He could see three patients, but the far corner bed which his father occupied was surrounded by a screen. As he watched, the screen was pulled back and wheeled away. Daniel could see his father lying on his back, chest rising evenly as he breathed. His face held a ghostly pallor, and the bones seemed to stick through the skin.

"I'm Mr. Kirschbaum's son," Daniel said, grabbing the arm of the doctor as he left the ward. "What's his condition?"

"Resting comfortably."

"Will he be all right?"

"Of course. He's suffered a very mild heart attack. He'll just have to take things easier in the future, that's all."

How much easier could his father take life? Daniel wondered. Isaac never went out of the house as it was. What was he supposed to do now? Stay in bed for the entire day and never move a muscle?

"Is it all right if I go in and speak to him?"

The doctor nodded. "Try to keep it quiet and short. He needs rest right now."

Forgetting about his mother who continued to sit in the corridor, or Moishe who would be trying to find out where he was, Daniel entered the ward and quietly pulled up a chair beside his father.

"How are you feeling?"

Isaac made a disgusted face. "All this fuss over a little bit of indigestion."

"You haven't got any indigestion. You didn't get to eat anything in Wheeler's last night."

"Okay, a chest cold then, not indigestion. But never mind about me." Isaac tried to sit up in bed. Daniel pushed him back gently. "How about you? How's that lump on the back of your head?"

"Don't worry about it. It's going down," Daniel replied. "I think that cow hurt you more than she hurt me. Why did you have to get so worked up about it?"

"What did you expect me to do?" Isaac countered. "Clap with the rest of those turncoats?"

"I'd have disowned you if you had." Daniel smiled at his father's question. Isaac could not be feeling that bad if he could manage to make jokes. "Why didn't you let Ma call the doctor when you first felt ill last night?"

"Ah, you know what your mother's like. First sneeze and we get ten specialists lining up outside the door, all counting on us to build their new swimming pools in time for the summer." He struggled to rise again; a second time Daniel pushed him back. "What's going to happen to you about last night?"

"I'm publishing an apology in the *Times.* To everyone, Hammersley, company members, patrons."

"Good," Isaac said in approval of the decision. "That's the right thing to do. I'm proud you thought of it."

Daniel laughed drily. "I didn't have much choice in the matter. Hammersley decided it for me. It was either that or kiss goodbye my career at the Grand."

Isaac chuckled. "The man's got you under his thumb. And I think he knows what's best."

"Maybe."

"Anna got us a cab home last night, you know. Don't forget to pay her back. She's a nice girl, Daniel."

"I know. She even wrote the apology for me."

"Because you would never have done it yourself?" Isaac guessed.

Daniel nodded. "Apologies still come hard, Pa." He leaned over the bed and kissed his father on the forehead. "Get some rest. I'll take Ma home and we'll look in again later in the day."

Daniel left the ward and went outside to his mother. Moishe had arrived and was sitting alongside Yetta, reading a newspaper he had bought in the kiosk downstairs.

"I'll wait a few hours and then call Jack," Daniel told Yetta. "There's no sense in him flying in, but he should be told what's happening with Pa."

Moishe suddenly held the newspaper aloft, startling Daniel. "Here you are, Danny boy. Fame at last. Real fame!"

"What?"

Moishe showed him the review of the previous night's performance. The story centered around the fracas in Wheeler's, with a quote from Hammersley explaining that the episode had been provoked by Claudia Rivera holding onto a note for an unnecessarily long time to make Daniel look bad. Daniel grinned as he read the article. Hammersley had been true to his word. He had spoken to the critics. The article finished by commenting that Daniel Kerr was establishing himself as a wit as well as a singer. He might even find new challenges in *opera buffa*—comic opera—once he had recovered from Claudia Rivera's knock-out punch.

"Very funny," Daniel said. He passed the newspaper to his mother who wanted to read the article.

"Do you want me to stick around?" Moishe asked.

Daniel thought about it before shaking his head. "Just drop us off at the house. I'll be able to cab it around for the rest of the day."

"Your father's going to be all right?"

"Sure. Nothing a bit of rest and proper attention won't cure. Thanks for all your help."

Moishe drove Daniel and Yetta to Van Cortlandt Park before going home to the Village. Taking into account the one-hour time difference between New York and Chicago, Daniel waited until almost midday before calling his brother. It was like speaking to a stranger. Jack had made a life for himself in Chicago and came east only once a year, during the fall. It was a duplication of his relationship with Tommy Mulvaney, Daniel decided. Grow up and you split. Sometimes he wondered how he still managed to remain friends with Moishe.

After assuring Jack that their father was all right, Daniel exchanged news politely and hung up. Then he called Anna. She promised that she would come over right away.

That evening Isaac was looking better and feeling brighter. Color had returned to his face. The bones no longer seemed so prominent. He sat up in bed, eyes alive with pleasure as he surveyed his visitors.

"They know who you are," he whispered to Daniel, pointing to the other three beds in the ward. "I told them who my son was. Now I can tell them who you are as well," he added to Anna.

Daniel glanced around the ward. The other patients were surrounded by visitors. He was grateful. As much as he liked the adulation that went with his career, he did not want to see a hospital ward transformed into a celebrity parade. "The doctor says you should be able to come home within a week. Do you want to go down south, to Miami, for a month?"

"No. I'll be fine in the Bronx. I'll get my strength back, and when spring comes I'll be able to get out some more."

Daniel turned to his mother. "Do you want to go to Miami? Until the weather breaks?"

"I think it would be an excellent idea, Mrs. Kirschbaum," Anna cut in. "This cold won't do your husband any good once he gets out."

"He doesn't want to go," Yetta replied stoically. "How can I go if he doesn't want to?"

"If you say you'll go, he'll go as well," Daniel pressed. Why did everything still have to be decided by a big conference, another Yalta? "I'll get the train tickets for you, make the hotel reservations, everything. All you'll have to do is go. Okay?"

"Why not?" Yetta shrugged. "Who needs the Bronx in the winter?"

"Pa, you're going to Miami to convalesce. No arguments."

Isaac reached out and grasped his son's arm. "No arguments."

Daniel stayed in the house long enough to be certain his mother was all right, then he took Anna home in a taxi. Only after she had invited him in for a drink did she notice his disheveled state, the torn trousers, the skinned hands.

"What did you do?" she asked.

"I took a dive on the ice this morning. Almost broke my neck."

"Did you forget to take a shower as well? You're reeking enough to be Rivera's twin."

Daniel wrinkled his nose in self-disgust. He was still wearing yesterday's clothes, and he hadn't even cleaned his teeth in the panic of the morning.

"You'll find a spare dressing gown hanging up in the bathroom. Give me your apartment key. While you're taking a shower, I'll get a cab over there and pick up some fresh clothes for you. You stink like last week's garbage."

Unprotestingly, Daniel handed over his apartment key. When she left, he drew himself a scalding hot bath and sat luxuriating in it for almost half an hour. It would take Anna the better part of an hour to get to the Village and back, and sort out clothes for him. Why was she bothering anyway? She could just as easily let him go home by himself, to clean up there.

He thought about his father in Montefiore Hospital. No matter how he tried to look at the situation, he felt guilty, responsible for his father's heart attack. If that scene in the restaurant had never taken place, his father would have been all right. At least he approved of the apology that would appear in Tuesday's *Times.* Funny how Isaac had been right, that apologies were still hard to force out. Not as difficult as they had once been, perhaps, but tough all the same.

He dried himself off briskly, cleaned his teeth with a new brush he found in the medicine cabinet and looked on the back of the door for the spare dressing gown. It was made of heavy wool, but to Daniel's horror it was bright pink and far too small. Probably it looked fantastic on Anna, but Daniel was not certain that tightly fitted pink was really his style. Still, if he was to avoid walking around the apartment in the nude, it would have to do.

Anna returned fifteen minutes later, a small leather suitcase in her hand. "Pink's your color, Daniel. Suits you like a dream. But I think you'd be better off wearing these." She set the suitcase on the table and opened it, pulling out a pair of gray trousers, a sportcoat, a roll-neck sweater, underwear and socks. "Where's the stuff you took off?"

Daniel pointed to a chair. "Don't worry about it. I'll pack it all away."

"Like hell you will. It's going down the incinerator."

"The suit as well?" he asked in disbelief.

"Why not? Unless you think torn trousers are going to be the fashion rage one day." Without another word, she started sorting through the clothes, removing money and keys, wallet and comb. With the exception of the topcoat, gloves and shoes, she threw everything down the incinerator in the hallway.

"Now, what would you like to drink?" she asked brightly on her return to the apartment.

"Got any pink champagne?" Daniel gestured at the dressing gown. "To go with this creation."

"Funny man." She went to a cabinet and took out a bottle of cognac. "For medicinal value." She poured some in a snifter for Daniel, but only took tomato juice for herself. "You still feeling guilty about your father?"

"How do you know?"

"It's pretty obvious, Daniel. Every thought you ever have runs right across your face like a newspaper headline. You'd be a lousy poker player."

Daniel stared moodily into the snifter of cognac before replying. "I can't seem to get rid of the feeling that I'm the one who put him in Montefiore."

If he expected any sympathy from Anna, he was disappointed. "Daniel, you can't say that you weren't warned about starting anything with that fat cow. Sometimes you've got to think of people other than yourself. For one thing, I'm not sure I like the idea of seeing my favorite tenor get smacked across the head with a bottle. And I'm damned sure that Mr. Hammersley wouldn't approve of any of his artists going out in sub-zero temperatures without a scarf or a hat. Unless you're planning to sing an off-key bass the next time out."

"I never thought about it because I was in such a hurry to get out this morning," Daniel admitted lamely. He drank some of the cognac. It burned a pleasant fire throughout his body. Coupled with the hot bath, it was the first time he had felt warm all day. Anna was right. He was probably going to get a cold; he'd done everything possible to deserve one. Not that it really mattered at the moment. He had no performances for almost three weeks. He could afford a cold. He moved on the chair and felt the dressing gown begin to open. Quickly he pulled it closed.

"Would you feel more comfortable if you changed?" Anna asked. "I promise I'll turn my back. Won't even peek."

"I'll use the bathroom." Daniel picked up the fresh clothes and went off to change. Anna called after him that she would make something to eat. When Daniel emerged five minutes later in the trousers and roll-neck sweater, Anna was in the kitchen, carefully watching over two steaks under the broiler.

"Can you make salad?" she asked.

"Does anyone make salad?"

"Where do you think it comes from then?"

"A deli?" he guessed. "That's where I always get my food from."

"It shows, Daniel. It shows. If you've split the seams on my dressing gown, you can buy me another one." She turned the steaks over and concentrated on the salad. "Do you ever cook for yourself?"

"Coffee," he replied.

"Marvelous diet. Grow strong on that," she said sarcastically. "Here, make yourself useful and take this inside." She handed him the bowl of salad. "How do you like your steak?"

"Large." He returned to the kitchen, found knives and forks and set the table.

"Why did you ask where my family came from last night?" Anna queried while they ate.

He looked up in surprise from his plate. "I told you. I was just curious about the name Markowitz, that's all."

Anna didn't say anything for a while. She toyed with her food, and then staggered Daniel by asking, "Were you checking to see if I came from a Russian background? Because of Lucy?"

Daniel slowly set down his fork and stared open-mouthed across the table. "Who told you anything about that?" he gasped. "Hammersley?" No, it couldn't be. The general manager knew that Lucy had killed herself, but he was not aware of the details. He didn't know anything about the child. Martinelli? No again. He and Anna had only crossed paths once, on Daniel's debut in *Manon Lescaut* four years earlier. They hadn't even spoken to each other.

"Your father," Anna said. "He told me about three months ago."

"Why? What business was it of his?" Daniel exploded, forgetting that his father was lying in a hospital bed.

"It came out in a conversation, that's all," Anna explained. "We were talking about the production of *Tosca* that the Grand had scheduled, with you and Rivera. Your father was worried about whether you'd be able to handle Cavaradossi. I asked him why, and he told me."

Daniel's flare-up of anger at his father subsided. "Why did you wait this long to bring it up?" he asked Anna.

"I didn't bring it up at all," Anna replied quietly. "You're the one who did."

Daniel switched subjects so swiftly that he left Anna foundering. "I just had a bath. If I go out there now, I'll catch pneumonia."

"What?"

"You've got a guest for the night. See?" he added proudly. "I'm thinking about other people by taking care of my health."

Anna smiled as she understood. "Good. It's about time."

At nine the following morning, Daniel took a taxi with Anna to the Grand Opera House. While Anna waited in the reception area, Daniel kept his appointment with Hammersley. The general manager read the letter of apology which Anna had prepared on Daniel's behalf and nodded approvingly.

"Excellent," he declared. "I'll get our publicity department to push this out to the *Times.* Let me assure you, Daniel, that I'm greatly relieved you've decided to follow my advice." Hammersley called in his secretary and gave her the letter, instructing her as to its disposition. When she had left, he continued talking to Daniel. "As you may have noticed, I managed to speak to the critics about Saturday's unhappy episode. The emphasis of all the stories was on the fight, not on your short note. Perhaps it's just as well that you did bait Rivera. It took everyone's attention off the obvious."

"Except that it put my father in the hospital with a heart attack."

"Oh?" Hammersley's eyebrows rose a fraction. "I'm terribly sorry to hear that. How is he?"

"Not too bad, considering. A few weeks rest and he'll be all right again. I'm sending him down to Florida when he gets out of the hospital."

"Good idea," Hammersley concurred. "But to happier events. Now that you've decided to stay with the Grand, perhaps we can talk about next season."

"Could we leave it for another time? Anna's waiting outside."

"Bring her in," Hammersley invited. "It concerns her as well."

Daniel called Anna into the office. They sat down facing Hammersley. "We've been doing the current production of

Bohème for so many seasons that I think it's becoming a little jaded," Hammersley said. "It's time for a new one."

Listening to Hammersley, Daniel felt the excitement building up within him. He perched on the edge of the chair, hands clasped tightly together. Hammersley noticed the effect his words were having and smiled.

"We're planning an entirely new *Bohème* for next season's opening night. New production, new sets, everything. Do you want Rodolfo?"

"Do I?" Daniel was out of the chair in his eagerness to snatch up the role. Of all the romantic tenor parts, Rodolfo was the choicest. He had never sung the role; suddenly he wanted it more than anything else in the world. "You bet I want Rodolfo!"

"And we can write you in for Mimi?" Hammersley asked Anna.

She nodded.

"Good." Hammersley clapped his hands in satisfaction. "We want this to be a *Bohème* that will be remembered by everyone. Although not, I hope, for the same reasons our *Tosca* will be."

"Tell me something," Daniel asked. "Did anyone ever write an opera where the tenor and soprano lived happily ever after?"

Hammersley scratched his head. "Daniel, it's Monday morning. Very early on a Monday morning, in fact. Why are you asking me such a question?"

"Because the situation's just arisen. As soon as this season is over, Anna and I are getting married."

Hammersley leaned back in the chair, his face blank, then smiling as he accepted the news. "That's marvelous. Absolutely wonderful. My congratulations to the pair of you." He picked up his telephone and called for the secretary; he had something else he wanted the Grand's publicity department to work on.

After leaving the opera house, Anna took a cab to her voice teacher for her regular instruction period while Daniel returned to the Village to get his car fixed. Once the battery was charged, he went to a travel agency to confirm tickets and hotel reservations for his parents in Miami. Then he picked up Anna. Together they drove to the Bronx.

"Shouldn't we call on your mother first?" Anna suggested as they stopped outside Montefiore Hospital.

"Later. I want to tell my father first. We'll go to the house afterwards." He led the way into the hospital, happily surprised to find his father sitting up in a chair, talking animatedly to the man in the next bed. Daniel was certain he knew what Isaac was talking about.

"Feeling better?" he asked Isaac.

"When can I get out of this place?" Isaac protested. "I don't need to be here any longer with all these sick people."

"Think I might join you if there's a spare bed anyplace around." Daniel felt awful. His head seemed to have swollen to twice its normal size and he had difficulty in breathing through his nose. Yesterday's folly in the snow and ice was beginning to exact its toll. "I've booked your tickets to Miami so you can't back out."

"Fine. Let me go now. I'm ready."

"Only after your doctor says so." The words came from Anna. "You've got a couple of big dates coming up this year, so you've got to be healthy."

"What big dates?"

"An opening night *Bohème* with Daniel in November," Anna replied. "An entirely new production."

"What else?"

"And a standing-room-only date under the *chuppah* in April," Daniel finished off. "Get better because there'll be no room for wheelchairs."

"A *chuppah?*" Isaac pointed at his two visitors. "You two?"

"Us two. Now are you going to get some rest?"

"Does your mother know yet?"

"We're on the way there now."

"Good. Tell her soon, otherwise she'll feel left out. Go on, go!" He shooed them away. As they passed through the ward door, Isaac called back his son. "Daniel this might sound funny, but believe me it's no business to make fun of."

"What do you want, Pa?" Daniel asked uncertainly.

"Do everyone a big favor this time. Make sure you tread on

the glass."

Tuesday's New York *Times* carried the public apology from Daniel, alongside a story concerning the impending marriage of two of the Grand's brightest stars.

He considered it fortuitous that he had a cold. It allowed him to stay in the apartment for the entire day, reading telegrams and answering calls about the apology and the story. Of the two dozen cables he received concerning the apology, not one criticized his action. He had, the common message read, proved himself to be a gentleman, rising above the antics of an unpopular Italian prima donna. Daniel decided to include the cables in his scrapbook.

Midway through the afternoon, Martinelli telephoned from Milan. The story of the apology had been sent over the wire and eagerly picked up by the Italian press. Daniel had taken the only proper course, the doctor stressed. His action had been honorable. When Daniel told him excitedly of his plans to marry, Martinelli promised that he would create time off from his practice to attend.

By evening, Daniel's eyes were streaming and his nose was raw from wiping. Anna had called twice. The first time she had offered to come around and nurse him. Daniel had put her off, fearful that her own performance in *Norma* that week would be imperiled by exposure to his cold. She had told him to drink plenty of hot liquid. The second time she had called was to find out if he was following her instructions.

Late that evening, when Daniel was preparing to go to bed, Moishe turned up. The probability of catching Daniel's cold didn't bother him. All he could think of was that Daniel had risen above the boring role of opera singer. He was now a national celebrity, a man who had his name plastered all over the New York *Times*. When Daniel inadvertently mentioned that the story had been sent over the wire and picked up in Italy, probably elsewhere, Moishe's delight was unbridled. He would have braved flu and pneumonia for this.

At last, he had in Daniel what he had always dreamed of: a marketable product.

Chapter Four

"Hey, Danny boy! Happy new house!" Moishe lifted his glass high in the air to make the toast.

Daniel looked up from the drink he was holding and gazed absent-mindedly at his friend. As much as he tried to avoid it, he could not help being fascinated by Moishe's head. It was almost as shiny as the lenses in his glasses. The baldness Daniel had first noticed four years earlier had spread like an epidemic. All that was left of Moishe's hair was a ring around the crown, a monk's tonsure. No small wonder that Moishe was still unmarried, Daniel decided uncharitably; what girl would want a thirty-seven-year-old lawyer with a head like a cue ball?

"Thanks," he finally replied to Moishe's salute.

Moishe came closer and sat down next to Daniel. "Didn't no one ever tell you that comparisons are odious?" he asked.

"Who says I'm comparing anything?" Daniel challenged.

"Be goddamned hard for you not to be."

Daniel knew Moishe was right. He found it impossible to stop making comparisons between Lucy and Anna. He supposed it was the natural thing to do. If you didn't compare, how did you know where you stood? Whether you were better off than before or not? There was no doubt about that. Every comparison he had made had been favorable. This time he had broken the glass on the first attempt, shattered it to dust with the heel of his shoe. The four-day honeymoon he'd stolen in Niagara Falls with Lucy looked shabby when compared with the two-week luxury cruise he had taken with Anna in the Caribbean before picking up the Grand's annual tour in Denver. He and Anna had been celebrities on the cruise ship, just as they had been feted on their return to the Grand's tour. The company's publicity department had worked overtime on the pair, two star-struck lovers whose romantic duets on stage contained more than just mere acting.

It wasn't only that Anna was a different person from Lucy.

Daniel knew his own character had a lot to do with it. He'd also changed. He'd grown up at the Grand. The opera company had been like a finishing school for him. He had learned how to cope with others, learned how to care for others. He often wondered how successful his first marriage might have been had he entered into it with the perspective he now possessed.

He looked away from Moishe to see Anna walking across the living room toward him. The long pale green dress she wore shimmered with every movement of her body.

"What mischief are you two hatching up?" she asked suspiciously.

"Nothing. Nothing at all." Daniel smiled up at her. "Just doing a bit of reminiscing, that's all. Deeds done and best forgotten."

"Oh? Anything I should have known about before I said yes to you under the *chuppah?*"

"We were trying to put together a list of the places that never asked us back for a return engagement," Moishe joked. "We had to stop when we ran out of fingers and toes."

Anna laughed at Moishe's answer. She'd heard countless stories of their club dates, and each tale was more embroidered than the last, the drunks more obnoxious, the premises more seedy. The only club date Daniel had never mentioned was the Deuces Wild, the night Lucy had died; that he would continue to keep as his own secret.

"They never realized the treasures they were passing up," she said. She took Daniel's arm and pulled him up from the chair. "You're going to have to reminisce by yourself for a while, Moishe. Daniel can't ignore his other guests and sit here to shoot the breeze with you all day long."

"Sure" Moishe nodded. "Catch you later."

Daniel allowed himself to be led through the French windows into the back garden. A huge, multi-colored marquee was set up in the center of the lawn. Inside, a red-jacketed barman dispensed drinks to the seventy guests who had been invited to the housewarming party. Primly attired waitresses in black dresses and white starched aprons carried trays of appetizers to the groups of people who stood talking on the lawn and patio. A chef—complete with a tall white hat—basted steaks over a sizzling barbecue.

The housewarming had not been Daniel's idea. If anything, he had been firmly set against having any kind of a celebration to mark the possession of the new house in the northern New Jersey town of Teaneck. He'd been through the performance before and held no desire to take the same route again. It had been at the housewarming in Paterson that they had first noticed Rachel was unwell. Again those damned comparisons! he thought. No matter how hard he tried to avoid them, they kept on cropping up. Anna had wanted a party, though, to show her friends and colleagues how well she had settled down to suburban life, so Daniel had given her one.

The early evening August sun sent long shadows spilling across the carefully manicured lawn, and the temperature was steadily dropping from its high of seventy-nine degrees reached during the afternoon. Through a crowd of people, Daniel spotted his father sitting on a lawn chair with a plate balanced on his knees. The summer months had done him good, following the six weeks he'd spent in Florida after he had been discharged from Montefiore Hospital. Isaac had more color in his cheeks than Daniel could remember seeing for a long time, and there was a spring to his step that belied his recent heart attack. But what would happen in another couple of months when fall began, with winter not far away? Would his father lock himself away in the house again and pray that he survived until the spring? Daniel looked around the garden for his mother but he was unable to see her. Probably stuck in the middle of a group of people, he decided, playing to the gallery until she bored them. Maybe it would be better all around if he moved his parents out of New York altogether. Where would he put them? In New Jersey, somewhere close enough to keep an eye on his father? Or should he send them down to Florida permanently?

"Daniel, don't you think you should spend some time with Mr. Hammersley and Robin Duguid?" Anna whispered. "Politics."

Daniel glanced to where the Grand's white-haired general manager stood. He was talking quietly with a tall, dignified-looking man in his late thirties, clean shaven, with a high brow that made his light brown hair appear to be receding. Daniel, Anna and the new house might have been the day's main objects of attention, but Hammersley had managed to dim some of their luster by springing the party's major surprise. During the summer months, rumors had permeated the structure of the Grand—and found their way into the press—that Hammersley wanted to retire and return to his native England. Everyone associated with the company had treated the rumors as just that. Hammersley had neither said nor done anything to confirm or refute the gossip, as if—like the performer he had once been—he was enjoying the Machiavellian atmosphere the stories were creating.

Until today, when he had arrived at the house by taxi with a guest of his own—Robin Duguid. Hammersley had introduced Duguid as the man who would take over the reins as general manager of the Grand Opera Company of New York at the beginning of the new season in November. Duguid's credentials, as vouched for by Hammersley, were impeccable. For the past four years he had been with the San Francisco Opera Company, working as an assistant to the company's founder and director, Gaetano Merola; before San Francisco he had managed small companies in Seattle and Vancouver, from where he originally came. Duguid was both experienced, Hammersley said, and young enough to push through his own innovative ideas.

Both Daniel and Anna had been shocked by Hammersley's announcement, as had other members of the company who were present at the party. Where did that leave the season's opening night *Bohème?* Daniel had asked. The new production that Hammersley had proudly planned? Eager to dispel any uncertainty, Duguid had assured everyone that the season would run as it had been planned. Any changes he instigated would come at a later date. Even with his assurances, however, the party had taken on a more somber note.

"Having a good time?" Daniel asked conversationally as he joined Hammersley and Duguid.

"Splendid," Hammersley replied. "A thoroughly enjoyable party. Much health and happiness in your new home."

"Thanks a lot. You?" he asked Duguid.

"It seems to be a very pleasant area. Perhaps not as pretty as San Francisco, but nice all the same."

Daniel stole a look at Anna out of the corner of his eye, trying to gauge her reaction to the remark. He was uncertain whether Duguid had just offered him genuine praise or a left-handed compliment.

"How did it ever get a name like Teaneck?" Duguid asked. "Is that an Indian name?"

"I don't know," Daniel admitted. He had asked the same question of the real estate agent through whom he had bought the house shortly before he and Anna were married at the end of the New York season. The agent hadn't known either. Not that the agent's ignorance had deterred Daniel from buying the five-bedroom brick house. As well as being a desirable area, Teaneck was equally convenient to either New York or Paterson, where Daniel continued to conduct the Jewish High Holy Day services. He had once punned to Anna that singing at Temple Isaiah was his "*Shabbatical.*" It was true. Despite the work involved, he continued to find the peace he had first discovered that day he had left Lucy alone in the house and sat by himself in the temple until the janitor had wanted to lock up. The money the temple gave him for his *Rosh Hashanah* and *Yom Kippur* appearances did not mean a thing to him. Each year he wrote down the full amount on a check and sent it off to the United Way.

The immensity of the house had been dictated by his and Anna's needs. They both required privacy for practicing. With five bedrooms there was no way they could continually be under each other's feet. And when they decided to have children—Anna had said that as she was starting late, she wanted the first child in one hell of a hurry—all those rooms would not go to waste.

"What kind of name is Duguid?" Daniel asked in response to the question about Teaneck. "Sounds like the kind of name a philanthropist should have."

Duguid smiled thinly at the comment. "My father was a Scot. Do you still think it's a philanthropist's name?"

Daniel didn't know what to say.

"Mr. Hammersley tells me that you'll be doing some work in

Europe next year," Duguid continued.

"I'm considering an offer to sing Turiddu next spring at the Royal Opera House in Covent Garden," Daniel replied. "That would be after the Grand's New York season is over, of course."

"Just as long as it doesn't interfere with the tour," Duguid pointed out. "You're quite an attraction."

"Rest assured, Mr. Duguid. I wouldn't let that happen."

Daniel's contract specified that he could take engagements with other houses as long as they did not conflict with the Grand's schedule, but he was always to be available for the tour that followed the close of the New York season. His private thoughts, however, were the opposite to the words he spoke to Duguid. He hated the tours. Weeks spent crammed together in a train while the sets rolled along behind on flatbeds, like the circus come to town. Feted like conquering heroes by local committees in towns you would never dream of visiting. Dragged to parties in this house and that by wealthy community leaders who had guaranteed money for the tour and wanted their pound of flesh in return.

No matter how hard he tried, Daniel could never bring himself to understand what prestige there was in playing host to a company of opera singers, most of whom could think of nothing other than their next meal or their last performance, providing it had been a memorable one. But the tours helped to keep the Grand solvent and to pay his own salary, so he knew he should not complain too loudly. And he realized that the minor players—on small salaries and even thinner expense accounts—looked to those free meals as their main sustenance.

The last tour had not been so bad. He and Anna had a sleeper reserved for themselves. Daniel had bribed an amazed waiter—amazed because touring opera companies were notoriously cheap when it came to tipping—to serve them their meals in the compartment. Whatever laughter had been generated by their spending most of their traveling time in their own compartment had been small payment for being spared the tedium of the never-ending card games and gossip sessions that passed the journeys.

"I'm relieved to hear you say that," Duguid observed. "Now that Bing's knocking the Met into shape, we must stand doubly alert to prevent the Grand from slipping."

When Daniel went the rounds of his other guests, his mind was preoccupied with Robin Duguid. Liking or disliking the man didn't enter into it, although Daniel wondered how he would respond to a general manager who was only a couple of years older than himself. Would he command the same respect that Hammersley had?

Daniel supposed he resented the manner in which Duguid had turned the housewarming into his own launching party. To a degree it was Hammersley's fault for bringing him along. Hammersley should have known better. But what was he to do? In all decency, he could not have left Duguid out in the cold when the appointment had just been announced by the Grand's board of management, and the man was in town.

"A bit overbearing, isn't he?" Anna murmured, reading Daniel's thoughts. "He didn't seem very happy about you doing *Cavalleria Rusticana* at Covent Garden."

"There isn't much he can do about it," Daniel answered. "I'm entitled to take other engagements as long as they don't interfere with my work at the Grand."

Anna gazed at him with increased interest. "Has something else cropped up that you haven't told me about?"

"Well . . ." He hesitated, debating whether to tell her. "Moishe mentioned an idea before, when we were sitting talking in the living room."

"Ah, so that's what the pair of you were plotting. What scheme is brewing under that gleaming dome?" Sometimes Anna felt that Moishe had been included as part of the *ketubah*, the Jewish marriage contract. She knew that Daniel regarded him as a talisman as well as a friend, but that did not stop her from viewing Moishe's ideas with a healthy dose of skepticism. "Let's hear the latest."

Daniel took a deep breath. "Moishe knows someone . . ."

"Who knows someone else," Anna continued as she guessed the next line. "Go on."

"That's about it. There's a movie producer called Joel Pomerantz who's trying to get together the money for a musical based on the life of Al Capone."

"Capone?" Anna almost shrieked. She backed away from Daniel and burst out laughing. "Did you say Al Capone?"

"Quiet!" Daniel hissed as heads turned in their direction. He was frightened of being overheard. He was still concerned about Robin Duguid and the impending change in the Grand's management. As he had told Anna, there was nothing the general manager elect could do if he took operatic engagements elsewhere. But Duguid might decide to put his foot down and establish his authority immediately if he learned that Daniel was thinking about accepting a role in a musical movie.

Anna was already in bed when Daniel came upstairs. She watched him undress before going into the bathroom to clean his teeth and gargle. The house was full of cigar and cigarette smoke, a memento of the guests who had stayed long into the night. Despite the open windows, the smell refused to disappear, clinging to the drapes and upholstery. Neither Anna nor Daniel smoked, and she knew the exposure had irritated his throat.

"Tell me more about this Al Capone scheme," she said when Daniel returned from the bathroom.

"It's a musical based on a very simple formula. English-language light opera for want of a better description. A musical centered on the life of Capone, or a part of it, is a two-edged sword. Capone's still a folk hero to a lot of people, mostly Italians. You link that with the Italians' love of music by throwing in some strong numbers and you've got a ready-made audience. Anyone else who pays to see the movie will be gravy."

Anna could not help laughing at the idea. The whole scheme was preposterous. Only Moishe could have thought it up. And only Daniel would have listened. "There's a third edge to this sword you're talking about, Daniel," she finally managed to say. "And I think you've forgotten what it is."

"Oh? What's that?"

"The very sharp edge that will come slashing down across the back of your neck if you even think about appearing in something like this. I'm damned sure that even Mr. Hammersley wouldn't let you get involved in a madcap scheme like this, and you're one of his favorites. God only knows what Robin Duguid would think. Anyway, what part in this award-winning movie would you play?"

"Nothing's been decided yet," Daniel answered, ignoring Anna's disapproval. "The whole idea's up in the air while the producer tries to bankroll it. All I'm asking right now is that you don't laugh."

"Why not?" She began to giggle, unable to control herself. A vision of Daniel wearing a chalkstripe suit, two-tone shoes and a gray homburg while he carried a tommy gun under his arm and sang something rousing and ferocious like "Di quella pira" from *Il Trovatore* was too much to bear straight-faced.

Daniel slid into bed beside her and turned off the lamp on the night table. "Do you know what the biggest box office hit is going to be next year?" he asked.

"The *Capone Chorale?*" she baited him. *"Dillinger's Duet?"*

Daniel enjoyed the banter. Anna had a knack for the absurd, a way of removing the tension from any situation so that it could be discussed on a rational basis. With Anna around, Daniel knew there was little chance of his becoming pompous or taking himself too seriously like some of the other tenors he knew. Basses and baritones hardly ever seemed to be afflicted by the problems from which most tenors suffered as a matter of course. Tenors were an operatic breed apart—insecure, perpetually worried about their voices, their looks, their weight, as demanding as any neurotic prima donna whose pet dog or cat was not allowed onstage during rehearsals. It wouldn't happen to him, though. He had Anna always ready with a sharp pin to prick any promising bubbles.

"It's a movie with Mario Lanza called *The Great Caruso.* You've heard Lanza sing, right?"

"Sure." Anna raked her memory for a moment before coming up with the names of movies. *"That Midnight Kiss* and *The Toast of New Orleans."*

"That's it. This guy has a natural, God-given voice. But he's never seriously sung opera in a big house. Never will, either."

"How do you know?"

"Because he refuses to take any direction. Says he hasn't got the time to mess around with learning from the bottom while he can be making money in the movies."

"That sounds like someone I used to know, someone who didn't have the time to take any minor roles." She sat up in bed as she became more interested. "Who told you all this about Lanza anyway?"

"I bumped into Bob Merrill from the Met in the Russian Tea Room the other day. He mentioned that he'd once recommended Lanza to his own teacher, but he didn't want to know anything about studying. Yet this guy with an uneducated voice is going to be busting box offices wide open for the next few years."

Anna listened patiently, waiting for Daniel's enthusiasm to wane. When he had finished, she spoke quietly. "Daniel, you said it yourself. Lanza's going to be in *The Great Caruso*. The story of an operatic tenor. Lanza's a matinee idol with a voice who can make a movie like this; he'll be upgrading himself. You're thinking about going in the opposite direction, an operatic tenor going into a dubious musical movie. The Grand will never buy it. They'll argue that you're bringing down the tone of the house by appearing in such a thing, and they'll be right."

"I'll make a fortune if the movie's a hit."

"Great! You'll be the richest out-of-work lyric tenor in the country. Singers of your reputation don't make musical comedies."

"It's not a musical comedy," Daniel argued. "It's just a musical."

"Daniel!" She reached out in the darkness and hugged him tightly, rejoicing in the warmth of his body. "Al Capone's life set to music has to be a comedy. Very black comedy maybe, but comedy nevertheless."

Daniel lay still for a moment, breathing evenly, his arms around Anna. Then he said, "Should I tell Moishe not to bother?"

"Tell him whatever you like. Just keep a watchful eye out for Duguid."

He snuggled in closer, pressing his knee in between Anna's

thighs. "I've just had an idea that's even funnier. Nothing to do with Moishe."

"What?" She wrapped her legs around him, imprisoning him, arching her back in anticipation as he pressed against her.

"We're opening *Bohème* in twelve weeks, right?"

"So?" She could feel his teeth nibbling gently on her ear lobe. The teasing sensation sent shivers streaking down the length of her spine.

"You know that scene in the first act, where Rodolfo's sitting alone in the garret after Marcello, Schaunard and Colline have split for the Café Momus?"

"Yes." His mouth left her ear and began working its way down to her neck. "What about it?"

"There's a knock on the door. Rodolfo opens it and sees Mimi. First time they've ever laid eyes on each other," Daniel said.

"That's right." She closed her eyes and trembled in delight as his tongue traced delicate patterns on her breasts.

"Think what a scream it would be if Mimi was pregnant. Say three months gone. And no one in the audience had the faintest idea that Rodolfo was the louse responsible."

"I might be sick," she said. "How would you like me to throw up all over you while you're singing 'Che gelida manina'?" Her stomach muscles tensed as Daniel continued his downward journey.

"I thought morning sickness only happened in the morning," he murmured.

"What will Mr. Duguid say when I cry off after *Bohème* because I'm pregnant?" Anna asked. "He'll have to recast for the remainder of the season."

Daniel chuckled at the question. "He'll look at me with jealousy in his unphilanthropic Scottish eyes. And I'll have to start making love to sopranos who outweigh me by fifty pounds."

"You think such a sacrifice would be worth it?"

Daniel didn't answer. He simply took her hand and guided it down, breathing raggedly as her long fingernails trailed tantalizingly across him.

* * *

Moishe telephoned two weeks later to arrange a lunch date between himself, Daniel and the movie producer. When Anna answered the call, there was no need for her to tell Daniel who it was. The expression on her face—and the way she pointed her index finger at her temple—made it clear the caller was Moishe.

"What do you want?"

"I've lined up Joel Pomerantz for a lunch meeting."

"Who Pomerantz?" Daniel asked; he'd already forgotten the man's name.

"Joel. The producer I told you about from Carmel Studios. He wants to get together with you, to talk about the project."

Daniel turned to look at Anna standing beside him. She was making faces, mouthing the words "Say no." Daniel grinned at her. "Where do we meet?"

"Katz's on East Houston Street. About twelve-thirty tomorrow."

"Where did you say?" Daniel demanded, unable to believe what he had heard.

"Katz's. You know, on the corner of Ludlow."

"I know where Katz's is. You're buying lunch, I take it."

"Yeah." Moishe sounded baffled. "How did you know?"

How did I know? Daniel repeated to himself. Because only a cheap sonofabitching lawyer like Moishe would pick a place like Katz's for a business lunch. Rub shoulders at the same time with diamond peddlers and the bums from the Bowery; share a pickle with them. "Haven't you got any class?"

"The guy wanted a good deli, for crying out loud."

"There's a million classier ones in the city, you cheap *mamzer*."

"Are you coming or not?" Moishe wanted to know.

"Yeah, I'll be there." He hung up and turned to Anna. "Katz's, would you believe?" He still could not believe it himself. Movie careers did not start in Katz's. Jewelry deals, yes. Indigestion, yes, when you gave in and ate too much. Maybe even the occasional bank robbery. But never a movie deal. Unless the guy who was handling your end of the deal was a pennypincher like Moishe.

Anna let a triumphant smile cross her face. "Does that tell

you something about the idea then?" she asked quietly.

"It tells me Moishe's cheap. But I knew that already. Look, what harm can it do if I go along and say nice to meet you to this guy?"

Anna knew there was no way of dissuading Daniel so she gave in. "I suppose not. But one sandwich only, and no knishes," she warned. "I'm the one that's supposed to get fat, not you." Since the housewarming party, she had come down on Daniel like an avenging angel, cutting down his calorie intake until he feared he would waste away. In two weeks his weight had dropped eight pounds to two-sixteen. Anna wanted it down to two hundred at least, maybe even one ninety-five. If he were to be the father of the child she was certain she was carrying, she wanted to make damned sure he would be a healthy one.

Daniel gazed at her through reproachful eyes. What was the fun in going to a deli if you weren't allowed to eat? All tenors were large; that power had to come from somewhere.

"Daniel, please think carefully before you let yourself get talked into signing anything. Don't pay too much attention to what Moishe says. Think of your career first. If you're doubtful, talk it over with Mr. Hammersley and Robin Duguid before you make any decisions."

"I promise." He held up his right hand like a man taking the Oath of Allegiance. "Only one sandwich, and no commitment without clearing it first."

The promise to Anna about only one sandwich was forgotten as soon as Daniel sat down. The corned beef had melted in his mouth like butter; the pastrami would be insulted if he didn't try that as well. What the hell! he decided. Anna would never know; he'd make up for his indiscretion some other time.

He bit into the second sandwich with all the relish of a gourmet savoring the most exquisite delicacy. Satisfied, he looked across the table at Joel Pomerantz.

The movie producer reminded Daniel of a German shepherd dog. Pomerantz had a sharp pointed face, large, oddly shaped ears that seemed to stand away from his head and watchful brown eyes. He had a habit of punctuating every few words with a grin, drawing his lips back from teeth that were so white and perfect they had to be false. "We're calling the movie *South Side Serenade,"* he said. The grin flashed on and off his face like a light switch being flicked. "Obviously we've got to catch the feeling of the Capone era in Chicago and at the same time put across the message that it's a musical."

"Great title, eh?" Moishe commented. "What do you say, Danny boy?"

"Not bad," Daniel acknowledged. He took another bite of the sandwich while he waited for Pomerantz to continue.

"We've already got Diane Orsini to play the part of Capone's mistress."

"I never knew she could sing," Daniel said. A spray of crumbs erupted from his mouth, scattering across the table. He hadn't thought that Diane Orsini could act either, the two times he had seen her on the screen. She was always being touted as the hottest sex symbol since Mae West, bleached hair, icy blue eyes and a bust that would have made three-dimensional movies a public outrage. In both movies Daniel had seen, she had played a gangster's moll, wiggling across the screen in obscenely tight dresses, flaunting her proudest possession at the camera. No wonder Pomerantz had cast her in the role.

"We'll be dubbing her in," Moishe interrupted.

"We?" Whose side was Moishe on? Had he decided already that Daniel would take the part?

"The studio, I mean," Moishe said quickly. "The studio will be dubbing her in. Joel needs a name to set the ball rolling. But you'll be doing most of the singing; all the big numbers."

"Yeah, that's right," Pomerantz agreed eagerly. Again the smile flickered on and off. "The entire movie will be a vehicle for your voice, for Daniel Kerr. Opera singers in movies are big business right now. Look at Mario Lanza."

"Mario Lanza's not an opera singer," Daniel pointed out as he remembered his discussion with Anna. "He's a matinee idol who happens to possess a good, natural voice."

"Same difference," Pomerantz said, not wanting to be drawn into a battle of semantics in a field about which he knew next to nothing. "Are you interested or not?"

"There are a few other points I'd like to discuss first," Daniel said. "I'd like the opportunity to read the script."

"Of course. Goes without saying."

"And I'd like to check out the music, make sure it's suitable for me. Who's writing the songs for you, anyway? Berlin? Porter?"

Pomerantz flashed the grin yet again and waved a hand in the air. "What do you take me for, a goddamned novice? You're an opera singer so I'm going to get you opera-type music. Do you think I'm going to pay good money to get a score written when there's ten tons of uncopyrighted junk floating around? Beautiful music! The kind of stuff you know already. I've got good writers putting in English words. I'm modernizing those opera songs."

"Arias," Daniel corrected him. Then he leaned back in the chair and began to laugh. "You're a character, you know that? You want me to play a musical Al Capone, which is preposterous to begin with, and sing English transpositions of famous operatic arias? You're crazy." As usual, Anna had been right. Another one of Moishe's scatterbrained schemes. Why had he even considered meeting Pomerantz? He should have known better. If Moishe was involved, it had to be on a lunatic level. And for his troubles he'd have a guilt complex about eating that second sandwich.

Moishe watched his friend cautiously. He felt embarrassed, having dragged both parties together only to see Daniel laughing at Pomerantz's proposal. But he thought he recognized a way to wipe the grin off Daniel's face. "Danny boy, don't laugh too hard. If you accept, and we agree on any musical changes you want, it's six weeks work for forty grand."

The laughter vanished. "How much did you say?" Daniel gasped.

Pomerantz repeated the figure. "For six weeks shooting, that's all. Plus a percentage of the profits. I'll leave you a copy of the script so you can make up your own mind." He pulled open the heavy briefcase on the floor next to his legs and tossed a bulky brown envelope onto the table. "The songs are in there, everything that you'll need to decide."

Daniel decided not to open the envelope until he arrived

home. He would read through the script with Anna and get her opinion before forming his own. "There's no way I can put six weeks together until next summer," he said. "When the New York season ends, I'm doing a *Cavalleria Rusticana* at Covent Garden, followed by the Grand's spring tour. Maybe June or July." He said nothing about hoping to be a father around that time; that would remain his and Anna's secret until they were ready to tell everyone.

Pomerantz nodded. "Maurice here already told me that. We've got a lot of details to iron out first, but I'd like a decision from you by the beginning of November. You should know by then whether you're interested or not."

"Fine." Daniel set the envelope down on the empty seat next to him and concentrated on eating again. He didn't feel like laughing anymore. Forty thousand dollars was a sum of money he could not afford to pass up. On top of that he would have the final word on the music. He could write his own ticket.

Anna's face reflected a mixture of amusement and interest as she put down the final page of the script for *South Side Serenade*. "I know I should be laughing at this entire thing," she said, "but it contains some very good ideas. What they've done with the music is clever."

"I know." Daniel had been happily surprised when he had read the script. The plot was simple, a period in Capone's life when he had wrested control of Chicago from the other mobs until he had made himself king of the heap. The strength of the movie was contained in the music, twelve numbers for Daniel to sing including the complete "M'appari" from Flotow's *Martha*—turned into a love song entitled "Those Smiling Eyes"—and portions of some Donizetti and Verdi arias. Daniel wondered what Martinelli would think of him putting commercial English lyrics to the words of the composers he idolized.

"What you have to ask yourself now, Daniel, is whether this is going to be beneficial to your career," Anna said.

Daniel nodded. "I've got to look at it as being part of my career," he said. "Everything I do or sing is part of my career.

That one song 'Those Smiling Eyes' will leap into the hit parade. You accompany me on the piano and see how it sounds."

"I know how it will sound," Anna said. "And I'm with you. But you have other considerations. When are you going to speak to Mr. Duguid about this? To Hammersley as well? It's common courtesy to tell them both that you're thinking about this."

Daniel told her that he did not have to tell anyone yet. He had until the beginning of November to make up his mind. He would know one way or the other before the opening night *Bohème* which would mark Robin Duguid's first official function with the company. Daniel was certain that there would be no problems should he decide to take work outside of opera.

"You've made up your mind already, haven't you?" Anna said.

"It shows?"

"Does it ever!"

Daniel tried to compose his face, to leave it so blank that no one would know what he was thinking. It was an impossible task. The screen was beckoning to him with promises of fame outside the world of opera. He knew it was a summons he would never be able to ignore.

Chapter Five

Opening night required tuxedos for men and long dresses for women employed by the Grand Opera Company, from the most anonymous ticket taker to the highest-paid, most celebrated singer. Roger Hammersley had always insisted on the tradition as a gesture of respect for the patrons who would dress up in their finest for this annual social occasion. Robin Duguid, in his first act as general manager, had decreed that the practice would be continued.

Standing in front of the full-length mirror in the bedroom, Daniel studied his reflection carefully. He decided his father would approve of the new tuxedo. It had been brought home from the tailor only two days earlier, after Anna had decided that Daniel's old suit could no longer be altered enough to fit him. Since the summer, he had lost twenty pounds and he looked and felt better than he had in ages. Despite the occasional lapses when he cheated on his diet, there was no need tonight to cinch in his middle with a cummerbund as there had been last year. The middle had almost disappeared. Just as long as the loss of weight had not affected his voice. If it had, no one had noticed anything at rehearsals.

Anna stuck her head around the bedroom door and watched him quietly for several seconds while he continued his self-admiration. "Have you quite finished?" she asked eventually. "Or should I call the Grand and tell them to hold the curtain for you?"

"Athletic-looking, that's the way I'd describe myself," Daniel said, patting his stomach. "I look like a model for a clothing company."

"Sure you do," Anna agreed. "Outsized clothing. Come on or we'll be late."

The housekeeper Daniel had hired a month earlier was waiting by the front door with their coats. Daniel took his own while the woman helped Anna into hers. Outside, he gave his new Cadillac a minute to warm up, then he headed on Route 4 for the George Washington Bridge and New York.

"When are you going to tell Duguid?" Anna asked.

"Tonight. After the performance."

"You're pushing your luck," she warned.

Daniel disagreed. "The man's had plenty of other things to occupy his mind without me wasting his time." He had purposely refrained from telling the new general manager that he had agreed to take the role in Joel Pomerantz's production of *South Side Serenade.* He was waiting for the most favorable moment, and what moment could be more favorable than tonight? Robin Duguid would be walking on clouds tonight. The season's opening. The smash hit of a new *Bohème.* And his own beginning as the man in charge of the Grand. Psychologically it would be the best time to strike. Duguid would be so buoyed up that he would find it impossible to say no. As the final applause died away, and Duguid was besieged by well-wishers, Daniel would tell him.

A week earlier Daniel had undertaken a screen test that Pomerantz had arranged in New York. He had sung "Those Smiling Eyes" to Diane Orsini who had been flown in from the West Coast. The test had been successful even if his first encounter with Diane Orsini had not. She immediately made it known that she was put out by having to fly across the country to test with Daniel, whom she kept referring to as "Mario Lanza's understudy." She had done her best to put him off while he was singing; yawning, poking a finger into her ear and even turning her back on him. Her antics had no effect on Daniel. As Moishe had once so rightly pointed out, if he could take on the Leishman brothers, he could take on the devil himself.

After the screen test, Daniel had taken Moishe, Pomerantz and Diane Orsini to Sherry's, the Metropolitan Opera House's restaurant for dinner. The Met had opened its season earlier than the Grand, and Daniel's appearance in Sherry's brought him a lot of attention from Met patrons who wondered if he was planning to join the company—and from at least one aging, concerned tenor who was wondering the same thing. Daniel had enjoyed the attention. Here, even in a competing house, he was known and respected while Diane Orsini was nothing more than his guest. She sat sullenly throughout the entire meal. Daniel had also enjoyed signing the contract which Pomerantz had brought with him, and accepting a check for twenty thousand dollars; the remaining twenty thousand would be paid on completion of shooting.

"And when are you going to tell anyone about us?" Anna asked. "Duguid knows and that's about all." She had already told the new general manager that she was pregnant and would be unavailable for the remainder of the season.

"Tonight," Daniel replied. He pulled up to the bridge toll booth and handed across a dollar bill, waiting for change. "I'm going to tell everyone tonight. I'm going to tell them everything. By tomorrow morning we'll be the most talked about couple in the whole wide world." He reached out and squeezed Anna's arm fondly.

"For all the right reasons, I hope," was her response.

Once all the pre-performance anxieties had been eased—finding his parents to give them tickets, making certain that Rodolfo's costume had been altered to fit his new slim figure—Daniel forced himself to relax. He'd taken two quick shots from the half bottle of rye he brought from home, and now he sat back in the chair, eyes closed while the make-up artist went to work on his face. At Duguid's insistence the beard had come off. Rodolfo, the new general manager maintained, was always clean-shaven. He might be a starving, idealistic artist but he was not a scruffy existentialist. Daniel had considered arguing the point purely on principle, but he had given in. He wanted Duguid on his side when it came time to broach the subject of *South Side Serenade.* Anyway, he knew the beard would have no place in the movie so he might as well get rid of it now and score points with Duguid at the same time.

As the make-up artist finished his work, Duguid entered the dressing room. Like everyone else he was wearing a tuxedo with the added touch of a white carnation on the left lapel. To Daniel, though, the tuxedo seemed out of place on the general manager. Only when he remembered that Hammersley had always worn white tie and tails for every production—not just opening nights—did Daniel realize why. Duguid had toned down the general manager's image.

"Come to wish me good luck?" Daniel asked. "No need to. I carry my own." He pulled out the gold chain from beneath his shirt and displayed the bent nail to Duguid. "Anna gave it to me years ago." Without waiting for an answer, he stood up, walked to the wall and rested his elbow against it while he cupped his hand to his ear. This was the only way he could hear how his voice sounded. Satisfied with a few scales, he switched to the first lines of the fourth-act aria which he would share with the baritone playing Marcello, "O Mimi, tu piu non torni." From his position by the dressing room door, Duguid watched impassively.

"I understand you had dinner in Sherry's last week," Duguid said when Daniel finished vocalizing.

"That's right," Daniel answered cheerfully. Enough people had recognized him there; word had to get back to the Grand. "That's not against the rules, is it?"

"No." Duguid shook his head in firm denial. "I'm just a bit curious about the contract you signed while you were there, that's all."

"It wasn't for the Met, so don't worry." Despite his easy answers, Daniel began to feel uneasy. Duguid had something—or he thought he did—so why the hell didn't he come right out and say what he wanted? The few dealings Daniel had shared so far with the new general manager had all been straightforward. Why was he beating about the bush now?

"Let me assure you that your deciding to sing with the Metropolitan Opera Company would not perturb me in the least," Duguid said. "Although I think you'd be a fool to give up your career with the Grand."

"So what's the problem then?" Come on, man, Daniel thought irritably. I've got to go out there in a few minutes. Quit making me tense.

"I also think you'd be a damned fool to appear in garbage like *South Side Serenade.*"

Daniel flinched as the name of the movie was tossed at him. "Who told you anything about that?"

"You have an excellent press agent."

For the first time Daniel noticed that Duguid was carrying a rolled-up newspaper. The general manager held it out. A story on the show business gossip page was outlined in red ink.

Stunned, Daniel read the article. Carmel Studios had acquired the services of Grand Opera Company tenor Daniel Kerr to sing the lead in their forthcoming production, *South Side Serenade*. The story even mentioned where the contract had been signed—at Sherry's—and quoted Joel Pomerantz as saying that Carmel Studios was gearing up for a no-holds-barred, head-on clash with MGM and Mario Lanza; and with Daniel Kerr, Carmel would come out on top.

"I think you could have had the decency to mention this to me," Duguid said quietly.

Daniel took a few seconds to recover from the shock of seeing the news in the paper. "I was going to," he said shakily. "Tonight, after the performance, when you'd officially taken over as general manager."

"Were you really?" Duguid asked, his voice icy. "Or were you going to wait until the end of the season? Or even later, until after this, this"—he seemed stuck for the right word—"piece of garbage had been shot. And then presented it as a *fait accompli?*"

"Hey!" Daniel protested. "Hold on just a minute! Aren't you running a bit fast? There's nothing in my contract that says I can't make a movie."

"True," Duguid agreed. "But there is one little clause that stipulates if you accept any undertakings the management deems to be detrimental to the reputation and welfare of the Grand Opera Company of New York, we will have grounds to consider discontinuing your contract."

Daniel heard a man's voice yelling that only five minutes remained until curtain. He didn't have the time to stand around and argue the finer points of his contract now. He had to get downstairs. "Why don't you wait till the movie's finished, Mr. Duguid. Then decide what to do."

"I would rather avoid an embarrassing catastrophe than have to apportion blame afterwards," Duguid said.

"I've got to go," Daniel snapped. "If that curtain goes up and there's no Rodolfo, you'll have an embarrassing catastrophe all right. Your first night as general manager will be your last." Ignoring Duguid's presence, Daniel pulled the half bottle of rye from the dressing table drawer and swigged quickly. He hoped it would relax him before the curtain went up. Then he brushed past the surprised general manager and ran down the two flights of stairs to stage level. Anna was waiting in the wings, looking anxiously for him. When she saw him, she smiled in relief.

"Why are you so late?" she asked.

"I just had a massive fight with Duguid. Something slipped out to the press about *South Side Serenade*. It's in tonight's paper. Our new general manager"—he said the title caustically—"is not a happy man right now." Daniel looked out onto the stage where the singers playing Marcello, Schaunard and Colline were clustered around the pot-bellied stove in the middle of the garret set. From the way they were laughing quietly, Daniel guessed that someone had just told a joke; he wished he'd been out there to share it.

From the auditorium came the sound of applause as the conductor appeared and took his place on the rostrum.

"Tell me all about it later," Anna whispered. She pushed him out onto the stage. As he turned back to say something, the overture began. There was no time. He walked quickly to the center of the stage and took his position as the curtain began to rise.

He knew he had never sung better in his entire life than he had in that first act.

The knowledge made Daniel proud. And to a certain degree it made him sorry. In a way, tonight was his swan song because it would be at least one full season before he sang again with Anna. It was as if knowing that she was pregnant had changed his voice, increased its power and its sensuality, made it more caring.

Anna's response to his "Che gelida manina" had been breathtakingly voluptuous, from the simple beginning where she told him her name to the final lines of their love duet which carried high up to the ceiling of the auditorium, reaching into every corner to fill its space with sweetness.

The effect was not lost on the opening night audience. From the way they applauded—calling the two main characters back in front of the gold curtains again and again—the audience realized that it had been allowed to share in a magical moment, an instant in musical history that went far beyond the realms dictated by composer and conductor. The audience had witnessed an event, a *Bohème* first act that would never be surpassed.

When the applause finally died, Daniel slipped through the curtain and rushed up the stairs. He slammed the dressing room door and picked up the phone.

"Moishe! It's Daniel. Did you see what Pomerantz has done?"

"The story?" Moishe asked.

"What else? I'm getting shit from the new guy here."

"Why?" Moishe sounded puzzled.

"Because I hadn't damned well mentioned it yet."

"Jesus Christ," Moishe muttered. "Why the hell not?"

"I was saving it for after tonight's performance. Why did Pomerantz rush to get it into the papers?"

"Because he wanted it to coincide with your opening night," Moishe tried to explain. "He thought it was timely."

"Why didn't anyone bother telling me?" Daniel wanted to know. "Give me Pomerantz's number."

"He's on the Coast."

"Just give me the number." Moishe did. Daniel broke the connection and called the operator, asking her to put him through to Los Angeles. When Pomerantz's phone rang unanswered for fully a minute, Daniel slammed down the receiver in disgust.

A woman's voice called his name. He spun around to find Anna waiting behind him. She asked what had happened with Duguid.

"I don't know yet," Daniel answered, his mind still full of Pomerantz and what he would like to do with the man. "He wants to see me after the performance."

"I thought we were seeing your parents then, to tell them about our news."

Daniel laughed bitterly. "I might have some other news for

them instead."

"Daniel, take it easy. Don't slam any doors behind yourself. You might want to go back through them."

After the performance, Anna sat in Wheeler's with the Kirschbaums. She had not told them anything, preferring to wait until Daniel arrived. The meeting with Duguid had been going on for fifteen minutes. Anna was uncertain whether that was a good sign or not. Looking at it optimistically, she decided the new general manager was at least listening to Daniel's side of the story.

People stopped by the table to offer congratulations on Anna's performance as Mimi. They did not know yet that it would be her one and only role of the season. The Grand would publicize that information the following morning. Anna smiled graciously at each compliment but her expression was automatic, an extention of the acting she had performed on stage. She was too preoccupied with Daniel to put her heart into accepting praise. She had told him all along that his timing was wrong, but he had insisted that tonight would be the best time to publicize the start of his movie career. He should have informed Duguid immediately about his plans to make the movie, not have the man read of it, secondhand, in a newspaper. As general manager, Duguid was entitled to know what his artists were planning. Letting it come on him as a surprise was like a slap in the face, as if Daniel wanted to show that he did not care about the man's feelings.

"Where is he?" Isaac asked. He was becoming anxious. Daniel never took this long after a performance to come down; he was always early, wanting to hear the applause that would ring out when he entered Wheeler's. Especially tonight, when he had opened the season in a new production.

"He's in an urgent meeting with Robin Duguid, the new g.m.," Anna replied, trying to make her voice dismiss the concern she felt. "There's a contract problem that Daniel wants to get sorted out."

"Money?" Yetta asked hopefully.

"No, not money." Anna did not try to explain further.

"What then?" Yetta pressed.

"It's a personal problem, something in the contract he doesn't like. If Daniel wants you to know about it, he'll explain it when he come down."

"Oh, I see." Yetta became subdued and Anna wondered if she had offended the older woman. Had the short replies seemed rude?

"He's not in any kind of trouble, is he?" Isaac asked gently.

"Not that I know of," Anna replied. Either Daniel's father was more intuitive than she had given him credit for, or else she was doing what she always claimed Daniel did—wearing her feelings in plain view.

When Daniel finally entered the restaurant five minutes later, his face was devoid of expression, like a man sleepwalking. The broad smile of pleasure he usually wore after an outstanding performance was missing. Anna feared the worst. He pulled out a chair and sat down. Before he could say anything about the meeting, Anna cut in.

"Can we book you as babysitters for next June onwards?" she asked her in-laws.

Isaac forgot that he had been worrying about his son. His face exploded into a beaming smile and he leaned across the table to grasp Daniel's hands. "Is that what your big important meeting was all about? It took you so long to tell your new boss that Anna was going to be a mother?"

Daniel looked blankly at his father, apparently mystified. Anna replied for him. "Tonight was my only performance of the season, but no one else knows that yet. I'm taking off the rest of it. Daniel was telling that to Mr. Duguid."

"That's what you call a personal problem?" Isaac exclaimed. "A contract problem, something Daniel doesn't like? That's not a problem. That's magnificent news!"

Daniel looked at Anna. She nudged his thigh under the table. He got the message and remained silent, content to let Anna do the talking. Following the lengthy meeting with Duguid, Daniel had more than enough to fill his mind.

For the second time in less than a year, his career at the Grand was on the line. It was as simple as that. Unlike the last time, though, when a public apology had served to soothe everyone's ruffled feelings, there was no easy avenue of escape. He was involved in a clash of wills. Duguid wanted him to back out of his contract for *South Side Serenade* and forget about the movie. Against Daniel's arguments that his appearing in the movie would have no adverse effects for the Grand, Duguid had bent as far as to say that the company would not object if Daniel's voice was used on the sound track; they would have serious reservations, however, if he appeared in the movie as he would be doing both himself and the company a disservice. Daniel had resisted stubbornly. He needed the movie to establish himself in another entertainment field. Opera was a love. He enjoyed it, just as he took pleasure in his cantorial singing. Never could it pay the kind of money that a popular movie could. Never could it give him the kind of thrilling reward that a hit song might.

To close the meeting, Duguid had told Daniel that the company's board of management did not expect him to reach a decision immediately. The general manager suggested that Daniel think very carefully about the matter and be prepared to make his choice by the end of the New York season. Only Daniel's mind was made up already. He would continue with his plans for the movie. If he continued to turn in the kind of performance he had in tonight's *Bohème*, the Grand would never let him go. They would not be able to afford the luxury of principle.

"What about next season?" Yetta asked Anna. "The child will be a few months old by then. Will you be coming back?"

"I'll probably take that season off as well," Anna admitted. "We haven't decided yet."

"You can always hire a nurse to look after the baby," Yetta suggested. "Are you sure you can afford to be away for two seasons?"

Anna stopped to think about the question, uncertain how her mother-in-law meant it. That long without singing, or that long without making money from singing? She decided to be charitable. "I'll be able to make my comeback whenever I decide to. I've waited a long time for my first child and I want to nurse it myself."

"If I had a career like yours, I would never let anything stand in my way," Yetta said.

Anna smiled as she recognized the sniping tone in Yetta's questions. "My career only came first until something better came along." She knew of the friction that had existed between Daniel and his mother, until he had decided the best course was to simply pretend to tolerate her for his father's sake. She could understand why.

"Daniel, are you all right?" Isaac asked suddenly, switching his attention from his wife's conversation with Anna to his son.

Anna turned to look at Daniel. He was staring down at the tablecloth, apparently unaware of what was taking place around him. She knew that she would not have to ask him how his meeting with Duguid had gone; the result was imprinted on his face. "Daniel, your father's talking to you."

He lifted his head abruptly, blinking in surprise like a man rudely awakened from a deep sleep. "Sorry, I was thinking about something else. What did you want?"

Isaac regarded him oddly. "I was wondering if you were all right, that was all. You look tired."

"I am," Daniel confessed. "I'm shattered. Would you be very upset if we called off dinner? I'll run you back to the Bronx, then I want to get home and sleep."

Isaac agreed readily, eager to believe that only fatigue was affecting his son. Yetta, though, did not seem pleased by the prospect of having her evening cut short. She had dressed up to the teeth for tonight's opening. She had been spinning tales of it for weeks to her friends. Who would be there. Whom she would meet. To be shunted off home early was not an agreeable prospect. "Haven't we even got time for a cup of coffee and a pastry?" she protested; that could always be expanded among her friends to a banquet, a feast where she was surrounded by opera lovers who all wanted to meet Daniel Kerr's mother.

"Daniel's feeling exhausted," Anna said quickly. "So am I. It's been a very hectic, very exciting day for the pair of us." She wanted Daniel out of the restaurant as quickly as possible, before he could say or do anything that would publicize the argument she knew had taken place with Duguid. "Would you mind very much if we left now?"

Isaac stood up immediately and pushed back his chair. "Of

course not. Come on, Yetta. We're leaving."

Yetta surveyed the still empty table unhappily. "First we get invited to dinner and then we don't get any dinner," she muttered. "What kind of invitation is that to give a person?"

"Just be glad you're getting a lift home," Daniel shot back as he transferred his smoldering anger at Duguid to a more readily accessible target. "I don't feel like eating anything tonight, okay? If you want to stay, suit yourself. But you'll have to get a cab home."

"Don't you want to be seen with us?" Yetta asked. "Are you such a bigshot now that you're ashamed to be seen with your parents?"

"Of course he's not," Anna said. "He's just tired, that's all. You try standing in front of the lights for two hours, wearing all that make-up and costumes. See how you feel." She pushed Daniel toward the restaurant exit as she tried to get the ball rolling. A man reached out to stop him, to ask him about the story that had appeared in the newspaper. Daniel pushed straight past as if he were not there. Anna followed, smiling apologetically, whispering that Daniel did not feel well.

Outside the opera house on West Thirty-fourth Street, Daniel breathed in deeply, letting the cool fresh air slowly work its miracles. His head cleared and he thought back to the meeting with Duguid. What would he have done had the roles been reversed? He tried to put himself in Duguid's position, imagining one of the company's singers aproaching him with a similar problem. He'd understand, he decided. He would know how important an opportunity like this was to an artist. That was the whole goddamned trouble. Duguid had never been a performer. Hammersley would have understood better, but Duguid would never know the feeling if he lived to be a hundred and fifty. He'd always been an administrative man, unable to relate to the pressures and problems of artists.

No matter how Daniel tried to view the situation, he failed to see any conflict between his work at the Grand and appearing in *South Side Serenade*. The two worlds would complement each other, not conflict. And he'd have the best of both worlds—he'd be a popular singer while enjoying a career as a lyric tenor. What was so wrong with that?

"Daniel, are you going to get the car or should I call a cab for all of us?" Anna asked as she watched him anxiously. She'd never seen him like this before, withdrawn, moody.

Daniel snapped out of his reverie. "Would you drive? I don't feel up to it."

She gave him a long, searching gaze and said, "I think I'd better." Taking the keys, she went to the parking lot while Daniel remained outside the opera house with his parents.

"Are you sure everything's all right?" Isaac queried. "This isn't the way you normally celebrate wonderful news like you gave us before. What's the matter?"

"I'm tired, Pa. That's all. Dead beat." He was relieved when he saw the Cadillac's headlights coming out of the parking lot. More than anything else, he just wanted to go home and go to bed.

"Okay, buster, what the hell happened back there?" Anna switched to a B-movie aggressive tone as she tried to shake Daniel out of his depression. She looked at the Kirschbaum's house, saw the front room light come on and steered the Cadillac away from the curb. "What did Duguid say that's got you so down in the mouth?"

"He's given me until the end of the New York season to make up my mind about what I want to do. Opera or movies."

"In other words, if you take the movie role you're finished at the Grand. Is that it?"

"That's what he thinks. But he's wrong."

"Daniel." Anna dropped the gravelly aggressive tone and became serious. "I know what you're thinking and it's you who's wrong, not Duguid. You are not bigger than the company. They can always replace you. Look how easily they replaced a tenor called Cesare Scarlatti in *Manon Lescaut.*"

"You're a fat lot of help."

"Do you want me to tell you that you're right when you're wrong?" she asked. "I won't."

"You wouldn't stand by me on this?"

"I'll stand by you on everything. But my loyalty doesn't stop me telling you what I think."

Daniel stared gloomily through the windshield. Some

opening night, he thought; some new production. Blackmailed by Duguid on his first full day on the job. Was it blackmail? he wondered. Of course it was. And on top of everything else, it had blunted what should have been the joyous occasion of telling his father about Anna and the child. He should have sent Isaac home overjoyed. Instead, he had sent him home hungry and bewildered.

"What do you think I should do?" he asked Anna.

"You've made up your mind to ignore Duguid, haven't you?"

"He's giving me until the end of the season to reach a decision. Or, as he so succinctly put it, the moment I set foot on the set of *South Side Serenade* my future at the Grand ends."

"Daniel, call Moishe first thing in the morning. He got you into this mess, with quite a bit of assistance from you. Now he can help to get you out of it. Otherwise there'll be no Markova and no Kerr in next season's productions."

Daniel supposed he could blame the entire mess on Moishe but that would not be at all fair. Anna had hit the bull's eye when she'd said that he'd assisted Moishe. Sure Moishe had waved the magical lure of Hollywood in front of his ambitious eyes like a wand, but he'd been the one who had grabbed at it. He'd wanted a crack at the movies, the opportunity to show himself and everyone else that whatever Lanza could do, he could do a damned sight better. He'd wanted the chance so much that he hadn't even stopped to consider how it would affect his standing with the Grand. Now he'd found out. "If worst comes to worst, I could always go back to being a cantor, I suppose. Full time," he remarked drily.

Anna spared a moment's concentration from the road to glance sideways at him. "If that's what you really wanted to do, I'd say go do it." Then she added, "You know something, Daniel? I think you'd really like to be a cantor again."

"Sure I would. When I'm old and gray and too fat and lazy to do anything else." He closed his eyes wearily and tried to sleep for the remaining few minutes of the journey. He'd call Moishe first thing in the morning and let him straighten everything out. Anna, as usual, was the voice of reason, the moderating force in his life that kept him firmly on the narrow path. *South*

Side Serenade would be a risky gamble, at best a dubious long shot. And the stakes might turn out to be considerably higher than he could afford.

Moishe shook his head emphatically as he faced Daniel across the desk in his office on West Forty-fifth Street. "You signed a contract, Danny boy. It's been witnessed, it's binding. There's no way out of it for you. You're committed to making *South Side Serenade,* like it or not."

"What do you mean I'm committed?" Daniel asked belligerently. "You're acting as my agent on this deal with Pomerantz. I'll give you the four grand you'll be out of from my pocket. Just get me out of it!"

"I can't, for Christ's sake! Will you get that through your thick skull? And that's a lawyer speaking, as well as an agent and a friend. I must have spoken to Pomerantz five times since you told me you wanted out of the deal. He won't let you out of it. He got his bankroll by showing your name on the contracts. He's got too much invested to let you back out on him now." Moishe had been aghast when Daniel had called him that morning after *La Bohème* and insisted he get the contract invalidated. On Daniel's urging, he had telephoned Joel Pomerantz at Carmel Studios and explained Daniel's position, that he might lose his Grand Opera Company contract if he went through with *South Side Serenade.* Pomerantz had been adamant. Daniel had signed the contract, accepted and banked the check. He was legally bound to appear in *South Side Serenade.* If he backed out now, Carmel Studios would have no alternative but to sue for damages to cover the prospective losses of cancellation or recasting. The amount Pomerantz had mentioned to Moishe had been a staggering half million dollars.

"What made you all of a sudden decide that you wanted to stick with opera and not try a musical?" Moishe demanded as he tried to understand what had brought about Daniel's abrupt reversal.

"I was never forced to make a choice before. Only when I had to pick one over the other did I realize what I wanted to do!" Daniel shot back.

"So now I suppose you're going to blame me for getting you involved with Pomerantz. Is that it?" Moishe asked acidly.

Daniel opened his mouth to say something, then thought better of it. Moishe was giving him a lesson in truth. Or maybe they'd just known each other for too long. Moishe realized how Daniel's mind worked, how he would throw any blame right onto Moishe's head.

"No, I'm not blaming you," Daniel said at last. "I'm blaming myself and no one else. I should have done a bit of thinking before I signed Pomerantz's bit of paper. I should have asked a couple of people what they thought."

Moishe listened to what constituted an apology. He felt he had to offer something himself. "Maybe your new general manager will thaw out by the time spring comes around," he said hopefully. "Right now he's chafing at the bit. He's just been made number one and everything that goes with it, so he wants to show the entire world right off that he runs the Grand. You were the first target to pop into his sights so he picked you off. Come the time they start shooting *South Side Serenade* he might have changed his mind about you. So wait as long as possible before you tell him that you're not going to back out. He might surprise you."

"Sure he'll surprise me," Daniel muttered without any real conviction. "Sure he'll change his mind."

South Side Serenade had better be the biggest blockbuster since *Gone With The Wind*. Otherwise he'd be out in the cold with nowhere for shelter.

Chapter Six

London in April was damp and chilly. A cold, gray, persistent drizzle formed a semi-opaque curtain across the city, dulling the edges of buildings, transforming the roads and sidewalks into greasy pools.

Coat collar pulled up and a heavy woolen scarf drawn tightly around his neck, Daniel left the Park Lane Hotel and walked slowly along Piccadilly toward Piccadilly Circus. More than ninety minutes remained before he was due at Covent Garden for the final rehearsal of *Cavalleria Rusticana.* He would use the time to window shop, to reacquaint himself with the city he had not visited for more than six years.

He had arrived in London the previous day, flying in from Idlewild after appearing in the Grand's last *La Bohème* of the season. Reporters had met him at London Airport and he had happily answered the inevitable questions. Yes, he was thrilled to be appearing at Covent Garden for the first time. That's right, it was in England that he had been given his first real break and he was delighted to be back. Yes, his wife, the Grand Opera soprano Anna Markova, was expecting a baby in a couple of months. The reporters had been kind to him. They had mentioned his commitment to *South Side Serenade,* but no questions had been asked about his problems with Robin Duguid and the Grand. Not that Daniel had really expected any. The rift between himself and the management had been kept quiet. So far, anyway. Duguid was content to sit back and wait for Daniel to make his move, one way or the other. If Daniel chose to put the company first, Duguid would be delighted; if he decided to forego his contract at the Grand, Duguid was certain he could find other tenors to fill in. But Daniel knew he could go only one way. His sole course of action was to present himself in July for the start of shooting *South Side Serenade.* And then Robin Duguid would undoubtedly throw the book at him; in his very gentlemanly way, of course.

As soon as he had arrived at the Park Lane Hotel from the airport, Daniel had put through a call to Anna. Although the housekeeper was there to help her, Daniel was anxious about leaving Anna alone in New Jersey. Even in her advanced state of pregnancy he had wanted to bring her with him, for herself and for his own sake. She would be his companion, his encouragement when he trod for the first time on a strange stage. Anna had declined. She was perfectly capable of coping at home for the few days he would be away. Besides, she told him, she was so far gone that she was convinced she looked awful and did not want to be seen in public.

Daniel had also called Martinelli in Milan. After explaining that he had to rush back to the States the morning after the Covent Garden performance, he had extracted a promise from the Italian doctor to visit London. When he had ended the conversation, he felt elation about seeing Martinelli and relief that he would have someone he knew in the audience. And with the way Martinelli felt about him, Daniel knew he would have to be disastrous to draw anything but praise.

He crossed the busy Piccadilly Circus junction, stopping long enough to look up at the statue of Eros, then began to walk slowly along Shaftesbury Avenue. A record store attracted his attention. His *Un Ballo in Maschera*—recorded under Toscanini with Claudia Rivera—was displayed prominently in the window. So was the *La Bohème* he had made with Anna following the Grand's opening night. Thrilled to see it already on display, Daniel entered the store. A sales clerk asked if he could help. Daniel pointed to the display of *Bohème* records, wanting to know how they were selling. When he explained who he was, the sales clerk called over the manager. Daniel left the store ten minutes later after making a promise that he would return on Friday afternoon and autograph the covers.

There was an added spring to his step as he crossed over Charing Cross Road and entered Long Acre. He was surprised to see how much the city had changed since he had been stationed there during the war. Bomb damage still showed, but most of it had been cleared and built over. He knew that if he went down to the dock area, though, he would find plenty of reminders of the bombing raids.

Fruit and vegetable warehouses were still open as he entered the Covent Garden area. Daniel could not resist a broad smile as he approached the opera house. The Grand was on West Thirty-fourth Street, the Met was on Thirty-ninth and Seventh, and The Royal Opera Company performed in the middle of Covent Garden fruit market. When you left the house after a performance, he had been told, you had to pick your way through trucks unloading produce as the market went through its busy period. At least, you never lacked for fresh fruit on the way home.

Because of the tightness of his schedule, Daniel had missed the first two rehearsals of *Cavalleria Rusticana*, which would share the bill with *Pagliacci*. The end of the New York season coincided almost exactly with the beginning of the Covent Garden season. There had been some reservations that one rehearsal would not be enough for Daniel to pick up any traits peculiar to the London production. Daniel had replied that he had played Turiddu enough times to be at home anywhere. He hadn't missed much by being absent from the first two rehearsals, he decided. Neither had been with the orchestra. The first hadn't even been in the opera house. It had taken place in a room across the street from the opera house; only the principal singers had been present—an understudy had stood in for him—and chairs had been used for scenery. The second rehearsal, at least, had been held on the Covent Garden stage, and the chorus had been involved.

He stopped outside the opera house to look at the calendar of events, curious to see who else was appearing during the season. His eyes drifted down to his own name and then he did a double take. Thank God he was doing *Cavalleria Rusticana* and not *Pagliacci*, he thought when he saw the cast in the accompanying opera. The role of Nedda in *Pagliacci* was being sung by Claudia Rivera.

When he entered the opera house, he was greeted by the company's musical director, who showed him around. Daniel was duly impressed. Covent Garden was older than the Grand, more ornate. The acoustics were marvelous, the sounds bouncing back at him from the furthest points. He decided that he would enjoy singing at Covent Garden, especially when he knew that Claudia Rivera would be watching him.

After three hours of rehearsing, Daniel's anticipated enjoyment was wearing dangerously thin. His throat felt like a sheet of sandpaper and he was starting to cough. He was sure that the overlong rehearsal and the dampness of the city were combining to affect his voice. How much longer was that damned musical director going to keep everyone rehearsing?

"That last scene one more time," the musical director called out. "After the *intermezzo.* It's still not right."

Daniel grimaced at the mezzo-soprano playing Lola, making certain that his feelings were well known. He had two major arias in that last scene—"Viva il vino spumeggiante" and "Mamma, quel vino è generoso." If he carried on singing like this, he'd have no voice at all for the performance in two days time. "Do they always drag these rehearsals out?" he whispered to the woman.

"Until it's right."

"It is right, for crying out loud." His voice sounded abnormally loud and he realized he had dropped his tactful whisper in favor of his normal tone. The acoustics were too good, and his petulant statement reverberated around the auditorium.

The musical director clapped his hands. "Is something the matter, Mr. Kerr?"

Daniel turned to face the man in the darkness of the auditorium. "How many more times are we going to go over this piece? It sounds fine to me."

"Perhaps it does," the musical director replied. "To you. But not to my ear. One more time, please."

The scene began again and Daniel willed himself to be patient. He felt out of place as it was, being the only American on stage. And no one had warned him that the English company dressed for rehearsals far more casually than did the Grand. In New York, you felt you had to wear a suit and tie for each rehearsal. In London, the style of clothing was dictated by comfort. The suit Daniel was wearing clashed with the sloppy, shapeless sweaters and baggy trousers of the English cast. But what the Royal Opera Company lacked in sartorial style it certainly made up for in lengthy rehearsals.

By the time Daniel went offstage with the baritone playing Alfio for the duel, he had made up his mind. He was adamant; this was the last rehearsal he would do. If the rest of the company didn't have it right by now, he couldn't give a damn. That was their problem, not his. Even with the two extra rehearsals they'd had, they couldn't put it together.

"Was that to your satisfaction?" he asked pointedly into the blackness where the musical director was sitting.

"From your attitude, Mr. Kerr, I would assume it has to be," the man remarked sardonically. "You may step down. We'll have one more go with your understudy filling in."

Exasperated, Daniel took off his jacket, rolled it up into a ball and threw it into the wings where it was caught by the stage manager. "Okay, one more time." His voice was sounding hoarser with each minute and he was sweating uncomfortably. Please God, get these frogs out of my throat by Friday night, he prayed silently. As much as he wanted to call it quits, there was no way he could walk out of the rehearsal now. Opera gossip was like an underground newspaper. Word of his refusal to continue with the rehearsal would reach everywhere. His difficulties at the Grand were already troublesome enough without having the reputation of temperamental tenor added to them.

When the rehearsal finally ended, Daniel nodded a curt farewell to his fellow artists and quickly left the opera house. He had to walk back to Charing Cross Road before he could find a taxi. After giving the driver an address, he slumped back in the seat and closed his eyes. God, his throat felt raw, like he'd swallowed a gallon of sulphuric acid. He'd better take something quickly, otherwise he'd sound like a cement mixer on Friday night.

The journey slipped past in a dream, until the taxi stopped outside a newly built row of anonymous, red brick houses. "Here you are, guv," the driver said. "This is the address you gave me." He managed to make the statement sound defiant, as if expecting his passenger to claim he'd been taken to the wrong place. After all, what wealthy-looking American would want to come to a street like this?

Daniel shook himself awake. "Thanks. Will you wait a few

minutes for me?"

"Sure. Don't bother me none. Meter's still running."

Daniel stepped out of the taxi and looked around. The buildings were unfamiliar to him, modern two-story council homes where once had stood old-fashioned, tall private houses. He wondered if the taxi driver could be mistaken until he looked along the street and recognized the public house on the corner. No, the driver had made no error. This was where he had been that Sunday morning with Harvey Berman, the chaplain from Chicago, and the family he was convinced he'd found in London. The old houses were gone, replaced with council homes, subsidized housing. Daniel stepped closer and tried to see through the communal hallway into the back garden where he had played ball with the boy that morning. There was no garden. Tarmac greeted his eyes. Children's swings and roundabouts. Slides and see-saws. It was a playground for the neighborhood kids.

"You looking for somebody, mister?"

Daniel turned around to see a woman standing behind him. Her hair was in curlers and she wore an apron over a faded blue dress. Suspicious of a stranger loitering on the premises, she had left her home to investigate.

"I'm trying to find an old friend. Phil Berman. Do you know him? He used to live here during the war."

The woman gazed at him, uncertain about the American accent, about his cashmere coat. "Don't nobody live around here from that time," she finally said. "These places are all new. Buzz bomb landed in the street and destroyed everything that was here before."

"I know. Thank you very much." He walked past her back to the waiting taxi, asking himself why he had bothered coming to this street. Had he really expected to find Phil Berman still living there? Or was it because he was so alone in the city that he needed someone he knew—no matter how vaguely or from how long ago? And if he had found Phil, what would he have said? That he'd seen his wife and child die?

"Where to now, guv?" the driver asked.

"Park Lane Hotel." He'd have a drink and try to get some sleep. Sleep would be the best cure of all. It wasn't only the sore throat that was bothering him; it was the huge time difference as well. That's what had made him irritable at the rehearsal. He had been so tired that he'd almost fallen asleep on his feet. No wonder his voice had sounded hoarse. Pleased to identify the source of his trouble, Daniel resolved to apologize to the musical director when he saw him next.

Back in the hotel room, he ordered a bottle of scotch and some ice. When it arrived, he poured a generous measure into the glass and sat back in an easy chair to relax.

When the telephone rang ninety minutes later, the bottle was almost half empty and Daniel was fast asleep in the chair. He woke sluggishly at the insistent double ring of the bell and looked around the room in bewilderment while he struggled to remember where he was.

"Yes?"

"Daniel Kerr?" a clipped voice asked.

"Who is this?" He sounded terrible. His words were slurred, hard to form. His throat ached. The whiskey had not done any good at all.

"Roger Hammersley. I had hoped that you might contact me when you knew you were coming to Covent Garden."

"I was going to," Daniel lied. He'd forgotten all about Hammersley. The man had left the Grand less than six months earlier to return to England and Daniel had already pushed him out of his memory. "Any chance of getting together for dinner sometime?" he asked, trying to make up for his lapse. "Say Friday. Spend the afternoon together and have a bite before the performance? I'm flying back on Saturday, otherwise I'd suggest then."

"That sounds excellent," Hammersley concurred. "I'll meet you at the Park Lane."

"Do you remember Enzo Martinelli from Milan?" Daniel asked, eager to prolong the conversation as he sought to hold onto a familiar voice.

"Your mentor with the scalpel?"

Daniel grinned at Hammersley's choice of words. "That's him. He's coming over for the performance. The three of us can have dinner together."

"That would be nice. I'm sure you'd like to tell us all about the trials and tribulations of an opera singer trying to break into grade-B films."

"How do you know about that?"

"I still have contacts at the Grand, Daniel. Friends who keep me informed of what's going on, even if you don't. By the way, your voice sounds terrible."

"I've just woken up and I've got a lousy cold."

"Look after it. See you Friday."

Daniel replaced the receiver and picked up the bottle again. He poured himself another large drink, undressed and crawled into bed, certain that he would feel better in the morning when his body had been given the rest it needed to adjust to the time change.

Martinelli arrived the following evening to take up the reservation Daniel had made for him at the Park Lane Hotel.

To Daniel, the Italian never seemed to age. The hair was still as black as he first remembered it, the body still as spare. Only the eyes and mouth had changed. Tiny crow's feet had crept in, almost indiscernible until Martinelli smiled.

Daniel was unable to hide his joy at seeing Martinelli. He had not left the hotel all day, eating his meals in the room, trying to find something in the newspapers he had ordered to interest him. With the exception of Hammersley, whom he would not see until the following day, he knew no one in the city and had never felt so lonely, so cut off. He missed Anna especially and kept wishing that she had accompanied him. After a few hours' separation during the course of a normal day, he was always glad to get home, to be with Anna again. The knowledge that he would not see her for a few days was almost unbearable. To make matters worse, the cold had intensified. He had wondered constantly whether he should call Covent Garden, beg off the commitment and book himself on the first plane back to Idlewild. The musical director had said that there was an understudy available. Good, let him play Turiddu. As he was about to lift the receiver and place the call, he had realized it would be a long time before the Royal Opera Company asked him back again.

"You look awful," was Martinelli's greeting when he visited Daniel in his room. "What's the matter with you?"

"A cold."

"Let me see your tongue."

Daniel obeyed. Martinelli saw the covering of white fur and told Daniel to close his mouth. "What kind of medication have you been prescribing for yourself? It smells like whiskey."

Daniel admitted that it was. He had finished off the bottle he had started the previous night and opened another.

"You are a fool," Martinelli said. "Alcohol is for sore muscles, not a sore voice." He left the room and was gone for twenty minutes. When he returned, he was carrying a thermometer which he stuck in Daniel's mouth.

"How is Anna?" he asked conversationally. "Getting big?"

Daniel nodded. "Fine," he mumbled through the thermometer. He had spoken to her in the early afternoon. The sound of her voice, so clear despite the thousands of miles separating them, had served to make him feel even more lonely and depressed. He'd never been away from her this long before. Wherever he had performed, she had always been nearby, ready with encouragement. Without her for the first time, he realized how desperately he relied on that support. Now she couldn't travel and he was on his own, like a small child left at school by himself for the first day. It was frightening. And the knowledge that he'd be on his own in Hollywood as well, when the time came to film *South Side Serenade*, only served to deepen his misery.

Martinelli removed the thermometer and checked the reading. "A hundred and one. You will live." He called room service and ordered a bowl of boiling water. From his pocket he pulled out a brown paper bag which bore the name of Boots, the drugstore chain. When the bowl of water was delivered by a curious maid, Martinelli tipped the contents of the brown paper bag into it. Immediately the strong smell of eucalyptus smothered the room. Martinelli forced Daniel's head over the bowl and covered it with a towel.

"Breathe deeply through your nose. You can stay like that for five minutes." He watched Daniel for a few seconds, then he began to scout around the room. When he found the opened bottle of scotch, he poured it down the basin.

"What are you doing?" Daniel called out from beneath the towel. He tried to look around, but his eyes were streaming.

"Saving your performance for tomorrow night. Saving your career." Martinelli pulled away the towel and helped Daniel to stand upright. "Since when did you start drinking like this?"

Daniel wiped his eyes with the wet towel. "Since I came down with this cold yesterday," he answered. "What the hell do you think I am, an alcoholic?" His voice felt better. His nose was clear and his throat seemed more comfortable. The eucalyptus and the steam had done their work. He felt fit enough to go on stage right now and sing Turiddu.

"What was wrong with trying cough syrup?" Martinelli asked.

"I never thought about it." Daniel sat down heavily on the edge of the bed and breathed deeply through his nose. The entire room was full of steam. The mirror was misted over and condensation clung in tiny drops to the windows. "Did you come to London to hear me sing or to give me a lecture?"

Martinelli's face tightened into a stern frown. "Both, if necessary. The scalpel I gave you on your debut at the Grand was not the only one I possess."

"Why did you pour away the scotch?"

"Because you are not to drink anymore. At least, not before tomorrow night. After that, you may do whatever you like. But I will not allow you to disgrace yourself at Covent Garden while I am in the audience."

Daniel pushed himself up from the bed and glared angrily at Martinelli. He'd been prepared to sit and listen to the Italian until now, but he'd overstepped the bounds of friendship. He owed the man, sure; but he wasn't certain he owed him this much. "When did I ever disgrace myself before? Tell me that?"

Martinelli's face relaxed and the smile that Daniel remembered took the place of the frown. The sharp, aquiline features softened and warmth returned to the brown eyes. "I never said you did. I am just ensuring that tomorrow night will not be the first time. Too many other artists have ruined their careers by relying on drink to solve their problems. I would not like my own personal discovery to be among that number." Martinelli poured away the inhalation and threw the sopping wet towel into the bath. "Do you feel up to eating anything?"

"Feed a cold, starve a fever?" Daniel queried, the spark of anger forgotten.

"A fallacy," Martinelli replied. "If you feed a cold, you will have to starve a fever later on. Settle for something light. A salad or an omelette."

"Sounds great." Daniel went into the bathroom to clean up, ready to go downstairs with Martinelli for dinner.

While they ate, Daniel told Martinelli all that had happened since he had signed the contract to appear in *South Side Serenade.* Martinelli said nothing, listening intently until Daniel had finished. Then he laid down his fork and slowly shook his head.

"Do you dream, perhaps, that you are another Mario Lanza?" he asked gently. "Gigli, Bjoerling never did these things. No serious opera singer would even consider starring in a musical movie of this nature while he is at the peak of his career. Movies, yes; by all means. But not something like this. You would make a mockery of your entire art." He stared across the table at Daniel, trying to understand what had made him take such a step.

"Quit looking at me like that," Daniel said defensively. "You're making me feel like I've got the plague."

Martinelli took no notice. He continued staring as he asked, "Are you quite prepared to abandon your operatic career for this film?"

"Why the hell should I abandon anything?"

"Because if you do not abandon it, it will surely abandon you. I hope, for your sake, that the film is an enormous success. That you make a vast sum of money from it. That you become famous in Hollywood. Because you will not be able to go back."

"I couldn't get out of it even if I wanted to," Daniel tried to explain. "The studio says they'll sue me. We start shooting in a little under three months, and if I'm not there, I'll have their lawyers chasing me."

"So let their lawyers chase." Martinelli made it sound ludicrously simple.

"And just where am I supposed to come up with the kind of money they're threatening to sue me for?" Daniel asked. "Have you got a spare half million dollars you can lend me till it's over?"

Martinelli pondered the question for a long moment.

"Congratulations," he said at last, with just the finest trace of sarcasm in his voice. "You seem to have succeeded in digging a splendid hole for yourself." He thought about adding that success had gone too quickly to Daniel's head; that he thought he was above sensible behavior. He refrained only when he realized how low Daniel already felt about the situation. "I think you should pray for this studio to go bankrupt, or that they should decide not to shoot this film at all. Not only would that get you out of an awkward position, but it would also put you in the novel situation of being able to sue the studio for breach of contract."

Daniel recognized the humor in Martinelli's statement and began to laugh. Thank God he had company tonight. He was frightened to even think what might have happened had he been alone again. Martinelli would see him through. And with Hammersley also there tomorrow night, he'd have no trouble in knocking them dead at Covent Garden.

Martinelli went to his room shortly before eleven, claiming fatigue from the full day of travel. Daniel sat in his own room for almost half an hour, fully dressed, knowing he would never sleep. The performance was still twenty hours away, but the familiar tension was creeping in. He clasped his hands together, closed his eyes and tried to pretend that Anna was with him. Anna with her special way of making his nervousness disappear, just as she always did before a performance. The jokes, the soothing conversation, the way of making him laugh at himself, at his worries.

Anna! That was it! He'd call her. He had already spoken to her once today so she would not be expecting a second call. He'd surprise her and help himself at the same time.

He dialed the operator and told him to place the call. Then he sat back and waited, his anticipation heightening. Ten minutes passed and the anticipation turned to anxiety. Why hadn't the operator called back yet? Impatiently he dialed again. The operator explained that he was trying to find a clear circuit. It might take up to an hour to complete the call. Did Daniel wish to cancel it? No, he answered. He did not. Keep trying. He had placed the call and keyed himself up to speak to Anna. Nothing was going to stop him now.

As the wait lengthened, he called room service. A night

porter knocked on the door. Daniel ordered another bottle of whiskey to replace the one Martinelli had poured away. When the man told him that the bar was closed, Daniel offered him five pounds. The porter looked first at the large white note and then at Daniel's face before saying he would see what he could do.

At half past one, when the operator finally called back, Daniel had drunk his way through a third of the bottle of Johnnie Walker the night porter had brought him. The bowl of ice had turned to water without a cube being taken from it. Daniel was drinking the whiskey straight.

"Hello?" Daniel answered the phone on the second ring, speaking uncertainly, his mind dulled. Who was calling him at this time of night? Who even knew he was staying at this hotel?

"Your call to the United States," the operator said. Suddenly Daniel remembered. A confused jumble of whirs and clicks attacked his ear, then he heard Anna's voice.

"Anna, it's Daniel. I'm in London."

"What?" She struggled to hear him. "What did you say?"

"I said I'm in London. How are you? I miss you."

"Daniel, are you all right?"

"I'm fine. I just wish you were here. I need you with me."

There was a long pause before Anna asked suspiciously, "Daniel, have you been drinking?"

"Me?" he asked in surprise. He looked in amazement at the glass in his hand and placed it on the dressing table. "No, I'm just lonely, that's all. And I've got a rotten cold, that's why I sound so bad. I'm frightened it's going to affect my singing tomorrow night."

"For God's sake, Daniel. Go to bed. You'll be out on your feet tomorrow if you carry on like this."

"I'm sorry." He was confounded to feel the warm trickle of tears that dribbled down his cheeks. He was crying. For himself. Crying because he was alone and no one wanted to keep him company through the long night. Not even Anna. She didn't want to talk to him. She wanted him to go to bed.

"Why don't you want to talk to me?" he asked plaintively. His head felt swollen again. The inhalation had worn off. Or maybe the whiskey had overwhelmed it. He hadn't drunk that much, or had he? He picked up the bottle and stared hard at it, trying to see exactly how much had gone. It could not have been full when the night porter brought it up, he finally decided. The man must have raided the bar for an open bottle.

"Daniel, listen carefully to me. I want you to go to bed right now and get some sleep. I'll see you on the weekend when you get home. Good night."

He heard the connection being broken, and the tears of self-pity increased to a deluge. Now he had no one to talk to at all. Wait a minute. He'd try Moishe. Moishe would be glad to hear from him. He'd be thrilled to get a call from England. So would Isaac! Daniel decided to call up everyone whose number he could remember. He'd show them that he hadn't forgotten them.

Mind made up, he got back to the operator and gave him the numbers of Maurice Waterman and Isaac Kirschbaum, instructing the man that if he could not get through to one, he should try the other.

When the operator called back an hour later with Moishe's connection, only two inches remained in the bottle of Johnnie Walker. Daniel was lying across the bed in a drunken stupor, breathing heavily, too far gone for the bell to ever reach him.

He moaned in his sleep, struggling to free himself from the two steely claws that grasped his shoulders. His legs were moving slowly, dragging him across the floor. His arms were hanging limply by his sides.

Daniel wished the dream would go away. He didn't want to dream. He wanted to sleep, to experience a long dreamless slumber that would leave him refreshed before the big performance at Covent Garden. Turiddu needed to rest before he sang.

He wasn't moving anymore. He was lying still again. Better. Much better. But he wasn't in bed. He was lying on something cold and smooth. Like a slab. A slab? Mortuaries had slabs. He was lying on a mortician's slab. He must be dead. But how? Turiddu was killed in the opera, but it was all in play. It was an act. So if it were all an act, what was he doing lying on a cold slab?

A stream of freezing water cannoned into his face, down his chest and legs. The dream vanished abruptly. In its place was Martinelli's voice, shouting, cursing, cajoling as he held Daniel under the cold shower.

"*Vergogna!* Are you mad, an *imbecille?* What happened to you?"

Daniel tried to force open his eyes. The stream of icy water slammed them shut again. He struggled and fought blindly against Martinelli's unrelenting grip, desperate to get out of the bombardment of water. But he was no match for the combined offensive of both Martinelli and his own aching head.

After a minute, Martinelli turned off the water and helped Daniel to his feet. The clothes in which he had fallen asleep were soaked through, ruined beyond redemption. Martinelli's shirt and trousers were also saturated. The Italian doctor did not seem to care. All his attention was focused on Daniel. He sat him down gently on the bathroom stool, watched him warily for a moment to be sure he would not fall off, then walked quickly to the telephone. Five minutes later, a maid appeared in the room, holding a tray with orange juice and coffee. She looked at the table, at the glass lying on the floor. When she peeked into the bathroom and saw Martinelli briskly slapping Daniel's face back and forth, she put down the tray and ran from the room. Martinelli hardly even noticed her.

"Drink this." He dropped two large white tablets into a glass of water. They fizzed angrily as Martinelli held the glass to Daniel's mouth.

"What is it?" Daniel asked. The bubbles tickling his nose made him feel nauseated.

"Something to make you feel better." Martinelli grabbed Daniel's nose and squeezed it shut. As Daniel gasped, the Italian poured the effervescent liquid down his throat. Daniel gagged against it. Martinelli refused to take away the glass. It was choke or swallow. Daniel yielded, then gulped frantically as the bubbles sent his already tortured stomach into instant rebellion. He lunged past Martinelli to the commode and retched painfully until nothing more would come. Martinelli watched impassively.

"Now drink the orange juice," Martinelli said. "Slowly."

Daniel climbed unsteadily to his feet and took the tall glass of freshly squeezed orange juice that Martinelli was holding out. The taste cleared his mouth, but his head continued to ache abominably.

"Do you feel better?" Martinelli asked, satisfied that the orange juice would not follow the Alka-Seltzer down the toilet.

"I feel terrible. What time is it?"

"Ten. You are due to sing in another ten hours."

Daniel shook his head to refute the statement. The pain inside his skull increased to battering ram proportions. "I'll never be able to. I'd better call them and cancel, give them time to warn the understudy."

"You will do no such thing," Martinelli said. "You will sing tonight. But first you will put on some dry clothes and we will go for a walk in the fresh air. Before you sing, you have to clear your head."

Daniel took one look at the stern expression on Martinelli's face and decided not to argue. It would be easier in the long run to do as the Italian said.

The black taxi stopped outside the Park Lane Hotel and a man wearing a bowler hat and a beige Great British Warm topcoat stepped out. He began to walk toward the hotel lobby when he noticed the two men pacing up and down the sidewalk, strolling in the brisk April afternoon air. He stood for a moment, watching, then he went over to join them.

"Expanding your lungs for tonight's performance?"

When Daniel looked around, Roger Hammersley stepped back in shock. Daniel's eyes were red-rimmed. His face was white and puffy and his breathing was labored. Hammersley knew that he would never be able to sing that night.

"Good Lord! What happened?"

Martinelli answered. "He was looking for courage for tonight's performance in a bottle of whiskey. Instead, he found a hangover."

Without another word, Hammersley grasped Daniel's free arm and began to walk with him, talking over his head to Martinelli. "When did you find him like this?"

As if Daniel was not there, Martinelli explained how he had waited for Daniel to meet him at breakfast. When he had not shown up, he went to the room, where he found him stretched across the bed, fully clothed and out to the world.

"Has Covent Garden been notified yet?" Hammersley asked.

Martinelli shook his head. "He will sing tonight. He will not let us down."

"Impossible," Hammersley asserted. "He can't even talk, let alone sing. I'll call in for him. They know me there. I'll make up a story that he's ill. They'll believe me."

Again Martinelli shook his head. "You will be doing Daniel a disservice, Mr. Hammersley. If he does not sing tonight, he might never sing again."

"What?" asked Hammersley in disbelief. "You'd better explain that."

"You should know already. Whenever Daniel sang before, Anna was always with him, either in the cast or watching. Tonight will be the first time he has sung without her presence."

"That's the reason for the whiskey?" Hammersley asked dubiously.

"Yes. To give him the courage to sing without her. And if he fails this time, this first time by himself, he might never be able to find the courage to try again."

Hammersley still had difficulty believing what the Italian was saying. During the five years he had worked with Daniel at the Grand, he had never lacked confidence. Usually, the opposite was true. Daniel had suffered from overconfidence, the certainty that he would never put a foot wrong, never miss a note, never forget a line or bungle a cue.

"I think, perhaps, that he fooled you as well, Mr. Hammersley," Martinelli continued. "Daniel needs perpetual encouragement, someone ready to pat him on the back the entire time." Martinelli had seen it at the hospital in Hitchin when he had been forced into tricking Daniel into participating in the concert by putting him in a position where he could not back out. And when he had rushed from the hall at the end of the scheduled recital and had to be bullied into returning for an encore. "In New York he always had Anna to push him. Here, he has nobody and he fell apart." Martinelli turned around and started to walk Daniel back toward the hotel. "Do you know what I learned he was doing at one o'clock this morning?"

"What?"

"Placing telephone calls to the United States. He was that desperate to speak with someone he knew. Anyone, it did not matter who, just as long as they would tell him how marvelous he was and what a success he would be at Covent Garden."

"I see," Hammersley murmured. "I guess we'd better start telling him that ourselves. Maybe we can salvage this evening's performance for him."

The telephone rang at four o'clock, just as Martinelli and Hammersley had managed to get Daniel to start vocalizing. The first minute sounded terrible. Hammersley wanted to drown out the noise, clasp his hands over his ears until Daniel ceased the travesty of the sweet voice he had heard on stage at the Grand.

"Keep going," Martinelli urged. "It can only get better."

"What about the phone?" Daniel asked. "Maybe it's something important." Anything to stop vocalizing. He knew how terrible his voice sounded; the more he pushed it, the worse it would become.

Hammersley answered the telephone, watching while Martinelli continued to make Daniel vocalize. God, Hammersley thought; if he sings like this tonight, he'll empty the house quicker than a fire alarm.

"Were you supposed to be at a record shop in Shaftesbury Avenue this afternoon?" Hammersley asked. "The manager's on the line, saying you had agreed to autograph some copies of the *Bohème* you and Anna recorded."

Mention of Anna immediately brightened Daniel's frame of mind. Until he remembered the promise he'd made to the record store manager. "I forgot all about it."

"Get dressed," Hammersley said. "We're going down there now."

"All of us?"

"All of us," Martinelli confirmed.

When Daniel marched into the record store fifteen minutes later, accompanied by Hammersley and Martinelli, a small crowd of customers was waiting. In one corner of the store a table had been erected; on it were neatly piled stacks of *Bohème* and *Ballo*. The manager, white-faced and clasping his hands in nervous despair, only relaxed when he saw Daniel.

"Thank heavens you're here, Mr. Kerr. That sign in the window"—he indicated a white cardboard placard that announced Daniel Kerr, of the Grand Opera Company of New York, would be in the store from four until five to autograph records—"aroused a lot of interest. We'd have been faced with a mutiny if you hadn't turned up."

"I'm sorry I'm late. I wasn't feeling very well." Daniel waited for either Hammersley or Martinelli to show him up as a liar. They did not.

"If you'll sit over there"—the manager guided Daniel to the table in the corner—"we can get going."

"Thirty minutes and no more," Martinelli told the manager. "Mr. Kerr has a performance at Covent Garden tonight."

"Who are you?"

"His voice teacher," Martinelli lied. "Mr. Kerr is just recovering from a bad cold and we do not wish to take any chances."

"Of course," the manager nodded.

Daniel made himself comfortable behind the table. The first thought to cross his mind when he picked up a pen was to draw glasses, a beard and moustache on Claudia Rivera's Amelia on the sleeve of *Un Ballo in Maschera*.

"Don't you dare," Hammersley whispered as soon as he recognized Daniel's intention. The Grand's former general manager decided it was a good sign. If Daniel had the alertness to remember his feud with the Italian soprano, he was feeling better.

"Just a thought," Daniel murmured. He did not know whether it was the brisk walk from the hotel or the work that Martinelli and Hammersley had forced him through in his room, but he was feeling better. Much better. All he needed now was something to eat and he'd be as fit as he had ever been.

He signed record covers and thanked the customers automatically while he let his mind drift back to the previous night. He must have been mad, drinking like that, feeling sorry for himself. Why had he ever allowed himself to feel so miserable when all these people were waiting to boast that Daniel Kerr had personally autographed their records?

They got him back to the Park Lane Hotel just after five.

Martinelli immediately sent down for sandwiches and a pot of tea heavily laced with honey. Then they began to work in earnest. Daniel vocalized in one-minute spurts, stopping for five minutes to drink the tea, starting over again. Three times hotel staff knocked on the door to check that everything was all right, their polite method of letting the room's occupants know they had received complaints from other guests about the noise. The manager showed up the next time to say he would throw out the three of them if the noise did not cease. As sympathetic as the hotel was to Mr. Kerr's need to rehearse, the other guests could not be disturbed.

The prospect of being evicted from the hotel and thrown out into the street made Hammersley decide it was time to leave for Covent Garden. They could finish their work in the dressing room.

"I have to call Anna first," Daniel said as they were about to leave.

Martinelli sensed that the fear had returned. "You will never get through in time. We dare not be late."

"I don't care. I've got to speak to her. I haven't called her yet today. She'll worry."

Hammersley saw a way out of the predicament. He gave instructions to the hotel switchboard. They were to call Mrs. Kerr in New Jersey and give her the number at Covent Garden where Daniel could be reached. She was to call him before the performance started. The arrangement seemed to satisfy Daniel.

When they arrived at the opera house, they were greeted by the musical director. After making a fuss of Hammersley, who had once sung with the company, the musical director informed Daniel that the soprano who was to have sung Santuzza in *Cavalleria Rusticana* had gone down with a heavy cold. Daniel's reflection that she had probably caught it from him during the rehearsal two days earlier was cut short when the musical director imparted additional news concerning the performance.

The soprano who was singing Nedda in *Pagliacci*—which shared the bill with *Cavalleria Rusticana*—had offered to fill in.

Daniel would be playing opposite Claudia Rivera.

Chapter Seven

Daniel sat perfectly still in the chair while the make-up man put the finishing touches to his face. Off to one side sat Hammersley and Martinelli, silent as they watched.

Hammersley was now certain that Daniel's voice would not let him down, and he was amazed how his opinion had changed. Daniel was still young and possessed an incredibly strong constitution that had enabled him to shrug off the effects of the previous night's bender. Six hours earlier, when he had arrived at the Park Lane Hotel to find Daniel being forcibly walked by Martinelli, Hammersley would have wagered everything he owned that Daniel would be unable to sing that night. Now it was thirty minutes to curtain time and the voice was as strong and as clear as he had ever heard it.

What did concern Hammersley was the way Daniel would react to singing with Claudia Rivera. Hammersley understood with painful clarity what Daniel must be thinking. That Claudia had only offered to sing Santuzza for the opportunity to cut him up again. This time in front of the sophisticated Covent Garden audience where she had sung many times before. All Daniel would remember as he stood onstage with Claudia would be how the soprano had held onto her note during the Grand's production of *Tosca* and thrown him to the hisses and catcalls of the audience. And, of course, there was the additional matter of a bottle of champagne across the back of the head, Hammersley ruefully recalled.

The telephone in the dressing room rang. Hammersley reached out a hand to answer it. He listened to the switchboard operator and then his face broke into a happy smile as he recognized Anna's voice asking for Daniel.

"Anna, my dear. This is Roger Hammersley. How are you?" He turned away from Daniel and lowered his voice. Perhaps Daniel's insistence on speaking to Anna before the performance would reap benefits Hammersley had not imagined.

If anyone could influence Daniel's behavior, it would be Anna.

"We have a little problem here, Anna," Hammersley said quietly. He looked sideways and saw Martinelli staring curiously at him. When he glanced toward the dressing table he saw that Daniel's eyes were closed, relaxing under the make-up artist's steady touch. Quickly Hammersley related how Martinelli had first found Daniel at the hotel, the second drinking bout, the tension, the gnawing anxiety that he was alone—all followed by the unexpected pressure of singing again opposite Claudia Rivera.

Anna listened, her mind in a confused whirl. Even the baby's insistent kicking inside her went unnoticed. She could hardly believe what Hammersley was saying. It didn't seem to make any sense. She had suspected that Daniel had been drinking when he'd called her the previous night. One drink, maybe two. That was nothing new. He had a couple of quick drinks before every performance. But an entire bottle? What Hammersley was saying was an unwelcome revelation. This surely couldn't be Daniel—to empty a bottle by himself and not give a damn about his performance. The tension she could understand; he was like that leading up to every performance. So were thousands of others. Drinking this heavily was something new.

"Let me speak to him," she said finally.

"We were hoping you would," Hammersley whispered. Then he added in his normal voice. "Glad to hear you're feeling so well. Don't forget that I expect an invitation to the christening."

"There won't be a christening."

"Of course, I forgot." Hammersley laughed heartily. "For you," he said to Daniel. "Anna to wish you good luck."

Daniel took the call. "Anna?"

"Hi. You feeling better?"

"Fine!" he exclaimed. "Why shouldn't I be?"

"You didn't sound too bright when you called last night."

"Last night?" Daniel asked, momentarily confused. "Did I speak to you last night? When?"

"About midway through the bottle, I'd guess, from the way you sounded."

He fell silent at her reply.

"You worried the life out of Moishe as well. He called me this morning. Said the operator called him with a transatlantic phone call and nobody was there when he got connected."

"What about my father?" Slowly Daniel began to remember the calls he had ordered.

"Did you call him as well? Were you that down on yourself?"

"Guess I must have been."

"Your entire fee for singing at Covent Garden's going to be wasted on phone calls," Anna chided him gently. "Listen, I understand you're singing opposite Claudia Rivera. She's filling in as Santuzza."

"Yes." The single word came out hesitantly, almost grudgingly.

"Are you worried about it?"

"Why should I be?"

"In case she tries to upstage you again?" Anna did not wait for an answer; she carried right on talking. "Have you seen her yet?"

"No. I don't want to either."

"Don't be stupid, Daniel. She offered to sing the part for one reason, and one reason only. Because she's a professional and did not want to see a production ruined because another singer couldn't keep a date. You should be grateful that she stepped in and made the offer, otherwise you'd be playing opposite an understudy who'd make you look awful. So don't go out there and make a fool of yourself by trying to put one over on her."

"What if she tries something on me?"

"She won't." Anna wished she felt as confident as she sounded. "She evened the score last time. Just go out there and sing like you've never sung before." She blew him a kiss and hung up.

"Ready?" Hammersley asked cheerfully.

Busy thinking over what Anna had said, Daniel did not hear the question. Was Anna right?

"Daniel, are you ready?" This time it was Martinelli who spoke. "You have just got time to finish your exercises before you are due on stage."

Daniel snapped out of it, his mind firmly made up. He knew how to conduct himself. He would give Claudia Rivera, Covent Garden, everyone who was out there a performance they'd never forget. He'd do it for Martinelli and Hammersley. For Anna as well. Without their care, their worry, their help, he would never have made it out of the hotel room. He would have lain on the bed, drowning in self-pity until someone came to tell him that his reservation at the hotel had expired and would he please leave so that the chambermaid could prepare the room for the next guest.

"Good evening, Mr. Kerr. I hope your manners have improved since the last time we met."

"Hi, Claudia. How are you doing, old girl?" Daniel walked right up to the soprano as they waited in the wings, grabbed hold of her and gave her a loud, resounding kiss on the cheek. "Been looking forward to working with you again," he lied.

Somehow the smell didn't bother him anymore. To some degree, the tail end of the cold protected him. Mostly, though, the reason was the role Claudia was playing, a nineteenth-century Sicilian peasant girl. If nineteenth-century Sicilian peasant girls didn't stink of sweat and garlic, Daniel reasoned, who did? Claudia was playing the role perfectly; even to the smell.

The soprano was taken aback by Daniel's friendly greeting. Tenors had never kissed her before. Especially one she had embarrassed and then leveled with a champagne bottle.

Still holding the woman, Daniel looked around at other members of the cast and winked; he was in charge and he wanted everyone to know it. "You know what people have been telling me?" he whispered in Claudia's ear. "That you only offered to sing Santuzza so you could make a fool of me again. That's not true, is it?"

"I do not know what you are talking about!"

"Good. Unless you want to sing Nedda in *Pagliacci* on crutches, you'd better watch the conductor. One long note and I'll throw you right across the goddamned stage. You hear me?" He moved to kiss her again. Instead, he bit the lobe of her ear. She shrieked loudly enough to be heard out in the auditorium and struggled to break free. Daniel maintained his grip; he hadn't finished yet. "And none of this standing in front of me crap, either. You take one step in front of me and I'll kick you so hard you'll wind up in the front seats."

Claudia paled at the threats. No one had ever spoken to her like this. First he had kissed her, then he had threatened her. She had expected gratitude for filling in. Instead, she was being promised harm. He was mad.

"You got a claque out there tonight?" Daniel asked. "You'd better pray they don't upset me." The claque was the only thing Daniel feared. No matter how well Claudia behaved herself on stage, he would be unable to control her paid supporters. If she had already instructed them to jeer him, there was little he could do about it. Unless he could persuade Claudia to change her orders before the opera began. "I get booed just once out there tonight and you're going to wind up on some violinist's lap with his bow shoved right up your ass."

He let go of her finally. She stepped back immediately, face white with fear, breathing unsteady. She turned and waddled away, avoiding the eyes of those who had witnessed the scene. Daniel guessed that she was going out to the auditorium to find her claque leader and change her instructions. When she returned five minutes later, just as applause sounded for the conductor's arrival, she marched straight up to Daniel.

"You need have no fears, Mr. Kerr. My claque will be silent tonight."

Daniel smiled at her. "I'm sure the violinists and the people in the front seats will be glad to hear that. *In bocca el lupo.*"

The last of the crowd had gone when Daniel, Martinelli and Hammersley left by the stage door on Floral Street. The sound of trucks and the shouts of men greeted them as the Covent Garden fruit market went through its nightly business.

Martinelli slapped Daniel joyfully on the back as they walked among crates of fruit being unloaded. "You have never sung better!" he shouted above the market's din. "Congratulations!"

An orange rolled loose along the sidewalk. Daniel kicked happily at it, a small boy again playing in the streets. The orange skidded along the concrete and thudded into a wall, splitting skin, spraying juice. He knew he'd sung well. He didn't need Martinelli to tell him that. After the final scene, the audience had refused to let him go. They had called him back time and again for more bows until he thought his back would remain bent.

Above his performance, though, he was proud of how he had pushed aside his problems, the loneliness, the drinking. He'd forced himself to fight back with the strongest weapon at his disposal, his own voice. There had been no defense against it, from the audience or from Claudia Rivera. She had known it, too. After the performance—during the interval between *Cavalleria Rusticana* and *Pagliacci*—she had knocked on the door of his dressing room while he was changing. His earlier threats were forgotten as she complimented him on the performance. Daniel had responded in an equally gracious manner, praising her for standing in for the indisposed Santuzza; he had even stayed to watch the production of *Pagliacci*, applauding Claudia as loudly as her own claque.

The evening did not serve to make him like Claudia Rivera; her egotism and her personal hygiene still left much to be desired. It did make him aware, though, of what a consummate professional she was. It was a trait to be admired, to be learned.

"Do you realize now what a fool you've been?" Hammersley asked. He managed to make the question sound like a fond remark, a father trying to guide a wayward son.

"Sure." Daniel felt so exuberant about his performance that he would agree to anything.

"And what an even bigger fool you'll be if you go through with this stupidity in Hollywood," Hammersley continued. "Get a doctor to sign you off ill. Do anything, but get out of it. I know Robin Duguid. I recommended him for the Grand appointment because I thought he was the best man for the job. Don't cross him, Daniel. Because if you ever want his help, you'll have to crawl back on your hands and knees."

Daniel said nothing. To argue now would destroy the euphoria he was feeling. And he would depress himself again; he could not afford that.

"Are you listening to a single word I'm saying?"

"Of course." Daniel stopped to kick another orange lying on the sidewalk. This one burst against his shoe, splattering his trousers. He pulled out a handkerchief to wipe the juice before it could dry on the fabric.

They reached Shaftesbury Avenue and Martinelli waved down a passing cab. Back at the Park Lane Hotel, Daniel waved aside suggestions of a late night snack and went straight up to his room, ordering a call to Anna in New Jersey. He wanted to tell her of his success, how he had come through it, turned disaster into triumph.

The connection was made almost immediately, as if to make a mockery of his previous night's efforts. As the words flowed from him—describing the performance to Anna, the way he'd cowed Claudia Rivera and her compliments afterwards—he did not give a moment's thought to Martinelli or Hammersley. His earlier gratitude to those who had helped him went unrecalled.

When Daniel's flight from London touched down at Idlewild the following evening, Moishe was waiting at the airport. First Daniel called Anna to tell her he was home, then he got into the car.

"Next time you call make sure you stay on the goddamned line," Moishe grumbled as they drove away from the airport. "You've got no idea how big an idiot you feel when you're waiting for a phone that's not answered and it's not even you who made the call."

"I forgot about it, it took so long to get through."

"What the hell did you want anyway?"

Daniel searched quickly for a reply; obviously Anna had not told Moishe what had happened in London. "I just got to thinking about Joel Pomerantz and *South Side Serenade*, that's all. Have you heard anything from Carmel Studios?"

Moishe nodded. "He's been on to me. Checking that you'll be out West once the Grand's tour is over and Anna's had the baby."

He would be checking, Daniel thought sourly. Pomerantz won't let go of me now that he's got his claws in. Goddamn! I was a stupid son of a bitch to sign that contract. Duguid will let me go, though. He won't be like Pomerantz.

Daniel did not look forward to seeing the Grand's general manager when the tour started in four days' time. They would be in each other's pocket for three weeks—in Cincinnati, Denver, Dallas, New Orleans, Miami and Atlanta—but Daniel knew that Duguid would never mention *South Side Serenade*. The general manager's mind was made up already on how he would handle the situation. He would wait for Daniel to set foot on Carmel's lot and for the cameras to begin rolling. Then, like a patient cat sitting by a hole in the wall for the mouse to be brave enough to stick its head out, he would pounce.

Daniel asked Moishe to make a detour to his parents' home in Van Cortlandt Park. He stopped in long enough to tell Isaac of his success in London and show him the review from that morning's London *Times*. At his father's suggestion, he left the review in the house for Isaac to show Yetta when she returned from visiting friends whom she was regaling with tales of the three months they had just spent in Florida. At Daniel's insistence, his parents had gone south again for the winter. Daniel did not think his father could have stood another New York winter, although the periodic heart check-ups were encouraging. Still, what strain could there be on his heart when he did next to nothing all day long?

Anna was waiting when Daniel arrived home, a bright maternity smock, if not actively hiding her condition, at least pleasantly disguising it. The housekeeper had prepared dinner, but Daniel felt too tired to eat. His body was still on Greenwich Mean Time. The day contained five hours too many for him and he felt as if it were three or four in the morning. He had been up early to see Martinelli off at Victoria Station for the long trip back to Milan, had a late breakfast with Hammersley and then gone to London Airport to catch his own flight. He had stayed awake during the entire flight; the abuse to which he had subjected his body and the lack of sleep were now combining to take their toll.

Realizing how exhausted Daniel was, Moishe refused the offer of dinner, claiming he had eaten at the airport while waiting for Daniel's flight to arrive. He was also tired, he said; if they'd excuse him, he'd like to go home.

After Moishe had left the house to drive back to New York,

Daniel sat in the living room with Anna. He put fresh logs on the fire and watched the flames dance merrily before he sank down in an armchair. The warmth of the fire settled him. It was time to talk, time to unwind after the exertions of the trip.

"Daniel, do you ever stop to think that you've got other people to consider? Not just yourself?"

The question startled him. It was not what he had been expecting. He had been looking to Anna for support, not an attack. "What do you mean?"

"You're living your life for your own enjoyment. No"—she shook her head while she tried to think of the words she wanted—"I don't mean that."

"What do you mean, then?"

"Whenever the slightest thing goes wrong, you immediately start looking around for a crutch, someone to lean on. You don't know what to do. You're hopeless at handling awkward situations."

He knew what she was driving at. "I had nothing to do," he broke in. "I was bored out of my mind. That's why I had a couple of drinks."

"It's not the drinking. It's the way you"—she paused again—"use people." Daniel opened his mouth to argue, but she held up her hand. "Please let me finish what I'm saying, Daniel. You do use people. Whether you realize it or not, you've been using them all your life. After you'd wiped yourself out in London, Mr. Hammersley and your friend Enzo went through hell and high water to get you straight in time for your performance. But you never mentioned them once to me on the phone after you'd got back to the hotel from Covent Garden. It was all you. You'd conquered the world all by yourself."

Daniel sat quietly, listening to Anna's criticism, thinking of what he could say in his own defense.

"They were both worried out of their minds about you. Mr. Hammersley told me everything that had happened to you in London. The drinking. The loneliness. They weren't helping you for their own benefit. They were doing it for you, so you wouldn't show yourself up in front of the Covent Garden audience. I think they'd both be very hurt if they knew you thought so little of their efforts. I know damned well I would."

"I appreciated what they did!" Daniel burst out. "I know how hard they worked to get me fit. It's just that in the excitement I forgot. You can't imagine how high I was, Anna! Even Rivera came into the dressing room to congratulate me!"

Anna raised her hands to her ears to block out his words. "There you go again! That's exactly what I'm talking about! You're only thinking of yourself, about what you did, how you did it all on your own without any help from anyone else. Everyone has helped you in this business. Me. Mr. Hammersley. Your friend Enzo. Even Moishe. And you're convinced that you've done everything by yourself."

"Well, I have!" Daniel protested. "I'm the one who stands up on the stage and sings. I'm the one the people come to see and hear. I'm the one who gives the performance."

Anna stared at him in desperation. She knew she could never hope to make him understand. She'd learned that a long time ago and still she tried to change him, to make him accept the fact that others were also responsible for his success. How could she hope to change him when he'd been this way all his life, having others to help him. There had always been others, she understood that. Daniel had told her about Fat Benny, how his uncle had opened all the doors for him, leaned on someone here, called in a favor there to make the way to the top easier for Daniel. And she had continued the tradition, although the paths she had cleared had been for Daniel's confidence; a timely word of encouragement, a promise to stand by him. How far would he have gotten had it not been for other people? she wondered. He seemed to accept their help as if it were his due. He took it for granted, certain that it would always be there and he would never need to acknowledge it.

She stood up and walked to the window. Bathed in the light spilling out of the living room, she could see daffodils in the front garden, trees beginning to blossom. She felt at one with them. When they bloomed, so would she. Another few weeks and she would be a mother.

Forgetting that Daniel was in the room with her, she let her hand stray down to her swollen stomach, caressing the child that slumbered within. She would need Daniel's help when the child was born. She'd need his support. But what help would he be able to offer? He would need her more than ever once he began shooting *South Side Serenade.* If ever his world was to cave in around him, it would be then, when what he had tried to ignore for five months finally happened. He would be home for the first three weeks after the child was born—enough time to be present at the *bris* if it were a boy—then he would be off to Hollywood. He would need encouragement there as he had never needed it before.

Anna wished fervently that he had sought the advice of others before he had signed the movie contract, that he had been straightforward with Robin Duguid. If he had been honest with the general manager, all this trouble could have been avoided. She was certain that Duguid did not want to lose Daniel any more than Daniel wanted to leave the Grand. They were like two immovable objects, two implacable armies pushing each other to see which would yield. And neither would. What worried Anna most was how the clash would leave Daniel. If his confidence could be destroyed simply by the knowledge that he was performing in a strange city for the first time, what would happen to him once he realized that the carpet had been pulled from underneath him at the Grand Opera Company, from where his strength came?

Mistaking Anna's silence for anger, Daniel stood up and joined her at the window. "Who do I apologize to first? You? Moishe? Hammersley? Enzo?"

He was like a child, as naive as the baby inside her. She turned around and smiled warmly at him, unable to resist his innocence. "No one, Daniel. You are the way you are and nothing in the world can change it. But try to remember sometimes that other people help you as well. Let them know you appreciate their efforts. Show them. Let them share in your happiness."

He put his hands on her shoulders and kissed her forehead. "Okay, I promise."

And she knew he would forget the promise as soon as his next triumph occurred.

Other than greeting Daniel when he joined the tour party at

Pennsylvania Station, Robin Duguid did not say a word. The matter of *South Side Serenade*, by tacit agreement, was left unmentioned. Duguid had too many other things on his mind.

He had just completed his debut New York season with the Grand and was embarking on his first tour. A string of successes, starting with the new production of *La Bohème*, lay behind him. Not that Duguid had been totally responsible; much of the work for the season had been accomplished by Hammersley before he had passed over the reins. The tour cities were eagerly awaiting the new Grand. Opera committees in the scheduled cities had raised more money than ever before to ensure the Grand's performances. Special functions for cast members had been planned. Most of the company wre dreading it.

Daniel walked along the coach, past the card games that were already in progress and found his seat. Junior members of the company respectfully mentioned his success at Covent Garden and Daniel received their praise graciously. He didn't expect any compliments from his equals—they were incredibly objective when it came to someone else's work—but it was nice to hear the junior singers, who, no doubt, one day hoped to take his place, praise him. Not that he tried to be friendly with any members of the cast. He made a point to keep his relationships within the company on a strictly professional basis. The card games, the riotous behavior and partying were not for him. He had an image to protect both within the company and outside. The problems he knew would arise when he started on *South Side Serenade* need not be fueled with scandalous memories of his previous behavior with the company.

As the train pulled out, Daniel took a sheet of paper from his pocket and began to read. On it was printed a list of boys' names. He hadn't yet chosen one for the child Anna was carrying, the baby he was certain would be a boy. He'd told Anna it would be a boy. He'd told his father. They had both said the same thing in reply: just pray that it's healthy and never mind what sex it is. Deep down, though, he prayed for a boy. He deserved a boy this time. Last time he had fathered a girl, and the memory still burned within him. With a boy, nothing could go wrong.

His eyes flicked over the list, reached the end and started again from the top. Dissatisfaction surged through him that no name had arrested his attention. God, there were enough from which to choose. He moved down the list of A's. Past Barry and Basil. Basil? What the hell kind of name was that for a kid? What kid wanted to be tagged with a moniker like Basil? He'd have every right to kill his parents for calling him that, and no judge in the country would convict him.

He moved further down the list. At Benjamin he stopped. Benjamin. Ben. Benny. Did he want a son called Benny? Maybe not Benny, although other kids—even grown-ups—would probably shorten Benjamin to Benny.

He'd call the kid Benjamin.

He'd show Anna that he cared about the contributions made to his life by other people.

Chapter Eight

Daniel was right, just as he had known he would be. The child carried by Anna was a boy, a chubby healthy son who would be named Benjamin after Fat Benny, whose gold watch Daniel still wore. There would be another Benny in the family. Not a Fat Benny Kirschbaum, but a Benny Kerr.

Memories of the Grand's successful tour slipped from Daniel's mind as he hurried around to inform everyone of the birth of his son. He was a father again! He'd waited so long—too long—and now it had happened. He busied himself making arrangements, happy to lose himself in an ecstasy he could share with everyone. He took Moishe out to a celebration dinner and told him he was the child's godfather. He made arrangements for the circumcision that would take place in the hospital. Work, his career, the problems he'd face because of *South Side Serenade* were all pushed aside. They could take a back seat for a while. Anna and his son came first.

Between visiting Anna in the hospital, Daniel supervised the decorators while they finished the nursery that awaited Benjamin—Little Benny as Daniel constantly thought of him. The nursery was on the second floor of the house, in the furthest corner where the sounds of voice and piano would never be able to penetrate. His son would be able to sleep undisturbed through the most rigorous practicing; even Daniel's most piercing top-C would never unsettle him there. Daniel had checked on that already, stationing a bemused painter in the nursery with the door shut while he sang part of "Di quella pira" at the top of his voice, aiming for sheer, shattering power instead of musical quality, blasting the two high notes in the aria. The painter had come down shaking his head, saying that Daniel's voice was barely audible. At other times, under other circumstances, Daniel would have felt insulted. This time he was happy.

On the eighth day, the hospital room was crowded. Daniel

watched in fond amusement as Isaac reveled in the role of grandfather. Clustered around the bed, watching, were Yetta, Moishe, Harry Feldman and people from Temple Isaiah in Paterson. Despite his father's urging to watch as the *mohel* performed the ritual operation, Daniel screwed his eyes tightly shut. He heard a short, sharp cry, followed immediately by a happy chuckling noise as Isaac dipped a finger in a glass of wine and brushed it lightly across the baby's lips.

When Daniel forced himself to open his eyes, it was as if nothing had happened. The baby was cooing contentedly; everyone standing around the small, linen-covered table where the *mohel* had operated, was smiling. Daniel felt ashamed that he had closed his eyes until he saw Moishe turn away, eyes blinking rapidly behind his glasses, face changing color. Some godfather you are, Daniel thought, forgetting about his own qualms; too queasy to even hold your own godson for his *bris*.

A nurse came to take away the baby and suddenly the room seemed to empty. Daniel arranged for his parents to be driven back to the Bronx, then he sat down on the edge of the bed, hardly noticing that Moishe still remained in the room, sitting quietly on a chair in the corner.

Anna reached out and took Daniel's hands, holding them gently between her own. "Is that how a Manrico or a Radames would behave?" she chided him smilingly. "Closing his eyes just because he was afraid to look?"

"I'm only Manrico on stage," he reminded her. "Watching a *bris*, I'm just like anyone else. Ready to chuck up."

"And your big brave friend over there's even worse." She nodded to the corner of the room where Moishe sat, his face still devoid of color. "He watches and almost passes out."

Daniel swung around to look, surprised to see that Moishe was still in the room. "You feel all right?" he asked.

"Someday someone's going to report every *mohel* to the cops for child abuse and molestation," Moishe murmured weakly. He continued to feel nauseated, although he was certain that any pain the child had felt could have been only momentary. "Anyway"—he brightened up considerably—"that kid's going to be proud that his old man's a big movie star."

Moishe's words, aimed at cheering himself, had the opposite

effect on Daniel. The excitement of the *bris* was over and Daniel's defenses were down. Mention of *South Side Serenade* darkened his joy, forced him to think of Duguid and the Grand, the threat to terminate his contract once shooting began. He had to go through with the movie; there was no way out of it for him. But was there a way out for Duguid? Daniel had never wondered that before. Had the general manager found an avenue of escape for the threat he had made? Had he found a way to save face? Or was he still as intent as ever about letting Daniel go?

"Moishe." Ann spoke quietly. The smile had left her face. "If you're feeling better, why don't you go on home?" She looked at Daniel sitting silently on the edge of the bed, knowing what had dampened his mood. She could not blame Moishe; he had only said something he thought was innocuous. He was not to know how deeply Daniel was worried by the prospect of making the movie.

"Another couple of minutes," Moishe said. "I'll be all right by then."

"Go now. The fresh air will do you good." Her voice was sharper. "Please. I want to be alone with Daniel."

Puzzled, Moishe looked at Daniel sitting on the bed. Daniel made no move, staring morosely at the blanket covering Anna. Moishe shrugged his shoulders, got up from the chair and patted Daniel on the shoulder. "Be in touch, Danny boy." He kissed Anna on the cheek and left the room.

"Will you stop worrying?" Anna pressed. "The worst hasn't happened yet and for all you know it might never."

"I know." He managed to raise a semblance of a smile. "I just feel kind of flat, that's all. One round's over—the baby, the *bris*, the tour, everything. Now I've got to lift myself for the next round."

"You will," she assured him. "Now, hadn't you better get home to see that the decorators have done all you wanted? I'm out of here in a couple of days, and I don't want to see paint brushes lying around the house. Unless you want Benjamin to be a housepainter."

"Got to be a damned sight easier than trying to make his living as a lyric tenor!" Daniel joked.

Anna felt better, happy to see that the mood had passed. She would feel happier still once the movie was out of the way and the dust had settled. Seeing Daniel kept on tenterhooks while he worried was worse than anything that could befall him once Duguid had made his decision.

The first day Anna was home, Daniel spent hours on end in the nursery, sitting by the sleeping child, watching intently. Every cough, every movement startled him; every time his son would change his breathing pattern, he was ready to rush out of the room and scream for Anna. He tried to convince himself that he was worrying needlessly. It couldn't possibly happen a second time. Anna didn't come from a Russian family. There was no chance. And still he maintained an anxious vigil on the child.

That evening the housekeeper peeped into the nursery and saw Daniel fast asleep in the armchair by the crib. Quietly she tiptoed downstairs to call Anna. For fully a minute Anna stood in the nursery doorway, watching. Then she prodded Daniel awake.

"Okay, buster. Your time's up. If we need a watchdog, we can hire a nurse."

"For what?' he asked groggily. "A nurse for what?"

"To keep an eye on the baby. Fathers play with their sons; they don't spend the entire time in the nursery watching over them." She led him outside, guiding him to their bedroom. "If you constantly worry about that child, you're going to make yourself ill," she told him sternly. "Benjamin is a perfectly healthy baby, so will you please stop standing guard over his crib like a vulcher on a death watch? You're making a nervous wreck out of me."

"Does it show?"

"Does it show?" She laughed at the question. "I've told you before that every thought you have stands out on your face like an illuminated sign. Stop it now."

"Okay." A gleam came into his eyes as he pulled her down onto the bed beside him. "I read somewhere that there's a great cure for being a nervous wreck."

"How would you know?" She snuggled close to him. "If it's

so good, why haven't you tried it on yourself?"

"Can't do it by yourself. You need a partner, and there's been no one available for the past few months."

"I'm glad to hear that. Anyway, I've been busy, or hadn't you noticed?"

Daniel grinned, the worry about his son eased. Anna had saved him again, dissipated his tensions and anxieties by understanding them. "I saw you'd put on a few pounds, but I figured that was because you'd stopped singing. The easy life was making you fat and lazy."

"The nerve of the man!" Anna exploded. "Just make sure I don't put on a few pounds again right now. Benjamin and you are the only kids I can handle at the moment."

The heat smashed into Daniel like a solid fiery wall as he walked the short distance from the airport terminal in Los Angeles to the waiting Cadillac limousine sent by Carmel Studios. Behind him trailed Moishe and a redcap carrying the suitcases of both men. When Daniel had asked Moishe in New York why he was coming with him, Moishe had replied that he was protecting his interests by ensuring that Daniel arrived on time at Carmel Studios; ten percent of Daniel's forty thousand dollar fee was more than enough of an incentive for Moishe to leave his law business for a few days and pay his own fare out West.

"Pomerantz has set up a press conference tomorrow morning," Moishe said as the Cadillac left the parking lot. "Wants to introduce you to everyone."

"If I'm awake." The flight in the TWA Constellation had taken twelve hours and Daniel felt numb, even worse than he had felt after the two transatlantic flights he'd taken. He wanted to sleep around the clock.

"You'll be awake," Moishe told him. "After the press conference, you can take the weekend to relax, then shooting starts on Monday."

Daniel nodded automatically, his mind half on what Moishe was saying—although he'd heard it a dozen times before—half on Anna whom he would not see for six weeks, until *South Side Serenade* was finished and in the can. Anna had driven him to the airport that morning to meet Moishe, and he had felt like crying as he watched her drive away, back to Teaneck and Little Benny. He could swear the kid was growing already. Three weeks old and as alert as a sentry, wide blue eyes that followed you everywhere you went. Was going to be a big kid as well. A real bruiser. Just as long as he didn't turn out to be another Benny in size as well as in name.

"Are you listening to a word I'm saying?" Moishe demanded. He jabbed Daniel in the side with his elbow.

"Sure," Daniel lied. "Every single word."

Convinced that Daniel had not heard a thing, Moishe started to repeat what he had said. Daniel cut him off. "Where are we staying, anyway?" he asked. He hadn't even thought about it. Moishe was supposed to have taken care of all those arrangements.

"The Chase. You've got a five-room suite there."

The trip began to look better to Daniel. A five-room suite in a luxury apartment hotel was more like it. Maybe there was something in this movie business after all; accommodations like that sure as hell beat where you stayed on the Grand's tours. "Generous of Carmel to foot the bill for a place like that."

"They're not," Moishe said, dispelling any misapprehensions. "You are. One thousand a month."

"Moishe, for Christ's sake!" Daniel yelled. The chauffeur glanced in the rearview mirror to learn the reason for the explosion from the back seat. "Whose idea was that? I don't have to live in a place like The Chase. If I'm paying, I can live in a small place."

"Hollywood rule number one," Moishe said evenly. "If you live small, you are small."

"Thanks. With my money, you're a bigshot!" Daniel stared out of the window as the Cadillac passed along a street of white Spanish-style ranches. He supposed Moishe was right and he had to make some kind of impression on these people; show them he was their equal and not some country bumpkin singer just up from the farm or wherever they thought opera singers came from. But one day his friend would surprise him by telling him beforehand of something he planned to do.

Surprise him? He'd kill him with the shock!

He began to think about Anna again. What was she doing now? On the East Coast, it would be ten in the evening. The baby would be asleep. Anna would be listening to the radio or reading; maybe she'd be playing the piano. Since she'd stopped singing at the Grand, she had taken more interest in the piano, using it to relax. Daniel grinned as he remembered the difficulty she'd encountered in getting close to the keyboard during the final months of her pregnancy. He'd told her to try growing her fingernails longer so she could reach the keys.

Once they arrived at the hotel, Daniel went straight up to the suite, leaving the baggage and checking-in formalities to Moishe while he ordered a call to New Jersey. Waiting for the operator to ring back, he looked around the suite, surprised when he found a mixed case of bourbon, scotch, gin and brandy in the small kitchen. "Where does this stuff come from?" he asked Moishe the moment his friend appeared.

"Don't worry about that. I ordered it ahead of time for when you entertain."

"You paid?" Amazement tinted Daniel's question.

"It goes on your tab."

"Get rid of it," Daniel said. He remembered the fiasco in London, the night porter who had raided the bar so he could get stinking drunk. He didn't want any repetitions; he didn't want to drink again as long as he lived.

"You have to entertain," Moishe protested. "Everyone does it."

"I'll do my entertaining by singing. Now, get it out of here and off my tab."

Moishe shrugged helplessly and looked for a bellboy to remove the case of liquor. The telephone rang and Daniel answered it.

"Everything all right?" he asked Anna.

"Why shouldn't it be?" Her voice was like music to his ears. In the madness he could already sense was Hollywood, the sound of Anna's voice was like a lifeline thrown to a shipwreck victim. "Or are you having premonitions now?" she asked.

"Of course not." He told her about the press conference set

for the following morning and promised to call her once it was over. "Love you," he whispered, waiting for her to respond before he broke the connection. Then he turned to Moishe. "What about some food? I'm starving."

"No sweat," Moishe answered grandly. "I'll get some sent up for us. What do you want?"

And Daniel saw more additions going onto his tab.

Daniel and Moishe were finishing a breakfast of lox and scrambled eggs the following morning when there was a double rap on the door of the suite. As if expecting a caller, Moishe leaped up to answer and came back with Joel Pomerantz. Daniel finished off the remaining forkful of food and got to his feet.

Pomerantz was wearing the grin that Daniel remembered from their first meeting in Katz's on Houston Street. "Glad to see you've arrived," the producer said, shaking hands too heartily for Daniel's liking. "Thought we were going to lose you for a while back there. Happy that Mr. Waterman finally got everything straightened out."

Daniel assumed that Pomerantz was referring to the threat that Carmel Studios would sue if he backed out of the deal.

"Hope you're fighting fit and raring to go," Pomerantz continued enthusiastically, "because this morning we're going to introduce Carmel Studios' newest star—Daniel Kerr—to the press. By the time our publicity people have finished with you, no one's going to be talking about Mario Lanza anymore. Your name will be on everyone's lips instead. What do you say to that?"

Daniel decided he had nothing to say to that. You don't carry on a jovial conversation with the guy who had threatened to sue you into the poorhouse, he decided; you just kept your distance and hoped that you could get through whatever ordeal he'd planned in as professional a manner as possible. Finally faced with the prospect of beginning his movie career, Daniel found himself wishing for the comparative sanity of the world of opera.

"See? He's speechless," Moishe said, covering quickly for Daniel who stood mutely in the center of the room. He could guess what was running through Daniel's mind. In all the years he had known him, Daniel had never been one to forgive easily; to forgive at all, for that matter. Moishe knew that the threatened lawsuit was still burning ulcers in Daniel's gut. He also knew that he would have to stick around longer than he had originally intended to make certain Daniel did not run out of the production.

"I'm not speechless," said Daniel eventually. "I just want to get on with this thing. In case anyone's forgotten, I've got a wife and tiny baby waiting for me back home. I'd like to get back to them as quickly as possible."

"You will, you will," Pomerantz assured him. "Six weeks and it'll be all over. If it runs longer, you get overtime. And think about this—by the time *South Side Serenade*'s been shown all over the civilized world and you've had a couple of big hits out of it, you'll have made more money than you could ever have hoped for by singing opera. You won't have to worry about sending your kid to college. You'll be able to *buy* him a goddamned college."

"Sure," Daniel said, unconvinced.

"Get your jacket on and let's get out of here," Pomerantz said. While Daniel put on a pale blue seersucker jacket, part of a complete wardrobe he'd bought for the trip west, Pomerantz crossed to the suite's entrance and rapped unobtrusively on the door before returning to the living room. Less than a minute later, a loud, prolonged knocking came from the door.

"Must be for you," Pomerantz said to Daniel.

Puzzled, Daniel straightened his jacket and went to answer the door. As he opened it, a woman's high-pitched voice screamed "Daaahling! Welcome to Hollywood!" A pair of arms were thrown around his neck and lips pressed against his own; a smothering perfume threatened to suffocate him. He was barely aware of the camera flashbulbs that popped off blindingly in his eyes as he fought to free himself.

When he managed to step back, he recognized Diane Orsini, platinum blonde hair falling down to her shoulders, dressed in skin-tight pink trousers and a blouse that pushed her capacious bosom almost up to her neck. Behind her stood three photographers and a group of men and women whom Daniel assumed were reporters. Moishe had warned him that there would be a press conference, but he hadn't said anything about Pomerantz arranging it to take place in the suite.

"Here he is, folks!" Pomerantz boomed. Daniel was surprised that the producer had such a strong voice when he wanted to use it. A pip-squeak like that should have a soprano, not tones that belonged to a Chaliapin, a giant. "Straight from the Grand Opera Company of New York City, Daniel Kerr!"

"What the hell is this?" Daniel whispered angrily to Moishe. "That picture comes out with that broad kissing me and Anna's going to fly straight through the roof!"

"Relax, will you?" Moishe said. "This is for publicity, something to get your face and name in the papers. Without it you're dead before you even start."

"You going to quit that longhair stuff if you click in *South Side Serenade?*" one man yelled. He pushed himself to the front of the crowd and repeated the question, his face only inches from Daniel's while he waited aggressively for the answer.

The reply came not from Daniel but from Pomerantz. "What are you talking about, if?" Pomerantz yelled back at the reporter. "Daniel Kerr's going to be the biggest name in musical pictures after *South Side Serenade.* And you can use that for collateral!" While he let the reporters digest his claim, he hissed at Daniel. "MGM's already shitting in their pants and we haven't even shot an inch of film yet."

"Why don't you let them quote you on that if you're so sure?" Daniel shot back.

"Hey, come on! We've all got to get a living out of this world. Be serious, will you?" Pomerantz turned back to the waiting reporters and photographers. "Why don't you get a couple more shots of Daniel and Di together, the most important pairing this town's ever going to see. Go on, Di," he urged the girl. "Get friendly."

Diane sidled closer to Daniel and draped an arm around his neck, brushing his face with her lips. "I never knew an opera singer before," she murmured huskily in his ear. "And I mean knew in the old-fashioned biblical way, you get what I mean?" The animosity she'd felt toward him in New York had gone. If what Pomerantz was claiming was true, this guy wasn't going to be Mario Lanza's understudy for long. He'd be a name to reckon with, a star in his own right. Besides, he wasn't that bad-looking. Tall. A bit tubby, but so were many of the men she'd been with. A bit of fat never hurt, just as long as there was enough muscle underneath to swing a hefty hammer.

"Blondes don't do nothing for me," Daniel hissed back, smiling all the time at the cameras that continued to record every detail. If Anna ever got to see any of these pictures, she'd laugh, he was certain of that. But his father would not. Nor would his mother; she'd be convinced he was having an affair with this celluloid sex symbol, always eager to think the worst about anything or anyone. Most of all, it was Robin Duguid's reaction about which he worried. If Duguid ever saw these pictures, it would be the final nail in Daniel's coffin.

"I'm not a natural blonde," Diane Orsini giggled. "But only my best friends know that." She stared at him inquisitively. "You want to be one of my best friends?"

"Sorry, I don't like sloppy seconds." He shrugged her off and gave his full attention to the reporters. So far only Pomerantz had answered all the questions. Maybe Daniel could salvage something for himself out of this three-ring circus of a press conference if he was given the opportunity to make the right replies.

"Mr. Kerr, what made you take a role like this?" a woman asked. "A lyric tenor of your stature taking a chance on a movie like this is unusual, to say the least."

Daniel felt like reaching out and kissing the woman. She knew what a lyric tenor was; most of these other creeps wouldn't be able to tell the difference between a soprano and a bass. Maybe he could score a few points here. "Because I firmly believe that beautiful music has a place on the screen as well as on the stage. Perhaps the words will be different, but the music will be the same."

"He's being modest!" Pomerantz called out and Daniel resisted the impulse to punch the producer in the mouth. "He's too shy to say that his voice is too good for opera. That it belongs on the screen where millions can appreciate it instead of a couple of thousand stuff-shirted creeps who probably need hearing aids."

"Shut up, you imbecile!" Daniel muttered with as much vehemence as he could muster. "You can't speak for me."

"Can't I?" Pomerantz replied threateningly. "You read your goddamned contract better. Carmel Studios can publicize you any way they see fit."

"Shy men are always queers," a woman's voice whispered from the other side of Daniel. "Maybe that's why you can sing so high . . . because you've got no balls."

Daniel swung around from Pomerantz to see Diane Orsini standing on the other side, finger resting against her lips as she gazed at him mischievously.

"Can get you fixed up with a nice fellow," she offered. "Anything to make your stay here more pleasant."

Daniel let a broad grin creep across his face. Making certain that no one else could see, he mouthed, "Screw you, baby." He was beginning to recognize Diane Orsini as a Claudia Rivera, but without even the faintest vestige of class or sophistication. Maybe Carmel Studios was not the Grand, his home turf, but he was damned certain he could take care of Diane Orsini.

"If I let you try it once, you'd never go back to men." She put her arms around him again and kissed him firmly on the lips. Although the gesture of affection was done for the photographers' benefit, Daniel could feel the tip of her tongue trying to force open his lips. He yielded. As her tongue snaked triumphantly between his teeth, he clamped down hard enough to pinch but not to draw blood. Diane jumped back, hand to her mouth in shock and pain, eyes blazing.

"You sonofabitch!" she cursed.

With ease, Daniel ducked the blow that whistled toward his face and laughed loudly as Diane's open hand cracked into the doorjamb. The woman's anguished scream filled the hall. While the photographers made the most of their unexpected good fortune, Moishe grabbed the opportunity to pull Daniel off to the side.

"Are you mad? That's your co-star, for God's sake!"

"Tough shit. Maybe Pomerantz'll fire me."

"With a million-dollar lawsuit he'll fire you." Moishe broke off as the producer came over to them, leaving the press to surround an indignant Diane Orsini, who was giving vent to her fury at Daniel.

"I'm warning you, Kerr." It was as if he had read Moishe's thoughts. "You screw up this movie with behavior like that and I'll sue you for everything you've got!"

Daniel drew himself up to his full height, dwarfing the producer. "My behavior is that of a professional. You'd just better keep a chain on that bitch."

Pomerantz swung around angrily to the reporters surrounding Diane Orsini. "Okay, folks," he shouted, pushing his way through. "Question time's over. We've got to get down to some work around here." He reached Diane and said something quietly to his blonde star. No one overheard the words, but they seemed to have the desired effect. Diane simmered down and allowed herself to be led away. Daniel turned around and returned to the suite. Behind him he could hear Moishe close the door, cutting out the din from the hallway.

"Jesus, Danny, what are you trying to pull? Do you want to get us sued for every penny? You can't get away with shit like that."

"What did I do?" Daniel wanted to know. "Tell me what I did that was so terrible? Tell me as a friend, an agent and a lawyer."

"You've got to bow to these people if you want to get on here. When you're a big name, you can get away with whatever you like, but right now you've got to knuckle down and do whatever Pomerantz says."

Daniel picked up the telephone to place a call to Anna. More than ever, he needed her sanity before he lost his own. As he waited for the switchboard to make the connection, Pomerantz entered the suite. He stood in front of Daniel, oblivious to the fact that he was on the phone.

"Shooting starts Monday morning at six sharp. A car will be coming to pick you up. Make damned sure you're ready." Then he stormed out of the suite to tend to his wounded star.

The first week's shooting was murder on Daniel. Because of the five o'clock call each morning in order to reach the lot by six, he could not shrug off the feeling of sluggishness. Lines were continually fluffed; simple scenes had to be shot over and over again.

Before coming west, Daniel had never realized how little he knew about acting. He'd never given it any thought. On stage, his singing alone carried him to success. The acting involved was basic with little room for delicacy. Fights and action scenes were carefully choreographed so as not to interfere with complicated musical cues. On camera, though, the style of acting he used at the Grand brought forth hysterical screams and a perpetual torrent of abuse from the director.

"Subtlety!" the man kept shrieking. "Be subtle, for Christ's sake! Do you know the meaning of the word? This is a movie, not a goddamned pantomime!" And Daniel continued to use the exaggerated style of acting he employed on stage.

Each mistake on Daniel's part gave Diane Orsini an opportunity to laugh maliciously at him. When they broke up for lunch on the fifth day, she passed by him and said, "Maybe they can find you a role as a homo next time out. You should be able to play that without any need for acting." Daniel simply glared at her, too tired to even think of fighting back.

Moishe kept him company in the studio commissary during the lunch break. Daniel pecked unhappily at his food, appetite dulled, while Moishe watched pensively. He'd got him this far and he'd be damned if he was going to let Daniel quit now. Moishe was booked on a flight back to New York that night as he could no longer afford to neglect his law business. It was now or never with Daniel as far as he was concerned. "Keep at it," he encouraged. "Once you get to the singing bits, you'll knock them all on their asses."

"If I ever get that far." The songs came right at the end when the studio would fill in all of the musical scenes in one long burst. In truth, it was only the thought of recording the songs that kept Daniel at all interested in *South Side Serenade*. It was the one point on which he agreed with Joel Pomerantz, that "Those Smiling Eyes" would leap straight into the hit parade. It had to; nothing could stop it. And more than anything else, Daniel wanted a hit record to add to his trophy list, the opportunity to show the entire country that he was just as good as Lanza.

A middle-aged man stopped by the table. Daniel recognized him as one of the extras. "Mr. Kerr, I'd like to say something to you."

"What is it?" Daniel wondered what other insults were about to be heaped on his head. Maybe he'd think twice about hauling off and slugging Diane Orsini or Pomerantz, but he would have no hesitation in sticking this little squirt on his back. Almost unconsciously he clenched his fists underneath the table, ready to lash out.

"We don't get paid too much, Mr. Kerr, so . . ."

"What?" Daniel asked, his fists relaxing. "What are you talking about?"

"Us extras. All these scenes we have to replay get us overtime. We want to thank you for lousing them up."

Suddenly Daniel began to laugh. He threw back his head, filling the entire commissary with the sound of his laughter. Heads turned in his direction, but all he could think of was the man standing in front of him. His wooden, heavy-handed acting was having an effect he had never even considered. No wonder everyone was getting so upset with him. He was costing the studio a fortune with each scene he screwed up.

"Knock it off," Moishe warned, embarrassed by the stares that were sent his way.

Daniel gained control of himself and looked at the man who continued to stand meekly by the table. "How about if I turned up late a few mornings as well? Would that help you?" he asked.

"Great, Mr. Kerr. Fantastic."

"You've got my word on it. You're going to get the biggest paycheck you've ever seen." Daniel burst out laughing again as the man walked away to join his friends at a nearby table; heads went down as he quietly imparted the good news.

"Pomerantz will kill you if you pull shit like that," Moishe muttered darkly.

"There's nothing in my contract about causing delays through ineptitude," Daniel retorted. "Or not turning up because I'm sick. I've read that damned contract so many times since the press conference that I can recite it off by heart. This whole goddamned bunch thinks I can't act. Well, they're right.

And it's going to cost them money to find out just how right they are."

As they walked back to the set after lunch, a uniformed guard approached Daniel. "Telegram for you, Mr. Kerr." He handed Daniel a Western Union envelope.

"Thanks." Still chuckling over the extra's request, Daniel slit open the envelope. He read the words quickly and his face turned white. When he looked at the message again, his mouth slowly formed the words as if he were unable to read without moving his lips.

"What is it?" Moishe asked.

"Here!" Daniel snapped savagely. "You read the goddamned thing. It's all your fucking fault anyway!" He threw the telegram at Moishe and strode off angrily toward the set.

Moishe picked up the piece of paper. His eyes first hit the signature block of Robin Duguid, then they took in the complete message area:

DANIEL KERR CARMEL STUDIOS HOLLYWOOD CALIFORNIA

WAS WILLING TO OVERLOOK YOUR FORAY INTO MOVIES IN HOPE YOU WOULD RETURN TO YOUR SENSES STOP NEWSPAPER PICTURES OF YOUR RELATIONSHIP WITH MISS DIANE ORSINI MAKE THAT IMPOSSIBLE STOP BECAUSE YOUR BEHAVIOR NOT IN BEST INTERESTS OF GRAND OPERA COMPANY WE ARE HEREBY TERMINATING YOUR CONTRACT STOP REGRET THIS EXTREME STEP BUT YOU LEAVE US NO ALTERNATIVE STOP GOOD LUCK IN THE MOVIES STOP ROBIN DUGUID.

Chapter Nine

The first telephone call Daniel made from his dressing room was to Anna. For once he did not pester her about the baby. Instead, he read out the contents of Duguid's cable. Anna waited until he had finished before informing him that an identical cable had been delivered to the house. Duguid was taking no chances on Daniel not knowing of his decision.

Next, Daniel called Duguid at the Grand. The general manager was icily polite.

"Mr. Duguid, it's Daniel Kerr."

"Good afternoon, Daniel. How are you?"

"I'm upset, how the hell do you think I am?" Daniel burst out. He closed his eyes and took a deep breath, willing himself to calm down; he could not afford to antagonize Duguid now. "I just received your cable."

"Where?"

"At Carmel Studios. It's a bit of a blow," Daniel added unnecessarily.

"Self-inflicted, I might point out," Duguid said. "As I mentioned in the cable, I was willing to live and let live as long as you maintained a certain discretion while you followed this path. Unfortunately, those newspaper pictures of you cavorting with that woman have forced my hand."

Daniel gripped the receiver harder as he forced himself to remain cool. "It was a set-up, Mr. Duguid, believe me. A stupid publicity stunt, that was all. She was waiting for me outside my suite with all the photographers. The studio arranged it. I never had a chance."

"I'm very sorry, Daniel, but there's little I can do about it now. You've chosen the path you wish to follow, and I hope you have success. Goodbye."

There was a soft click in Daniel's ear and the line went dead. Angry and frustrated, he called the Grand again. When he identified himself, Duguid's secretary said that the general manager had just been called away to an urgent meeting and would not be available for the remainder of the day. Perhaps Daniel would like to try again on Monday morning?

Daniel slammed down the receiver and stormed out of his dressing room. When he saw the other members of the cast happily talking away the remainder of the lunch break, he spun around and headed toward the parking lot. The Studebaker Carmel had loaned him for his stay in Hollywood—Moishe had demanded a Cadillac but had settled willingly for less—was parked close to the exit. Daniel revved the engine savagely. Wheels spinning, the Studebaker tore out of the parking lot, past the guard on the gate and headed toward Los Angeles. The bizarre thought that the extras would have a field day flashed across Daniel's mind. Good! He was glad that someone could make capital out of his misery.

He drove blindly, his mind only seeing the cable that Duguid had sent. He couldn't believe it. He'd kidded himself all along that it would never happen, that Duguid was only bluffing, that he'd find a way at the last moment to avoid the inevitable. The Grand couldn't do without him, he'd told himself repeatedly. Now Duguid had proved that they damned well could.

He saw a bar and slammed the Studebaker to a juddering halt. Inside the bar, he forgot about the way he'd told Moishe to get rid of the liquor. He needed a drink now more than ever. He called loudly for a bourbon. Almost before the bartender had set down the glass, Daniel had emptied it, calling impatiently for a refill. The bartender eyed him curiously before pouring another measure. Then he moved away to the other end of the bar, leaving Daniel alone.

Daniel drank the second bourbon more slowly, letting his mind wander over the ramifications of Duguid's act. Duguid was bent on proving that the opera house could exist without him, but could he exist without opera? It was the Grand that had made him. Without it, he would never have been approached for this part in *South Side Serenade*. Christ, why had he ever been fool enough to accept it? Everyone had warned him against doing it, but he'd gone blithely on, disregarding the advice of people who knew a damned sight more than he did. He looked bleakly into the glass as he remembered throwing the cable at Moishe and shouting that it was all his fault. He knew damned well it wasn't. He had nobody to blame but himself. His own ego had pushed him into it, and now he was out of work; or out of the work he loved more than anything else. He didn't want movies. He didn't want a hit record. He couldn't care less about proving he was better than Lanza. All he wanted was the chance to walk once more on the stage of the Grand and thrill people with his voice.

"Another one?" the bartender asked.

Daniel glanced at his glass, surprised to find it empty. "Sure. Keep them coming."

"Whatever you say, mac."

As the afternoon wore on, more people entered the bar. Daniel took no notice of them, too intent on pondering his own problems, a nightmare that had suddenly become reality. At one point he made up his mind to try calling Duguid again. The general manager would be home by now. Daniel knew the phone number of his apartment in Manhattan. Duguid would answer the phone himself; there would be no way of his avoiding speaking to Daniel. When he stood up to use the pay phone someone was already there. By the time the call was finished, Daniel's determination had waned.

"You all right, mac?" the bartender asked as he passed Daniel's seat.

"Course I'm all right." Daniel did not realize how distorted his words were. "Gimme another one."

"You sure you want another one? Or would you rather I called you a cab to take you home?"

"Gimme another drink!" Daniel declared fiercely. "I've got the money to pay!" He pulled a roll of bills out of his pocket and slammed it onto the bar; money fluttered onto the floor. "Fill me up till that runs out."

"Put your money away," the bartender said quietly. He bent down to pick up the bills that had fallen on his side of the bar. "I'll get you a cab."

"I don't want a goddamned cab!" Daniel yelled. Customers turned at the noise. "I want another drink!"

"Not here, pal. Not today."

Daniel's rage at himself found an easier target. He leaned across the bar and grabbed the man by the shoulder. "Gimme another drink, you stinking sonofabitch! Do you know who I am?"

The bartender turned around slowly, his gaze disdainful as he looked at Daniel's hand on his shoulder. "I don't give a shit who you are, mister. Get your hand off me and get your ass out of this bar before I call the cops."

"You can't talk to me like that! I'm Daniel Kerr!" The fury reached boiling point and spilled over. Daniel swung an ill-aimed punch at the bartender. The man stepped back and Daniel flopped across the bar, gasping for breath as his chest slammed into the fixture. The bartender raised his own hand to strike back before deciding it was unnecessary. He left Daniel straddled across the bar while he telephoned for the police.

A minute passed while Daniel lay across the bar. His chest hurt like hell; he was sure he'd busted a couple of ribs. Above the pain, though, he knew he had to get out of the bar. The cops were coming. That was all he needed. He pushed himself to his feet, standing unsteadily.

"Hold him!" the bartender yelled.

Daniel felt hands restraining him as other customers tried to keep him from leaving. Fear of staying and being arrested gave him strength. He lashed out with his hands and feet, hearing yells of pain and surprise. Suddenly there was a clear space between himself and the door. And freedom. He dove toward the door as the bartender vaulted over the bar, a sawed-off baseball bat in his hand. Daniel saw the club swing toward his head, ducked, and then slammed a short right at the bartender. This punch hit home. Coupled with the bartender's forward impetus, the blow was devastating. Daniel's fist smashed into the man's solar plexus. The club went flying through the air to shatter the bar's front window, spilling glass over the sidewalk. Daniel's shoes crunched broken glass as he ran from the bar, swung open the Studebaker's door and started the engine. Figures erupted from the bar. He heard the sound of sirens and floored the gas pedal.

The Studebaker screeched away from the curb. Ahead Daniel saw a black and white patrol car tearing toward him. He swung the car in a wide, fast u-turn, without realizing that he'd just made the chase easier for the policemen. Horns blasted as traffic in both directions took evasive action. Daniel held his hand down on the horn to clear a path. He had to get back to the lot, had to get back to the movie. They'd protect him there. He was a star. Without him the movie couldn't continue.

There was another patrol car coming from the opposite direction. Its siren drowned out the sound of the Studebaker's horn. Too late Daniel recognized the police driver's intention as the approaching patrol car cut across traffic and positioned itself in Daniel's path. Daniel went rigid in the seat, foot jammed down on the brake. At the last moment, he yanked the steering wheel sideways and cannoned broadside into the police car.

"We were worried sick about you!"

Moishe's voice battered through the waves of pain and dizziness that surged unmercifully through Daniel's head. "What the hell happened to you? You're lucky you weren't killed, you damned lunatic, driving like that!"

Daniel looked around the white-painted walls of the police station. Uniformed figures moved around as if unaware of his presence. He looked at Moishe and Pomerantz standing in front of him. Moishe seemed anxious, Pomerantz furious. "How did I get here?" Daniel mumbled. He felt terrible. He didn't even know what time it was or how long had passed since he'd been in the crash.

"The cops called us," Pomerantz answered sharply. "And they called the papers at the same time. I've got a good mind to throw you out and sue you for what you've cost us in shooting time and bad publicity. You're going to be in all the papers tomorrow. Carmel star in drunken brawl, car chase, smash-up. You name it, you did it. Very nice!"

"I did all that?" For the life of him Daniel could not remember exactly what had happened. All he could recall was the moment of impact, when he'd slammed sideways into the police cruiser. "Was anyone hurt?" He was amazed to find himself in one piece.

"No, and you're goddamned lucky," Pomerantz answered. "Because you didn't kill anyone, I'll be able to square it away. But you're paying for the damage you caused, make no mistake about that."

Damage? Daniel shuddered as he thought about it. The Studebaker, the cop car; and whatever he'd done during the fight he was supposed to have had. A picture of a window shattering as a club went through it filtered into his memory and he shuddered again. "What time is it?" he finally asked.

"Just after six," Moishe muttered. "I've missed my flight as well, thanks to you. Now I've got to wait till tomorrow. Asshole!"

Daniel got to his feet. "Can we go?" he asked. "Or do the police still want me?"

"We can go. Right back to your suite where you can sleep it off until tomorrow morning. And if you're not on the set by six A.M. tomorrow, you're going to be sued for every penny you ever make. And this time I mean it! Understand?"

Daniel looked at Moishe, who nodded grimly. Pomerantz watched while Moishe held Daniel's arm, guiding him outside. Then he followed, shaking his head.

Daniel telephoned Anna from his suite early the following morning before he left for the lot. News of the drunken fight and police chase had made the late editions of the New York papers. In one, there was even a quote from Robin Duguid saying he was sad to witness a singer of such undisputed brilliance following such a path, but as Daniel was no longer with the Grand, there was nothing he could do about it.

"What about my father?" Daniel asked. "Have you spoken to him?"

"He called a little while back," Anna replied. "He was very upset. He says you should never have gone to Hollywood in the first place."

"Great," Daniel muttered. With the exception of Anna, he didn't have a single supporter left in the entire world. And she probably, rightfully, thought him a fool anyway. He supposed he could always try for the Met when he returned to New York. No; it wouldn't work. No doubt there was a loyalty between the two houses, and Bing would look the same way upon his antics as Duguid did.

He'd have to make his peace with Duguid. But how, for Christ's sake? How?

Maybe he'd make a million from *South Side Serenade* and be able to retire, be able to tell them all to go to hell in a handcart. Some hopes, he reflected bitterly. If he managed to get off the Carmel lot without owing money, he'd be more than satisfied.

Chapter Ten

When he returned to New Jersey after completion of *South Side Serenade*, Daniel could not believe how much Little Benny had grown. He was certain he was not looking at the same child he had left just seven weeks earlier, and he was annoyed with himself that he could have allowed so long a period of his son's life to pass without being there to share it. Thick brown hair covered the baby's head, and his cheeks were so chubby that even the most confirmed baby-hater would find it hard to resist pinching them. Daniel picked up the child and lifted him high into the air, laughing as Benjamin spread his arms like a bird in flight.

"Put him down," Anna said. "You're scaring the living daylights out of the poor kid. That's why he's waving his arms around like that."

"Of course it's not. He's enjoying it."

"Like hell he is," Anna contradicted. Gently but firmly she took the baby from Daniel's hands and set him back in the crib. Then she went downstairs, leaving Daniel alone in the nursery with his son.

Daniel pulled a chair up to the crib and sat staring in fascination. Occasionally he would tickle Benjamin's hand, amazed at the strength contained in the minute fingers as they clutched at his own and refused to let go. How could he have let himself stay away for seven weeks? Forty-nine days, each second of them absolutely irreplaceable. Even the photographs Anna had taken at every opportunity and the stories with which she had regaled him during their twice-daily telephone conversations could never even remotely compensate him for his absence. But now he was back and nothing would ever drag him away again. Not that Joel Pomerantz of Carmel Studios would ever want him back. No matter how much money *South Side Serenade* made—if it made anything at all—Pomerantz would never call him again. In addition to the three thousand dollars he had paid for damages to the two cars and the bar, Daniel had cost the studio a small fortune in overtime. He had made no friends there, unless he counted the extras who had reaped a golden harvest in salary because of his clumsiness.

Benjamin fell asleep and Daniel tiptoed out of the nursery. When he went downstairs, Anna asked about his plans. The Grand was already rehearsing for the next season, and Duguid had been quoted liberally in the press about his efforts to replace Daniel in the productions for which he had contracted. In some instances, European tenors were being brought in for single appearances; otherwise, young, upcoming singers would substitute. The cost of the changes was astronomical, Duguid had said, but expense was of secondary importance where such a matter of principle was involved. He had the unequivocal support of his board of management and major patrons. The Grand Opera Company of New York would continue without the services of Daniel Kerr.

"I've got to see Duguid, I suppose," Daniel told Anna. "Maybe a face-to-face confrontation will do the trick."

"Call him soon and set up an appointment," Anna suggested. "He probably knows you're back from California, and he'll be waiting to hear from you. The longer you leave it, the tougher it's going to be to patch it up."

Although Anna continued to offer her wholehearted support to Daniel, she was far from confident that he would have any success with Duguid. Intentionally or otherwise, Daniel had made the general manager look small. Duguid had retaliated by proving beyond any doubt that he was the master of the company and nothing or no one would be allowed to dispute his authority. He had stuck to his threat of firing Daniel. Now that he had gone so far as to publicize how he planned to replace Daniel, Anna could not see any real hope of him changing his mind. He was determined to teach Daniel a lesson and to let others benefit from the example—even if it meant hurting both himself and the company.

Early the following morning, Daniel dialed the Grand. Duguid's secretary placed him on hold for several minutes, then she said yes, the general manager would be able to see him that afternoon. Her tone was frosty and distant, and Daniel held out no great optimism for the meeting.

At three o'clock that afternoon he entered the opera house, forcing himself to walk quickly and confidently up to the offices, determined to show everyone that he had not come to beg. He noticed the difference immediately. Office staff who had always fussed over him now looked in another direction, embarrassed by his presence. When he tried to strike up a conversation as he waited for Duguid to see him, his attempts met with no success. It was as if he were suffering from leprosy; no one wanted to take a chance on catching it.

"Mr. Duguid will see you now."

Daniel entered the familiar office. Duguid was sitting behind his desk, head bent low as he scribbled in pencil on a sheet of lined yellow paper. He made Daniel wait for almost half a minute before he finished writing and looked up. "How's Anna and the baby?" he asked conversationally.

"They're fine, thank you," Daniel answered automatically. He had expected that to be the opening question. Duguid was a gentleman to the last.

"You look well, too," Duguid said evenly, referring to the deep, even suntan Daniel had achieved. "The West Coast must agree with you."

"Not really, Mr. Duguid." It was time to get down to the reason for the meeting. "I've learned that I'm much happier on the East Coast."

"I see." Duguid looked down at the piece of yellow paper on the desk. "What do you plan to do now? Have you decided yet?"

"I was hoping we could talk about that today."

"Oh?" Duguid looked up again, his face devoid of expression, giving Daniel no clue to his feelings. "I'm afraid that the Grand no longer has a place for you, Daniel. However, I'd be more than happy to furnish references if you decide to work somewhere else. With your talent, though, I would imagine that any references I could offer would be merely redundant."

Daniel clenched and unclenched his fists while he willed himself to remain calm, to maintain the confident manner he had promised himself he would show. Duguid was goading him.

He was in a position of power and he was rubbing Daniel's face in it. "Mr. Duguid, I do not wish to work with another company. My entire professional life centers around the Grand."

Duguid sighed sadly. "Daniel, I thought I had made the company's position perfectly clear in both the telegram I sent to you and during the phone conversation that followed. Your antics in Hollywood—whether they were of your own making or a publicity stunt over which you had no control—forced my hand irrevocably. And there was that unfortunate business with the police. The Grand does not have a position for an artist, no matter how good, who puts his personal aggrandizement above the overall welfare of the company. I'm tremendously sad that it has come to this pass, but we have no other option open to us."

Daniel could feel the tears starting to burn behind his eyes. Not tears of pain and sorrow. Or regret because he had done wrong. They were tears of rage and frustration. Duguid was cutting his throat for him and there wasn't a single thing he could do but sit and watch it happen.

"Try putting yourself in my position, Daniel." Duguid dug through a drawer and pulled out a large brown envelope from which he shook a batch of newspaper clippings. "If you were general manager of a prestigious opera house, would you continue to employ a singer who behaved as you did?" He pushed the clippings across the desk to Daniel.

This was the first time Daniel had seen the stories in the New York newspapers. Anna had made certain there were none about the house when he returned from Hollywood. He picked them up, curiosity overcoming anger. There were several pictures of Diane Orsini throwing her arms around him, and there were garish, exaggerated stories of the fight in the bar and the ensuing collision with the police car, turned into a hundred-mile-an-hour drunken chase. Numbly he read each story, looked at each picture before letting them slip from his fingers.

Duguid watched him carefully. "Daniel, even if I wanted to take you back I couldn't. My hands are tied. The Grand's board of management has professed disgust with your behavior. On top of that, the productions for the coming season are all settled. Every role is filled. There's nothing I could offer you at this late stage."

Daniel picked his head up and gazed stonily across the desk at Duguid. "I guess I wasted my time in coming to see you."

Duguid pursed his lips in thought. "Perhaps. And perhaps not. At least you've realized where your priorities should have been."

"But that doesn't buy the groceries, does it?" Daniel said.

"I'm afraid not. Are you in financial difficulties?"

"Money's no problem, Mr. Duguid."

"Good. What will you do now?"

Go home and cry, Daniel thought. But he'd be damned if he'd let Duguid know he felt that way. He had entered the building with his head held high, and he was going to leave it the same way. His grief was private. "I don't think I'll have any trouble in finding other engagements, Mr. Duguid. My agent's already got a number of offers. Concerts. Clubs. I can sing anything. Anywhere."

"I'm delighted to hear that." Duguid sounded as if he were genuinely pleased. "No doubt we'll be running across each other again in the future. Good luck." He held out his hand. Daniel looked at it for a long moment, debating whether to accept it. Finally he did.

"I enjoyed the season I spent with you, Mr. Duguid. I think it was my best season. Good day." He turned around and walked quickly from the office. Duguid watched the door swing slowly closed before he returned his attention to the piece of lined yellow paper on top of his desk. He read it through several times, the letter he was thinking of sending to Daniel. It was not a letter of forgiveness; it was a letter setting out the terms under which forgiveness could be made and Daniel reinstated with the company.

Like Daniel, Duguid had refused to let his true feelings show during the meeting. The pronouncements he had made to the press had been for public consumption only. He wanted Daniel back as badly as Daniel wanted to be back. There were no upcoming singers even near Daniel's class, and the European tenors Duguid had booked at short notice were of limited ability. Daniel had a place in the hearts of the Grand's followers. He was local talent, a direct link to the New York audiences.

Uncertain how to deal with the problem, Duguid had spoken with Hammersley in England. Flattered at having been brought into the dispute, Hammersley had recalled the uproar in Wheeler's following the production of *Tosca*. He had suggested to Duguid that a public apology might be in order again. Duguid had accepted the advice, but he had decided to hold off setting out the terms for forgiveness until he could gauge Daniel's attitude. What he had just witnessed during the meeting made him decide not to send the letter. Apart from what could be construed as a token attempt at regret—saying that his professional life centered around the Grand—Daniel had not seemed in the least contrite. If anything, he had been cocky. Overconfident that he would be taken back.

Duguid rolled up the piece of yellow paper and tossed it into the trashcan. He had made up his mind that Daniel could stew in his own juices for a while. It might do his oversized ego a world of good.

Daniel waited until he reached the comparative privacy of his car, then he hammered futilely at the steering wheel with his fists. All that crap about his agent getting him work, concerts, club dates. Duguid had seen right through it. He must be sitting up there laughing now over Daniel's obvious lies.

He didn't want concerts or club dates. He didn't want any other kind of work. All he wanted was the chance to go back on stage in the roles he loved best, and Duguid was not going to offer him that chance. He banged on the steering wheel again while he wondered what an opera singer did when there was no opera company that wanted him.

When his temper had subsided, he started the car's engine, shifted into gear and headed north. Who said that no other company wanted him? What the hell! He'd try the Met! He'd walk in there and take them by storm. He'd make Duguid squirm by throwing in his lot with the opposition.

Parking the car on West Thirty-ninth Street, he recalled

that other time of desperation when he had stopped by the yellow brick building to look at the *Il Trovatore* sets and the man in the frayed suit had denied him entrance to the opera house. This time he was going in by the front door and no one would stop him until he'd got right through to see Rudolf Bing. And he'd walk out of there with the promise of a contract. See what Duguid and his goddamned board of management did about that!

Reaching the offices, he stated that he wanted to see Rudolf Bing. Asked the reason by a surprised middle-aged woman, Daniel could think of nothing to say other than he wanted a job, to which the woman replied that the Met did not give "auditions just like that." When Daniel finally identified himself, the woman said that Mr. Bing was away for a week; perhaps Daniel would like to make an appointment for when the general manager returned. Daniel mustered enough courtesy to thank her and left the building.

Back in the car, he wondered what to do next. Go home? And tell Anna what had happened? That he was out of work? He decided instead to drive up to the Bronx and visit his parents. He had not seen them since he had returned from California; now seemed as good a time as any to let his father in on the grim news as well.

It was a mistake. Whereas Anna had made certain that no trace of the newspaper stories remained in the house, Yetta Kirschbaum had clung onto them as if they were made of solid gold. "A nice time you had in Hollywood," she greeted Daniel when she opened the front door. "I'm glad you changed your name to Kerr and didn't leave it as Kirschbaum." She carried on talking without giving Daniel the chance to say anything. "How am I supposed to feel when I see pictures like this? Read stories like this?" She led him into the living room, where the same newspaper clippings Duguid had showed him were proudly displayed on a table, alongside family wedding pictures.

Daniel ignored the display. "Where's Pa?" he asked.

Yetta paused only long enough to tell Daniel that Isaac had gone out for a walk. Then she started all over again. "You're lucky you have a girl like Anna. Me? I would have left home when I heard about the things you were doing."

"I wasn't doing anything. What time will Pa be back?"

"How should I know? Sometimes he meets his friends in the park. A nice day like this he plays some cards. Why did you have to get involved with this woman?" She pointed at a picture of Diane Orsini. "All my friends who know you're my son think you're messing around with a *shiksa*, and you're in trouble with the police because you're a *shikker*."

Before Yetta's horrified gaze, Daniel picked up the pile of clippings and tore them into shreds, dumping them into the trash bag in the kitchen. "Why did you do that?" Yetta yelled after him.

"I thought you were ashamed of them!" he shouted back even more loudly. "Don't keep anything you're ashamed of!" He slammed the front door and walked toward the park.

When he found his father, Isaac was playing chess with another elderly man, sitting under the shade of a maple tree so intent on the game that he did not even notice Daniel standing behind him. Daniel watched his father make a move, then he clucked his tongue in disapproval. "Two question marks for that one."

Isaac's eyes lit up when he recognized the voice. He turned around on the seat, looked at Daniel for an instant and then stood up to clasp him around the shoulders and kiss him on the cheek.

"When did you get back?"

"Yesterday."

"Your movie's all finished?"

Daniel nodded. "Thank God."

Isaac introduced him to the other man playing chess, then excused both himself and Daniel. "I give you the game!" he called in farewell. "What's the news with the opera company and your Mr. Duguid?" he asked anxiously as he walked with Daniel from the park, back toward the house.

Daniel debated whether or not to lie. Anna had told him how upset Isaac had been about Duguid's statement to the press. It might be a kindness to hide the truth from his father. Later he could pretend to come down with some illness that would keep him from singing and then his father might never know. Wild fantasies prevailed in his mind as he sought to disguise the truth from Isaac.

"Well?" Isaac pressed. "Have you been to see your Mr. Duguid? Did you make it up with him?"

"No, Pa. I saw him but I didn't make it up. I'm not with the Grand anymore."

Isaac fell silent and walked with his head bowed. As much as he rued his folly for himself, Daniel regretted it twice as badly for his father. What did the old man have now? One son was a thousand miles away. And the son who had remained close—who had brought him pride and joy through singing—had deeply disappointed him. Isaac had nothing.

"So what do you plan to do?" Isaac asked. "Are you and Anna all right for money?"

"Of course we're all right for money." Why did everyone have to keep asking if he was solvent? Just because he'd lost the job didn't mean he was broke. And if he'd said he desperately needed money, what would Isaac have done? Sold the house that Daniel had bought for him and moved back to an apartment?

"But you've got to do something with your life," Isaac said. "You can't just sit back and be idle. What will you do?"

"I wish I knew, Pa. I thought about trying the Met but that wouldn't work. I even went in there before, but the general manager, Mr. Bing, was unavailable."

"Try again," Isaac suggested.

Daniel shook his head. "After the way I've fallen out with Duguid, the Met wouldn't touch me. Guess I'll have to go back to being a full-time cantor again." He said the last sentence lightly, trying to coax a smile onto his father's troubled face.

"You know something, Daniel?" They reached the edge of the park and looked up and down the road before crossing. "Ever since you got involved in this opera business, I've had a dream."

"What about?"

"It was *La Juive* that killed Caruso. The strain of performing it. It's a very difficult role. I always wanted more than anything else to see you in the role of Eleazar, because I know in my heart that you would have done it better than Caruso. I've pictured it a million different times. And maybe, when the baby's bigger, Anna as Rachel." He reached out and grasped Daniel's hand. "Looks like it was just an old man's foolish dream, eh?"

Daniel felt a lump grow in his throat. He gulped a couple of times, forced it back so he could speak. "The only reason you have dreams is so you can sit back and watch them come true," he finally replied. "Stick around so you can see this one come true as well." Empty words to speak, he realized. Easy promises to make. Daniel knew it, and he was certain Isaac knew it, too.

"Then you'd better start doing something about it soon, Daniel," his father said. He led the way into the house, holding open the door for his son. "Were you serious about what you said before, going back to being a *chazan?*"

"Who knows? I've got to do something." He spotted his mother in the kitchen. The garbage can was on the sink counter and Yetta was sorting through the torn-up scraps of paper, trying to piece them together.

"Will you look at her, Pa?" Daniel said. "I tore up all that newspaper junk about Hollywood, and she's busy trying to stick it all back together again."

"Sure I am!" Yetta shot back, surprised at the sound of Daniel's voice because she had not heard the front door open. "I want you to remember all those terrible things that happened to you there."

"Yetta, Daniel doesn't need anything to remind him," Isaac said quietly. "He's paying enough for it."

"How's he paying?" Yetta wanted to know. "I'm the one who's paying. People look at me with pity in their eyes because they know I'm Daniel Kerr's mother. Better I should have died giving him birth than have to suffer this."

Very deliberately Daniel turned away from his mother and patted Isaac gently on the shoulder. "I'm going home. If I stick around here I'll say something we'll all be sorry for. I don't need it; neither do you."

Understanding, Isaac followed him to the front door. "Don't forget what I told you about *La Juive,* Daniel. I don't have that much longer for you to sort yourself out. I don't care whether you sing it with the Grand, with the Met or with some tiny company that doesn't even pay you. But please God, I get to hear you sing it just once."

Daniel bent low and kissed his father. "You will. Don't worry about it."

While he drove back to Teaneck, Daniel tried to place his thoughts into some semblance of order. Top priority was finding something to do until he could get back into opera. Sure, there would be overseas offers, recording contracts should he want them. And *South Side Serenade* would be out the beginning of the year. But none of those could fill the loss left by Duguid's decision.

He needed something to fill his time completely.

As usual, he would be conducting the High Holy Day services at Temple Isaiah in Paterson. That was something to anticipate, but it would only last for a few days. Even if he did decide to return to being a full-time cantor—and he knew there would be no shortage of offers—the work would not have the same appeal, the same fulfillment that he gained from singing at the Grand.

Then he realized there was one occupation that would pass the time as sweetly as singing. He would be a full-time father to Little Benny. He would spend more time with his son than any father ever spent with any kid before.

Chapter Eleven

The Grand Opera Company opened the following season with Giacomo Puccini's *Turandot*, the first production attempted by Robin Duguid that was totally free of any influence from Roger Hammersley's tenure as general manager.

When the production had been planned originally, the tenor lead role of Calaf had been given to Daniel. It was a natural role for him, giving full rein to his strong, vibrant voice. At the time he had been offered Calaf, he had admitted that he was overjoyed; it was a role he wanted to sing above most others. But on opening night, instead of commanding the audience's attention from the center of the stage, he was merely a member of that audience, sitting in the orchestra stalls with Anna, who continually pressed his hand in sympathy with his biting disappointment.

While he listened, he tried to pick holes in the performance of the tenor who had been given his part. He knew it was his frustration and self-directed anger that prodded him to seek flaws in the substitute singer. Some of the mistakes he was convinced he spotted were nonexistent. Only by continually telling himself that the tenor was not as good as himself, however, was Daniel able to sit through the first two acts. In the third act, when Calaf began to sing "Nessun Dorma," Daniel could take no more. He stood up and apologized his way along the row until he reached the aisle. Then he walked quickly out of the auditorium and stood in the lobby until the performance was over and the crowd began to spill out. Stares of recognition were cast in his direction; greetings hailed his presence. He ignored them all while he waited for Anna, vaguely annoyed that she had not followed his example by walking out in the middle of the act.

"You should feel ashamed of yourself," she laced into him when she joined him in the lobby. She kept her voice low so that no one would be able to overhear, but her anger was evident. "If you didn't want to listen, you should have damned well stayed at home!"

"I couldn't take it anymore," Daniel protested. "That should have been me up there. I'd have done a better job." She was right; he shouldn't have come, he reflected. He'd have done himself a favor by staying home and looking after Little Benny. He certainly would have gained more pleasure out of it. Attending the opening night had been Anna's idea. It was the best place to meet Robin Duguid, she'd said. To catch the general manager off guard. To get even the faintest hint that soon Daniel would be forgiven for his sins and welcomed back into the fold. If the opening night performance was a good one, Duguid would be in an expansive mood. Then would be the best time to face him.

"Do you want me to cancel our reservation in Wheeler's?" Anna asked.

"No." If he had managed to sit through almost the entire opera, he could find the strength to eat in Wheeler's. The best chance he had of arranging an accidental meeting with Duguid was in the restaurant. Taking Anna's hand, he led her into Wheeler's. The maître d' greeted them effusively and showed them to their table by the window overlooking West Thirty-fourth Steet; he treated them like valuable customers rather than former artists with the Grand.

Daniel sat down heavily in the chair that was held out for him and gazed through the window onto the street. Cars were being driven up to the Grand's entrance to pick up passengers. Tonight those people in the cars would be talking about another tenor, Daniel thought. And later on, when the maître d' brought around the reviews contained in the early editions of tomorrow's papers, he'd be dropping them off on someone else's table, making some other singer feel that his own personal oyster had just been popped open to reveal the biggest, brightest pearl in history. Daniel envied that man for his youth and enthusiasm. And he pitied him for his innocence, his inability to recognize the pitfalls that might beckon to him in the future.

Daniel turned from the window as the ovation he had once

received rang out for the tenor who had substituted for him. Trying to demonstrate how magnanimous he was, he joined in. The simple action of applauding another singer brought an approving glance from Anna. She stretched a hand across the table and gripped his wrist lightly. "They'll soon be doing it for you again," she whispered confidently. Her eyes sparkled with the reflection of the restaurant's ornate chandeliers, and for a moment Daniel allowed himself to believe her words; it was easier that way.

"Keep telling me," he said. "Say it often enough and maybe it'll come true." He returned to staring out the window, using the pane of glass as a mirror to see who else entered the restaurant. When he recognized Robin Duguid among a group of people, he did not turn around. The last thing he wanted was for Duguid to think he was waylaying him.

The general manager looked around Wheeler's, nodded politely to several diners, then spotted Anna and Daniel. Excusing himself from his own party, he made his way quickly over to the table for two by the window.

"I'm delighted you could make the opening night," he said. "What did you think of it?"

Daniel was uncertain how Duguid meant the question. Before he could decide to be charitable and tell Duguid it was one of the finest productions of *Turandot* he'd ever heard—even if he had walked out in the middle of the final act—Anna answered.

"Very enjoyable, Mr. Duguid. You've every reason to feel proud. It was the most enjoyable opening night I can recall. Probably because I was watching it in comfort and not working," she added brightly, which drew an approving chuckle from the general manager.

"Thank you. How's the baby?"

"Growing at an alarming rate," Anna replied. "We'll soon be bringing him along for an audition. He's got a pair of lungs you wouldn't believe, holds a note for an hour or more."

Duguid smiled. "Perhaps we'll be able to find him a slot as Cio-Cio-San's son in *Butterfly*." He looked around for an empty chair. While his back was turned, Anna gestured at Daniel, urging him to become involved in the conversation. If he was serious about working his way back into Duguid's plans for the Grand, sullen silence was not the way to go about it.

"I was meaning to telephone you during the week," Duguid said, pulling a chair up to the table and sitting down. Daniel's heart quickened until he realized the general manager was addressing his words solely to Anna. "With the baby getting bigger, you must be thinking about resuming your career by now. Obviously I'd prefer that you resume it with the Grand."

"Daniel and I have been discussing it," Anna answered, determined to drag her still-silent husband into the conversation. How did he hope to show his repentance to Duguid if he didn't open his mouth? "Definitely for next season."

"I'm glad to hear that." There was no mistaking the genuine sentiment in Duguid's voice. "Just tell me when you're ready and I'll start arranging for your return." He switched his attention to Daniel. "How about your movie? That's coming out soon, isn't it?"

Daniel blinked in surprise at the question, amazed that Duguid would even mention *South Side Serenade*. "Six weeks," he murmured. "There's a simultaneous opening in New York and Los Angeles."

"Which one will you be attending?"

"New York. I've had more than my fill of Los Angeles."

Duguid nodded as if he understood Daniel's meaning. "And the songs?" he queried gently.

"The sound track's due out about a month later. After they see how the movie goes."

"I must admit I'm quite looking forward to hearing the music. Should be really exceptional." He nodded again, and Daniel did not know whether he was being sarcastic or just complimentary. In the end, he decided that Duguid was simply being his gentlemanly self. "You'll have to excuse me now, but I have some people waiting." He stood up and replaced the chair at the table from which he had taken it. "Don't forget, Anna. The moment you decide you're ready to come back, let me know. Nice to see you as well, Daniel. Enjoy your meal."

Daniel seethed while he watched Duguid walk away. The guy hadn't given him any kind of opening to use; not even the slimmest hint that he wanted Daniel back at the Grand with Anna.

"Why not send him a couple of tickets for the opening?" Anna suggested. "He might appreciate the thought."

Daniel continued to gaze after Duguid, willing the general manager to turn around and recognize the beseeching expression in his eyes. Duguid did not. He rejoined his party and sat down, involved in their company. "Yeah, he'd appreciate the thought all right," he eventually muttered. "He'd think I was stringing him along, poking fun at him. He's no more interested in the movie or the sound track than I am in doing missionary work in Africa."

"Then I'll send them to him."

Daniel allowed a long weary sigh to escape. "You do whatever you like." He looked around for the waiter. What he wanted more than anything was a drink, a real drink that would make the throbbing in his stomach go away. Anna would never allow him to have one, though; he'd have to make do with a bottle of wine instead.

Anna sent two tickets to Robin Duguid which he gracefully declined, stating prior commitments as his reason for refusal. If Anna was disappointed by the rejection, Daniel was not. He had expected no different response. Duguid would not be caught within five miles of the opening of *South Side Serenade*, a musical that featured a man who had been one of his leading tenors. Perhaps he'd sneak in when the movie was on general release, at a small theater where no one would recognize him; but he would never dare go where the spotlight was certain to fall on him.

South Side Serenade never went on general release.

A preview for critics scheduled a week before the movie's double opening had been panned mercilessly, including one review that claimed it was the biggest mistake Carmel Studios had ever made. Daniel was particularly chagrined when Carmel subsequently slashed the promotional budget that had been allocated to the movie.

When Daniel went to the New York opening—accompanied by Anna, his parents, who had put off their annual Florida trip until February to attend the opening, and Moishe—he fidgeted uneasily in the seat for the entire two hours of the performance. His voice sounded fine and there was a sustained round of applause after "Those Smiling Eyes" to the tune of "M'appari," but he could sense the first-night audience moving just as restlessly as he was. Even from his own subjective viewpoint, wanting to believe it was good, the movie was a disaster, nothing short of an amateurish parody of the type of film that had pushed Mario Lanza to instant fame. Daniel closed his eyes in relief as the credits came up at the end. He could almost hear the MGM top brass laughing themselves sick at Carmel Studios' puny challenge. The same top brass who had been intimidated to the point of panic, as Pomerantz had said.

The applause that greeted the end of the film was nothing more than polite. Daniel remained rooted in the seat, too embarrassed to stand up and take any credit. He wondered what Diane Orsini was doing over in Los Angeles. She'd stand up, that was for certain. She'd jump to her feet and wave around that oversized bosom, convinced that she'd just seen herself in the finest movie ever made. Regretfully Daniel conceded that every warning given to him had been well-founded. He had no place in this business.

"Sorry, Danny boy," Moishe whispered as they left the cinema in an ominously silent group.

Daniel clapped him sympathetically on the shoulder. "No fault of yours. Just bad judgment on my part."

"But that one song sounded great," Moishe carried on. "Even if the movie's shit, that number'll make the top twenty."

Daniel grinned, his mood momentarily lightened by Moishe's enthusiasm. "I guess I should feel like a pitcher who got one strike-out while giving up ten grand slams. I'll have something to remember when I'm back on the farm team again." He turned to his father. "Let's have your two cents' worth."

Isaac made a disparaging face. "You want the truth or do you want to hear something nice? Daniel, it will take you twenty lifetimes to live this down. You've made yourself look like a fool."

"Anyone else got anything to add?" Daniel asked. He could not understand why he was sounding so cheerful about the whole thing. It was nothing short of a tragedy and he was beginning to feel good about it. It was relief, that was it. He was grateful that the damned thing was over and done with. Now he could get on with living again.

"I think what your father said sums it up pretty well," Anna replied. "You swam a mile out of your depth and you almost drowned. Now you need artificial respiration."

"You offering to give it to me?"

Anna shook her head. "It's a job you've got to do on your own. Come on, let's get something to eat and go home."

They selected a restaurant far away from the cinema. Even if Daniel had managed to come to terms with his own private catastrophe, he did not want to be recognized by anyone who might have seen the movie. That embarrassment would no doubt come later. Right now he wanted to fend it off for as long as possible.

Within four days, *South Side Serenade* was playing to half-empty movie houses on both coasts. After ten, it was brutally shoved aside and forgotten.

The recording company which was to have released the sound track debated the situation before deciding not to throw good money after bad. The sound track was abandoned.

Moishe visited Daniel in Teaneck to relay the latest bad news. Daniel accepted it stoically. There was no point in displaying animosity. He had resigned himself to *South Side Serenade* being one of the biggest bombs of all time, along with everything associated with it. He wondered how Duguid would react to the news. Would he laugh? Or would he just shake his head and congratulate himself because he had been right?

When Moishe left, Daniel went upstairs to the nursery and played with his son for half an hour. He took pleasure in changing the baby, proud that unlike many fathers, he was not above this necessary chore. Next season Anna would be singing again, and he'd be running the house. It would be his job to look after the child. Little Benny couldn't be left to the care of the housekeeper.

"Your old man's out of work, and he hasn't got a prospect in the world," he said quietly to the uncomprehending baby he held on his lap. "Are you ashamed of him? Do you want to change him in for a later model?"

The baby gurgled happily and Daniel smiled.

"Listen to your old man, kid. Don't grow up to be a movie star. Unless you've got a wife who can work to support you." He laughed loudly, startling the child. "Don't be a singer, either. Be something smart and sensible like a lawyer." He thought about Moishe and shook his head. "Don't be a lawyer either. Just marry a rich girl, then you won't have to worry." With the utmost care, he placed the child in the crib, straightened the covers and went downstairs to find Anna in the kitchen.

"I've decided what I'm going to do," he announced grandly.

She looked up from the pie crust she was rolling. "About time. What is it?"

"It's a secret. I'll let you know when it happens."

"Have you been smuggling a bottle up to the nursery?"

He forced his breath on her. "Nothing, see?"

"So what are you going to do?" She finished off the piece of dough and placed it carefully on top of the apple pie.

"Take this season off to begin with."

"Very good." She carried on with preparing dinner, convinced that Daniel was not going to make any sense. The act he kept putting on to show how little he cared was becoming more extravagant with each airing; half the time he seemed to be rambling. It was a problem he would have to solve for himself, though. Following the conversation in Wheeler's with Duguid, Anna had been to see the general manager to discuss her return to the company for the next season. During their meeting, Duguid had made no mention of Daniel other than to say he was sorry the movie had failed. At no time had he asked Anna what Daniel planned to do; it was as if he had washed his hands completely of his wayward tenor.

"Aren't you even going to try and guess?" Daniel asked, wanting to keep the conversation alive.

"I'm too busy," Anna replied. "When you decide, you'll let

me know." She looked up sharply as Daniel took his coat from the closet. "Where are you going?"

"Over to the Bronx. To see my father."

"Daniel, dinner will be ready in an hour. There's a roast in the oven. You can't go out now."

He didn't take any notice of her protest. "You eat. Leave mine in the oven. I won't be home late."

She watched in despair as he left the house, then she popped the apple pie into the oven. She would wait for him to come back and hope he didn't return so late that the meal would be ruined. Would he even bother going to the Bronx to see his father? Or would he abandon the idea the moment he passed the nearest bar? She supposed she could leave Benjamin in the housekeeper's care while she toured around, seeing if she could spot Daniel's Cadillac in front of any bars. That was no use, though, she finally decided. Even if she found him, what could she do? Make a fool of herself by going into the bar and trying to persuade him to leave?

After half an hour she telephoned the house in Van Cortlandt Park. Yetta Kirschbaum answered. Yes, she said, Daniel was there. He was eating dinner while he and his father talked and listened to records. Anna put down the phone, went to the oven and took out the apple pie and the roast. Without a second thought, she threw the whole lot into the garbage. Then she went into the living room and turned on the television set. She'd kill him when he got home, she silently promised herself. She'd strangle him with her bare hands, smash in his skull with the rolling pin she'd been using on the apple pie crust.

Gradually her anger subsided. It was probably the best thing he could do, talk with his father. Maybe Isaac could make more sense out of what Daniel needed, be better able to give him the right advice. If Daniel would listen to advice from any quarter. At one time Anna thought she knew how Daniel's mind worked. Now she was no longer so certain. Despite the nonchalance he worked so hard to affect, this latest upset had taken away his drive, cut his legs out from underneath him. He had cushioned himself against losing his position with the Grand by being so certain that *South Side Serenade* would be a smash hit, open the doors for a new career. His optimism had been shattered, and Daniel was left to face the irrefutable truth that singing with the Grand was the only work he really wanted.

What disturbed Anna most was that Daniel had stopped practicing. While he had continued, his vocalizing had been a positive force. The sound of his voice ringing through the house had assured her that he was keeping trim like an athlete, always ready for that moment when Duguid picked him again for the team. His decision to stop seemed to Anna like he had given up the battle, resigned himself to believing that he would never return.

She telephoned the Kirschbaums again and asked to speak to Daniel. In the background she could hear a man's voice singing "Celeste Aïda." She thought she recognized Richard Tucker. They must both be sitting there, Daniel and his father, listening to records, discussing the techniques of different singers. And they would both be agreeing that Daniel was better than any of them. If only someone had once had the courage to tell him that he wasn't. He'd spent his entire career being told by everyone—herself included—that he was brilliant. How could he not believe it?

Instead of Daniel coming to the phone, it was Isaac. He told Anna that his son had just left, as she rang. Anna asked if Daniel was on the way home. Isaac replied that he believed so. Anna thanked him and put down the receiver, willing herself to be patient until Daniel returned.

Daniel got home twenty-five minutes later. When she showed him the food she had thrown into the garbage can, he looked sheepish and explained that his parents had been sitting down to dinner when he arrived. He'd suddenly felt hungry. Her anger at him was tinged with relief that he had not stopped off at a bar.

"I'm going back to being a *chazan*," he said. "I talked it over with my father. I'll still be welcome in Paterson on a full-time basis."

"Is that really what you want?" she asked, knowing it was not. She guessed Daniel had mentioned the idea to his father, and Isaac, thinking Daniel really wanted it, had encouraged him.

"It'll have to be, won't it? Until Duguid decides that I've done my time. If he ever decides that."

"Daniel, for Christ's sake!" Anna's voice rose high above the level she'd intended as her frayed nerves began to show. "What do you expect Duguid to do? Come crawling to you? Begging you to go back? Let me tell you something. There's only one Grand Opera Company, but there are a thousand tenors who can sing Rodolfo. Now you figure out who should go crawling to whom!"

"What do you mean by that?" In Anna's outburst Daniel recognized the erosion of her support.

"I mean exactly what I say. You need Robin Duguid a darned sight more than he needs you." Tears sprang hotly to Anna's eyes as she, too, realized that she was pulling away the prop she'd promised him. She was betraying his trust, but how long was she supposed to put up with his refusal to face reality? "Daniel, you're driving me crazy, you're ruining us, splitting us apart with your selfishness." She watched him wilt under the barrage of words and felt ashamed of the savage delight that pulsed through her. She should have acted like this ages ago, cut Daniel down instead of pampering his ego. It would have done him more good than all the encouragement she'd offered. It would have made him see the truth.

Anna found it impossible to hold back now. It felt like floodgates had been opened; a safety valve finally turned to let out dangerous pressure in the system. "I also want to go back to the Grand, Daniel. It's my career, too. But I'm suffering because you've got me worried sick about you all the goddamned time!" She paused only for the shallowest of breaths. "Each time you walk out of that front door, I'm not sure whether you're going to come back under your own steam or whether you'll have to be pulled out of a bar!"

"Wait a minute!" he finally managed to yell back. "Do you think I'm a wino, is that it? It's the pressure that's doing it to me, that's what! And you'd think I'd get a little bit of help from my wife, wouldn't you?"

Anna put her hands on her hips, threw back her head and laughed. "Pressure? Do you think no one else suffers from it? Believe me, any pressure you've got right now is of your own making."

Unwelcome parallels began to form in Daniel's mind as he faced Anna, stunned by the ferocity of her assault. One moment it was Anna he saw, the next it was Lucy and her attack on him after he had been relieved of his job at the B'nai Yeshurun in Washington Heights. Lucy had told him almost the same, accused him of mooning around at home instead of getting out and making things happen for himself. Why had he married an opera singer the second time around? Didn't he learn enough of a lesson from the first miserable encounter?

Anna finally lowered her voice after realizing too late that the housekeeper upstairs in her room must be hearing every word of the argument. "Daniel, if you want to go back to being a *chazan*, go ahead. If you want to be a bus driver, go ahead. Do whatever you want to do. But please, for my sake, for Benjamin's sake, do something before you drive us all into the madhouse!" With that, she turned around and ran up the stairs. Seconds later, Daniel heard the bedroom door slam.

For the better part of fifteen minutes, he walked aimlessly around the living room while he ran the argument through in his mind, trying to spot what had triggered it. His eating out and causing Anna to throw away the meal she had been making? No. That he wanted to be a cantor again? He shook his head in bewilderment. Women, he thought; there was never any way of knowing which way they'd turn. No rhyme or reason to their actions. She'd stuck by him all this time, and now, when he had reached a decision, she was turning on him. Who could understand that kind of logic?

He walked across to the old mahogany secretary that he'd brought over from the Greenwich Village apartment and pulled out the scrapbook. If Anna didn't want to stand by him anymore, the words of praise the critics had written would give him all the support he would ever need. They'd show him he was right in waiting for Duguid to come to him. How could anyone who had received the acclaim he had be shut out of any opera house? Sooner or later, Duguid would realize it. He'd want Daniel back, and he would return on his own terms.

Reviews passed before his eyes as he read and reread of his

many triumphs. Had any other lyric tenor gone back to being something like a cantor while he waited for the right opportunity to arise? Or had they chased endlessly after a general manager like Duguid until they were patted affectionately on the head, well-trained dogs that had learned to obey their master's bidding? He wasn't a well-trained dog. Duguid could contact him, otherwise it would be the Grand's loss and Temple Isaiah's gain.

He fell asleep in an armchair. After a while, the scrapbook dropped to the floor, its noise muffled by the thick broadloom, and he slumbered on undisturbed.

At breakfast the following morning, Anna passed no comment about the previous night's argument. Daniel ate sullenly, then went upstairs to play with Benjamin before showering. Shortly after ten o'clock, he walked through the entrance of Harry Feldman's real estate office in Paterson.

"Pleasant surprise," Feldman exclaimed when he saw Daniel. "Business or pleasure?"

"Business." Daniel pulled up a chair and sat down opposite the temple president. "How would you like a former opera singer as your full-time *chazan?*" He made the offer grandly, as if he were giving Feldman his greatest opportunity ever.

Feldman sat still for a moment while he thought over the question. He knew all about Daniel's troubles with the Grand; everyone in the congregation did. "What about the *chazan* we've already got?" he asked. "What do I do with him? Give him a month's pay in lieu of notice and say it's been nice to know you?"

Daniel opened his mouth to answer, then closed it again. He'd expected Feldman to jump at the offer; he hadn't counted on a negative question in return. "I'm a million times better than he is. You know it and so do I."

"Sure you are," Feldman acknowledged. "You've got one of the most beautiful voices I've ever heard. And so you should because you're an opera singer. That's where you belong. In an opera house."

"I've had enough of opera," Daniel protested. "It's full of frauds, people who clap you on the back and stick a knife in you the next moment. I want to get back to what I love most of all." He was forced to struggle hard to find the right words. He'd figured out what he would say to Feldman, just as he'd figured out how the temple president would jump at it. Only Feldman had not been shown the same script. He wasn't jumping. He wasn't even walking slowly toward Daniel's offer. "How come I'm okay to sing for you on *Rosh Hashanah* and *Yom Kippur*, but you don't want me back on a regular basis?"

"Because you're a celebrity. A celebrity as *chazan* for the *yomtovim* is a big draw," Feldman explained, although he did not know why he was bothering. Daniel knew why they hired him for the High Holy Days. "The *chazan* we've got now is singing for a living. Sure his voice isn't as sweet as yours, but he's doing it to support his family. And we can rely on this guy. He won't leave us the moment something breaks in his major field, because being a *chazan* is his major field."

"I told you, Harry, I'm finished with the opera. Too many sharp characters, too little sincerity. I want to be a full-time *chazan* again."

Feldman chuckled deeply. It annoyed Daniel even more than Anna's laughter had. "Who are you trying to kid?" Feldman asked. "You'd jump straight back into your so-called world of frauds the moment the opportunity arose. We'd be without a *chazan* again, and no one would touch us with a ten-foot pole because of the way we threw out our regular guy to make room for one of your whims. Besides, I don't think the *shul* can afford any more of those contracts your crazy lawyer friend would throw at us. I hate to think what his special clauses would be now."

Daniel stood up and loomed over Feldman's desk. "Is that so? You just wait until next *Rosh Hashanah* and see what kind of crowd your regular *chazan* draws. All by himself. Because I won't be there to give your services a touch of class."

To his further annoyance, Feldman continued to laugh. "Daniel, do me a favor and get out of here before you ruin the day for me. Go back to your opera company, to your wife, to your baby. Just leave me alone. I've got work to do."

Daniel stormed out of the door and walked blindly back to where he had parked the car. Now they were laughing at him as

well. He was an object of ridicule.
They could all go screw themselves!

Robin Duguid was poring over the Grand Opera Company's books with the accountant when his secretary entered the office to announce that a gentleman was waiting to see him.
"He doesn't have an appointment, Mr. Duguid. But he says that it's very urgent."
A brief expression of annoyance flitted across Duguid's face. He believed in appointments, just as he believed in running his personal and business life to a determined routine. Without it, you were lost. Routine, to Duguid, was the lifeline to sanity in a particularly insane business. "Who is it and what's it all about?" he asked testily.
The secretary held out a business card.
Duguid took the card and scrutinized it. The expression of annoyance returned when he saw the words attorney-at-law under the name of Maurice Waterman. Lawyers always meant trouble. "Who is this Mr. Waterman?"
The secretary took a deep breath. "He says that he represents Daniel Kerr."
Duguid nodded in sudden enlightenment. He had met Moishe at the housewarming party when Hammersley had introduced him as the Grand's next general manager. "Tell him I can spare five minutes," he said. "In about half an hour if he wants to wait that long." He turned back to the balance sheet.
The secretary returned to the reception area and passed Duguid's message onto Moishe. Moishe accepted it without any fuss. He had spent hours summoning up the courage to call on Duguid; he might as well wait for the man to find the time to see him.
Moishe thanked the secretary and sat back while he wondered exactly what he was doing in the opera house. Guilt hadn't pushed him into making the visit. He had done nothing to feel guilty about. Daniel had accepted Joel Pomerantz's proposal for making *South Side Serenade* with his eyes wide open. Sure he might have been temporarily blinded by seductive visions of a rapid escalation to Hollywood stardom,

but he was still old enough to recognize his own best course.

Like hell he was.

Despite any rationalization, Moishe knew he did harbor guilt feelings. Daniel could always bring them out in you, like your mother. He was a big kid, that was all. You could push him this way and that just as long as the direction appealed to his ego; he'd walk down any dark tunnel if there was the slightest chance of finding applause at the end of it. And somehow he always made you feel you were to blame if something went wrong, even through his own fault. The only time Daniel did not try to pass the buck was when something turned out to be successful, and then he had done it all on his own.

Moishe sighed as he identified himself in the role of martyr. Daniel had blamed him for enough things before now; he should be used to it. It was his own fault as much as it was Daniel's because he usually accepted the blame and tried to find ways of correcting a situation. If you wanted to remain friends with a guy like Daniel, you had to be willing to carry the can for him. Did he want to remain friends? he suddenly asked himself. What was the point of even thinking about it? He'd been friends with Daniel for so long, helping him out of one jam or another, that life without him seemed almost unthinkable.

"Mr. Duguid will see you now, Mr. Waterman."

Moishe looked up at the secretary, then down at his watch, surprised to find that twenty-five minutes had slipped away while he had been thinking over his long relationship with Daniel. He must have covered everything in those twenty-five minutes, the first meeting on the way to Joey Bloom's hotel in the mountains, through Larry Kahn and the radio station to the present time. Smiling at the memory, Moishe followed the secretary into Duguid's office.

"Mr. Waterman, nice to meet you again." Duguid walked around the desk to greet his visitor, then he tempered the welcome with an immediate, "I can give you five minutes and no more, I'm afraid. You've caught me at a very busy time."

"Thank you." Moishe was uncertain whether he had the time to sit down or not. Duguid pointed to a chair and Moishe took it. "I've come here on Daniel Kerr's behalf, Mr. Duguid."

"Yes?"

"He wants to come back to the Grand. He wants to sing here again."

"Has he told you this?" Duguid began to look vaguely interested in what Moishe had to say.

"No. But you can see it. It's driving him nuts being out of here. It's not doing his family life any good either."

"The last time I saw Daniel was in Wheeler's after our opening night production of *Turandot,*" Duguid interrupted, "and I didn't get the impression he wanted to return. If anything, I received the opposite impression. Daniel couldn't seem to care less about the Grand."

"He keeps it bottled up inside of him," Moishe said quickly. "That's the reason I'm here. To ask on his behalf what he's got to do to come back."

"I see. So you're the errand boy, is that it?"

"Hardly," Moishe answered and called himself a liar immediately. Of course he was the errand boy, even if Daniel had not sent him. He'd been Daniel's errand boy from the moment he'd first met him. "He doesn't even know I'm here."

Duguid studied Moishe for a long moment. "If I set out the conditions and you relayed them to Daniel, would it make any difference? Would he accept them?"

Behind the thick glasses, Moishe's eyes widened as he saw a ray of hope in Duguid's words. There were conditions. Which meant the Grand would have him back. "I believe so, Mr. Duguid. I just think he's too embarrassed to come here and ask you himself."

"Embarrassed? High and mighty is a more accurate description," Duguid pointed out. "Never mind," he added quickly, as if he regretted allowing his personal opinion to slip out. "Mr. Waterman, Daniel Kerr has never shown the slightest remorse for the way he acted. He made a fool out of himself, which he's perfectly free to do. But at the same time, he dragged the name of this opera company through the mud."

"No one knows that more than Daniel does." When Moishe saw Duguid sneak a look at the clock on the wall, he realized he was wasting time. Half of his allotted five minutes had passed and still he had not made any inroads. To hell with diplomacy, he decided, and asked straight out: "What does Daniel have to do to return to the Grand?"

"The hardest thing of all," Duguid replied.

"What's that?"

"He has to apologize to me."

"That's all?" Moishe asked, amazed at the simplicity of the reply.

"That is all." Duguid stood up. "Now if you'll excuse me, Mr. Waterman, I have an opera company to manage. Thank you for dropping by. I found our talk most enlightening."

Moishe stood up, shook Duguid's hand and left the office in a happy daze, a man who had discovered gold. Daniel was on the way back, and Moishe had found out the magic words, the open sesame for him.

By the time he reached the street, Moishe's euphoria had all but disappeared. The words would be anything but magic. Duguid hadn't been kidding when he'd said Daniel had to do the hardest thing of all. Getting Daniel to apologize for anything was like trying to squeeze blood out of a rock.

Chapter Twelve

Moishe glanced nervously at the hands of his watch as they neared twelve-thirty. Any minute now he'd hear Daniel's voice outside, informing the receptionist that he had an appointment with Mr. Waterman. And Moishe didn't know what to tell him when he came in.

Following the meeting with Robin Duguid, Moishe had called Daniel. Instead of coming right out and admitting he had been to see the Grand's general manager, Moishe had suggested lunch the following day to discuss a business deal in which Daniel might be interested. Daniel had pressed him for details but Moishe had declined. There was no point in telling Daniel over the phone. Daniel would probably resent his intrusion, tell him to look after his own affairs. Face to face, though, he might have a better chance of explaining why he had been to see Duguid.

"Hi, I've got a lunch date with Mr. Waterman." Daniel's voice filtered through Moishe's closed office door. Moishe stood up, straightened the jacket of his dark gray suit, slipped on his topcoat and prepared to leave.

The door opened and the receptionist stuck her head inside. Moishe nodded and came out to find Daniel standing by the woman's desk, huddled up inside a navy blue cashmere coat. The heavy coat made him look like an overstuffed teddy bear, and Moishe knew it wasn't just the coat that made him appear so bulky. Daniel had been trying to eat away his troubles again. Either that, or he was picking up all the extra calories from booze. As Yetta Kirschbaum had once been alarmed to discover, Moishe could see physical similarities between Daniel and his Uncle Benny.

"What's doing, Moishe?" Daniel greeted him. He enjoyed using his friend's familiar name in front of the receptionist, certain that it shocked her prim and proper outlook on how a lawyer should conduct his business.

"Not too much. What do you say to a bite on West Forty-seventh Street?" Now that the diamond business had all but moved from Canal Street to West Forty-seventh Street between Fifth and Sixth Avenues, Moishe liked to frequent the area. The constant nonstop bustle of activity never failed to fascinate him.

Daniel fell into step as they headed down the stairs to the street. "Why walk all the way over there?" he complained, although it would take no more than five minutes. "There's a good place downstairs. Great corned beef."

Moishe knew Daniel was referring to the Irish bar a few yards away. He shook his head firmly. "I don't like drinking at lunchtime. Kills the afternoon for me."

"Who said anything about drinking?"

"I thought it might come up." Moishe shoved his bare hands deep into the pockets of his coat and started to walk eastward toward Sixth Avenue. Daniel followed sullenly, his bright mood at anticipating Moishe's latest piece of lunacy already dampened. Since Harry Feldman had turned him down for a full-time cantor's position with Temple Isaiah, Daniel had been in a state of numb depression, wandering around the house, going out for long, aimless drives which more often than not finished up in local bars, or sitting idly with Little Benny. Hearing Anna practice only served to make Daniel more despondent. Everyone was following a rewarding career while he was being squeezed out on all sides. When Moishe had called and mentioned a business deal, Daniel had sensed another wild scheme which, if nothing else, might temporarily relieve the monotony. Now Moishe wouldn't even have a drink with him.

The delicatessen into which Moishe led the way was crowded with lunchtime traffic from the diamond district. Anonymous men filled the tables, talking and eating simultaneously as if unwilling to allow a single second of the day to pass without accounting for it. Two overworked waitresses scurried among the tables, carrying orders from the counter, dirty plates, cups and cutlery back to the kitchen. Daniel found little to appeal to him in the activity that captivated Moishe. He stared moodily around the delicatessen, wishing they had gone to the bar instead.

"Let's get out of here," he pleaded. "It's too crowded for me. I feel claustrophobic."

Moishe ignored the request. He spotted two men leaving a table and immediately pushed his way through. He and Daniel reached it one step ahead of two other men and sat down quickly, claiming the territory. "What do you want to eat?" Moishe asked.

Deciding to make the best of an unavoidable situation, Daniel scanned the menu and selected a pastrami sandwich on rye and potato *latkes*. Moishe settled for only a sandwich and sat back, waiting for the order to be delivered.

"Okay, what's all this secrecy about?" Daniel asked impatiently. "What's so big that you wouldn't mention it on the phone?"

Moishe passed a hand across his shining head while he debated how to answer. He decided on a delaying tactic. "How's Anna? Benjamin?"

"Fine. They're fine. Just like they were when you asked me last night." Daniel sounded like he was grumbling. "You didn't drag me all the way down here to ask me that. What do you want?"

"Why are you so edgy?"

"Edgy? You're crazy."

The order came before Daniel could say any more. He watched helplessly as Moishe started on the sandwich, without making any attempt to explain the reason for the meeting.

Moishe's jaw worked automatically as he consumed the sandwich. Then he turned his attention to a bowl of pickled cucumbers in the center of the table. Only when the coffee arrived did he decide to end Daniel's wait. "You working at all?"

"You know damned well I'm not. What ideas have you got?"

"What about Feldman and Temple Isaiah?" When Daniel had mentioned returning to the temple, Moishe had not thought much of the idea. Those days were over for Daniel. Being a cantor would be a stopgap measure at best, something to keep him occupied until another opportunity opened up.

"I didn't bother in the end," Daniel lied. Moishe didn't have to know that Feldman was not interested, that he'd seen right through Daniel's reason for asking.

"You want to go back to the Grand?" Moishe asked quietly.

If he had lit a firecracker under Daniel's chair, he could not have received a sharper, more startled response. "Do I?" Daniel almost leaped to his feet, spilling coffee onto the table as his hand knocked against the cup. "If you know how I can do that, let me in on it!"

Moishe took a deep breath and pushed his glasses to the top of his nose. "I met Robin Duguid yesterday," he began.

"Where?" Daniel wanted to know. "How? Did he have anything to say about me?"

Moishe held up a hand for Daniel to stop. "I didn't meet him by accident."

Daniel looked confused. "What do you mean you didn't meet him by accident? Did you go up there to see him? To his office at the Grand?" The questions were tinged with disbelief.

Moishe nodded. "I went up to his office. He gave me five minutes. It was all I needed."

"Needed for what?"

"To find out his conditions for allowing you back with the company."

Daniel stared across the table, at first uncomprehending. Then his face reddened as his anger grew. "You asked Duguid what he wants me to do before he'll allow me back? What goddamned business is it of yours?"

"Do you want to go back or not?" Moishe snapped.

"Of course I damned well want to go back! But I'll do it my way when I'm good and ready. I don't need other people sticking their noses in for me!"

"What is your way? Eating yourself sick until you're the size of a zeppelin?" Moishe injected his own anger into the questions as he tried to deflate Daniel's dangerous complacency. "Drinking yourself into a sponge?"

"Is that what Duguid said about me? Or is that just your expert opinion?" Daniel demanded loudly. A waitress passing by the table looked nervously at the two men as their voices rose.

"All Duguid said is that he wants a personal apology from you. Nothing more. That's his sole condition for allowing you back. Seems reasonable to me."

"An apology for what?"

"For making a fool of yourself and denigrating the company."

Daniel pushed back the chair and stood up. In one furious motion, he pulled on the cashmere topcoat and started to stride away from the table. When he had gone five yards, he swung around, face almost crimson, finger shaking with rage as he pointed it at Moishe. "You see him again!" he shouted across the delicatessen. "You tell him he can kiss my ass! The same goes for you, too! You keep your face out of my goddamned business from now on! You've cost me too much already!"

Moishe shuddered and closed his eyes as if the simple action would make all the curious faces in the delicatessen disappear. When he could bear to open his eyes again, Daniel had disappeared. The delicatessen was back to normal, the momentary disturbance swallowed up and forgotten in the normal run of activity.

"Anything else for you, honey?" the waitress asked as she cleared the table.

"Just the check," Moishe muttered. He leaned back in the chair while he tried to decide what to do next. The most attractive alternative was to drop the matter altogether. If Daniel was hell bent on hanging himself, no one had the right to stop him. He had picked up the pieces for Daniel too many times already; maybe they were better off being left where they fell.

Two minutes later, after he had paid the check and left the delicatessen, Moishe was exploring other possibilities, and by the time he reached his office, his mind was made up. He'd give it one more try. If Daniel accused him of sticking his nose where it wasn't wanted because he had seen Robin Duguid, God alone knew what he'd accuse him of once he'd spoken to Anna.

The housekeeper answered the phone and asked Moishe to

wait. Anna sounded surprised and worried when she came on the line. Daniel was meeting Moishe for lunch; was something wrong?

Using the barest minimum of words, Moishe explained what had happened during his meeting with Duguid and what had followed when he'd tried to tell Daniel that Duguid wanted nothing more than an apology to heal the wounds.

"Why do you stand by him?" Anna asked when Moishe had finished.

The unexpected question floored Moishe. He'd asked himself the same thing dozens of times and had never yet come up with a satisfactory answer. "I need a regular dose of aggravation," he replied flippantly. "Daniel makes me realize how sane the rest of the world is."

"Or maybe you're like all of us," Anna suggested, "and you care more about him than he does himself."

Moishe smiled thinly at Anna's words. It was the story of Daniel's life for as long as he'd known him. There had always been someone around to help Daniel to his feet; he found himself wondering where Daniel would have wound up if he'd been on his own. "Will you talk to him about it?" he asked.

"I guess I don't have much choice, do I? You've dropped the ball fair and square in my lap."

"Thanks. You might have more luck than me."

"Don't bet on it." Anna started to put down the receiver, then she stopped. "Are you still there, Moishe?"

"Yes."

"Thanks for calling. I mean it. Thanks a lot for everything."

Daniel did not return home until almost eight in the evening. Anna did not have to be told where he'd been; she could smell it on his breath. She asked if he had eaten, and he replied he'd had dinner in the city. Then she questioned him about the lunch date with Moishe.

"Some *meshuggeh* idea he's got," Daniel shrugged off the question. "You know what Moishe's like. I can do without his brainwaves."

"Is an apology to Mr. Duguid so crazy?"

Daniel's eyes narrowed. "Who said anything about an

apology to Duguid? Oh, I get it. Bigmouth called here, did he?"

"Right after you screamed at him in the delicatessen. Is that all your beautiful voice is good for now, yelling abuse at people who try to help you?"

Daniel stamped away. Anna grabbed him by the arm and spun him around with a force she never knew she possessed. Her eyes were blazing when she looked into his face. "If you're so desperate to kill yourself, why do it the hard way? Why don't you just take a loaded gun and blow your brains out? Put us all out of our misery!"

"Leave me alone, will you?" He tried to escape from her grip. She held on tenaciously, refusing to let him go. She didn't have to be a psychologist to know that Daniel was purposely punishing himself by holding out against Duguid. Punishing himself for some wrong—real or imagined; she didn't know—by refusing to take what he wanted most. Perhaps it was his own way of exacting retribution against himself for *South Side Serenade*, because he'd known all along he was doing the wrong thing. When he'd hurt himself enough, he'd look around and decide it was time to stop. Then and only then would he go to Duguid. Or would he just carry on because he was bent on destroying himself completely?

"Daniel, you might hate yourself right now, but do you care about me? Do you care anything about Benjamin? Do you?"

"Of course I do!" he snapped back.

"Then will you damned well start acting like you do?"

"I am not apologizing to Robin Duguid or to anyone else!" he shouted. "He can come to me!" With a savage tug, he tore himself loose of Anna's grasp and stormed out of the house, leaving the front door wide open to let in the wintry wind.

When he returned home after midnight, a strange car was sitting in the driveway. Daniel got out of the Cadillac and examined the blue Chevrolet, curious to know what it was doing there. He saw the New York plates and realized it belonged to Moishe.

What was he doing in the house? Hatching up more mischief with Anna?

The knowledge that Anna was still awake sobered Daniel. He

had expected her to be sleeping when he returned, but the living room light was shining in the darkness of the street. Anna would be in there with Moishe; they were ganging up on him now. They'd both want to know where he'd been. He wasn't ashamed to tell them. He'd been sitting in a bar in Hoboken, down at the water's edge, drinking and talking with seamen. They had made more sense to him than his own family and friends.

"What the hell are you doing here?" he growled when he saw Moishe sitting alone in the living room. "Where's Anna? Upstairs?"

"She's not here, Daniel."

Daniel did not seem to notice it was one of the few times Moishe had ever called him by his full name. "What do you mean she's not here?"

"Nobody's here but me." Moishe stood up, ready for the onslaught he knew would greet his next words. "Anna's taken Benjamin with her. I drove them and your housekeeper to a hotel in New York. They're not coming back."

"What? You slimy, four-eyed sonofabitch!" Daniel closed the gap in two large strides. Moishe saw the punch coming and tried to duck. He never had a chance. Daniel's right fist grazed the side of his face and sent him staggering backward, knocking his glasses into the air. As Moishe tried to regain his balance, Daniel brought over the left. It smacked solidly into Moishe's mouth, splitting his lips, mashing them back onto his teeth.

The sickly-sweet taste of his own blood was adrenalin to Moishe's system. He swung his arms furiously, aiming blindly in Daniel's direction, aching to feel his fists pound savagely into flesh. Years of frustration, years of playing straight man to Daniel's clown, lent energy to the wild punches. Daniel stepped back in amazement, dodging the punches with ease. If he had not been so mad at Moishe, he'd have laughed. Moishe wasn't a scrapper. He was a bookworm, a milquetoast. He'd fight you with words. With jokes. With cunning. Never with his fists.

"You self-centered bastard!" Moishe yelled at the indistinct figure in front of him. He whirled his arms like a windmill and landed a glancing blow on Daniel's shoulder. "Don't you ever think of anyone but your fucking self?"

Another punch thudded into Daniel's arm as he stood perfectly still, at last providing a target that Moishe could identify without his glasses. Daniel moved only to dodge the roundhouse right that whistled dangerously toward his head, then he grabbed hold of Moishe's arms, pinioning them to his sides. "Hold on, will you, for Christ's sake? You'll kill yourself!"

"Since when do you fucking care?" Moishe lashed out with his foot, surprising Daniel as the shoe thudded painfully against his shin. "Since when are you concerned about anything but your own damned self? You couldn't give a shit about anyone! About Anna! About me! Even about Lucy!" The foot swung again and Daniel jumped back, releasing Moishe's arms in his haste to dodge the kick.

"You killed Lucy because you didn't give a shit about her!" Moishe screamed.

Black rage enveloped Daniel at the accusation. Feet planted firmly on the ground, he slammed his fist into Moishe's face. The punch landed just below Moishe's right eye and toppled him backward. He sat down in the middle of the carpet, spitting blood from the earlier blow. He shook his head and tried to lever himself up.

Daniel looked down at him, suddenly horrified by what he had done, even more frightened that Moishe would struggle to his feet to continue the fight. "Don't get up, Moishe. Please."

"Fuck you! I'm not jumping out of any windows just to please you." With an almighty shove, Moishe staggered to his feet. "You didn't like hearing the truth about Lucy, did you?" It was torture to form the words. He didn't care because he knew hearing them would hurt Daniel even more. Whoever wrote that sticks and stones could hurt your bones but names would never harm you was full of crap. Moishe knew the taunts he was yelling were going through Daniel like red hot knives. "You think Lucy jumped? You pushed her!"

"Shut up!" Daniel yelled. "Do you hear me? Shut up before I kill you!"

"Now you're trying to do the same thing to Anna. I won't let you. That's why I took her away. One Lucy was enough!"

Daniel's fist exploded like a shell burst in the center of Moishe's face. Arms flailing for balance, Moishe fell across an armchair, tipped it over and hit the floor with a sickening crash. A groan escaped from his mouth as the breath was driven out of him. His body wriggled sluggishly like a crushed worm.

"Moishe?" Daniel's head cleared. "Moishe?" He ran across the room and knelt down beside the prostrate figure. "Are you all right?" He turned Moishe's face upward and felt sick when he saw the smashed lips and nose, the large bruise that was already puffing up the right eye.

Moishe groaned again. No recognition showed in his eyes. His breath erupted in ragged, painful gasps. Daniel stood up slowly, unable to tear his terrified gaze away from the destruction he had wrought. He could not believe he'd done it. Couldn't understand why. Just as he was unable to comprehend why Moishe would throw up all those terrible lies about Lucy. Daniel felt like a man living through a nightmare which had somehow managed to make itself real, found the back door of his mind to invade his very existence.

He spotted Moishe's glasses lying on the carpet and picked them up. One lens was smashed. "Here's your glasses," he said quietly, kneeling down again. "I'll pay to get them repaired."

Moishe's eyes blinked and Daniel stepped away. He stopped by the living room door long enough to look back once more, willing himself to believe that Moishe was all right. Then he fled from the house, dived into the car and tore up the street in a protesting scream of skidding tires.

Lying on the floor, still dazed by that final blow, Moishe was barely aware of the sound of the Cadillac accelerating along the street. He was confused, trying to piece everything together. The fight—if a fight it had been—and his own screaming rage at Daniel. For the first time since that night in the Deuces Wild in Harlem, when he had jumped on the back of the man attacking Daniel, Moishe had resorted to violence. He'd lost, but what had he expected to do against someone of Daniel's physique? Using fists was almost second nature to Daniel. Winning, though, had been a secondary concern to Moishe. Most importantly, he had shown Daniel that he wasn't scared of standing up to him.

He reached out for the glasses and slipped them on. The smashed lens covered his puffy eye. As he struggled to his feet, leaning heavily on the overturned armchair, a staccato hammering came from the front door. Unsteadily Moishe walked toward the noise. He opened the door a crack and saw a police officer standing outside, face illuminated by the porch light.

"Mr. Kerr?"

Moishe shook his head. "He's not here," he mumbled through swollen lips. He ran the tip of his tongue along his top teeth and felt jagged edges; two of them were broken.

The police officer peered closer, suspicious when he saw the smashed spectacles, bleeding nose and mouth. "Who are you?"

"I thought I was a friend of Mr. Kerr. I guess I was mistaken." He opened the door wider and allowed the policeman into the house.

The policeman looked around the living room, noticing the overturned chair, the total disarray. "We had a report of a disturbance. A neighbor complained."

Despite the pain, Moishe managed to smile. "Your disturbance just left."

"Everything all right?" the police officer asked. "Nothing you want to tell me?" He hoped there wasn't. It was a cold night and he wanted to get to the all-night diner half a mile away for a cup of coffee and a cigarette.

"Nothing at all," Moishe said, to the man's relief. He held the front door open and followed the policeman out.

Daniel pressed down the bell on the front door of the house in Van Cortlandt Park. All the lights were out, but his parents would hear him. He'd keep on ringing the damned bell until they woke up.

Ten seconds passed, and he added to the noise by banging on the door with his clenched fist. A light came on in the front bedroom. Drapes were pulled back. Daniel saw his mother's face peering out into the night. He stepped back and waved for her to open the door. The drape fell back into place and other lights began to glow. He rang the bell again and the door opened. Yetta stood facing him, dragging a heavy woolen dressing gown around herself.

"What's the matter, you wake everyone up this time of night?"

"I want to speak to Pa." He pushed his way past Yetta and walked into the living room.

Yetta followed him, annoyance at being woken up yielding to curiosity. She thought she'd smelled liquor on his breath as he'd walked past her.

On the stairs, Daniel heard his father's slippered tread. He waited for Isaac to enter, then said, "Anna's left me. Taken the baby and cleared off."

"What?" The single word of disbelief came simultaneously from both Isaac and Yetta as they stared in horror at their son.

"She's gone to some hotel in New York. Moishe took them and the housekeeper."

"How come Moishe?" Isaac asked.

"Because . . . oh, I don't know," Daniel finished lamely. He'd caught himself just in time from heaping all the blame on Moishe's shoulders, just like he always did. "I suppose Anna called him up while I was out."

"Where were you?" Yetta asked. "In some bar?"

"Yes, I was," Daniel replied belligerently. "Is there something wrong with that?"

Isaac rubbed the sleep from his eyes and tied up the belt of his dressing gown. "Why did she leave you?"

"Because I've been making her life a goddamned misery, I suppose." He turned angrily on his mother. "That's what you're waiting to hear, isn't it? That I've been on the skids ever since I got slung out of the Grand?"

"From your own mouth you admit it," Yetta said. "Why should I say anything?"

"Which hotel?" Isaac asked quickly. He felt dizzy at being woken up. An argument between his wife and son would only make him feel worse.

"I don't know. Moishe was waiting for me at the house. He told me he'd taken them, but he wouldn't say where."

"Why did you come here?" Yetta asked. "If you're so concerned about Anna and Benjamin, why aren't you trying the hotels?"

Concerned! Moishe had used the same word, asked him why he was suddenly concerned about anyone else. Now his mother was using it. "Do you think I don't give a damn about anyone either?" Daniel snapped at her. "Yeah, that's it! You're just like Moishe. You all think I couldn't give a shit about anyone but myself."

Yetta stood her ground silently at the outburst, but Isaac was shaken. "Is that what Moishe told you?" he asked quietly. "Or did Anna tell him to say that?"

Daniel turned on his father, ready to attack him as well. He couldn't. The strength seemed to drain right out of him, leaving his body weak and limp.

"You've been friends with Moishe since you were fourteen," Isaac pointed out. "It's part of a friend's duty to tell the truth, as painful as it is. If he tries to protect you from the truth, hide it from you, then he's not a real friend."

Confronted by his father's reasoning, Daniel slumped into a chair. Before his eyes danced an image of Moishe staggering back from that final punch, the shattered face, the smashed glasses on the floor. How long had Moishe bottled up his feelings? Kept them inside as he had struggled to maintain the friendship? Tonight they had spilled over. Moishe had seen all along what Daniel had refused to acknowledge. That he was hurting everyone—not just himself—in his selfish quest for vindication at the Grand. He'd driven Anna to distraction, left her despairing just as surely as he had left Lucy in torment. After giving up trying to communicate with him, Anna had turned to Moishe, hoping that he would be able to make Daniel understand.

"Pa, will you come out with me? Try a few hotels? Persuade her to come back if we can find her?"

Despite his own weakness, Isaac nodded. "I'll get dressed."

He turned away to trudge upstairs to the bedroom when Yetta called him back. "You'll do no such thing. It's freezing cold outside and you're not going to make yourself ill because of his foolishness. There's the phone." She pointed to the instrument. "Let him phone the hotels. You don't have to go out with him."

Isaac opened his mouth to argue, but Daniel saw the sense in his mother's suggestion. "Okay, Pa. You pick the hotels from the directory and I'll call them."

"You sure?" Isaac asked, relieved that he would not have to go out.

"Sure." Daniel already had the receiver in his hand.

Watching, Yetta nodded her approval. "I'll make you some coffee," she offered. "You might be here a long time."

From the window of her room in the Statler Hilton on Seventh Avenue, Anna looked out over Penn Station and thought about the phone call she'd just had from Moishe. His words had been almost inaudible, a sudden attack of toothache, he'd explained. He'd told her that he'd waited until Daniel arrived home and informed him that Anna had left with Benjamin and the housekeeper. Moishe made no mention of the fight, or of the police coming. He finished up by saying that Daniel had left in the car.

Anna turned her gaze to the crib the hotel had provided. Benjamin slept soundly, undisturbed by the night's panic; the housekeeper, too, in the suite's other bedroom. Anna supposed Daniel would come looking for her. She wished him luck. She'd taken steps to prevent his discovery of where she was by registering in the name of Wasserman, a nice little touch suggested by Moishe.

Daniel. She repeated his name quietly while she wondered what to do. Leaving him permanently never crossed her mind. She knew she would go back to the house in Teaneck, to Daniel. But before she returned, she wanted him to suffer a dose of the medicine he'd been handing out. Eating humble pie might do him a world of good, give him a more honest perspective. Perhaps he would have had a better outlook already if he had struggled the way she had, started with smaller parts until she'd attained a reputation by hard work. It had all come too easily for Daniel. Now, faced with a real crisis, he did not know how to cope.

She remembered writing that first letter of apology for him. She'd be damned if she'd do it again.

* * *

Isaac Kirschbaum felt the first twinges of pain in his chest when he read out the eighteenth hotel for Daniel to try. He excused himself and went upstairs to the bedroom for his white pills. Yetta was sleeping, having divorced herself from the crisis. Isaac looked at her still form for an instant before slipping one of the pills under his tongue and quietly returning downstairs. He was just in time to hear Daniel ask one night clerk if the hotel had anyone registered under the name of Anna Markova, Markowitz or Kerr. Again the answer was no and Daniel slammed down the receiver in disgust.

"I bet that sonofabitch is putting her up at his apartment," he cursed, totally oblivious of his father's discomfort.

"So call there and find out." Isaac settled carefully into a chair, the Manhattan telephone directory balanced on his knees. He did not approve of his son's language, especially when it concerned Moishe. How long would it take Daniel to realize that in Moishe he had one friend he could trust?

"No. Give me another hotel." He watched his father trace the names with his forefinger, seeming to take forever. "Come on, Pa! We haven't even done twenty yet!"

"Daniel"—Isaac closed the book and let it drop heavily to the floor—"all of a sudden I don't feel so good."

"What?"

"I just took a pill. It hasn't helped." Even as he spoke, Isaac's face grew paler.

"Do you want another one?"

Isaac pointed to the ceiling. "I don't think I can manage the stairs. I left the pills in the bedroom."

Daniel's senses sharpened. He forgot all about the phone calls to the hotels, all about Anna and Benjamin. He leaped from the chair and took the stairs three at a time, feet pounding with the urgency of his fear. Forgetting that his mother was asleep in the room, he turned on the light.

"What's going on?" Yetta asked, sitting up in bed.

Daniel didn't bother to answer. He searched feverishly through his father's clothes until he spotted the small brown bottle on the night table. He grabbed the bottle and raced from the room. Yetta climbed out of bed, put on her dressing gown and followed him downstairs in time to see him uncap the bottle and pass a pill to Isaac, who hastily slipped it underneath his tongue.

"What's the matter?" Yetta screamed. "Are you killing him as well with your madness?"

Daniel spun around. "I didn't do anything!"

"What do you mean you didn't do anything? You dragged us all out of bed in the middle of the night, got your father all excited, with his heart and all. And you did nothing?" She stepped closer. Isaac's eyes were closed as he fought against the constriction in his chest. Yetta wasted no time. She picked up the receiver and dialed the local doctor. Too bad if he was asleep; he got paid to heal, not to sleep.

The doctor arrived within fifteen minutes, jacket and topcoat thrown hastily over his pajama top. He checked Isaac's pulse and heartbeat, then peered into his eyes.

"Nothing to worry about," he assured Yetta and Daniel. "Just to make sure, though, I'll get him to a hospital." He used the phone to call for an ambulance, then returned to the patient. Color was returning to Isaac's face. His breathing had evened out, as if the pills had finally achieved their objective.

"Is it another attack?" Daniel asked.

"A spasm, that's all. But they can check him out far better in the hospital than I can here. Heartbeat and pulse seem normal."

The ambulance from Montefiore drew up outside the house ten minutes later. The doctor followed the attendants outside while Daniel remained in the living room with his mother. "I'll come by for you in the morning," he said. "We'll both go to see him."

"Before you go near him again, you make sure you've sorted out this business with Anna," Yetta warned.

It came as something of a revelation to Daniel that after all these years, his mother was really concerned about his father.

It was almost dawn when Daniel arrived home. He put the Cadillac away in the garage next to Anna's car and started for the house. Surprise struck him when he saw the open front door and deepened when he stepped inside the house. Chairs were overturned, furniture was in disarray. Then he remembered the fight with Moishe. This must have been how he had left the house, and Moishe had gone immediately afterward, forgetting to close the door.

Then Daniel looked at the mantelpiece over the fireplace. Two heavy silver candlesticks given to him and Anna as wedding presents had disappeared. Suspicion darkened his mind and he began to explore further. Other ornaments were missing, the silver *bucha*, with which he made *Kiddush* every Friday night, silver dishes, an inscribed gold plate which had been presented to Anna and himself after their opening night in *La Bohème* the previous season. He ran upstairs to the master bedroom. Drawers had been pulled out, the mattress pulled off the bed. Anna's jewelry box had been rifled. His gold cuff links were gone. And worst of all, Fat Benny's gold watch was missing.

The house had been burglarized.

Without looking any further, Daniel returned downstairs, straightened one of the chairs and sat down. Then he leaned back and simply stared blankly ahead in the silent room, his mind replaying the day's events—and Moishe's accusations—until he was numbed by them.

Chapter Thirteen

At seven the following morning, Moishe was frying eggs in the small kitchen of his apartment when the phone rang. He turned down the gas and answered. When he recognized Daniel's voice, he made himself ready for a continuation of hostilities by pushing his spare pair of glasses up to the bridge of his nose.

"What do you want now?" He would have done better to stay watching the eggs. This sonofabitch was going to ruin his breakfast as well. He ran his tongue across the two broken teeth and tenderly touched his broken nose.

"I want to apologize for last night," Daniel said meekly.

"You do, do you?" Moishe didn't know whether the feel of his own injuries, the obscured vision through his closed eye or Daniel's humility was giving him the courage to be aggressive. It didn't matter. On the phone he could say whatever he liked and not risk getting his lights punched out. "What makes you think I give a shit whether you're sorry or not?"

"Because I need your help."

"Huh?" Moishe couldn't help himself. This wasn't Daniel talking. It was Daniel's voice, sure, but the sentiments did not belong to him.

"I need your help," Daniel repeated. "I want to know where Anna and Benjamin are. My father's in the hospital again. And on top of all that, you didn't close the door when you left last night. The house got cleaned out."

"Got what?" Moishe was glad Daniel was miles away because he could not stop himself from letting out a satisfied laugh.

"Cleaned out. Robbed. You left the door open and someone walked off with half the house."

"Serves you goddamned right, asshole."

"Never mind about that. Just tell me where Anna is."

"I can't."

"You can't or you won't?"

"Won't, then. Not till you straighten yourself out with your stupid opera company. I promised Anna I wouldn't."

Daniel considered threats and discarded them. Moishe wasn't scared of him; he'd proved that the previous night. "Screw you, too, buddy." There was a long pause, then Daniel said, "Listen, I'm going to Montefiore to see my father this afternoon. He's in there because he got upset over Anna . . . over me. I don't want to see him before I've got everything straightened out."

"Then you'd better start off by seeing your friend Duguid. Because that's the only place for you to start." And Moishe hung up the receiver.

Daniel sat back in the chair and wondered what to do next. He supposed he should call the police about the burglary but the loss of material possessions was furthest from his mind. The loss of his family concerned him most. And the loss of Moishe as a friend. Not that he didn't deserve to lose them all. He'd gone out of his way to alienate everyone, that was for sure.

An apology, that's what Moishe said Duguid wanted. A simple apology. What was so terrible about that? Did it make him any less of a singer to apologize? Any less of a man?

Daniel recalled that Duguid liked to be first into the office every morning. He liked the feeling of having the opera house almost to himself at least once a day, even if only for a few minutes. Probably a dreamer, Daniel had once decided. Stands up on the stage when there's no one present and pretends he's Rodolfo or Canio. Pretends he's me.

Dreamer or not, this would be one morning Duguid would be disappointed. Because Daniel would be there before him.

Robin Duguid walked along the corridor from the reception area to his own office and stopped dead when he saw Daniel standing by the door. He recovered quickly and produced the key to his office.

"Good morning, Daniel. Something I can do for you?"

"Yes, sir. I'd like to talk to you if you can spare me a few minutes."

"Come in." Duguid led the way into the office and pointed to a chair. "Make yourself comfortable." He hung up his coat and sat down behind the desk, facing his visitor. There was no need to ask what Daniel wanted. Duguid could tell. Following the visit Duguid had received from Moishe, Daniel could be in the office for only one reason. The rebel had finally realized his error and had come to ask forgiveness. In his moment of triumph, Duguid knew no sensation of righteousness. All he could feel was relief.

"I'd like to come back to the Grand, Mr. Duguid."

"Yes?" The general manager made up his mind to offer no help. The apology had to come from Daniel, without any assistance from anyone else.

"I made a mistake with that movie. I wanted to get out of it, but I couldn't without getting entangled with a million lawsuits." Daniel hesitated and looked hopefully across the desk. Duguid's expression was cool, an indication that Daniel had not gone far enough.

"I want to apologize for the way I let the company down, Mr. Duguid. And to ask you to consider lifting your ban on me."

Duguid pursed his lips thoughtfully. "Thank you, Daniel. I promise I'll consider it."

Daniel debated whether to add anything else. As far as he was concered, he'd said more than enough already. Nonetheless, he could see that Duguid remained unconvinced of his sincerity. He supposed he could throw himself on the general manger's mercy, tell him about his father's hospitalization, about Anna taking the baby and leaving him. But his pride had suffered enough already; he had no intention of dragging himself even lower.

"Yes," Duguid repeated. "I'll consider it."

"I promise there'll be no repeat performances," Daniel blurted out.

For the first time in the meeting, Duguid smiled. "I'm certain there won't. From what I saw of your reviews for *South Side Serenade*, Carmel Studios wouldn't touch you again."

"They weren't very good, were they?" Daniel admitted. He began to find it easier to talk. The bridge between himself and Duguid had been crossed, the apology made. Now they were talking as equals. "They even killed the soundtrack."

"So I heard. A pity, because I would rather have liked to hear the music, to learn whether it's possible to anglicize and modernize opera," Duguid admitted. He stood up and Daniel followed suit, convinced that the meeting was already at an end. No doubt Duguid would inform his board that Daniel had made amends. Then there would be a message—probably a letter because Duguid believed in formality—asking him to come in for contract discussions regarding next season. Daniel didn't even know what productions were being planned for next season. Anna would, though; she'd be making her comeback then. Anna. He had to see her as well, tell her about the meeting with Duguid, persuade her that he had done enough.

As he started to walk toward the door, Duguid called him back. "On the subject of reviews, you might have noticed that our *Turandots* haven't been faring very well either."

Daniel stopped and turned around, stomach twisting, praying that his mind was not playing tricks by imagining what was not there. "I didn't read them," he lied.

"They were terrible, take my word for it." Duguid smiled thinly as he saw through Daniel's denial. Of course Daniel would have read them; and he would have laughed over them. Duguid was glad to see the tact in Daniel's answer; it was another sign of his sincerity. "You will sing Calaf for this Saturday's matinée performance."

Daniel understood how much the offer meant to Duguid. *Turandot* was the general manager's first solo production at the Grand. Although the opening night performance had received reviews that were polite more than complimentary, the two performances since then had been panned. Critics had complained that the young tenor singing Calaf possessed a voice that was too thin. Furthermore, the Saturday afternoon performances were broadcast live on the radio. Duguid wanted the best at his disposal for the broadcast; with one outstanding performance, he would be able to salvage the production from the previous ravages of the critics. "Thank you, Mr. Duguid. I can handle the role. I won't let you down."

"I'm certain you won't." Duguid held out his hand to seal the bargain. "The last time we shook hands it was on a rather somber note. This time we're both happier in our minds that an honorable settlement has been reached. Welcome back."

Daniel grabbed the hand, scared that it might be withdrawn

and the offer with it. His apology had been accepted, his return assured. All he had to do now was convince Anna.

He left the opera house and drove the few blocks north to Times Square. The receptionist in the law office recognized him and asked him to take a seat while she checked whether Mr. Waterman was busy. Daniel fidgeted awkwardly while he waited. Finally the woman reappeared and told him to go in.

Moishe was staring out of the window, his back to the door. Hearing Daniel enter he turned around. Two purple eyes gazed out mournfully from behind the spare pair of glasses; one eye was almost completely closed. "See what you did, asshole!" he greeted Daniel. "And this!" He stepped closer to Daniel and touched his nose gingerly, to show where it had been broken. "I'm going to need a goddamned nose job, thanks to you. And this as well!" He opened his mouth to display the two broken front teeth and the battered lips. "Serves you right you got robbed. Pity they didn't take you as well."

Daniel held up his hands in a gesture of peace. "I'll pay to get your teeth capped," he promised. "I'll pay to get your nose straightened. Don't worry about it."

"And the glasses you smashed. Don't forget the glasses. Those frames set me back a fortune."

"I'll buy you a hundred pairs of glasses, a whole store! Just tell me where Anna is."

"What about Duguid?"

"I just came from there. I'm in *Turandot* for this Saturday's matinee performance."

Moishe studied Daniel's face, searching for the truth.

"If you don't believe me, call the Grand and ask!" Daniel grabbed the phone. Fingers fumbling in their haste, he spun the dial.

"Grand Opera Company box office," a woman's voice answered.

"Who's in *Turandot* for this Saturday's matinee?" He held the receiver between himself and Moishe so they could both hear.

"Just a moment, sir, I'll check." The woman came back an instant later. "There's been a cast change, sir. Daniel Kerr will be returning to sing Calaf."

"Thank you."

"Statler Hilton," Moishe said. "She's registered under the name of"—he began to smile—"Anna Wasserman."

No wonder he'd had no luck the previous night when he'd called the Statler Hilton. Anna Wasserman. What was it, a private joke on Moishe's part? Or wishful thinking? "Thanks, I'll speak to you later."

"What about your father?" Moishe called after him.

"I'm going up there right after I've seen Anna. I'll take her with me. That's the best medicine he could get."

"Good luck!" Moishe called out. He meant it. The unpleasantness of the night was over. If it had taken getting the hell beaten out of him to set Daniel straight with his career and Anna, it was worth it. He called out to the receptionist to set up an appointment with the dentist. If Daniel was paying, Moishe wouldn't settle for having the broken teeth simply capped.

He'd have gold.

Anna was playing with the baby when she heard the urgent rapping on the door. She put down the child and listened carefully. The knock did not sound like someone from the hotel. Or Moishe; he would have telephoned. It could only be Daniel.

"Yes?" she called out.

"Anna, it's me. I want to speak to you."

"Who told you I was here?"

"Moishe. I've been to see Duguid. Everything's straightened out."

Wanting to believe him, she opened the door. He pushed in gently and put his arms around her. She was surprised to see tears glistening wetly in his eyes. Then he looked past her to his son. "I've come to take you all home," Daniel said. "And to say sorry for the way I've been carrying on."

"What about Mr. Duguid?"

"I saw him first thing this morning. We're friends now. I'm in *Turandot* this Saturday."

"The radio broadcast? That's only three days away. You'd better get your voice in shape, make sure you know the role. There's no time for rehearsals. We'll start as soon as we get back to the house," she said quickly, her enthusiasm mounting.

Daniel shook his head and told her they first had to go to the hospital. She looked shocked when he explained that his father had been taken ill again.

"Whenever I have a bust-up, he's the one who always suffers."

Then he told Anna that the house had been burglarized while he'd been out searching for her. She started to grin, then covered her face with her hands as laughter rippled through her.

"Thank God we're insured," she finally managed to say.

"We're not. I forgot to renew the policy."

She laughed even harder.

Once the housekeeper had been sent back to New Jersey with the baby in a taxi, Anna and Daniel drove up to the Bronx. They picked up Yetta and continued to Montefiore Hospital. Isaac was sitting up in bed, looking cheerful when they entered. He saw Anna and waved excitedly, beckoning for her to come closer.

"You malingering again?" she asked brightly. "A young man like you spending all this time in bed! Shame on you!"

"Ah!" Isaac said in disgust. "I'm protesting, that's all. When Daniel sings again, I'll get out of bed to hear him."

"You'd better hurry up and find your clothes, then," Anna told him. "He's in the Grand's Saturday afternoon broadcast performance."

"*Turandot*," Daniel explained. "I had a meeting with Robin Duguid first thing this morning and we're all squared away."

"You sure you can step into the part after being away for so long?" Isaac wanted to know.

Daniel nodded instantly. Despite the confident way he'd assured Duguid he could handle the role, the same anxieties were plaguing him. He'd be damned if he'd let his father know, however.

"Good," Isaac said. He turned to the man in the next bed. "I won't be in this lousy place come Saturday, but you make sure you listen to my son, Daniel Kerr, on the Grand Opera broadcast. Okay?"

The man looked bemused but said he would.

Chapter Fourteen

Isaac had to be helped by Anna and Yetta to his seat in the circle on Saturday afternoon. The doctor had been loath to discharge him from Montefiore. Isaac had argued and had finally signed a waiver of responsibility. He still felt weak and could not walk without the aid of a cane. Nevertheless, he was determined not to miss his son's return performance.

He sat down and looked around the almost empty auditorium. Only a scattering of people had so far taken their seats. The performance was not due to begin for another forty-five minutes, and Isaac was struck by the awesome silence of the opera house when it was empty. It allowed his imagination to play tricks, to lift the heavy gold curtain and impose his own characters on the stage, in his own opera. He could see Daniel playing Eleazar in *La Juive*, with Anna as Rachel. Closing his eyes, Isaac offered up a prayer to God that he might live long enough to see that production. It was just a wish, though. One that he felt would not be fulfilled. Daniel had never made any serious mention of wanting to perform the role. It was a killer. Look what it had done to Caruso! And the Grand, to Isaac's knowledge, had never discussed the feasibility of resurrecting it.

If they did a production of *La Juive*, it would have to be soon, Isaac knew. He'd kidded Daniel about it. Told him he'd have to hurry with the part if he wanted his father to see it. Only it wasn't really a joke. Despite the way he'd walked out of Montefiore Hospital, telling the doctor he felt as sprightly as a two-year-old, Isaac knew his heart was failing. He'd worked too hard, seen too much sorrow for it to be any other way. The other night hadn't helped either, although he would never blame Daniel for the second attack. Daniel had come to the one person he trusted the most, his father. How could a father refuse to help his son? He'd have gone willingly into the cold to search for Anna if Daniel had thought it would help.

Anna's voice intruded on his thoughts. "I'm going backstage to be with Daniel."

Isaac smiled at her. He knew how hard Anna had worked with Daniel over the past three days to prepare him for this return. She had told Isaac when Daniel had stopped vocalizing, ceased practicing in the depths of his depression. The sessions with Anna had been long and painful, with Daniel constantly complaining that he had lost his voice. Anna had persisted, going over the score again and again until she was satisfied. Daniel was like an athlete deciding to come out of retirement to run against the best in a mile race, and giving himself only three days to tone his body into peak fitness. Maybe he wouldn't win the race, but Anna had made damned sure he'd finish in style.

"Tell him I'm praying for him," Isaac said.

"I will." She walked away, leaving Isaac and Yetta alone in the circle, two solitary figures in the vastness of the auditorium. When she reached the exit, she looked back and could barely make out their shapes. She hurried to the dressing rooms and found Daniel sitting disconsolately in front of the mirror, already in costume and make-up.

"What's the matter?"

"Worried," was the one-word reply.

"What about?" She pulled up a chair and sat down next to him. "This is your big chance to kill them stone-dead. You've got no cause to be worried."

He turned to look at her, his face frightened behind the false beard and heavy make-up. "I'm more scared than ever of going out there. Scared I'll forget the words, miss a note, fall over a loose prop and break my neck. Everything."

"Don't be ridiculous. You wanted to come back. Now you're back. Come on, it's time to do your exercises."

Feeling like a man preparing for the scaffold, Daniel stood up and began to vocalize. Despite knowing his voice sounded almost as clear as it ever had, he could not shake off a feeling of impending catastrophe. Surely his vocal cords must have suffered from the abuse he'd subjected them to. Duguid should have given him more time, not just three days' notice. If something went wrong, it wouldn't be his fault but Duguid's.

Only it would be Daniel whom the critics would lambast. Or was that what Duguid was hoping for? That he'd make a fool of himself?

"It sounds fine to me, Daniel," Anna said, listening carefully. "Don't even think about the opera. Just think about afterwards, when everyone will be on your side again and *South Side Serenade* will have been forgotten."

Daniel grew more confident as he listened to her words.

"Think about Benjamin. He's waiting for you at home. He's expecting a hero to come back."

"And what about you?"

"Think about me as well. And your parents. Moishe, too."

Instead, Daniel thought briefly about the two shots of whiskey he'd always enjoyed before a performance. There was none today. Anna had made sure of that.

He stood in front of the mirror, thinking about what she had said. He breathed in deeply and puffed out his chest. The nervous tension still ran through his body, but now he knew how to cope.

At two o'clock, Moishe tuned in for the radio broadcast of *Turandot*. He didn't have the slightest idea what the words meant. He wasn't even sure about the story. All he wanted to do was listen to Daniel's voice, to learn if he could live through the holocaust he'd created for himself.

He held his breath as Daniel's voice first came from the radio speaker. The snatches of music, short duets, told him nothing. He waited patiently for one aria, "Non piangere, Liù," when he would be able to decide if Daniel had retained the quality.

When the aria began, Moishe sat up tensely, eyes closed, fists clenched as he willed Daniel to succeed. The voice coming from the radio started off uncertainly and Moishe cursed. Then it seemed to gather strength and sweetness as the aria continued. At last, it coalesced into the silver clear and vibrantly warm tenor that Moishe had always associated with Daniel.

"Sonofabitch!" he yelled triumphantly into the apartment, eyes gleaming in the triumph he felt for his friend. "That sonofabitch did it!"

He leaped off the chair and jumped into the air, yelling encouragement at the radio. He'd call Daniel that night and drive over to the house. They'd all have dinner together. It would be just like old times.

During the intermission preceding the third act, Isaac allowed his eyelids to droop. He sensed rather than saw other members of the audience moving about him as they went outside for refreshments or a smoke. He was too tired to move. He wanted to conserve his strength for the last act, the most enjoyable of the entire opera as far as Isaac was concerned. Daniel was beyond comparison with Caruso now. Caruso had died before Puccini wrote *Turandot.* For once, Isaac knew that his judgment would not be clouded with comparisons.

He heard applause as the conductor returned to his rostrum. The noise grew in volume as the conductor signaled the entire orchestra to stand. Isaac opened his eyes again, mind refreshed by the short rest. He glanced sideways at Yetta, whose eyes were riveted on the stage.

"Enjoying it?" he asked.

"He's lucky," Yetta said. "All that he did to himself and they've given him another chance. He should get down on his knees and thank everyone."

Isaac smiled and turned to Anna. "What do you think?"

"He's singing like an angel." He was—he was singing as well, if not better than she had ever heard him. He'd started hesitantly and she'd caught him looking toward the prompter's box a few times. Then he'd picked up strength, gathering it from the rest of the cast, the audience, the opera house itself, until he'd broken free of his bonds during "Non piangere, Liù."

Anna's description satisfied Isaac. He knew there were no angels, but if there were, they would sound like Daniel did this afternoon.

The curtain lifted and the final act began. Isaac felt the warm wetness of a tear beginning to form in his right eye. He made no attempt to stop its flow. It rolled down his cheek and caught the corner of his mouth. He could taste the salt. Too late he pulled out a handkerchief and dabbed at his eyes. With the passage of the first tear, the flow had grown. He put away the handkerchief and let the tears fall unchecked.

So what if people saw him cry? They'd seen him cry during *Bohème*. It wouldn't do them any harm to see him cry again.

The orchestra's triumphant refrain thundered in on the final *"Vincero!"* of "Nessun dorma" and Daniel did something he had never done before. Disregarding the discipline that had been drummed into him by Roger Hammersley, he faced the audience and took a solemn bow.

The audience responded to the unexpected action by increasing the volume of its ovation. Daniel glanced swiftly at the orchestra. The musicians had set aside their instruments and were joining in! Welcoming him home by sharing in the audience's applause! He caught the eye of the conductor. Daniel nodded and the man lifted his baton, ready to end the applause and continue the act.

Then, from somewhere in the circle, a woman screamed.

Anna clapped her hands enthusiastically when Daniel bowed. He'd broken the Grand's tradition and got away with it. Capped his successful return by doing what no one else dared to do. Accept applause by taking a bow. Her gaze strayed to Duguid's private box. The light in the box was on and Anna could see Duguid and his party. All were clapping; two of the women in the box were even standing, calling praise down onto the stage. Anna had known Duguid would let Daniel get away with the bow. The prodigal son had returned home duly repentant. He'd turned in a performance that would never be forgotten. And at the same time he'd shown that he still wasn't above tweaking a few noses.

She turned her head a fraction to look at Daniel's parents. Yetta was applauding, a formal action that held none of the spontaneity others were injecting into the ovation. It was a major aria, and major arias were always applauded; so Yetta was applauding. It was as simple as that. Then Anna looked at her father-in-law. At first, she was curious why he was doing nothing. She had heard him sniff, seen the tears start at the beginning of the act. The show of emotion was understandable.

She'd even felt like crying herself. Was Isaac so overcome now that he couldn't even clap his hands?

She looked closer. Isaac's cheeks were glistening from the tears, but his head was bowed as if he were praying. She reached out and took his hand. As she pulled it toward herself, Isaac's body toppled in the seat and fell against her.

It was then she screamed.

Robin Duguid stood uncomfortably in front of the closed gold curtain and looked out into the darkness of the auditorium. He was unused to such silence. Whenever he had walked out into this position before, his appearance in the spotlight had always been greeted with groans of displeasure because the audience knew he had to announce that a leading singer would not be playing the role advertised. The general manager only appeared with bad tidings.

"Ladies and gentlemen," Duguid began quietly, wondering if they could hear him in the rear of the balcony. "On April the twenty-fifth, 1926, when *Turandot* was first performed at La Scala, in Milan, the conductor was Arturo Toscanini. On that occasion, he laid down his baton in the third act after the death of Liù and said to the audience: 'Here at this point, Giacomo Puccini broke off his work. Death on this occasion was stronger than art.' Today, unfortunately, death is again stronger than art.

"As some of you may now be aware, Mr. Kerr's father has passed away during this performance. Although Mr. Kerr has professed willingness to continue with the final act, it is my feeling that it would be most respectful if we emulated Maestro Toscanini. Thank you all very much for listening to me. Good day."

Duguid stayed in front of the curtain while he watched members of the audience rise and begin to leave the suddenly silent auditorium. Then he turned away and walked quickly up the stairs to the dressing rooms.

Daniel couldn't feel a thing. From the moment he had heard the scream of horror from the circle, his world had collapsed. Even without knowing who had screamed, some inner sense had warned him that he would be affected.

There had been immediate consternation in the audience. The lights had come on and he'd looked up to the circle where his parents and Anna were sitting. He'd spotted the green of Anna's long dress as she bent over his father. Attendants had come cascading down the aisle. He had followed the drama from the stage, now part of the audience to another production. A man's voice—Daniel supposed it was one of the attendants—had yelled down that it was his father. He had jumped off the stage, rushed through the orchestra pit and raced up the stairs to the circle. A doctor was already there, a woman who had been sitting in the row behind. When Daniel pushed his way through the throng of people, the woman had looked at him with despair in her eyes.

He remembered telling Duguid that he would carry on. God knows how he would have managed it, though. He barely had the strength to return to the dressing room and fall into the chair. They would have had to carry him back to the stage. Duguid had rejected the idea immediately, before going onstage to announce the abrupt termination of the performance. Daniel was grateful to the general manager; it hadn't even crossed Duguid's mind to let the understudy complete the final act. If Isaac knew that his passing had been elevated to the level of Puccini's, he'd be thrilled, Daniel reflected.

"The ambulance has come."

Anna's soft voice made Daniel look up. Her face was tear-stained, a mirror of his own. He had made no attempt to check the tears that had started as soon as he'd arrived in the circle and seen the woman doctor's face. "My mother?" he asked.

"She went with him." Anna watched him warily, guessing the tumult in his mind . . . that Isaac's death had been caused by the way Daniel had behaved; or by the way she'd left him that night, taking the baby. Daniel always had to find a reason for everything bad that happened to him. Anna wondered which way he would swing.

He reached out suddenly, grasped her around the waist and buried his face in her breasts. She could feel him shake, feel the dampness of his tears as they penetrated the fabric of her dress. Before he could say a word, she knew he was taking the blame all on his own.

"That goddamned stupid movie!" he cursed. "All because I took that goddamned stupid offer! If I hadn't gone, none of this would have happened." His grip became tighter until it threatened to crush the breath out of her. She let him hold on, gazing up at the white-painted ceiling until at last she closed her eyes.

"Stop it, Daniel," she whispered. "Don't say that."

He didn't seem to hear her. He kept repeating over and over "That goddamned movie!" until at last the words became quiet, less distinct.

A knock sounded on the dressing room door. Gently Anna eased herself out of Daniel's arms and walked slowly to the door. "Who is it?"

"Robin Duguid. May I come in?"

Anna turned around to look at Daniel. His head was on the dressing table top as he sobbed quietly into his arms. She opened the door a fraction and looked out. "What do you want?"

"How is he?" Duguid tried to look past Anna. She blocked his view.

"Upset. Is it something important?"

Duguid shook his head. "Tell him if he needs anything to contact me. I'm sorry."

"Thank you." She closed the door and returned to Daniel. "I think we'd better go. Your mother also needs you."

Daniel raised his head from the table and looked at Anna through red-rimmed eyes. He understood that she felt the shock as deeply as he did and looked for some way to ease her grief; his own as well. Finally he pointed to Calaf's costume that he still wore and to the make-up on his face. "Do you think I should change before we go? Or should I go like this?"

A feeling of unity passed between them at his words. Anna held out both hands. He took them, brushing them against his lips. Thank God he had Anna. He couldn't even begin to think what this would be like without her.

The house in Teaneck was crowded. Daniel, his brother Jack who had flown in from Chicago for the funeral, and Yetta

Kirschbaum sat on small wooden chairs, accepting condolences from visitors.

The *shivah* period was in its third day. Evening prayers had just finished and everyone was sitting down. Cups of coffee were appearing, passed around as the housekeeper took charge of the kitchen. Daniel tried to spot Anna, wanting to ask her how the baby was. He could not see her and guessed she was in the kitchen, helping the housekeeper.

Since the funeral, Yetta had hardly spoken a word to him. When he had followed her to the hospital on the day of Isaac's death, she'd hysterically accused him of causing it. Anna had stepped in quickly, leading Daniel away, knowing how troubled he was already by the possibility. During the funeral—at the same New Jersey cemetery where Fat Benny and Tessie were buried—Yetta had remained aloof to all that was taking place around her. Daniel had cried. So had Jack. Tears were the only bond between them; otherwise they treated each other as strangers, polite exchanges of words about work and family.

Daniel looked up as a cup of coffee was passed to him. Moishe was acting as waiter, eyes still purple, nose swollen, teeth still broken. He gave a weak, encouraging smile as he passed across the cup and touched Daniel's hand lightly. Daniel nodded his thanks, knowing how grateful he should feel to Moishe. Old reliable. Always there when you needed him; and sometimes when you reckoned you didn't. The thought brought a slight smile to Daniel's face. Moishe had been waiting inside the house when they had arrived home on Saturday night. He had heard the commotion over the radio and rushed to the opera house to find that everyone had already left. No one could tell him which hospital Daniel had gone to, so he had driven to Teaneck to wait there, the offer to help in any way he could springing from his lips the moment Daniel and Anna arrived there.

"I'll take your mother home tonight," Moishe offered, as he had done every night. Yetta refused to stay in Teaneck. Both Daniel and Anna had insisted, but Yetta had firmly rejected the idea. She had her own home; she was perfectly capable of taking care of herself. The sentiment was new to Daniel's ears. This was a moment when his mother should be bringing into play every act she could, every frailty that would assure her of attention. Instead, she was backing away. He was certain he knew why. She did blame him for Isaac's death. It hadn't been just hysteria that had made her shriek at him in the hospital. She'd meant it.

Because of it, Daniel felt sorry for his brother. Not wanting his mother to be alone in the house, he had sent Jack with her each night. As a dutiful son, Jack had gone. Daniel knew he had not been happy about the chore. What would happen when Jack flew back to Chicago and his own family at the end of the *shivah* was anyone's guess, Daniel decided. He had a career to get on with again. Anna also had her career.

And they both had a child to share.

Part Three

La Juive

Chapter One

Richard Milhous Nixon and John Fitzgerald Kennedy were dominating the news again. Daniel was getting sick of the sight of the two names. No matter which newspaper he read, which radio program he listened to, which television station he watched, the names of the two presidential candidates plagued him. Even the New York Board of Rabbis was getting into the act now, according to the story on the front page of that Saturday's New York *Times*.

A man's religion had never been a factor in a presidential race before, Daniel thought, while he read about the rabbis deploring any attempts to inject religious conflict into the current campaign. To his memory, though, the country had never had a major Catholic candidate either. If Kennedy got the vote two months in the future, the country would have its first Catholic president. Good luck to him, Daniel decided, knowing he'd probably vote for the Massachusetts senator. Just give us all a break from the damned thing.

He flicked through the newspaper. Miami was getting slammed by Hurricane Donna. He wondered if his mother was all right and prayed that the weather did not get so bad that she would come back up north. He'd done the clever thing by shipping her off to Miami where she could sit and chatter all day long with other old women and stay out of his hair.

Kennedy and Nixon. There they were again, on page ten, a story about the television and radio debates they would have. What were the political campaigns of the country becoming? A three-ring circus?

Eager to escape, he moved on to the sports page, past the results from the Rome Olympics. A smile lit his face. The Yankees were doing it again, beating the Tigers, 4-1, to get within a half game of the league-leading Orioles. He'd have to take Benjamin to a Yankee game one of these days. The kid was old enough now to understand what was going on, and he had been promising him. He'd wait till Maris or Mantle hit one a mile, then he'd casually tell Benjamin about Ruth and Gehrig. How they used to bunt that far.

Thinking of Benjamin, Daniel put down the newspaper and left the den, looking for his son. The kid should be almost ready by now, all dressed up for his regular Saturday morning visit to the temple. Daniel did not understand where Benjamin had inherited his religious zeal; certainly not from himself or Anna. Although he no longer conducted High Holy Day services at Temple Isaiah in Paterson, Daniel attended services in the local temple in Teaneck. But he had never shown the ardent love for religion that his young son did. Ever since Daniel had first taken him, the kid had been turned on by the history of the Jews and by the tradition of their religion. Hebrew classes, which Daniel had loathed when he was Benjamin's age, were like an outing to the shore for his son. At nine years old he could stand up in the *shul* and take the service all by himself.

Daniel called Benjamin's name. His son's high voice came back from upstairs; he was still getting dressed. Daniel grinned. The kid was like this every *Shabbos* morning, a bridegroom making certain that every last detail was perfect before he finally met his bride. Still grinning, he returned to the den to continue reading the newspaper until Benjamin was ready.

He glanced quickly, disinterestedly, at some more stories. Nikita Khrushchev was on his way to New York to head the Soviet Union's delegation to the United States. The *mamzer* should take a *misse meshinah,* Daniel wished; drop dead before his boat ever docks in New York.

His attention was attracted by a British movie called *Carry on Nurse.* After perusing the report, Daniel decided not to bother seeing it.

A familiar face on page twenty-one startled his eyes. The three words, "Italian Operatic Roles" shrieked at him from the top left hand corner. Daniel stopped turning pages. A choking sensation enveloped him. A pounding started in his head and chest as he read the complete headline:

Jussi Bjoerling of Met is Dead;
Noted for Italian Operatic Roles

Bjoerling was dead at forty-nine, swept away in his summer home on the island of Siar Oe, in the Stockholm Archipelago, by the third of a swift succession of heart attacks.

Daniel felt dazed as he read and reread the lengthy story in the *Times*. The uncomfortable knowledge of his own mortality brushed against him for an instant and he shuddered. Bjoerling had been only four years older than himself. Now the voice that had thrilled a worldwide audience for thirty years was still.

He heard the door of the den open and looked around. His son stood in the doorway, sparkling clean, dressed in a short-trousered gray suit. "I'm ready to go, Pa."

Suddenly Daniel did not feel like taking Benjamin to the temple. He did not feel like moving out of the chair. He wanted to sit, to be alone with his memories, to think about the death of his contemporary, the man who had been one of his inspirations to become an opera singer himself. "Ask your mother to walk you down to the *shul*, will you, Benny? I don't feel so good."

Daniel felt guilty at disappointing the kid. At the same time, he knew he was robbing himself of one of the pleasures of being a father. He enjoyed the times he went to the temple with Benjamin, the short walk where they would talk about baseball, about school, about anything; it did not matter just as long as they talked. Then, in the temple, he'd get a huge kick out of witnessing his son's enjoyment, the total absorption in the service and everything around him. If he went this morning, though, Daniel knew he would be silent throughout the service, too caught up with the tragic news to communicate anything but grief.

"What's the matter with you?" Anna asked after Benjamin had relayed the message.

"This. Take a look at it." He held up page twenty-one for Anna to see. She sucked in her breath in shock as she read of Bjoerling's death.

"So young," she murmured. "Such a terrible waste."

Daniel understood what she meant. The *Times* report had not mentioned it, but the stories of Bjoerling's drinking problems were almost legendary. The insecurity that had plagued him, particularly toward the end of his career. The abrupt dives into the bottle as if he could find the answers there. Daniel had come close enough to know how it felt. He had been lucky, though. He had managed to make the return journey.

He heard the front door close as Anna left the house with Benjamin. From the kitchen came the noise of the housekeeper cleaning up after breakfast. Daniel paid no attention, his mind riveted on one subject. With Bjoerling gone, who was left? Tucker and Peerce, the brothers-in-law. Del Monaco. Bergonzi. Di Stefano. Himself. Three Italians and three New York Jews. And Gedda, a Russian-Swede. And soon how many of those tenors would be left? And who would take their places? More cantors? More Italians?

Roger Hammersley was also dead, another heart attack victim. So was Harry Feldman from Paterson; when he had died, Daniel had ceased to conduct the High Holy Day services at Temple Isaiah. Gigli was dead as well. Many of the father figures, the men Daniel had looked up to or tried to emulate had died during the fifties, just like his own father. Now Bjoerling had started off the sixties in the same manner. Daniel allowed himself the luxury of becoming maudlin while he wondered who would still be around when the seventies began. His mother? If she was, she'd be in her middle-eighties. Somehow the knowledge that Yetta Kirschbaum would probably die before the end of the decade did not bother Daniel. She was living in Miami with money he sent her each month in addition to her Social Security. If he saw her once a year, it was a lot. When she needed anything, she telephoned him. And when the Grand's tour encompassed Florida, she always expected free tickets to each performance so she could point Daniel out to her friends. Daniel felt that being on show like that was a small price to pay for not seeing his mother for the remainder of the year.

Daniel thought about Martinelli, retired from his practice in Milan. The last time they had met was two years earlier, when Anna and Benjamin had accompanied him to Milan where he had sung Radames in *Aïda* at La Scala. Martinelli had shared the honors of the performance after Daniel had insisted on introducing the doctor from the stage as the man who had been instrumental in making him select an operatic career. Martinelli had loved it; so had the audience and the Italian press. Now Daniel was forced to think about Martinelli in another, darker light. Would the last of the people who had been responsible for his career be alive when the sixties ended?

He thought about Moishe as well. Would that clown be around when the sixties passed into history? And finally, reluctantly, he focused on himself. Would Daniel Kerr be alive when the big ball dropped in Times Square to celebrate the birth of 1970? Of course he would; he laughed at his own fears. Life without himself wasn't possible. Then he realized that Bjoerling had probably thought the same thing only a year earlier, before the heart attacks had started to shake his faith.

Daniel's mood of weeping sentimentality changed slowly to regret. There was really so little time left and so many things to do. At forty-five, his life was well past the halfway mark and he had not done one tenth of the things he'd promised himself he would do. There were still countless roles he wanted to perform, places he wanted to visit, stages upon which he wanted to sing. He had started late, that was the trouble; he had let too many years elapse. If only he could have known earlier what he wanted to do with his life. All that precious time wasted, playing the clubs with Moishe. Even the years spent on the *bima* praising God had been wasted; he could see that now. He should have met Martinelli earlier, listened to him earlier. Or listened to his father, who had loved the world of grand opera just as dearly as the Italian did. Why did his final decision have to wait until a German flying bomb had dumped an American soldier into a hospital in Britain so an Italian doctor could explain the beauty of opera and start him on a road he should have taken a lifetime earlier? Even Lucy! Why hadn't he listened to what Lucy had tried to tell him?

He read the story in the *Times* yet again and recalled the occasions he had seen Bjoerling at the Met. The Swede had not possessed outstanding stage presence. Daniel, with the advantage of height, knew he possessed more. But the wondrous instrument of Bjoerling's voice had more than compensated for what he lacked in stature and dramatic talent. Each season had added even more style and technique to his singing, and somehow the voice had never showed signs of darkening, never achieved the downward movement toward the baritone range that affected so many tenors. Daniel knew his own voice was beginning to darken, becoming richer yet deeper. It was a natural, physiological transformation that came with age, affecting some more than others. He had made up his mind to quit if it showed signs of becoming too deep, like Caruso's had done. Daniel wanted to be remembered as a true tenor, not as a baritone changeling.

As he stood up the newspaper fell to the floor, its pages scattering across the carpet. Stepping carefully to avoid the pages, he walked to the phonograph. The recording he selected was Bjoerling's "E lucevan le stelle" from *Tosca*. This time Daniel did not seem to notice how much it resembled "Avalon." Nor did the music bring to mind Lucy's dramatic plunge from the window of the house in Paterson. He just thought of Bjoerling and of the story in the *Times*. The Swede had been scheduled to sing in *Manon Lescaut* the following month at the Met; now a replacement would get his big chance.

When the track finished, Daniel selected another. From the *Turandot* Bjoerling had only recently recorded with Birgit Nilsson and the Rome Opera House Orchestra and Chorus, Daniel played "Nessun dorma." No tenor had ever sung it like Bjoerling; not even himself. No tenor ever would again.

Anna returned from taking Benjamin to the temple to find Daniel still sitting in the den. Tears cascaded down his face.

"Hey, you've got a recital tonight." She tapped him gently on the shoulder. "Carnegie Hall's expecting Daniel Kerr, not Johnny Ray."

He felt her touch but could not tear himself away from the poignant memories aroused by the voice and the music. His father had died during "Nessun dorma." Now Bjoerling, too, was dead.

Anna tried again. "Daniel, you've got a recital tonight. Don't get yourself all upset." She had not seen him this despondent since the days of his fight with Robin Duguid and the Grand's management. He had lost a god, she realized that.

A fellow artist whom he had looked up to, whom he had tried to emulate because he thought he was the best.

"So I have." He wiped his eyes with a handkerchief and stood up to clasp his arms around Anna. "But I'm still allowed a brief period of mourning for a departed comrade, aren't I?"

"Sure you are." She stood on tiptoe to kiss him. The early morning sunlight shining in through the den window highlighted the gray that was spreading along the sides of his thick mane of hair. If she met him now for the first time, she knew she'd fall in love with him all over again. The only difference was that it would happen quicker this time. While other couples had drifted apart, she and Daniel had grown closer together, tied by more than just respect and love. They shared everything, their work, each other's experiences on stage. Anna knew that without Daniel she would be Laurel without Hardy, Crosby without Hope, me without my shadow; and she was strengthened by the knowledge that his devotion to her was just as fierce.

When she had first met him—the indignant novice who refused to make his operatic debut in anything but a lead role—she had been intrigued by his stubborn tenacity, the dogged determination to stick it out no matter what the cost. He had been a fighter, even if sometimes in his enthusiasm he picked the wrong causes to champion. Now he was approaching the level of a respected elder statesman, an established artist the new generation of singers could look up to, admire, use as their own inspiration, as Daniel had done with Bjoerling. Because of it, Anna loved him even more.

"What time will you be home from the city?" she asked.

"Around eleven, eleven-thirty." He was disappointed that she would not be accompanying him, but the housekeeper had been promised this particular evening off for months and the babysitter had come down with a cold the previous night. Daniel would give Anna's ticket to Moishe instead, make him sit through the recital.

"Will you eat dinner before you leave, or shall I hold it till you get back?"

"When I get back." He'd stop off at a delicatessen for a couple of sandwiches on the way in, or maybe he'd eat at the

Russian Tea Room.

"No snacks," she warned, reading his mind.

"No snacks." It amused Daniel that after all these years, Anna was still fighting the battle of his bulge. For her own sake, he allowed her to believe she was winning, although his weight never seemed to drop below two-twenty these days. It was his metabolism, he claimed. Even if she starved him on a diet of dry crackers and water, he wouldn't get any thinner. She accepted his story and knew all along that he was cheating. But if she hadn't managed to change him yet, she reasoned, what chance did she have now?

The gnawing possibility of his own death preoccupied Daniel throughout the entire journey to the city that evening. He knew the idea was preposterous. He should be laughing at the very thought. He was in the best of health. The last check-up, two months earlier, had assured him of that. Just watch your weight, the doctor had advised. He had nothing to worry about. Aware of the strain that being a lyric tenor put on the heart, Daniel watched his health carefully. Still, he could not bring himself to laugh. Reading in the *Times* of Bjoerling's sudden death—even if the Swede had suffered previous heart attacks—had guided Daniel's own mind down an unwelcome but inescapable avenue.

Death happened to everyone, sure; other than taxes it was the only certainty in life. He'd never worried about it before, though. The possibility itself was not so terrifying, he reflected; it was just the knowledge that he was thinking about it all.

He parked the car in a lot on West Fifty-sixth Street, stopped in at a delicatessen to pick up a pastrami sandwich and a cup of coffee and then hurried to Carnegie Hall, acutely conscious of the curious stares that followed his white tie and tails. Everyone probably thought he was a waiter at some restaurant. Maybe he'd have been smarter to wear a light topcoat or carry a change of clothes. After leaving the spare ticket for Moishe, Daniel made his way to the dressing room. He was very early, but he had decided on some last minute changes to the published program and needed time to go over them with the conductor.

A few minutes before the scheduled commencement of the recital at eight o'clock, Daniel stood in the wings and watched the conductor take center stage, his back to the orchestra.

"Ladies and gentlemen. By now you are all aware of the tragic passing of Jussi Bjoerling."

A slight murmur from the audience greeted the conductor's words. He waited patiently for silence.

"To honor the memory of this magnificent artist, Mr. Kerr will now open his recital with 'Cuius animam' from Rossini's *Stabat Mater*. Mr. Kerr asks that instead of applauding, you remain silent for one minute after the completion of the work." The conductor took up his position on the rostrum, baton raised. Daniel walked out solemnly from the wings.

Never before had he experienced a silence that was so complete. It would be so easy to believe that the auditorium was empty, that it was not filled with people who were expectantly waiting to hear him sing. The silence emanated a power of its own, an eerie, intangible force that reached out to embrace and smother him just as strongly as any enthusiastic ovation could ever do. For several seconds he allowed the utter quiet to sweep over him, to lull him. This reverential silence alone was homage to Bjoerling. Every member of the audience, the orchestra, the Carnegie Hall employees, were sparing a few moments of their own lives to remember one man. Many, like Daniel, had seen Bjoerling at the Met. Others, less fortunate, had heard him only on record. Now they were all joined as one to show their respect for the man who only two days earlier had been the world's outstanding tenor, but who was now only a treasured memory.

Daniel moved his head a fraction in a signal to the conductor. The baton fell and the slow, dramatic sound of Rossini's music filled the hall. "Cuius animam" was a work Daniel had never sung before, never thought he would sing although he was familiar with it. As a boy, he had sung "Ave Maria" in the school choir, but since his first days in the B'Nai Yeshurun choir under Kawolsky, he had never performed Christian liturgical music. The Latin words sounded strange to his ears, felt strange to his lips. The unaccustomed repetition of words and lines took up all of his concentration, did not allow him time to think how he sounded.

One member of the audience forgot about the conductor's request for no applause. A single handclap rang out, embarrassingly loud, as Daniel ended the hymn; it was just as abruptly terminated as the culprit remembered where he was. The pistol-shot of noise only served to make the following silence even blacker, more awesome. Daniel bowed solemnly, turned to his left and walked offstage. Behind, he left total quiet. From the wings he looked back onto the stage at the silent orchestra, at the mournful blackness of the auditorium. The king had died and his subjects were paying homage to his memory. In sixty seconds, the crown prince would appear triumphantly to take his rightful place on the vacant throne. The man who had sent Daniel a cable on his debut saying "Now I know who you are" had stepped aside to leave the path clear for his successor.

At the end of the minute, the conductor's baton rose and dropped once more. The orchestra moved sweetly into the introduction for "M'appari" from Flotow's *Martha*, the aria that was to have started the recital originally. Daniel walked out from the wings, head held high to meet the overwhelming applause that almost drowned out the music. He bowed formally to the conductor, to the audience. The new king's coronation had begun.

The recital continued as planned with arias from *La Bohème*, *Tosca*, *Turandot*, *Carmen*, *Un Ballo in Maschera*, *Pagliacci*, *Cavalleria Rusticana* and *Faust*, along with a selection of Neapolitan favorites, interspersed with orchestral arrangements. Shortly before ten-thirty, when the recital was due to finish, Daniel walked off into the wings again, leaving the stage to the conductor.

"Ladies and gentlemen. As Mr. Kerr opened this recital with 'Cuius animam', he wishes to close it with another religious work. From the Jewish *Yom Kippur* service—the Day of Atonement—Mr. Kerr will sing . . ."

Even before the conductor could finish the sentence, the applause began to ring out. In the wings, Daniel chewed his top lip thoughtfully, wondering if he was doing the right thing.

Seven years earlier he had made a recording of Jewish religious music that was still selling steadily, but he had never taken his cantorial background into the concert hall before. "Kol nidre" was a classic, easily on the same level as "Cuius animam" or the "Ingemisco" from Verdi's *Requiem;* still, he hesitated about doing it. Too late now, though. He had made the decision during the intermission and the conductor had just announced it. He walked slowly back to his position at the center of the stage, head bowed, working himself up to the emotional level he needed for the hymn. There would be no orchestral backing here. He would be on his own, just like when he had conducted services in the temple, his voice against everything else while he beseeched the Almighty.

"*Kol nidre ve-esoray . . .*"

Never had a temple or a congregation been more receptive to his voice as was his Carnegie Hall audience at that moment. An entire mass of people hung on his every note. Gentile and Jews together prayed with him that all sins committed by them would be forgiven, all forced vows overlooked. He would be singing "Kol nidre" again soon enough, part of a congregation while he watched another cantor lead the service. *Yom Kippur* was only three weeks away. He would be praying to be inscribed in the Book of Life for the following year. The prayer seemed to take on more meaning. He had never thought about it before. It was automatic that he would be inscribed in the Book of Life. He was too young not to be. After Bjoerling, Daniel knew he had to pray. There was nothing automatic about it anymore.

The audience refused to let him go. Daniel, happily, refused to leave. After the two encores he had decided upon before the start of the performance—"O Paradiso!" from *L'Africaine,* and "Ah! lève-toi, soleil!" from *Roméo et Juliette*—Daniel conferred hurriedly with the conductor. Then he stood at the edge of the stage and looked down at the front row.

Requests were called up to him. He smiled and nodded at each suggestion, undecided which one he would sing. Then he decided against all of them. He would do an encore just for himself, a selection of his own choice. He returned to the conductor for another discussion. The conductor nodded approval and passed the message on to the orchestra. A shuffling of paper followed as the musicians found the score.

Daniel stood in the center of the stage while he listened to the long, slow introduction to the aria he had chosen. More than anything, he wished his father were out front. Isaac would have appreciated this particular aria more than anyone. Perhaps he was not appearing in a full production of *La Juive*, but singing "Rachel! quand du Seigneur" was as close as he would ever likely come.

As he began to sing, he wondered how many of his audience had heard the aria before. It was a first for him; probably a first for most of his listeners as well. To his knowledge, other than Caruso, only Gigli had recorded it. It was almost an unknown.

"What the hell was that last thing you sang?" Moishe wanted to know when he met Daniel in the dressing room after the performance.

"From *La Juive*. Any the wiser?"

Moishe shook his head. "That was a nice gesture you started off with, that business with Bjoerling. I think the audience appreciated it."

"Did you?" Daniel asked. Whenever he spoke to Moishe, he had difficulty tearing his eyes away from the flashing gold teeth in his friend's mouth, the constant reminder of the havoc he had created that night. Moishe had never mentioned the incident. He'd locked it away in whatever part of his mind he kept unwelcome memories; or maybe he'd forced himself to forget all about it. Whenever he opened his mouth, though, Daniel was reminded.

The gold teeth shone as Moishe grinned. "Kind of struck me as the president elect finding something nice to say about the guy whose job he's just taken, if you want to know."

"Struck me the same way." Daniel stood up and gave himself a final inspection in the mirror. "Doing anything now?"

"What have you got in mind?"

"Come home with me for a bite to eat. Anna's preparing a late dinner. Stay over the night."

Moishe weighed up the offer. "Sure, why not?"

"Here's the keys. Pick up the car from the lot and meet me outside. I don't want to walk around looking like a penguin anymore."

Moishe took the keys and told Daniel he'd see him in ten minutes. When he drove up to the main entrance of the hall, he saw Daniel gladly signing autographs for a large group of fans. He honked and Daniel waved at him to wait. He signed another dozen pieces of paper that were pushed at him before climbing into the car.

"Will Benny still be awake?" Moishe asked

Daniel checked the dashboard clock. "I hope not. If he is, there's something wrong." He looked sideways at Moishe, just in time to catch the flicker of disappointment. "You'll see him in the morning before he goes to Hebrew classes." Prompted by Moishe's interest in the child, Daniel decided to satisfy his own curiosity. "How come you never got married?"

"Never found anyone who could stand me, I guess." Moishe kept his eyes fixed on the road while he answered quietly.

"You never thought about it?" Daniel pressed. Moishe would have made some kid a good father. He always made a big fuss over Benjamin whenever he saw him, spent a lot of time with the kid, brought him presents by the armful.

"I thought about it once or twice," Moishe admitted. "Long time ago."

"So what happened?"

"The girl wasn't thinking the same thing. Who wants to take a skinny, four-eyed, bald-headed bastard like me home to meet the family?"

Moishe laughed as he spoke, as if he found the whole idea a huge joke. To Daniel's ear the sound was forced. He remembered once thinking the same thing about Moishe and felt guilty. "It's still not too late."

"I'm too settled in my ways now." Moishe guided the car off the George Washington Bridge onto Route 4 and picked up speed. Motels and gas stations flashed past as they left Fort Lee.

"Don't you ever get lonely?"

Moishe took his attention off the highway for the instant it needed to turn around and glare at Daniel. "Hey! What's with the sudden third degree?"

"I'm interested, that's all. You've stuck your face in my affairs often enough. I'm repaying the favor."

"You needed help from time to time."

"Are you saying you don't?"

Moishe made no reply and Daniel decided to let the subject drop. Somehow he had exposed a nerve. Perhaps Moishe had been turned down a couple of times and it continued to rankle him. Or was he jealous of Daniel for his family life? At first, the idea seemed absurd. The more Daniel thought about it, however, the more plausible it became. After all, under what name had Moishe registered Anna and the kid when they'd left the house that time?

"Are you interested in meeting someone?" Daniel asked out of the blue.

The front of the car veered slightly as Moishe's hands involuntarily jerked the steering wheel. "What the hell are you trying to do? Play *shidduch*-maker?"

Daniel ignored the frightened questions. "Anna's got some single girlfriends. Do you want to meet one of them?"

"I don't know." Moishe hesitated, uncertain whether he wanted this conversation to continue.

"What harm can it do, for crying out loud? The worst that happens is that you spend a couple of hours with one of them. You don't have to see her again if you don't want to."

Moishe lapsed into silence. Daniel did not know whether he was thinking about the prospect of a blind date, or whether he was scared dumb by it.

An hour after he had gone to bed, Daniel continued to lie awake, thinking about Moishe who was asleep in the guest room. How many times had Moishe gone to bat for him? Plenty. Now he had the opportunity to return some of that friendship, whether Moishe thought he wanted it or not. How come he'd never realized it before, that Moishe was frightened of women, frightened of meeting them, frightened of being alone with them? If it were not for Daniel's company, the guy would be a hermit, a scared, lonely man who had built up a defense of bluster.

"You sleeping?" Daniel whispered to Anna.

"I was trying to." She rolled over to face him in the darkness. "It's damned near impossible with you tossing and turning all night long. What's the problem?"

"Moishe. Have you got any single friends who are looking for someone?"

"Why do you want to fix him up?"

"Why not? I'm as miserable as sin. Why shouldn't he be?"

Anna dug him playfully in the ribs with her elbow. "Are you sure he wants to get fixed up?"

"He doesn't know what the hell he wants. If we show him a nice girl, he'll want to get fixed up."

Anna closed her eyes in thought. "There's Lena," she finally said.

Daniel considered the suggestion, a middle-aged secretary who had never been married. "Too aggressive," he decided. "She'd scare the living daylights out of him. Anyone else?"

"Helen Silver?"

"Helen?" The idea appealed to him, a young attractive widow in her late thirties with a daughter who attended Benjamin's school. Her husband had died three years earlier, and Anna had done as much as anyone to help her through. She came to the house at least once a week for dinner and often kept Anna company while Daniel was away. Moishe would like Helen, a soft, gentle soul who would not frighten him away. He just hoped that Helen would like Moishe. "Think she'll be interested?"

"I'll ask her around for lunch tomorrow. It's supposed to be fine so we can eat outside. Does Moishe have any clean clothes with him?"

"I'll run him back to the city first thing in the morning." Daniel began to smile as he thought over the idea. What would Moishe say when he learned he'd been fixed up?

The smile turned to a throaty chuckle and Anna asked what the joke was. He did not try to explain. All he could think of was that the day had started on a bad note but it was finishing brightly.

Chapter Two

The bat swung freely in Moishe's grip, lifting the white plastic ball high into the air. In slow motion it reached the peak of its climb and began to drop, twisting lazily in the light breeze. Glove raised in optimism rather than confidence, Benjamin circled under the spinning orb, lips stretched tightly in concentration, brown eyes alert.

From a chair on the patio, Daniel observed the scene with amusement. His kid was never going to play in the Yankee outfield, that was for damned sure. Moishe had been shagging flies for all of ten minutes and Benjamin had only caught two. Three, if you counted the attempt that had skipped twice out of the clutching glove and had been snatched finally as it made contact with the lawn; charitably, Moishe had called it a fair catch. Even as Daniel thought about it, Benjamin made a despairing grab at the ball. It hit the end of the glove and bounced away into a flower bed. Benjamin charged enthusiastically after it, and Daniel winced as he watched a rhododendron shrub being hammered almost flat beneath his son's pounding feet.

"That's enough!" Daniel called before more damage could ensue. Anna took enough pride in her garden to go wild when she saw her flowers flattened, and he would take as much of the blame as Benjamin. "You've got to get ready for *cheder!*"

The boy climbed out of the flower bed, dropped the bat in the middle of the lawn and ran into the house to clean up. Moishe followed, face covered in sweat but smiling happily.

"Great kid you've got there." He picked up his jacket from a chair and slipped it on.

"You want to try getting one of your own," Daniel said. He did not begrudge Moishe the time he spent with Benjamin. The kid enjoyed it every bit as much as Moishe did. But now was as good a time as any to get Moishe in the proper frame of mind for meeting Anna's friend at lunchtime.

"Where do you buy them?"

"You don't. Or didn't anyone bother explaining that to you?"

Moishe laughed. "What's the big deal about my going back to the apartment to change? Why can't I stay like this?"

"Because by lunchtime you'll be smelling worse than the Hackensack River." Would he be better off by letting Moishe continue to wear old clothes? That day he had proposed to Anna he'd needed a bath and a change. Helen might take pity on Moishe if she saw him like this, figure here was a man who needed someone to look after him. Or maybe she'd stick a clothes pin over her nose and run a mile. "We'll drop Benny off at *cheder*, then I'll run you home."

They entered the house to find Anna sitting at the kitchen table while she read the Sunday *Times*. Both she and Daniel had been disappointed to learn there was no review of the previous night's Carnegie Hall recital until they realized they had the early edition which had gone to press before the performance ended. Above all, Anna had wanted to read what the critics had thought of Daniel's rendition of "Rachel! quand du Seigneur." She had been delighted that Daniel had decided spontaneously to include the aria from *La Juive* and wondered if there was any point in using a good review to persuade the Grand's management to stage a revival of Halévy's opera. There had been talk about the Grand giving Daniel an entirely new production for the following season to celebrate his fifteen years with the company. *La Juive*, she believed, would be perfect for him. Daniel, however, was not keen on using the opportunity of a new production to revive *La Juive*. Although he had experimented with the aria, he thought the opera was too heavy for him, too taxing, both physically and mentally. To keep Anna happy, he had promised to talk to Robin Duguid about the possibility when he met with the general manager the following week.

"See you in a couple of hours," Daniel told Anna. "I'll drop Moishe off home and then come back. Give you a hand getting the lunch ready." He winked at Anna as he spoke, keeping his face turned away from Moishe.

"What's the big occasion anyway?" Moishe demanded.

"Why do I have to go home and get changed?"

"Because none of my clothes will fit you!" Daniel laughed.

"Don't take any notice of him," Anna advised. "We've got some friends coming over this afternoon, that's all. We thought you might like to meet them." She had called Helen Silver while Moishe had been playing in the garden with Benjamin. At first, Helen had been wary of the unexpected invitation. Only when Anna had stressed the intensity of Daniel's friendship had Helen agreed to meet him.

"You're not trying to fix me up with some broad, are you?" Moishe asked suspiciously.

"What?" Daniel choked back another burst of laughter. "There's no one we dislike that much."

"I find a measure of consolation in your abuse." Moishe kissed Anna on the cheek, said he'd see her later and went looking for Benjamin.

"You think he'll be mad when he finds out?" Anna asked.

"No. Helen's probably one of the first women he's been introduced to in years. Inside his puny chest, his little heart will flutter wildly and he'll fall hopelessly in love."

"I know," Anna replied. "That's what worries me."

Moishe returned just after one in the afternoon, his arms loaded down with a football uniform, helmet and ball for Benjamin. "Baseball season's almost finished," he called out cheerfully. "Time for a new game."

"What did you do?" Daniel asked in amazement as he surveyed the pile of equipment. "Raid a locker room?"

"Stopped off on Canal Street. Where's Benny?"

"Upstairs. Getting changed. Come out back, there's someone we'd like you to meet."

Still clutching the football gear, Moishe allowed himself to be led through the house into the back garden. Chairs were set out on the patio; drinks and appetizers crowded a small table. Moishe saw Anna talking to a petite blonde woman whom he had never seen before. On the lawn behind them, a young girl played with the white plastic ball Benjamin had been using that morning.

"Where are the rest of your guests?" Moishe asked. He

looked around anxiously, hoping to find more people.

"You're looking at them," Daniel answered. He stepped in behind Moishe to cut off any avenue of escape. A sheen of perspiration started to appear on top of Moishe's head. Daniel knew it had nothing to do with the heat. "Helen Silver, meet Maurice Waterman."

Moishe dropped the football equipment onto the ground, jammed his glasses to the top of his nose and stuck out his right hand. "Pleased to meet you," he mumbled.

Helen pushed herself up from the chair, an action that combined grace with an economy of movement. Watching and comparing, Daniel wondered whether he and Anna had been too smart. On appearances, Moishe and Helen were a total mismatch. Moishe was ungainly, awkward, obviously disconcerted by the sudden appearance of the woman. Helen was neat and confident, elegant in a bright cotton print dress while Moishe looked slovenly, his trousers rumpled, shoes scuffed.

"Anna's been telling me a lot about you, Maurice. Or is it Moishe?" Helen asked as an afterthought.

"His friends can call him . . ." Daniel began before he saw Anna's warning glance and fell silent.

"Moishe's okay," Moishe said. He grasped the woman's hand uncertainly. The greeting over, he dropped to his knees to gather up the football equipment. A sharp movement startled him. He looked up to find Helen kneeling beside him on the concrete, helping. "I can do it," he protested. "I don't need any help, thanks."

"All this stuff's for Benny?" Helen asked, taking no notice of Moishe's protests.

"Yes." He collected the last piece of padding and stood up. To his dismay, Daniel and Anna had moved back into the house, leaving him alone on the patio with this strange woman. On the lawn the little girl continued to play, unaware of the trauma that Moishe was experiencing. Desperately he tried to think of something to say. He felt embarrassed at being left alone with Helen Silver. At the same time he was angry with Daniel and Anna for putting him in this position. He'd been taken; he knew that now. Offered the chance to meet a few friends of Daniel and Anna and then set up.

"You must think a lot of Benny," Helen said, recognizing Moishe's awkwardness and finding it appealing. "Daniel was telling me how you were playing with him this morning."

"He's my godson." Moishe glanced around, spotted the little girl on the lawn and recognized his salvation. "Is that your daughter?"

Helen nodded. "Susie!" she called out. "Come over here and say hello to Mr. Waterman."

The little girl dropped the ball and ran obediently toward her mother. Very formally, she offered Moishe her right hand. "How do you do, sir?"

Despite his own discomfort, Moishe could not resist a smile at the little girl's primness. "I do pretty good. How about yourself?"

The girl looked at him oddly before releasing his hand and running back to the ball.

"Looks like I scared the hell out of her," Moishe said regretfully.

"Oh, I doubt that." Helen sat down in the chair again, delicately crossing her legs. "Daniel tells me you're a lawyer. Where's your practice?"

"Manhattan."

"Do you specialize in any particular field?"

"Just in paying the rent and keeping some food in the fridge." Moishe was surprised to realize he had made a joke and the woman was smiling. "Not really. I handle everything. But I do a lot of immigration work, visas, green cards. I suppose you could say I specialize in that."

"I've heard about your immigration work from Daniel. He says he owes you quite a few favors."

"What do you do?"

"Schoolteacher. I went back to it a couple of years ago, after my husband died."

"Your husband?" Moishe appeared lost.

"He died from a heart attack. He was only thirty-nine."

"I'm sorry."

The little girl wandered back from her game for a second and looked at Moishe. She stood perfectly still on the edge of the patio, finger to her lips while she studied him. Moishe waved at her. She turned around as if to run again, then stole another furtive glance at him. This time Moishe made a face and she laughed happily.

"So much for scaring the hell out of her," Helen said.

Just then Daniel reappeared, carrying plates from the kitchen. He began to set the table on the patio, every so often looking at Moishe and Helen while he tried to gauge the situation. When he returned to the kitchen, Anna asked him what was happening outside.

"He hasn't run away yet."

"Has Helen?" Anna asked, and they both laughed.

Daniel realized he should feel guilty about the way he had dropped Moishe into what was obviously an uncomfortable situation for him. Instead, he felt amused. Moishe had stuck him in enough awkward messes by trying to help him. It was only fair that he retaliate. Anyway, he was doing it for Moishe's own good. As long as he kept telling himself that, there was no way he was going to feel guilty.

By late afternoon, Moishe was in his shirtsleeves, playing on the lawn with the two children and obviously enjoying it. Daniel sat in a lounge chair on the patio, watching, convinced finally that he had done the right thing.

"Has he asked her out yet?" Anna wanted to know.

Daniel twisted his head around to see where Helen was. Satisfied she was out of earshot, he replied, "One thing at a time. She might not want to go out with him."

"She does."

"How do you know?"

"She told me she thinks he's sweet. He likes kids and they like him. That's very important to her."

Sweet? Moishe Wasserman sweet? "Where's the wedding going to be?" Daniel asked, giggling like a kid himself. It was a new sensation, introducing two total strangers to each other and watching them hit it off. It made him feel good.

"Give them a chance, Daniel. And don't go opening your big mouth about it either. Let them do whatever they want."

"Okay, I promise." He clapped a heavy hand over his mouth, like one of the three wise monkeys.

Later on, when Daniel suggested the six of them go out to

dinner, he was surprised to hear Moishe reject the idea. "Helen's already agreed to come out for dinner with me tonight," he whispered after pulling Daniel off to the side. "Would you mind very much if we took a raincheck on you and Anna?"

"Not at all. You like her, eh? You're not so mad anymore about being fixed up."

"She's not bad."

Daniel could not resist turning the screw. "She's got a lovely house, Moishe. Play your cards right and you could move out of that solitary confinement cell in the Village."

"How far are you and Anna planning on taking this thing?" Moishe asked, frightened as possibilities opened up in his imagination.

Daniel just laughed.

"Can you do us one favor for tonight?" Moishe asked.

"Sure. Anything."

The laughter died when Moishe asked Daniel to babysit Helen's daughter while they went out for dinner.

Daniel's poignant tribute to Jussi Bjoerling dominated the reviews of his recital that appeared in later editions of the Sunday newspapers. Needlessly, he carried copies when he went to his meeting the following week with Robin Duguid, certain that the general manager would have seen the notices already.

"A wonderful gesture of respect," Duguid acknowledged when Daniel entered his office at the Grand. "You had the opportunity to do the proper thing and you did it."

Everyone seemed to be telling him that. It was fate again, that same force of destiny that Roger Hammersley had once said intended Daniel to make his operatic debut as des Grieux and not the lamplighter. Fate had decreed that Daniel would have a Carnegie Hall recital scheduled for the day he read of Bjoerling's death. It would be his respect, his sorrow, that would make the headlines; his name would be prominent.

"And the world's a magnificent tenor poorer," Daniel said in reply. "To tell you the truth, Mr. Duguid, reading that obituary scared the living daylights out of me." Even after nine years with Duguid, Daniel could not bring himself to call the general manager by his first name. Only four years separated them in age, and since Daniel's return to Duguid's good graces in *Turandot*, a professional friendship had flourished between the two men, nurtured by a common desire to see the Grand succeed and a respect for each other's abilities. Intentionally, Duguid kept himself socially aloof from the members of the company, but during the tours he would often pass the traveling time by playing chess or talking with Daniel. Nevertheless, Daniel felt more comfortable keeping the relationship on a formal level. Duguid was in charge of the company and should be treated accordingly; familiarity would only erode his authority.

"I doubt if you were alone in your fear," Duguid said. "His death frightened a lot of people. When a man of forty-nine dies at the very peak of his career, it makes a lot of his contemporaries take a long, hard look at themselves. What did you learn?"

Daniel's pride was tickled to hear Duguid refer to him as a contemporary of a singer like Bjoerling; the Swede had won enough triumphs to fill an entire career before Daniel had even decided to become an opera singer. "I learned that there are still plenty of roles I'd like to do."

"I see. Was that why you included 'Rachel! quand du Seigneur' in your Carnegie Hall recital?" Duguid asked. "To see how it was received? Whether it would be worth using a good review to push for a full production?"

"Have you been talking to Anna?"

"Why do you ask that?"

"Well"—Daniel felt uncomfortable, as if he had overstepped the mark—"there's talk about offering me a new production to celebrate my fifteen years with the company. Anna seems to think that *La Juive* would be a fine choice."

Duguid mulled over the suggestion. "What about you? What do you think?"

"I don't know," Daniel admitted. "*La Juive* has got a lot of sentimental pull for me. It was my father's favorite of all Caruso's works. I grew up listening to Caruso sing that aria. But"—he let the word hang suggestively—"it's far heavier than anything I've taken into my repertory so far."

"It's a very powerful opera, Daniel. But it's not a very popular one. We were thinking, instead, of *La Gioconda.*"

Daniel seemed relieved. He had not been enthusiastic about tackling *La Juive.* As Duguid had said, it was not a popular work. Off hand, Daniel could not even remember when he had last heard of it being performed. Maybe Caruso had been the last one to sing it. He had only mentioned it for Anna—and for his father's memory. Now Duguid had removed the responsibility of taking the matter further. The role of Enzo Grimaldo was much easier. He had sung it before. Even a new production would not need the vast amount of work that would be required to learn *La Juive.*

"We're also hoping Anna will appear with you in this production," Duguid continued. "She's due for a new production even more than you."

Daniel smiled at the general manager's comments. Although Anna kept her appearances to a minimum and never went on tour anymore—preferring to be a full-time mother instead of a full-time soprano—Anna had been with the company longer than anyone else.

"See if you can have a word with her, Daniel. Persuade her. Get her in the right frame of mind for when I contact her next week. There aren't so many top-level sopranos that we can afford to let Anna's talents go to waste in the wilds of New Jersey."

"I don't think she'd be very thrilled to hear you say she was wasting away. Being a mother's a very serious business for Anna." Daniel knew he would have no trouble in getting Anna to appear with him in the production. She would support him to the hilt. It would be an honor for her as well; she'd share the glory of the new production with him.

"I'm sure it is," Duguid agreed. "How's Benjamin? Is he showing signs of following in his father's footsteps?"

"Hardly." Daniel had to laugh as he remembered the kid playing with Moishe on the lawn. "The only thing he does worse than sing is catch a ball."

"Not to worry," Duguid concluded philosophically. "There are many other ways to earn a living."

Sure there are, Daniel thought. But not one of them is anywhere near as rewarding and exciting as this one.

After finishing the meeting with Duguid, Daniel headed up to Moishe's office, eager to learn how his friend was progressing with Helen Silver. Anna had spoken on the phone for almost half an hour with Helen the previous evening, two teenaged girls eagerly exchanging gossip about their newest dates. Daniel had ribbed Anna about it. He'd told her she was too old to be spending hours on the phone talking about men; nevertheless, he wanted to find out how his machinations were working out.

He entered Moishe's office, unannounced by the receptionist. Moishe looked up in surprise and tried to sweep two framed photographs off the top of his desk and bundle them into the drawer. Daniel was quicker. He grabbed Moishe's hand and, to his friend's embarrassment, picked up the photographs. One was of Helen; the other was of Helen and her daughter.

"Leave them on the desk," Daniel said. "What do you want to hide them for?"

"Helen wanted me to have them," Moishe said defiantly, determined to prove to Daniel that it was not his idea. He came out from behind the desk and Daniel noticed that his shoes were shined to a high gloss, his trousers were pressed and his shirt was crisp, well-laundered.

"Like hell she wanted you to have them. You asked her for them." Daniel knew that much from Anna.

"All right, so I asked her for them! Is there a law against it?"

"Of course not. When are you seeing her again?"

"Tonight," Moishe answered proudly. "I'm going there for dinner."

"Are you taking her more red roses?"

"Who told you about that? Is my life going to be a gossip column item from now on?" Moishe demanded.

Daniel sat down heavily on a chair, his body shaking with helpless laughter. There was no fool like an old fool! Thank God he'd got it all out of his system early on and could concentrate on more important matters, be able to see the world without having his vision clouded over by dreams of wild love. Although what Helen could see in Moishe was beyond him. Getting on well with kids must be more important than he'd ever realized.

He dreamed that night, shadowy images that drifted in and out of his subconscious, fleeting, tantalizing, as he tried to reach out and grasp them. He dreamed of death and of life. Of those who had gone and those who remained.

His father appeared, the lined face solemn, an admonishing finger raised. The lips moved. No sound came to invade the silence of the dream, but Daniel knew the words his father was speaking. "You had the chance to sing *La Juive* and you let it go. It might never come again." Daniel heard his own voice screaming in reply, "I don't want anything to do with an opera where a father watches his daughter boiled alive! I've already lost one daughter. Can't you understand that?"

Isaac's face disappeared. Another took shape in its place. Fat Benny, whom Daniel could have helped and had not. Slumped beside a hot dog stand in Yankee Stadium while the crowd which had just witnessed one bloodletting stopped to gawk in fascination at another. If only he had been more concerned with his uncle's welfare instead of his own indignation, he could have helped Fat Benny, helped him to live long enough to see his nephew succeed on stage.

Who else had been disappointed by him? At one time or another, he'd let down everyone; his irresponsible actions had caused grief to those he loved and respected.

He dreamed of Moishe. If one person had stood by him, it was Moishe. His support had been as strong as Anna's. The dream brightened momentarily as he recalled their hapless journey back from the hotel in the mountains when they had first met. Then it darkened again as memory made an unwelcome visit to the final act of that meeting in an apartment on Park Avenue, figures in uniform, the crashing sounds of explosions in a confined space and a woman's vengeful, hysterical screams. But he was paying Moishe back, wasn't he? Helping his friend to share in a relationship that would bring him contentment if he'd let it. He began to laugh as the final, fragmented sequence of the dream found Moishe standing under a *chuppah* with Helen. The idiot was wearing mismatched socks!

Bright light penetrated his eyelids. Through them he sensed a shadowy figure looming over him.

"Daniel? Daniel?"

He recognized Anna's voice, calling quietly as she tried to wake him. Slowly he opened his eyes and looked around. The light on Anna's night table was shining. Anna was kneeling on the bed, staring at him anxiously.

"Were you having a dream?"

"I think so." He sat up, dazed by the abrupt return to consciousness. "Why do you ask?"

"You were shouting. And all of a sudden you began to laugh."

"What was I shouting?" For the life of him he could not remember a thing. The dream had vanished like a mist when the morning sun burns through it.

"Something about a daughter, that was all I could understand. And then you started laughing. Daniel, you frightened me."

"I'm sorry." As he moved to kiss Anna, he felt his pajamas sticking uncomfortably to his body; he was soaked through with sweat. "Shouldn't have had that grilled cheese sandwich before I went to bed," he joked feebly. "Cheese always gives me nightmares."

"You didn't have any. Unless you sneaked down in the middle of the night to raid the refrigerator."

"Would I do a thing like that?"

"Damned right you would. Where are you going now?" she asked as he clambered out of bed.

"To take a shower and put on fresh pajamas. I'm sticking to myself." He padded softly across the carpet to the *en suite* bathroom and ran the water almost cold.

Anna was asleep, a comfortable bundle under the covers, when Daniel left the bathroom. Without turning on a light, he crossed the bedroom and tiptoed downstairs to the kitchen. As he opened the refrigerator door, a flash of vivid blue light blinded him. He blinked furiously, rubbing his eyes with his hands. By the time he had regained his sight, the kitchen light was on and Anna was sitting in a chair, a camera and flash on the table next to her.

"Sleepwalking?" she teased.

"I thought you were in bed."

Anna began to laugh delightedly. "Stage prop, Daniel. Nothing more than a bolster shoved under the blankets. Do you really think I'm that shapeless?"

Four weeks later, after a whirlwind courtship that Daniel witnessed with a mixture of amusement and amazement, Moishe turned up at the house late one night with a request.

"Will you be my best man, Danny boy?" he asked before he even passed over the doorstep.

Daniel pulled the dressing gown tighter around himself, the initial annoyance at being pulled out of bed to answer the door after eleven o'clock yielding to pleasure. "When did you pop the question?"

"Just now. I left her at the house and came right over here to reserve your services."

"I assume she said yes."

"Damned right she did. So did Susie."

"You asked them both?" Daniel put the kettle on the gas and hunted for cups; at this time of night, instant coffee would have to do.

"I had to."

"So when's the big day?"

"January." Moishe paced from one end of the kitchen to the other, hands clasped behind his back while he recounted how he had gone to Helen's house that night for dinner and had ended up by asking her to marry him. "I never thought I'd get married, Danny boy. You can't even begin to know how I feel." He turned around and walked in the other direction. "I owe you, kiddo. I owe you."

"Be happy and quit wearing out the kitchen floor and you'll have paid the debt," Daniel told him. "You thought about what you're going to do yet? What *shul* you're getting married in? Reception? Junk like that?"

"Helen wants to get married in the local shul. And . . ." Moishe seemed to lose some of his enthusiasm. ". . . we're going to have the reception in the house."

"Nice." Daniel made a big show of making two cups of coffee. As an afterthought, he added another cup, then went upstairs to wake Anna. She'd want to be in on this as well; in fact, she'd be miffed that he'd found out before her.

"What is it?" she wanted to know.

"Moishe's downstairs. The nervous bridegroom."

"Bridegroom?" She sat up in bed, suddenly alert.

"He just asked Helen the big question and got the right answer. They're getting married in January."

"I'm coming down."

"I thought you would. Coffee's all poured. By the way, I'm the best man."

"I always thought you were."

As he walked out of the room, he saw Anna pick up the bedside phone and spin the dial to call Helen. He knew he shouldn't have poured the third cup; it would be stone cold by the time she got downstairs.

Moishe had not touched the coffee when Daniel returned to the kitchen. He was still walking nervously across the floor. At the sound of Daniel's footsteps, he spun around.

"Danny, I need a favor."

"Ask."

"Can you lend me a thousand bucks? It's for—"

Daniel held up a hand. "I'm not interested in what it's for." He left Moishe alone in the kitchen, went to the mahogany secretary and pulled out his checkbook. When he returned, he was holding a check for one thousand dollars. "Is that enough?"

"Fine. Thanks. I'll pay you back as soon as I can."

"Don't worry about it." He stuffed the check into Moishe's top pocket. "Now drink your coffee and relax, will you?"

While he watched Moishe pick up the cup, Daniel wondered why he needed the money. Despite saying he didn't want to know, he was curious. Honeymoon? It did not seem to make any sense. Moishe's law practice must be making money. Or was it? Hadn't Moishe said that he and Helen planned to hold the reception in the house and not in a hall?

Anna entered the kitchen, rushed up to Moishe and kissed

him on the cheek. Coffee splashed all over the floor. No one paid any attention to the accident. "Helen says you're going to be our neighbor," Anna exclaimed.

"Maybe the real estate taxes will come down," Daniel muttered. "Bad elements moving into the district." It still didn't seem to make any sense to him. Helen had the house; it was paid for, surely, by the insurance her late husband must have taken out. He decided to talk to Anna about it once Moishe left.

Through Anna asking Helen, Daniel learned a lot of things he had never known about Moishe. With the exception of Daniel, Anna and his receptionist, Moishe had no one to invite to the wedding. He was lonelier than he had ever admitted. And he was broke. The law business on West Forty-fifth Street barely made enough money for him to pay his way. Helen told Anna of clients that never paid, of cases Moishe took without ever having a hope of collecting his fee; he accepted cases because he felt sorry for people. Moishe did not have the money to pay for a reception. Neither did Helen. That was the other thing Daniel learned. Claims under the mortgage insurance policy and life policy her husband had carried had been denied. Her husband had failed to inform the insurance companies that he had suffered from rheumatic fever when he was a child. He had died from a heart attack, and the companies, on finding out about the rheumatic fever, had said the risk would have been greater had they known. So Helen was struggling to pay the mortgage while bringing up her daughter on a schoolteacher's salary.

Daniel listened to Anna's information with a feeling of helpless disbelief. Helen's problems did not shock him as much as Moishe's straits. He had known Moishe for thirty years; why hadn't the idiot said something?

"He's crazy. I would have helped him."

"Maybe he's too proud to ask for help," Anna suggested.

"That's not pride. That's stupidity. I'm going to call him right now. Tell him he can have whatever he needs."

"Don't you dare," Anna warned. "You'll make him feel small. If he needs anything he'll ask, just like he did with the thousand dollars."

"Then why the hell did he never ask before? I know what to do. I'll call that thousand bucks his wedding present. That'll help him out."

"That won't help at all. It'll just embarrass him even more. He'll pay you back and you make sure you take every penny. Don't shove your wealth and success down his throat. You'll choke him."

Daniel recognized the wisdom in Anna's words. Nonetheless, he continued to feel terrible. He had to do something for Moishe. Hadn't Moishe done enough for him? If it had not been for Moishe, who knew what would have happened to his marriage, to his career? He was the one friend Moishe had; a friend couldn't stand idly by and do nothing. "What about if we arrange the reception for them?" he suggested. "Instead of letting Helen arrange it at the house, why don't we organize a big do for them? Hire the hall, the caterers. Spring it on them as a big surprise."

Anna shook her head. "They don't have that many people to invite." Lines appeared on her forehead while she concentrated. Then she raised a hand in the air, fingers trembling with excitement, eyes sparkling. "I've got the perfect idea, Daniel. You'll have to do it, but for God's sake be tactful. If you're not, you'll lose Helen and Moishe as friends."

Daniel listened to Anna's idea and his face creased up into a huge grin. Hell, next to this, the thousand dollars he had been willing to give Moishe as a present paled into insignificance.

There weren't many people in the temple the Sunday afternoon that Moishe and Helen got married.

Daniel arrived early to ensure the flowers he had ordered were in place. A nice little touch, he decided; nothing that could make Moishe offended. Wasn't it part of the best man's duty to see that everything went smoothly?

Anna arrived with Benjamin and Susie, Helen's daughter. Benjamin was dressed in blue silk trousers and a pristine white shirt with ruffled collar and cuffs while Susie wore a pale blue frilly dress; as pageboy and bridesmaid they made a fine pair, standing in the still empty temple, holding hands to encourage each other. Daniel reckoned Benjamin would enjoy himself over the next couple of weeks when Susie stayed with them.

The kid would have company his own age. They'd be with each other at school and in the house; a couple of childhood sweethearts.

Moishe had bought a new suit for the occasion, a dark blue pinstripe from Brooks Brothers. Daniel had never seen him looking so smart. While he waited under the wedding canopy for Helen to be escorted in by an uncle who was giving her away, he glanced around nervously. "Who arranged for all the flowers?"

Daniel admitted that he had. "Got to have something attractive in here to make up for you." He reached an arm fondly around Moishe's shoulders and hugged him tightly. "Got a fast car with the engine running waiting outside. Say the word and I'll smuggle you out of the state."

"You think I want that?"

"No. You'd be a fool if you did. You're doing the best thing you've ever done. Except you should have done it a long time ago."

"I didn't meet anyone a long time ago."

"That was your own damned fault."

Moishe took off his glasses and wiped the lenses. His eyes were moist, and a vein in his temple throbbed to a regular beat.

"Nervous?" Daniel asked unnecessarily.

"Bet your ass I am. Look what I'm giving up."

"What?" Daniel reached out to straighten Moishe's tie, which was threatening to slide around to the side of his neck. He changed his mind and left it alone; maybe Moishe would be better off retaining some of his slovenliness. "A shoebox of an apartment? Talking yourself to sleep every night? Being as lonely as a leper?"

"You'll take good care of Susie, won't you?"

"Like she was our own daughter. What are you worrying about?"

More guests entered the temple and took their seats. Moishe glanced around, uncertain of himself as he hesitantly acknowledged their smiles. "I never told you this before, Danny, but I was jealous as all hell of you."

"Of me?" What was Moishe trying to do to him? Alleviate his own anxiety by throwing it on someone else's shoulders? "In God's name, why? Because I sang?"

"No. Nothing to do with that. I still don't understand half that crap you wail from the stage. I was jealous of your family. Of the fact that you had someone. You always had someone. You made friends easy. I never did."

"Okay, so you've changed. Now we're equal. You've got a family just like me." He tried to switch the subject by asking Moishe who were the people in the temple; anything to make him relax. If he carried on like this, he'd be in tears by the time the ceremony began. So would everyone else.

Moishe refused to be sidetracked. "You know, if there's anything I can ever do for you . . ."

"You've done more than enough for me already. Now will you just shut up so we can get on with this thing?" To his relief, he saw the rabbi take up his position. He pushed Moishe around to face the rabbi, then glanced behind as the temple door opened and Helen entered on her uncle's arm. Daniel felt in his pocket to make certain he had the ring. His fingers came in contact with a bulky envelope, the present he would give to Helen and Moishe during the reception. Moishe might be a lot easier in his mind if he knew of the envelope's contents. The idea of such a gift had been a stroke of genius on Anna's part. Daniel knew he would never have thought of it. He'd have gone ahead and told Moishe to forget about the thousand bucks, probably made him feel about an inch tall. Anna's suggestion had been more subtle. It would raise a few tears, protests that they shouldn't have done it. But it would be appreciated. And it would remove a lot of the headaches from the new marriage.

Daniel's eyes shifted downward as Moishe fidgeted nervously. Typical, he thought. The guy buys his first new suit in years and the trousers don't talk to the shoes; the cuffs of the pants finished a full half inch above his shoe tops. Daniel felt himself beginning to laugh and choked it back. The dream had been right. The stupid *klutz* was wearing one dark blue and one light blue sock!

Forty people attended the reception held in Helen's home. Moishe walked around in a semi-daze as if he could not believe he was married. Helen took the duties of hostess on her own shoulders, compensating for her new, bemused husband.

"Got lots of little white envelopes?" Daniel kidded. "Just

like a *bar mitzvah.*"

"A couple," Moishe answered. "And tea services, things like that."

"Stick this with your collection." Daniel pulled the heavy envelope out of his pocket, glad to be rid of it at last. Moishe regarded it questioningly. "Helen will probably understand it more than you will, although it's written in the kind of gobbledygook only a lawyer would appreciate."

Moishe balanced the package in his hand, gauging the weight. "May I open it?"

"Sure. You're going to have to open it eventually, so do it now." Daniel gazed into Moishe's face, wanting to treasure the expression that would come when his friend recognized the contents. Moishe peeled back the flap and pulled out the contents.

"You son of a bitch!" Tears sprung to his eyes, just as Daniel had known they would. "What the hell did you go and do a thing like this for?"

"Because Anna and I wanted to. And do you know what kind of a performance it was to track down the little old lady who held the mortgage on this place?" Gently he pried Moishe's fingers off the title to the house and the documents that settled the outstanding mortgage. A little over eleven thousand dollars had been outstanding. With one signature on a check, Daniel had wiped off the entire amount and given Moishe and Helen a clean start to their marriage.

Moishe looked around the room, past the buffet table from which guests were helping themselves, past Helen talking to some friends. Finally his eyes settled on Benjamin and Susie, two children lost in a world of adults, standing solemnly while they witnessed what went on around them. "Looks like a perfect match," he said. "Maybe you and me will be in-laws yet."

"God forbid," Daniel muttered. "Not that I've got anything against Helen and Susie, but you I ain't too sure about. I'm not even certain whether I'm happy we're living in the same town now. Come on!" He slapped Moishe on the back so heartily that his glasses almost flew off. "Be the good host and look after your guests."

Chapter Three

Even before he had asked Benjamin what he wanted for a *bar mitzvah* present, Daniel knew what the answer would be. The kid was so hyped up about being a Jew that he could ask for only one thing. So sure was Daniel, he even had a bet with Anna on the answer. And he won a dollar.

Benjamin wanted a trip to Israel. Following his *bar mitzvah,* he wanted to spend the entire school summer vacation in the country. He wanted to visit every site mentioned in the Old Testament that was encompassed by the modern boundaries. He wanted to walk where Abraham, Isaac and Jacob had walked, to live on a *kibbutz,* to worship where Moses had worshipped. In the end, he settled for two weeks split between West Jerusalem, Tel Aviv and Natanya, the longest that Daniel could afford to be away.

The trip was a first, also, for his parents, one of the many things Daniel had always meant to do but had somehow never accomplished. They didn't even need a guide book. Ever since Daniel had told Benjamin they would be making the trip, his son had been avidly consuming every tourist pamphlet, every book, every scrap of information he could about the country, adding to his already vast store of knowledge. The child became the guide, and Daniel swore he could see his son growing up in those two weeks.

An alert *Daily News* photographer recognized Daniel as he passed through the airport on the return journey. Smiling at the camera, an arm each around Anna and Benjamin, Daniel explained the reason for the trip. The photographer jotted down the information before turning away in search of other celebrities. Daniel dimmed Benjamin's joy at the recognition by telling him not to bother looking for the photograph the following day; the newspaper had more important pictures to print.

He was wrong. The *Daily News* carried the photograph the following day on its show business page. Daniel would not have known about it had not Moishe read the paper. He brought the copy around to the house that evening. Daniel, in turn, gave the clipping to Benjamin to begin his own scrapbook.

The woman started appearing outside Benjamin's school the week he began the fall term. When he first mentioned her to his parents, neither Daniel nor Anna paid much attention, thinking she was probably the mother of one of the other children. Only after the woman had appeared three more times in the space of two weeks, and sought Benjamin out to speak to him, did Daniel take notice.

"She said she knows you, Pa. She saw your picture in the *News*," Benjamin said. "She knows you."

"She didn't give a name, nothing like that?" Why was he getting worked up over this, some woman who'd spoken to Benjamin outside school three times? Lots of people knew him; lots of people must have seen the family photograph in the *News*. What was so strange about that? "None of the other kids know who she is? Like she doesn't belong to one of them?"

"Did she speak to anyone else?" Anna wanted to know. "Who was you with today when you left school?"

"Just Susie. She ignored Susie completely. She came up to me and said I should say hello to you for her." He looked hopefully at his father to explain the mystery.

"What did she look like?"

Benjamin made a face. "She was old."

That did not mean much. Anyone over twenty was old to Benjamin. "What color hair did she have?"

"Blonde. Very stiff, like she sprayed loads of gook all over it. And her face was all lined."

Listening to her son, Anna decided to call Helen. Maybe Susie would be able to offer a better description. "Do you think we should tell the police?" she asked Daniel after Benjamin had gone to his room.

"What the hell for? It's just some harmless, crackpot old woman. Doesn't mean a thing." Nonetheless, he decided to walk Benjamin to school and pick him up each day. He would see for himself who this strange blonde woman was. And what, if anything, she wanted from him.

A week of fruitless journeys passed. Each morning Daniel took Benjamin to the school gate and waited until the children had been called into class. At lunchtime, while Daniel was in the city rehearsing for the coming season, Anna or the housekeeper would act as escort. Daniel made certain he was back from the city to collect Benjamin at the end of the afternoon session. He even had to cut one rehearsal of the opening-week production of *Il Trovatore* to be there. After explaining the reason to Robin Duguid, the general manager overlooked the unusual behavior and filled in the role of Manrico with an understudy for the rehearsal.

On the eighth day, as Benjamin rushed out of the school toward his father, he abruptly stopped in mid-stride, eyes suddenly wide, finger pointed. "There she is, Pa!" he yelled. "That's the woman!"

Daniel swung around, determined to get to the bottom of the mystery. He caught just a glimpse of the woman from the back—wearing brown slacks and sweater with blonde hair piled high—before she dived into the passenger seat of a blue Mercury which sped away from the curb immediately. The car was too far away for him to read the number; all Daniel could make out was that it was a New York plate. If he had been right and it was some crackpot old woman, why had she taken off like that? He'd been wrong all along. He did have something to worry about.

"We're going inside." He grabbed Benjamin by the arm and pulled him into the school building. He passed Susie and didn't even recognize her. "Where's the principal's office?"

Benjamin led the way. Daniel confronted a startled secretary and demanded to speak to the principal. The woman looked from Daniel to Benjamin, whom she knew by sight, then asked what the problem was. "Mr. Palmer is in a meeting right now."

"I'm not interested in what he's doing," Daniel growled. "My kid's being molested outside this school by some woman and I want to get to the bottom of it."

"I see, Mr. . . . ?"

"Kerr. Daniel Kerr."

"Just a moment, Mr. Kerr. I'll check if Mr. Palmer can see you."

"Don't bother. I'll check myself." Dragging Benhamin behind him, Daniel pushed past the woman and barged through to the door to the principal's office. Four startled faces turned around at the noisy intrusion. The principal pushed himself to his feet, face reddening with indignation.

"What is the meaning of this?"

"Mr. Palmer?"

"Yes. Who are you?"

"I'm this boy's father. Three times in the past couple of weeks he's been accosted outside this school by some woman. I want it stopped."

"Perhaps you'll come outside with me, Mr. Kerr." He excused himself to the three people present and led Daniel and Benjamin into the secretary's office. The woman picked up her purse and left. "Now what's this all about, Mr. Kerr?"

Briefly Daniel told the principal what Benjamin had told him, finishing off with the incident of the blonde woman leaping into the Mercury. The principal asked why Benjamin had never notified any of the school staff before. Daniel replied that they had never thought it worthwhile. Until today, when the woman had caught sight of him and fled.

"Did you get the number of the car?"

Daniel felt foolish when he had to say no. "Just a blue Mercury with New York plates. Maybe a sixty-two. Two people in the car, the blonde and a driver."

Palmer picked up the phone and dialed the local police. "If they're heading back to the city, perhaps we can get them stopped at the bridge. We can settle this here and now." He got through and passed on the information. "The Port Authority police will be on the watch for the car. If it hasn't gone through yet, we might get lucky."

"Can I wait here?"

"Surely. I'll just break up that meeting and we can have the office to ourselves." He went back into his office. Moments later, the three people who had been sharing the meeting came out. Palmer asked Daniel and Benjamin to wait in his office.

The telephone rang fifteen minutes later. Palmer picked it up. "Teaneck police have checked Route 4 from here through to the bridge. They've seen nothing of a blue Mercury with two people in it that answers your description. Port Authority police have also come up with nothing. Are you certain the car had New York plates?"

"Of course I'm certain," Daniel said irritably. "I'm not that blind that I can't tell the difference between an orange-and-blue plate and a black-and-beige one."

"Pity you didn't get the number."

"Isn't it? So what are the police going to do?"

"I don't think there's very much they can do, Mr. Kerr. If the matter had been brought to our attention before we might have been able to do something. But now I'm afraid we're helpless."

"Well, you'd better stop being helpless damned quick!" Daniel roared. "Because my kid's not coming back to this school until you've got some kind of security system around here." He lowered his voice. "Come on, Benny, we're going home."

Palmer rushed to reach the door before Daniel. "Mr. Kerr, please try to understand that I'm the last person who would want anything to happen to one of our pupils." His tone was placatory, the words carefully chosen. "Ultimately, I'm responsible for everything that happens here. But you must realize that what we do now will be from scratch."

Slowly Daniel simmered down as he realized that his own rage was even more dangerous than the blonde woman in the blue Mercury. If she was dangerous at all. Of course she was! Otherwise why had she taken off like that when he had turned to look at her?

"I'd suggest that you take Benjamin down to the police station. In the meantime, I'll try to find out if there are any other children who saw this woman. Between them, they might come up with a reasonable description for the police artist. Then, at least, the police will know whom they're seeking."

"I will. Thanks." Daniel offered his hand apologetically. "Sorry if I was rude. I'm just worried."

Palmer took the hand which Daniel held out. "Of course, Mr. Kerr. Let's all hope we can solve this riddle quickly."

* * *

The local police were as helpful as they could be. Benjamin, Susie and three other schoolchildren who claimed they had seen the blonde woman at one time or another offered their descriptions. The artist came up with three different sketches and the children argued among themselves about which one was correct. They turned it into a game until finally the sergeant who had organized the meeting told Daniel he thought that nothing could be gained by continuing it. Regretfully, Daniel was forced to agree with him.

"Who do you think it is?"

The question came from Moishe, brow lined in thought, head shining dully as it reflected the light in the center of the living room. He shared the couch with Helen, while Daniel sat in a straight-backed chair. Anna was in the kitchen making coffee; upstairs, Susie and Benjamin played.

"If I knew that, we wouldn't have this problem, would we?" Daniel shook his head in exasperation as he struggled to think of a reason why any woman would be interested in either him or Benjamin. He had called Helen when he got home from the police station to arrange a meeting for that evening. Between all of them, they might be able to force a reason to surface. It was all well and good for the local police department to make sure a man was posted at the school when the kids came and went, but what about the rest of the time? Was Benjamin going to have an escort for everything he did? Every time he played in the park, went to the public library, or went to the temple on Friday night and Saturday morning, would a police officer be tagging alongside?

"Is there an old girlfriend you've been keeping quiet about?" Helen joked, desperate to lighten the oppressive atmosphere.

"No." Daniel dismissed the idea with uncharacteristic curtness, failing to see any humor in it. There was nothing to laugh about when his son was being threatened.

"And the police still think it's just some crank," Moishe murmured. "Some nut with nothing better to do."

"Why would some crank come all the way over from New York just to pester me?" Daniel demanded of Moishe.

"Beats the hell out of me." As much as he was concerned for Benjamin, Moishe was also worried how it would affect Susie. She wasn't his own flesh and blood, but he cared for her just as strongly as if she were. He'd watched the girl grow up for four years now and bitterly regretted that he had not been there for the first nine, and even before. All the favors he had ever done for Daniel, all the times he'd stood by him, had been paid back with any interest due by the introduction to Helen. Before he had met her, Moishe could not even conceive what it would be like to share his life with another. After he'd met her, he couldn't bear to think what it would be like any other way.

The door opened and Anna came in carrying a tray with four cups, coffee pot, cream and sugar, and homemade cheesecake. Very pointedly she indicated the smallest portion of cake. "That's for you," she told Daniel.

"No. I don't want any. Just the coffee'll do."

Anna regarded him oddly. He was more worried about the mysterious blonde than he was showing. Any other time he would have battled for a bigger slice; this time he was passing it up altogether. "I'll confess to you all now," she said. "I invented this mysterious blonde just to put Daniel off his food. How else could I make him lose weight?"

The sound of Moishe's and Helen's laughter passed right over Daniel's head. He hadn't even heard what Anna had said to start them laughing. All he could think of was the woman. If he had to go over to New York himself and check out every blue Mercury registered in the state to find out what was going on, he'd damned well do it.

The tension was increased another notch the following morning. The mailman brought two letters addressed to Daniel. One was a telephone bill. The other, with his name and address printed on the envelope in clumsy block capitals, contained the page from the *Daily News* with the photograph taken at the airport circled in red and an accompanying sheet of white paper. On the paper, letters cut from different publications spelled out, "What a happy family. You don't deserve it."

Furiously Daniel crumpled the envelope and its contents into a small, tight ball before he remembered that the police would need to see them. Not that they would be able to learn much; he was certain of that. Anyone who took the trouble to write in block capitals and then use letters cut from magazines for the message would surely avoid leaving fingerprints on the paper. That's if fingerprints could be left on paper to begin with. Hell, he was out of his depth here. He was struggling against something he didn't understand. For a reason he didn't understand.

He debated whether or not to show the letter to Anna. He could take it straight to the police and not give Anna additional worries. There seemed little point in making her as upset as himself. Then he realized she would be even more upset if she knew he was keeping anything from her.

"You've got no idea what any of this means?" Anna looked at the New York postmark on the envelope. She was more perplexed than worried, confused as to why anyone should go to these lengths to harm them. Was this the price of fame—that any nut who could read enough to look up a celebrity in the telephone directory could start pestering them? She had argued years earlier with Daniel about having their phone number and address unlisted, but he had insisted on its inclusion in the Bergen County directory. He was a public figure, he had reasoned, and if people wanted to contact him, they should be able to. The idea to make himself accessible had been good. Daniel had enjoyed talking both to fans and aspiring singers who wanted advice. But now nuts were getting through. Accessibility was suddenly a peril.

"Do you think if I knew what it meant, I'd be standing here?" Daniel asked in return. "I'd be out there with someone's neck between my hands." He clenched his fists, subconsciously relishing the sensation of having the blonde woman's throat in his grip.

Anna watched him carefully while she tried to gauge the turmoil she knew was raging inside him. Whatever it was, whatever grudge, real or imagined, that this woman held against her family, she wished it would come to a head before it wrought havoc with Daniel.

Easing the heavy sword from its scabbard, Daniel stared pensively at the shining blade. From dressing rooms on either side he could hear fellow artists loosening up their voices for the performance of Verdi's *Il Trovatore*. He fingered the dull edge of the blade; no sense in having it sharp in case he got carried away during the performance and took someone's head off by mistake. He knew whose head he'd like it to be. Visions of a bloody head with blonde hair bouncing across the stage into the orchestra pit briefly lightened his mood.

Three more letters had followed the first. They had

contained originals of old reviews, even one from his debut as des Grieux in *Manon Lescaut* from the New York *Times.* The police had jumped on that one. They had checked with the *Times* morgue and with libraries in New York to see if they had records of anyone checking out that particular issue. The replies had come back, all identical. No library in the city had a record of anyone asking for that particular copy of the *Times.* Also, all their copies were intact; nothing had been ripped out. Whoever was plaguing Daniel had been holding the grudge for a long time. Long enough to have collected the reviews from almost twenty years before.

At least the pestering of Benjamin at school had ceased. Daniel was grateful for that. Obviously, the perpetrator had decided to alter the method of attack and use the mails to unnerve him. That had one advantage. Using the mails made it a federal matter, although Daniel seriously doubted if the FBI had enough spare time to go chasing after some lunatic woman who was making a nuisance of herself.

Not much point in dwelling on it, Daniel decided. Whatever will be will be. Whoever's behind it will get an even bigger kick if I go out there and blow a note to hell and back. He stood up, attached the scabbard to his belt and left the dressing room. He met Robin Duguid in the corridor outside, as the general manager was making his rounds of the dressing rooms to wish his artists good luck. When he spotted Daniel, his face became serious.

"Anything new on your phantom letter writer?"

"I wish you hadn't mentioned it, Mr. Duguid. I'm doing my best to try not to think about it."

"I'm sorry. I didn't realize."

"Not your fault. Nothing new. Every so often I get another old review in the mail. The cops think whoever's behind it has had it in for me since day one in this business. Now they're digging through their scrapbooks to send me a few reminders. I just wish they'd send something that could give the cops a clue."

"Anything I can do to help?" Duguid asked gently as he accompanied Daniel downstairs to stage level.

"Come up with a motive."

"I wish I could." Duguid clapped Daniel on the shoulder in a rare gesture of closeness. "Good luck."

The blonde woman was winning her war of nerves. During the second act, Daniel forgot a line. He looked around blindly, mouth gaping, face blank while he prayed silently for assistance. The panic was contagious. Instead of calling out softly, the prompter shouted with enough force to be heard halfway around the auditorium.

When Daniel came off for the intermission between the second and third acts, he spoke to no one. If he still kept a bottle in the dressing room, he would have emptied it without a second thought. Duguid was sympathetic. He knocked gently on the dressing room door and stood just inside. "Do you want me to go onstage and say you've been taken ill?"

Daniel glared moodily into the mirror while he shook his head. *Il Trovatore* was an opera, like so many others, where the tenor could rescue a mediocre performance with a powerful third-act aria. In this instance it was "Di quella pira." Daniel, as the insurgent leader, Manrico, would stand at the front of the stage, sword raised valiantly aloft, and rouse his followers to storm his enemy's castle. "I'll make them forget that blunder," he promised Duguid.

The general manager smiled at his tenor's confidence. "That's what I was expecting you to say. Go blow their eardrums out." He patted Daniel on the shoulder and left the room.

Daniel continued to stare in the mirror until he heard the call go out that only five minutes remained to the beginning of the third act. As he prepared to leave, the telephone rang. It was Anna. The tactics had been changed yet again. First it had been Benjamin, then the newspaper clippings and the old reviews had started to arrive. Now, whoever was plaguing them had turned to the telephone. When it had rung three minutes earlier, Anna had answered it to hear the first-act duet from the *La Bohème* she and Daniel had recorded fourteen years earlier. As she listened, the speed was changed, first fast and then slow. When Anna screamed, the receiver at the other end was put down.

Daniel felt sweat begin to bead on his brow. Someone was turning the screws, and there wasn't a damned thing he could do about it. "Call the cops," he said. "And call the phone company. Better still, get the cops to do it. Maybe they can get some kind of permanent trace on the line, listen in if this nut calls again."

"Daniel, I'm frightened." It was the first time Anna had ever admitted fear. Daniel knew how deeply frightened she was.

"Don't worry. I'll finish off this third act and come straight home. Call Moishe. Get him to come and sit with you."

"All right." She blew a kiss into the mouthpiece and hung up.

Daniel walked slowly down to stage level, his face wet and ashen. People asked if he was feeling all right. He nodded brusquely. He would feel better once the third act began and he immersed himself again in the character of Manrico, ready to redeem his poor performance so far.

A popular tenor's performance can recover from many ills. He can compensate for a frigid start with later sweetness and warmth and his audience will welcome him back into their hearts. A forgotten word or line can be forgiven in the time it takes to draw the next carefully controlled breath and come back with a cluster of high notes that will shake the chandeliers. But no tenor ever recovers from a cracked high-C.

Daniel knew he was going to fall short of his high-C in "Di quella pira" even before he tried to reach for it. He wasn't into the part at all. He wasn't Manrico trying to save his mother from being burned at the stake. He was Daniel Kerr, trying to sing while he was worried stiff about some nut who had singled out his family for an experiment in psychological terror. Some nut who was doing a damned good job . . .

The high-C cracked. Daniel felt his throat closing up as he went for it. Where before his voice had soared effortlessly, now it faltered. He sounded like a man choking, drowning, a final scream for help that turned into a weak gasp as the waters closed over him. His eyes bulged. His mouth froze in a wide, helpless circle. His lungs burst and his heart stopped. The sword, held so proudly aloft moments earlier, clattered from his hand onto the stage. Daniel stared down at the conductor's concerned face, at the blackness of the auditorium where the audience sat, all witnesses to a catastrophe instead of the expected triumph.

Was the blonde woman out there even now? Watching and listening to the havoc she had created? Was this her triumph? The objective of the terror campaign? To be on hand when he tried to hit the top and collapsed? Was she the friend of someone who wanted him out of the way? Doing a more frightening version of what Moishe had once done for him with an Italian tenor named Cesare Scarlatti?

A shocked gasp exploded from the audience as realization finally hit home. Their hero of countless productions had been vanquished. It was time for another hero. The heavy gold curtain dropped down in the middle of the scene. Daniel spun around and walked quickly into the wings. He passed his double, the understudy dressed up as a second Manrico, all ready to go on. Duguid had sensed problems and had been prepared for it. While he watched the understudy take up his recently vacated position in the center of the stage, Daniel heard Duguid's voice in front of the curtain, telling the audience that Mr. Kerr had been taken ill and would be replaced by tenor Paul Lankau. Daniel did not wait to hear any more. When the curtain rose and the orchestra began again with the introduction to "Di quella pira," Daniel was racing up the stairs to the dressing room. He did not even spare a sympathetic thought for Paul Lankau, his understudy, who had been flung into the lion's den without the least protection, forced to sing a "Di quella pira" without the slightest recitative to ease himself into the part.

When Duguid reached the dressing room, Manrico's costume was already on the floor in an untidy heap and Daniel was clambering into his trousers.

"Are you all right?"

"Yeah. I'm going home." He realized that Duguid did not know about the phone call Anna had taken, the distorted playing of the duet from *La Bohème*. While he continued dressing, he related the story. Duguid nodded understandingly.

"Daniel, if you want a leave of absence from the company, for God's sake say so. You went on just before when you know damned well you shouldn't have." Daniel opened his mouth to speak in his own defense. Duguid held up a hand. "I know what you're going to say. That the audience paid to hear you sing Manrico. That's the risk they take when they book, whether you'll be in the part or not. Instead, they heard you give what was probably the worst performance of your entire career. You cheated everyone, yourself included."

Daniel saw no sense in arguing with Duguid. The general manager was right in everything he said. Daniel had cheated everyone. He'd cheated himself by turning in a performance so bad he'd never be able to forget it; and he had cheated his audience by offering them second rate when they had come to expect only the finest.

"Do you want a leave of absence from the company?"

"I think I'd better." He slipped into his jacket, paused long enough to make sure he had his car keys and wallet, then grabbed his topcoat. "I'll give you a call tomorrow. Let you know what's happening."

As he clattered down the stairs toward the stage door, he heard the sound of voices. The performance was continuing without him. It would have to remain that way until the police got to the bottom of this mess. Daniel prayed that it did not take so long that the audience would forget him.

The house was full when he arrived; the entire world seemed to have congregated in his living room. Benjamin and Moishe sat talking quietly. Anna, eyes red but dry, sat alone on the couch, hands clasped on her lap as she talked to two men Daniel had never seen before. They introduced themselves as FBI agents. A Teaneck police officer was also present, representing the local municipality.

"Mr. Kerr." The senior of the two agents addressed him, a man with graying hair and blue eyes that somehow managed to remain warm. "I'm Jack Regan. I'll be handling the case from now on. From talking to your wife"—he indicated Anna, still sitting on the couch—"I'd suggest that we monitor all your phone calls in future."

"What about changing the number?"

"That would just avoid the issue, sir. We'd like to trace where the calls are being made from; that way we can get a lead on whoever is behind this campaign against your family.

We've already notified the phone company. And for your personal safety, we'll be leaving an agent in the house." He motioned to the second man.

"Guess you'd better watch your personal calls from now on, Danny boy," Moishe called out. The words brought an involuntary grin to Daniel's face; even Anna laughed.

"I doubt if we'll be listening in on those, sir," Regan remarked drily.

"If you want juicy calls, try eavesdropping on some of the deals he tries to pull over the phone," Daniel shot back. "Your ears would drop off." He was pleased to see Moishe's face redden.

"What was the name of your friend who was with the FBI?" Anna asked suddenly. "You know, the one we met in the Village that night before we got married? The one you promised to send tickets to."

"Tommy?" Daniel asked, surprised that Anna should remember. "Tommy Mulvaney. Either of you guys know him?"

Regan nodded. "He's with the New York office, a senior investigator."

"Where do you work out of?"

"Hackensack. You know Mulvaney well?"

"Used to," Daniel admitted, shamefaced. "We were friends as kids. Then kind of drifted apart."

"When I run into him the next time, I'll let him know you're still alive." The agent turned to the local cop. "Anything you want to ask?"

The police officer shook his head.

"Okay, then, Mr. Kerr. I'll be taking off. Your housekeeper's kindly made up a room for my man. He'll be living with you for a while. Just treat him like one of the family."

"Does that mean you can claim him as a tax exemption?" Moishe wanted to know. Laughter rocked the room, dissipating the tension and anxiety that had greeted Daniel only a short while earlier.

Moishe was the last to leave, standing by the front door while Daniel thanked him for coming around. Not only had he supported Anna until Daniel arrived home, he had also acted as a release valve for the pressure with his inane jokes. After watching Moishe drive away, Daniel returned inside. He checked that the FBI agent was comfortable before looking in on Benjamin who was already in bed.

"You're going to have an escort when you go to school tomorrow," Daniel promised. "You'll be the talk of the school."

"Do you think I'm the one who's in danger?" his son asked. "Or is it Ma and you?"

Touched by the intelligence and consideration of such a question, Daniel was uncertain how to answer. "I hope that none of us is in danger," he replied at last. "The cops seem to believe we're just facing some crank who picked on us. With the forces we've got on our side now, they should pick them up soon."

"I wish I'd taken more notice of that woman those times she spoke to me," Benjamin said wistfully. "Then she might be out of our hair already."

Daniel chuckled at the sentiment. "That's a problem Moishe will never have," he joked. "Good night." He turned off the light and left the room. In the hall, he passed the FBI agent on the way to the bathroom.

"Anything you need?"

The agent shook his head. "Nothing at all, thanks, Mr. Kerr. I'm being looked after here better than in my own home. Sleep well."

Daniel entered his own bedroom. Anna was waiting for him, sitting in the chair by the dressing table. They were alone at last, and she could ask him what had happened at the Grand. He had arrived home much too early to have completed the performance.

"I blew the 'Di quella pira.' Cracked the high-C."

"What did Mr. Duguid say?" Anna knew she did not have to ask the question; the answer was already obvious.

"He dropped the curtain, and then went onstage to say I'd been taken ill. They picked up the third act again from 'Di quella pira' with my understudy."

"Did you see Mr. Duguid afterwards?"

Daniel nodded. "He insisted that I take a leave of absence until this thing blows over. He says I'm harming myself more than anyone else by persisting."

"He's right. How do you feel?"

"Rough. And mad. I'd like to get hold of the sonofabitch behind all this. What the hell did we ever do to deserve all this crap?"

"Daniel, have you really combed your memory? Are you sure there isn't someone with good reason to hold a grudge against you? You know, you did some pretty wild things in the old days."

"You mean Pomerantz? Still mad at me because of what I cost Carmel Studios?"

"Pomerantz. Anyone. What else did you get up to?"

"What's the point of going back before then? No one holds a grudge for twenty or thirty years."

"Then why have we been singled out? Daniel, it's terrifying to know that someone out there"—she waved vaguely at the bedroom windows—"is jerking us around like a puppet on a string."

"Ah, there are more nuts out than in," Daniel said as he tried to assure Anna. "The cops'll nail this one as well. Quit worrying about it."

"And what about you? You're not worried? You're so calm that you blew a high-C for the first time in your life."

"That wasn't fear. That was age. I'll be fifty soon." He pulled off his shirt and stood in front of the full-length mirror, sucking in his stomach. "There. That's not bad for half a century, is it?"

"Now let it out," Anna told him. "You won't be able to see your feet."

A knock on the door made Daniel hastily throw on a dressing gown. The FBI agent stood outside, bedsheets and pillow bundled up in his arms.

"Mr. Kerr, I think it would be better if I slept downstairs on the couch. Good night."

"Good night." Daniel closed the door and continued preparing for bed. He decided to shower. The make-up from the aborted performance was still on his face and he could smell the sweat on himself. Fifteen minutes later, when he emerged from the bathroom, Anna was sitting up in bed.

"I was wondering whether you'd notice," she greeted him.

"That I smelled?"

"No. That you were still wearing Manrico's face. God knows what that man from the FBI must have thought when you came marching in looking like that."

"Or just now," Daniel added. "Seeing me all ready for bed with a pound of heavily applied make-up on my face. Thanks for telling me."

"There's probably a standard police officer mentality that thinks all artists are freaks and should be accepted as such," Anna said. "You didn't disappoint them."

Daniel slid into bed, reached across Anna and turned out her light. As he pulled back his hand, Anna grasped it. "Daniel, I don't want to go to sleep. I'm frightened."

"You and me both," Daniel admitted. "The only one who's not scared out of his wits is Benny. He's more worried about us than anything else."

"Talk to me."

He put his arms around her, closing his eyes for an instant while he tried to remember Anna as he had first known her. She'd had a body that was kept as fit and lithe as any athlete's. Years of being a singer, of being a wife, of being a mother had taken their toll. Anna was heavier, with comfortable folds of flesh that he could grasp where before there had been only skin. Her hair, like his own, had streaks of gray, and she had taken to wearing glasses for reading. She had considered having her hair tinted to remove the visible signs of age, only to decide against it after making the appointment. An old man like you would look peculiar with a young girl on his arm, she'd told Daniel. People will think you're out with your daughter, not your wife. Daniel found it comforting that Anna was content to age gracefully with him. The gray hair did not have to be there; nor did the lines that were showing in her face. She could have them camouflaged, removed. Daniel was grateful that she had chosen not to.

"What shall we talk about?"

"Anything. Anything at all. Just as long as it's not this hell we're being put through."

He kissed her tenderly on the forehead, feeling her snuggle closer to him. Slowly he moved downward, caressing her eyelids, the tip of her nose, her lips. Anna moaned softly and pressed against him. There was no need to talk.

Chapter Four

The reason for Daniel's leave of absence somehow reached the press. Newspapers were sympathetic, atoning to some degree for the doubts critics had expressed about the continuation of his career when he had been replaced in *Il Trovatore* by the understudy. Questioned by reporters, Daniel had admitted that threats were being made against his family, adding that the FBI and local police were adopting protective measures to combat the menace. Jack Regan, the agent heading the investigation, came down hard on Daniel for his tactlessness. Then, when nothing happened for a month—no phone calls, no letters, no visitations—Regan told Daniel that his error might have been advantageous. Publicizing what the police were doing had probably forced the crank to seek new victims to harass.

The police and federal agents decided to end their vigilance. Daniel and Anna agreed, relieved, wanting to believe that the campaign of terror was over. No reason had existed for it to commence; similarly, for no reason, it had finished. Daniel met with Duguid and made arrangements to return to the Grand. Duguid decided to make him wait a further two weeks, until the next scheduled production of *Il Trovatore* in which he was to have starred. He had left the company with Verdi's opera. It was only fitting that he should return in the same role. He would dispel any doubts about his voice and simultaneously set to rest any rumors that the threats plaguing his family had been nothing more than a cover-up for his failure to sing.

Publicized beforehand in the press, Daniel's return to the Grand was an unqualified success. A ten-minute, foot-banging, hand-thrashing ovation greeted his "Di quella pira." At the end of the final act, the audience—his audience—refused to let him go. They called him back again and again until at last he raised his hands in the air, as he'd seen Joe Louis do those many years earlier at Yankee Stadium.

In Wheeler's, the post-performance atmosphere was festive—July the Fourth, Thanksgiving and Christmas all rolled into one. Daniel played the gracious host to Anna, Moishe and Helen. He had wanted Benjamin and Susie to attend the performance also, but they had school the following day and could not afford to go to bed at three in the morning. Susie was staying over at the house with Benjamin, watched over by the housekeeper, and would go straight to school in the morning.

Fans who stopped by the table to compliment Daniel on his performance were greeted with open arms. Autographs were scribbled on linen napkins. Robin Duguid stopped by to offer his congratulations yet again, staying long enough to chat with Anna about putting in more time with the company. Gently she rejected his persuasion. One production each season was all she would allow herself.

The party broke up just before two-thirty, when Moishe complained that he had to go to work in a few hours. Daniel's offer to drop him at the office on the way home met with muttered obscenities.

"Don't forget to set your alarm," Daniel told Moishe when he dropped off his passengers. "You don't want to take a chance on oversleeping."

"I'll wake you up just as I leave," Moishe said sourly.

"You just try and your head'll get to the office half an hour before the rest of your body does." Still full of pleasure from the performance and the following celebration, Daniel laughed loudly. "Glad you're not handling any cases for me in the morning. See you."

When they reached their own house, Anna waited under the front porch while Daniel put the car away in the garage. He took the key from her and opened the door softly. The lower hall light was on and as he closed and bolted the door, he heard Anna gasp.

"What . . . ?" He spun around just in time to see Anna raise her hands to her mouth as she tried unsuccessfully to stifle a scream of terror.

By the light spilling from the hall into the living room, Daniel could see two figures tied to chairs, hands bound behind them, mouths covered with white adhesive tape. Susie and the housekeeper. The television was still on, a late-night movie sending light and dark shadows flickering across the room. Benjamin was nowhere in sight.

Daniel lunged into the room and tore the strip of tape from the housekeeper's mouth, unaware of the pain the violent action must have caused. "What happened?"

The woman gulped, straining against the bonds that held her to the chair. As Daniel struggled to free her, she blurted out that two men had come to the house shortly before ten o'clock. When she had answered the door, they had pushed their way inside, tied her and Susie to chairs and . . .

"And what? Where the hell's my son?" Daniel snapped off the last of the ropes. The woman staggered to her feet, stumbling as her circulation-deprived legs refused to take the weight. He dragged her upright and pushed her into an armchair.

"They took him with them," the housekeeper mumbled.

Daniel's expression was grim as he watched a technician dust the chairs that had held Susie and the housekeeper for fingerprints. Come on, you sonofabitch, find something! Anything! Even a smudge, he prayed for, a minute clue that could be quickly identified and would lead to the apprehension of the men who had stolen Benjamin. Two men only, Susie and the housekeeper had told the police and FBI agents who had flocked to the house. No sign at all of a blonde woman.

Daniel spared a moment to think of Anna, lying upstairs under a strong sedative, blissfully asleep. She'd screamed like a madwoman when she realized what had taken place. When the screaming had stopped, the crying had started, continuing until Anna had no more tears left, only dry, choking sobs as she blamed herself for not being in the house that night. Daniel had called a doctor who lived three houses away. The man had come right over and administered a shot. When Anna woke up, she'd remember and cry again, but that wouldn't be for a few hours yet. Daniel wondered how the experience would affect Susie and the housekeeper. Susie had been sent home as soon as the investigators had finished with her, picked up by a flabbergasted Moishe who had been woken up to be told about the abduction.

"I'm afraid all we can do is sit and wait now, sir," said Regan, the FBI agent with graying hair and blue eyes who had led the investigation into the nuisance letters and phone calls.

"What?" Daniel had not heard a word; he was too busy thinking about Benjamin, whether the kid was all right, where he was.

Regan repeated his statement. "It's a very unusual case, Mr. Kerr. With kidnapping, the victim is normally abducted and a ransom demand follows. Here, you and your family have been harassed for some time, like you were being warned something was going to happen. I'll be frank with you. I'm wondering if we're going to get a ransom demand at all."

Daniel pondered the agent's words. Someone had yanked the kid, not for money, but for some other reason, all tied in with those letters and phone calls.

"Are you a rich man, Mr. Kerr?"

"I suppose so." Personal wealth was the furthest thing from his mind. He would give away the whole bundle and start again from scratch if it would get his son back. "What happens should a ransom demand come through?" He preferred to stick with that possibility; money, at least, was a motive he could comprehend.

"Well, the choice is up to you." Regan stopped talking as the telephone rang. He motioned for Daniel to pick it up. Simultaneously he lifted an extension that had been installed early that morning.

"Yes?" Daniel could barely force himself to utter the single word.

"Danny? It's Moishe. What's happening?"

Daniel breathed out heavily, relieved that it was only Moishe. And at the same time disappointed. "Nothing. Where are you?"

"Just got in the office. Anything I can do?"

"Pray."

"I already did."

Daniel believed him. "Thanks." He saw Regan waving at him to get off the line. "Moishe, I'll speak to you later."

"Okay. Good luck."

"Stay off the phone," the agent warned. "Just in case a call should come through."

"What were you saying before about the choice being mine?"

"Either to pay whatever ransom they want and hope to get your son back that way, or let us handle the drop and try to nail whoever's behind it."

"Which way ensures my son won't be harmed?"

Regan shook his head sympathetically. "There's no guarantee about anything. We prefer that we're allowed to handle it. But it's your son who's involved so the choice is yours."

Daniel didn't need to think it over. "If I can raise the cash, I'll pay to get my son back. You can worry about catching the bastards responsible afterwards."

Regan glanced through the living room window as a gray Chevrolet pulled up outside the house to join the cluster of automobiles already there. A man wearing a heavy camel coat and a snap-brim hat pulled low over his eyes walked quickly from the Chevrolet up the path to the front door. Before the bell could ring, Regan left Daniel and went to open the door.

"Hi, Cherrybum."

"Hi, copper." There wasn't the faintest trace of pleasure in Daniel's voice as he greeted Tommy Mulvaney. It might just as well have been a total stranger standing in front of him. Benjamin's abduction had drained him of all emotion but fear. "What are you doing here?"

"Helping out if I can. I saw the report and came right over." He let his eyes drift over Daniel, then he smiled. "You haven't changed a bit, Cherrybum. You're still fat enough to make a damned good plate blocker." He clapped Daniel on the shoulder and wandered away to watch the man dusting for fingerprints.

"You've got the big hitters going to bat for you," Regan said. "If anyone can direct this case, Mulvaney can."

Daniel nodded absently while his eyes followed Tommy. The guy had turned out just like his old man, a solid, uncompromising face, hardly an ounce of fat on the body. Only the hair had changed, the bright, angry ginger fading to a salt-and-pepper mixture of red and gray.

Tommy came back and pulled Daniel aside. "Where's Anna?"

"Upstairs. Sleeping."

"You've got no idea who's out to get you?"

"None."

"Has Regan explained the procedure to you?"

"That I can pay up or leave it in your hands. If there's a ransom demand."

Tommy nodded. "What do you want to do?"

"What will get my kid back for me?"

"If I knew that . . ." He left the sentence unfinished.

"What about the blonde woman who started all this?" Daniel assumed that Tommy knew the history of the case, right back to Benjamin being pestered outside school.

"Do you know how many blue Mercurys there are? Sure we've got people looking for a blonde driving one with New York plates, but don't get your hopes up over that. The only line we'll get is when the kidnappers contact us."

"How long does that normally take?"

"Depends. Some do it immediately because they want to get it over with as quickly as you do. Others? Well, they take their time to build up the suspense."

Daniel forced himself to ask the question from which he had been hiding. "Even if I pay, is there a guarantee . . ."

"That you'll get your kid back in one piece? I wish I could tell you yes, but I can't."

"Thanks for being honest."

Tommy gave him a sardonic smile. "That's what we're supposed to be. If we're not, who is?"

Anna awoke shortly before midday. When she ventured downstairs, her mind was still numbed by the sedative, but she remembered Tommy from the meeting more than fifteen years earlier in Greenwich Village. "How's your wife?" she asked, a question that Daniel had neglected.

Tommy grimaced. "She gave me an ultimatum about six years ago. Her or the job. I guess I took too long making up my mind."

"Any children?"

"Three. A boy and two girls. They're with her."

"Are you divorced?" Daniel asked, surprised.

"No. Just separated. She won't even mention the word—a good Catholic—and I don't see any point in getting one. We see each other weekends."

The telephone rang, a single sharp jangle that cut through everyone in the room like a winter wind. Daniel's hand jerked spasmodically as he reached out for the receiver. Tommy slammed his hand down on top. "Let it ring a couple of times, Cherrybum. Don't show them you're sitting on it." He strode to the extension, his eyes on Daniel, waiting for him to answer.

Daniel picked it up on the third ring. "Yes?"

"Mr. Kerr." A woman's voice. "Your son is well."

Daniel flicked a glance at Tommy, who nodded encouragingly. "Where is he?"

"Never mind where he is. You will only see him again if you do exactly as we say."

"Who are you?" Daniel asked stupidly in response to Tommy's mimed command to keep talking.

The question was ignored. "We'll speak to you again at five o'clock this evening." The call ended abruptly.

Tommy got through to the telephone company. There was nothing, no way of getting a bearing on such a short call. "Looks like we've got to wait."

"Do you think it was the blonde woman?" Anna asked.

"Who knows?" Daniel had never felt so helpless in his life. The joy and triumph of the previous night had turned sour, leaving him desperate and impotent, unable to do anything. He realized what course he had to follow. Tommy and Regan, the other FBI agent, had laid out the cards clearly. Either he could deliver whatever ransom the kidnappers demanded in the hope that Benjamin would be released, or he could let the FBI use the drop as a lead to cracking the case—which would probably endanger his son. Only one course appealed to him—give them whatever the hell they wanted just to get Benjamin back. He'd worry about the money afterward.

Five o'clock came and went without another phone call.

Tommy tried to ease Daniel's fears by saying he had expected it. The kidnappers were playing with Daniel, teasing him, psyching him up to such a degree of anxiety that he would do anything when they finally decided to reveal their terms.

Moishe arrived just before six, battling his way through the reporters camped outside the house, to offer any help he could. He knew of Tommy's presence from radio reports on the kidnapping. They shook hands formally, two men at a business meeting; old friendships could be continued at a later date.

The telephone rang many times with friends and colleagues anxious to learn what was happening. Daniel kept the calls short, explaining that the line had to be free. At seven-thirty, the call he was waiting for came through.

"Mr. Kerr."

He recognized the woman's voice immediately. "Where were you at five?" he demanded angrily. "You told me you'd call back at five!"

On the extension, Tommy raised a hand to caution him to remain calm. Then he dropped it. If Daniel got involved in an argument with the kidnappers, he might keep them on the telephone long enough to get a trace; anything was worth a try.

The woman took no notice of Daniel's furious questions. "We want two hundred thousand dollars for the return of your son. In cash. By midday tomorrow."

"Where the hell am I supposed to come up with that?"

"You're worth it."

"Not in accessible cash I'm not!" He looked around the room wildly, searching for ideas to prolong the call. "I'll need more time. I can't raise that much by midday."

"You'll have to. We'll call back at midnight with directions for the delivery."

"Ask to speak to your kid," Moishe mouthed.

"How do I know my son's all right?" Daniel asked the woman. "I want to speak to him."

"You can't."

"Lady, I'm not putting together ten bucks until I know my son's all right."

The woman hung up.

Tommy cursed quietly and fluently. "Let's see if we had any

luck this time." He called the exchange and shook his head. "Too quick again. Can you get that kind of bread?"

"From the bank. They'll loan me."

"How much do they want?" Anna and Moishe asked simultaneously.

"Two hundred grand. By midday tomorrow."

"I'm going outside to talk to the reporters," Tommy said. "Keep them off your back by giving them something to chew on."

Daniel watched through the bay window of the living room as Tommy answered reporters' questions. He had no idea what Tommy was saying; he just wished he had the answers himself.

By five minutes after midnight, Daniel knew he had to make the hardest decision of his life. Do it Tommy's way, or the way he wanted to. The woman had called at precisely midnight to ask Daniel if he had arranged for the money. Daniel said he had, in used fifties and twenties. The bank manager would have it ready for him at ten-thirty the following morning. The woman had then specified that the money was to be delivered to a drive-in movie in Little Ferry, four miles away from where Daniel lived. The movie lot was abandoned for the winter, and the surrounding area was deserted enough for any police tails to be spotted. If the pick-up man was satisfied that whoever made the delivery had not been followed, the woman had said, he would accept the ransom. If not, the pick-up would be aborted and the woman promised Daniel he would never see Benjamin again.

"I'm a father, too, Cherrybum," Tommy said softly. "I know exactly what you're thinking right now. Do you want us to handle it, or do you want to make the drop yourself and hope for the best?"

Daniel did not know how to answer. He had dreaded this moment, when the life of his son would hang on his words.

"Do it Tommy's way," Anna said quietly. "We have no guarantee of Benjamin's safety even if we do it their way."

Tommy didn't wait for Daniel's opinion. As far as he was concerned, Anna had spoken for them all. "We'll set the place up. The only thing remaining now is whether you want to make the drop yourself, with us keeping watch, or you'd rather one of my men did it."

"I'll do it." The offer came from Moishe. "Give me the directions and the money and I'll make the drop. They take one look at me, and they'll know I'm not a cop."

The comment brought a smile to the faces of the people in the room. Tommy asked Daniel for a large suitcase he could use. "We can fix it up, plant a homing device that'll give us an idea where they go. We don't want to follow too closely in case they tumble onto us."

Daniel went upstairs for the suitcase. When he came back down, Tommy was briefing Moishe on what he had to do.

Moishe set out from the house at eleven thirty-five the following morning. The suitcase containing two hundred thousand dollars was locked in the trunk of his car. The instructions were clear. He was to enter the empty drive-in, drop the suitcase in the garbage container close to the entrance and leave immediately. Six FBI agents in three vehicles had already staked out the drive-in, and local police had been warned to give the vicinity a wide berth.

Daniel remained in the house with Anna, Tommy and another agent. The two FBI men showed no signs of the anxiety that was eating away Daniel's stomach like acid. He guessed they were used to the tension, hardened professionals, men who had been through it a thousand times in a thousand similar situations.

A radio transmitter on the table next to Tommy crackled into life. One FBI team disguised as a telephone repair crew had seen Moishe entering the drive-in. "There's something wrong. Another car's just pulling in behind him."

"What kind of car?"

"A dark blue Mercury with New York plates. Just the driver, a male Caucasian."

Daniel sat bolt upright in the chair, his hand clasping Anna's at the mention of the blue Mercury. The agent read off the license plate and Tommy told the other man in the living room to run it.

"Stay with it," Tommy advised the stake-out man. For the

first time a tremor showed in his voice.

"Why have they changed their plans?" Daniel asked. "Moishe was supposed to drop off the money in the garbage container. He wasn't supposed to be met."

"I don't know. Maybe they've been following him all the time. Maybe they had the house staked out, just like we're doing to the drop-off point. They saw a man leave with a suitcase so they followed to make sure Moishe wasn't being tailed by us."

Suddenly a babble of voices erupted from the transmitter, shouted words about suspects and deliveryman and shooting. Tommy grabbed the transmitter. "Move in!" he snapped. "Pick him up!"

"What happened?" Daniel asked.

"They forgot the rules, Cherrybum. The guy in the Mercury just shot your buddy and tried to run with the suitcase."

"Where are you going?" Daniel screamed as Tommy ran toward the front door.

"Where do you think? Down there."

Daniel forgot all about Anna as he leaped after Tommy. "Not without me you're not!"

Tommy and Daniel arrived at the drive-in moments after an ambulance had whisked Moishe off to the hospital. Regan was waiting and Tommy demanded to know what had happened. Twenty yards away, past a line of audio hook-ups for the movie, Daniel could see a man in handcuffs.

Regan related the events in a dull monotone; he might just as well have been reading off a shopping list. "The suspect was waiting by the entrance. As Mr. Waterman drove in, he followed. Mr. Waterman got out of his car with the case, intent on depositing it in the garbage container. When the suspect tried to take the case from him, Mr. Waterman put up a struggle. The suspect then pulled out a gun and fired one shot."

"How is he?" Daniel burst out. "Moishe. What happened to him?"

Regan seemed to notice Daniel's presence for the first time.

"It was a flesh wound. The bullet just nicked his left shoulder. If you ask me, Mr. Kerr, your friend fainted the moment he saw the gun. He was already on his way down when the suspect fired. We came out before he could fire again."

Daniel's head dropped onto his chest and a sigh of relief shook his frame. Until he remembered Benjamin. He grabbed Tommy by the arm and pulled him around. "What happens to my son now?"

"I don't know. All we can do is grill this guy. If we get nothing out of him, we have to go back and wait for another phone call." He turned to Regan. "What have you got on the suspect?"

Regan didn't have to consult any notes. "Name's Paul Fulford. Address 73-12 Thirty-seventh Avenue, Jackson Heights. An apartment. We're checking out his sheet now."

Daniel followed Regan and Tommy across to the handcuffed suspect, who was being guarded by two more agents. On the ground next to the man was the suitcase containing the money.

"Has he been told his rights?" Tommy asked. One of the agents nodded. Tommy directed his attention to the suspect. "You want to help yourself? Or do you want to protect your friends?"

The man said nothing.

"Kidnapping is a capital crime. Do you know what that means? You can burn for it. Is that what you want, while your friends get off scot free?"

"I don't know anything about any kidnapping. I was trying to grab that guy's suitcase, that's all."

"With a gun?" Tommy asked sarcastically. "You needed a gun for that?"

Watching, Daniel felt the fury of his own temper building up inside him. He shoved his way between Regan and Tommy and lunged at the handcuffed man. "Where's my son?" he bellowed. "What have you done with my son?" Before any of the federal agents could make a move to stop him, he pounded a huge fist into the man's face and sent him staggering backward. Unable to break his fall with his hands, the man crashed awkwardly to the ground, skinning his face on the hard, frozen earth.

Hands grabbed Daniel's shoulders, lifting him as he tried to dive onto the prostrate figure. He shook himself free and pounced again, fists still flying. One punch hammered into the concrete ground. Daniel never felt the spasm of pain that flashed up his arm. All he knew was the blind, hopeless rage that consumed him. The man on the ground knew where his son was being held. That man could stop his son from being harmed. "Tell me where he is, you bastard! Before I kill you!"

Hands grabbed him again, this time like steel claws which yanked him upright. "Knock it off, for Christ's sake!" Tommy yelled. "We want a suspect for questioning, not a goddamned corpse!"

"He knows where my kid is!" Daniel screamed back.

"He's not going to tell you anything if you split his head open and spill his brains on the earth. Will you listen to reason?"

One of the agents interrupted the argument with news about the suspect. "He owns a bar on Northern Boulevard in Queens. No record at all. The Mercury's registered to him."

"No record?" Tommy asked. "Are you sure?"

"Not under his own name. Clean as they come."

Tommy turned to face the suspect. The man was slowly getting to his feet. Blood was trickling from his nose and one side of his face was badly scraped. "Fulford, you help us and I promise you the judge'll let you down lightly. You've got no record and my word'll help."

What did letting down lightly mean? Daniel wanted to know. Five years? Ten? No matter how much the guy helped, Daniel did not want to see him let off. He'd put Anna and Benjamin through misery and torment; why the hell should he be treated leniently?

A crowd had gathered, attracted first by the sound of the shot, then by the flurry of action in the deserted drive-in theater. Local police had to be called in to keep onlookers at a distance. Tommy decided that the area was becoming too public. He gripped Fulford by the arm and steered him toward the fake telephone repair truck. Police officers cleared a path through the crowd. Tommy shoved the handcuffed suspect into the back of the truck and slammed the door on him.

"You ever hear of the nice-guy-bad-guy routine?" he asked Daniel.

Daniel stared at him blankly, unable to understand.

Tommy explained briefly. "A subject is interrogated by two men. One's reasonable while the other wants to break every bone in the suspect's body. It's a psychological deal. I reckon you're the most believable bad guy around here right now. We're going for a ride." He told Regan to get in and drive. Then Tommy climbed in the back of the truck with Daniel.

As the truck began to move, Tommy opened up. "We're taking a trip, Fulford. By the time we're finished, you're either going to tell us where the Kerr kid is, or you're going to be carried out of here in a bag. Take your choice." He sat back against the wall of the truck while he let the words sink in. Daniel watched carefully, looking for his cue. Not that he needed one. He didn't need any kind of cue to launch himself across the confined space and slam the bastard's head to pulp against the wall.

"Where do you want me to go?" Regan called from the driver's seat.

"Go on 46 back toward the Bridge. Keep it slow." Satisfied that Regan was going in the right direction, Tommy turned back to Fulford. "Tell me where the kid is. Otherwise I'm going to let his father loose on you."

"I don't know anything about any kid."

"He's all yours, Cherrybum."

Daniel crouched in the low space. His hands shot out and caught Fulford around the neck. Four times in quick succession Daniel smashed the man's head into the side of the truck. Each blow was accompanied by a scream of pain. In the front, Regan glanced in the mirror to see what was happening, then he looked back at the road.

"That's enough!" Tommy called out. Daniel moved back and Tommy confronted Fulford again. "That's just a taste of what you're going to get. When we were kids, this guy beat the hell out of me with a baseball bat. That's nothing to what he'll do to you. And we'll swear on a stack of bibles that you were trying to escape. That you jumped out of the back of the truck and bounced on the road a few times." Tommy heard the radio but paid no attention.

Regan's voice came from the front. "There's been another phone call to the house. The woman. Says the bagman's late and if he doesn't get back in half an hour, they're going to dump the kid."

Daniel pushed Tommy out of the way. "Where's my kid?" His clenched fist crashed into Fulford's face. The suspect's head bounced sickeningly off the side of the truck. Tommy made no attempt to intervene, as if he had realized that Daniel's way was now the only way. Time was the most important factor now.

"Where's my kid?" Daniel's fist slammed into the man again. His knuckles were bruised and bloody, throbbing with pain from where he had hit the frozen ground before, but all he knew was the release of the fury that had been boiling up inside him like a volcano since the blonde woman had first appeared. "Where is he? Where are they holding him?"

Tommy pulled back Daniel's arm as he was about to strike again. Fulford's head was hanging loosely. A froth of blood covered his nose and mouth. As he breathed, red bubbles formed and burst obscenely. "He's going to beat you to death and I'm not going to raise a finger to stop him," he warned quietly. "Unless you tell us what we want to know."

The man tried to say something. A gurgling came from his battered mouth and he spat out blood. "Empty apartment in the Bronx. University and One Fifty-ninth."

"Move it!" Tommy shouted to Regan. "University and One Fifty-ninth! Call in more units!" Regan sent out the call and put his foot down on the gas pedal; as an afterthought, he called the house to keep the agent posted there informed.

"Will we get there in time?" Daniel asked.

"Easy," Tommy replied. "Other units will be there before us." He turned to Fulford. "Who else is in the apartment? How many?"

"Two," the man mumbled painfully. "Man and a woman."

"Names?"

Daniel felt the truck pick up speed as Regan headed toward the George Washington Bridge."

"Jack Harris."

"The woman?"

"I don't know her name."

"You don't know her name?" Tommy asked incredulously.

"She came into my bar a few times. Felt us out, Jack and me, to see if we were interested in this job." The man's voice became clearer. "Said we could keep all the money. She didn't want any part of it."

"What did she want?"

"She wanted him." The man nodded at Daniel.

"Why did you shoot the guy who made the drop? Why didn't you keep to your part of the bargain and let him drop off the money in the garbage container?"

"The broad was planning on stringing it out. I was going to take the money, and she'd call you to say the money wasn't where it was supposed to be. She'd threaten to have the kid killed. Then she'd call again to say we'd got the money but now it wasn't enough. She told us maybe we could end up with half a million between us this way."

"Were you going to let the kid loose?"

"I don't know what she'd planned. I never meant the kid any harm, honest. You've got to believe me. I didn't mean to hurt the guy who made the drop either. I never thought a skinny runt like that would put up a fight."

Tommy turned around to look at Daniel. "Someone's sure got it in for you, Cherrybum. Got it in for you so much that they're not even interested in the money. Any ideas?"

Daniel shook his head. He must have made enemies along the way. Everyone did. But no one, surely, would strike back this fiercely. He thought about Moishe and asked Tommy to check how he was. Regan called the agent stationed at the hospital.

"Your pal's all right. A graze, nothing more. He'll be home by tonight."

"Thank God for that." Now all he had to worry about was Benjamin.

Chapter Five

Anna sat quietly in the living room, willing herself to remain calm. From time to time she looked at the federal agent who had been left behind. He had answered the telephone when the woman had last called, and had relayed the information to Tommy Mulvaney. Anna had been unable to help but overhear the urgent message. When he had realized what he had done, the agent tried to cover up. But Anna knew the truth. The dreadful knowledge from which she had tried to hide had made itself felt. Her son's very life was in danger.

She felt cold, encased in a block of ice, unable to think or act. The role of operatic heroine had invaded reality, all the tragedies in which she had ever starred had combined into one greater tragedy. Only now there was no comforting knowledge that when it was all over, she would stand in front of the gold curtain and accept ovations, flowers. The ending to this particular production had not been written yet. The composer was penning in the notes while he went along, changing in mid-stroke to give another twist, another dimension to the performance. Or—the most chilling possibility of all—had the final act already been written? Was Benjamin even now dead?

"Are you all right, Mrs. Kerr?" the agent asked, concerned at her silence. "Is there anything I can do for you?"

"Just get my son back to me."

The agent laid a reassuring hand on Anna's arm. "Try not to worry, Mrs. Kerr. They know where he's being held. They're on the way there now. They'll get him out."

Anna searched the man's eyes as she tried to find the truth. She saw nothing; the certainty in his voice had not reached his eyes.

"Can't this thing go any faster?" Daniel snapped at Tommy. "We're crawling along, for Christ's sake. We'll be too late!"

"We're doing seventy-five," Tommy replied as the truck

streaked across the bottom level of the George Washington Bridge. From somewhere a flashing red light had appeared on the truck, accompanied by a strident siren to clear its path; inside the truck, the clamor was amplified tenfold. Daniel looked around and saw the bloody face of the man who had shot Moishe. Tommy had handcuffed him to the pipe leading from the gas filler to the tank. With each bump and jolt he swung around drunkenly, his unprotected head banging violently against the side of the truck. Daniel could not care less.

Four-hundred yards from the apartment where Benjamin was being held, Regan turned off the siren and the light. The sudden silence was eerie. Daniel felt as if he were in an aircraft and his ears had just popped under pressure. He dug his fingers into them as he tried to clear the blockage, wanting to hear more than just the truck's straining engine note and the noise of other traffic. Without the piercing sound of the siren, the urgency had disappeared; and with it the chance to save his son.

"Up there." Tommy pointed past Regan's shoulder at a corner apartment block. "There are four cars there already."

Daniel saw a lot of cars. He could not tell which ones belonged to the FBI. A man dressed in Con Edison overalls stepped from the sidewalk into the road and waved the truck to a halt.

"We're evacuating the building," he called in through the open window to Regan.

"Won't that tip them off?" Daniel asked.

"Give us some credit, Cherrybum," Tommy replied. "They won't even know what's happening until we go in there." He switched his attention to the man in Con Ed overalls. "Can you see into the apartment at all?"

"We've got a lookout across the street." The man pointed to another apartment block; a man was on the roof with a pair of binoculars. "He hasn't been able to see inside though. They've got sheets or something over the windows."

"Okay." Tommy reached inside his jacket and withdrew a revolver. "Let's get this thing over with."

Daniel started to follow him into the building, but Regan

blocked the way. "Hey! I'm going with you!" Daniel protested.

"Nothing doing, pal," Tommy said. "You stay right here."

"But—"

"I told you, nothing doing. This is our job, not yours." He dismissed Daniel and led the way into the evacuated apartment building. Powerless, Daniel watched him go, followed by six other men. Regan stayed behind, alternately watching Daniel and the people who had gathered around the entrance to the building as they sensed something happening.

"Go on, beat it all of you!" Regan hissed. "You're putting a kid's life in jeopardy."

The crowd did not move. Regan edged toward the nearest people, waving his hands. In the instant it took the federal agent to make the move, Daniel darted into the building's doorway, looked around to orient himself and pounded heavily up the stairs. Behind, he could hear Regan's desperate shout for him to stop. Screw you! Daniel muttered. No one's keeping me out of something like this. That's my kid they're holding in there, and I want to see what happens.

As he reached the third floor, heart pounding, breath ragged, he recognized one of Tommy's men, pressed flat against a wall while he waited for a signal. The man turned at the sound of Daniel's heavy steps. Anger flashed across his face and he waved furiously with his hand for Daniel to keep back. Daniel stopped for an instant, then ran to where the agent stood.

"Get the fuck out of here!" the man spat out. Further down the hallway, Daniel could see Tommy and three of the other men; two men were still out of sight and he guessed they were hiding somewhere, ready for action.

"I'm not going anywhere," Daniel growled.

The man made no further attempt to argue. His attention was on Tommy, who raised a hand in the air, then made a sharp cutting motion. One of the agents with him lifted a foot and slammed the door at the lock. Wood splintered. The door flew back and slammed against the wall with a noise like a bomb exploding. Tommy dived through with two other men hard on his heels. Shouts echoed along the narrow hallway. Daniel waited fearfully for the sound of shots. There were none. He rushed forward, charging into the apartment after the last of the agents. Confusion greeted him. Two agents held a man over a table; one had a gun jammed into his ear while the other searched him. Another two agents, their backs to Daniel, were grappling with a blonde woman. The bitch who had made the calls, molested Benjamin outside the school, threatened to kill him. Tommy stood in the center of the room, the revolver back in its holster, supervising.

"What the hell are you doing up here!" he yelled as he recognized Daniel standing in the doorway.

"Where's Benny?"

"In the bedroom." Tommy turned back to the two men who were struggling with the blonde. She was kicking and clawing like a fury. One man already had a deep red furrow down his cheek. Daniel ignored it all as he raced into the bedroom. A figure was crouched in the corner, mouth gagged, hands and feet tied. Daniel stared before he recognized the trussed-up parcel as his son. He leaped across the intervening space and scrabbled furiously with the ropes that bound Benjamin, fingers fumbling in their haste to release him. A noise from behind made him turn.

"Try using this." Tommy held out a pocket knife. Daniel slashed through the gag, then attacked the ropes that bound Benjamin's hands and feet.

"You all right?"

The boy tried to speak. A dry croaking sound came from his mouth. Tears welled up in his eyes and dribbled down his cheeks.

Why? Daniel wanted to scream. Why did these animals pick on someone who'd never harmed a soul? Gradually he forced himself to be calm, to ease Benjamin's anxiety by displaying none of his own.

"She said I was going to be killed, Pa," Benjamin finally managed to say. "Even if you paid what they wanted, she was going to kill me." He started to cough and more tears sprang to his eyes. Daniel waited. "She said they were going to leave me here after they left. I'd starve to death before anyone found me."

"No one's going to hurt you, Benny." Daniel could feel tears beginning to burn his own eyes. "We're taking you home right now. Your mother wants to see you. When we get downstairs, we'll call her. You can talk to her. Tell her you're all right." He helped Benjamin to stand up, watching in pain as his son hopped from one foot to the other as he fought against the agony of returning circulation. Tommy stepped forward to help, taking one arm while Daniel held the other.

They reentered the living room. All six agents who had entered the building with Tommy were present. The situation was under control. The man was sitting on the floor, hands cuffed behind his back. The woman, blonde hair awry, make-up smeared grotesquely, was being held by two men. Daniel stood in front of her and looked hard into her face. She was in her fifties, lines on her forehead and around her mouth. He could swear he had never seen her before in his life.

"What did I ever do to you?" he asked. "What?"

She laughed harshly. The sound sent shivers down Daniel's spine. Then she spat at him, striking him under the right eye. He made no attempt to retaliate. The saliva dripped down his cheek like another tear. "I hope you crawled," she whispered. "Writhed like I did when you killed my father, you bastard!"

The woman's words had more effect on Tommy than on Daniel. He grabbed hold of her chin and jerked her face around. "Joey Bloom's daughter!" he exclaimed, voice full of wonder. "Joey Bloom's daughter, Linda!"

"Linda?" The single word came out as a whisper, and Daniel stared at her in disbelief.

"Linda," the woman said, a malicious edge in her voice. "I waited years for this. It was worth waiting for. Just as it'll be worth rotting in prison for. It would have been worth dying to get even with you, you sonofabitch!" She spat at him again, hitting his coat. "I hope you burn in hell!"

"Get her out of here," Tommy said. He'd seen enough. Any second now Daniel would lose control of himself, and this time Tommy was not sure he could handle him. The two men holding Linda began to move. Daniel motioned for them to stay, but let Regan take Benjamin outside.

"Why did you wait all this time?" he asked. "And why my kid? Why not me?"

She regarded him coldly, debating whether to administer the ultimate injury by refusing to answer his questions. "I watched you climb, Daniel, and I wanted you to fall off the ladder so badly that it burned a hole in my gut. Then I decided you'd fall harder once you got right to the top. So I waited. And I collected the ammunition I'd need to make your life a misery."

Daniel listened, unable to find a reply to the hate in Linda's voice. The first girl he'd ever been with, ever made love to. He knew he should be yearning to strangle her right now. He had been until he found out who she was. Instead, he could feel nothing toward her, no animosity, no anger. That had died. If he felt anything, it was pity.

"When I saw that picture of you, your wife and kid coming back from Israel, I knew how to hit you."

"But why Benny?"

"Because I wanted you to live with it afterwards. Just like I had to live with the memory of being there when you got my father killed."

"Take her away," Tommy said. This time Daniel did not try to stop the two agents who guided Linda out of the apartment, down to one of the waiting cars. He was exhausted. His own anger he could have coped with, understood. But how could he comprehend a woman who had nurtured a hatred for twenty-seven years?

"Come on." Tommy put a hand on his shoulder and led him toward the hallway. By the door, he stopped. "Hey, Cherrybum, I've got something for you."

Daniel looked up expectantly. He saw Tommy's fist swing through a short arc before it impacted just below his left eye. He stumbled backward, his own hands raised to defend himself.

"What the hell was that for?"

"For not staying downstairs when I told you to. You could have screwed up the whole deal by rushing up here the way you did." He began to laugh when he saw the anger looming on Daniel's face. "Besides, how in the name of heaven do you hope to claim self-defense for what you did to that guy downstairs when you haven't got a mark on you? Him with his head smashed in and you without a scratch!"

As Daniel comprehended, he dropped his hands. Self-defense. He had to have some mark on him, otherwise no one would believe it. Tommy didn't have to hit him so hard, though. The sonofabitch had put enough into the punch to knock out an ox.

Tommy's fist flashed through the air again and slammed into the same spot. Daniel spun around and collided with the wall. "That's for what you did to me with a baseball bat when we were kids," Tommy called out over his shoulder as he left the apartment. "Now we're quits. Come on down and look after your kid."

Daniel clawed at the wall for balance. He felt his eye, relieved to find it was still in the socket. That Irish bastard could still hit, even if he was past fifty. Slowly he followed Tommy down to the street. There was no sign of Linda or the man who had been with her in the apartment. Only Tommy and Benjamin remained outside the building. Regan was off to one side, pushing back a crowd of onlookers who wanted to see what the commotion was about. He was telling them they could read all about it in the newspapers that evening.

"Some shiner that guy gave you," Tommy said. "No wonder you hauled off like you did."

Benjamin's eyes opened wide in fright as he saw the rapidly swelling bruise under his father's left eye. He could not make up his mind whether it had been there before. "What happened, Pa?" He ran toward Daniel and threw his arms around him.

"Some other guy did it. Earlier. When we went to drop off the money they wanted."

"What did you do to him?"

"Your father almost killed the guy," Tommy answered. "We had to drag him off, kicking and screaming." He accompanied the words with a smile and Daniel could not help joining in. "Isn't that right, Cherrybum?"

"That's right. No one hits your old man and gets away with it, Benny. And no one takes off with you and gets away with it either."

"About time you made that call," Tommy reminded him.

"Otherwise Anna's going to be going out of her head with worry."

While the seconds ticked past, the last vestiges of hope passed from Anna's breast. Either they had not found where Benjamin was being held, or—and the thought was even more frightening—they had found him and did not want her to know.

What did a mother do when she lost her only child? And when she was too old to ever hope for another? Daniel already knew how it felt for a father to lose his child. He'd been through it once already. He'd know how to cope. No; she changed her mind. He might cave in completely, be powerless to shrug off another tragedy. What would she do to numb the loss? Throw herself wholeheartedly back into her work? Lose herself in the embrace of the stage, of opera? Robin Duguid would like that. He was always trying to persuade her to become more involved with the Grand. For someone, at least, her own tragedy would present a silver lining.

The telephone rang. The FBI agent's hand reached out to lift the receiver before the first ring could end. He listened for a few seconds. "For you," he said, passing the receiver to Anna.

She searched his eyes for the truth. Did he know already what the call was about? And couldn't bear to tell her himself? "Yes," she said hesitantly into the mouthpiece."

"Ma? It's Benny."

"Where are you?" How could she speak so calmly? Was she acting, using lessons she'd learned from the stage?

"I'm with Pa. I'm all right."

The receiver dropped from Anna's hand, bounced on her lap and thudded dully onto the carpet. The agent started from his chair. He stopped when he saw Anna's closed eyes, the rhythmic movement of her chest as she sobbed quietly in relief. He got up from his chair and walked quietly from the room.

Daniel visited Moishe at home that evening to find his friend sitting up in bed, apparently well. As Regan had said, it was a graze, nothing more serious. Moishe insisted on displaying the bandages that swathed his left shoulder, all the while telling Daniel how it felt to face a man with a gun, to see the orange flame spurt out, to feel hot metal burn through flesh. While he listened, Daniel glanced at Helen. Every few words, she would pretend to dab tears from her eyes. Suddenly cast in the role of hero, with his picture in the newspapers and on television, Moishe was embroidering the story more with each telling.

"Who told you to go for the guy?" Daniel asked. "Have you been reading Dick Tracy again?"

"What would you have done if it had been my kid?" Moishe retorted. "If it had been Susie? You wouldn't have done the same thing for me?"

Daniel was too tired to argue. Today had seen the most strenuous performance of his life and he was mentally and physically shattered. He had spent almost an hour talking with reporters. Tommy had claimed another two hours of his time. Now he knew he had to go home to Anna and explain why a middle-aged blonde woman would organize a kidnapping against his son. That would be the most difficult part of all. He had kept Linda from Anna all this time; now that she had surfaced, Anna was entitled to know the connection. "I guess I'd have done the same thing," he finally admitted.

"I hear you did some job on that guy who shot me," Moishe said, wanting to keep the excitement alive. "Beat him black and blue."

"Look what he did to me first." Daniel pointed to his discolored eye, already convinced that Tommy had not been responsible. "Besides, if someone tried to shoot me, wouldn't you have done the same thing?"

"Only if he was chained up," Moishe replied honestly.

"He was."

While Moishe stayed in bed, Helen walked Daniel downstairs to the door. "You know he thinks the world of you, don't you?" she said quietly. "He wouldn't have volunteered to deliver the money for anyone else. Even for me, I don't think."

Daniel thought about her words and smiled. "Moishe and I have known each other for too long, I guess. He's had so much practice in going to bat for me that it's got to be a habit."

"Moishe wouldn't have it any other way."

On the doorstep, Daniel kissed Helen on the cheek. "Neither would I. But don't tell him that."

During the short journey home, Daniel reached his decision. He would be completely open with Anna about Linda. They had been married for too long, shared too much for it to be handled any other way. He would tell her about Linda and Joey Bloom. He'd leave nothing out. How he had first met Linda in her father's hotel. The relationship between them. Then Fat Benny's murder, and how he had used Linda to trap her father. The whole episode had been closed more than seven years before he had met Anna, so what did it matter anyway?

Anna listened carefully to Daniel's account of his experience with Linda. It had little effect on her. She was just grateful that it was all over and that Benjamin was safe. If anything, she could not help sharing Daniel's sentiments, feeling sorry for Linda, sorry for a woman who had stored and nourished her hatred for twenty-seven years.

"What a terrible waste of a life," she said when Daniel finished speaking. "To spend it like that, plotting to wreck someone else's life."

"I'm glad you can feel sorry for her."

"Don't you? Or is it going to help you if she goes to jail for the remainder of her life?"

"You know something? Pity's all I did feel when I recognized her in the apartment. First confusion. Then, when I realized who she was and why she'd done it, pity. I wonder if Tommy can do anything to her if we don't press charges." The idea appealed to him. "They can get the guy who shot Moishe for attempted murder. Probably nail that other clown for something. But I wonder if there's any sense in sending Linda to prison for the rest of her life."

Anna was amused by Daniel's change in attitude. "Before you were ready to kill. Now you're thinking about forgiving and forgetting."

"Not forgetting." He shook his head vehemently. "Just forgiving. I'm getting too old to be vindictive anymore. I'm grateful that Benny's safe and sound. I don't want revenge because I can see what it did for Linda."

"Why don't you ask Benny?" Anna suggested. "See what he thinks."

"Good idea," Daniel agreed, pleased with it. Benjamin had been in the eye of the storm. He should be the one to decide what course of action to follow. Daniel got out of the chair and went upstairs, followed by Anna. He knocked tentatively on the door of Benjamin's room, scared of waking his son if he was asleep. When a voice called out to enter, Daniel and Anna went inside. Benjamin was sitting up in bed, reading.

"Hi, how do you feel?"

"All right, I guess." Benjamin set the book on the night table. Daniel glanced at the cover and saw it was Leon Uris's *Exodus*. The kid must have read it half a dozen times by now; he kept on going back to it as if it were the Bible.

"We want to talk to you, Benny. We want to ask your advice."

"What about?" The boy seemed disturbed at the prospect of adults coming to him for advice.

"That blonde woman. What do you think should be done to her?"

"She'll go to prison, won't she?"

"Is that what you want to happen to her?" The question came from Anna.

Benjamin looked confused as he pondered the question. He didn't have the answer and his face showed it. "I don't know. When I was in that room, all tied up, I wanted to kill them all. For what they were doing to me. And to you."

Daniel nodded, understanding his son's emotions. They had been his own. "And now?"

"Now I don't really care. It's over and I want to forget about it. I just don't ever want to see that woman again."

"Okay, Benny, you won't." Daniel leaned over the bed and kissed his son on the forehead. "Good night. Get some sleep."

Downstairs, he faced Anna. "I'm going to call Tommy and tell him to forget about Linda. Let the poor bitch go free for all I care."

"What if she tries something again?"

"Do you really think she would?"

It took Anna only a moment to decide. "No." She threw her

arms around Daniel and hugged him tightly. "You're just a big softie, you know that? A big soft teddy bear. And I love you for it."

"Get off," he protested, embarrassed that the housekeeper might come down and see Anna plastering his face with kisses. "We're middle-aged. We're not supposed to be acting like this."

"There's a little scrap of paper somewhere that says we can act any way we damned well like. Unless you want to let me go free as well."

"You've got some hopes."

"That's what I thought." She became serious again. "Don't forget when you speak to Tommy to mention those two tickets you offered him a million years ago. He might want them now."

If Daniel were in front of him now, Tommy knew he would have no hesitation in closing his other eye to knock some sense into him. The whole idea was preposterous, wanting to let the woman go.

"You listen to me and you listen good!" Tommy yelled into the phone. "That woman is going for trial with the other two. And she's going to be convicted with them. Nothing's going to interfere with this case."

"But, Tommy . . ." Daniel knew it was hopeless to continue. The whole idea was crazy, asking Tommy if he could let Linda go free. He and Anna were so overcome with relief at getting Benjamin back that their minds were clouded by a charity that didn't belong in the situation. "Hasn't the poor bitch suffered enough? What's the point of sending her to prison?"

"Who the hell said anything about prison?" Tommy demanded. "Kidnapping's an offense punishable by the death penalty."

"What?" Daniel was horrified.

"Don't worry too much about it. We don't execute many people these days."

"But can't you just let her go and forget about it?"

"Cherrybum, get this through your thick skull, will you? If you pull out on us, Uncle Sam's going to take a good, hard look at you. He'll want to know why you don't want to press kidnapping charges, why you're backing out. With a person in your position, there can be only one reason. There was no kidnapping. You needed publicity, that's the reason. Maybe your career's in trouble, who knows? But you needed some good, sympathetic publicity so you arranged to have your son kidnapped."

"What? That's crazy! You know it's not true."

"Sure I know it's not true. But you can't afford to be charitable because there are a whole gang of people who'll think you fixed the whole thing. And I wouldn't blame them."

"What will happen to her then?"

"Life. Don't feel sorry for her, Cherrybum. She was a loser. Came from a family of losers. Just be thankful you got out of it okay. You hear me?"

"I hear you." The euphoria of finding his own solution had been disintegrated by Tommy's cold realism. If it were not so serious, it would have been funny, setting himself up for an investigation by trying to show mercy to Linda. She would have had the last laugh after all.

"So forget all about this crazy idea. We'll let you know when we need you."

"Hey, don't hang up!" Daniel remembered what Anna had told him. "Do you want a couple of tickets for a performance? I'm doing *Il Trovatore* again before the end of the season."

"You're doing what?"

"Never mind. It was just an idea. Be speaking to you, copper." He replaced the receiver and went upstairs to Anna.

Chapter Six

"Pa! Wake up! Wake up!"

Like a tornado in full, destructive flight, Benjamin burst through the door of his parents' bedroom to send it slamming back against the stop.

"What time is it?" Daniel asked groggily as he struggled to shake off slumber and sit up. Next to him, Anna poked fists into her eyes, trying to force them open. "Is the house on fire? It had better be." He saw his son standing over the bed. The kid was already dressed in jeans and a T-shirt. Perhaps it was late, and he and Anna had slept through the alarm.

"Six o'clock."

"What?"

"Six o'clock," Benjamin repeated. "Turn on your radio, quick! There's a war on!"

A war? Everyone knew there was a war on. Vietnam. Why was the kid getting so excited about it all of a sudden? Because he figured he might get drafted in a few years? Daniel reached out to flick on the bedside radio which was tuned to an all-news station. He didn't have to wait long. While Benjamin perched excitedly on the edge of the king-sized bed, Daniel and Anna listened to the announcer read out the latest information from the Middle East. Claims and counterclaims from Israeli and Arab spokesmen—all to Daniel's ears exaggerated. On the one hand, the Arab air forces claimed to have shot down hundreds of Israeli planes during major air battles; on the other, the entire air forces of Egypt, Syria and Jordan had supposedly been destroyed by the Israelis on the ground in the opening minutes of the war. Daniel felt giddy as he listened. Egypt was claiming its army was cutting across the thin waist of Israel in a drive to join up with the Jordanians, while the Israelis said they were pushing into the Gaza Strip and the Sinai.

"What do you think is happening?" Benjamin asked. "Who's telling the truth?"

"Who do you think?" Daniel asked back. He wasn't sure himself, but he'd be damned if he let his son know that.

Benjamin looked from his father to his mother and back. "I don't know. The Israelis, I hope."

"So do I." Daniel swung his feet clear of the bed and stood up, pulling the cord of his pajama trousers tight as he felt them slipping. Like everyone else, he had followed the events of the past weeks with close, anxious attention. The threats by Nasser, the blockading of the Straits of Tiran, the ever more ardent flirtation with war. He had relaxed when the Israeli government had said it would try to seek a peaceful solution. If the Israeli claims of wholesale destruction of Arab air power were to be believed, the Arabs had also relaxed.

"Where are you going?" Anna asked.

"Downstairs. Make some coffee. Come on." He put his arm around Benjamin's shoulders. "We can listen downstairs. Give your mother some peace and quiet."

By six o'clock that evening, Benjamin was arranging fund-raising activities through the local Zionist group to which he belonged, and Daniel had agreed to perform three concerts during the coming two weeks to raise money for Israel. He felt as if he had been in the middle of an explosion, like that time in London when the buzz bomb had landed a hundred yards away. Jewish organizations had called him up to ask if he'd perform in benefit concerts. Carnegie Hall had already been booked for one; so had the Grand. In the end, he stopped answering the telephone. There were only so many hours in his day; he could not do anymore.

Benjamin arrived home after ten-thirty, eyes blazing with excitement. In his hand was a Manischewitz *gefilte* fish jar, full of money, coins and bills. While Daniel watched, fascinated, Benjamin counted the money out on the kitchen table. It amounted to one hundred and thirty-five dollars and twenty cents, all made from knocking on doors in the neighborhood. Seven other boys of Benjamin's age had gone out that night; they expected to have more than one thousand dollars to send to Israel.

"When can we go there again, Pa?"

"How about we pack our bags and go right now?" Daniel asked, trying to keep his face straight.

"Can we?"

"Get out of here," Daniel laughed. "One, there's a war on right now. Two, you're in the middle of school. Maybe in the summer, if this thing has quieted down." He had meant to answer if Israel won but could not bring himself to say the words. No such doubt existed in Benjamin's mind. The kid was convinced that Israel would emerge victorious. To dampen that ardor would be nothing short of sinful. Daniel, also, was beginning to feel confident. That evening, the most comprehensive news report had emerged from the war zone, and it appeared that Israeli claims to have destroyed the Arab air forces on the ground were true. Perhaps they'd reach the Suez again. Perhaps . . .

"Do you think they'll take the old city of Jerusalem?" Benjamin asked, reading his father's thoughts.

"Be something, wouldn't it?" Daniel answered with a huge grin.

"Pa, make me a promise. If they take the old city, we'll go there this summer. I want to see the temple."

"I promise." He pointed to the money on the table. "Let's check that and I'll sign for it. We can talk about going to Israel in the morning."

With a brightly colored *yarmulke* perched dangerously on top of his thick brown hair and a *tallis* draped around his shoulders, Benjamin merged into the Saturday-morning crowd of shirt-sleeved worshippers thronging the Western Wall of the temple and disappeared from view. The effect was not lost on Daniel and Anna, who stood at the back of the crowd, unwilling to be separated into the men's and women's sections of the makeshift synagogue that had been organized at the wall.

"He's one of them," Anna marveled. "We brought up a middle-class American kid, and he fits into a bunch of Israelis like he was born here."

"I know." Daniel did not find it amusing. He saw a time in the future when his son would not ask to be taken to Israel for a vacation; he'd just up and leave. The United States and luxury weren't for Benjamin. He wanted to work for his pleasure, his fulfillment, wanted to work for it in the land he'd dreamed about ever since the first time he set foot inside a temple. When that day came, Daniel knew he would not fight his son. If Israel was what he wanted, Daniel would be proud, not regretful. He wondered if Anna realized it yet. He thought about discussing it with her now but refrained. She was the kid's mother after all. Mention something like Benjamin wanting to live in Israel—far away from the warmth and safety of home—and Anna would have a fit. She'd need time to adjust to it; now was not the moment to spring it on her.

As he listened to the congregation chanting prayers, Daniel was overcome by a sudden thought. He had not conducted a temple service since Harry Feldman at Paterson had died. Because of Benjamin's involvement in the local Jewish community, he went as regularly as he could to temple, but leading the service had become a memory. He preferred to be one of the congregation. Here, in front of the Western Wall, all that remained of the biblical temple, Daniel wanted to take a service again. Here was where it had all started a hundred lifetimes earlier.

Taking a prayer shawl from the stack, he slipped it on and eased his way through the crowd of men to where Benjamin stood. His son looked up, surprised to see him.

"Thought you were just going to watch."

"What's the matter? You think you're a better Jew than I am?" Daniel challenged. "I tell you one thing, I'm a better *chazan* than the guy they've got."

"Go ahead," Benjamin invited. "Show them what it's all about."

Daniel did not need any further prompting. He pushed his way gently toward the front of the congregation. The man who was leading the service, a white-bearded chaplain in the defense forces, regarded Daniel with curiosity as he squeezed himself out of the front row. As he waited for a pause in the service, Daniel hoped the old man spoke English.

"I'm a *chazan* in the States," he whispered. He was certain enough people in Israel knew him, that the name of Daniel Kerr would be recognizable. He didn't use it. All he wanted right now was to be a cantor again. "Can I take a part of the service?"

"Surely." The chaplain accepted the request as a *mitzvah*, a good deed.

"I'll wait until the end of the service. The 'Adon olom,' if I may." On his way through the congregation, Daniel had decided which hymn he wanted to sing, the closing piece from the Sabbath and High Holy Day morning services. He'd use the tune he had always reserved for the High Holy Days, a slow, intricate melody that only a cantor with the utmost faith in his voice would dare to use.

"Very good."

Daniel made his way back to Benjamin. He looked toward the barrier separating men from women and spotted Anna. He waved and grinned triumphantly.

Benjamin seemed disappointed when he saw his father returning. "What's the matter, aren't you good enough for this house?"

"Bite your tongue. You'll hear me."

Toward the end of the service, Daniel moved again to the front. The bearded chaplain stepped aside and Daniel took his place on the raised dais. He faced the wall where an ark had been erected to hold the sacred scrolls of the Torah. He changed his mind. He would sing to his audience, his congregation, give them a finale they had not anticipated.

Heads in the congregation lifted at the sound of the new voice, a world removed from that of the chaplain who had been conducting the service. The voice was recognizable, known by Americans in the congregation who had heard it on religious recordings. Smiles of pride and pleasure appeared to lift the solemnity of the service as the Americans recognized one of their own.

It was the first time Daniel had ever sung in the open air. He had no acoustics to worry about, no sounds bouncing back at him. There would be no applause either. It didn't matter. He was enjoying himself, even experiencing some of the feeling of coming home that his son felt. The fine temples of the United States, the grandeur of the opera houses he had graced held little at this particular moment against this sensation.

Daniel did not sing with the congregation. He sang above it, far above, letting his voice ring full as he aimed for the optimum combination of sweetness and sheer power. He improvised, interjected higher notes than normal, wished that the hymn could last forever.

Worshippers had come that morning to the Western Wall to witness a miracle. They were not disappointed. The miracle was the voice they heard. At the end of the hymn, the chaplain grasped Daniel's hand and shook it enthusiastically. He was besieged by well-wishers. Worshippers told him they had seen him at the Grand, had heard him on records; some even embarrassed him by pulling out pens on the Sabbath and asking for his autograph. He declined. When he saw Benjamin, he grinned happily. "See? Your old man had them stomping in the aisles!"

"Mr. Kerr?" A middle-aged man pushed his way to the front of the crowd of admirers surrounding Daniel. "I'm Mordecai Katz, of the Hebrew National Opera."

"How do you do?"

Katz struggled to pull Daniel away from the crowd. Benjamin followed and they walked toward where Anna was waiting. "How long will you be staying in Israel, Mr. Kerr?" Katz asked.

"Another ten days." Daniel introduced Katz to Anna.

"That is a pity. As I listened to you before, I thought that perhaps you might be interested in appearing in Israel."

"That's something my agent would have to handle."

"Would you at least do us the honor of stopping by the company if you are in Tel Aviv?" Katz asked. "We have some interesting productions at the present time."

"*Lohengrin?*" Daniel did not understand why he attempted such a feeble joke.

Katz smiled thinly. "I doubt if you will ever hear Wagner played in this country, Mr. Kerr. Liszt, perhaps. He only wanted to give us our own country so we would leave his. Wagner wanted much worse done."

"I know. I'm sorry. Look, we'll be in Tel Aviv in a couple of days. I'll drop by and say hello." He shook hands with Katz and led Anna and Benjamin away.

"That was in bad taste, Pa," Benjamin chided him.

"Don't know why I said it. I got turned off Wagner a long time ago." He thought of Martinelli. Should he send the Italian a postcard showing the temple's Western Wall, inscribe it that his latest performance had been there? Maybe they could arrange their return flight with a stopover in Milan. He had not seen Martinelli since that night at La Scala nine years earlier, when he had dragged him onto the stage after *Aïda* to share in the acclaim. Martinelli had told him once that a cantor could never thrill his audience as a lyric tenor could. Well, he was wrong. And today Daniel had proven it.

"Want to stop off in Milan on the way home?" Daniel asked Anna.

"To see your friend Enzo?"

"I was just thinking about him."

"I'd love to." Anna linked arms with her husband and son, feeling secure and happy as she walked between the two men in her life.

Daniel only intended to spend a few minutes with Mordecai Katz at the Hebrew National Opera in Tel Aviv. He allowed himself to be shown around the opera house, nodding politely to everything Katz said, barely listening.

". . . In 1947, when the British were still here, we began with Opera Israel," Katz said. "The first performance was *Thaïs* by Massenet, with Edis de Philippe who, with her husband Eben Zohar, formed the current Hebrew National Opera nine years ago."

"That's right," Daniel said automatically. "Who's singing now with the company?"

"We had Placido Domingo with us for three years, until 1965 when he moved to the New York City Opera."

Daniel nodded. He wanted to get outside, back to Anna and Benjamin who were waiting in a restaurant. "If I can find the time, Mr. Katz, perhaps I'll drop in on one of your productions while I'm in Tel Aviv."

Katz was so thrilled that he did not even notice the boredom enveloping his guest. "I think you would like what we are doing," he enthused. "Especially our production of Halévy's

La Juive, such a fitting work for this company."

"*La Juive?*"

"Yes." Katz didn't understand the questioning tone Daniel put into the name. "Is there something wrong with that?"

"No. When is it?"

"Tomorrow night."

"Let me have three tickets, will you? I'll be here."

"Of course, Mr. Kerr. Of course. We will be delighted to have you and your party as our guests."

Daniel sat through the performance of *La Juive*, totally absorbed by the story. He did not understand French, the language of the opera. The libretto, written in Hebrew, was not much use to him either. All he understood was the one aria, "Rachel! quand du Seigneur," which he had chosen as his final encore at Carnegie Hall. Nonetheless, he found himself wrapped up in the role of Eleazar, the proud Jewish goldsmith in the Swiss town of Constance who sacrifices himself and his daughter in preference to bending to the will of the Church. Never before had he realized what a powerful role it was, far more dramatic than anything he had ever attempted.

"You want to do it, don't you?" Anna whispered as the audience called back the cast for curtain calls.

"Should I?" he asked uncertainly. He moved in the seat and found that his clothes were sticking to him. He had sweated as much during the opera as he did during his own performances. He felt as if he had sung every note with the tenor playing Eleazar. "Depends on whether a certain soprano would come out of semi-retirement to sing Rachel."

"It depends on a lot more than that, Daniel."

He knew exactly what she meant. The choice of productions was not his decision. It was Robin Duguid's, based on a very simple yet effective formula. Check what had done well over the previous couple of seasons and use them as staples—*Bohème*, *Tosca*, *Rigoletto*. Then start to fill out the production roster. Add a few daring ones, modern operas that would have limited appeal but needed to be aired to round out the repertory. Where would something like *La Juive* fit into that?

"I could do it better than that guy." He pointed toward the

stage, where the young tenor was taking another curtain call. "He doesn't have the depth Eleazar needs."

"Of course you could do it better." Anna wasn't trying to flatter him; that was an approach she had never used. She was telling the truth. Daniel was an established singer, a man who had held the spotlight for more than twenty years. He had the depth and experience needed for such a role.

"I'm going to talk with Duguid when I get back," he decided. "See if I can persuade him to revive it at the Grand." He leaned across Anna and directed his next words to Benjamin. "Whatever the Israelis can do, the Grand can always do better."

Before leaving Israel, Daniel sent Martinelli a cable with the flight number and time of arrival; he would be able to spend a few hours between planes in the city. When they landed in Milan, Daniel was surprised to find the Italian doctor was not there. Instead, he saw a smartly dressed young man holding up a piece of card with the name "Kerr" printed on it.

"Did Enzo send you?" Daniel asked.

"I am his grandson, Benito. My grandfather regrets that he was unable to meet you personally but he said he is looking forward to seeing you again."

"Benito, huh? Meet Benny." Daniel introduced Martinelli's grandson to Benjamin and Anna. They checked the baggage onto the onward flight, then followed the young man out to the parking lot. A rusty, beige Fiat 600 awaited them. Somehow they managed to cram themselves into the minute car. Daniel was almost crouched double on the front passenger seat. Benjamin and Anna shared the tiny back seat, squashed against each other, the sides of the car and the seats in front.

"How is your grandfather?" Daniel asked as the youth swung the car out of the airport and joined the stream of traffic. He closed his eyes as the tiny car abruptly changed lanes and cut in front of a heavy truck. The truck driver's irate blast on the horn was rewarded with a derisive wave of Benito's hand through the open sunroof and a stream of Italian invectives.

"Not very well, I am afraid," Benito replied, grinning as he glanced in the mirror to see the truck he had cut off. "His arthritis has become very bad."

"I didn't know he had arthritis."

"My grandfather is not a man to burden others with his problems. You will see how he is when you meet him."

Daniel wondered if Martinelli had got arthritis by sitting in a car like this for long periods of time. He knew if the journey did not end soon, he would never be able to stand up straight again. He'd be able to play Rigoletto without a costume that was tailored to make him crouch. Only Benjamin seemed to be enjoying the ride, laughing loudly as he described to Anna how he would tell his friends about his trip in a mobile sardine can.

They stopped outside an apartment block. Daniel helped Anna and Benjamin out of the confines of the back seat. "Come, Mr. Kerr," Benito invited. "We will meet my grandfather."

"What happened to the house he used to live in?" Martinelli had sent Daniel his address change, but he had never mentioned moving into an apartment.

"The house was too big for him alone. He moved into an apartment complex for older people. Here he is looked after."

Daniel was beginning to worry. The doctor had never mentioned any of this in his infrequent letters. Daniel knew Martinelli's wife had died, but never had the Italian admitted he was ill.

Benito rapped loudly at a door on the ground floor. A middle-aged woman answered, smiling pleasantly as she recognized the youth. He rattled off long sentences in Italian which Daniel did not understand. "My grandfather is awaiting you," Benito finally said. He led his three guests into the small apartment. Daniel glanced around as he walked through. The place resembled a hospital ward, everything neatly placed, everything plastic. The difference from the house Daniel had seen nine years earlier was staggering. The doctor had loved antique furniture. Here there was nothing old. There wasn't even the piano that Martinelli had loved to play.

"What is this place?" he whispered to Benito.

"It is a nursing home for elderly people. An old age home for people who have enough money to pay for their own apartment. My parents wanted my grandfather to be with us, but he refuses to be an imposition. He came here instead." He stopped talking as the woman opened the bedroom door. Martinelli was sitting in a chair by the window, looking out. When he heard the door open, he turned around. Daniel was shocked. The once black hair was a dirty gray. The face was heavily lined, a piece of dark, wrinkled leather. As Martinelli stood up with the aid of two metal sticks, Daniel could see how badly bent his back was.

"Daniel! Have you come to sing for an old man?" He crossed the room slowly, his movement restricted. Daniel started to go toward him but stopped when he felt Anna's restraining hand on his arm. He let Martinelli come to him.

"How are you, Enzo? What's with the sticks?"

Martinelli looked disparagingly at the two sticks which supported him. "She makes me use them," he said, glaring at the woman who had opened the door. "She runs my life for me. Do you let Anna run your life for you as well?"

The woman took Martinelli's words as a signal. She left the room; moments later, Benito followed.

"I'd be in a whole mess of trouble if I didn't," Daniel replied to Martinelli's question. "You remember Benny, don't you?" He pulled his son forward. "From nine years ago?"

"He was a child. Now he is a giant." Martinelli looked up and down the boy. "He is truly your son, Daniel. Is he going to be a singer like you?" He looked to Benjamin for the answer.

"I don't think so, Mr. Martinelli."

"He's going to be a farmer instead," Daniel cut in. "Working on a *kibbutz* in Israel. We've just come from there. We had to drag him away from the place, he didn't want to leave that much."

Martinelli laughed delightedly. "Your father worked with his hands, Daniel. You did not, but your son wants to. What can you do, eh?" He sat down on the edge of the bed and invited his three guests to make themselves comfortable. When Daniel told him they had only a few hours between flights, Martinelli could not hide his disappointment.

"I hoped to hear you sing at least once."

"What's wrong with those?" Daniel pointed to the stack of

opera records that were piled neatly next to a turntable. Each of his recordings he had inscribed and sent to Martinelli.

"A plastic disc with something that sounds like your voice. Come, Daniel. Perform a favor for an old man. A favor for your longest-standing admirer."

Daniel blushed. He didn't know how to refuse Martinelli's request. "Without a piano?"

"You do not need a piano. Your voice needs nothing."

"I'll sing for you what I sang at the Western Wall of the temple in Jerusalem," Daniel offered. "You won't understand a word of it, but it's beautiful."

Martinelli nodded happily. Glancing at Anna and Benjamin, who sat in rapt attention, Daniel began to sing "Adon olom." He kept his voice low; he was in a small room now, not in the open spaces surrounding the wall.

"Beautiful," Martinelli murmured when Daniel had finished. "What does it mean?"

"It praises God. Sabbath and High Holy Day morning services are terminated with it."

"And people go home with glorious music ringing in their ears." Martinelli closed his eyes as he envisaged it.

"Daniel's going home with *La Juive* ringing in his," Anna said.

"Oh?" Martinelli became alert again. "Your father's favorite. Did you see a production of it?"

"The Hebrew National Opera put it on. I was interested."

"Interested enough to try for it?"

"I don't know whether I'm equipped for such a heavy role," Daniel admitted. "I know I can do better than the tenor who sang Eleazar in Tel Aviv. Whether I can do it well enough to satisfy myself is another matter."

The years suddenly seemed to roll off Martinelli's face and body. His eyes became sharp and his hands moved quickly in time with his words as he said, "For a role like that, you have to understand the true meaning of tragedy. The meaning of irony. And the meaning of revenge. All that before you even sing a note. You are a Jew clinging stubbornly to your faith in the middle of Christian pressure to change." He assumed the role of teacher easily. Daniel sat down to listen, entranced as he had once been in a house with a thatched roof in the English countryside. "And your daughter, the light of your life, the sole reason for your existence, is the weapon of your terrible vengeance against those who despise you for your faith."

"The Israeli tenor didn't have that," Anna said. "He had a pleasant voice, but the drama was missing."

"What did you expect?" Daniel turned to face her. "He was a kid. I'm not. I can handle a role like that."

"Then go see Robin Duguid when you get back. Tell him you want to choose your own production. It'll be your twenty-fifth anniversary with the company in three years' time. The 1970-1971 season will mark your quarter century."

Faced with the direct challenge from Anna, Daniel's enthusiasm waned. He looked to Benjamin, who shrugged his shoulders; decisions like this were not his mete.

"Maybe Duguid will be against it as he was the last time." Daniel seemed to forget Martinelli's presence as he argued with Anna.

"You'll never know if you don't ask him. Besides, you'll have something big to celebrate in three years' time. You'll have leverage."

"I'll mention it to him." He glanced down at the watch on his wrist and was amazed to see that more than two hours had passed so quickly. "Guess it's almost time to say goodbye, Enzo. Sorry it was so short."

"Next time it will be longer. I am grateful that you remembered me." Martinelli struggled to his feet again. Daniel resisted an impulse to offer help; he did not want to injure the older man's pride.

"My grandson will drive you back to the airport. It was good to see you again, Daniel." He shook hands formally with Anna and Benjamin, then grasped Daniel around the shoulders and kissed him on both cheeks. Daniel could not help noticing the tears that misted the Italian's eyes.

Robin Duguid rejected the idea again when Daniel met him for lunch the week following his return from Israel. Duguid's argument against the production was the same one he had used seven years earlier. *La Juive* was too removed from the popular arena to be worth the new production the Grand would give Daniel to commemorate his silver anniversary with the company.

The last time Duguid had turned it down, Daniel had not been unhappy. He had been relieved. This time, though, the refusal did not sit well with him. He was determined to push for it; if not for his twenty-fifth anniversay, then he would aim for some later date. On the way home he stopped off at the library in Teaneck, where he began to peruse the section on opera, searching through the shelves of scores until he found what he wanted—the score for Halévy's *La Juive.* When he checked it out, the woman at the counter smiled knowingly.

"Will this be one of your next roles, Mr. Kerr?"

"Perhaps." He smiled back. If he put it around that he was studying the score, people might begin to talk. Rumors would spread. A push would start to get *La Juive* back into production.

By the time he reached his car, the idea had vanished. Robin Duguid would no more listen to gossip started by a librarian than he would to an astrologer's chart when it came to setting the Grand's production schedule.

A telegram was waiting for him at home. Anna had already opened the envelope and read the message. Wordlessly, she handed it to him. It was from Benito, Martinelli's grandson, in Milan.

"Regret to inform you that my grandfather passed away in his sleep last night." Daniel read aloud; the lump in his throat grew larger, more uncomfortable. "Your kind visit made his last days joyous ones. Thank you."

Chapter Seven

Shortly after the family had returned from Israel, Benjamin's personality underwent a transformation. Daniel was certain it had something to do with the trip, the visits to ancient biblical sites that had been impossible before the Six-Day War, the sensation of peace and homecoming they had all experienced while walking the gentle slopes of the West Bank. Benjamin became even more religious, aggressively so. Every morning he zealously put on *teffilin*, the phylacteries wound around his left arm and head. He started to talk incessantly about the Jews' right to the occupied territories, how they were not negotiable, how Israel would again be the master of the entire Middle East with the boundaries it had enjoyed in Old Testament days.

Daniel chuckled to himself while he listened to his son's theories. He recognized the young man finally coming to the surface, politically and socially aware, knowing what he must do to change the world to the way he wanted it. Anna found nothing to laugh at, though. Her son was beginning to mix with a new crowd, not the friends he had made in Teaneck and neighboring towns, but radicals in New York, where he would spend the evenings and Sundays.

"He's a kid," Daniel had argued when Anna first brought up her objections. "He's just finding out that he wants to change the system. Let him be."

"He's our son," she had replied. "Do you like the way he dresses now? The long hair, the denim jackets and jeans, like he belongs to some secret army? He's mixing with this bunch of bums in the city and I'm frightened he'll turn out like them. Is that what you want for a son?"

"I'll talk to him."

Talking to Benjamin did not help. Since his second trip to Israel, he'd found out what it really meant to be a Jew, he told his father. It meant you had to fight to stay alive, and there was only one country where you could continue that fight. Israel. If they gave in on Israel and negotiated with its enemies, they would all be lost. When asked about the group he mixed with in New York, he said he preferred it to the Zionist organizations he had belonged to in New Jersey. "They do more things over there. They act! They don't sit around talking."

"Act?" Daniel was mystified. "How do you mean act?"

"You'll see," Benjamin promised. "When the time comes, you'll see how they act."

Political literature began to adorn the walls of his room, posters from Betar, the right-wing Zionist group that included Menachem Begin among its alumni. One poster even Anna had to laugh at—a bearded *Hasid* complete with long *payis* emerging from a telephone booth in a Superman costume.

Anna was not alone in her concern. The same group that Benjamin had joined had attracted Susie. She would accompany Benjamin into the city for meetings whose purpose they refused to share with their parents. Their schoolwork suffered as they spent more time with their new friends in New York. From being childhood sweethearts the two had become co-conspirators. Both sets of parents got together one night to discuss their children's fascination with this new Zionist group—they assumed it was Zionist—but no decisions were made. Daniel was firmly set against restricting his son. The kid was flexing his muscles, that was all. He'd get over it. His schoolwork would pick up again.

Instead, Daniel tried a different tack. On Friday night, during the *Shabbos* meal, he gently steered the conversation around to the difficulties the Israelis were facing in controlling the occupied territories. Benjamin jumped in immediately, as Daniel knew he would, defending any actions Israel took to maintain its authority.

"Is that what your new friends teach you?" he asked quietly.

"When are we going to meet these friends of yours?" Anna asked. "You keep telling us all about them. All about what they teach you. But we never get to meet them. Are you ashamed of them? Ashamed of us?"

Daniel could see Benjamin was becoming flustered under

the assault. He pushed on. "Invite them over here for one of the meetings. You can use the house. Or don't they know enough to get out of New York?"

Benjamin turned red and raised his voice to his parents. "Do you want to see them? You come to the Soviet Mission on Sunday and you'll see them!"

"Why the Soviet Mission?" Anna asked.

"Because that's where the action's going to be. We're going to let the Russians know they've got a fight on their hands when they start with the Jews."

"What kind of fight?" Anna was scared of the belligerence that had suddenly asserted itself in her son.

"Since the Six-Day War, there's millions of Jews in Russia who have remembered they're Jews," Benjamin answered. His voice was lower but his tone was no less enthusiastic. "They've all renounced their Soviet citizenship and declared themselves to be Israelis. They are Israelis under the Law of Return and they want to be allowed to go there. The Russians won't let them out. Starting this Sunday, we're going to make sure that what happened to six million Jews under Hitler doesn't happen to three million more under the Soviets."

"Wait a minute." Daniel held up his hand, deciding it was time to bring this nonsense to a halt. "What kind of favor would you be doing Israel if you got three million Russian Jews dumped on them? Where the hell would they put them?"

"Where?" Benjamin repeated the word incredulously. "They'll build settlements. On the West Bank. In the Sinai."

"They're not going to keep those territories forever. They'll negotiate for peace and security with them."

"Of course they're going to keep them forever. They belong to Israel!"

Daniel fell silent, choosing to concentrate on his meal. He did not wish to carry the conversation any further. He was certain now that he knew what group his son and Susie had joined, and he was as anxious as Anna.

Benjamin came downstairs just before midday on Sunday, wearing faded army fatigues with all insignia removed. The *yarmulke* he had taken to wearing permanently was pinned to his bushy hair. Around his neck, dangling outside the fatigue jacket, was an oversized Star of David. Pinned to the jacket was a round badge that depicted the clenched fist thrust through a Star of David. Written underneath were two words. "Never Again."

"Jewish Defense League?" Daniel asked.

"You'd better believe it, Pa. We're going to let the world know that we care enough to fight. Before they do it to us all over again."

"Susie's going with you? Dressed up like that?"

Benjamin nodded. "I'm picking her up. We're getting the bus across the bridge to the 'A' train."

Daniel debated whether to offer his son a lift, then decided against it; he refused to be an accomplice. If Benjamin was that set on going to demonstrate, he could get there under his own steam. "What time does this shindig of yours start?"

"Three o'clock. Are you coming?"

"Maybe." He watched as Benjamin kissed Anna goodbye and left the house. Walking up the street, his back was ramrod straight and he swung his arms stiffly, like a marching soldier. That's what he is, Daniel reflected. Another one of King David's soldiers marching off to war. And to think I was worried about him being drafted to fight in Vietnam when he's old enough; he's going to find his own war long before then.

"Do you think there'll be any trouble this afternoon?" Anna asked as she watched through the window with Daniel.

"No." He forced himself to sound confident. "These kids don't mean any real harm. They're just letting off steam."

"You've got to do something to stop him, Daniel. Before it's too late."

"What can I do?" he asked helplessly. "He's found a cause he believes in. I should tell him to quit it?"

"What about when he wants to go over there to live?"

"We'll worry about that when it happens," Daniel replied curtly. And it's going to happen damned soon, he realized. He doesn't give a hoot about school anymore. All he cares about is Israel. Being a Zionist, supporting the country wasn't enough for him; he has to belong to this bunch of lunatics as well.

* * *

Daniel, Anna, Moishe and Helen stood in a small group on East Sixty-ninth Street, across from the Soviet Mission to the United Nations. Outside the mission, under the watchful yet amused eyes of police officers, some fifty youngsters paraded in a large circle. Many carried placards that read "Let my people go." Most of the youngsters were students but the hard-core phalanx of the group was composed of boys and girls dressed like Benjamin and Susie. They all wore the JDL badge and shouted the loudest.

"I think we were worrying for nothing," Moishe said optimistically after they had watched the protest for fifteen minutes. "They're just a bunch of kids fooling around." There had been no sign of trouble. The demonstrators had maintained an orderly formation. And there had been no evidence of any reaction from the Soviet Mission. Press photographers had stopped by to snap a few pictures and a camera crew from one of the New York television stations had shot some film.

"If this is all they were planning to do, you're right," Daniel agreed. "It depends on how set they are on getting some reaction out of the Soviets."

"No, this is it. They've had their say and they'll pack it in." As Moishe spoke the words, the lieutenant in charge of the police detail moved in and told the demonstrators their time was up. Obediently they dispersed. A scattering of applause broke out from the people watching. Daniel did not join in as he watched Benjamin and Susie cross the road toward them.

"Feel better now you've got it out of your system?" He looked at some of the other JDL members as they marched past him. Their ages were anywhere between sixteen and eighteen, he guessed; some looked as if they weren't tough enough to push their way past a paper bag, let alone sway Kremlin policy.

Helen reached out a hand to Susie. The girl recoiled as if contact with her mother was repugnant. Daniel noticed the shocked, hurt expression on Helen's face. She felt as Anna did, unable to understand the change that was overtaking her child.

"Are you coming with us?" Moishe asked quickly, wanting to gloss over the awkward moment. "Grab a bite to eat?"

Susie shook her head. "We've got a meeting first."

"Where?"

"At headquarters. To discuss what we achieved today. And make plans for the future."

"Just what did you achieve?" Daniel asked.

Benjamin answered. "We showed everyone we cared. That we're not afraid to stand up for our own people."

"Nobody even looked out of a goddamned window!" Daniel heard his voice rising, but he couldn't control it any more than he could control his son, stop him from associating with these religious fanatics who wanted to wield swords and spears again in the name of God. "That's how much you showed them!"

Benjamin refused to be cowed by his father's anger. "Wait till next time," he vowed. "Wait until you see blood. Theirs, not ours!" He backed away, turned around and began to run down the street after his comrades. Susie followed him.

"The young revolutionaries," Moishe commented. "Maybe we were like that at their age, only we've forgotten."

"The hell we were," Daniel muttered.

Anna went to bed early but Daniel waited up. He wanted to have this out with his son once and for all. Find out why he was getting mixed up with a gang of zealots, what he had to do to get Benjamin away from them.

A little after eleven, Benjamin arrived home. The JDL badge was still pinned proudly to his shirt as he swaggered into the house.

"How was the meeting?" Daniel asked. "Where do you meet anyway?"

"A loft in a building on Forty-second Street. And it was fine, just fine." He walked through to the kitchen. When he returned, he was holding a glass of milk and a peanut butter and jelly sandwich. The sight of his revolutionary son on such a diet brought home the ridiculousness of the situation.

"So what did you and your friends decide to do for an encore?"

"We're going to wait."

"Wait for what?"

"To see what the Soviets do. If they let our people go to Israel, we'd have won."

"And if they don't?" Fat chance of the Soviet Union taking any notice of today's puny parade, Daniel thought.

"Then nowhere in New York, nowhere in the whole United States and Canada is going to be safe for the Soviets. We've got people in Canada, too. Do you know what we are, Pa? We're the children of the holocaust. We learned. And what we learned we're going to put to good use. No one pushes the Jews around anymore while we're in business."

"Who drummed all this nonsense into your head? Meir Kahane?"

At once, Benjamin's expression changed from righteous anger to one of awe. "Pa, you should hear him speak. He rips into you. All he has to say are those two words, 'Never again,' and you realize what your existence is all about."

"I don't want to hear him speak. I don't like extremists, no matter which side of the field they come in from."

Listening to his father denigrate his idol, Benjamin became belligerent. "What did you do to save the Jews during the war? Eh? If Kahane had been here, plenty would have been done. For every Jew that died in a gas chamber, ten Nazis would have been killed!"

Under his son's tirade, Daniel began to feel guilty. He knew damned well he had no reason to; you didn't feel guilty when you were compared with a fanatic, even if he was your son's messiah. But what had he done? Got blown up while learning to play cricket with a young boy in someone's back garden on a sunny Sunday morning? "Your enemies aren't here, Benny. If Kahane wants to fight so badly, let him go to Israel and take his crazy organization with him."

"Where do you think we're going?" Benjamin shot back. "As soon as I've finished high school, I'm off. So is Susie. We're all going."

"Susie can do whatever she likes. So can the rest of that mob. But you're not going anywhere, young man."

"Who's going to stop me?"

"I will, that's who?"

"What for? So I can stick around to become cannon fodder in Vietnam? If I'm going to fight anywhere, it'll be for my own people, my own kind."

"You're going to stay here so you can go to college and learn something." Daniel heard footsteps and turned around. Anna had come downstairs, woken by the loud argument in the living room.

"Are you two going to come to blows or are you planning on settling this peacefully?"

"Ask your son," Daniel said sarcastically. "He's all ready to pack his bags and take off for Israel. Can't wait to pick up a gun and kill someone. It used to be kill a Commie for Christ; now it's kill an Arab for Kahane, the new messiah. The man who's going to lead the Jews back to what they owned in bible times. And lead them back four thousand years while he's doing it." He turned back to Benjamin. "What damned good do you think you're going to be to Israel? They need professionals, skilled craftsmen, builders of a country. The way you're heading right now, you won't even finish high school!"

"Then I'll be a farmer. I'll shovel chickenshit on a *kibbutz*. And I'll carry a gun for the country."

"What's the matter with you?" Daniel yelled. "You think farmers don't need a decent education? Israel's not the promised land you seem to think it is. It's not a place where you throw a few seeds into the ground and wait for a bountiful harvest to come up. Who the hell do you think figured out the irrigation systems that make crops grow in the deserts? High school dropouts like you and your crazy friends?"

Benjamin's aggressiveness, his dream of becoming a pioneer, wilted in the face of his father's angry logic. He stood in the center of the living room, looking around himself foolishly. His fingers toyed with the large Star of David dangling from his neck. Daniel watched him carefully, feeling the tension seep out of his own body; he had finally managed to make his son understand the realities of life.

"Do you want to go to bed and think it over?" he asked Benjamin quietly. "Make up your mind what you want to do?"

Benjamin nodded.

Daniel waited until his son began to climb the stairs, then called him back. "You finish high school and go to college. Study something you'll be able to use over there, for your own good and for Israel's good. Then I'll help you get over there.

But if you drop out of school, I promise I won't lift a finger to help you."

Benjamin nodded again before continuing on his way upstairs.

A period of quiet descended on the house. Benjamin continued to attend the meetings in New York, but he no longer brought his enthusiasm home with him. Daniel was grateful to see his son's grades improve, glad to see the kid was taking notice of him. Hell, Benjamin wasn't a kid anymore. Kids didn't talk about killing their enemies and making the world safe for their own kind. That was adult language; fanatic adults at that. Daniel supposed he should be grateful that Benjamin was only protesting Soviet treatment of Jewish dissidents; everyone else seemed to be taken up with the anti-Vietnam War crusade.

The truce ended when Benjamin learned that a Soviet ballet troupe would be putting on a performance of *Swan Lake* at the Grand, and that his parents intended going. For weeks he urged them not to attend, arguing that it was hypocritical to support Israel and then watch Russian dancers who were representative of a government that was oppressing the Jews. Daniel did not even bother to argue with him; he simply made it clear that he and Anna were going and nothing would change their minds.

On the night of the performance, Benjamin cornered his parents in their bedroom as they were dressing.

"Do you have to go tonight?" he asked yet again.

"What's it to you?" Daniel asked, continuing to tie his bow tie in front of the full length mirror. The topic had worn thin and he didn't want to argue anymore.

"You're paying money to see Russian dancers. Money that will be used to suppress Jews in the Soviet Union."

"We're not paying anything," Anna said, weary of the subject. "Robin Duguid gave us complimentary tickets."

"That doesn't matter," Benjamin shot back. "Just by your presence you're giving them support. Think what would happen if no one showed up. Maybe the Russians would get the message."

"Just like they got the message when you and your friends paraded outside the Soviet mission that time, eh?" Daniel asked. "You're flogging a dead horse, Benny. Give it up."

Benjamin changed tactics. He dropped his aggressiveness. In its place was an abject plea. "For my sake, will you stay at home tonight?" he asked quietly. "Just miss this one performance, that's all I want. Is that too much to ask? Too much to do for your son?"

Daniel breathed out loudly. "I'm sorry, Benny. We told Robin Duguid we'll be there. We've got to go."

Anna tried to humor her son. "We won't go to the next one," she promised.

Benjamin stared silently at his parents, willing them to change their minds. When he saw they were still bent on going, he left the room and ran downstairs. Seconds later the front door slammed after him. Daniel glanced at Anna and shrugged his shoulders. The kid was *meshuggeh*.

"Does it feel different to enter as a spectator?" Anna asked when Daniel held open the door to the Grand's lobby.

He grinned. "Feels easier. Maybe I'll even manage to fall asleep during the performance."

"Don't you dare," she warned. She knew that Daniel disliked sitting through a ballet and had come only because she wanted to see the performance. He would have given in willingly to Benjamin's demands that they miss out on the performance if it had not been for Anna. "Why do you think Benny got so upset?" she asked Daniel as they walked down the center aisle toward their seats.

"How would I know?" he answered. "I don't understand how that kid's mind works." They sat down and Daniel looked around. "So this is how it looks from the other side of the fence," he said in mock wonder. "Gee, I never would have guessed the curtain was that color." He grinned hugely when his words made nearby members of the audience turn in his direction and recognize him.

"Now you daren't go to sleep," Anna whispered. "You'll be talked about if you do."

"Let them talk." Daniel made himself comfortable and purposely closed his eyes. Seconds later, he grunted quietly when Anna jabbed him in the ribs with her elbow.

Daniel never got the opportunity to fall asleep. As the gold curtain rose on the first act, half a dozen figures in jeans and denim jackets erupted along the center aisle and began to converge on the stage. Daniel's first amazed thought concerned their style of dress. Who came to the Grand dressed this casually? And motorcycle crash helmets? What were they doing in motorcycle crash helmets? What the hell was going on?

A girl's voice next to him screamed "Never again!" He turned around in time to see an arm raised, a missile launched toward the stage. The dancers scurried to the safety of the wings as a plastic bag full of blood arced over the orchestra pit and splattered against the set.

All hell broke loose. Uniformed attendants and men in tuxedoes raced along the center aisle. Fights erupted. Women among the audience screamed in terror. Daniel jumped out of his seat and threw his arms around the girl who had thrown the bag of blood. She kicked and punched at him, surprising him with the ferocity of her attack. He let go and she raced away, back up the aisle, straight into the arms of one of the attendants. Savagely, the man tore the motorcycle helmet off her head. Daniel gasped in shock. The sight of Susie struggling vainly in the attendant's arms brought home to Daniel why Benjamin had been so hostile about his parents attending the ballet.

The performance was cancelled. While other members of the audience went to restaurants or drove home to talk excitedly about the incident, Daniel and Anna went to the police station where the demonstrators had been taken. They were both certain that Benjamin would be there.

They found him in the police station, sitting with Susie and four other members of the JDL, young boys like himself. Benjamin showed no surprise when he saw his parents. Daniel forced down his fury when he confronted his son.

"Are you happy now? I was a member of that audience. You embarrassed the hell out of me."

"Good!" the boy spat back. "You had no business being

there, supporting the enemies of the Jews!"

"Wrong! I had every business being there. I work there. I'm an artist. I was watching other artists work. Your kind of stupidity comes to a screeching halt when it affects my work."

"Is music sacred?" Benjamin demanded. Other members of the group who had been sitting sullenly began to take more interest in the argument. Susie cut in with, "Don't you know they played classical music at Auschwitz? That's how sacred it is. They played it while Jews burned."

"Does your mother know where you are tonight?" Anna asked Susie. She took in the rest of the group with a concerned gaze. "Do any of your parents know where you are?"

No one answered.

Daniel turned away and sought out the sergeant who seemed to be in charge of the situation. "What's going to happen to them?"

"Who are you?"

"I'm Daniel Kerr. I'm the father of Benjamin Kerr. I was in the audience at the Grand."

"They'll spend the night in the cells. We're notifying the parents. Tomorrow morning they'll go before the judge and set bail."

"What charges will there be? They're all still juveniles."

"So what? Assault. Creating a disturbance."

"Thanks." He went back to Benjamin. "You're going to spend the night in a cell. Maybe that'll knock some sense into you."

The prospect didn't bother the boy. If anything, it appealed to him. An even stronger bond would be forged between himself and the others, jailed for a cause they'd die for.

"Stick around here," Daniel told Anna. "I'm going to call Moishe and Helen; better I do it than the police. Then I'm going back to the Grand to try and see Duguid. He'd better hear it from me first that my son was involved in that disgraceful melée."

He asked the sergeant if he could use the telephone. When he got through to Moishe, he told him what had happened. Moishe stayed calm, but Helen went hysterical, screaming into the phone about the injustice of her daughter being kept overnight in jail. Daniel told Moishe there was no point in coming into the city. They'd all be released on bail the following morning. Finally he promised to stop off at their house on the way home.

Leaving Anna in the police station, he returned to the Grand. He found Duguid—still white-faced and shaken by the episode—in his office, talking with a heavy-set man whom Daniel did not know.

"I've come to apologize," Daniel said simply.

"For what?" Duguid asked, surprised by Daniel's unexpected appearance and the offer of an apology. He turned to the heavy-set man. "Daniel, this is Igor Radenko, the manager of the Soviet dance troupe. I'm sure you've heard of Daniel Kerr, one of this country's outstanding singers."

"Of course." The man stood up. "I am delighted to meet an artist of your reputation, Mr. Kerr."

Daniel acknowledged him briefly before returning his attention to Duguid. "My son, Benjamin, was one of the demonstrators."

"What?" Duguid stood up, mouth open in amazement.

"He was one of them. He's a member of the Jewish Defense League. He's at the police station now with the others."

Duguid sank back into the chair while the Russian's expression of greeting turned to one of hostility. "What do you want me to do, Daniel?" Duguid asked.

"What were you going to do?"

"Press charges, of course. I will not tolerate that kind of behavior in my house."

"Then go right ahead. It might teach him a lesson." Daniel moved toward the door, eager to get back to the police station and Anna.

"Daniel." Duguid called him back. "Thank you for coming by to tell me. I appreciate it."

"Good night." Daniel left the opera house and hurried back to the police station. The six JDL members were no longer in sight. Anna told him they had been taken away. Daniel checked with the sergeant on the time of the court appearance the following day. Then he drove back to New Jersey. Moishe and Helen were waiting nervously. Daniel could see Helen had been crying and he couldn't blame her. Anna seemed the calmest of them all, as if she had convinced herself that the entire episode was only a dream. Her son spending a night in jail, like a common criminal? It couldn't happen. But it had, and now they had to face up to it, decide what to do in the future to make sure it never happened again.

"Short of banning them from seeing these lunatics, what can we do?" Moishe asked.

"That wouldn't work." Daniel knew the quickest way to make Benjamin do something was to forbid him. Maybe he should encourage his son with this JDL madness, egg him on. Then he'd rebel against his father's wishes and revert to being conventional. Reverse psychology. Some hopes! With a normal kid it might work. Not with someone indoctrinated by these madmen.

"Do you think a night in jail will help?" Helen asked. "Bring them to their senses?"

"No way," Daniel replied. "They're reveling in it as if being flung in jail confirmed that they were right all along. They'll get a fine. And a record," he added sourly. "Why is it that I'm almost fifty-three years old and I haven't got a record? Yet my son—and your daughter—are going to have records by the time they're seventeen."

"You were lucky," Anna said. "No one ever caught you."

Despite his aggravation, Daniel laughed. Anna had hit the right spot. For what he had done in Los Angeles while tied up with Carmel Studios, he should have gone to jail for life.

Moishe followed Anna's lead, seeing they would get nowhere by beating their breasts. "If we need a good lawyer tomorrow morning, I know just the guy."

"I want those kids out of there," Daniel shot back. "I don't want to see them sent up for life!"

Daniel lay awake in bed, eyes fixed on the ceiling while he reviewed the events of the evening. One night in jail and they'll both be martyrs, he reflected. Brother and sister in idealism. Or is terrorism the word I'm looking for? Is this how terrorists start out, how urban guerrillas get their training?

What do they do next? Hijack a plane when they're not even old enough to get driving licenses yet?

Chapter Eight

Benjamin graduated from high school and started college, his mind made up to become an engineer. He wanted to work with his hands, to accomplish miracles with them. Others in his class talked of the dams they would build, the hydroelectric plants; the student who attended college with a *yarmulke* on his head dreamed of the bridges he would erect across the Suez Canal, the tanks and fighter aircraft he would design.

In his second year at college, news began to reach the American press of show trials in the Soviet Union for Jewish dissidents. Benjamin's group called an urgent meeting. The decision was taken to launch an anti-Soviet terrorist campaign. The first Daniel and Anna knew of it was when Benjamin and Susie were arrested in a sit-in outside the Soviet Mission.

"This has got to stop! Right this instant!" Daniel yelled at Benjamin after he'd bailed him out the following morning.

"It hasn't started yet! Can't you understand that?" Benjamin shouted back just as loudly.

"Sit-ins are going to change the world? Is that your answer? Harassing the hell out of Soviet diplomats by putting their phone numbers in ads for hookers?"

"You wait," Benjamin promised. "You'll see what we can do."

Daniel did not have to wait long. Two days later a bomb wrecked a car with DPL plates that belonged to the Soviet Mission. The Jewish Defense League proudly claimed responsibility. The following weekend Benjamin was arrested yet again, with Susie, for charging police barricades outside the Soviet Mission as they tried to force their way into the building. More fines followed, which Daniel paid. Benjamin's name began to appear in newspapers. The first couple of times he was identified as the only son of Grand Opera tenor Daniel Kerr; after that, he achieved a fame of his own. He was one of the leaders, one of the vanguard of Jewish belligerents who would do anything, risk anything to help their fellow Jews in the Soviet Union.

Colleagues offered Daniel sympathy. He refused to accept it. He didn't want sympathy from anyone for the way his son behaved. In some strange, inexplicable way he was coming to terms with Benjamin's ideals. He was becoming used to them, the furtive meetings of an organization in which the Federal Bureau of Investigation was interested, the sudden embarrassing, destructive strikes at the Soviets, the promise to protect Jewish lives and property. Once, even a sensation of pride touched him, the time that Benjamin showed him a press clipping that said the Soviet Union was allowing a handful of Jews to leave the country for Israel.

"We're winning, Pa! Can't you see that now?" Benjamin said exultantly. "They're giving in."

"Do you really think it's you and your pals who are doing it?"

Benjamin came back immediately with, "Who the hell else bombs their offices?" And Daniel realized, to a degree, that he was right.

The telephone rang late one night. Daniel answered it and listened carefully. When he replaced the receiver, his face was serious, the features tightly set.

"What is it?" Anna asked.

"I have to go out."

"This late? Why?"

"I'll explain later. It's about Benny."

For an instant Anna thought that he had been arrested again, until she remembered that he was in his bedroom, reading for an exam the following day. "He's here, in the house."

"I'll tell you when I get back." He called Moishe and told him to be in front of the house in ten minutes; he'd be by with the car to pick him up.

Daniel and Moishe drove in silence for thirty-five minutes until they reached an almost deserted street in an industrial section of Newark. Empty factories stared down at them; the shadowy figures of night watchmen making their rounds flitted into sight like ghosts. One other car was in the street, a late model Dodge, engine and lights off, a figure behind the steering wheel. As Daniel pulled in behind the Dodge, the driver's door opened and the man got out. Bent low, he hurried toward Daniel's car, opened the back door and climbed in.

"Hi, Cherrybum. Moishe."

"What's the big emergency, copper?"

"I'm doing you both a favor and I don't know why."

"Spit it out, Tommy," Moishe said.

"You've got a couple of crazy kids there. And they're running around with an even nuttier group."

"They're fighting for what they believe in." Daniel was surprised to hear himself defending Benjamin and Susie.

"Maybe. I just wish they'd do it somewhere else where it doesn't give my people headaches." Tommy lit a cigarette and rolled down the window to toss out the spent match. "Their big chief, Kahane, has split and moved to Israel. I'd suggest your two kids do the same. And damned quick."

"Why?"

Tommy ignored the question. "Have they got passports of their own? Valid ones?"

Daniel and Moishe nodded.

"Then get them on a plane out of here first thing in the morning. Before it's too late. Get them on a flight to Israel and let them stay there."

"For God's sake, why?" Moishe asked.

"Any day now there's going to be a whole bunch of Grand Jury subpoenas handed down. About an attempted bombing a few months back. Two of them have got your kids' names on them. It won't be fines this time. It'll be jail."

"Hey, come on!" Moishe protested. "Okay, they're a couple of hotheads. They might have got involved with the sit-ins, crap like that. But not bombings!"

"I'm just telling you what I know. Take my advice, be safe and get them the hell out of the country." Tommy opened the car door and slid out. He didn't look back as he jogged to the Dodge, jumped in and drove away. Only when he reached the intersection a hundred yards away did he turn on the lights.

"What do you think?" Moishe asked nervously.

"I think the man's giving us a break and we'd better do as he says." Daniel gunned the engine and sent the car streaking toward the intersection. Benjamin was probably in bed by now. Anna, too. He guessed that his son wouldn't mind being woken up to be told he was flying to Israel the following day. For an extended stay.

They all traveled to Kennedy in one car. The few pieces of baggage that Benjamin and Susie needed did not fill up half the trunk. Who needs suits and fancy dresses in Israel? they had asked. Jeans. Work clothes. We're going there to help build the country, not to dance. And to escape a Grand Jury subpoena, Daniel added quietly.

"Do you think the immigration people will stop them from going?" Moishe asked, worried by the possibility.

"I doubt it. The subpoenas haven't been issued yet. Might be a different story in a few days' time." He was more concerned with what Benjamin and Susie would do when they arrived in the country. They would be accepted as legal immigrants; that was no problem. And they had enough money for their immediate needs. But what about after that? Benjamin swore he knew people over there, members of the JDL who had already left the United States and were now working on *kibbutzim*.

Only Benjamin and Susie showed no signs of sadness when the flight was called. They were like two small children going off on vacation, eager to be on their way, enthusiastic about the sandcastles they would build once they reached the shore.

As the flight was called, Daniel grasped Benjamin and hugged him tightly. "Take care of yourself. Don't be in too much of a hurry to pick up a gun." Benjamin started to pull away but Daniel held on tightly. "What about that bombing?"

"It was a Soviet trade office, Pa," Benjamin whispered. "It never went off."

"But you did it?"

Benjamin nodded. "I made it and I planted it. I didn't make it too well."

"Were there others?"

Again, Benjamin nodded. "Some others went off, but we

never killed anyone. Only property."

Daniel gulped back a sob. His kid talking so casually about making bombs. What had happened? To him? To the world? "Go get your plane," he finally said, releasing his grip on Benjamin.

The four adults waited until the El Al flight took off, then they trudged slowly back to the car. No one spoke a word during the entire journey back to New Jersey. Once Daniel glanced in the rearview mirror and saw Moishe taking off his glasses to wipe his eyes.

Bombs, he thought. He's studying to be an engineer so he can build bigger and better bombs. And I'm the one who forced him to go to college.

The subpoenas calling Benjamin and Susie to appear before a Grand Jury arrived two weeks later, the same day as letters which told their parents they had settled into a *kibbutz* in northern Israel, a few miles from the Lebanese border. Benjamin was working on a building crew while he continued his interrupted engineering studies. Susie was working on a chicken farm.

Daniel passed Benjamin's subpoena over to Moishe. He was the lawyer; he could handle them. It was time, after all the excitement and anxiety, to get back to worrying about his own career.

Why should he have to worry? He had already reached the peak of his career. One of the finest lyric tenors in the United States, if not the world. Hadn't Robin Duguid introduced him as such to the manager of the Soviet dance troupe, that night Benjamin and his friends had run down the center aisle of the Grand and thrown bags of chicken blood at the Russian dancers, screaming "Never again!"

There was no longer any need to feel concerned, he decided. He could retire whenever he liked, although he would prefer to see it through until the 1975-1976 season, his thirtieth with the company. If he paced himself carefully, he could last out with plenty to spare. His voice had not darkened any more. In his thirtieth year he would still be fresh; and sound a damned sight better than some of the younger singers who were coming through.

Suddenly he knew why he was worried. It was easier to be anxious about himself than about Benjamin. With his own life, at least, he had some control. He could afford to worry because he could always find the means to solve the problems.

"Want to sell the house?" Daniel asked.

Anna looked across the living room in surprise. "What made you ask that?"

"We've been here a long time. Maybe we should make a move. Who needs a house this big when there's just the two of us?"

"What about when Benny comes back?"

Daniel laughed at the question. "He's not going to come back, is he? And even if he did, even if the impossible happened and he returned to this country, do you think he'd want to live with his old-fashioned establishment parents?"

The knowledge pained Anna. "Where would you want to move?"

"Maybe back into the city." Daniel had been thinking it over for some time. Without Benjamin, the house seemed like a mausoleum, empty, just like that night after his debut when he had sat alone for a few seconds in the vastness of the Grand's auditorium. It was full of shadows and echoes, a scrapbook he could look into whenever he felt the urge. He needed somewhere smaller, a place that took less work to run. He didn't even appreciate the garden anymore; the swimming pool hadn't been used since Benjamin had gone away. "We'll buy a co-op," he decided. "Somewhere nice on the East Side."

"Next you'll be wanting to move into a retirement village somewhere," Anna chided him. "Is a co-op in the city what you really want?"

Daniel did not answer the question directly. "Maybe after we come back from Israel next summer we'll look around. Who knows," he added, as if he had misgivings about his earlier words, "maybe Benny'll tell us he wants to come back." There wasn't much chance of it, he thought as Anna dwelt on the possibility. When they had been to Israel the previous summer, Benjamin had given them no hint that he would ever return to live. His Hebrew was as fluent as that of any native.

He'd put on weight, hard-packed muscle, and looked fitter and happier than Daniel had ever seen him before. He'd grown up, matured, accepted the responsibilities of being an adult. The talk was no longer of building a modern-day Jewish empire. It was of making peace with the Arabs and turning the entire area into a productive part of the world instead of a constant battlefield.

Daniel was used to the idea that his son would never return, just as Moishe and Helen had become accustomed to Susie staying out there. Anna was the holdout, the only one of the four to keep alive a hope that her child would come home. Daniel could never bring himself to argue with her; it was kinder not to quench that hope.

Chapter Nine

The two-week vacation to Israel Daniel and Anna had originally planned for the following year was rapidly changed to a two-month trip after Benjamin wired that he and Susie were getting married toward the end of the summer. Both sets of parents knew they had been living together in a two-room apartment in Beersheba after leaving the *kibbutz*. It was a subject left unmentioned. Even when Susie wrote to Moishe and Helen that she was expecting Benjamin's child, little was said. Without Anna's knowledge, however, Daniel wrote to Benjamin to ask if he planned to marry Susie; he was proud that he was still old-fashioned enough to expect such a progression of events. It was one of the few letters Daniel had written in the past few years. He preferred to use a telephone. If he thought a call would have helped this time, he would have done so, but he reasoned that the printed word would carry more impact. It did. The reply was the telegram announcing plans for the wedding.

Benjamin followed up the wire with a lengthy letter. Toward the end, like a postscript, he casually informed his parents that all his friends knew of Daniel Kerr—and he was certain his father would not mind staying over a few weeks after the wedding to conduct the *Rosh Hashanah* and *Yom Kippur* services at the local synagogue. Benjamin had already offered his services; and the offer had been immediately accepted.

"*Chutzpah!*" Daniel declared when he read the letter aloud to Anna. "Goddamned cheek to think I'm going to stay out there for six weeks after his wedding to sing for free at some little *shul!*"

"You know you'll love it," Anna told him. "You're a born showman. You'll sing anywhere, anytime someone gives you an invitation. And sometimes when they don't."

The first glance Daniel had of the synagogue where he would conduct the services was during Benjamin's wedding.

His initial reaction was one of skepticism. The place wasn't a B'nai Yeshurun or a Temple Isaiah, that was for sure. He doubted if it held two hundred people; even then they'd have to be crammed in like sardines. The temple was on one level, with the women's section separated from the men by nothing more imaginative than a rope. If he sang in this place as he used to sing in Paterson or Washington Heights, he'd blow every window clean out of its frame. He'd bring the walls down like Joshua with his trumpets at Jericho.

Susie made no attempt to conceal that she was five months pregnant when she entered the synagogue on Moishe's arm. Daniel stole a look at Helen and wondered what was going through her mind. Any other mother would have been screaming blue murder, hammering down our front door, he decided, telling us what a little bastard we had for a son, getting her daughter knocked up. Helen hadn't said a word and neither had Moishe. We're still the best of friends. What would have happened, though, if he had not written that letter to Benjamin? Helen and Moishe would have been grandparents without a son-in-law.

The *chuppah* was held up by four men, friends of Benjamin. The service was quicker than any Daniel had heard before. There was no English at all. Here, Hebrew was not only the language of religion. It was the language of the people.

An outdoor reception was held after the ceremony. Food and drink were abundant. Lively music encouraged even the most staid guests to dance. Daniel joined a circle, one arm around Moishe's shoulders, the other around Anna, and kicked up his legs to a *hora* tune. In the center of the circle, two teenaged boys did a *kezatske* with more flourish than any pair of Cossacks. A Jewish wedding's a Jewish wedding, Daniel thought; whether you're wearing a tuxedo in New York or an open-necked shirt like here.

"Never thought we'd be in-laws, did you?" Moishe yelled above the din. Sweat poured off his brow and glistened on his head as he worked at the dance, obviously enjoying himself.

"You don't know how many times I prayed it would never happen!" Daniel shouted back. The music ended and he came to a grateful halt. His shirt was soaked and he wanted a cold drink. He smiled broadly as he remembered the skinny kid who'd walked toward him along Grand Concourse and waved, forgetting he was holding a folder full of sheet music. *Golem,* Fat Benny had called him. Now the *golem* was his in-law. "You sure you and Helen can't stay any longer than a couple of weeks?"

"We have to get back. I'm not a big-time singer like you. I can't afford the time. We won't even be here when Susie has the kid," he added sadly.

"Neither will we." The Grand's season started two weeks after *Yom Kippur*. Daniel would have just enough time to get back for the final rehearsal of *Pagliacci*, his first performance of the new season. If he was lucky, he would be able to swing a few days to make another trip with Anna; otherwise, she would have to come out by herself to be with Benjamin and Susie when the baby was due.

All the jokes Daniel had ever heard about small towns that rolled up the sidewalks paled beside Beersheba on *Yom Kippur*; especially when the fast fell on a Saturday as well. The only sounds on the streets were the footsteps of worshippers on the way to the temple. A cloudless blue sky added to the purity of the day.

Daniel didn't miss the constant hum of the air conditioners he knew would be working in the temples back in the States, drying out the soaking humidity so that worshippers could pray for forgiveness in comfort. Here, the weather was dry. A perfect day that did not sap the strength from you.

He sensed that something was wrong around midday, when two men in uniform entered the temple. Not that there was anything unusual about that; soldiers prayed as well. These men, however, carried no prayer books, wore no prayer shawls. They held sheets of paper in their hands and walked quietly along the rows of seats, seeking out other men. Worshippers rose, folded their prayer shawls, set down their books and just as quietly left. Within five minutes, the congregation was halved. Puzzled, Daniel looked to where Benjamin sat; he wanted an explanation. He was just in time to see his son, tight-lipped, join the exodus.

A man came up to the *bima* and whispered to Daniel that Egyptian forces had crossed the Suez Canal in depth and attacked Israeli positions in the Sinai; simultaneously, Syrian armor in unprecedented strength had broken through the weak Israeli defense line strung precariously along the Golan Heights. The country had been caught unaware. Its much vaunted intelligence system had failed.

By two-thirty, Daniel was performing to a congregation of elderly men, women and children. Everyone of military age had been called away to their units. Sirens had sounded, followed by an all-clear. While he prayed, Daniel wondered where Benjamin was. He knew his son was a reserve officer with a tank unit, but he had no idea where he would be sent. Probably to the Sinai to face the Egyptians. The air force would take care of the Syrian thrust in the Golan. Would it be another six-day wonder? With everyone safely home by the end of the week? The prospect did not seem quite so probable this time. The Arabs had chosen their time of attack with care. When the entire country was in *shul*, the defenses at their weakest. The Israelis had not received the slightest warning. Their intelligence had let them down. This war would last longer. How many would die this time to protect the integrity of the tiny Jewish state?

How many, Daniel asked himself, of those who had just prayed to be inscribed in the Book of Life were already dead?

Late that evening, after *Yom Kippur* had finished, Daniel and Anna sat up with the elderly owners of the guest house in which they were staying. The man translated the latest radio bulletins for his visitors. There seemed to be fighting everywhere, and the guest house owner enthusiastically declared that soon, very soon, the Arabs would be pushed back even beyond the earlier boundaries. This time, he declared, the Jews would occupy Damascus, Cairo and Amman; they would wrest such a victory from their foes that the Arabs would not bother anyone again for twenty years.

Daniel tried to decide what to do. He was too old to fight, not that he would have been able to. He was an American, a visitor in the country. He could sing, though. He could entertain. He could be a Jewish Bob Hope in a time when entertainment would be appreciated tenfold. Anna could join him. They could form a team. He broached the idea to her and she agreed immediately.

His enthusiasm waned only when he realized he did not have the slightest idea how to put his scheme into operation. He asked the guest house owner, who recommended Daniel approach the local military command.

Two days later, after signing a release form that relieved the Israeli government of any responsibility for their safety, Daniel and Anna were performing in camps and military hospitals. Back in New York, Robin Duguid was studying a telegram which told him that Daniel would be unable to sing Canio in the season's first *Pagliacci*.

They had just completed a series of duets at the hospital in Jerusalem, finishing with "Un dì felice" from the opening act of *La Traviata*, when a man in uniform approached them.

"Mr. Kerr? Mrs. Kerr? I have some news for you."

Daniel looked into the man's dark brown eyes and knew even before a word was spoken that the information he had was bad. "Benny?" he asked.

"Your son. I am afraid he has been wounded in a battle in the Sinai."

"How bad?" Daniel took a deep breath and braced himself for the worst.

"His leg was crushed when his tank exploded. The doctors had to amputate."

Daniel heard Anna's terrified gasp. He reached out and gripped her wrist, trying to instill his own strength into her. "Where is he? Does his wife know?"

"He's in a military hospital in Tel Aviv. I will take you there. His wife is already with him."

Still holding onto Anna, Daniel followed the man out of the small hall, unaware of the puzzled stares from wounded soldiers that followed his abrupt departure. He was no longer interested in their wounds, in helping them over their injuries. His own son had been hurt; that was all he could think of.

The helicopter journey passed in a daze. A jeep with blue-painted lights met them at the landing pad and whisked them to the hospital. A doctor was waiting. Benjamin, he said, was sleeping under sedation. He had lost his right leg below the knee. Daniel felt himself go cold. Immediately he thought that his son was a cripple, a helpless shell who would have to depend on someone else for the remainder of his life. The doctor tried to explain that with the artificial limb which he would be fitted for once the wound had healed, he would be able to lead a normal life.

"Will he be able to run, to play baseball?" Daniel wanted to know. How the hell could anyone lead a normal life without two real legs? Was this where Benjamin's zest for religion, his Zionism had landed him? In a hospital bed while his lower leg was somewhere else? What did they do with amputated limbs anyway? Did they bury them? Burn them? Pickle them in formaldehyde so they could be interred at some later date with their original owner when he eventually died? Like the American Indians who believed they wouldn't go to their happy hunting grounds if their bodies were not intact?

"When can we see him?" Anna asked quietly. She had calmed down during the journey and now seemed more in control of the situation than Daniel. The doctor addressed his reply to her.

"Perhaps tomorrow. In the meantime, I am certain we can find you some accommodation."

"What about Susie? His wife?"

"She is also here."

"How is she?"

"Bearing up strongly. Accepting the news."

She would, Anna thought. Anyone who graduated from Meir Kahane's Jewish Defense League would not be turned off by an injury like this. They had all been prepared to die for what they believed in, and to accept the deaths of those close to them in the same cause.

They found Susie waiting calmly in a small anteroom. Her face was dry; no tear streaks marred the perfection of her skin. "He's going to be all right," she greeted her parents-in-law. "It's a below-the-knee amputation so he'll retain full use of the joint. They're much more serious above the knee."

A pregnant child speaks so unemotionally, Daniel marveled. Like ice. Devoid of all feeling. Was this the child who used to play ball on his lawn in New Jersey with Benjamin? "Have you seen him yet?"

Susie nodded. "After they took him to the ward. He was barely conscious but I know he recognized me."

Gradually their fears were eased by the girl's serenity. What right did they have to be frightened when their son's wife was so unafraid?

Accompanied by Anna and Susie, Daniel was allowed to see Benjamin the following afternoon. His son was in a large ward with twenty other men; burn victims caught up in the inferno of the Sinai front who groaned in pain even under the strongest sedation; limbless soldiers who, like the rest of the country, had been taken by surprise when the Arabs had attacked; boys who weren't even old enough to shave, with tubes sticking out of their bodies.

Benjamin was awake and alert. He managed to coax a weak smile onto his face when he recognized his visitors. Susie leaned over and kissed him. Anna stood nervously by the side of the bed. Daniel could not tear his eyes away from the flat spot underneath the sheet where a healthy man's right leg would be.

"What happened to you?" Daniel asked, forcing himself to speak.

"I didn't get out of the way. It was a New York-style mugging. We got jumped by four of the bastards."

"Where?" His eyes flicked from his son's face to the flat spot under the sheet again.

"Somewhere in Israel," Benjamin answered, giving the government's standard line for designating areas of military activity. "You know better than to ask that." He turned his eyes from Daniel to Anna. "Why so glum, old lady? It's not the end of the world."

"Not so much of the old lady," she warned, smiling in spite of herself.

"I hear you two were giving concerts," Benjamin continued. He propped himself up on his elbows, knowing he had to keep talking, anything so that his parents would not have time to dwell on his injury. "Someone told me the only reason we got reinforcements to the front so quickly was because of the pair of you. You both sang so badly you cleared all the camps and hospitals. Our reinforcements were really trying to emigrate."

"Benny, don't try so hard. We're not worried about you," Daniel lied. "So you can quit acting."

Benjamin lowered himself slowly and stared up at the ceiling. "You're both worried as hell. If not about me, then about this country. We got caught with our pants down and we got clobbered. We're not invincible, are we?"

"Who is?"

"We were. Until we got soft."

"You think you can stay on guard the whole time? Always combat-ready? Is that any way to live?"

"It is when you've got neighbors like we do. How much longer are you both staying for?"

"Till this thing blows over. A couple of weeks, I guess."

"It'll be sooner than that. As soon as we reverse the position, the United Nations will step in and blow the whistle. In the meantime, you keep on entertaining the troops. That was how you started out, wasn't it?"

"I was one of the troops." He looked sideways at Anna and guessed the question that was on her lips.

"Are you coming back home when this is over?" she asked.

Benjamin smiled at his mother. "I am home, Ma. You still can't understand that, can you?"

"I can," Daniel answered. "But I don't think your mother ever will."

The Egyptian Third Army was saved from obliteration by the United Nations after the Israelis crossed the Suez Canal to surround it. Benjamin left the hospital to return home pending being fitted for his artificial leg. Anna stayed on, wanting to be with her injured son and pregnant daughter-in-law. Daniel returned alone to the United States, after promising Anna he would be back when the baby was due.

The morning after he arrived home, still exhausted by jet lag on top of the exertions of the past three weeks, he telephoned Robin Duguid and asked to meet him for lunch. Duguid cancelled the appointment he already had and agreed.

They met in a quiet restaurant close to Central Park. Daniel told Duguid about Benjamin and the general manager sympathized. When Daniel told him he had wanted to stay on, to be with the soldiers, Duguid merely nodded, understanding that as well, the desire to be with the family rather than with the audience. From being youthful antagonists, they had progressed through the years to professional comrades, able to understand and appreciate each other's needs.

After lunch they walked in the park, enjoying the fall scenery. The leaves were turning and Daniel stopped to admire the colors, regarding nature with a new appreciation. He thought of Anna back in Israel; how was she faring? Duguid watched him thoughtfully for several seconds, then said, "Was there something else you wanted to talk to me about, Daniel?"

Daniel let Duguid wait for the answer until he had walked down to the lake and sat on one of the benches. When Duguid joined him, he said, "I think I'm nearing the end of the road. I want a little time for myself, for my family. I've given enough."

The admission caused no expression or word of shock from Duguid. It was as if he had been expecting such a decision. "Not this season, though, I hope."

"No, not this season. I wouldn't let you down like that." Daniel became quiet as he tried to imagine life without his work, the stage at the Grand that would no longer echo to his applause. "I was thinking about giving it another couple of years, making the '75-'76 season my last. That'll make a round thirty years with the Grand."

The sound of Duguid's gentle laughter made Daniel swing around in the seat. "What's so funny?"

"Coincidences, Daniel. Coincidences are funny. That was the season I set for my retirement as well. I'll be sixty-five then, a good age to slip gracefully away from the limelight. You know, we'll have been together for twenty-five years then. It'll be our silver wedding."

Daniel smiled at the comparison. "Our marriage had a stormy start, didn't it?"

"It did indeed. But we worked out our differences far better than some couples. What do you plan to do with your spare time?"

"Live, I suppose. Try to get in a few ball games. I used to be a great Yankee fan when I was a kid, and that doesn't seem so long ago." He looked down at his hands resting on his lap. "I suppose I'll split my time between here and Israel. Anna and I are moving back into the city, and Benny's going to be staying out there."

"Sounds good, Daniel." Duguid paused for a moment to watch two children under the care of their mothers try to launch a small sailboat from the edge of the lake. "Do you still want to sing *La Juive?* Have it as your finale at the Grand?"

"There's only one thing I want more, Robin." It took both men several seconds to realize it was the first time Daniel had ever called Duguid by his first name. They laughed together, almost embarrassed, at the destruction of the final barrier. "Above anything else I want to see my kid with both legs. That's not going to happen. I'll settle instead for singing *La Juive* in my final season."

Duguid clapped him on the thigh. "I'm going back to the Grand right now to begin making the arrangements. Two years should be enough time to make sure nothing goes wrong."

Daniel watched him walk away. When the general manager was lost to sight, he turned his attention to the lake, sharing the success with the two children as the sailboat floated triumphantly away from the bank.

Chapter Ten

Moishe pulled his plate away and sat back in the chair, hands massaging his swollen stomach. "I've eaten too much," he complained to Anna, "but it was too good to leave alone."

Anna laughed as she cleared away the plates from in front of Helen and Daniel. On the way into the kitchen, she looked through the living room window of the co-op apartment she and Daniel had bought when they'd returned to the city. It was still raining. Pedestrians scurried across the intersection of Park Avenue and East Sixty-eighth Street, dodging both cars and rain. She placed the dirty plates in the dishwasher and returned to the living room.

"Guess we should be going now," Daniel said.

Moishe looked up questioningly. "Going where?"

"Kennedy Airport."

"Kennedy? Why?" Helen asked.

"We're meeting an El Al flight. Some people we know are on it." Daniel smiled broadly as he witnessed the stunned expressions on Moishe's and Helen's faces. He wished he had a camera in his hand to capture them.

"Benny and Susie are coming in?" Helen managed to ask.

"And David," Anna added.

"What? When did . . ." Moishe spluttered.

"We wanted to surprise you," Anna said. "Daniel arranged it a couple of months ago. They're coming in for his final performance."

"They never said anything in their letters," Moishe said.

"Of course they didn't. We swore them to secrecy." Anna went to the closet and started bringing out coats. Moishe forgot all about his full stomach as he grabbed his coat, thrust his arms into it and looked impatiently at the others.

"Come on! What are we waiting for? We don't want to be late for the flight. What time's it due in anyway?"

"Seven twenty-eight," Daniel answered. "Don't worry.

We've got plenty of time."

"There might be traffic jams in this rain," Moishe called over his shoulder. He was already out the door and halfway down the hall to the bank of elevators.

The El Al flight touched down at Kennedy two minutes ahead of its scheduled arrival time. Daniel felt his stomach give the faintest tremor as he watched the word "arrived" click jerkily into place beside the flight number on the information board.

His kids were home! With a kid of their own. A son called David who was almost two years old. He had a grandson who was almost two! It didn't seem possible. The years didn't pass that quickly. But he knew they did. They'd flown by, clouds scudding across the sky, one moment on the far horizon, the next moment overhead, and then, in the time it took to blink, they were gone, racing, chasing each other out of sight.

"How long will they be in customs?" Anna asked.

"Maybe half an hour before they're through." Daniel looked past Anna to Helen and Moishe. Were they as thrilled as he was? So excited they could not stand still in one spot for more than ten seconds? He knew they were. They had surprise to contend with as well. Until an hour ago they had not even known Benjamin and Susie were making the long trip to New York for Daniel's finale. At least he and Anna had seen their grandson only a few months earlier when they had made their regular summer trip to Israel. Moishe and Helen had not been over there for more than a year. Daniel knew the child would have grown by leaps and bounds in just the few months since he had seen him. How would the other grandparents reconcile themselves to seeing a grandchild who had doubled in size and now walked and talked incessantly?

"Nervous?" Anna asked quietly.

"What do you think?" He kept his eyes fixed on the doors leading to the customs and immigration area, willing the El Al passengers to come through. On the edge of his vision he saw Moishe walk away and ask a question of one of the porters. He came back and told the group that the porter reckoned anywhere from ten to twenty-five minutes before the passengers came through. Daniel was grateful that someone else was struggling on the same tenterhooks on which he was impaled.

"This had better be your best performance ever," Anna warned. "Their first trip back in five years and they're doing it just for you."

Daniel did not have to be told. He knew. The new season opened in just a few days with Halévy's *La Juive*. The Grand had invested a small fortune on the sets. They were all new, designed from scratch. They had to be, because the company had none in its inventory. *La Juive* had never been performed at the Grand. It was a first. And, for Daniel, a last, a triumphant exit which would mark his thirtieth season with the Grand, and the end of a long, distinguished career. Both he and Duguid had spent hours trying to coax Anna out of retirement for the production. They had pressed her with the sentimentality of the occasion, how much her presence would add. She had declined. The role of Rachel, Eleazar's daughter, called for a younger woman. Besides, the work that was involved, not only in learning the score and rehearsing, but in trying to bring her voice back to something resembling its former beauty, would be awesome. She had not sung at the Grand for ten years. A comeback was not in her plans. *La Juive* would be Daniel's production, Daniel's triumph. The entire season would belong to Daniel. She would do nothing that might detract from his hour of supreme glory.

La Juive would be Daniel's only work of his final season. He would star in the opening night production, then in two more performances over the following six weeks. The third production, shortly before Christmas, would be his last. After that, *La Juive* would belong to someone else, and Daniel would become a spectator. All three of the performances had been sold out the moment tickets were released, and the final performance would be broadcast live on public television to allow millions more across the country to share in the historic occasion. Gala festivities were planned following the last performance. Wheeler's would be taken over for the night, and the Grand was paying the bill for anyone whom Daniel wanted to invite. Invitations had already been sent by the Grand to local dignitaries. Duguid was determined to make the evening a fitting climax to an outstanding career.

To make Daniel's final weeks even fuller, Benjamin and Susie had arranged to be in the States for the entire time, from before the opening night production until after Christmas, sharing their time between Daniel and Anna in the co-op apartment in Manhattan and Moishe and Helen in Teaneck.

A scattering of passengers began to drift through the doors from the customs area. Moishe darted forward to look at their baggage tags and came back smiling. He'd spotted the El Al stickers on the bags. The long wait was almost over.

Anna was the first to spot them. As the door opened to allow a large group of passengers through, she caught a glimpse of Susie pushing the baby in a stroller while Benjamin struggled with a baggage cart toward the customs inspector.

"There they are!" she shrieked. "I saw them!" Other people waiting for passengers turned around and smiled in amusement at her enthusiasm.

Before Benjamin and Susie could see the welcoming committee, the doors swung closed again, cutting off the view of the customs area.

"Relax, will you?" Daniel said. "Hysterics won't make them come out any quicker."

Helen answered. "You relax. We'll shriek."

The doors opened and closed four more times before Benjamin and Susie came through. Anna and Helen tried to press forward but their progress was impeded by the security railing. "Look how David's grown!" Helen cried. "He's not a baby anymore. He's a big boy!"

Daniel threw a swift glance at Moishe. He had never satisfactorily figured out how Moishe fitted into this scene. Did he feel like an outsider because Susie wasn't really his own flesh and blood? The huge, almost childish grin that spread across Moishe's face dismissed any doubts that Daniel had; no real grandfather could be getting more *naches* out of the moment than Moishe was.

Susie bent down and untied the harness holding the child in the stroller. She pointed to the four people leaning over the railing, but it was unnecessary. The child remembered Daniel and Anna from their visit a few months earlier, and anyone standing with them had to be all right. He waddled toward the group, arms outstretched, his diaper-distorted bottom sticking out like a soccer ball. Daniel reached over the barrier and lifted David high into the air. Then he handed him to Moishe, who held the child for an instant before passing him over to Helen and Anna.

Daniel turned back to the barrier. Benjamin came through and clasped his father around the shoulders. "No tears," Daniel warned sternly. "I promised your mother no tears." There were tears all the same. "How's the leg feeling?"

"Did you see me limp?"

"No," Daniel lied. The limp was there, slight but noticeable all the same. The artificial leg could never take the place of a real one. "What happened when you went through the security scanner in Israel?"

"It sounded like World War Three had broken out," Benjamin retorted. "I carry a doctor's slip, but they insisted on making me roll up my trouser leg anyway."

Susie kissed Moishe and Helen, then turned to Benjamin's parents. "You'd better be in good voice to drag me away from home for so long," she told Daniel. "The last time I heard you sing, you started a war all by yourself." She threw her arms around her in-laws and kissed them ecstatically. "Come on, let's get out of here and you can show me what's happened to good old New York while I've been away."

Daniel signaled for a porter to take the baggage to the car. Moishe carried the child, tickling him under the chin, while Daniel pushed the empty stroller. Benjamin, Susie, Helen and Anna followed, all chattering excitedly.

"Benjamin Kerr? Susan Silver?"

Three men in raincoats blocked the exit. Benjamin glanced at them uncertainly. "What is it?"

"We're federal agents," the leader of the three men said. "We have warrants for the arrest of you and your wife, the former Susan Silver."

Moishe slammed down the telephone receiver in a rarely exhibited display of fury. Behind the thick glasses his eyes blazed wildly as he turned to face the others. "They're bringing up that old shit from the JDL days! Can you believe that?"

"What specifically are the charges?" Anna asked. Purposely she slowed her speech. If she spoke slowly and clearly, thought carefully about each word, she would remain calm.

"Possession of a dangerous substance. Dynamite. They were conspiring to bomb some Soviet trade office."

"I know all about that." Daniel's admission brought shocked stares from Anna and Helen. "It never went off. What the hell are they trying to prove after all these years?"

Anna hissed at Daniel to lower his voice before the noise disturbed the child sleeping in the apartment's second bedroom.

"A hundred lunatics planted bombs in those days," Daniel said, dropping his voice. "Why pick on Benny and Susie?"

"Because they came back," Moishe replied. "The warrants have been outstanding all this time. Extradition attempts failed. The Israeli government wasn't interested. So the feds waited."

"How'd they find out?"

"I suppose their names were on the list when they came through immigration."

"The big book the inspector checks?" Daniel asked, remembering the procedure from when he traveled.

"That's the one. He must have tipped off the feds. Damn!" Moishe suddenly swore. "If you hadn't swung this whole thing as a big surprise this would never have happened!"

"What do you mean?"

"Because I should have known the warrants would still be outstanding, that's why! I'm a goddamned lawyer, remember? I got so worked up when you pulled the big surprise that I didn't even think!"

"So what do we do now?" The question came from Helen as she tried to settle her husband.

"There's a hearing tomorrow morning. I'll represent them. See if we can straighten this mess out. In the meantime, you call your pal Mulvaney and find out what the score is."

Daniel picked up the receiver, surprised to find it was still in one piece after the battering it had received from Moishe. He caught Tommy at home and told him what had happened at the airport. Tommy cursed.

"Didn't you realize any warrants we had against them were still valid, could still be served?" Tommy demanded. "What do you think we do with them, chuck them out with the garbage if we can't find anyone to serve them with?" There was a long silence while Tommy thought it over. From the second bedroom, Daniel could hear the baby's cries. They had woken David. He turned around to see Anna walking quickly from the living room to comfort the child. "I'll see you at the hearing tomorrow," Tommy promised. "Maybe we can come up with something there."

Daniel let the phone buzz in his ear for ten seconds while he tried to think of a plan of action. It would be like taking on Goliath. Just his luck the kids would miss the opening night *La Juive* as well. Hell, the way things were going they'd miss all three performances. They'd be able to read about the old man's grand finale in jail.

Anna returned to the living room, holding little David by the hand as he toddled behind her. Watching the child, Daniel's bleak mood lifted momentarily. The little tyke didn't even miss his parents; he was happy just as long as there was someone to play with him and feed him.

He put down the receiver and clapped his hands, laughing as David looked toward the noise and started to run in his direction. He lifted up his grandson and placed him gently on his lap, bouncing him up and down.

The joyful welcoming committee had been transformed into an apprehensive babysitting squad.

Daniel and Moishe met outside the courthouse the following morning. Each dreaded the approaching time for the hearing. Together they went inside where Tommy was waiting for them. He called them over to a corner and began a whispered conversation.

"Get hold of your lawyer."

"I *am* the lawyer," Moishe interrupted.

"You? Okay. It's an old case, we admit it. And it doesn't hold much water."

"Thanks," Daniel responded sarcastically. "So why the hell are your people bothering with it?"

"Sheer bloody-mindedness, what else? It's on the books so we've got to go with it. Your kids skipped the country to get out of an investigation. We tried to extradite them from Israel and got nowhere fast. Not that we expected to. So we nailed them when they stuck their faces back here again. It makes us look like we're on our toes."

"Three cheers for your public relations," Daniel muttered.

"Cut it out, Cherrybum. I'm trying to help."

"Sorry."

Moishe cut in quickly, sensing the fire that was smoldering inside Daniel, wanting to cut it off before it burst into open flame. "So what do you want?"

Tommy looked around nervously, as if frightened someone might be spying on him. His voice dropped even lower. "We don't like wasting taxpayer's money . . ."

"More public relations?" Daniel couldn't help himself.

"Yeah, more PR. Besides, the feeling among a lot of people right now is your kids should be given a medal, not arrested. Maybe we could come up with a deal."

"What kind of deal are we talking about?" Moishe felt more comfortable. The bargaining had begun and he was on firmer ground.

"Benjamin and Susie weren't the only outstanding cases stemming from the old JDL days," Tommy said. "There were a bunch of them."

"You want names?"

"Damned right we want names. You get those kids to cough up names that can tie up some of the other cases and we'll drop this one. I promise you."

Moishe thought over the proposition. He pulled Daniel away and shook his head doubtfully. "Can you imagine Susie or Benny finking on their pals to get out of this jam?"

"What if they don't?"

"The judge might throw it out of court anyway. Even Tommy said the FBI's case doesn't hold much water. We could plead for sympathy as well, Benny's artificial leg, your own fame."

"Supposing the judge doesn't throw it out of court, though? They'll wind up in jail."

"Then you and me had better get hold of them and make them spit out some names," Moishe decided. "Quick."

Daniel and Moishe faced Benjamin and Susie across a narrow table in one of the courthouse's detention rooms. In the corner stood Tommy Mulvaney, arms folded across his chest while he witnessed the heated argument.

"All they want is names?" Benjamin shouted. "Names? So they can throw other people in jail? What do you think I am, crazy?"

"Who says they're going to throw anyone in jail?" Daniel demanded. "They're just trying to tie up some other cases."

Benjamin slammed his open hand against his forehead. "Tie up some other cases, my ass! You're asking me to betray friends! Would you?"

Tommy coughed discreetly, a warning to keep down the noise.

"What will happen if we don't cooperate?" Susie asked.

"You'll get bail," Moishe answered. "Your passports will be confiscated and a trial date will be set. You won't be going home till David's almost *bar mitzvah*ed."

Susie paled at the information but Benjamin remained righteously irate. "I'm not doing it," he stated vehemently. "I'd rather spend time in jail than turn traitor."

"What about me, then?" Daniel asked. "If you couldn't give a damn about yourself, think about me. This is the final moment in my career, my grand exit, and you're going to louse it up?"

The sound of laughter rocked the small room. The four people at the table turned around to see Tommy convulsed, hands clasping his stomach.

"What the hell's so funny?" Daniel wanted to know.

Tommy pointed a finger in Daniel's direction while his mouth tried to form words. Finally he spluttered, "Jesus Christ, but you sounded just like your mother used to."

"What?"

"Guilt!" Tommy laughed. "Fill your kids with guilt!" He

burst out laughing again and turned to face the wall. His shoulders shook as more spasms tore through him.

Daniel lowered his head and grinned. Tommy was right. When he looked up again, he saw that the other three people at the table were also smiling.

"Did you lose any friends over there?" Tommy suddenly asked Benjamin.

"What do you mean?"

"During the last war. Did any of your JDL boys buy it?"

Daniel and Moishe stared uncomprehendingly at Tommy, but Benjamin seemed to catch on. "A few."

"Who had something to do with Soviet property over here being damaged?"

"There was Dov, Yehuda and Joel," Susie cut in, also seeing where Tommy was leading.

"What are their full names?"

"Joel Lerner, Yehuda Kahn and Dov Stein," Benjamin answered.

"You give me the details of what they did to Soviet property here and I'll call it a fair trade," Tommy offered. "I won't even put down that they're dead. The bureau can find that out when they try to extradite."

Finally Daniel understood. He got up from the chair, walked across to where Tommy stood and embraced him.

Two anxious, middle-aged men had arrived at the courthouse that morning. At midday, when they walked down the courthouse steps, accompanied by Benjamin and Susie, the anxiety had disappeared.

"Tommy got a postponement," Moishe explained. "Sometime during the next couple of weeks the charges will be quietly dropped."

Daniel clapped Moishe across the back, then he put his arms around the shoulders of Benjamin and Susie. The clouds had gone. His kids were back with him again and nothing would be allowed to mar those three performances of *La Juive.*

The atmosphere had built up slowly over the six weeks separating the opening night *La Juive* from Daniel's final performance at the Grand. A cauldron brought carefully to the boil by an expert chef, until at last the aroma of the dish was unbearably delicious and tantalizing.

The opening night performance had been a critical triumph for Daniel. The reviews had centered upon the revival of *La Juive*, commending Daniel for his fine portrayal of Eleazar, the proud, vengeful Jewish goldsmith who uses his daughter to gain a chilling revenge upon the Christians he despises. The second performance had, perhaps, been Daniel's most satisfying. It was one where he could relax the most, project himself into the role without thinking about opening night or his own closing. He had brought the house down.

As the third and final performance neared, he found himself falling prey to the nagging fears that had plagued him in the early moments of his career. It was ridiculous. He had no career to concern himself about anymore. One more performance, that was all. After that, he could gracefully retire.

Three hours before he was due at the Grand, he left Anna, Benjamin, Susie and his grandson in the apartment and went out for a walk. He needed to be alone. He wanted time to review the thirty-year career that would end that very night amid a wild, sentimental celebration. After tonight, his voice would be nothing more than a recording.

What do you do with a voice when you retire it? he asked himself as he walked south along Park Avenue. Ahead he could see the Pan Am Building all lit up in preparation for Christmas. Do I get a Christmas wish? Can I start all over again? With one difference. Let me know, dear God, everything that I know now so I won't make the same mistakes again. I'd be even greater the second time around.

Wishing for the chance to start all over again brought a smile to his face. He should be grateful that he had been given the opportunity to make it to the top just once. God had given him a gift, that's what everyone had always told him. He'd laughed at them. A gift! What else was it then if it wasn't a gift? A voice like this could be nothing else. It was a gift direct from heaven. God had looked down and fixed his gaze on a fat kid in the Bronx called Daniel Kirschbaum. You, my boy, are going to have a wonderful voice.

Before he realized it, he was at the Pan Am Building. He stopped to look around, watching people as they scurried from offices on their way home. This is what the gift had saved him from. A humdrum life in some office, bent over a desk until he retired at sixty-five with a gold watch. He'd sooner die.

A middle-aged man approached him hesitantly, peering into Daniel's face as he tried to decide whether or not it was the Grand Opera tenor Daniel Kerr. "Excuse me," he said timidly, "but are you Daniel Kerr?"

The simple fact of being recognized on busy Park Avenue brought home to Daniel all that he would be missing after tonight's performance. It wouldn't happen immediately. He'd slip gradually from the public eye. His recordings would still afford him recognition, but how long would it take before his pictures on the record sleeves bore little resemblance to himself? "Yes," he said to the stranger. "I'm Daniel Kerr."

The man offered his hand, more sure of himself. "I'm delighted to meet you, Mr. Kerr. My wife and I saw you in *Rigoletto* three seasons ago. We're big admirers of yours."

"Thank you." Daniel was at a loss for words. How do you reply to compliments you once took for granted, but which you might never receive again after tonight? "Thank you very much."

"We'll be watching you tonight, Mr. Kerr. On the television."

"Not in person?" Daniel didn't know why he asked the question. It sounded pompous and he regretted it.

The man shrugged his shoulders apologetically in case Daniel took offense that he would be watching *La Juive* on television. "You don't know how hard I tried to get tickets for one of the *La Juive* performances, Mr. Kerr. They were like gold. My father, rest his soul, always told me about Caruso singing *La Juive*. I'll be watching tonight to compare."

Daniel looked down and saw that he still held the stranger's hand. He could not remember taking it in the first place. "Your father probably knew my father. All I ever heard as a kid was Caruso in *La Juive* as well." He looked up from the clasped hands into the man's eyes. "Do you want a couple of tickets for tonight?"

"I can't afford the expensive ones."

"What's your name?"

"Benetti."

"Mr. Benetti," Daniel said grandly, "you don't have to worry about affording anything. Stop by the ticket office and there will be two tickets waiting for you." Before the surprised man could offer his thanks, Daniel added, "And wear a tuxedo. You're invited to my farewell party afterwards. Give your wife my regards and tell her I'm looking forward to meeting her." He turned around and walked away quickly, leaving the amazed man to stare after him, like a child watching Santa Claus soar off into the sky after leaving the present he always wanted.

Daniel arrived back at the apartment as gleeful as any child, eager to tell Anna what he had done. She questioned his charity, whether there were any tickets left; he had already given away more than his special allocation for the evening. Duguid will always find a couple more, he told her. Even if they have to stand in the back of the auditorium, it'll be all right. He hugged and kissed her on the lips, wanting her to share his own joy.

They left David with a babysitter and took a cab to the Grand, arriving ninety minutes before the performance was due to begin. Another last, Daniel thought, looking through the cab's dirty window; no more will I take a cab to the Grand as an opera singer, only as a member of the audience. When they arrived, he went immediately to the dressing room. The room had been gaudily decorated for the occasion. Streamers hung down from the ceiling. Gold and silver stars were plastered all over the walls. Piled in front of the mirror were letters and telegrams of congratulations. He leafed through them quickly, felt tears start to burn in the corners of his eyes as he recognized names, surrendered to sentiment. Even one from the White House.

The first president he had sung for was Harry Truman, that night Claudia Rivera had held onto her note in the final act of *Tosca* and sent him rushing shame-faced from the stage at the end of the opera. Memory made him smile; what had seemed so important then was now nothing more than an amusing moment. Since then, he had sung before every president, including a recital at the White House for John F. Kennedy. There was a wire from Gracie Mansion, signed by the mayor who would be present at the dinner later on in Wheeler's. Remembering the dinner, Daniel left the dressing room and rushed to the ticket office. Two seats in the fifth row of the orchestra had just been returned. Before they could be snapped up by the hopefuls on top of the cancellation list, Daniel commandeered them, telling the woman in the office to reserve them in the name of Benetti; they'd be picked up later on.

On his way back to the dressing room, he ran into Robin Duguid. Daniel stood and stared. The general manager looked like a reincarnation of Roger Hammersley, dressed impeccably in white tie and tails. When he saw Daniel gaping, Duguid smiled.

"Some more telegrams have arrived, Daniel." He handed over a thick bundle of Western Union envelopes. "I hope I get one tenth of this adoration when I call it quits at the end of the season."

"I'll send you one," Daniel promised. He wanted to sit and chat with Duguid, to share a few precious moments of this final night with the man he had hated and then learned to admire. The make-up artist cut short any time for reminiscing. Daniel sat back in the chair and watched. On went a long white beard and wig. Then the artist went to work on his face. Not much to do anymore, Daniel thought. Once I played a Cavaradossi or a Turiddu with hardly any make-up; now I can play an Eleazar the same way. He waited until the make-up man had finished, then turned to Duguid, who had remained in the room.

"What about tonight's program? I haven't seen a copy of it yet."

"I'll get you one." Duguid left the dressing room and returned less than a minute later. In his hand was the commemorative program for that night's performance. The cover was gold with black ink. Inside was the complete libretto of the opera, the cast, messages of goodwill from record companies and operatic organizations with which Daniel had been associated. He was interested in none of them. Quickly he turned to the first right-hand page and stared at the few words written there:

"This performance is dedicated to the memory of Isaac Kirschbaum."

"Thanks, Robin. That makes everything just perfect."

As much as he wanted to remember every note, every movement, every experience of his final performance, the first three acts slipped past Daniel as if he were sleepwalking. He was only vaguely aware of the subtle change in lighting that allowed the television crews from PBS to send the production live into homes across the country. A comfortable sensation of sadness enveloped him as the opera continued, as if he was finally realizing that the major portion of his life was coming to an end. After tonight, his time would be his own. To be with Anna. To be with his family.

The fourth act opened with Daniel watching from the wings, waiting for his cue. If he had so far failed to cling to one moment of his final performance, he would make no mistake with this act.

As Eleazar, he walked proudly onto the stage to be told by his enemy, the Cardinal de Brogni, that only by renouncing his faith could he save his daughter Rachel from death. Scornfully he rejected the offer, and swore that even though he and his daughter might die, he would be avenged on one Christian—the cardinal himself. The cardinal's daughter had disappeared as a young child, rescued from a fire in which the cardinal had believed she'd perished. Eleazar knew where she was but he would not tell. After pleading with him for the information, the cardinal abandoned the fanatic to his fate. For a sweet moment, Eleazar gloated over the doubt he had instilled in the cardinal's mind. Then his heart softened as he thought about Rachel, his own daughter, whom he was sacrificing.

The last encore Daniel had sung at Carnegie Hall on the night he paid homage to Bjoerling cast its spell for the final time over the Grand's audience.

"*Rachel! quand du Seigneur la grâce tutélaire . . .*"

Wheeler's had been rearranged for the gala celebration

following Daniel's final *La Juive.* It looked as if a wedding was planned, a *bar mitzvah,* a family affair. Four tables had been joined together to form one long top table, with other tables clustered in front of it. At the center of the top table sat Daniel and Anna, flanked by Benjamin and Susie, Helen and Moishe, Robin Duguid and a perplexed looking Tommy Mulvaney, who was still trying to make some sense out of what he had seen and heard. Talking to him after the performance, Daniel knew he had been right in never getting back to Tommy with the tickets thirty years ago.

He looked out over the tables and spotted Benetti, the man he had met by the Pan Am Building earlier that day. Benetti and his wife were at the same table as the Mayor of New York and a host of other dignitaries. Daniel caught Benetti's eye and raised his glass in a salute.

The maítre d' placed a bottle of Dom Pérignon on the table in front of Daniel. Attached to it was a small white card covered in dainty handwriting. Daniel read the note and laughed out loud. See how hard I prayed . . . Anna. He turned in the seat and kissed her, not caring who saw. Tonight was his night; he could do whatever he liked.

Speech followed speech. Fellow artists showered compliments on Daniel's head. The telegrams that had been waiting in his dressing room were read out. Each one was followed by a loud burst of applause; each round of applause seemed more sustained than the one preceding it.

Finally, Duguid stood up to the microphone, resting his hands on Daniel's shoulders. "Friends." The single word took in everyone. "We have witnessed tonight the farewell performance of a truly magnificent artist." Another round of applause greeted the statement. "I am proud that for twenty-five years I worked with Daniel Kerr. It wasn't all roses—anyone unlucky enough to have seen a movie called *South Side Serenade* will tell you that."

Daniel joined in the laughter which swept through the restaurant.

"Those of us who have been fortunate enough to share this night will treasure the memory. I treasure far more than that. I treasure the relationship I shared with Daniel. He is a dedicated artist and a dedicated family man; in this particular business, those two are sometimes hard to find in the same man." Duguid removed a hand from Daniel's shoulder and raised it to his mouth to cover a nervous cough.

"It's my privilege tonight to pass on to Daniel a memento of his thirty years with the Grand." He reached into his pocket and pulled out a small package. "Daniel, from the Grand Opera Company of New York; just so you won't forget us."

Daniel took the package and opened it. Inside was a minute but perfect replica of the front of the opera house on West Thirty-fourth, cast in solid gold. Inscribed on the base was the date, his own name and the title of the opera he'd chosen for his finale. He stood up, knowing he had to respond, but he could not think of a word. His eyes lingered over the familiar faces and his mind captured a million memories. From now on, when he came to Wheeler's he would be a guest, another member of the audience stopping in for a meal after the performance. It was time. Other tenors were entitled to get their bite at the cherry, to carve their reputations.

"Has anyone," he asked softly into the microphone, "seen the *Times* review for tonight's performance yet?"